ALSO FROM JOE BOOKS

Disney Frozen Cinestory Comic
Disney Cinderella Cinestory Comic
Disney 101 Dalmatians Cinestory Comic
Disney Princess Comics Treasury
Disney • Pixar Comics Treasury
Disney Darkwing Duck: The Definitively Dangerous Edition
Disney Frozen: The Story of the Movie in Comics
Disney Big Hero 6 Cinestory Comic
Disney • Pixar Inside Out Cinestory Comic
Disney • Pixar Inside Out Fun Book
Disney Gravity Falls Cinestory Comic Volume One
Disney Gravity Falls Cinestory Comic Volume Two
Disney • Pixar The Good Dinosaur Cinestory Comic
Disney • Pixar The Good Dinosaur Fun Book
Disney Zootopia Cinestory Comic
Marvel Thor: Dueling with Giants
Marvel Guardians of the Galaxy: Castaways
Disney Winnie the Pooh Cinestory Comic
Disney Descendants Wicked World Cinestory Comic Volume One
Disney Descendants Wicked World Cinestory Comic Volume Two
Disney Alice in Wonderland Cinestory Comic
Disney • Pixar Finding Nemo Cinestory Comic
Disney • Pixar Finding Dory Cinestory Comic
Disney Star vs the Forces of Evil Cinestory Comic
Disney • Pixar Finding Dory Graphic Novel
Disney Zootopia Graphic Novel
Disney Princess Comic Strips Collection Volume One
Disney Darkwing Duck Comics Collection Volume One

Don't miss our monthly comics…
Disney Frozen
Disney Darkwing Duck
Disney • Pixar Finding Dory
Disney Pirates of the Caribbean
Disney Princess
Disney Star vs the Forces of Evil

GRAVITY FALLS

CINESTORY COMIC

VOLUME 3

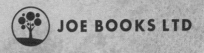

JOE BOOKS LTD

Published simultaneously in the United States and Canada by Joe Books Ltd,
489 College Street, Suite 203, Toronto, Ontario, M6G 1A5

www.joebooks.com

First Joe Books Edition: October 2016

ISBN 978-1-988032-92-4

Library and Archives Canada Cataloguing in Publication
information is available upon request

Printed and bound in Canada
1 3 5 7 9 10 8 6 4 2

For information regarding the CPSIA on this printed material, call:
(203) 595-3636 and provide reference # RICH - 613704

GRAVITY FALLS

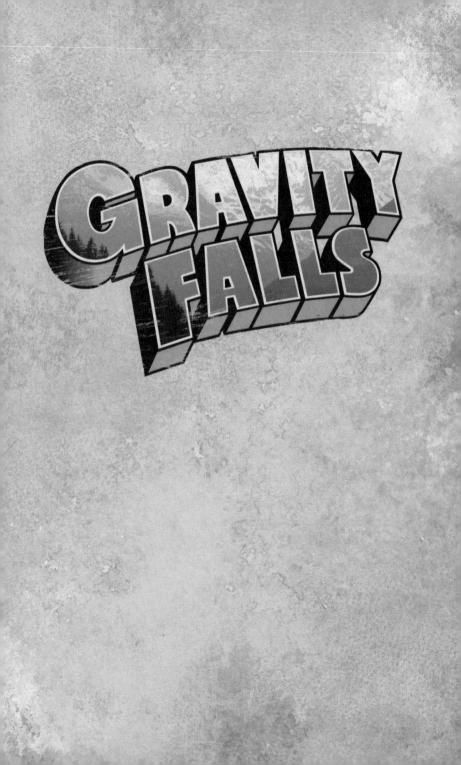

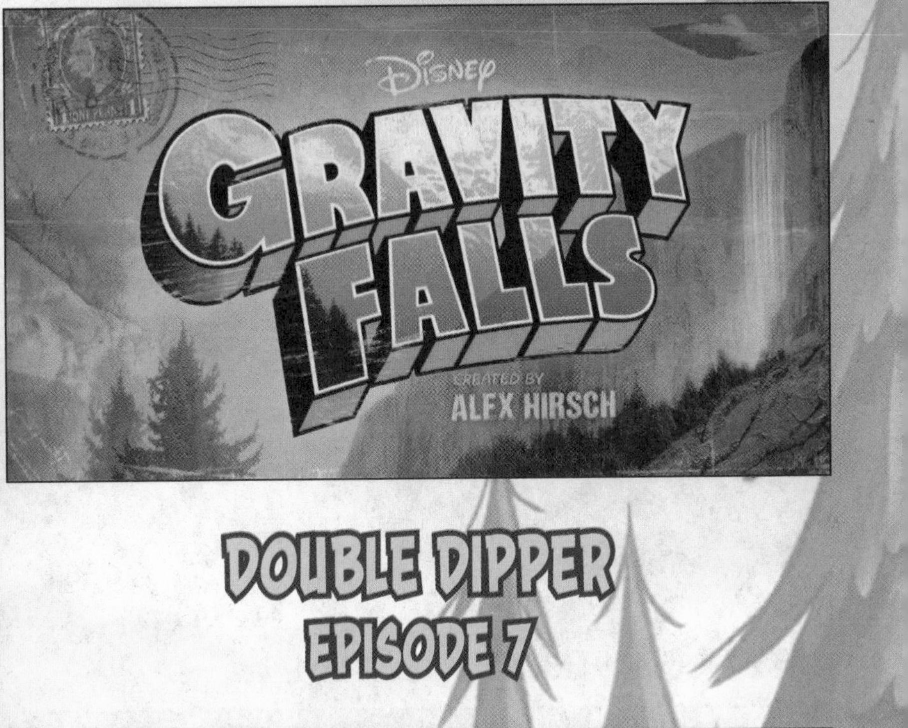
Disney
GRAVITY FALLS
CREATED BY
ALEX HIRSCH

DOUBLE DIPPER
EPISODE 7

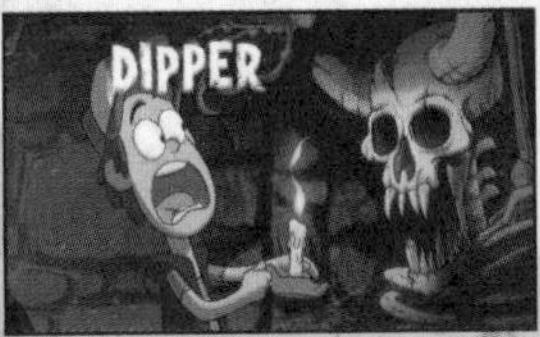
DIPPER

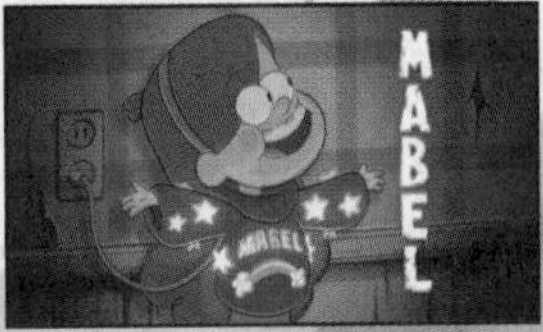
MABEL

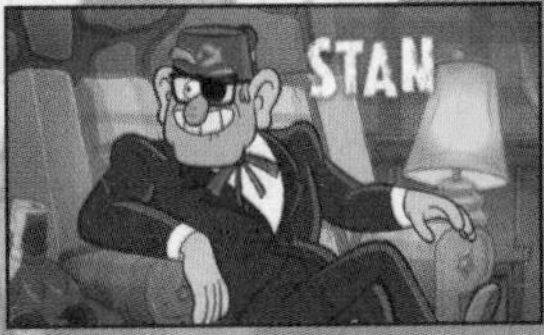
STAN

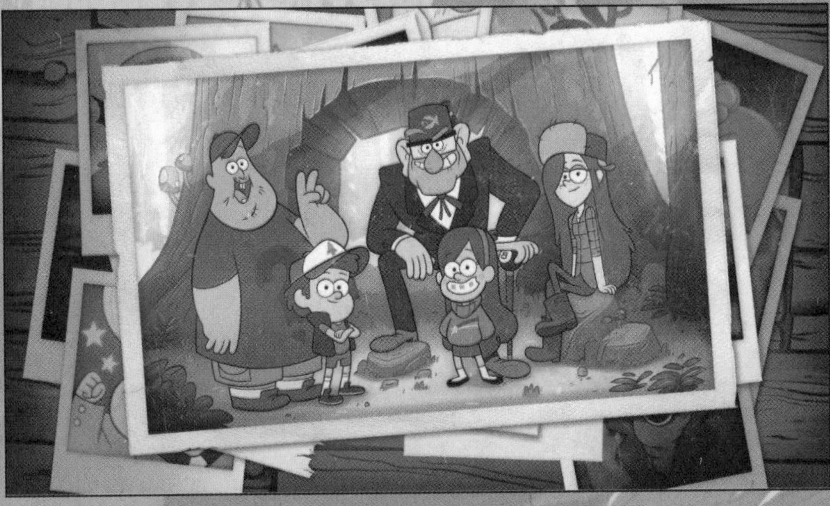

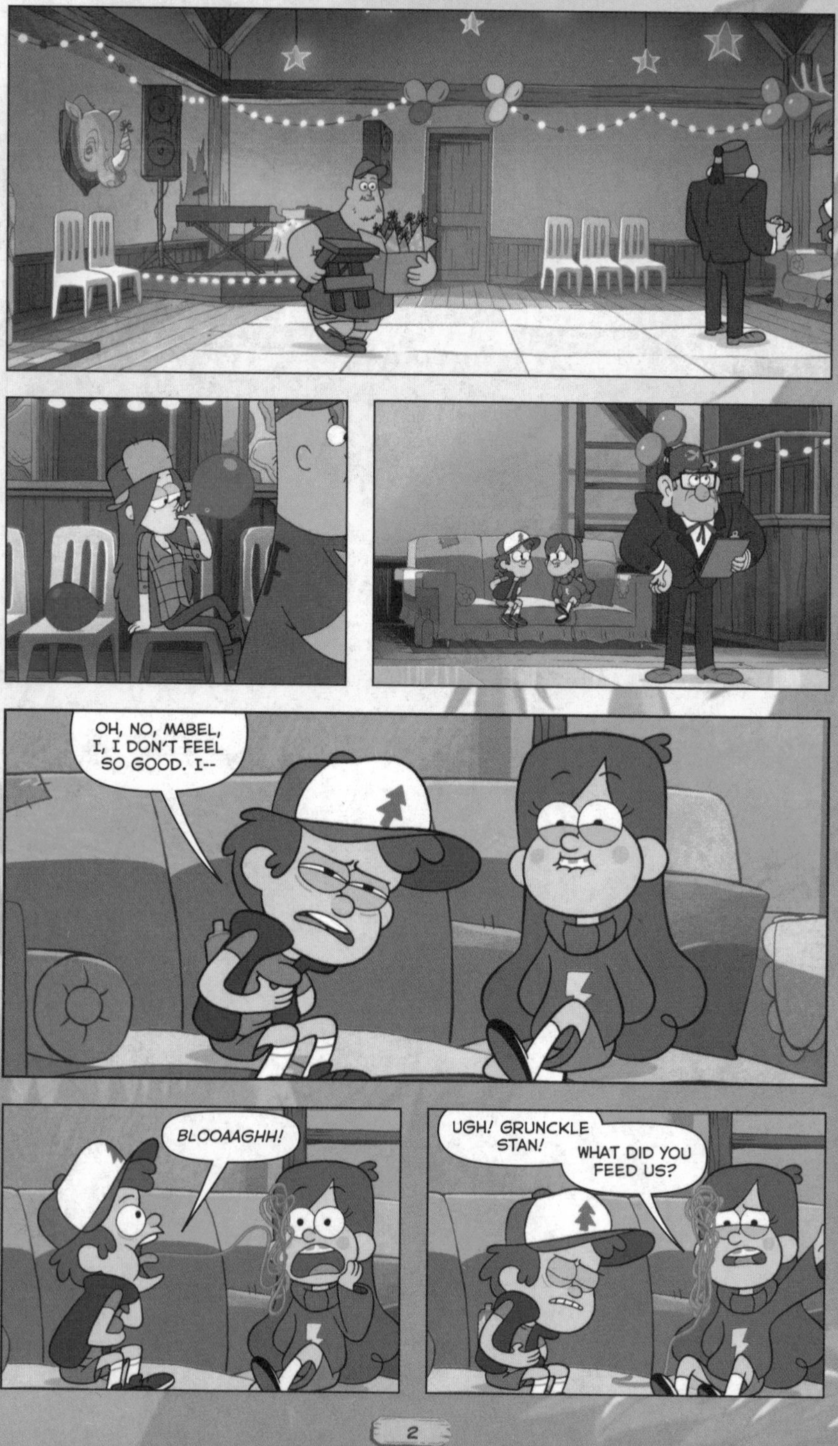
OH, NO, MABEL, I, I DON'T FEEL SO GOOD. I--
BLOOAAGHH!
UGH! GRUNCKLE STAN!
WHAT DID YOU FEED US?

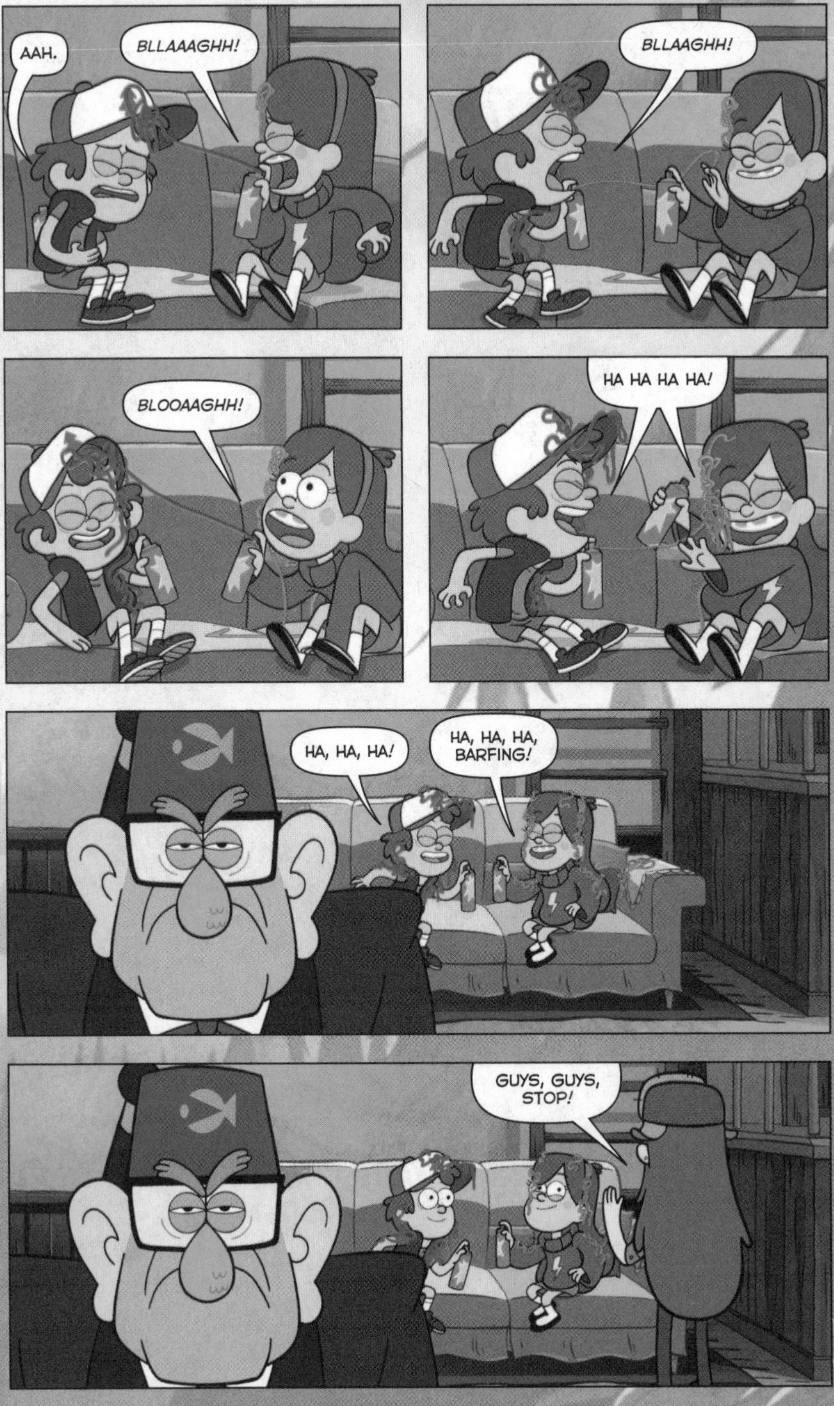
AAH.
BLLAAAGHH!
BLLAAGHH!
BLOOAAGHH!
HA HA HA HA!
HA, HA, HA!
HA, HA, HA, BARFING!
GUYS, GUYS, STOP!

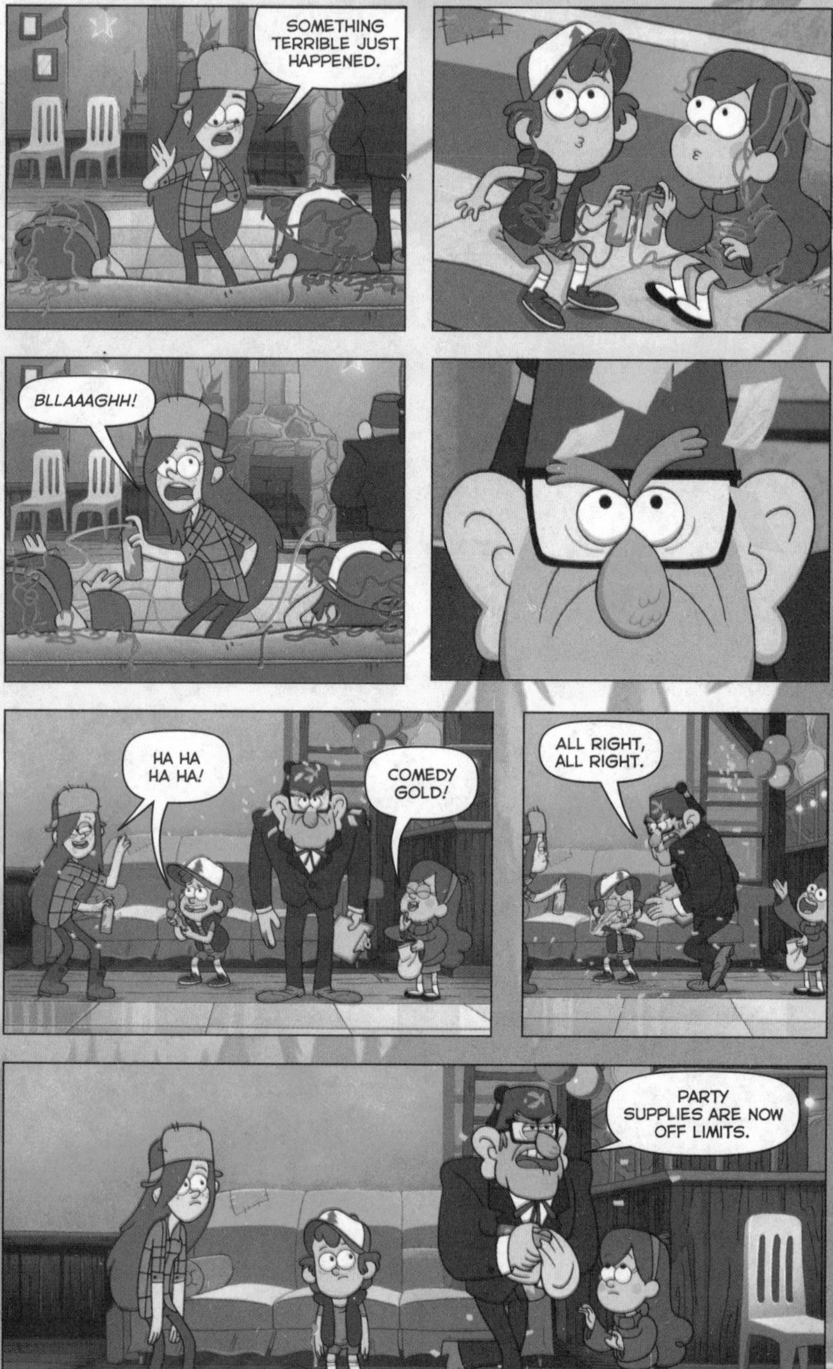
SOMETHING TERRIBLE JUST HAPPENED.
BLLAAAGHH!
HA HA HA HA!
COMEDY GOLD!
ALL RIGHT, ALL RIGHT.
PARTY SUPPLIES ARE NOW OFF LIMITS.

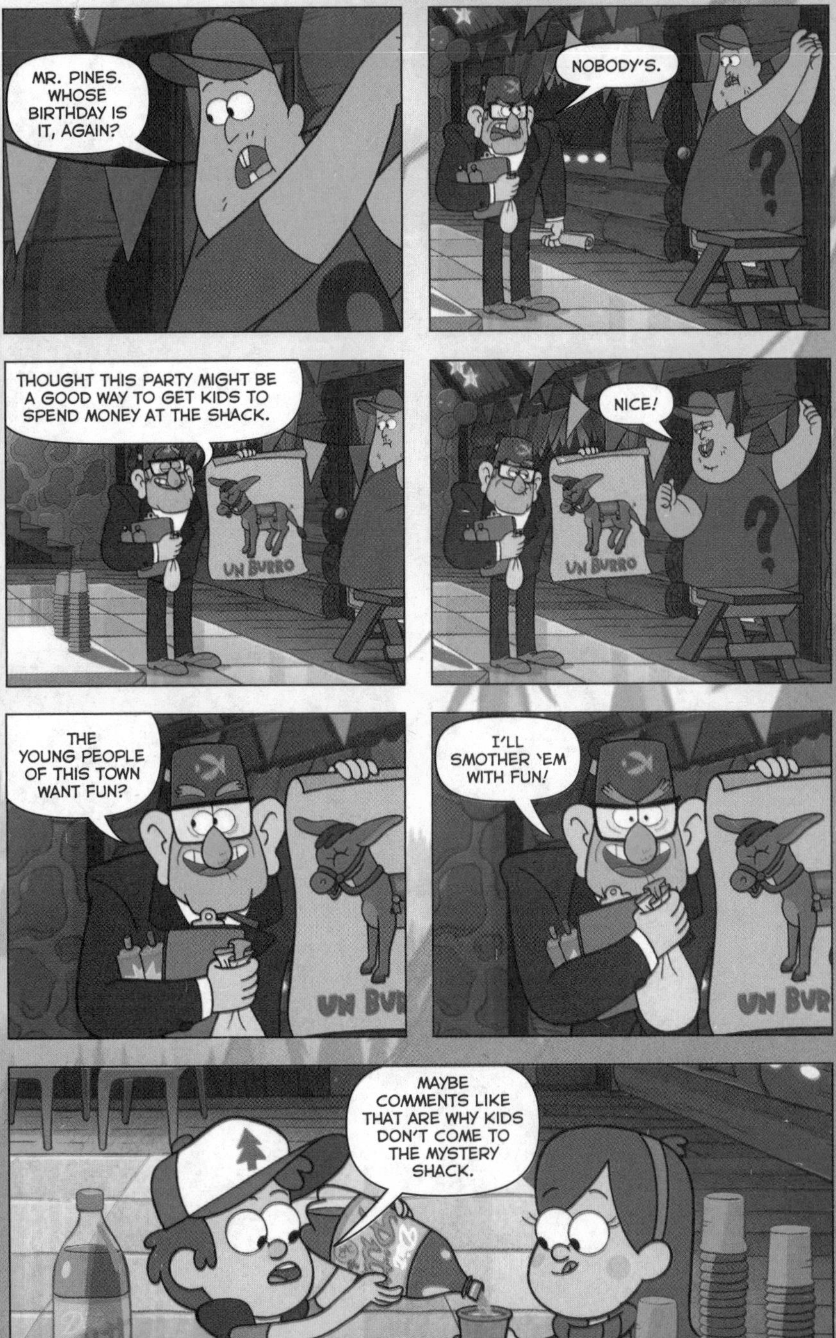
MR. PINES. WHOSE BIRTHDAY IS IT, AGAIN?
NOBODY'S.
THOUGHT THIS PARTY MIGHT BE A GOOD WAY TO GET KIDS TO SPEND MONEY AT THE SHACK.
UN BURRO
NICE!
UN BURRO
THE YOUNG PEOPLE OF THIS TOWN WANT FUN?
I'LL SMOTHER 'EM WITH FUN!
MAYBE COMMENTS LIKE THAT ARE WHY KIDS DON'T COME TO THE MYSTERY SHACK.

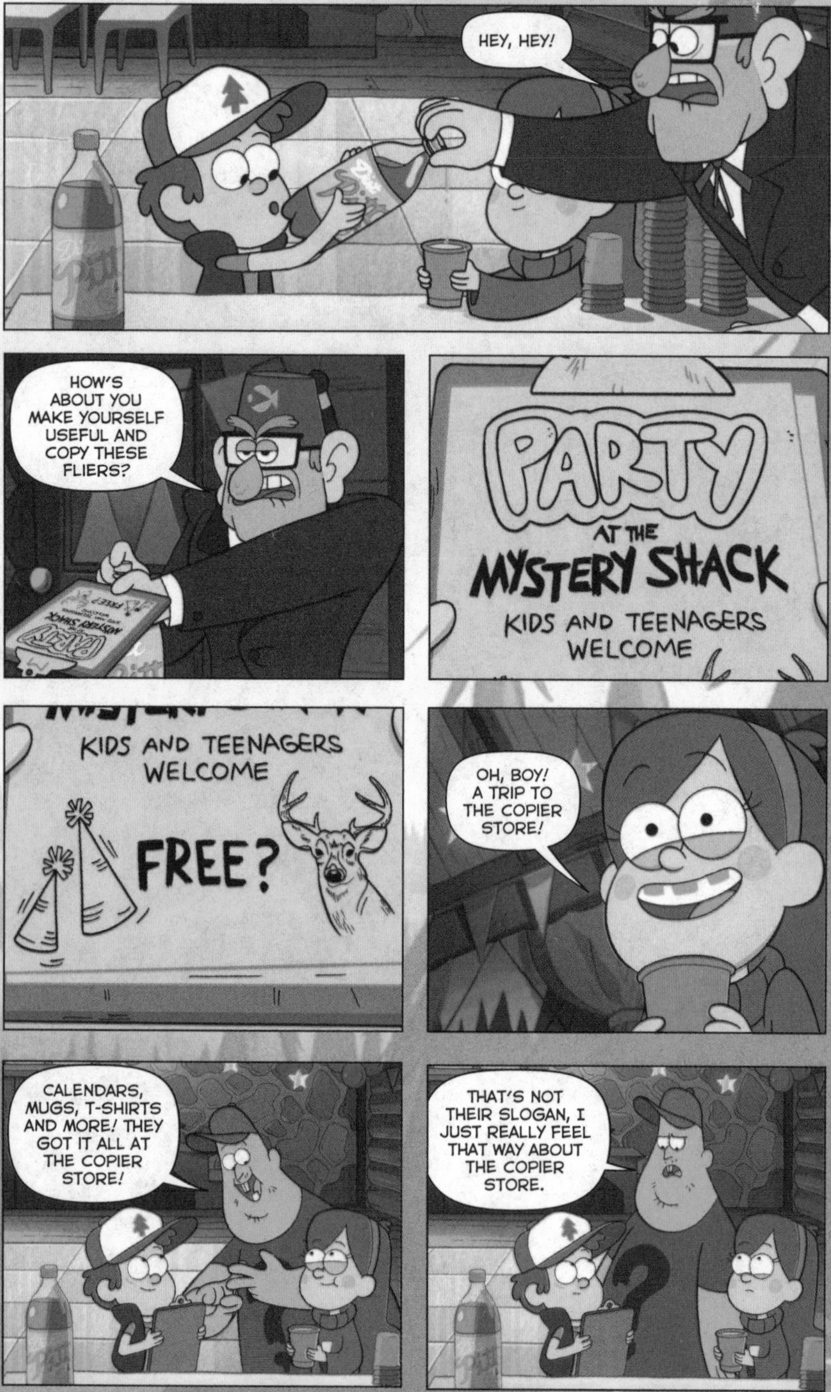
HEY, HEY!
HOW'S ABOUT YOU MAKE YOURSELF USEFUL AND COPY THESE FLIERS?
PARTY AT THE MYSTERY SHACK
KIDS AND TEENAGERS WELCOME
KIDS AND TEENAGERS WELCOME
FREE?
OH, BOY! A TRIP TO THE COPIER STORE!
CALENDARS, MUGS, T-SHIRTS AND MORE! THEY GOT IT ALL AT THE COPIER STORE!
THAT'S NOT THEIR SLOGAN, I JUST REALLY FEEL THAT WAY ABOUT THE COPIER STORE.

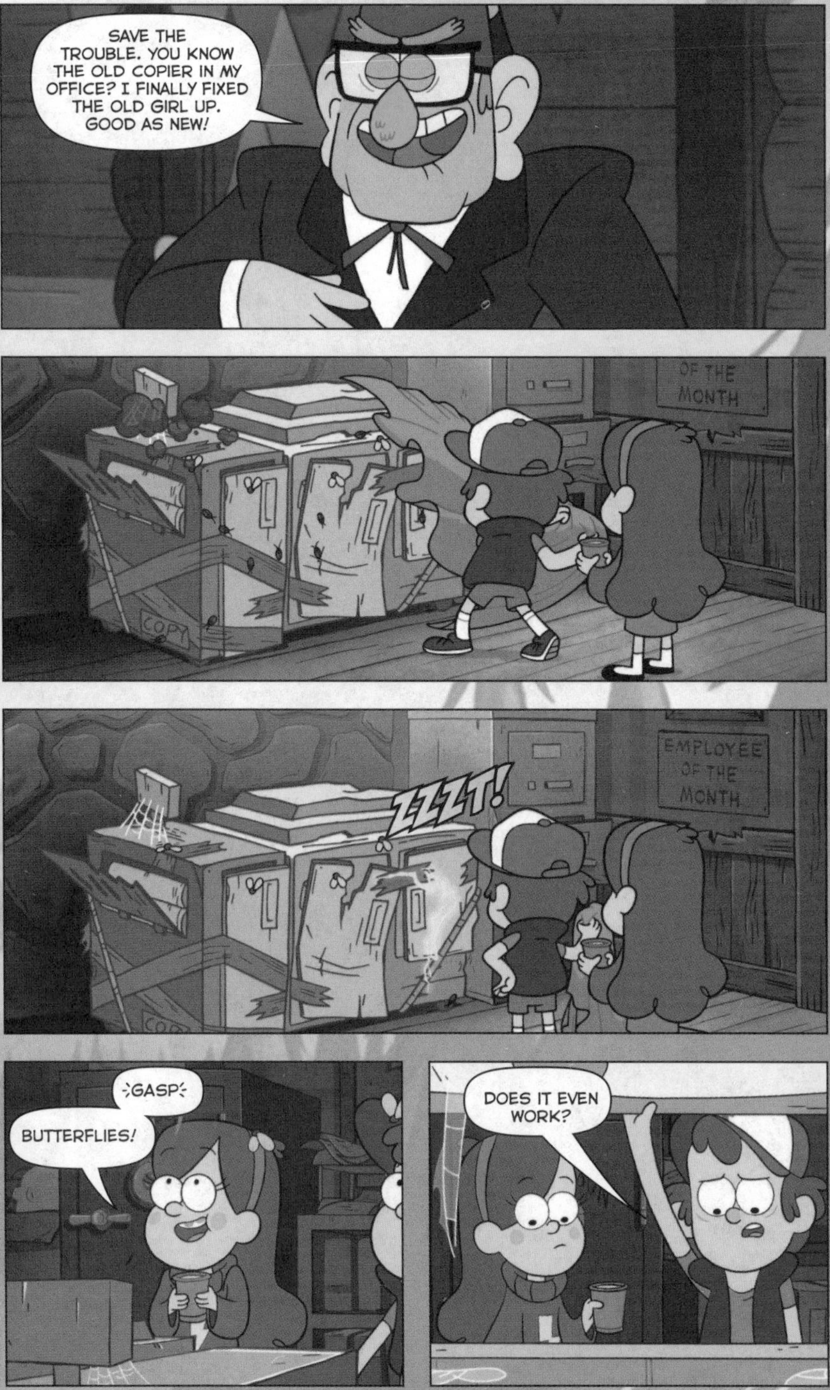
SAVE THE TROUBLE. YOU KNOW THE OLD COPIER IN MY OFFICE? I FINALLY FIXED THE OLD GIRL UP. GOOD AS NEW!
OF THE MONTH
COPY
EMPLOYEE OF THE MONTH
ZZZT!
GASP
BUTTERFLIES!
DOES IT EVEN WORK?

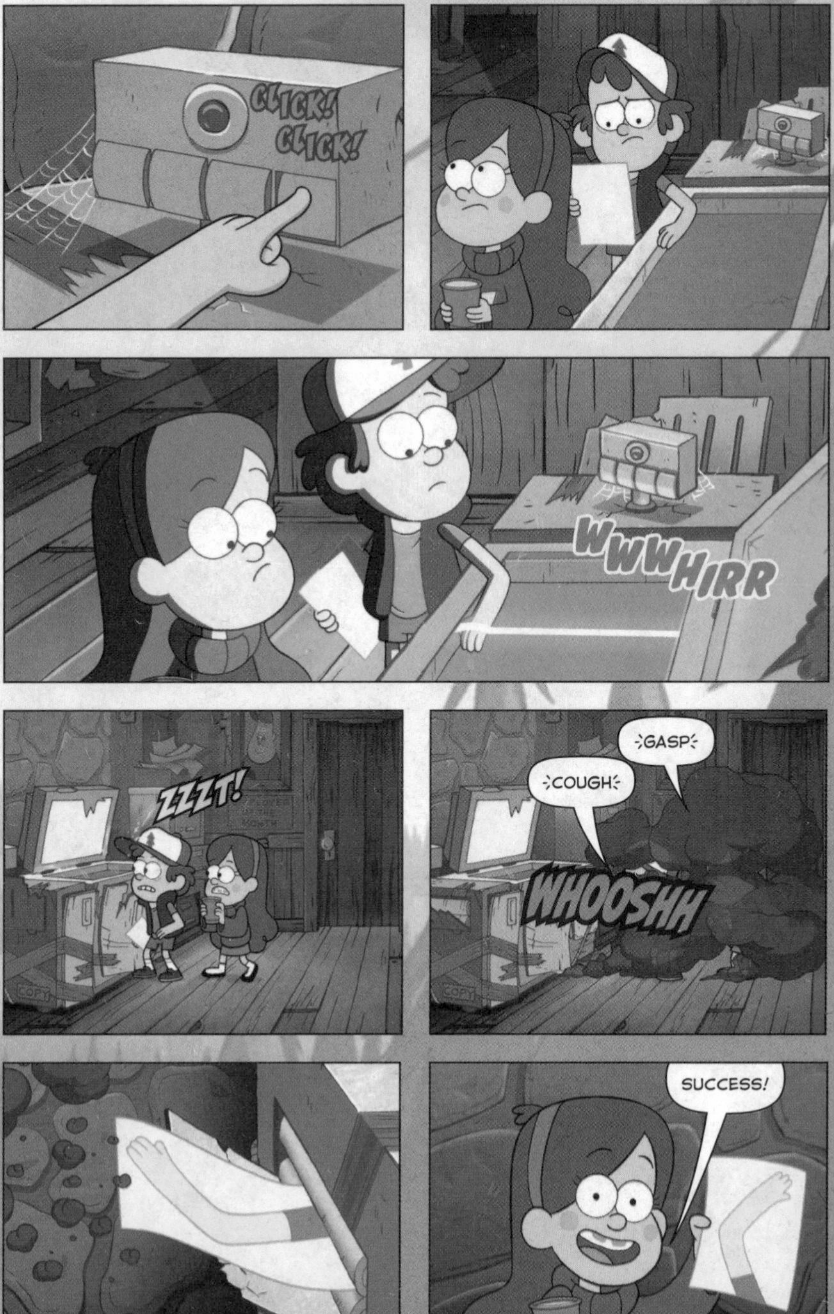

CLICK! CLICK!
WWWHIRR
ZZZT!
COUGH
GASP
WHOOSHH
SUCCESS!

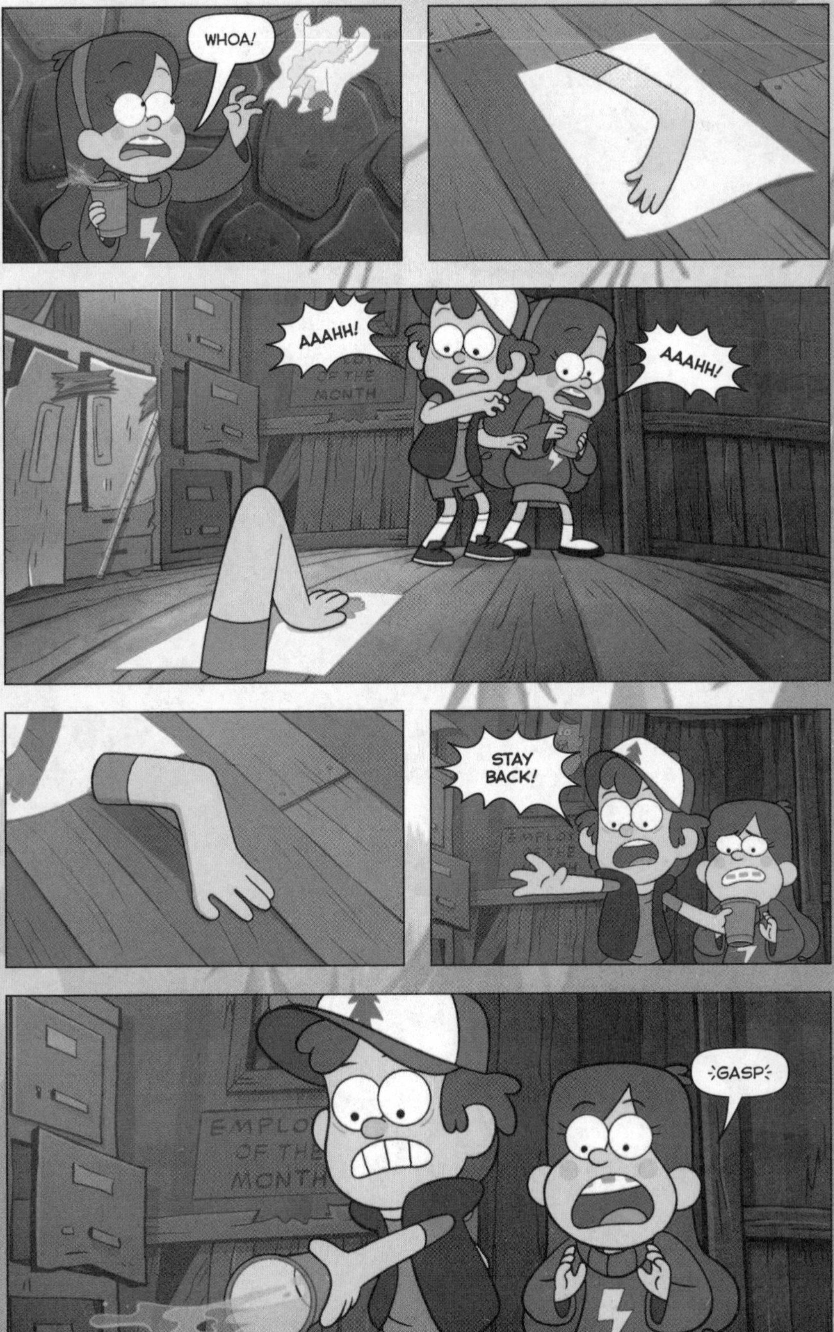
WHOA!
AAAHH!
AAAHH!
STAY BACK!
GASP

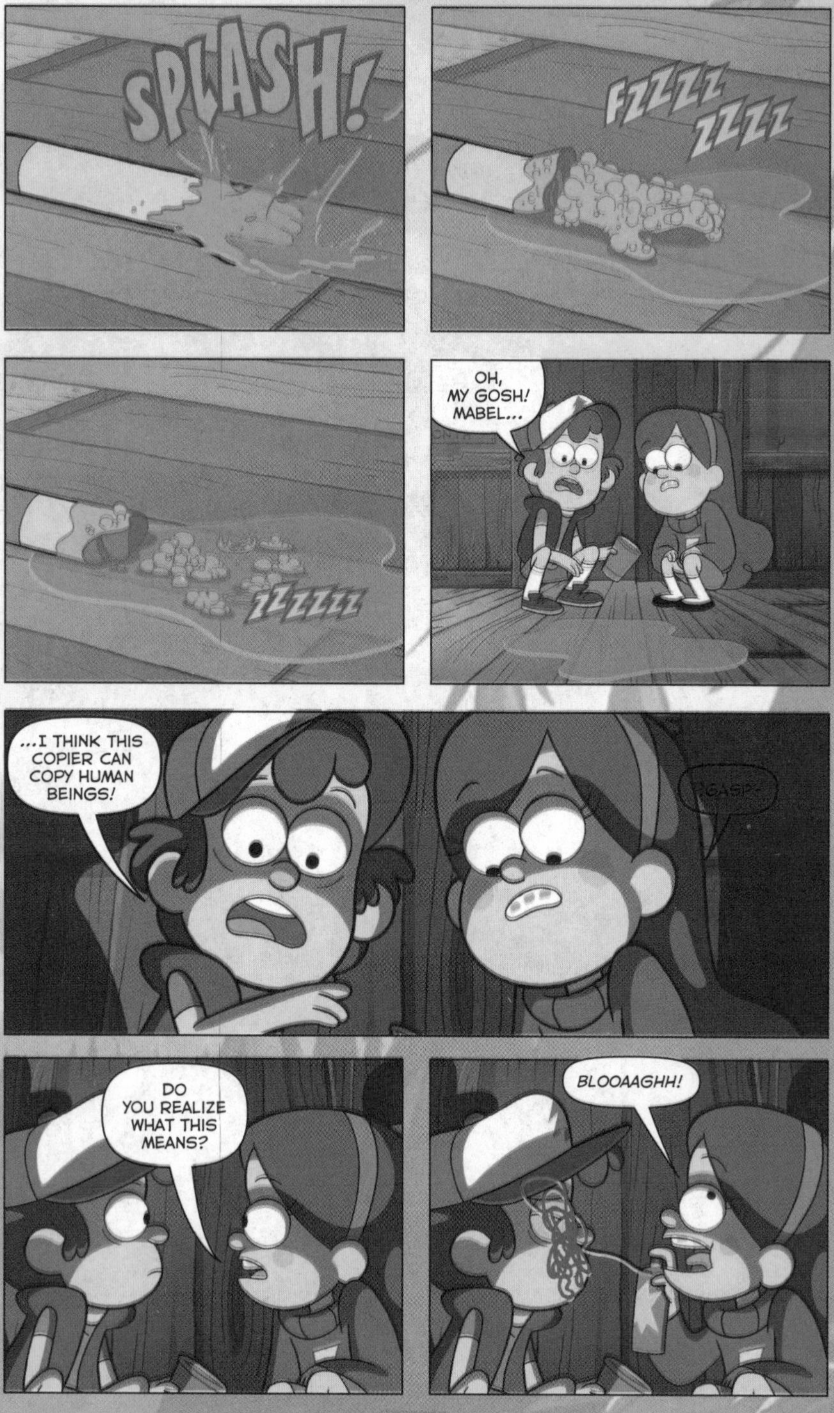
SPLASH!
FZZZZ ZZZZ
ZZZZZZ
OH, MY GOSH! MABEL...
...I THINK THIS COPIER CAN COPY HUMAN BEINGS!
-GASP-
DO YOU REALIZE WHAT THIS MEANS?
BLOOAAGHH!

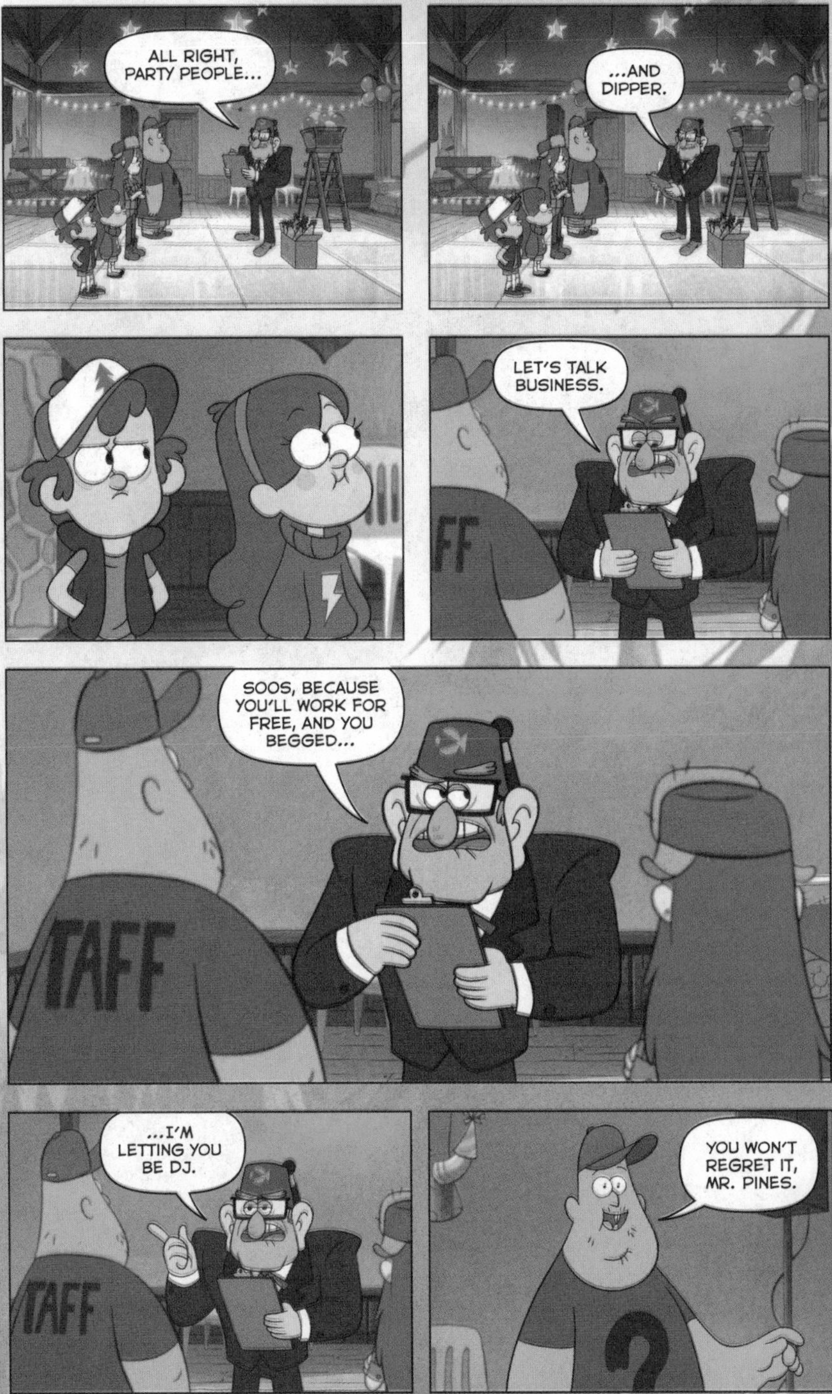
ALL RIGHT, PARTY PEOPLE...
...AND DIPPER.
LET'S TALK BUSINESS.
SOOS, BECAUSE YOU'LL WORK FOR FREE, AND YOU BEGGED...
TAFF
...I'M LETTING YOU BE DJ.
TAFF
YOU WON'T REGRET IT, MR. PINES.

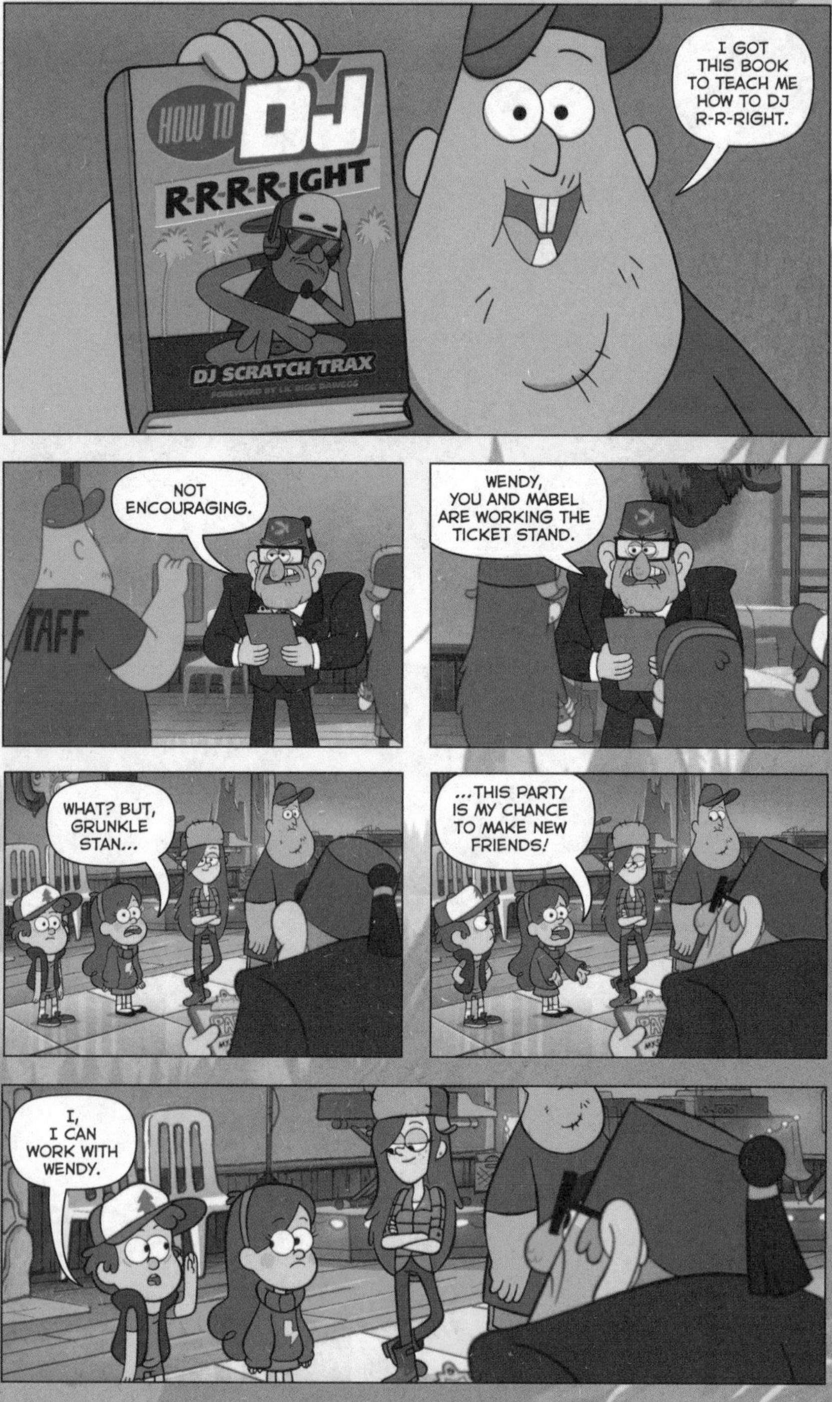
HOW TO DJ
R-R-R-RIGHT
DJ SCRATCH TRAX
I GOT THIS BOOK TO TEACH ME HOW TO DJ R-R-RIGHT.
NOT ENCOURAGING.
WENDY, YOU AND MABEL ARE WORKING THE TICKET STAND.
WHAT? BUT, GRUNKLE STAN...
...THIS PARTY IS MY CHANCE TO MAKE NEW FRIENDS!
I, I CAN WORK WITH WENDY.

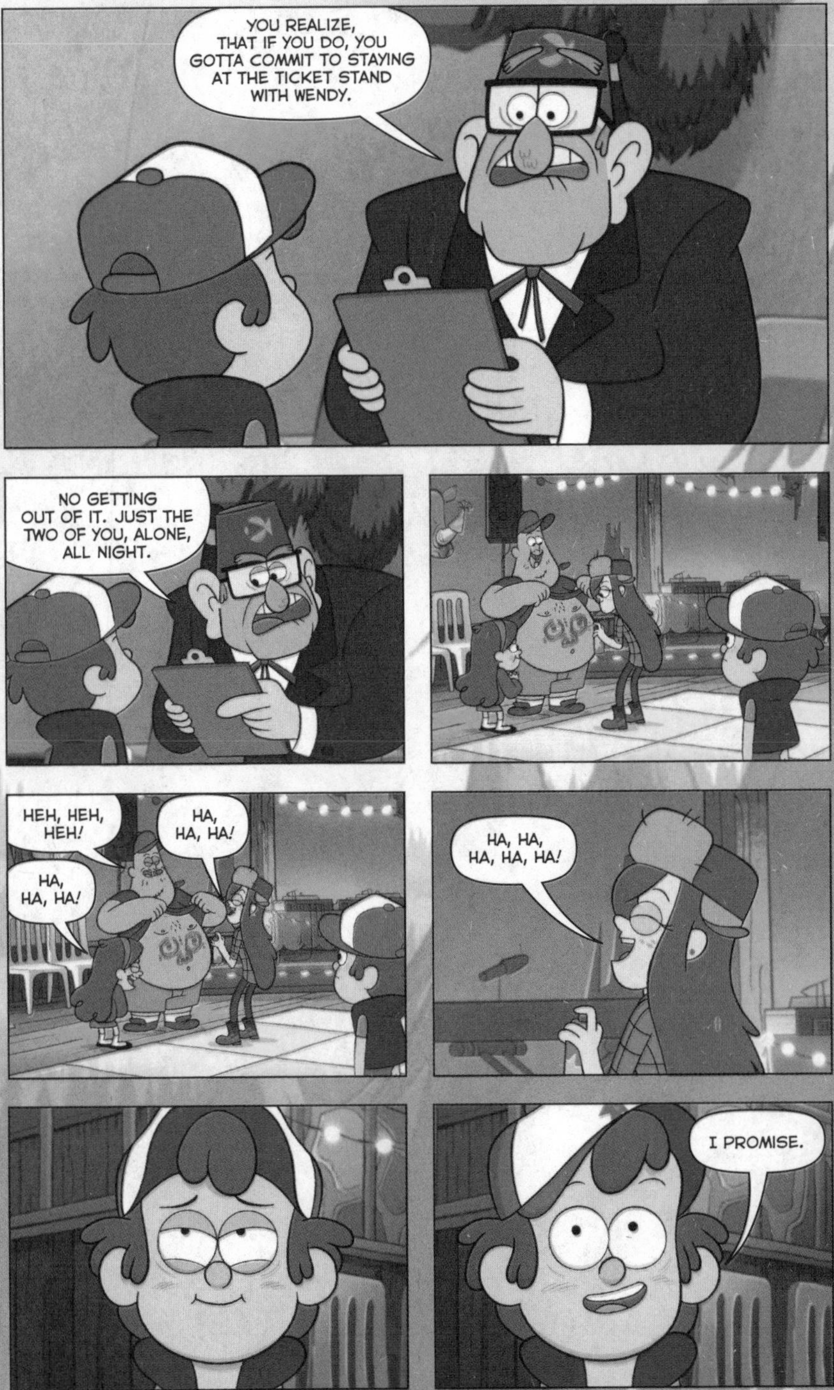
YOU REALIZE, THAT IF YOU DO, YOU GOTTA COMMIT TO STAYING AT THE TICKET STAND WITH WENDY.
NO GETTING OUT OF IT. JUST THE TWO OF YOU, ALONE, ALL NIGHT.
HEH, HEH, HEH!
HA, HA, HA!
HA, HA, HA!
HA, HA, HA, HA, HA!
I PROMISE.

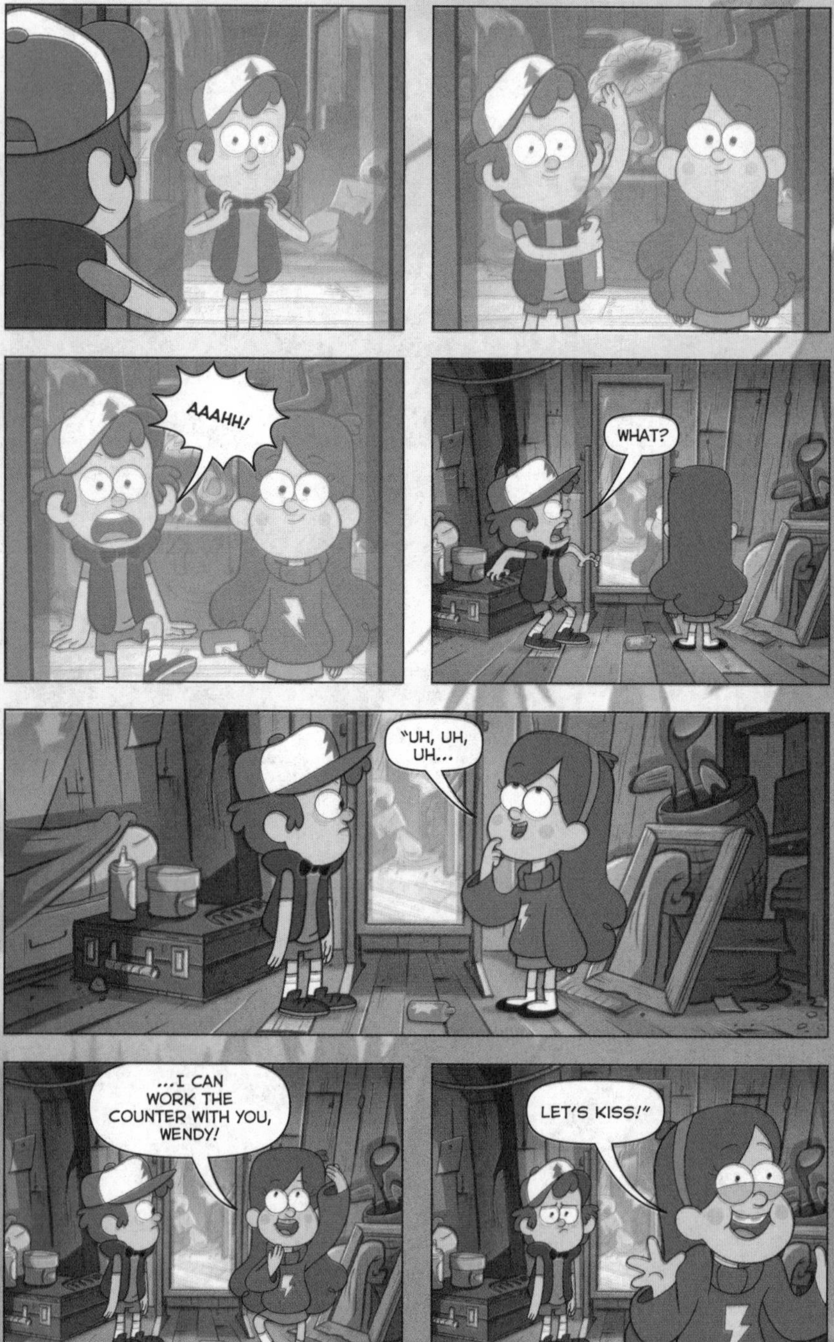
AAAHH!
WHAT?
"UH, UH, UH...
...I CAN WORK THE COUNTER WITH YOU, WENDY!
LET'S KISS!"

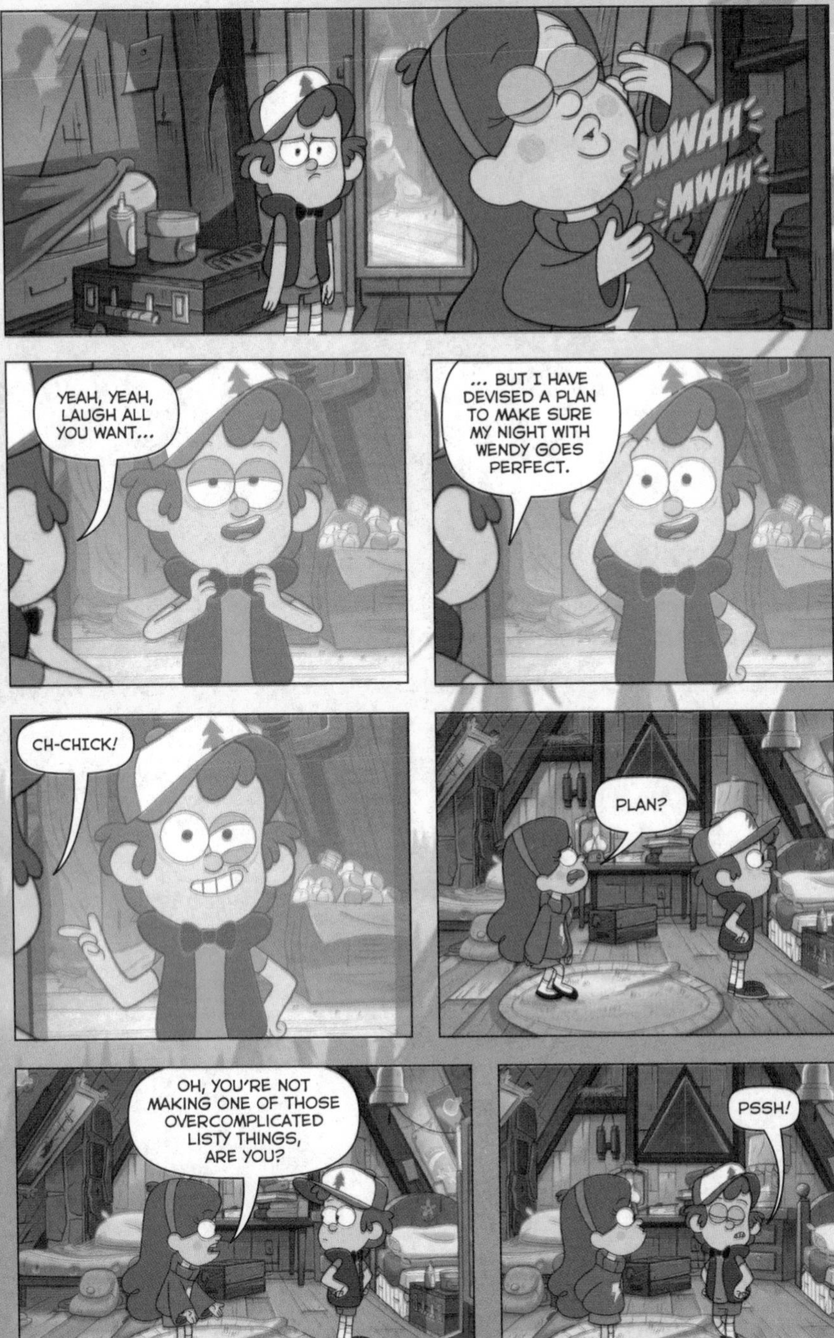
MWAH
MWAH
YEAH, YEAH, LAUGH ALL YOU WANT...
... BUT I HAVE DEVISED A PLAN TO MAKE SURE MY NIGHT WITH WENDY GOES PERFECT.
CH-CHICK!
PLAN?
OH, YOU'RE NOT MAKING ONE OF THOSE OVERCOMPLICATED LISTY THINGS, ARE YOU?
PSSH!

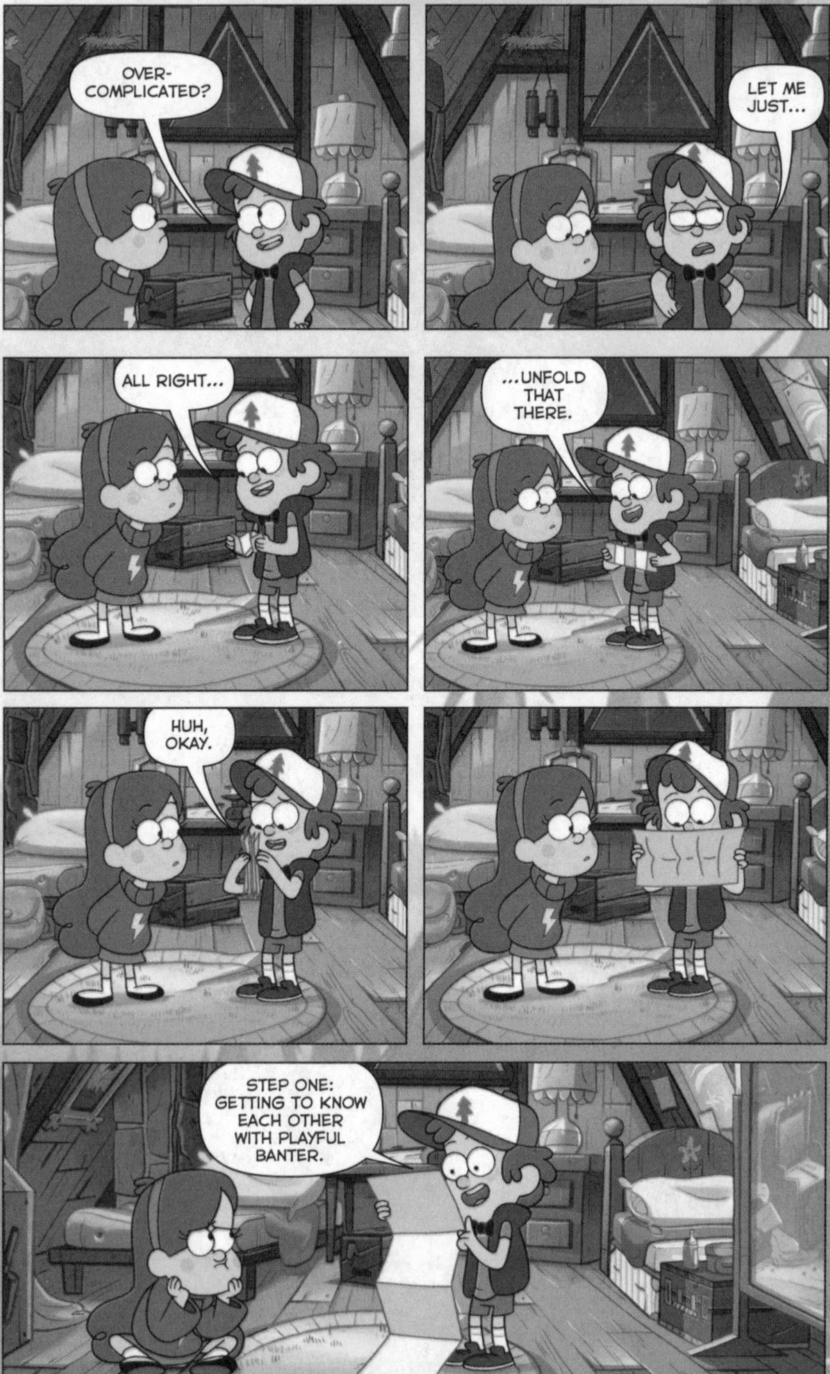
OVER-COMPLICATED?
LET ME JUST...
ALL RIGHT...
...UNFOLD THAT THERE.
HUH, OKAY.
STEP ONE: GETTING TO KNOW EACH OTHER WITH PLAYFUL BANTER.

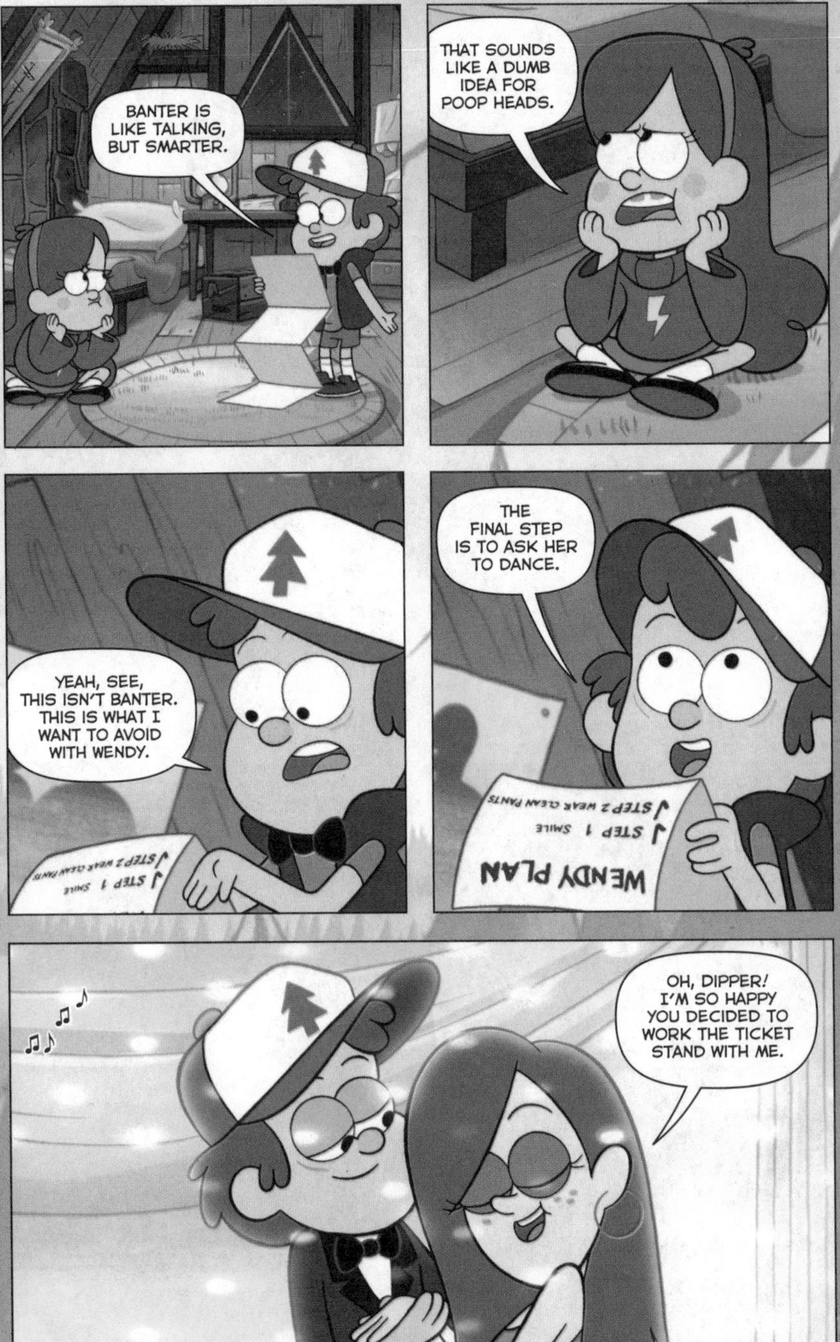

BANTER IS LIKE TALKING, BUT SMARTER.
THAT SOUNDS LIKE A DUMB IDEA FOR POOP HEADS.
YEAH, SEE, THIS ISN'T BANTER. THIS IS WHAT I WANT TO AVOID WITH WENDY.
THE FINAL STEP IS TO ASK HER TO DANCE.
WENDY PLAN
STEP 1 SMILE
STEP 2 WEAR CLEAN PANTS
OH, DIPPER! I'M SO HAPPY YOU DECIDED TO WORK THE TICKET STAND WITH ME.

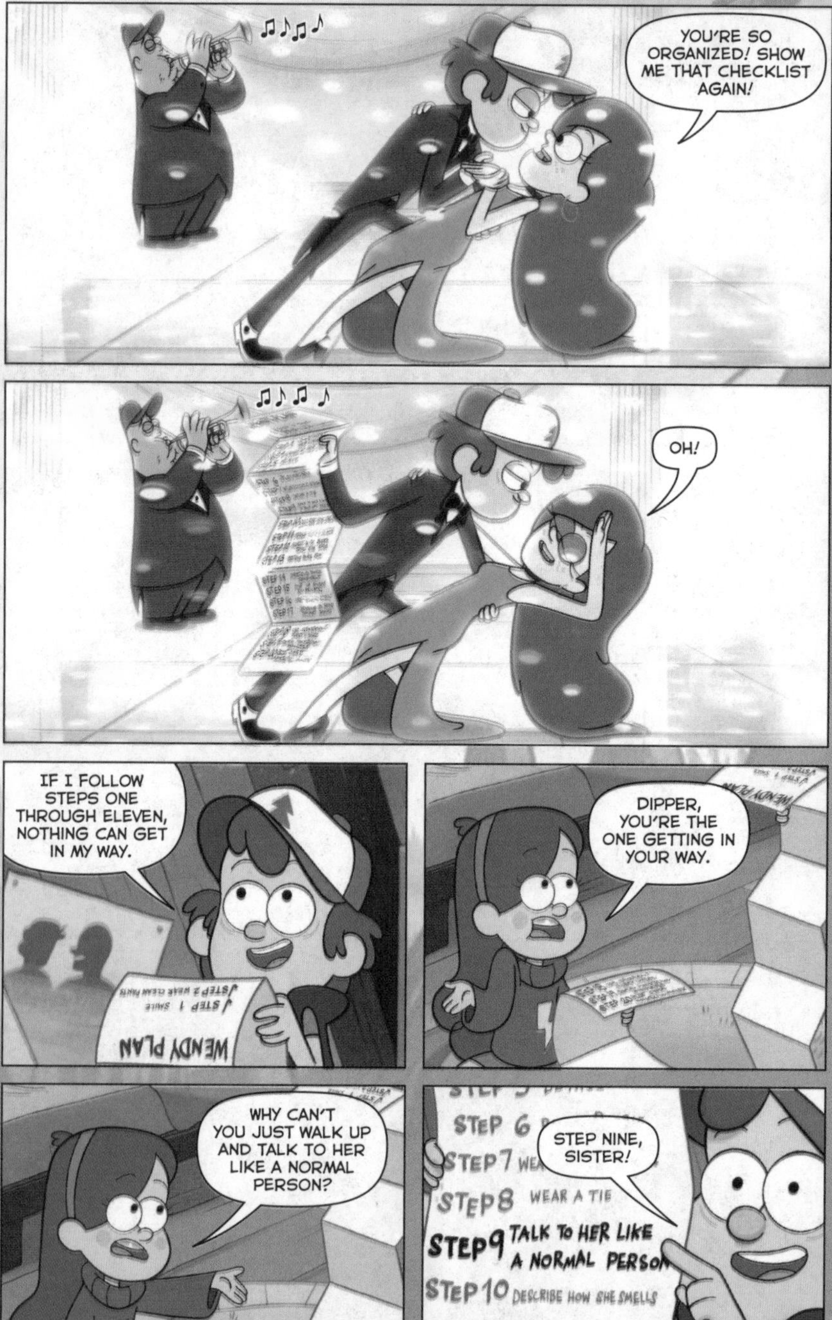

YOU'RE SO ORGANIZED! SHOW ME THAT CHECKLIST AGAIN!
OH!
IF I FOLLOW STEPS ONE THROUGH ELEVEN, NOTHING CAN GET IN MY WAY.
DIPPER, YOU'RE THE ONE GETTING IN YOUR WAY.
WHY CAN'T YOU JUST WALK UP AND TALK TO HER LIKE A NORMAL PERSON?
STEP 8 WEAR A TIE
STEP 9 TALK TO HER LIKE A NORMAL PERSON
STEP 10 DESCRIBE HOW SHE SMELLS
STEP 11 MAKE HER LAUGH
STEP 12 AGREE WITH EVERY-THING SHE SAYS
STEP NINE, SISTER!

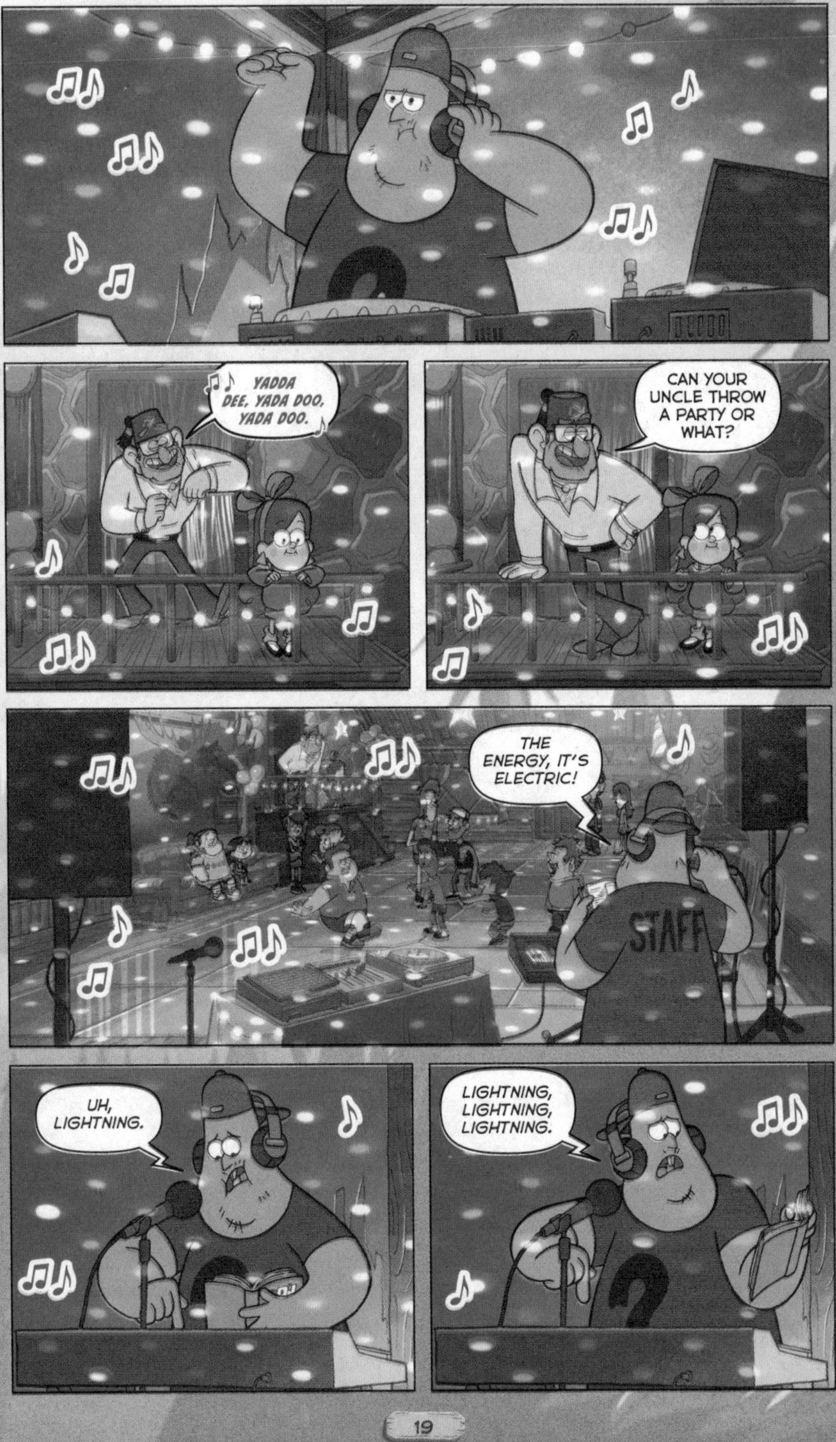

YADDA DEE, YADA DOO, YADA DOO.
CAN YOUR UNCLE THROW A PARTY OR WHAT?
THE ENERGY, IT'S ELECTRIC!
STAFF
UH, LIGHTNING.
LIGHTNING, LIGHTNING, LIGHTNING.

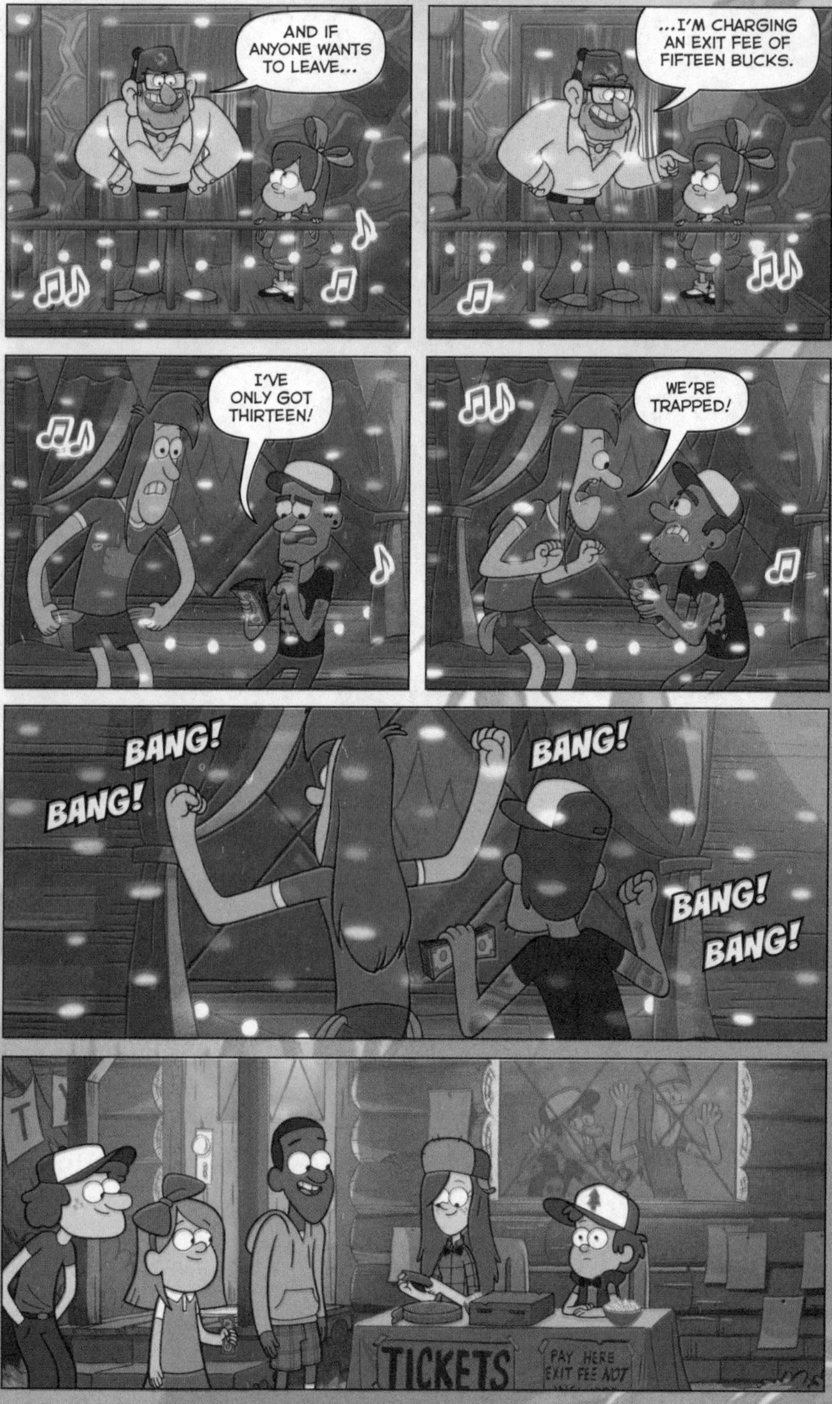
AND IF ANYONE WANTS TO LEAVE...
...I'M CHARGING AN EXIT FEE OF FIFTEEN BUCKS.
I'VE ONLY GOT THIRTEEN!
WE'RE TRAPPED!
BANG!
BANG!
BANG!
BANG!
BANG!
TICKETS
PAY HERE
EXIT FEE NOT

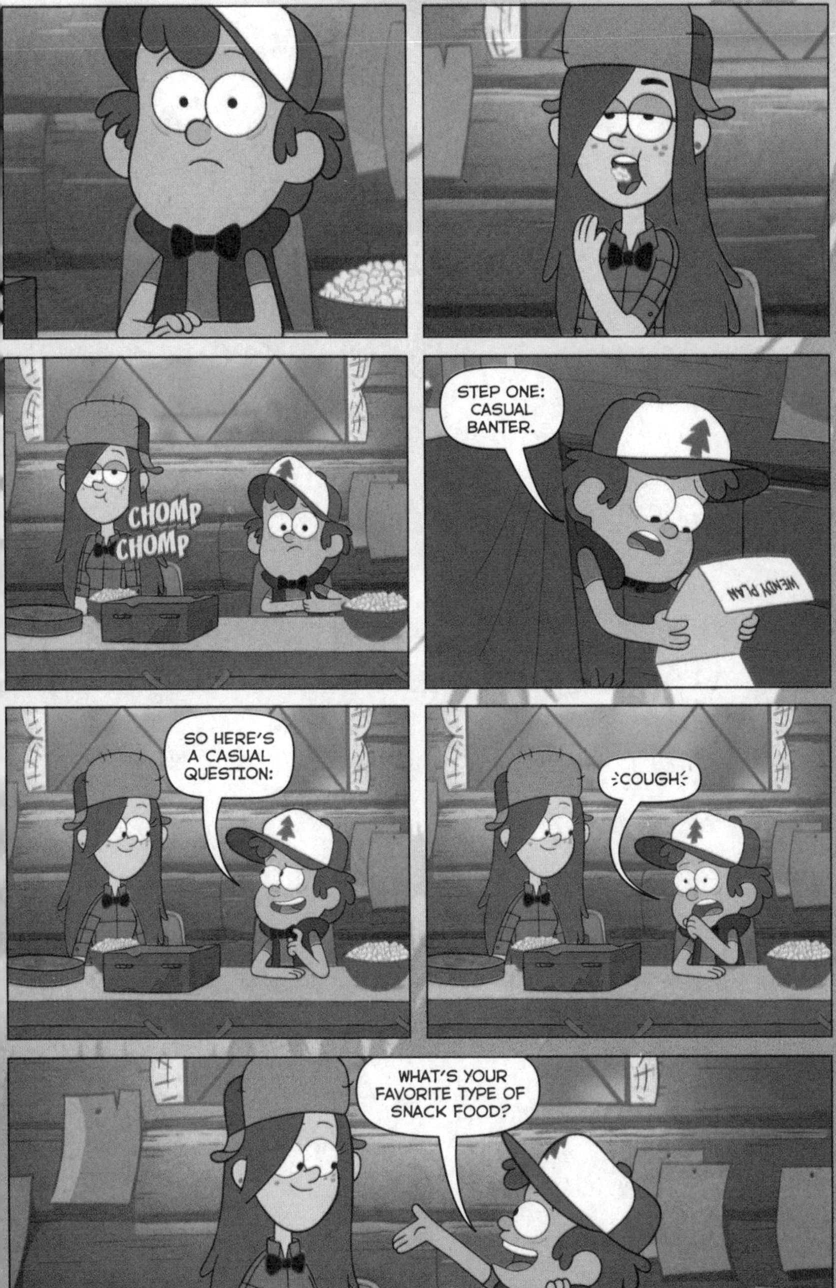
CHOMP
CHOMP
STEP ONE: CASUAL BANTER.
WENDY PLAN
SO HERE'S A CASUAL QUESTION:
COUGH
WHAT'S YOUR FAVORITE TYPE OF SNACK FOOD?

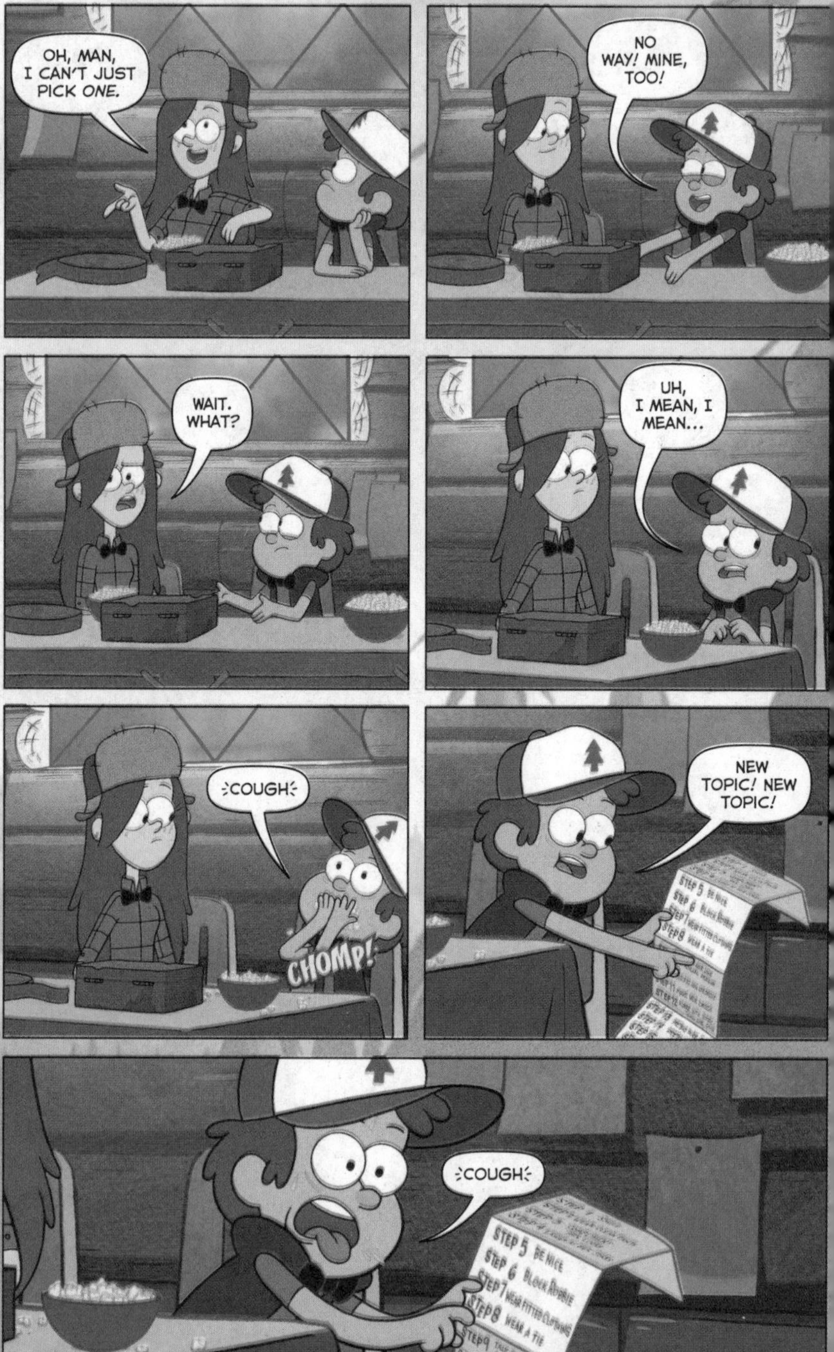
OH, MAN, I CAN'T JUST PICK ONE.
NO WAY! MINE, TOO!
WAIT. WHAT?
UH, I MEAN, I MEAN...
:COUGH:
CHOMP!
NEW TOPIC! NEW TOPIC!
:COUGH:
STEP 5 BE NICE
STEP 6 BLOCK ROBBIE
STEP 7 WEAR FITTED CLOTHING
STEP 8 WEAR A TIE

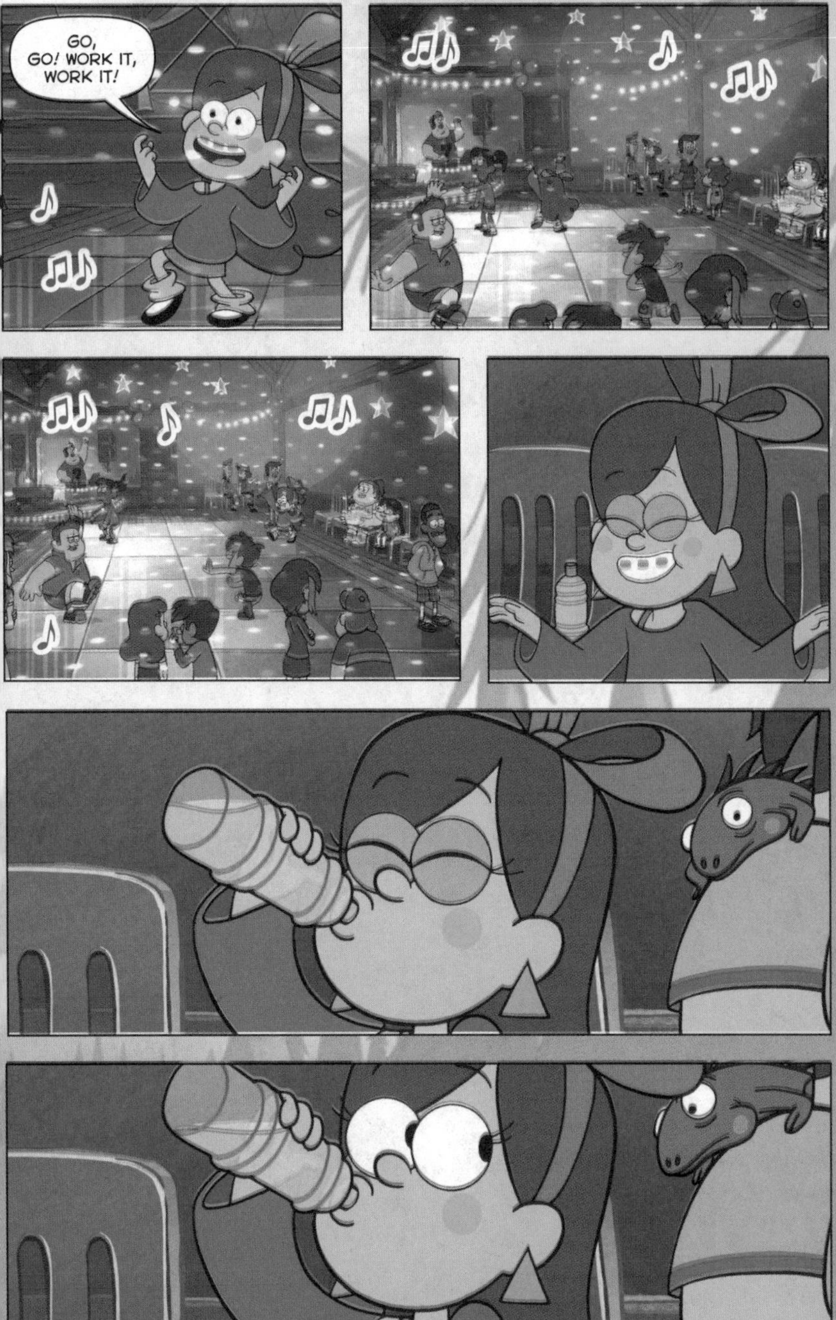
GO, GO! WORK IT, WORK IT!

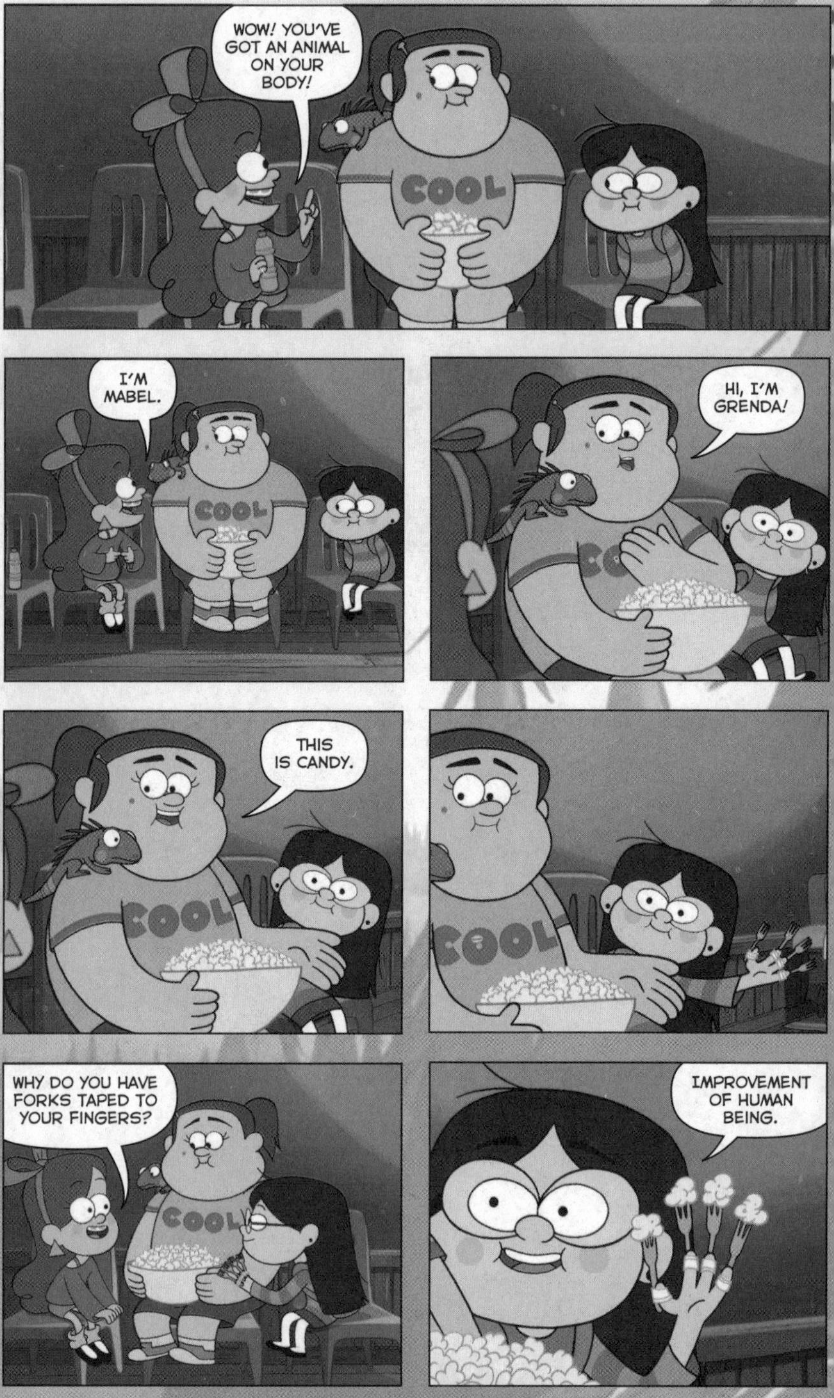
WOW! YOU'VE GOT AN ANIMAL ON YOUR BODY!
I'M MABEL.
HI, I'M GRENDA!
COOL
THIS IS CANDY.
WHY DO YOU HAVE FORKS TAPED TO YOUR FINGERS?
IMPROVEMENT OF HUMAN BEING.

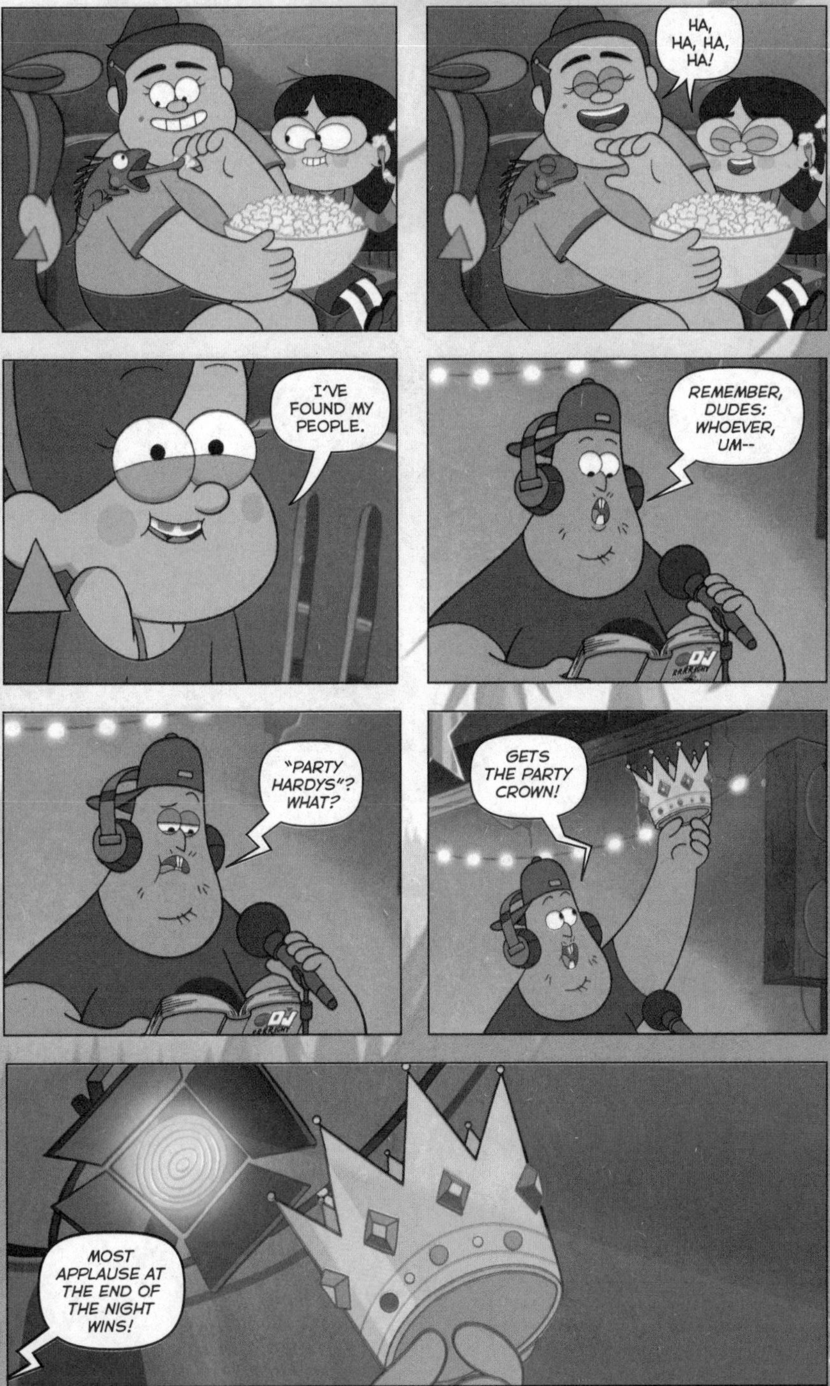
HA, HA, HA, HA!
I'VE FOUND MY PEOPLE.
REMEMBER, DUDES: WHOEVER, UM--
"PARTY HARDYS"? WHAT?
GETS THE PARTY CROWN!
MOST APPLAUSE AT THE END OF THE NIGHT WINS!

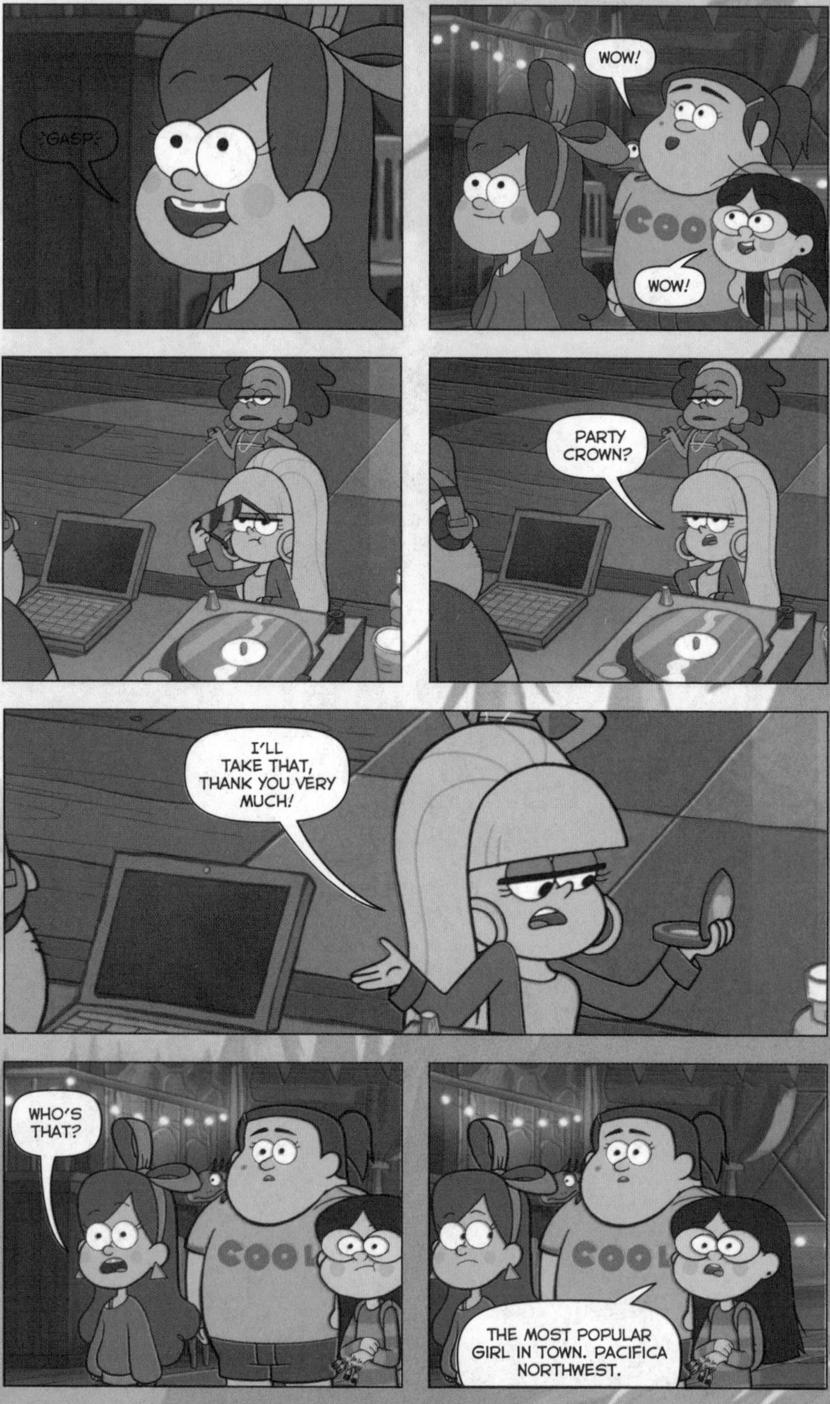
GASP
WOW!
WOW!
PARTY CROWN?
I'LL TAKE THAT, THANK YOU VERY MUCH!
WHO'S THAT?
THE MOST POPULAR GIRL IN TOWN. PACIFICA NORTHWEST.

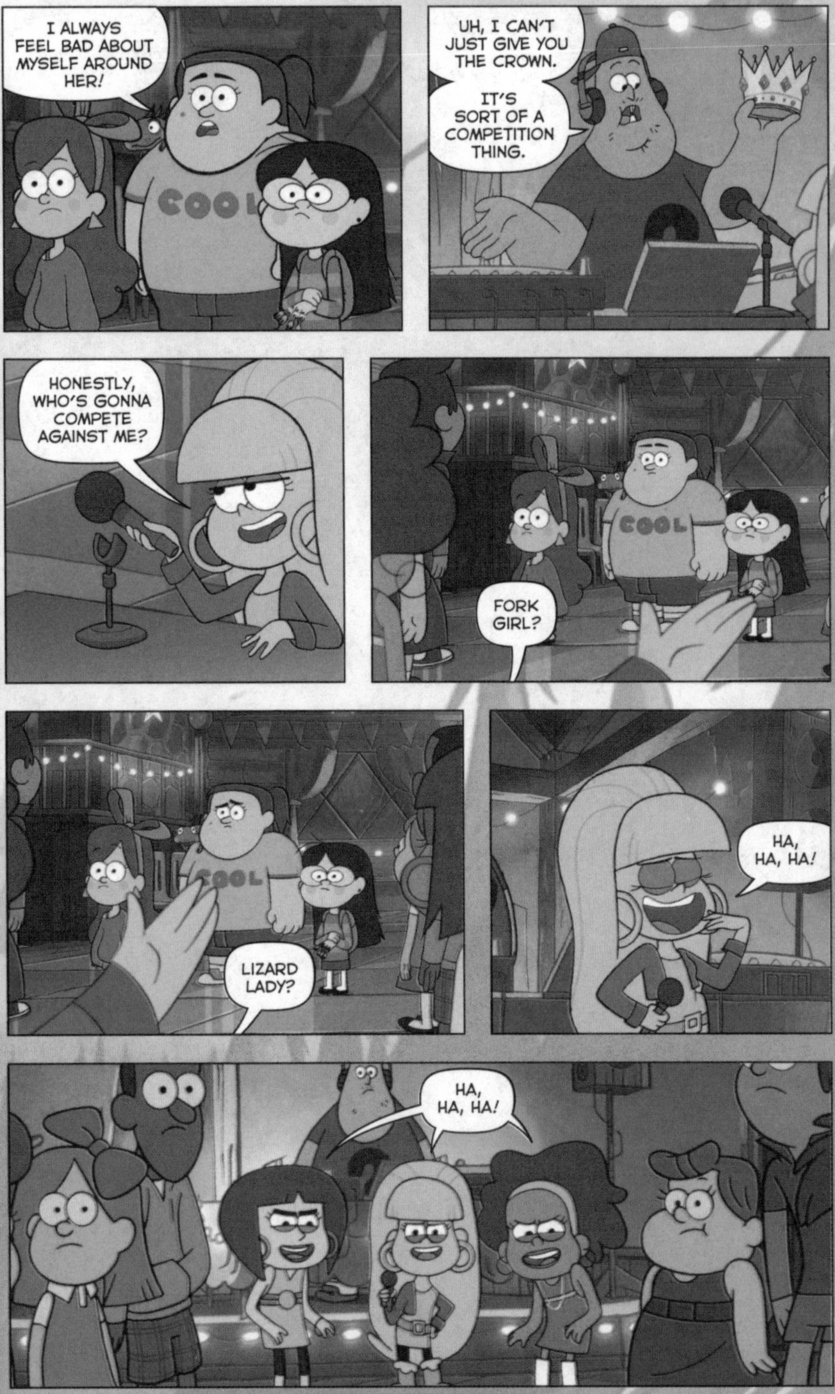
I ALWAYS FEEL BAD ABOUT MYSELF AROUND HER!
COOL
UH, I CAN'T JUST GIVE YOU THE CROWN.
IT'S SORT OF A COMPETITION THING.
HONESTLY, WHO'S GONNA COMPETE AGAINST ME?
COOL
FORK GIRL?
COOL
LIZARD LADY?
HA, HA, HA!
HA, HA, HA!

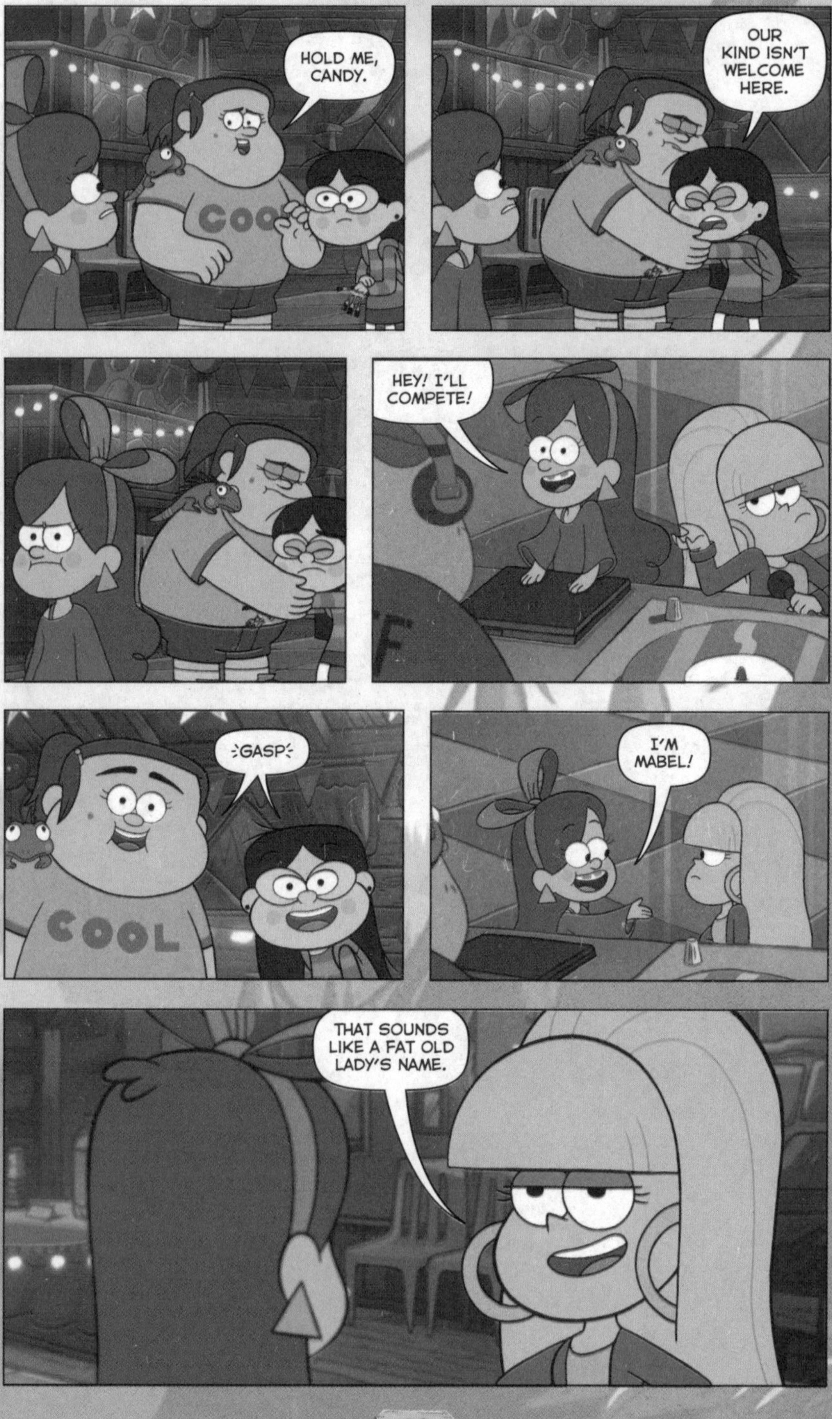
HOLD ME, CANDY.
OUR KIND ISN'T WELCOME HERE.
HEY! I'LL COMPETE!
GASP
I'M MABEL!
THAT SOUNDS LIKE A FAT OLD LADY'S NAME.

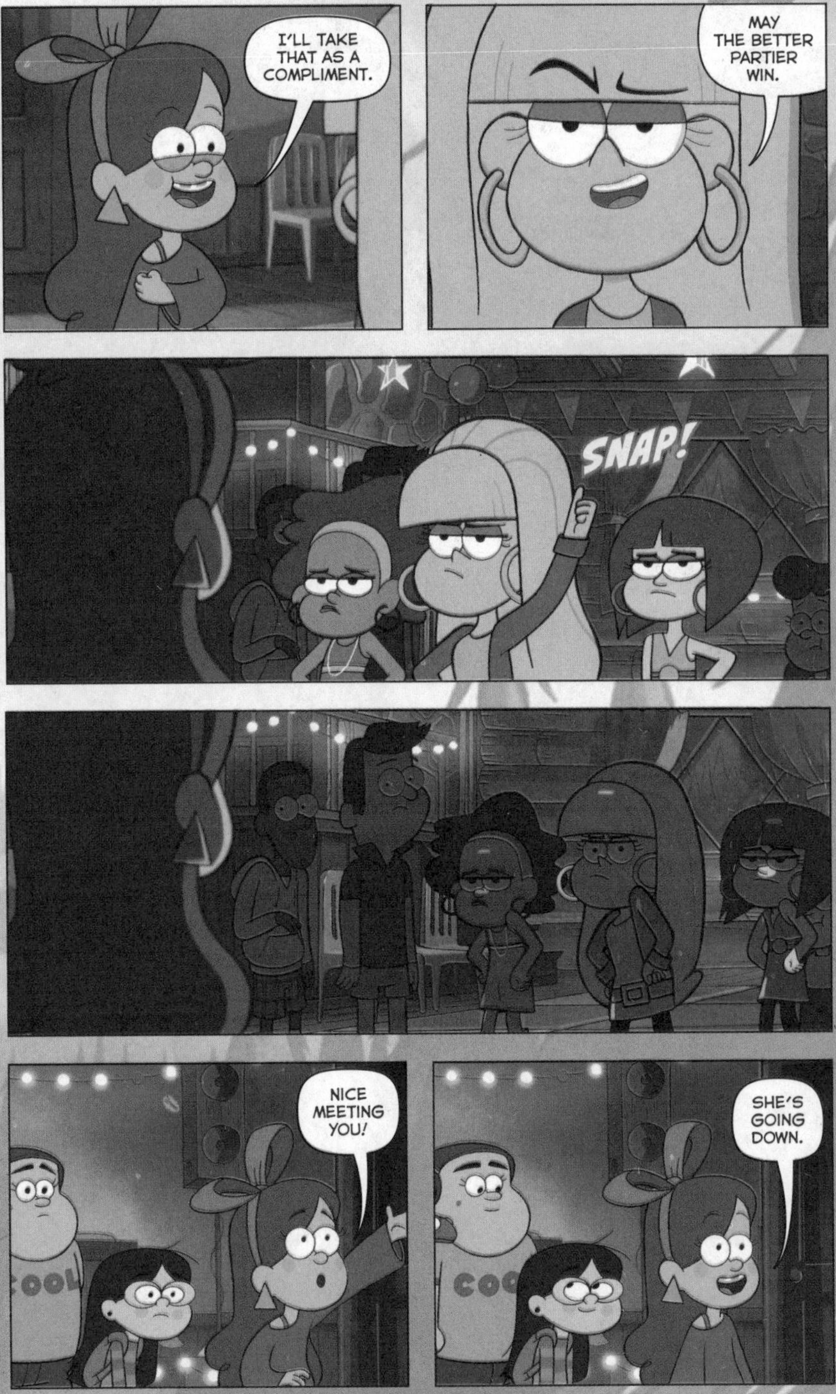
I'LL TAKE THAT AS A COMPLIMENT.
MAY THE BETTER PARTIER WIN.
SNAP!
NICE MEETING YOU!
SHE'S GOING DOWN.
COOL

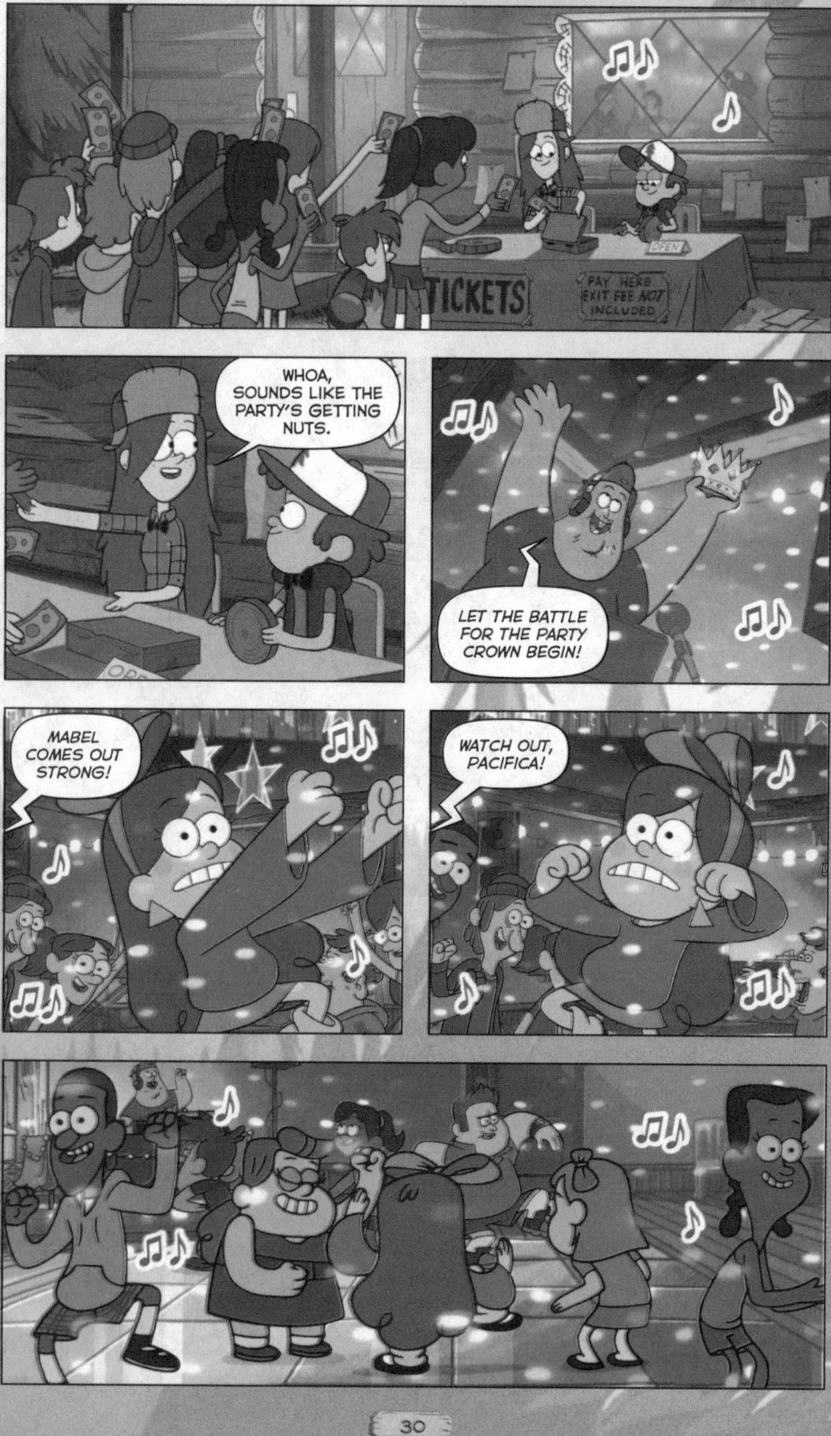
TICKETS
PAY HERE
EXIT FEE NOT INCLUDED
OPEN
WHOA, SOUNDS LIKE THE PARTY'S GETTING NUTS.
LET THE BATTLE FOR THE PARTY CROWN BEGIN!
MABEL COMES OUT STRONG!
WATCH OUT, PACIFICA!

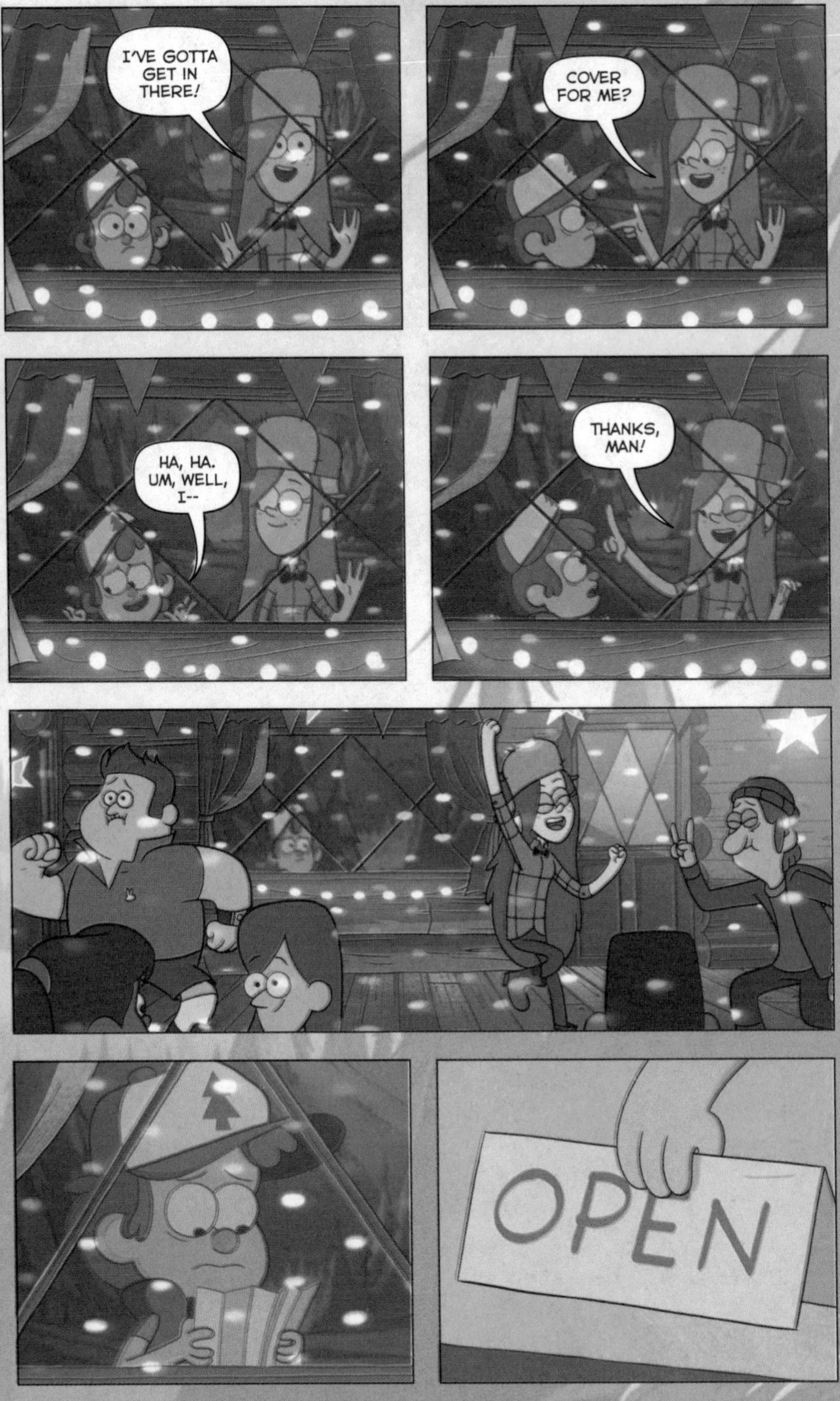
I'VE GOTTA GET IN THERE!
COVER FOR ME?
HA, HA. UM, WELL, I--
THANKS, MAN!
OPEN

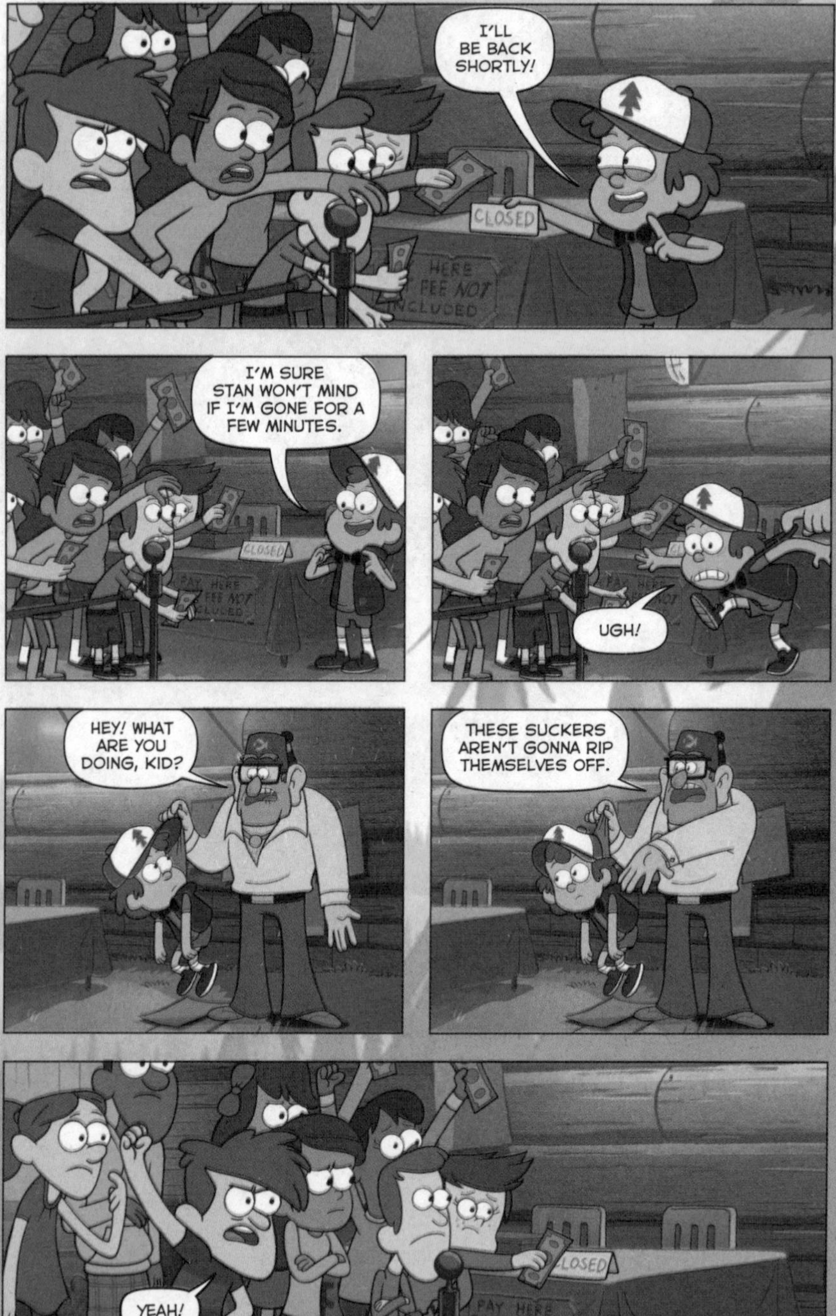
I'LL BE BACK SHORTLY!
CLOSED
I'M SURE STAN WON'T MIND IF I'M GONE FOR A FEW MINUTES.
CLOSED
UGH!
HEY! WHAT ARE YOU DOING, KID?
THESE SUCKERS AREN'T GONNA RIP THEMSELVES OFF.
YEAH!
CLOSED
PAY HERE
EXIT FEE NOT
INCLUDED

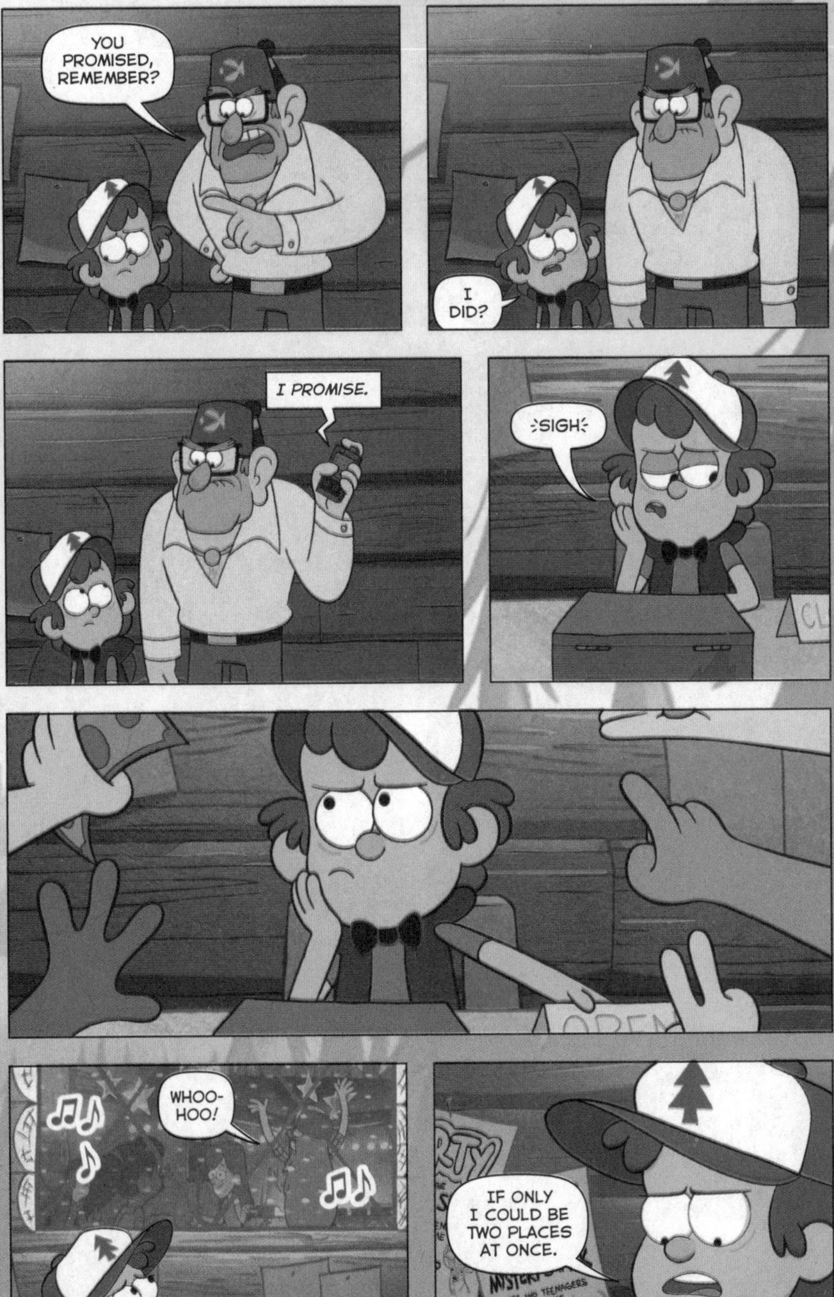
YOU PROMISED, REMEMBER?
I DID?
I PROMISE.
SIGH
WHOO-HOO!
IF ONLY I COULD BE TWO PLACES AT ONCE.
KIDS AND TEENAGERS WELCOME
FREE?

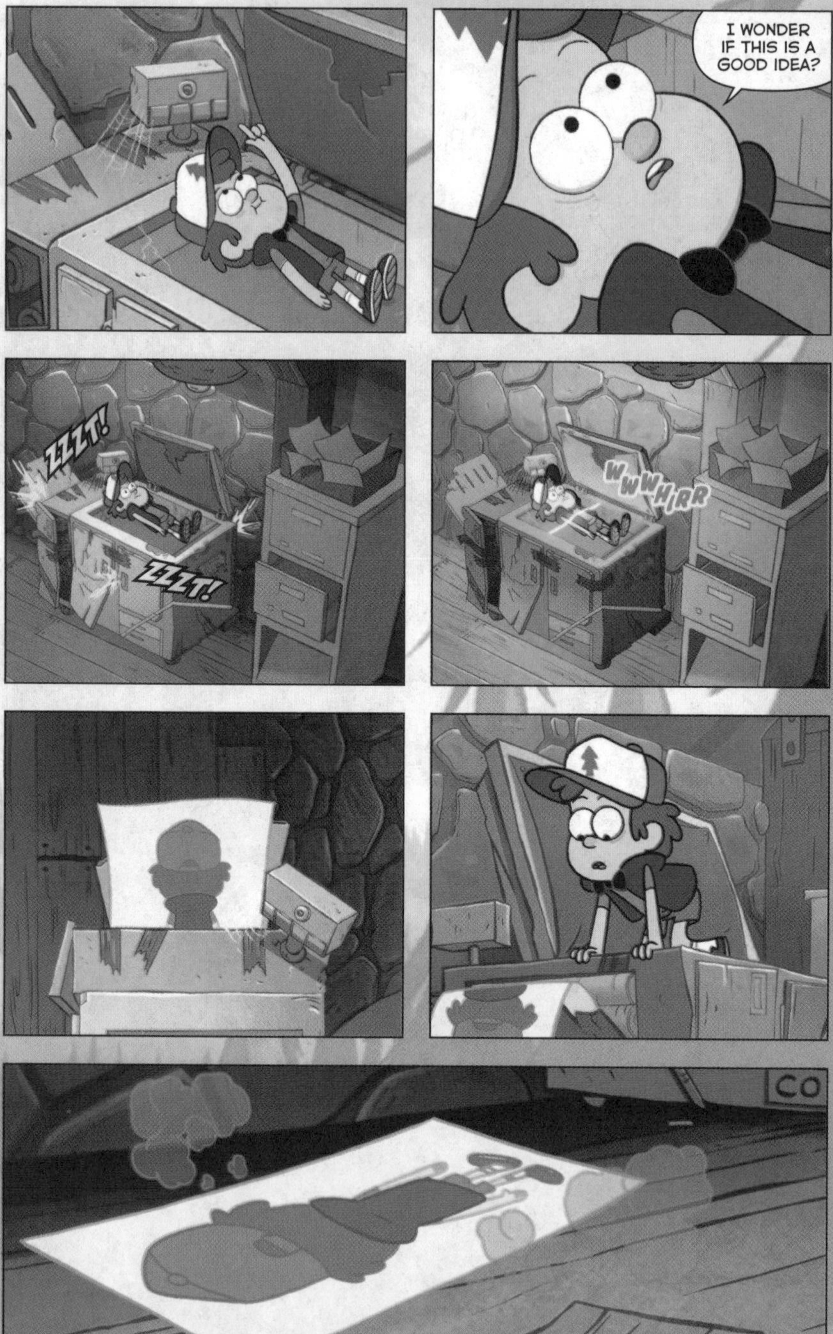
I WONDER IF THIS IS A GOOD IDEA?
ZZZT!
ZZZT!
WWWHIRR
CO

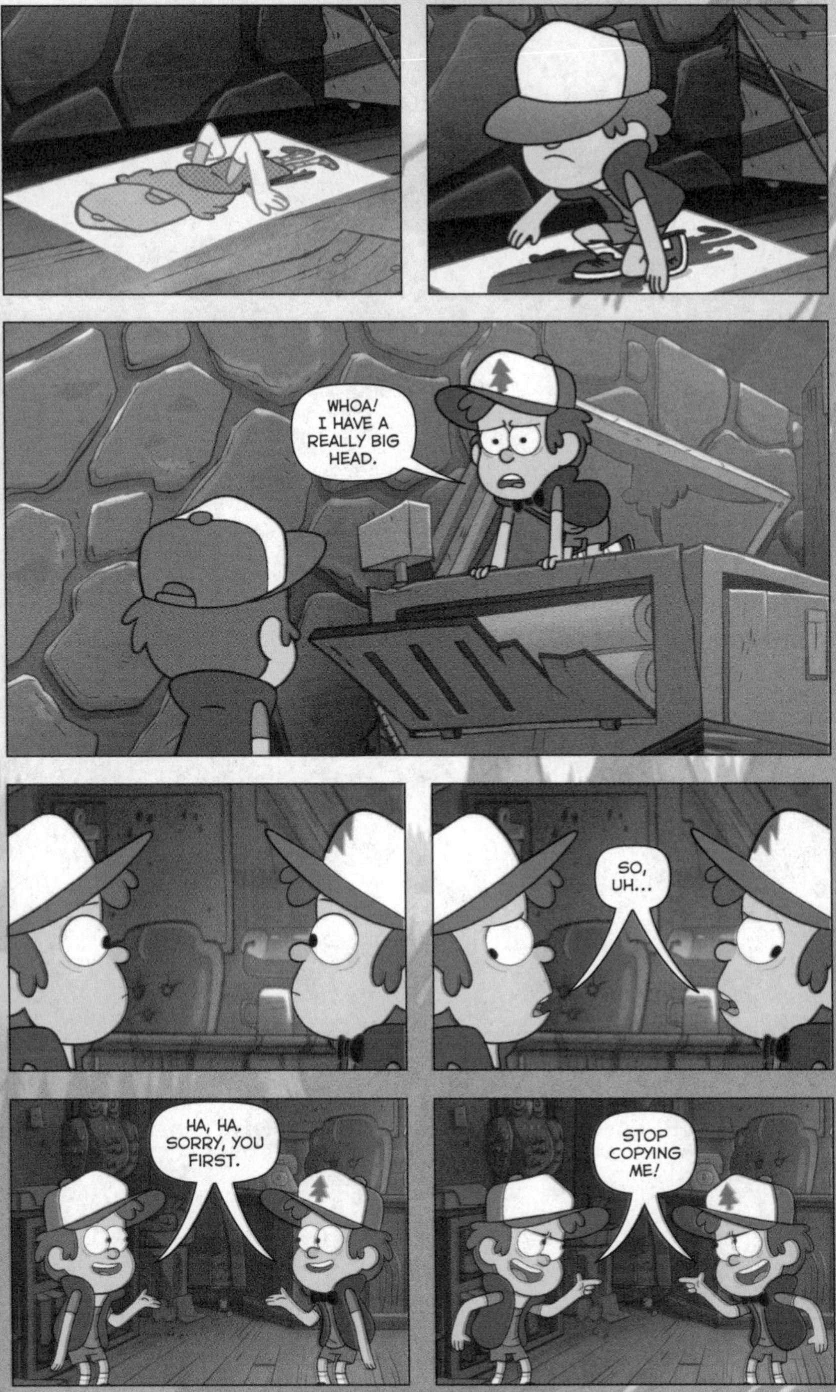
WHOA! I HAVE A REALLY BIG HEAD.
SO, UH...
HA, HA. SORRY, YOU FIRST.
STOP COPYING ME!

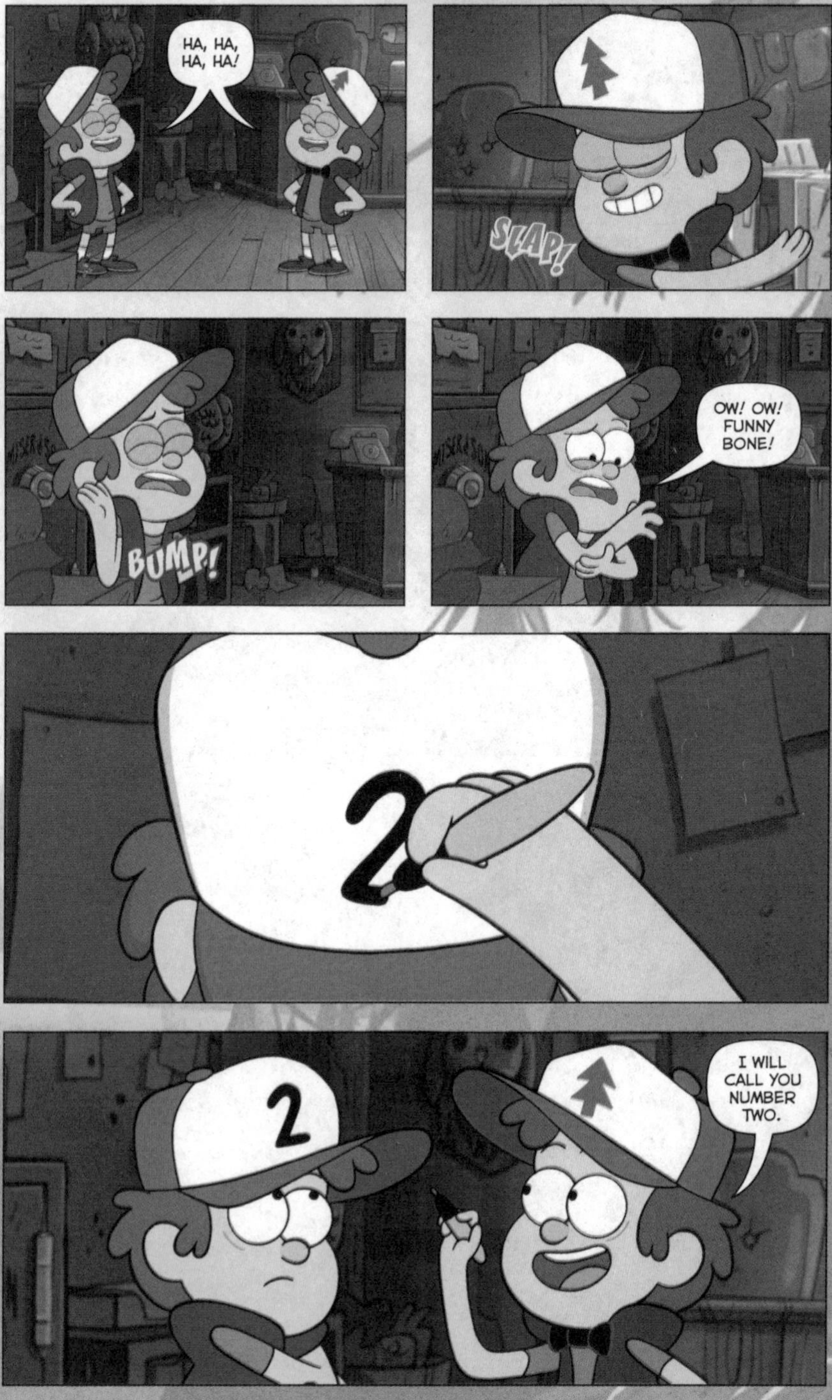
HA, HA,
HA, HA!
SLAP!
BUMP!
OW! OW!
FUNNY
BONE!
I WILL
CALL YOU
NUMBER
TWO.

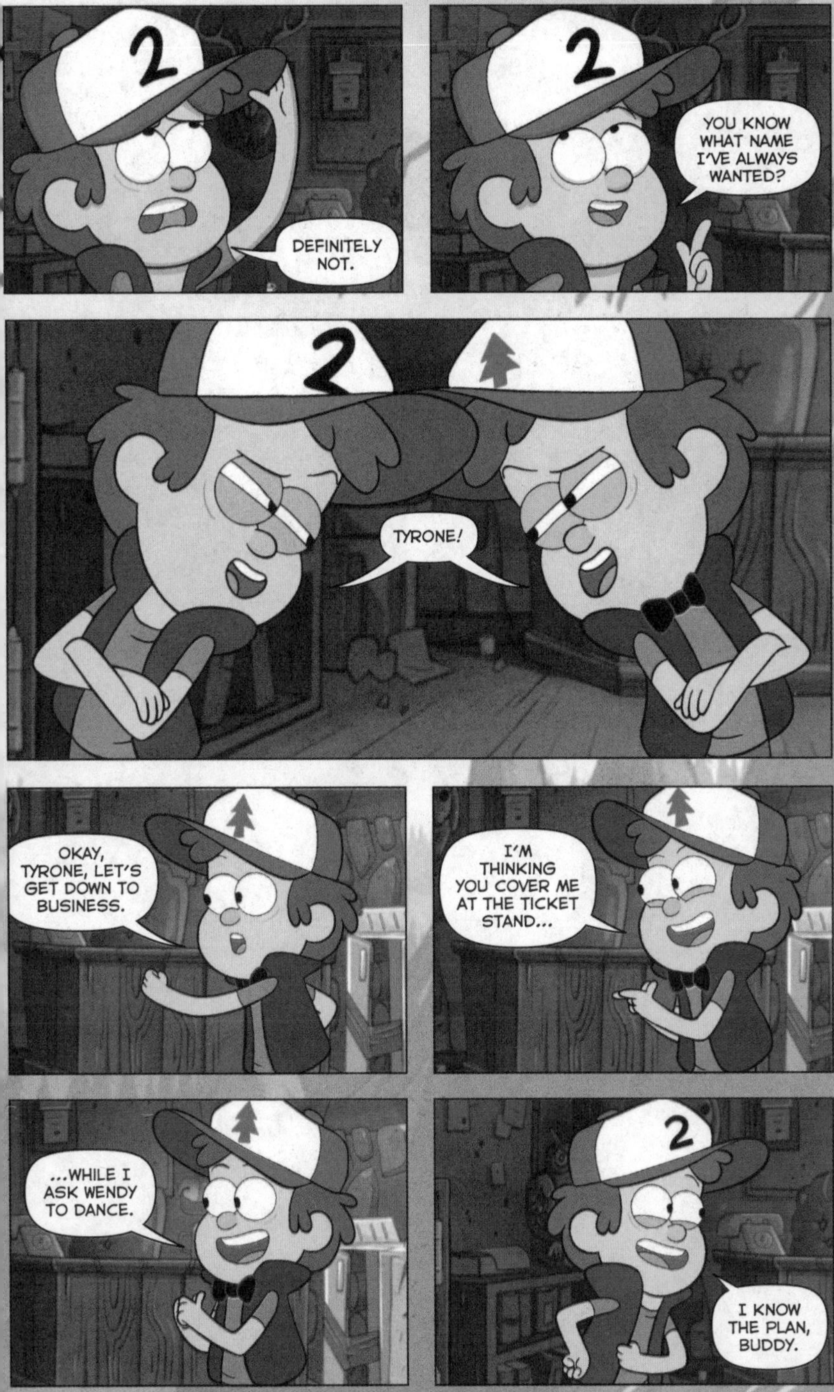
DEFINITELY NOT.
YOU KNOW WHAT NAME I'VE ALWAYS WANTED?
TYRONE!
OKAY, TYRONE, LET'S GET DOWN TO BUSINESS.
I'M THINKING YOU COVER ME AT THE TICKET STAND...
...WHILE I ASK WENDY TO DANCE.
I KNOW THE PLAN, BUDDY.

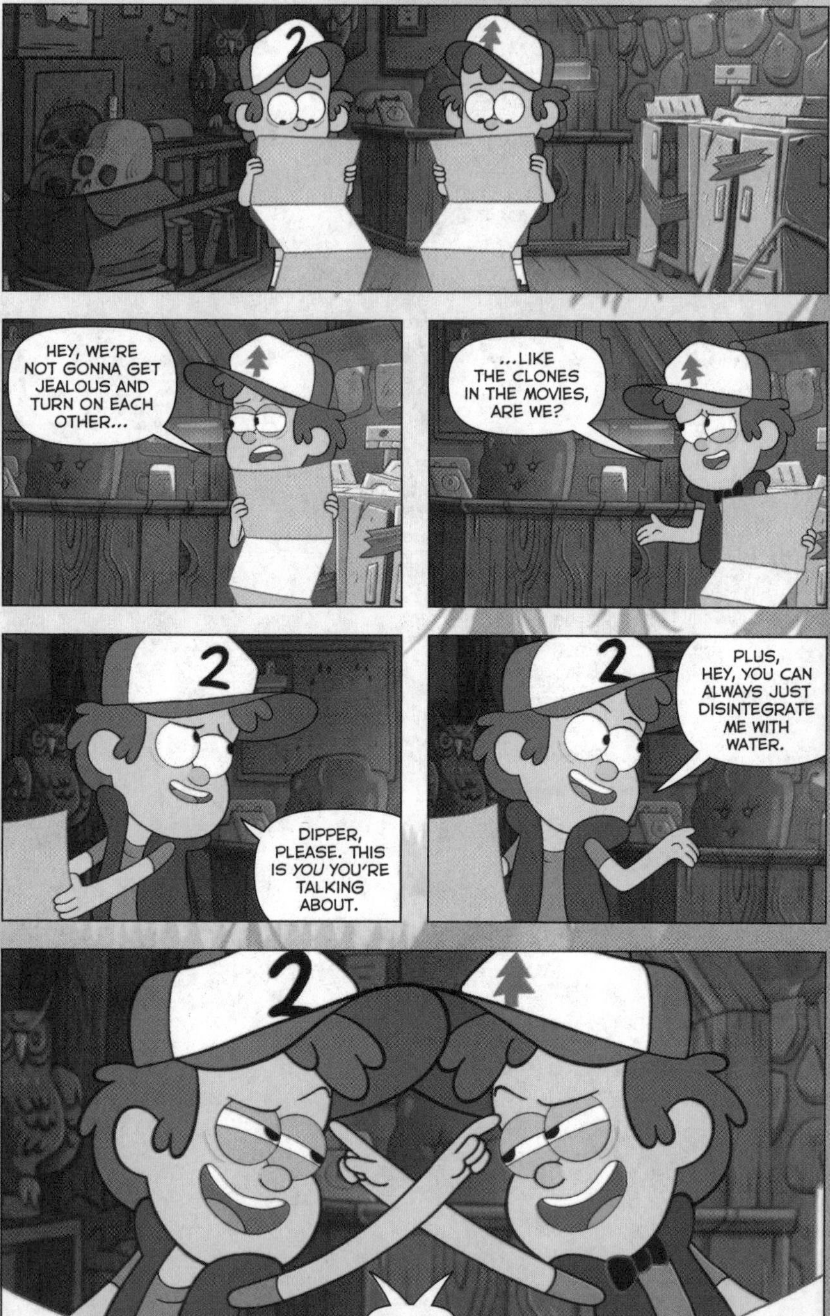

HEY, WE'RE NOT GONNA GET JEALOUS AND TURN ON EACH OTHER...
...LIKE THE CLONES IN THE MOVIES, ARE WE?
DIPPER, PLEASE. THIS IS *YOU* YOU'RE TALKING ABOUT.
PLUS, HEY, YOU CAN ALWAYS JUST DISINTEGRATE ME WITH WATER.
YEAH. YEAH!

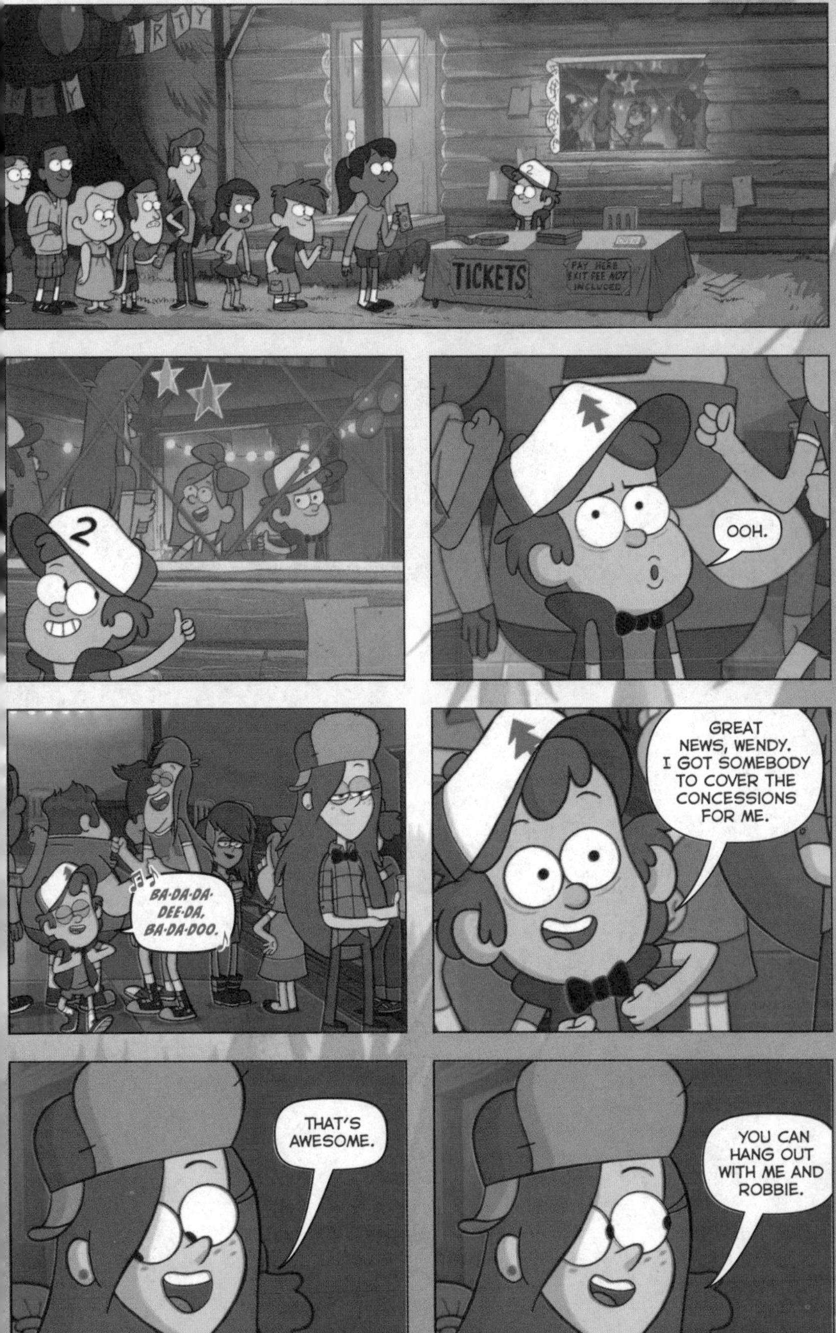
TICKETS
PAY HERE
EXIT FEE NOT INCLUDED
OOH.
BA-DA-DA-DEE-DA, BA-DA-DOO.
GREAT NEWS, WENDY. I GOT SOMEBODY TO COVER THE CONCESSIONS FOR ME.
THAT'S AWESOME.
YOU CAN HANG OUT WITH ME AND ROBBIE.

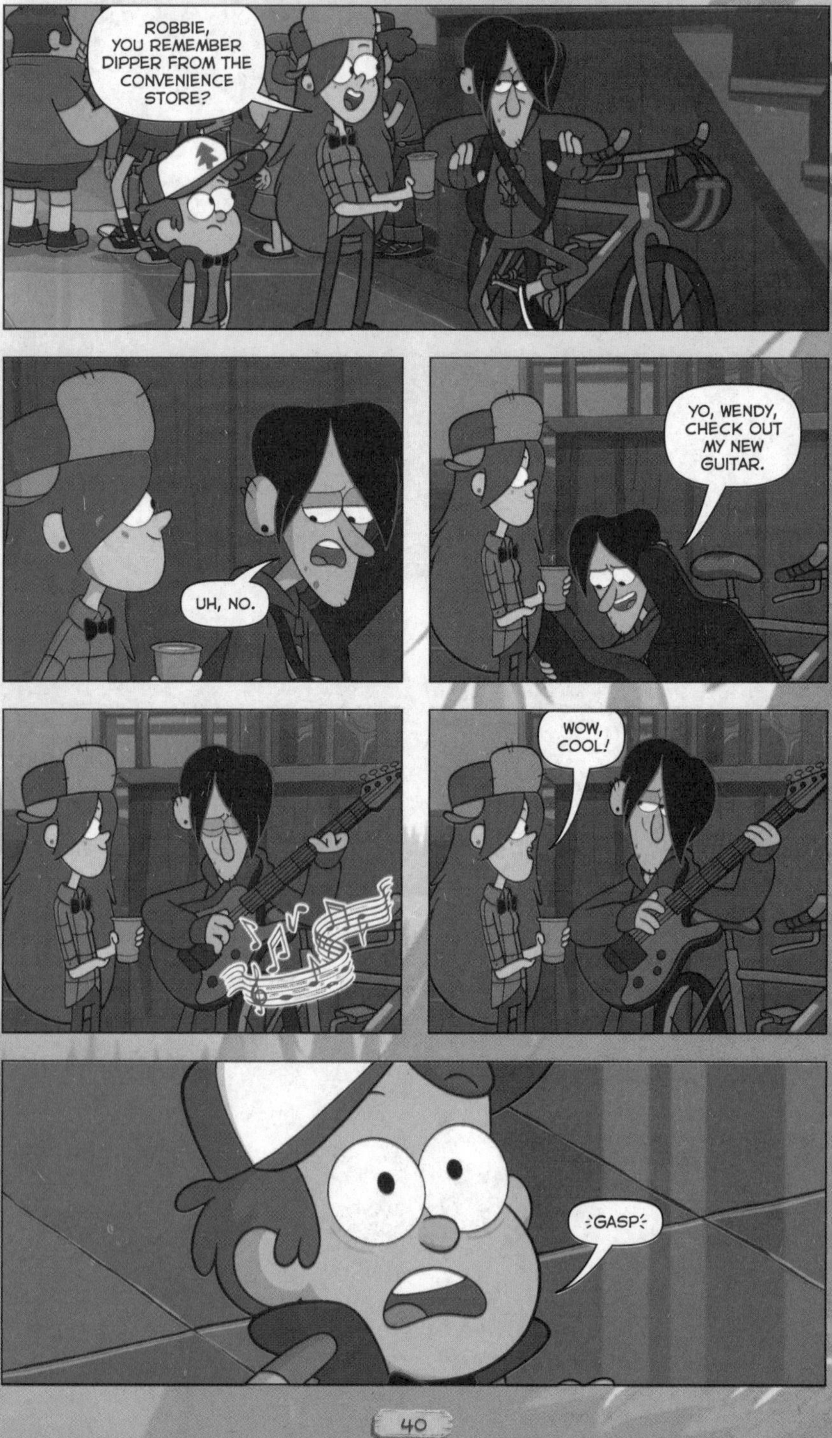
ROBBIE, YOU REMEMBER DIPPER FROM THE CONVENIENCE STORE?
UH, NO.
YO, WENDY, CHECK OUT MY NEW GUITAR.
WOW, COOL!
GASP

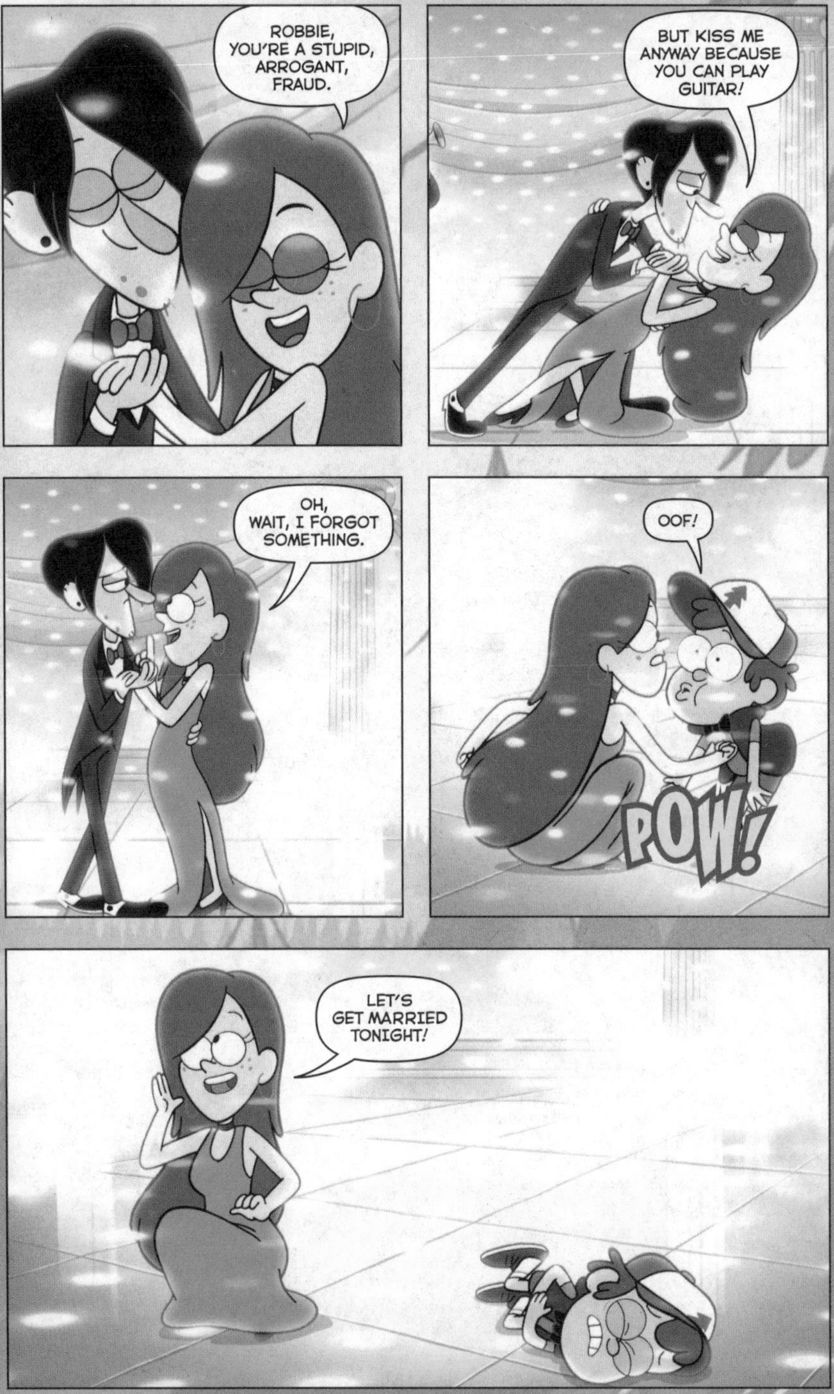
ROBBIE, YOU'RE A STUPID, ARROGANT, FRAUD.
BUT KISS ME ANYWAY BECAUSE YOU CAN PLAY GUITAR!
OH, WAIT, I FORGOT SOMETHING.
OOF!
POW!
LET'S GET MARRIED TONIGHT!

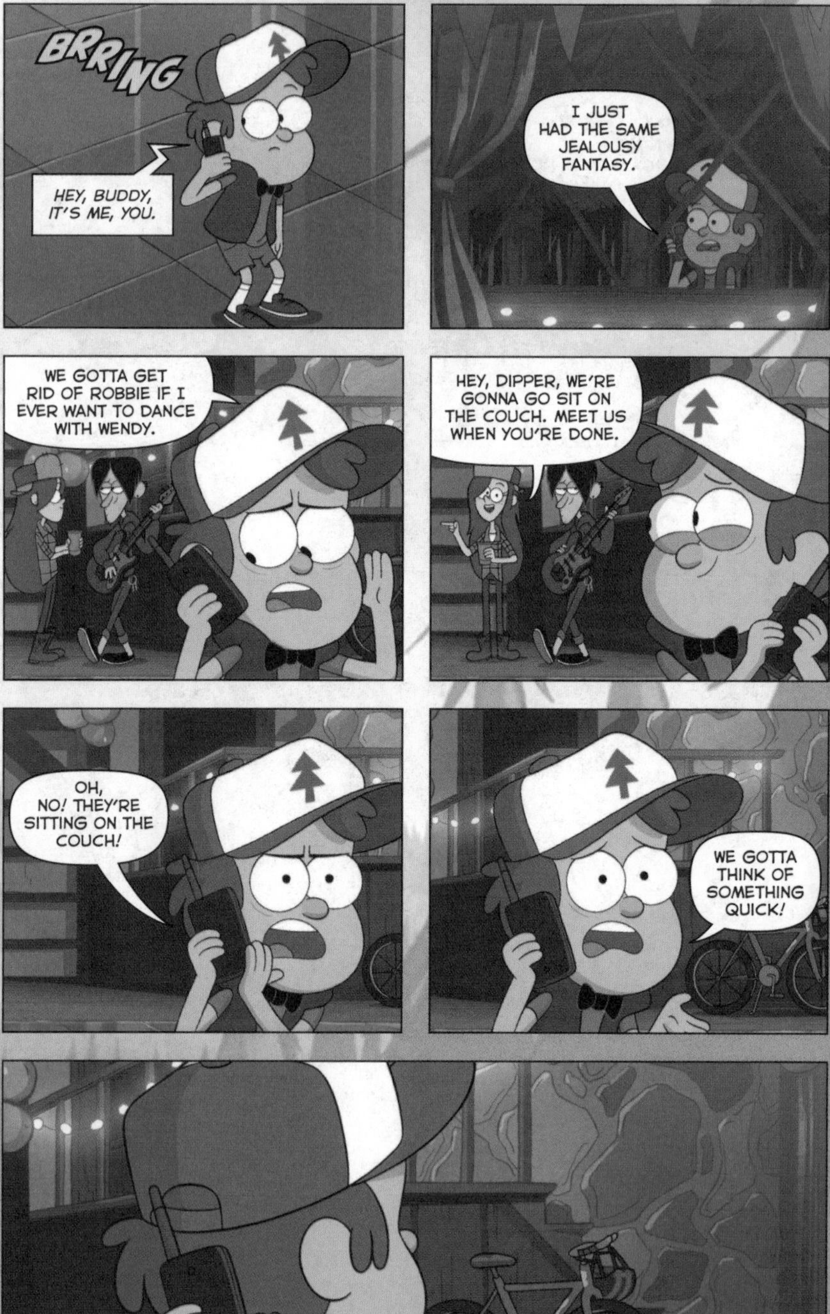
BRRING
HEY, BUDDY, IT'S ME, YOU.
I JUST HAD THE SAME JEALOUSY FANTASY.
WE GOTTA GET RID OF ROBBIE IF I EVER WANT TO DANCE WITH WENDY.
HEY, DIPPER, WE'RE GONNA GO SIT ON THE COUCH. MEET US WHEN YOU'RE DONE.
OH, NO! THEY'RE SITTING ON THE COUCH!
WE GOTTA THINK OF SOMETHING QUICK!

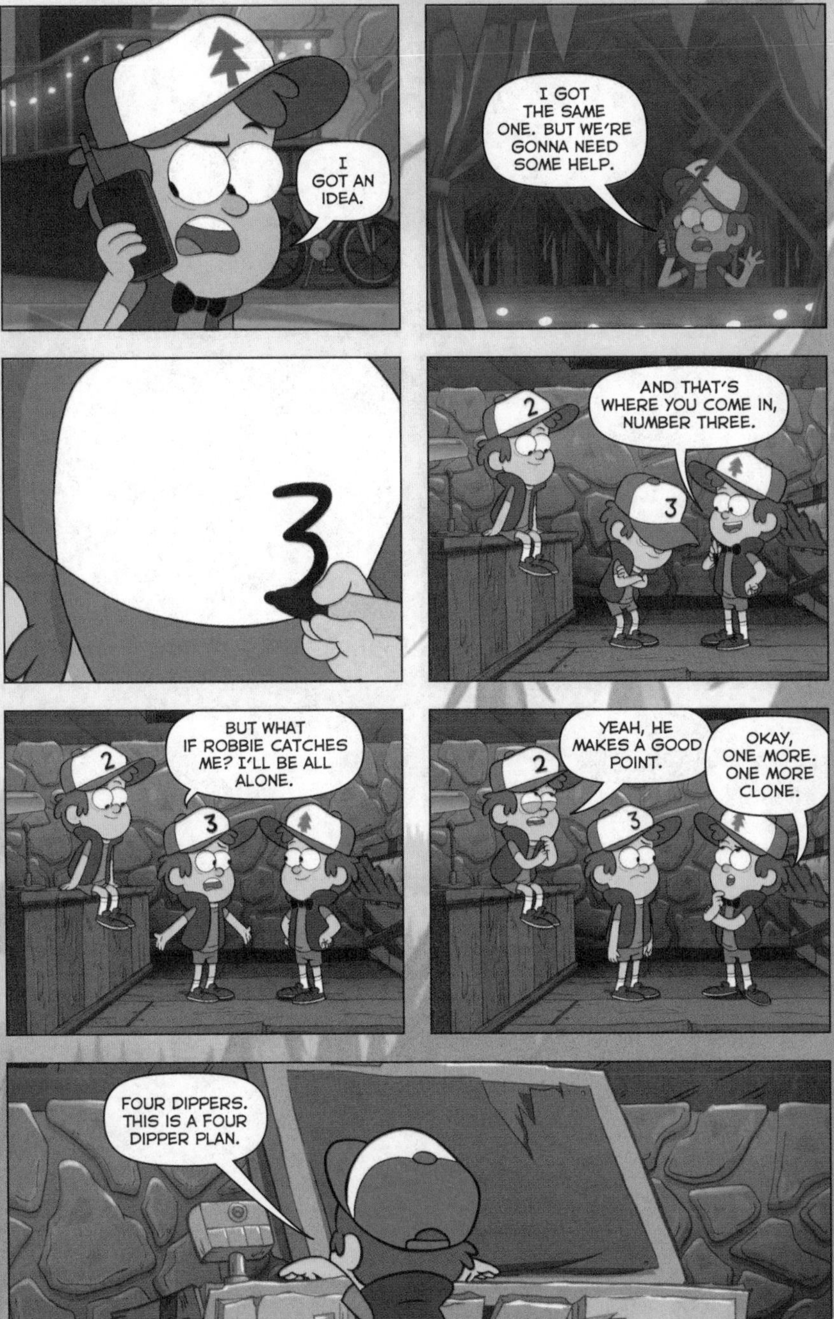
I GOT AN IDEA.
I GOT THE SAME ONE. BUT WE'RE GONNA NEED SOME HELP.
3
AND THAT'S WHERE YOU COME IN, NUMBER THREE.
BUT WHAT IF ROBBIE CATCHES ME? I'LL BE ALL ALONE.
YEAH, HE MAKES A GOOD POINT.
OKAY, ONE MORE. ONE MORE CLONE.
FOUR DIPPERS. THIS IS A FOUR DIPPER PLAN.

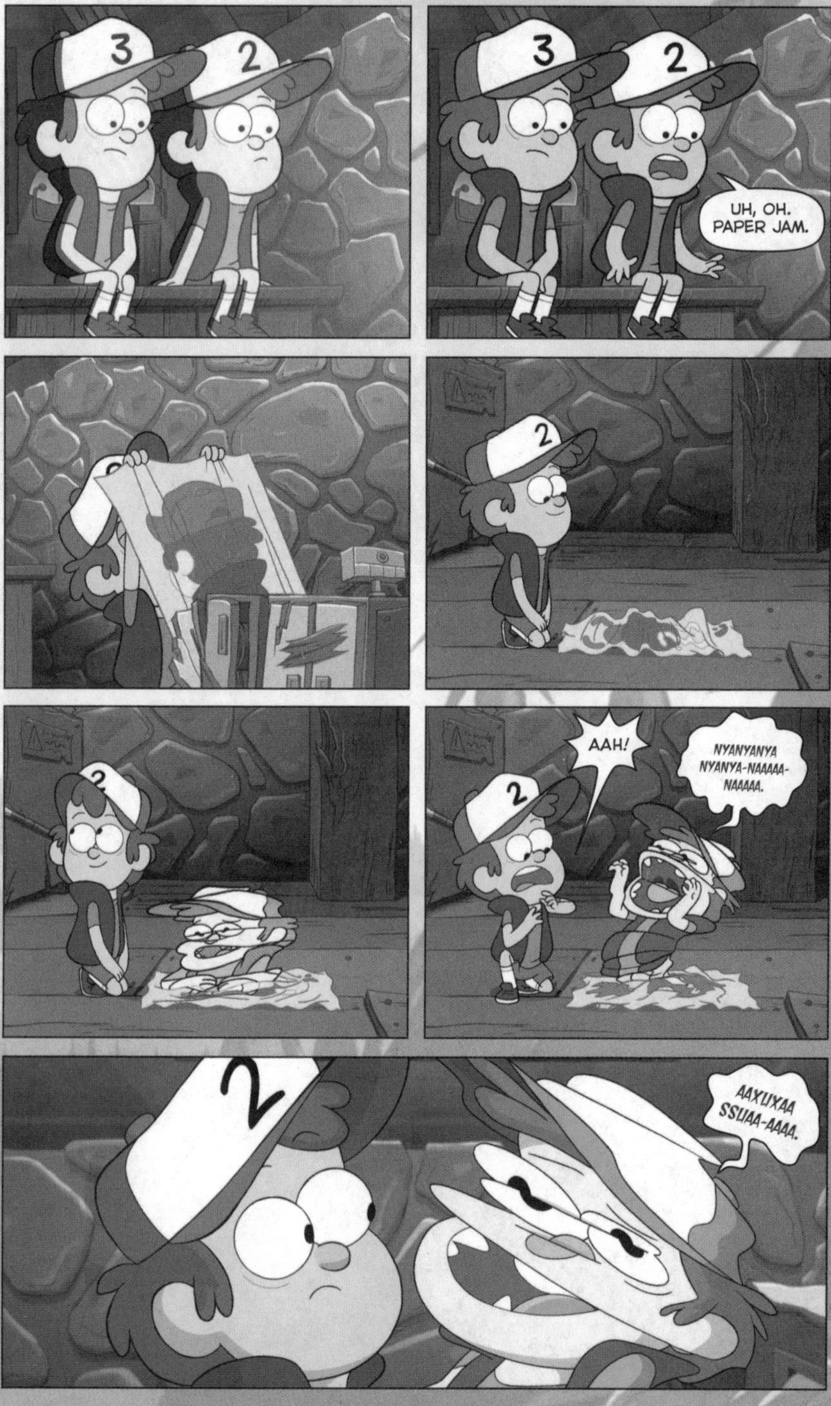
UH, OH.
PAPER JAM.
AAH!
NYANYANYA
NYANYA-NAAAAA-
NAAAAA.
AAXUXAA
SSUAA-AAAA.

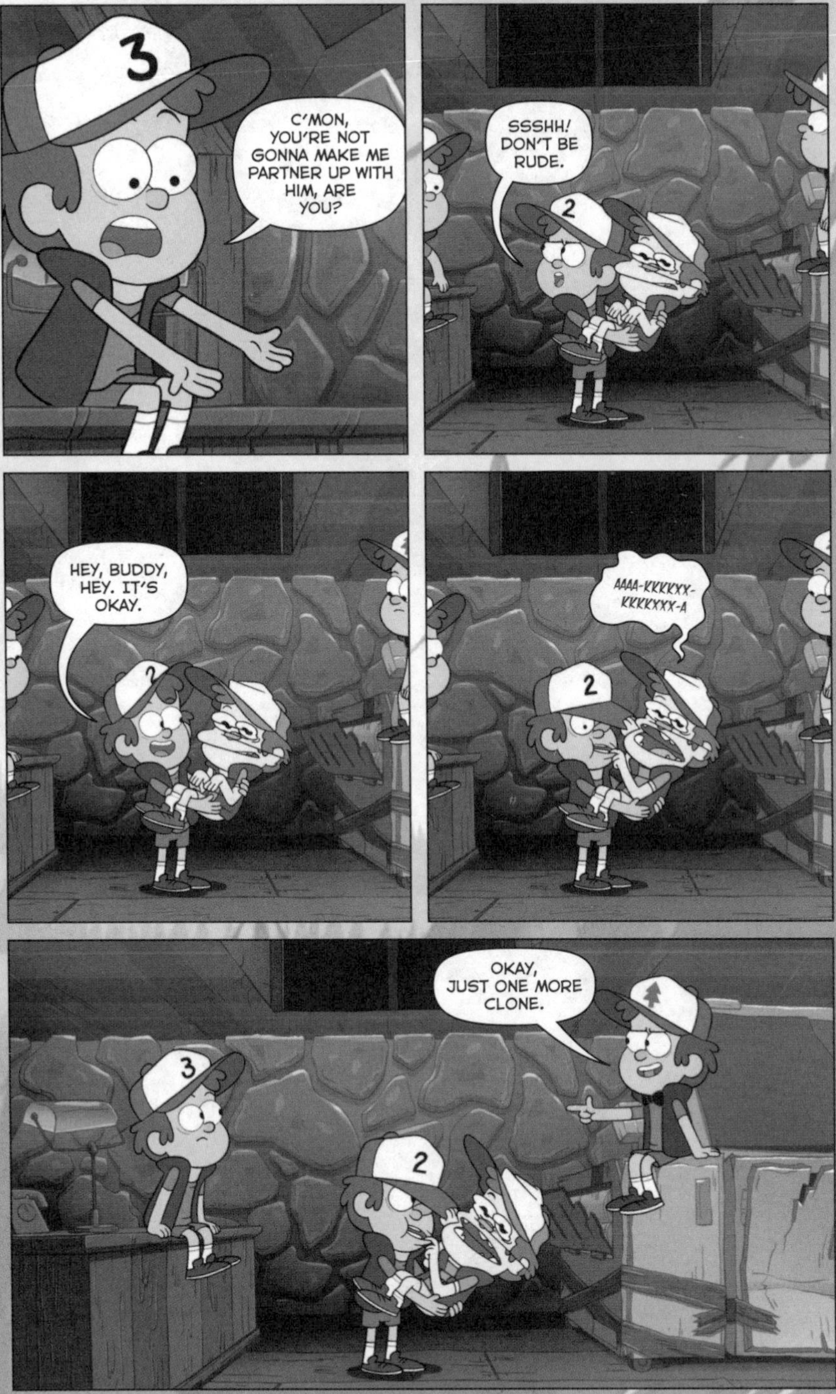
C'MON, YOU'RE NOT GONNA MAKE ME PARTNER UP WITH HIM, ARE YOU?
SSSHH! DON'T BE RUDE.
HEY, BUDDY, HEY. IT'S OKAY.
AAAA-KKKKXX-KKKKXXX-A
OKAY, JUST ONE MORE CLONE.

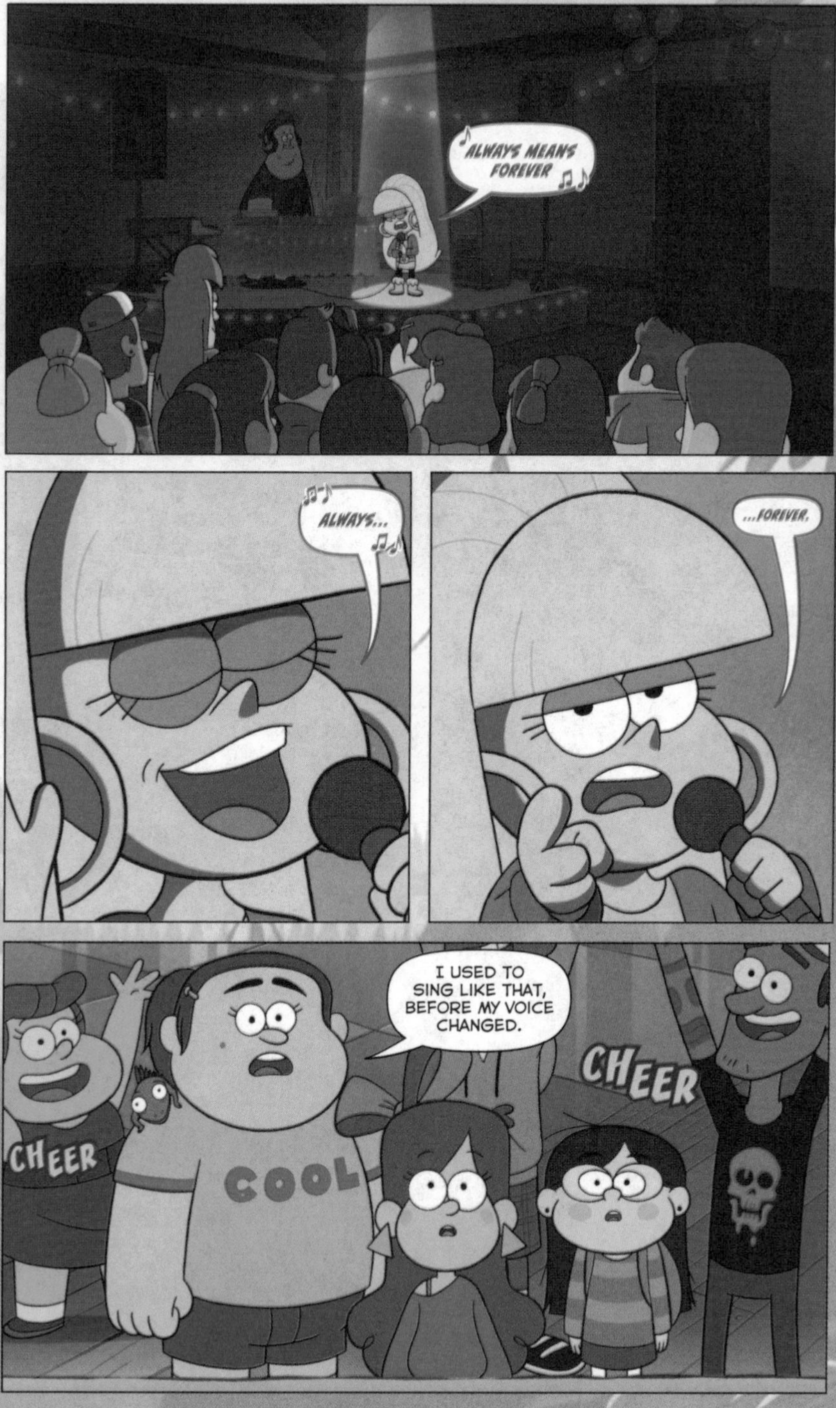
ALWAYS MEANS FOREVER
ALWAYS...
...FOREVER.
I USED TO SING LIKE THAT, BEFORE MY VOICE CHANGED.
CHEER
CHEER
COOL

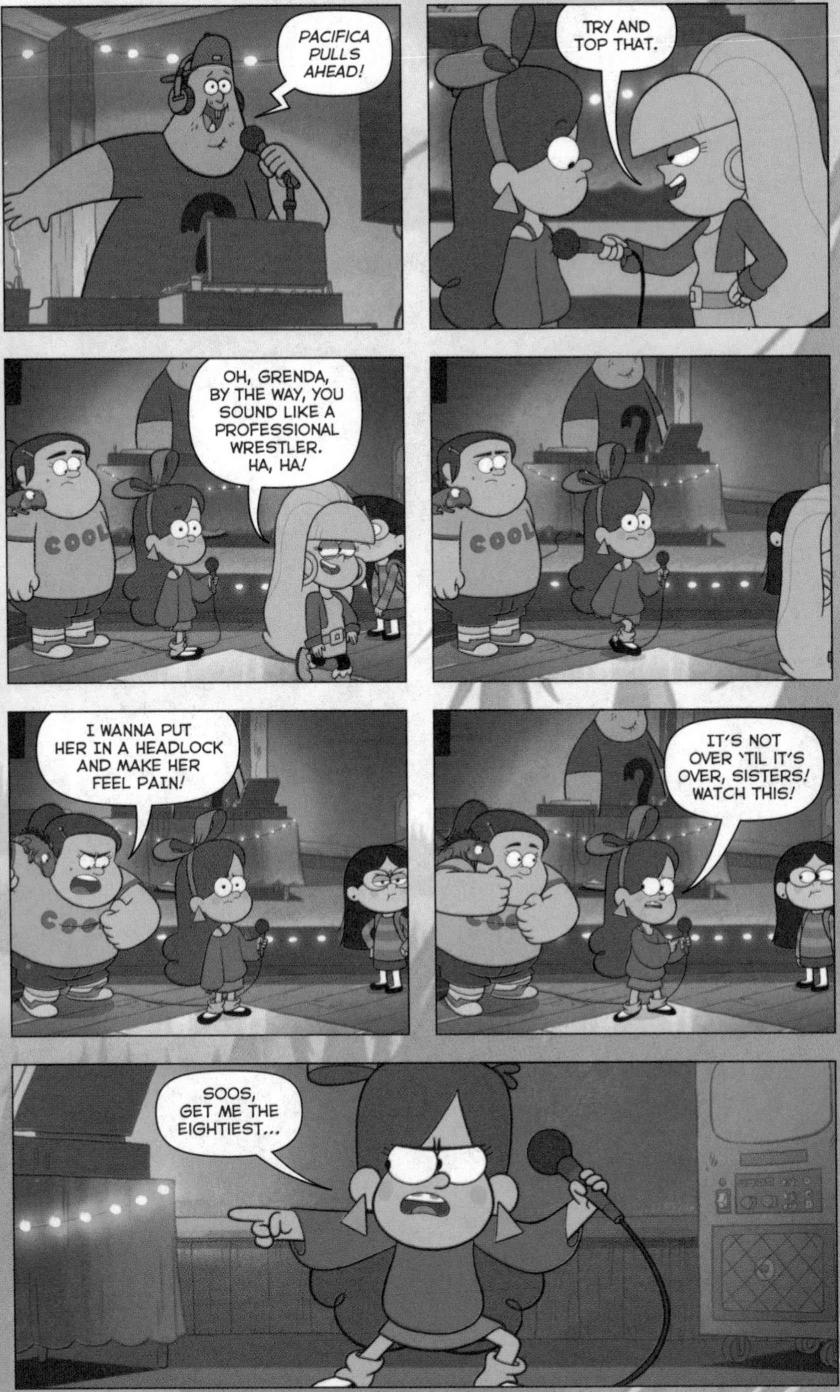

PACIFICA PULLS AHEAD!
TRY AND TOP THAT.
OH, GRENDA, BY THE WAY, YOU SOUND LIKE A PROFESSIONAL WRESTLER. HA, HA!
COOL
COOL
I WANNA PUT HER IN A HEADLOCK AND MAKE HER FEEL PAIN!
IT'S NOT OVER 'TIL IT'S OVER, SISTERS! WATCH THIS!
SOOS, GET ME THE EIGHTIEST...

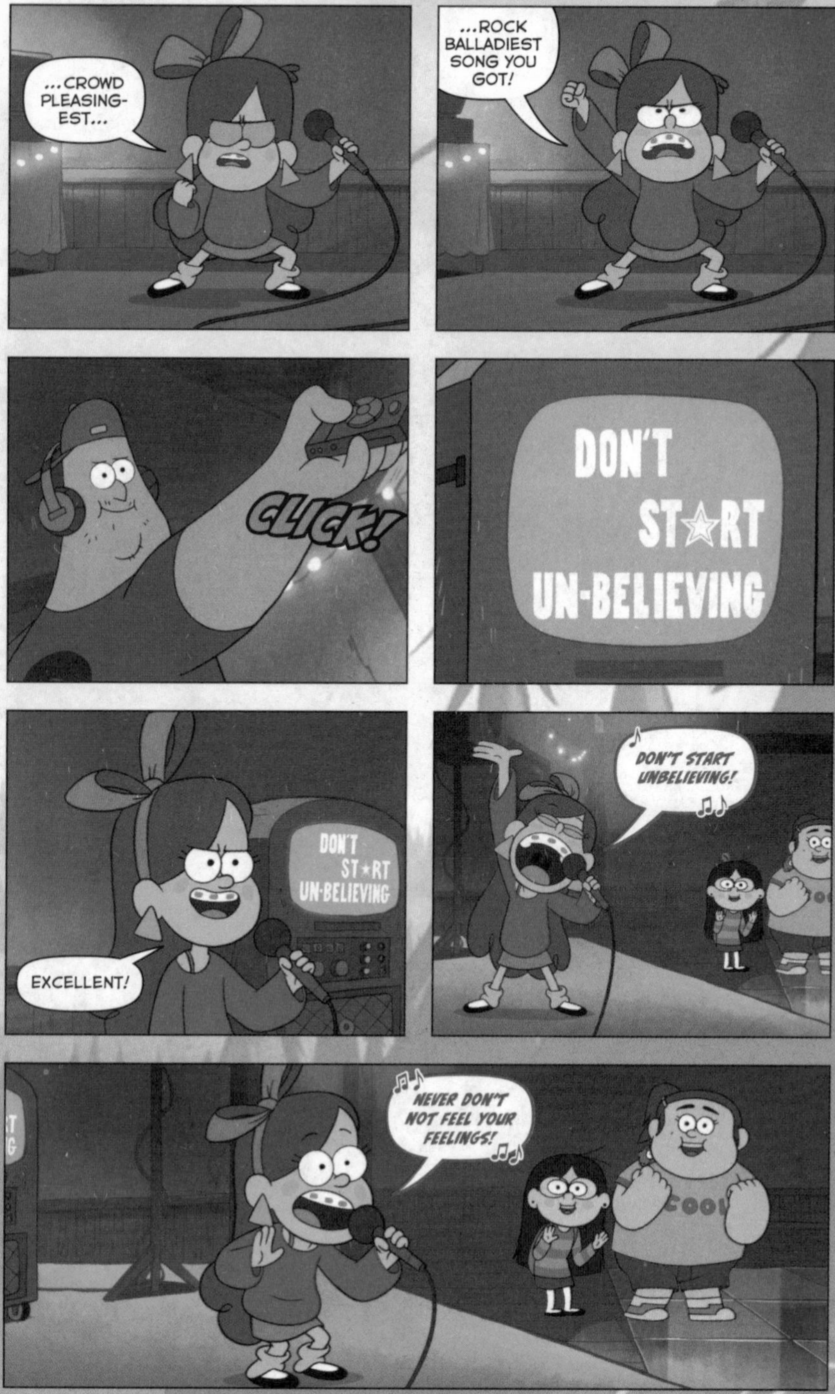

...CROWD PLEASING-EST...
...ROCK BALLADIEST SONG YOU GOT!
CLICK!
DON'T START UN-BELIEVING
DON'T START UN-BELIEVING
EXCELLENT!
DON'T START UNBELIEVING!
NEVER DON'T NOT FEEL YOUR FEELINGS!

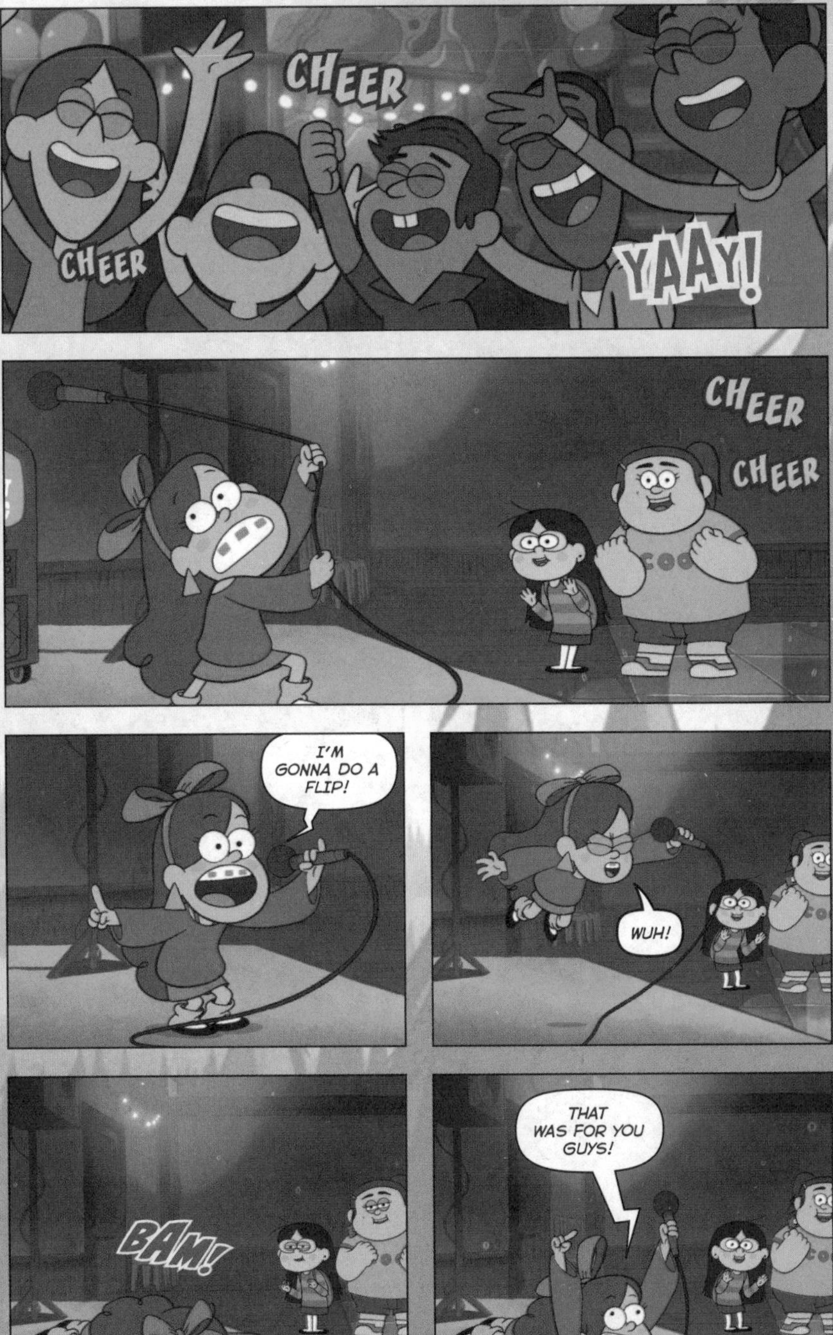
CHEER
CHEER
YAAY!
CHEER
CHEER
I'M GONNA DO A FLIP!
WUH!
BAM!
THAT WAS FOR YOU GUYS!

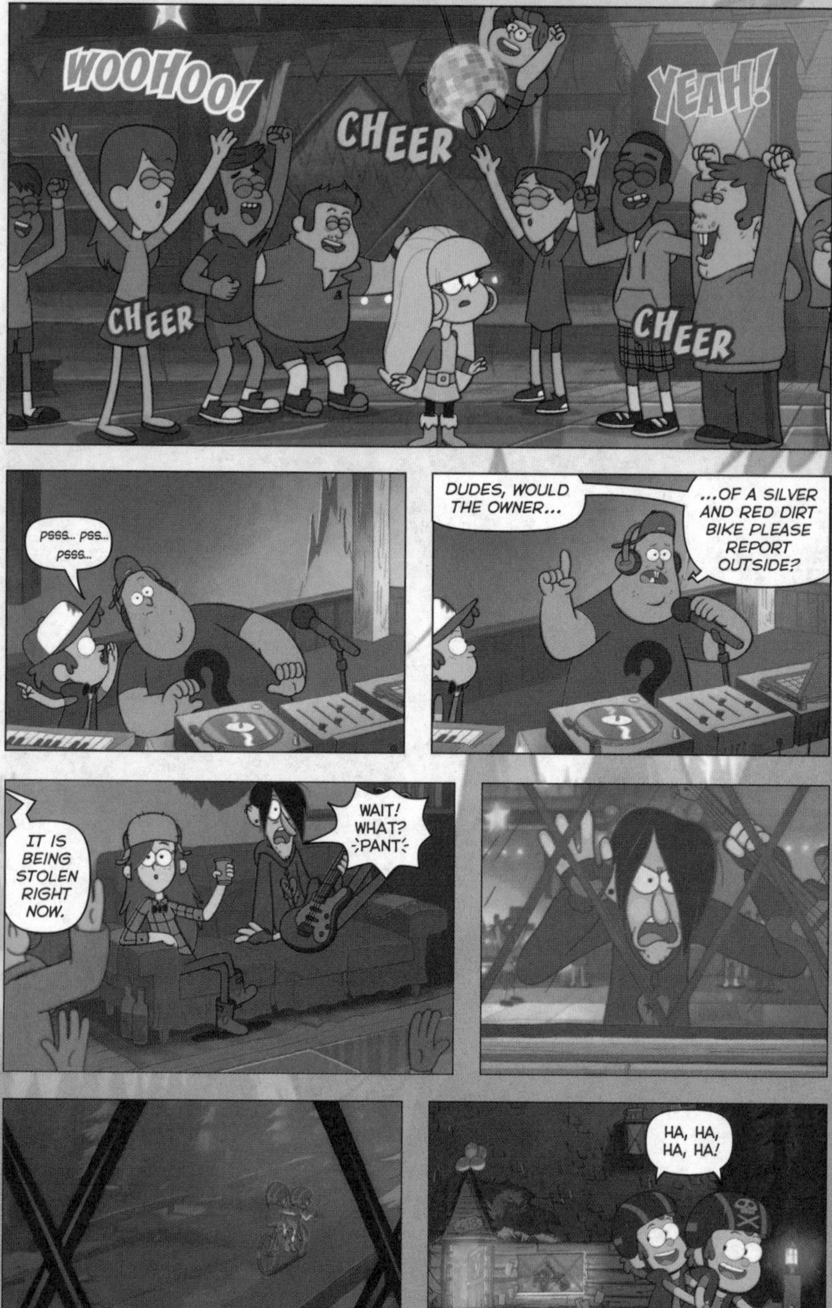
WOOHOO!
CHEER
YEAH!
CHEER
CHEER
PSSS... PSS... PSSS...
DUDES, WOULD THE OWNER...
...OF A SILVER AND RED DIRT BIKE PLEASE REPORT OUTSIDE?
IT IS BEING STOLEN RIGHT NOW.
WAIT! WHAT? PANT
HA, HA, HA, HA!

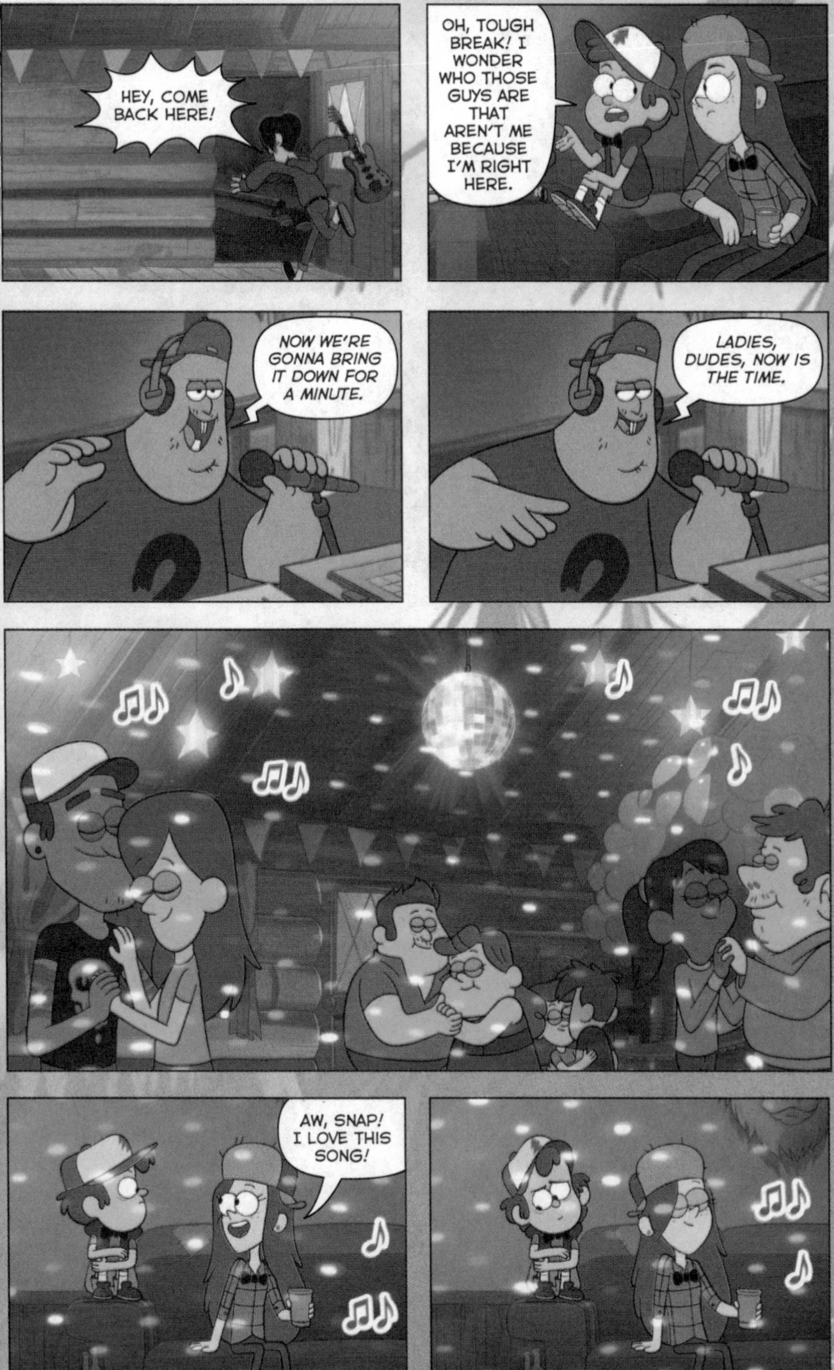
HEY, COME BACK HERE!
OH, TOUGH BREAK! I WONDER WHO THOSE GUYS ARE THAT AREN'T ME BECAUSE I'M RIGHT HERE.
NOW WE'RE GONNA BRING IT DOWN FOR A MINUTE.
LADIES, DUDES, NOW IS THE TIME.
AW, SNAP! I LOVE THIS SONG!

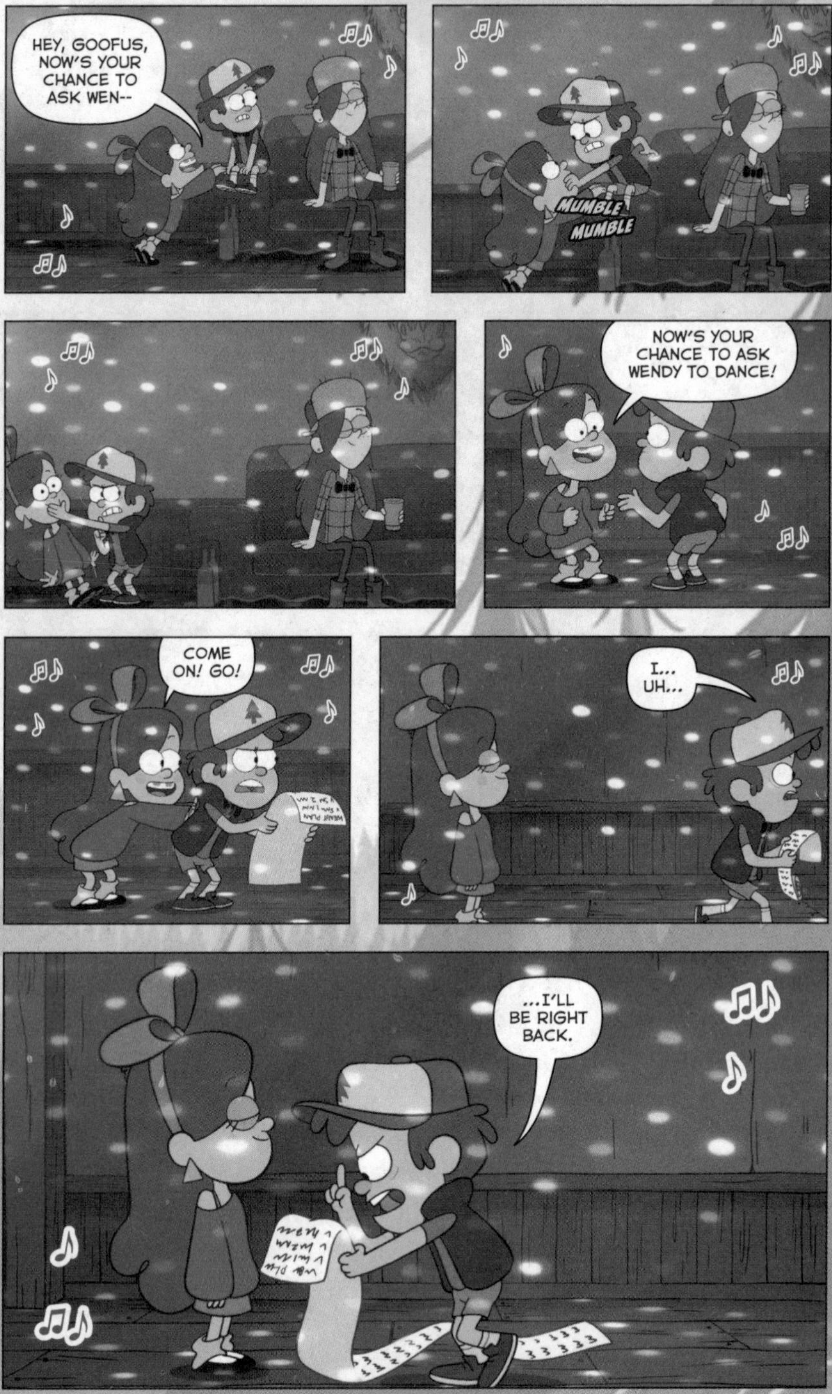
HEY, GOOFUS, NOW'S YOUR CHANCE TO ASK WEN--
MUMBLE MUMBLE
NOW'S YOUR CHANCE TO ASK WENDY TO DANCE!
COME ON! GO!
I... UH...
...I'LL BE RIGHT BACK.

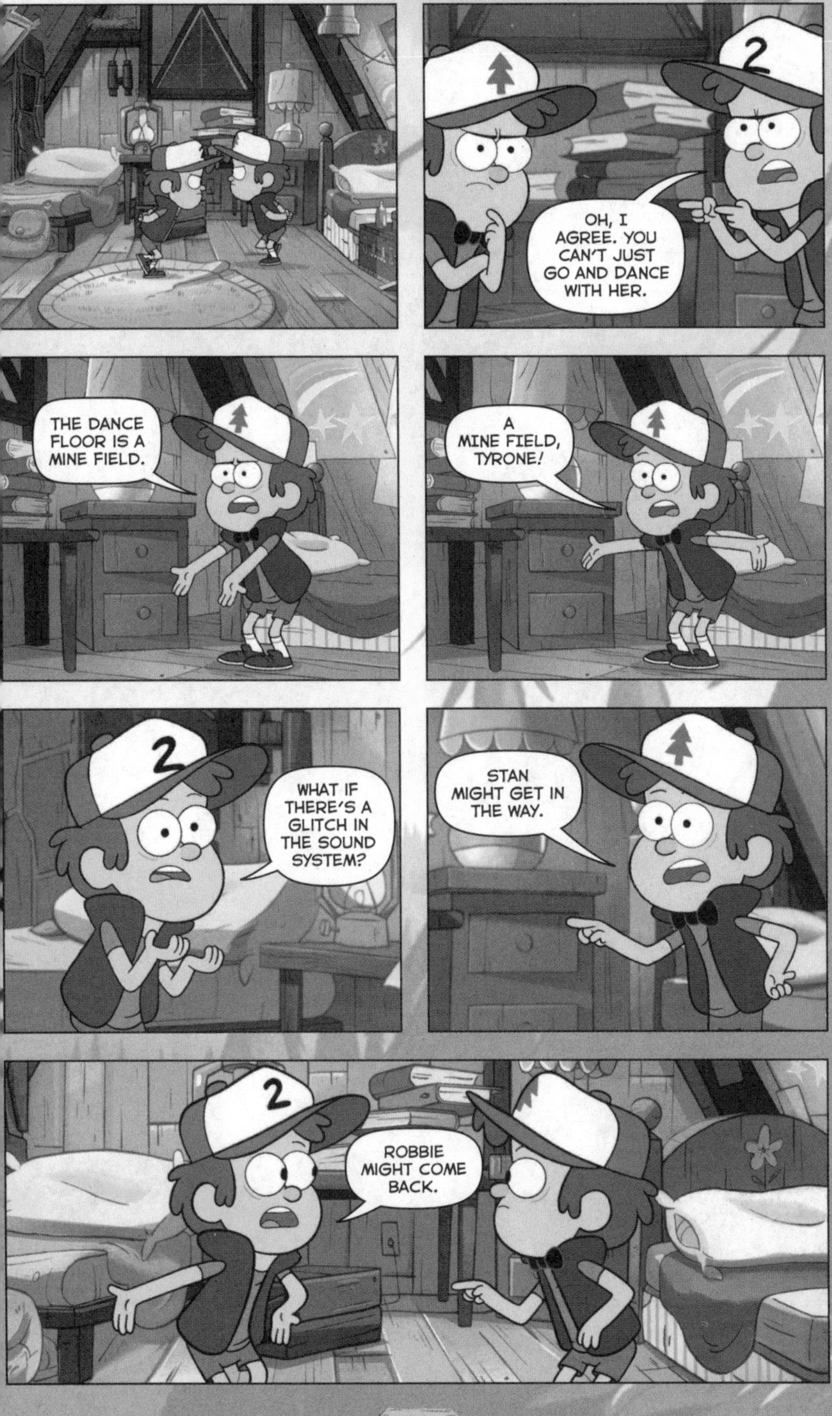

OH, I AGREE. YOU CAN'T JUST GO AND DANCE WITH HER.
THE DANCE FLOOR IS A MINE FIELD.
A MINE FIELD, TYRONE!
WHAT IF THERE'S A GLITCH IN THE SOUND SYSTEM?
STAN MIGHT GET IN THE WAY.
ROBBIE MIGHT COME BACK.

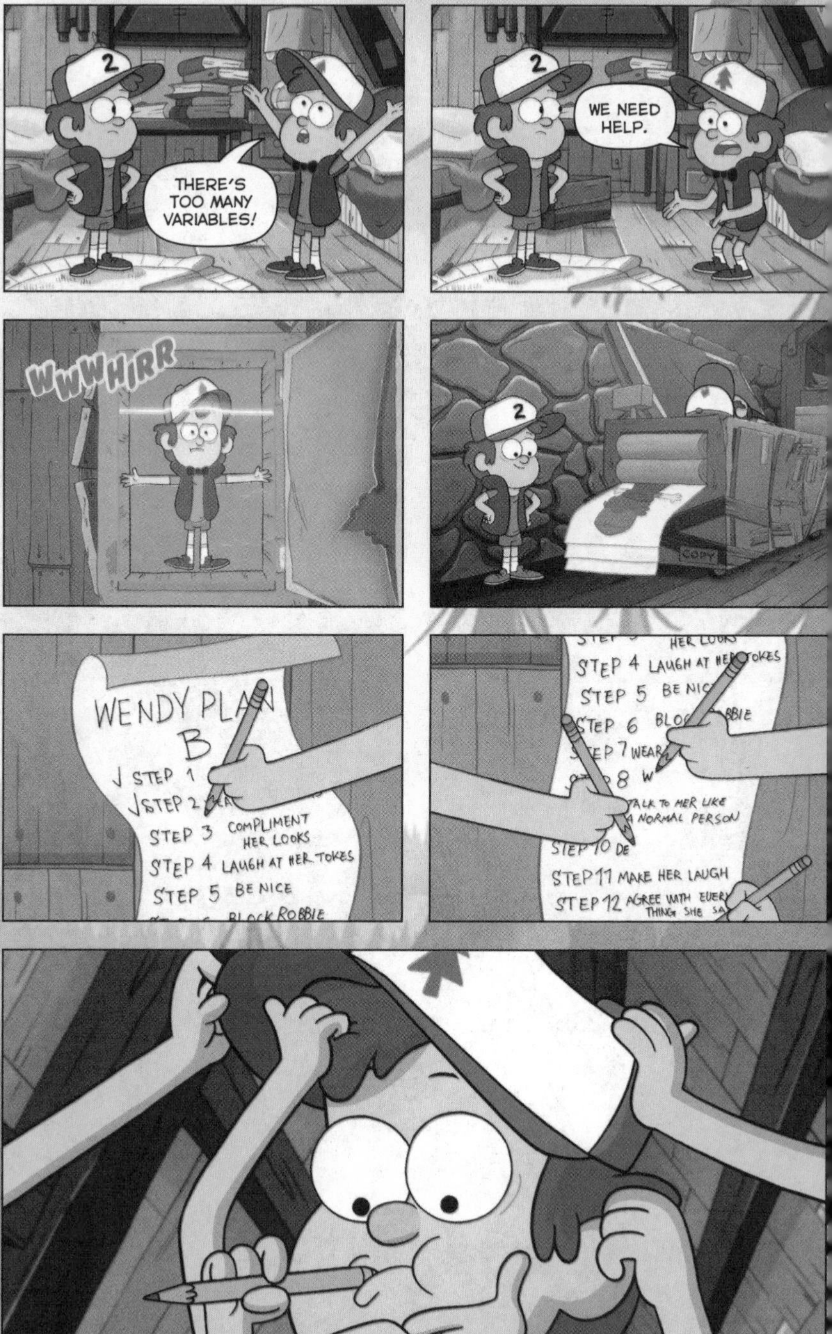
THERE'S TOO MANY VARIABLES!
WE NEED HELP.
WWWHIRR
COPY
WENDY PLAN B
STEP 1
STEP 2
STEP 3 COMPLIMENT HER LOOKS
STEP 4 LAUGH AT HER TOKES
STEP 5 BE NICE
STEP 4 LAUGH AT HER TOKES
STEP 5 BE NIC
STEP 6
STEP 10
STEP 11 MAKE HER LAUGH
STEP 12 AGREE WITH EVERY THING SHE SA

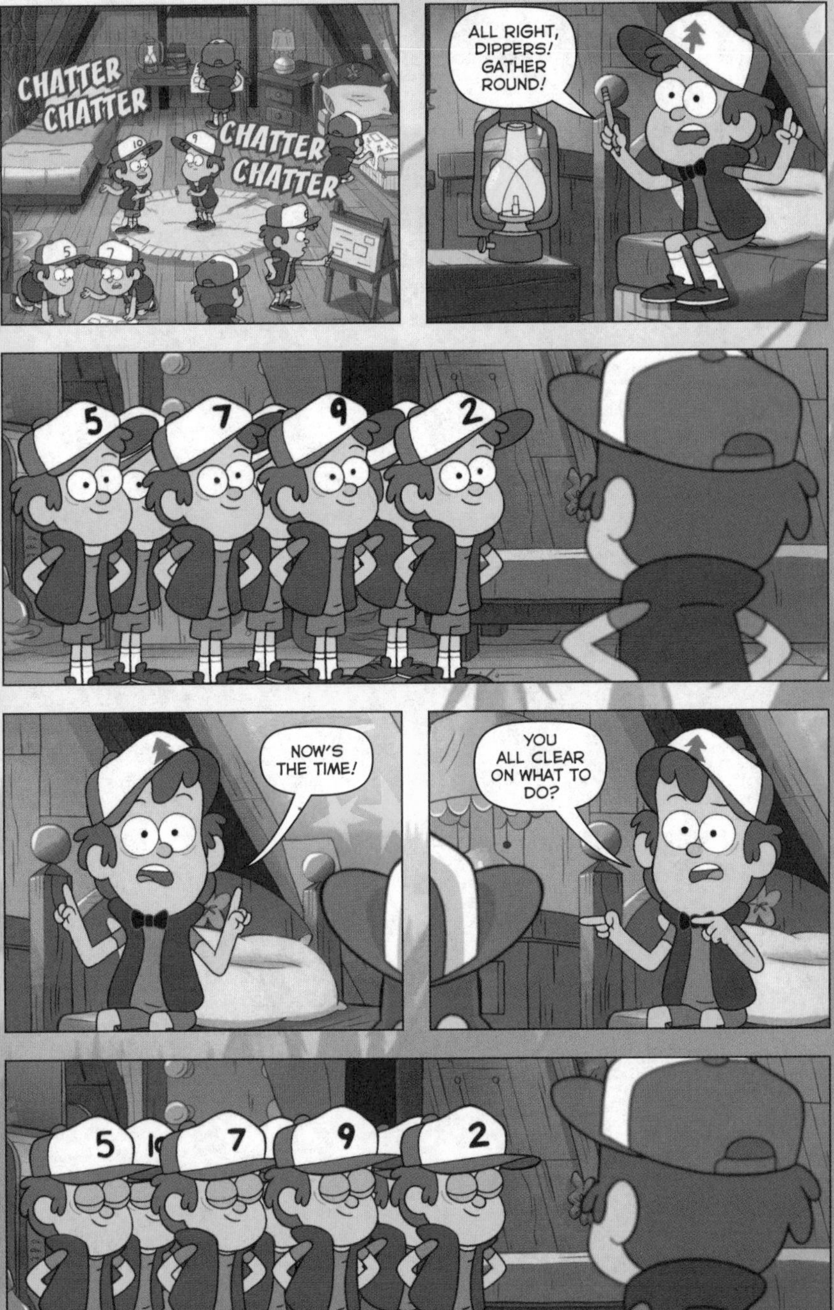
CHATTER
CHATTER
CHATTER
CHATTER
ALL RIGHT, DIPPERS! GATHER ROUND!
5
7
9
2
NOW'S THE TIME!
YOU ALL CLEAR ON WHAT TO DO?
5
7
9
2

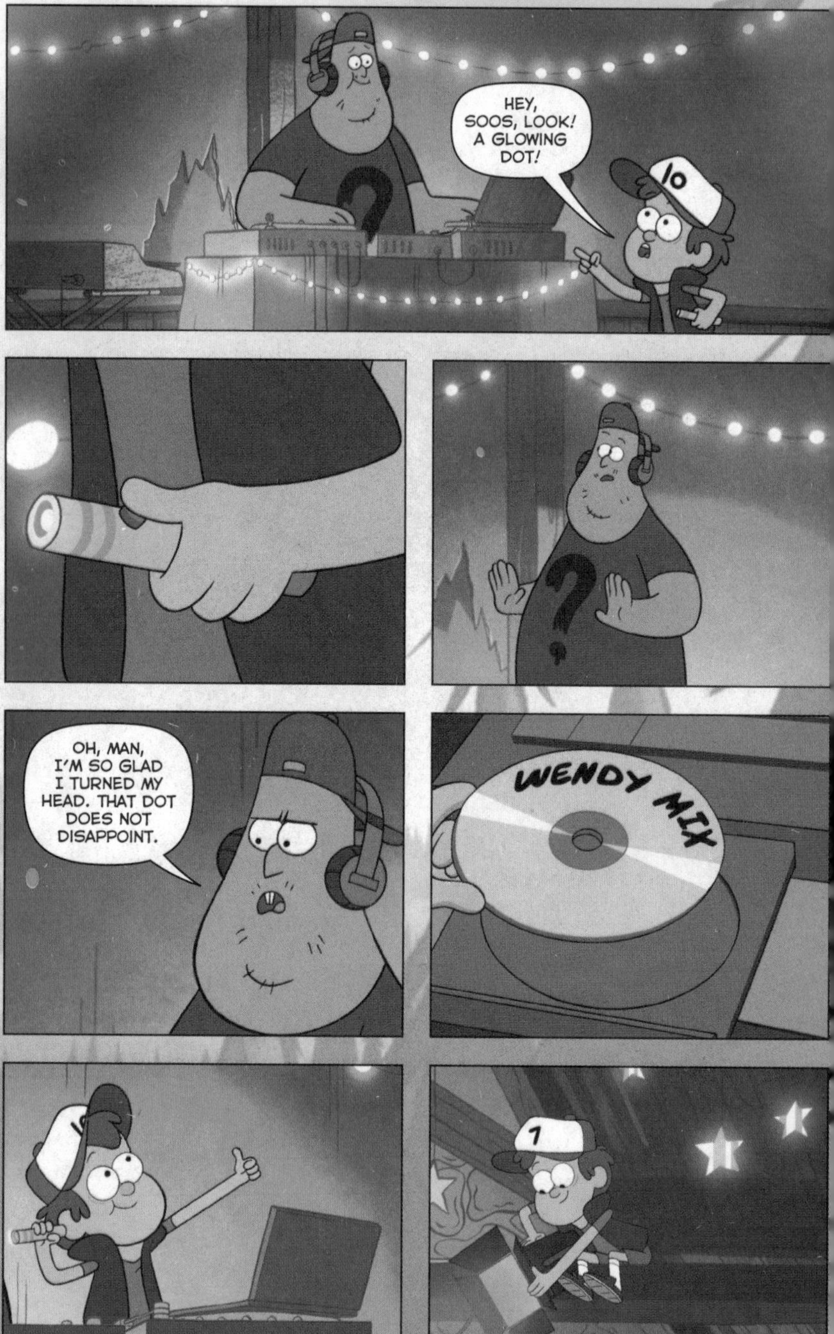
HEY, SOOS, LOOK! A GLOWING DOT!
10
OH, MAN, I'M SO GLAD I TURNED MY HEAD. THAT DOT DOES NOT DISAPPOINT.
WENDY MIX
7

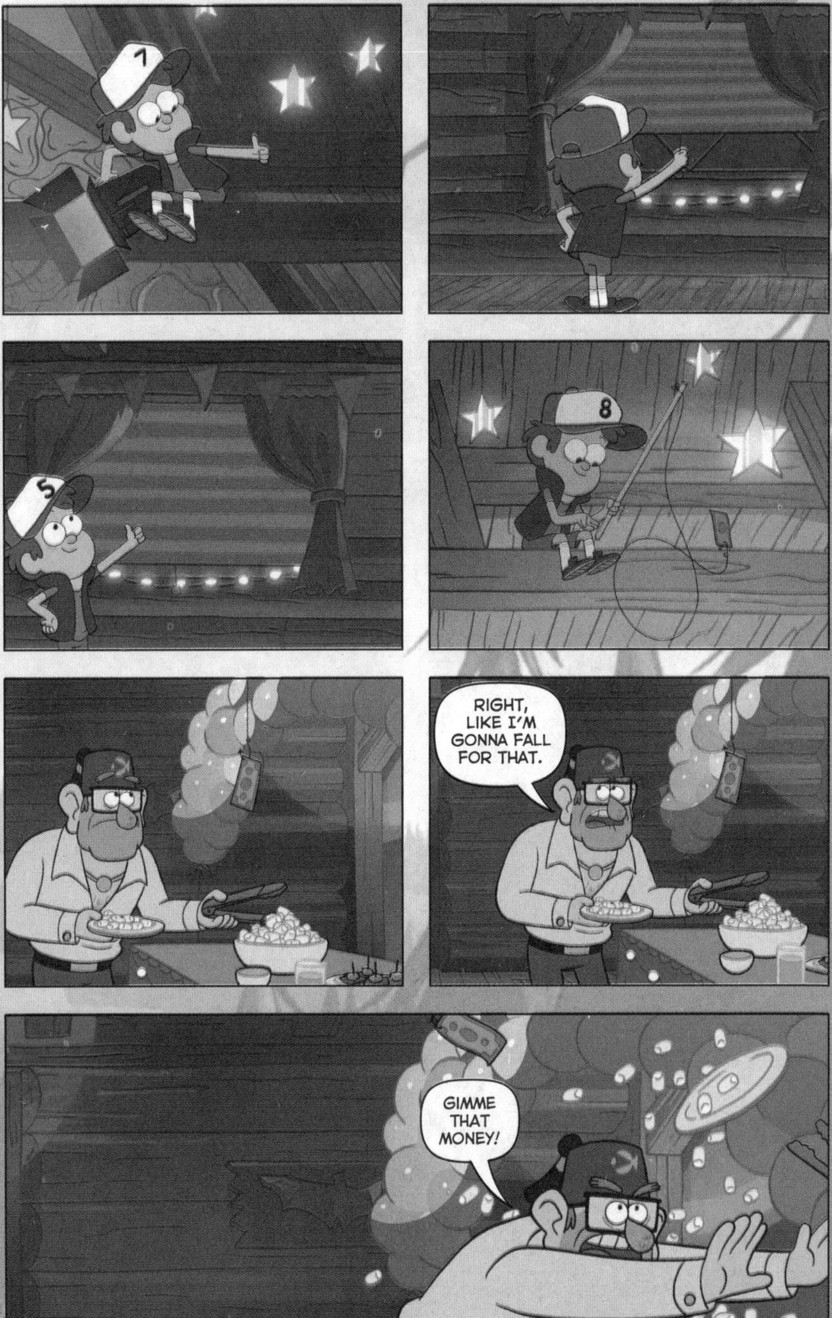
RIGHT, LIKE I'M GONNA FALL FOR THAT.
GIMME THAT MONEY!

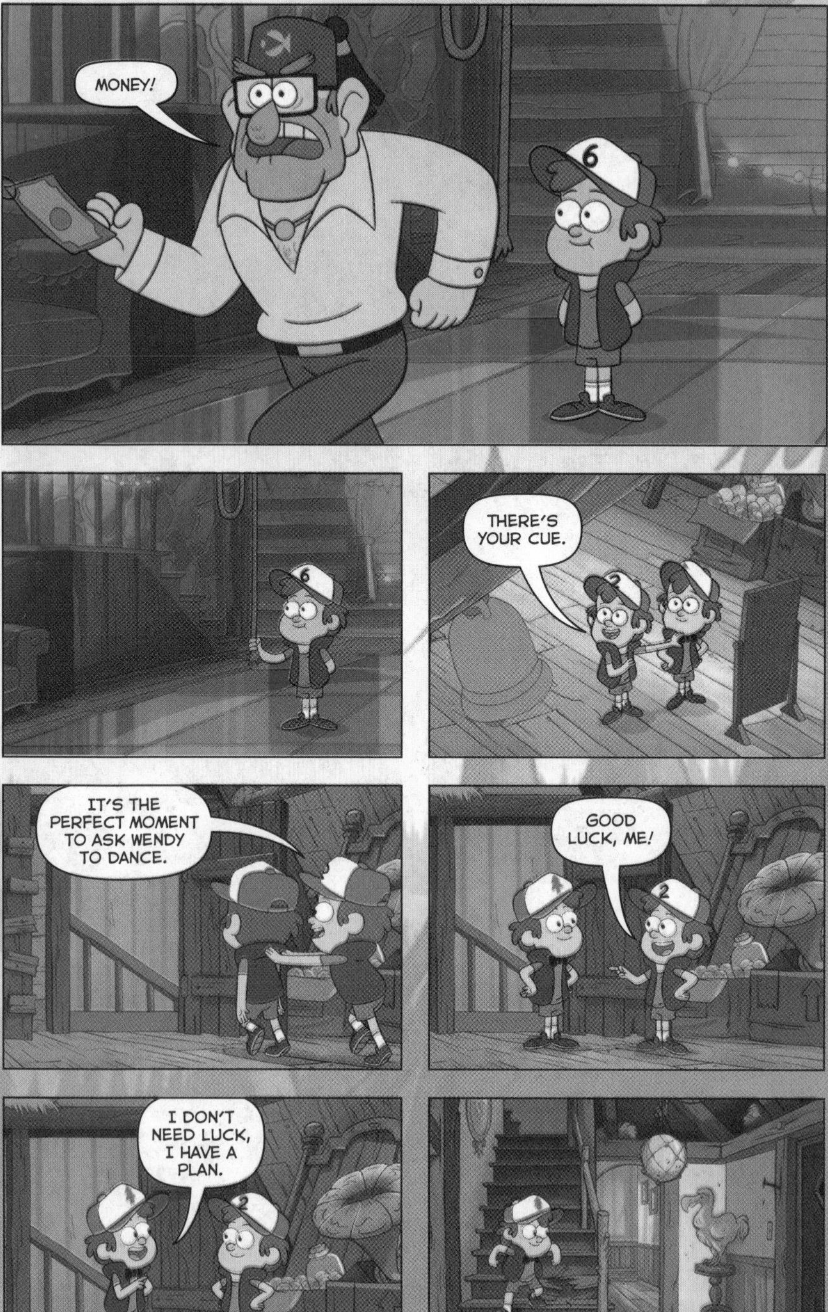

MONEY!
THERE'S YOUR CUE.
IT'S THE PERFECT MOMENT TO ASK WENDY TO DANCE.
GOOD LUCK, ME!
I DON'T NEED LUCK, I HAVE A PLAN.

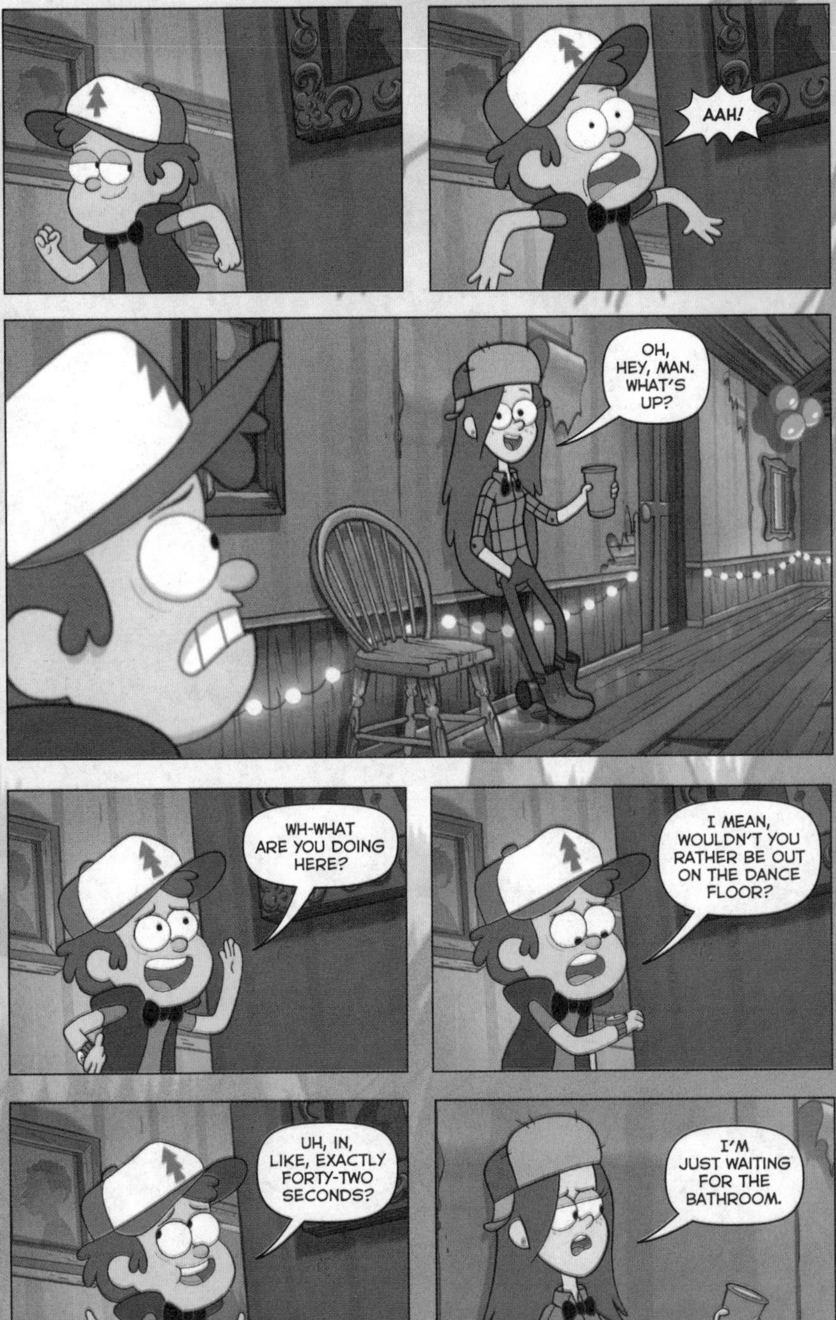
AAH!
OH, HEY, MAN. WHAT'S UP?
WH-WHAT ARE YOU DOING HERE?
I MEAN, WOULDN'T YOU RATHER BE OUT ON THE DANCE FLOOR?
UH, IN, LIKE, EXACTLY FORTY-TWO SECONDS?
I'M JUST WAITING FOR THE BATHROOM.

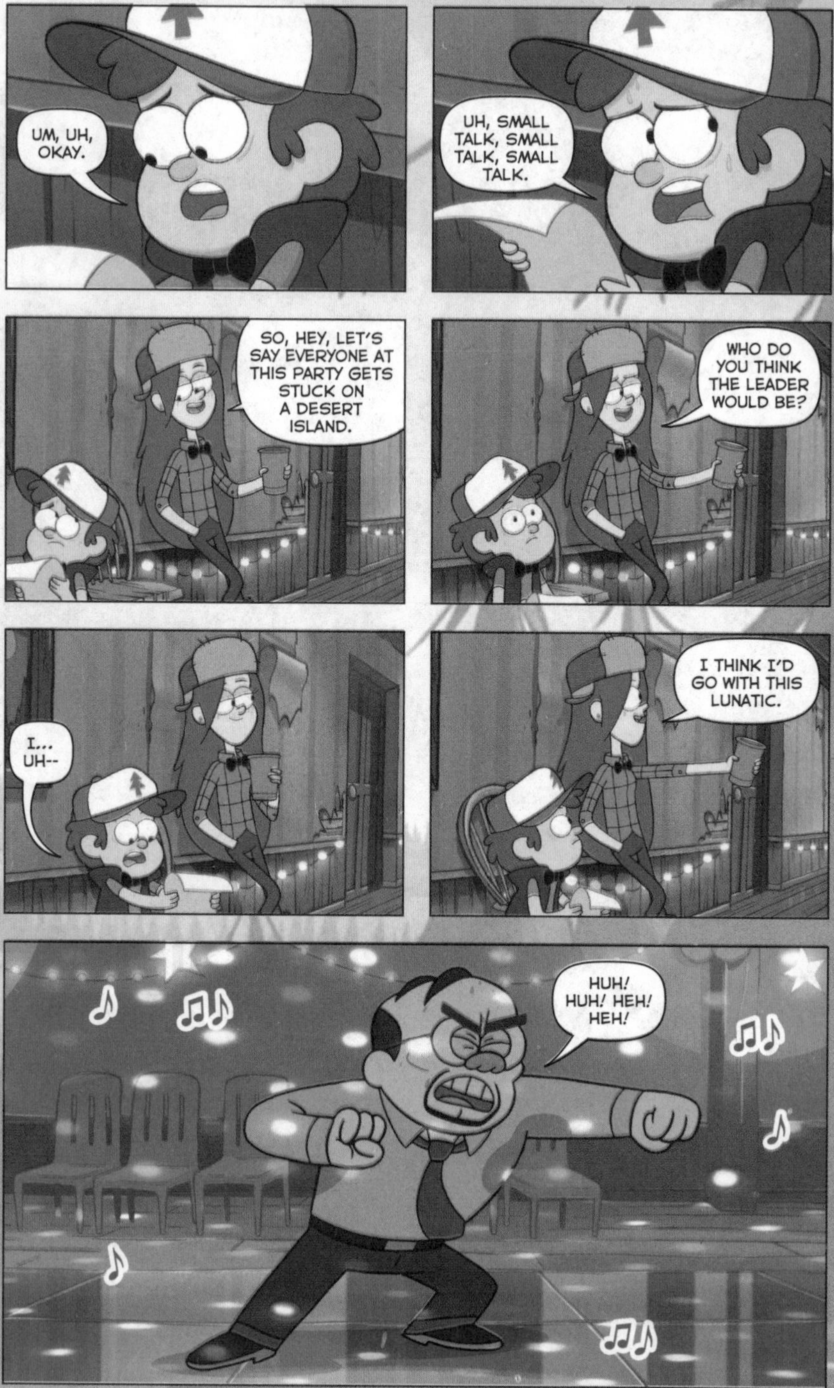
UM, UH, OKAY.
UH, SMALL TALK, SMALL TALK, SMALL TALK.
SO, HEY, LET'S SAY EVERYONE AT THIS PARTY GETS STUCK ON A DESERT ISLAND.
WHO DO YOU THINK THE LEADER WOULD BE?
I... UH--
I THINK I'D GO WITH THIS LUNATIC.
HUH! HUH! HEH! HEH!

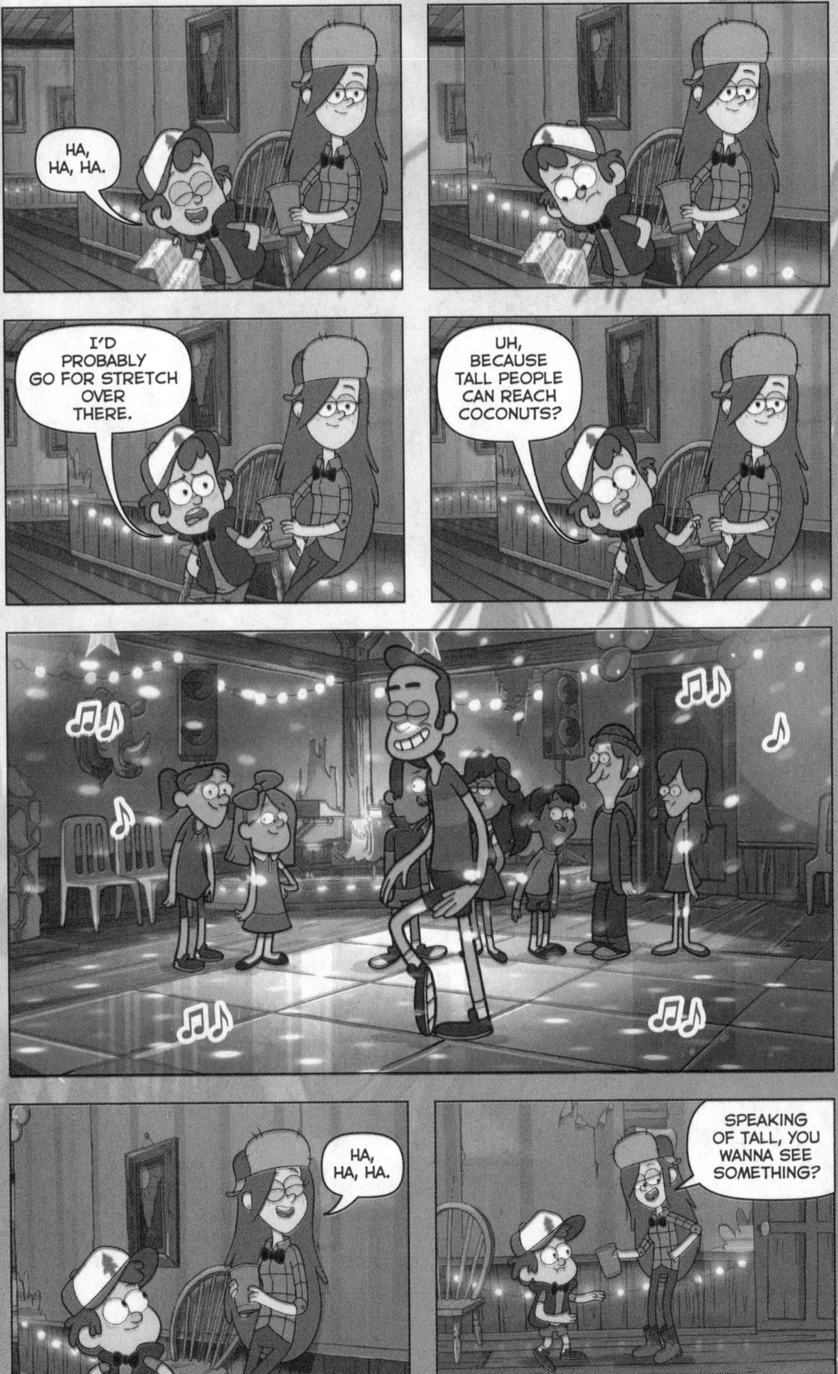
HA, HA, HA.
I'D PROBABLY GO FOR STRETCH OVER THERE.
UH, BECAUSE TALL PEOPLE CAN REACH COCONUTS?
HA, HA, HA.
SPEAKING OF TALL, YOU WANNA SEE SOMETHING?

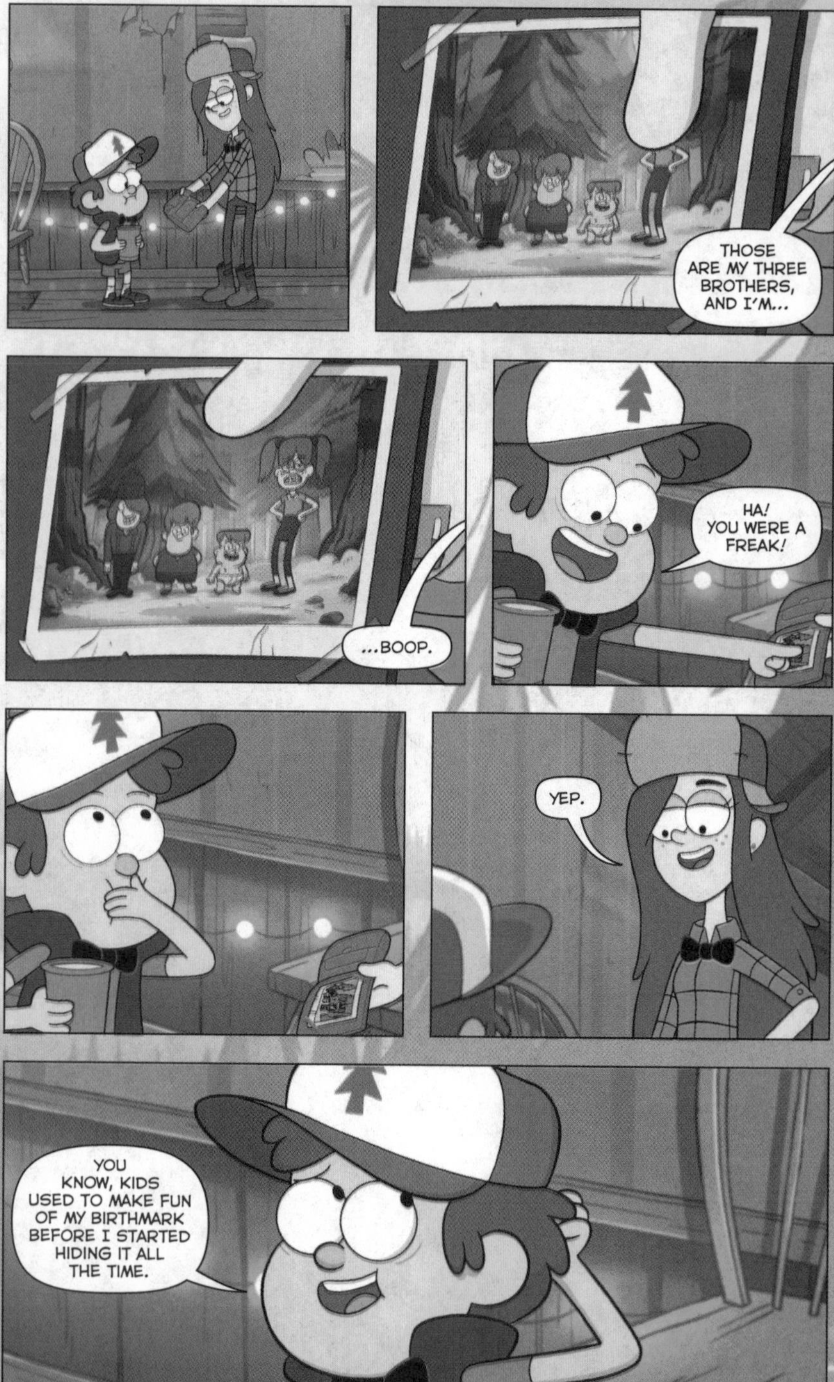
THOSE ARE MY THREE BROTHERS, AND I'M...
...BOOP.
HA! YOU WERE A FREAK!
YEP.
YOU KNOW, KIDS USED TO MAKE FUN OF MY BIRTHMARK BEFORE I STARTED HIDING IT ALL THE TIME.

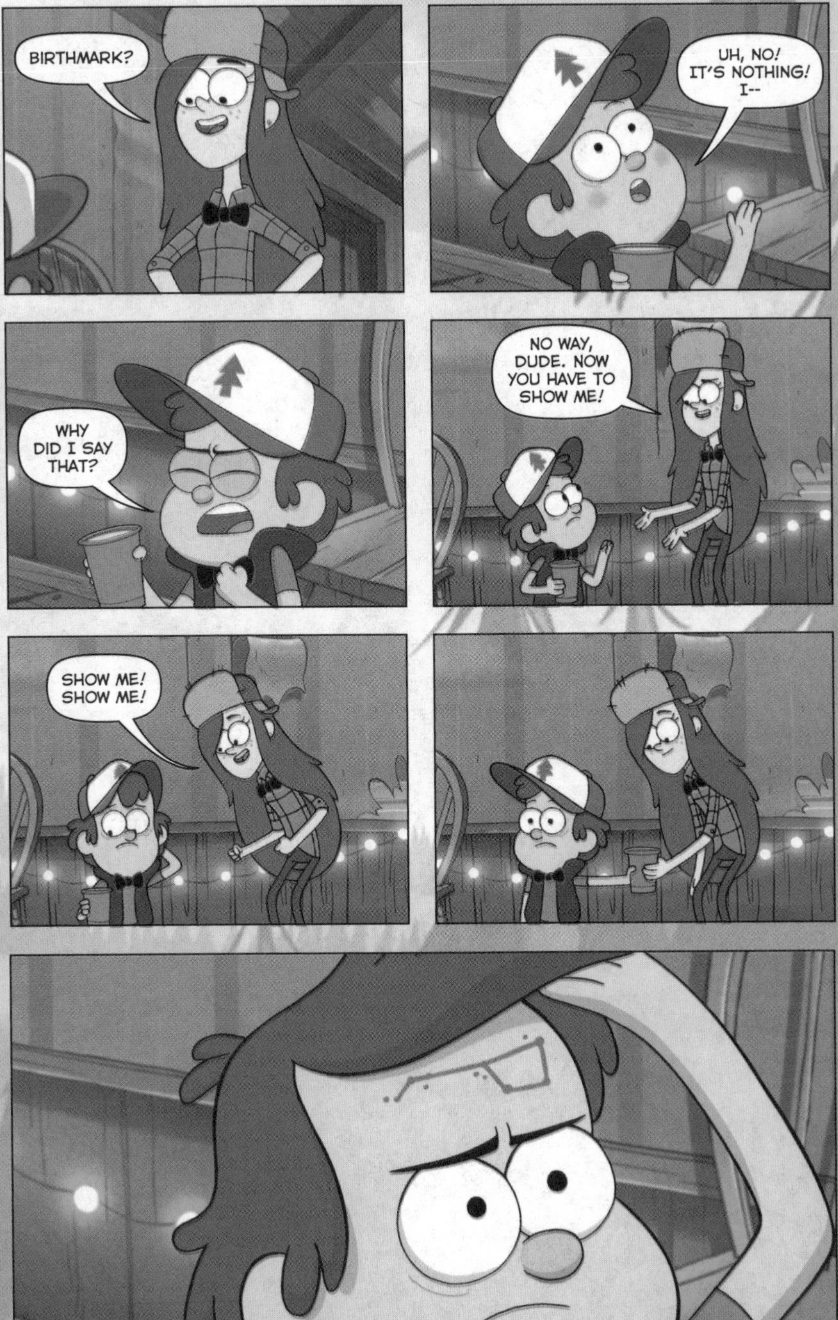
BIRTHMARK?
UH, NO! IT'S NOTHING! I--
WHY DID I SAY THAT?
NO WAY, DUDE. NOW YOU HAVE TO SHOW ME!
SHOW ME! SHOW ME!

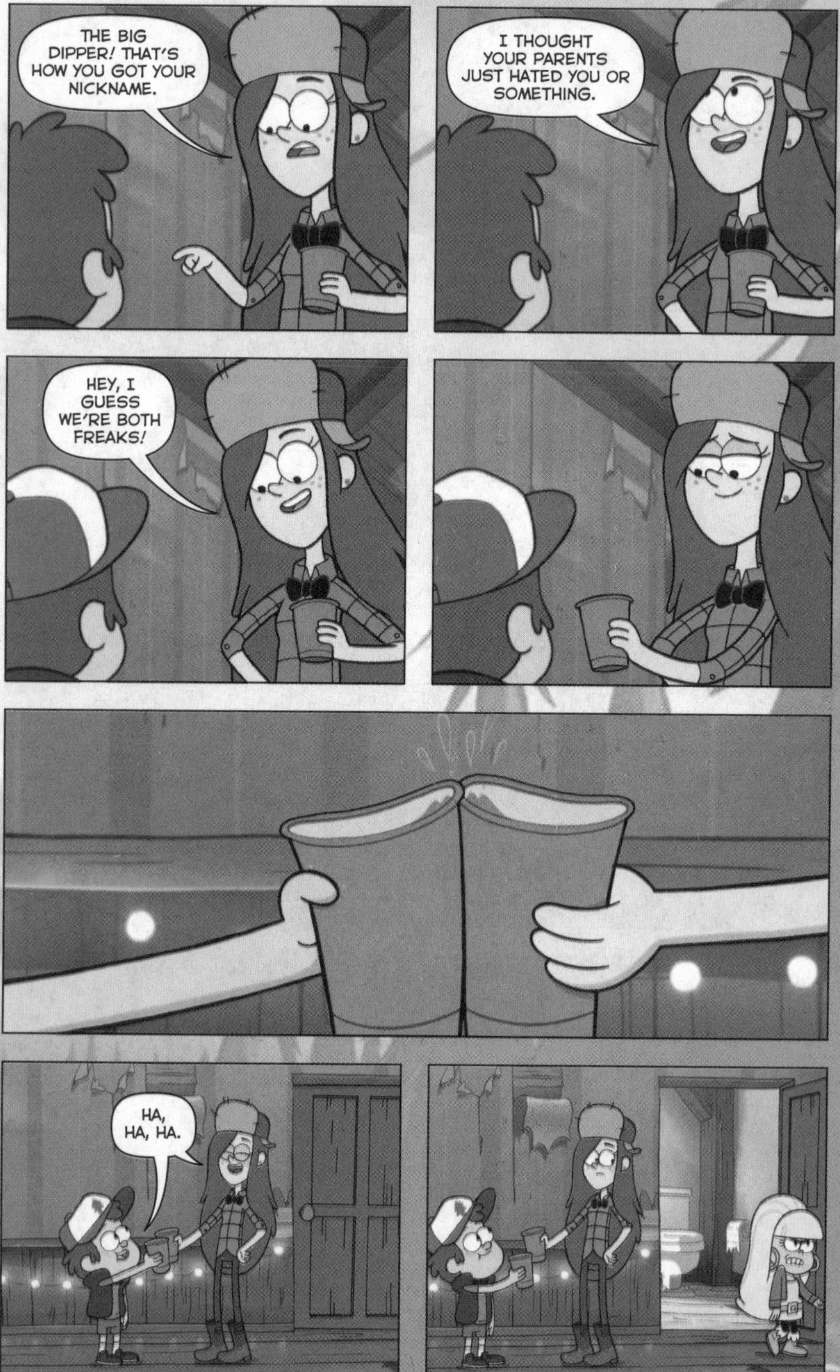
THE BIG DIPPER! THAT'S HOW YOU GOT YOUR NICKNAME.
I THOUGHT YOUR PARENTS JUST HATED YOU OR SOMETHING.
HEY, I GUESS WE'RE BOTH FREAKS!
HA, HA, HA.

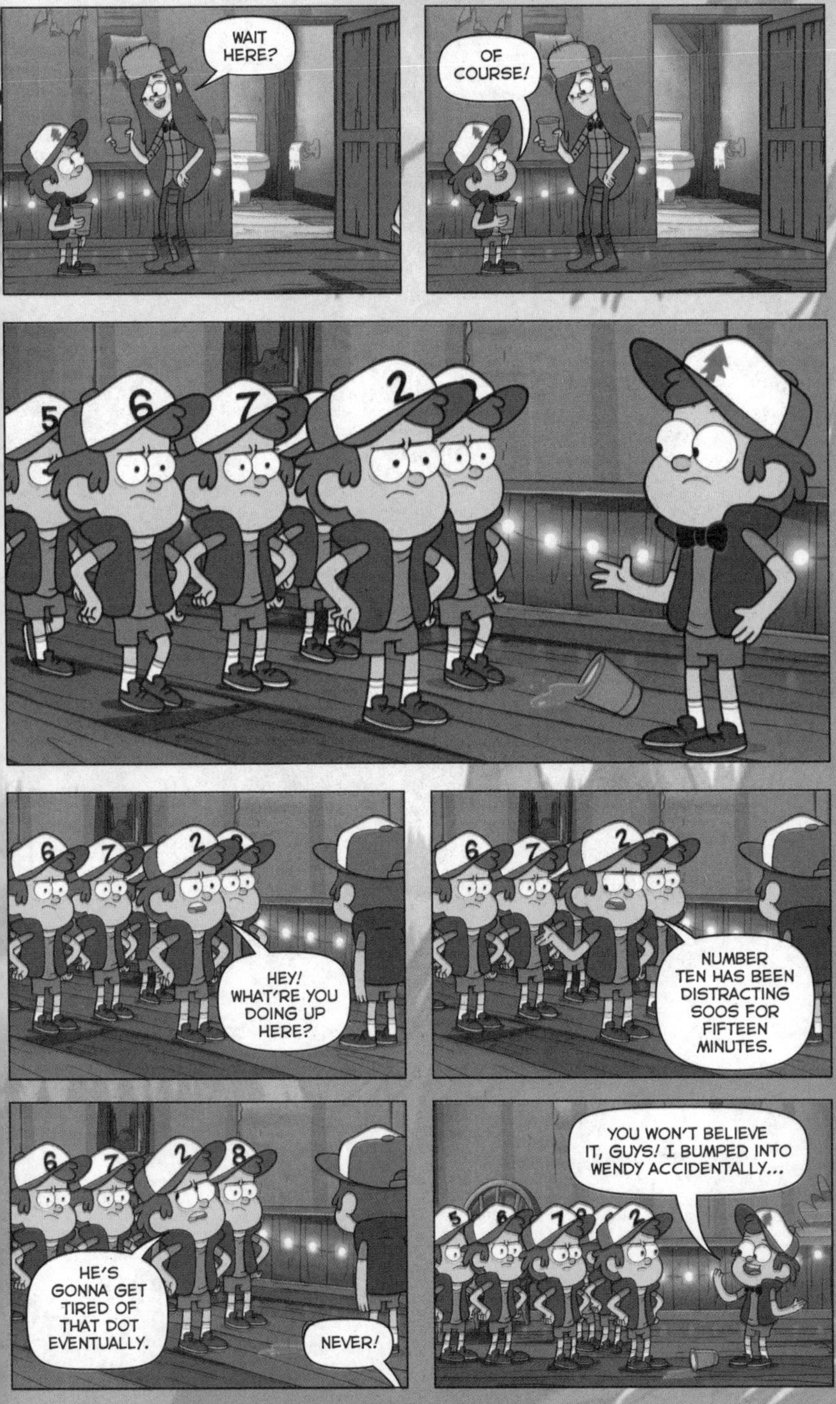

WAIT HERE?
OF COURSE!
HEY! WHAT'RE YOU DOING UP HERE?
NUMBER TEN HAS BEEN DISTRACTING SOOS FOR FIFTEEN MINUTES.
HE'S GONNA GET TIRED OF THAT DOT EVENTUALLY.
NEVER!
YOU WON'T BELIEVE IT, GUYS! I BUMPED INTO WENDY ACCIDENTALLY...

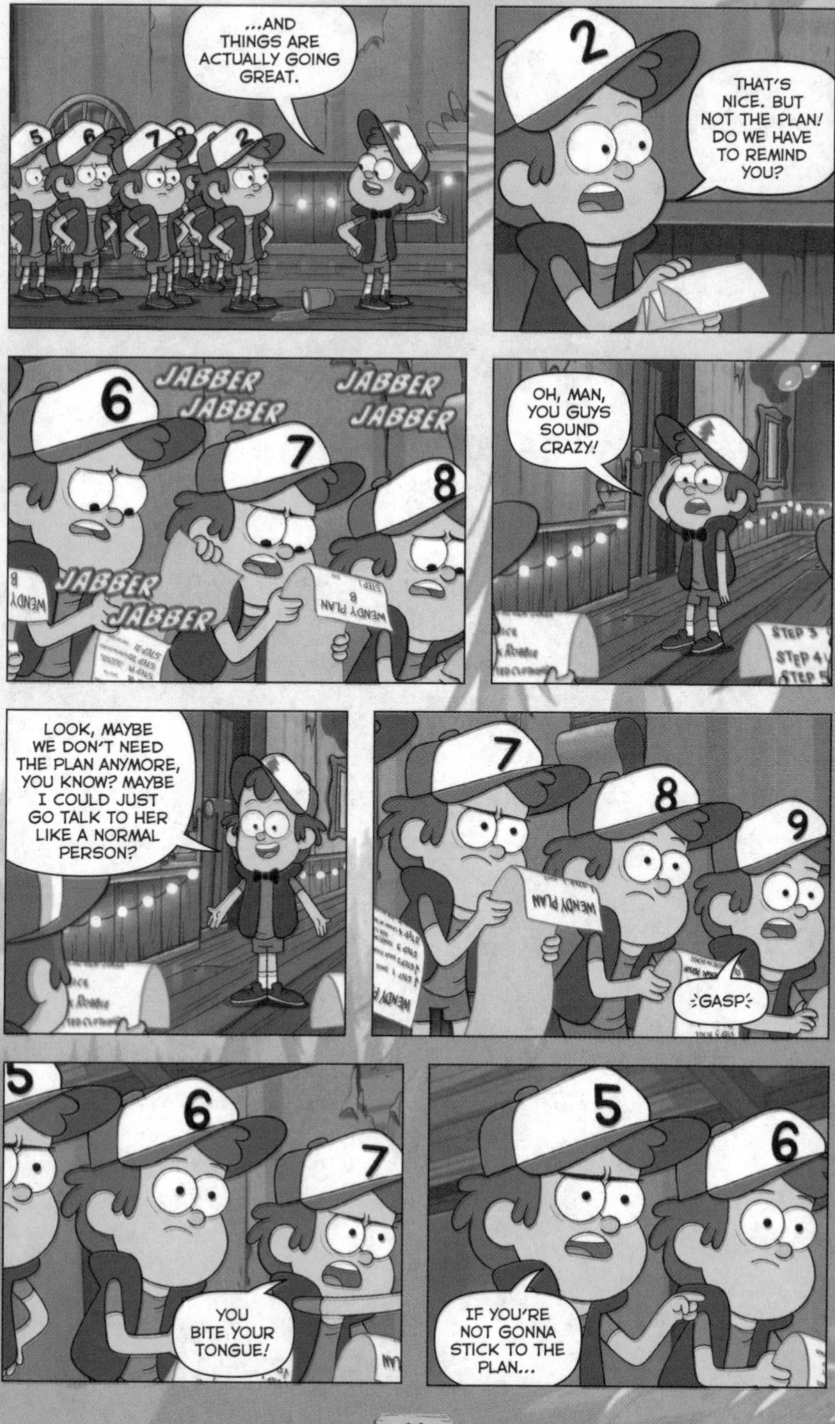

...AND THINGS ARE ACTUALLY GOING GREAT.
THAT'S NICE. BUT NOT THE PLAN! DO WE HAVE TO REMIND YOU?
JABBER JABBER
JABBER JABBER
JABBER JABBER
WENDY PLAN B
OH, MAN, YOU GUYS SOUND CRAZY!
STEP 3
STEP 4
LOOK, MAYBE WE DON'T NEED THE PLAN ANYMORE, YOU KNOW? MAYBE I COULD JUST GO TALK TO HER LIKE A NORMAL PERSON?
WENDY PLAN
GASP
YOU BITE YOUR TONGUE!
IF YOU'RE NOT GONNA STICK TO THE PLAN...

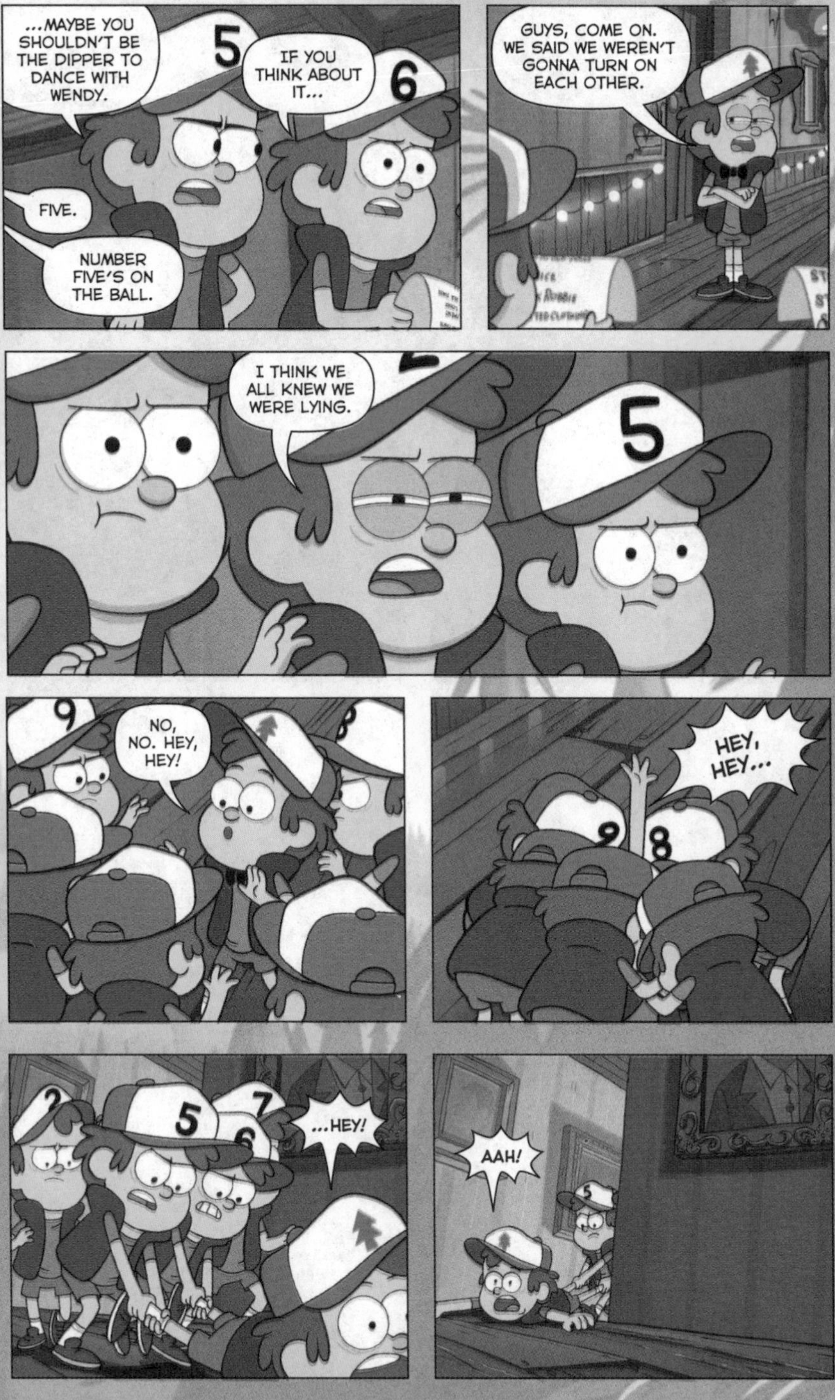
...MAYBE YOU SHOULDN'T BE THE DIPPER TO DANCE WITH WENDY.
IF YOU THINK ABOUT IT...
FIVE.
NUMBER FIVE'S ON THE BALL.
GUYS, COME ON. WE SAID WE WEREN'T GONNA TURN ON EACH OTHER.
I THINK WE ALL KNEW WE WERE LYING.
NO, NO. HEY, HEY!
HEY, HEY...
...HEY!
AAH!

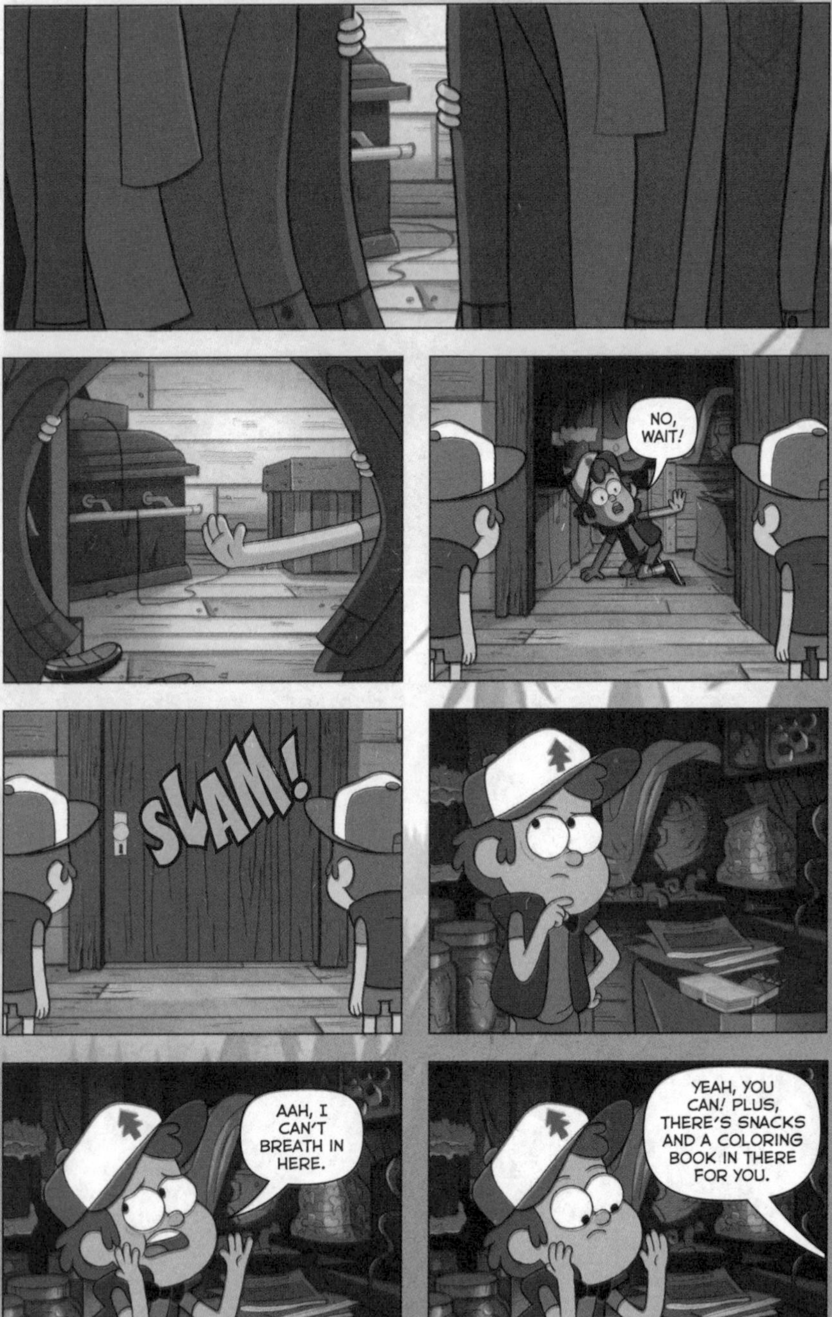
NO, WAIT!
SLAM!
AAH, I CAN'T BREATH IN HERE.
YEAH, YOU CAN! PLUS, THERE'S SNACKS AND A COLORING BOOK IN THERE FOR YOU.

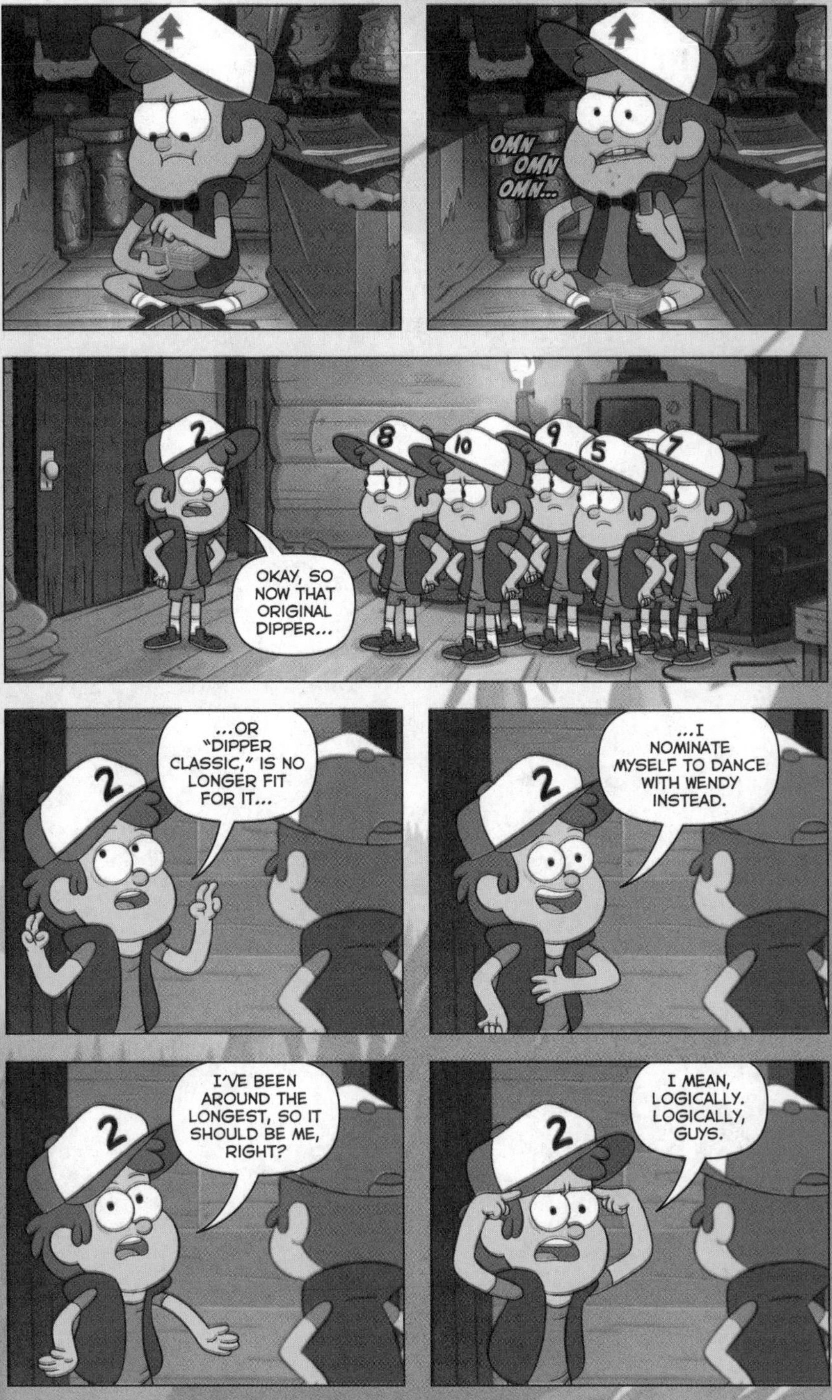
OMN
OMN
OMN...
OKAY, SO NOW THAT ORIGINAL DIPPER...
...OR "DIPPER CLASSIC," IS NO LONGER FIT FOR IT...
...I NOMINATE MYSELF TO DANCE WITH WENDY INSTEAD.
I'VE BEEN AROUND THE LONGEST, SO IT SHOULD BE ME, RIGHT?
I MEAN, LOGICALLY. LOGICALLY, GUYS.

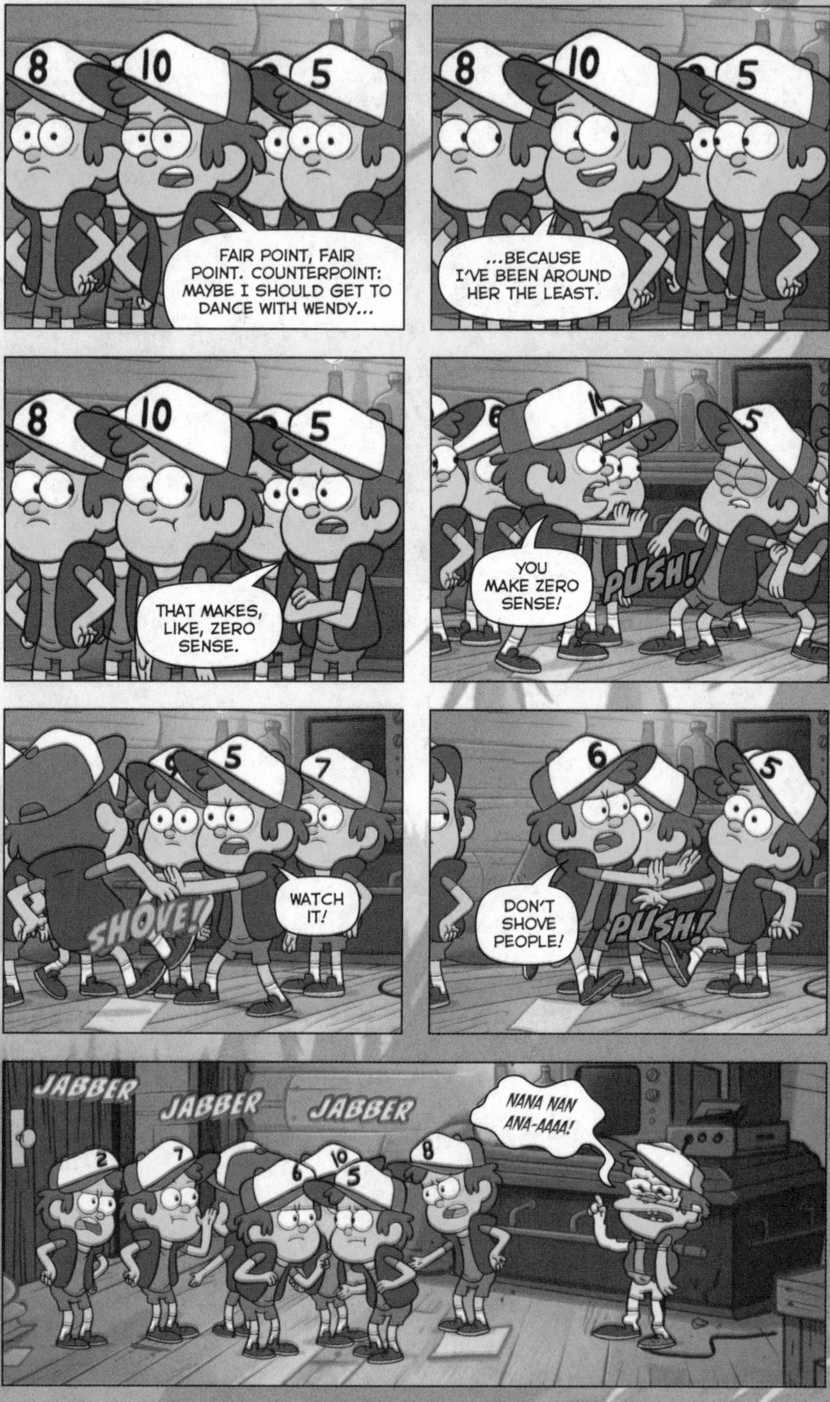

FAIR POINT, FAIR POINT. COUNTERPOINT: MAYBE I SHOULD GET TO DANCE WITH WENDY...
...BECAUSE I'VE BEEN AROUND HER THE LEAST.
THAT MAKES, LIKE, ZERO SENSE.
YOU MAKE ZERO SENSE!
PUSH!
SHOVE!!
WATCH IT!
DON'T SHOVE PEOPLE!
PUSH!
JABBER
JABBER
JABBER
NANA NAN ANA-AAAA!

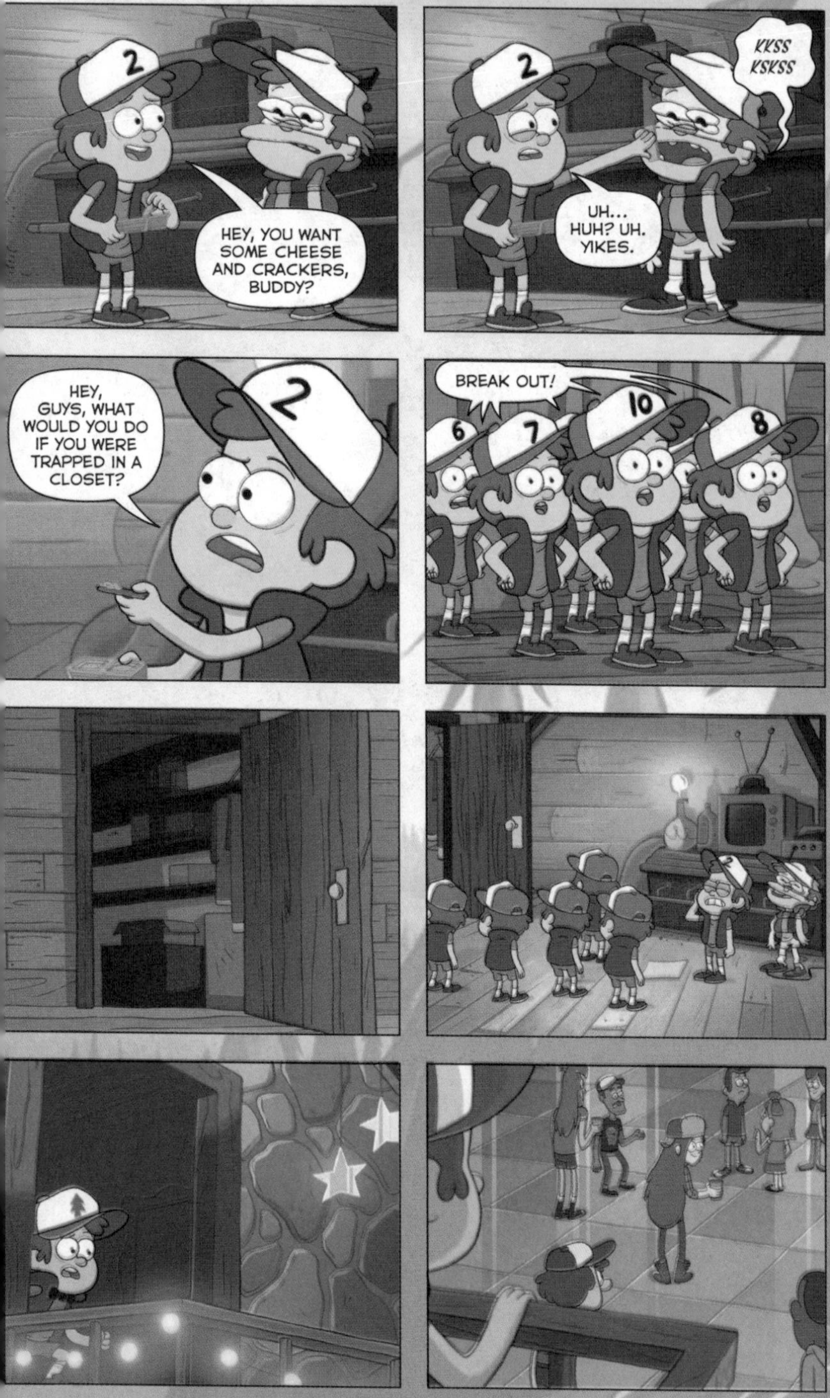
HEY, YOU WANT SOME CHEESE AND CRACKERS, BUDDY?
KKSS KSKSS
UH... HUH? UH. YIKES.
HEY, GUYS, WHAT WOULD YOU DO IF YOU WERE TRAPPED IN A CLOSET?
BREAK OUT!

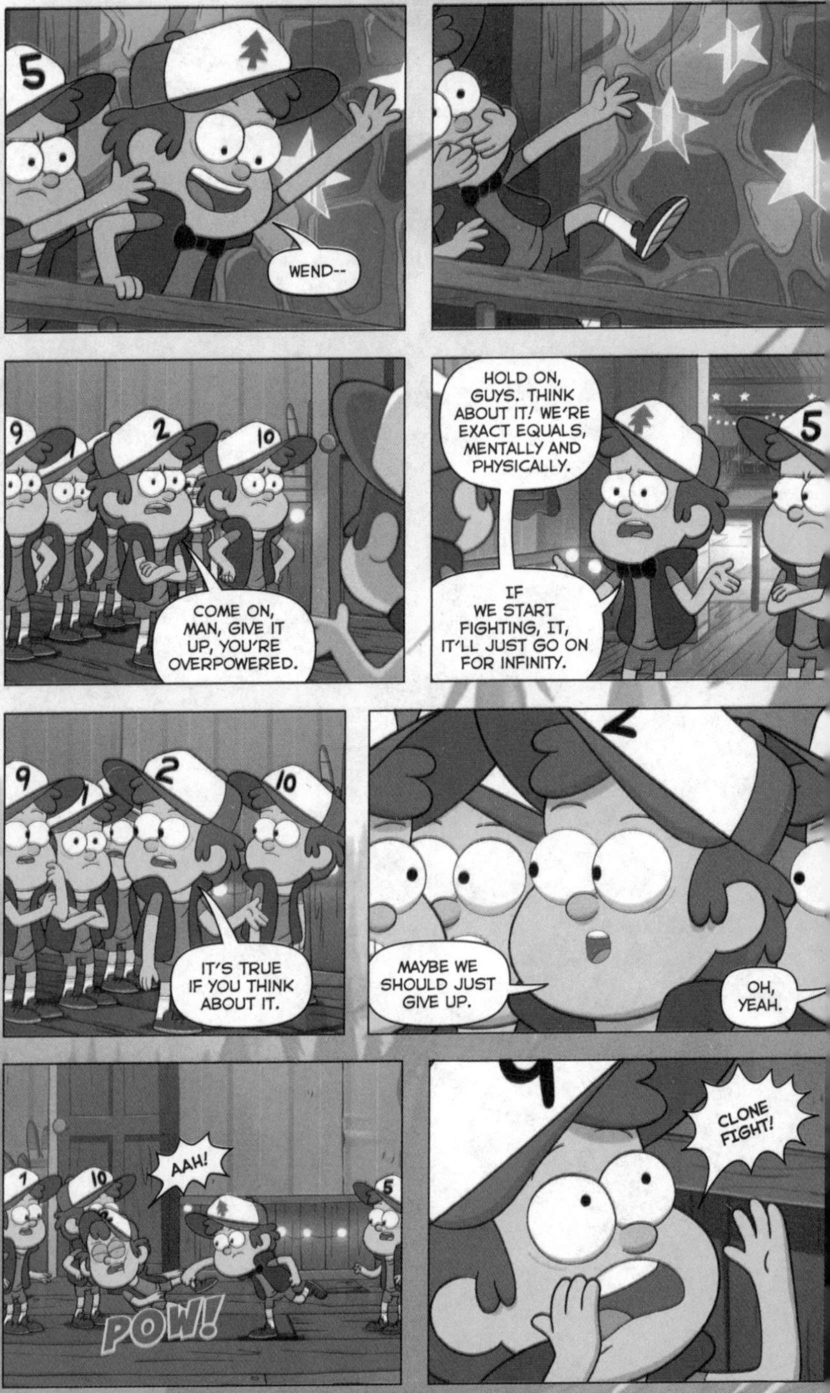
WEND--
COME ON, MAN, GIVE IT UP, YOU'RE OVERPOWERED.
HOLD ON, GUYS. THINK ABOUT IT! WE'RE EXACT EQUALS, MENTALLY AND PHYSICALLY.
IF WE START FIGHTING, IT, IT'LL JUST GO ON FOR INFINITY.
IT'S TRUE IF YOU THINK ABOUT IT.
MAYBE WE SHOULD JUST GIVE UP.
OH, YEAH.
AAH!
POW!
CLONE FIGHT!

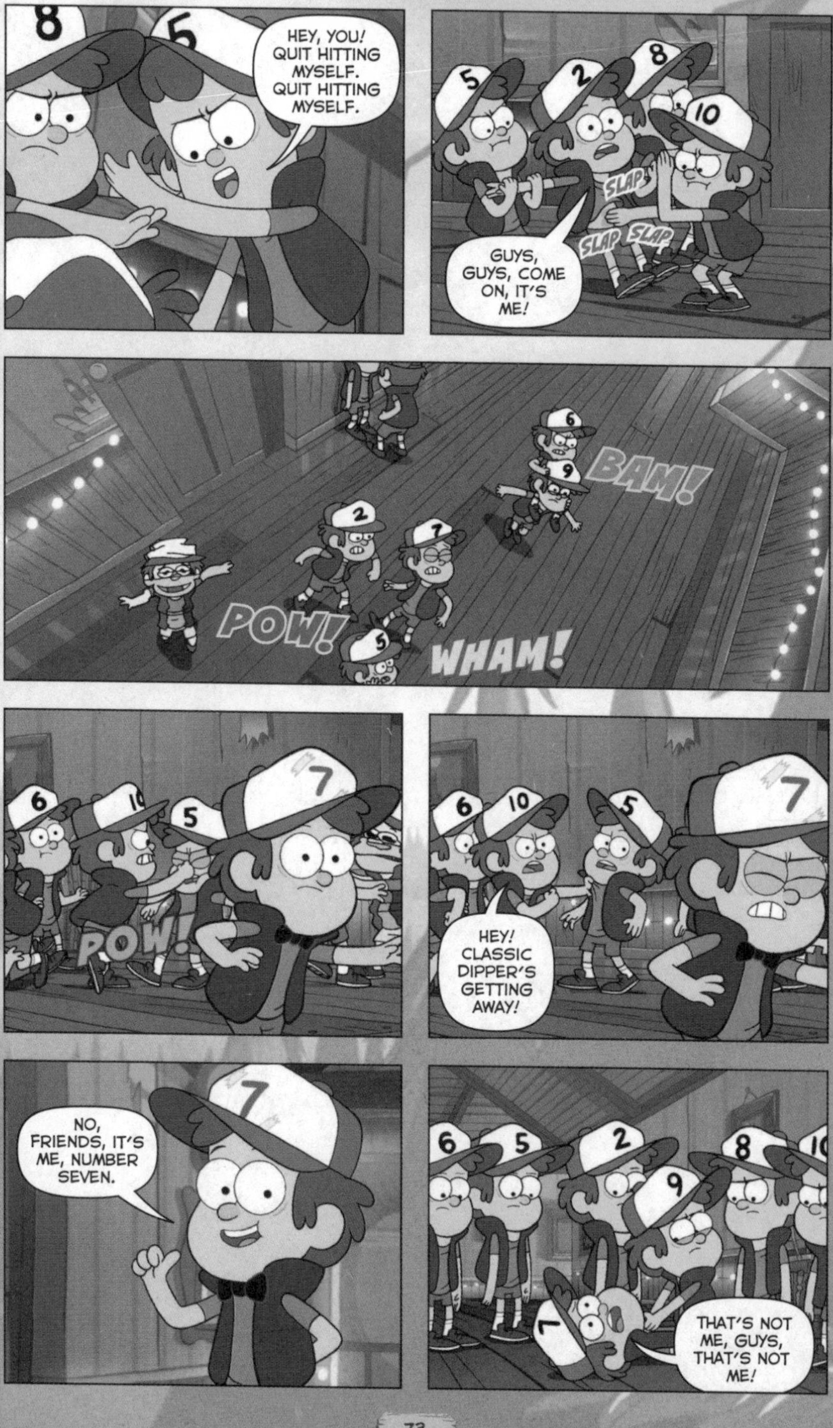
HEY, YOU! QUIT HITTING MYSELF. QUIT HITTING MYSELF.
SLAP
SLAP SLAP
GUYS, GUYS, COME ON, IT'S ME!
BAM!
POW!
WHAM!
POW!
HEY! CLASSIC DIPPER'S GETTING AWAY!
NO, FRIENDS, IT'S ME, NUMBER SEVEN.
THAT'S NOT ME, GUYS, THAT'S NOT ME!

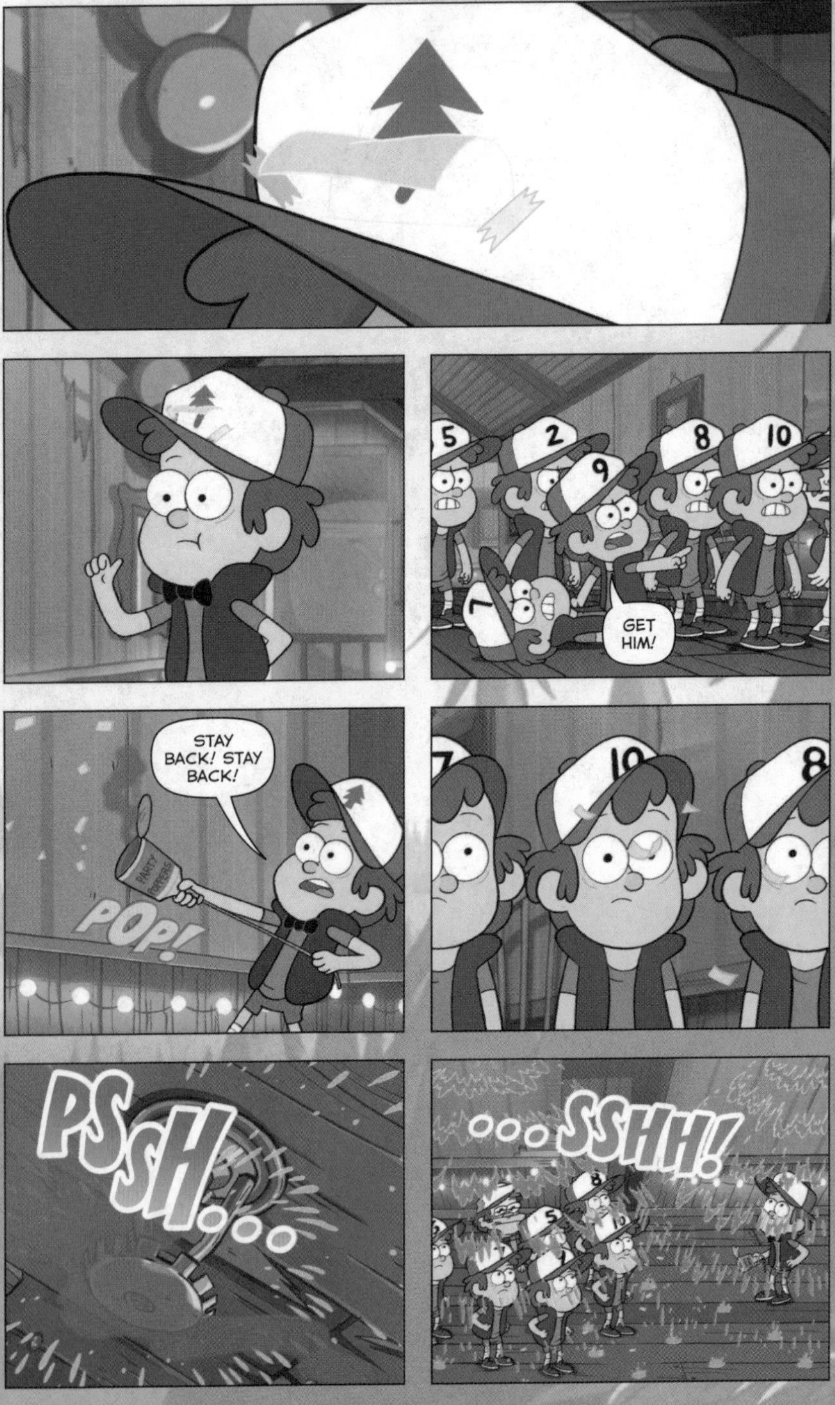
GET HIM!
STAY BACK! STAY BACK!
PARTY POPPERS
POP!
PSSH...
...SSHH!

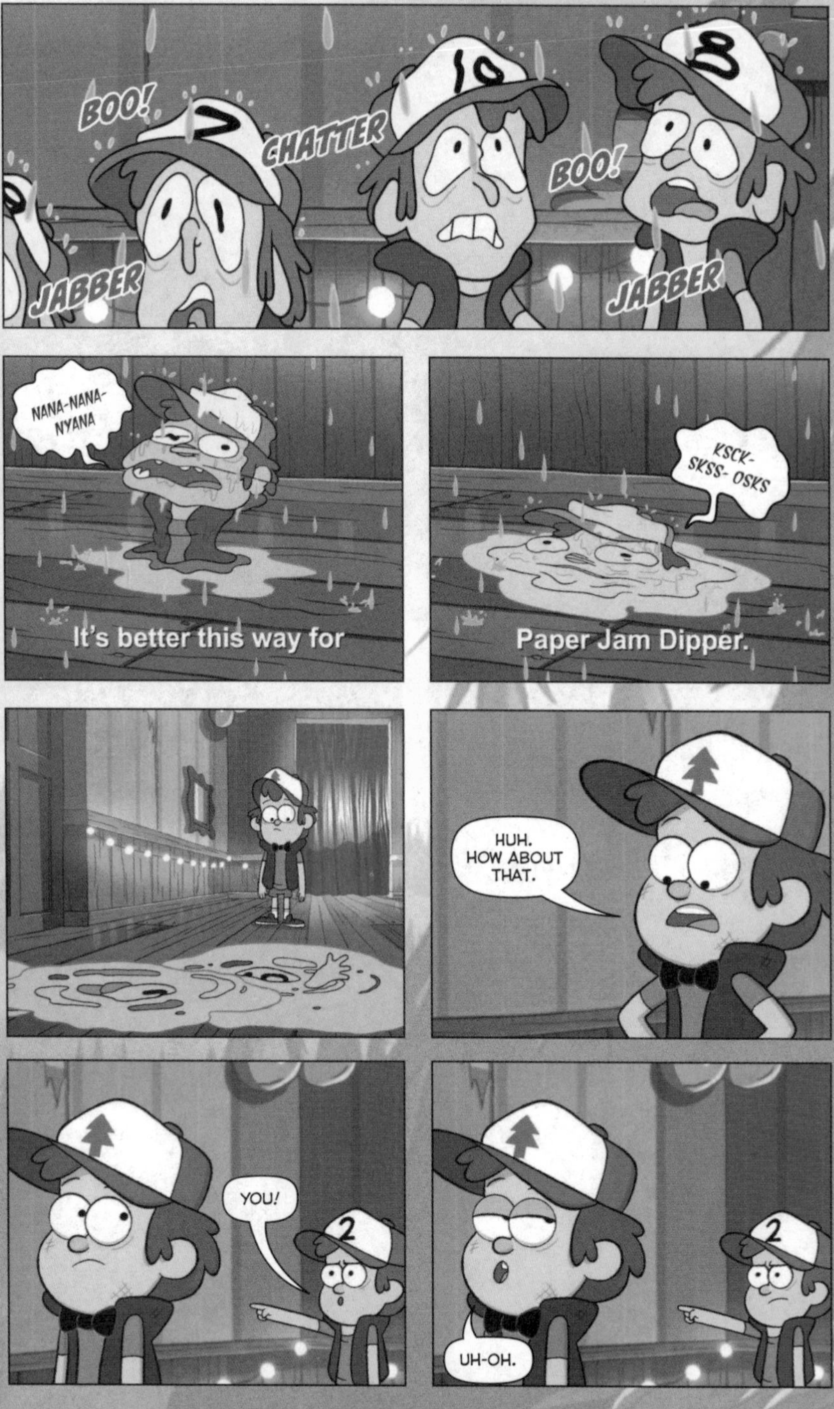
BOO!
CHATTER
BOO!
JABBER
JABBER
NANA-NANA-NYANA
It's better this way for
KSCK-SKSS- OSKS
Paper Jam Dipper.
HUH. HOW ABOUT THAT.
YOU!
UH-OH.

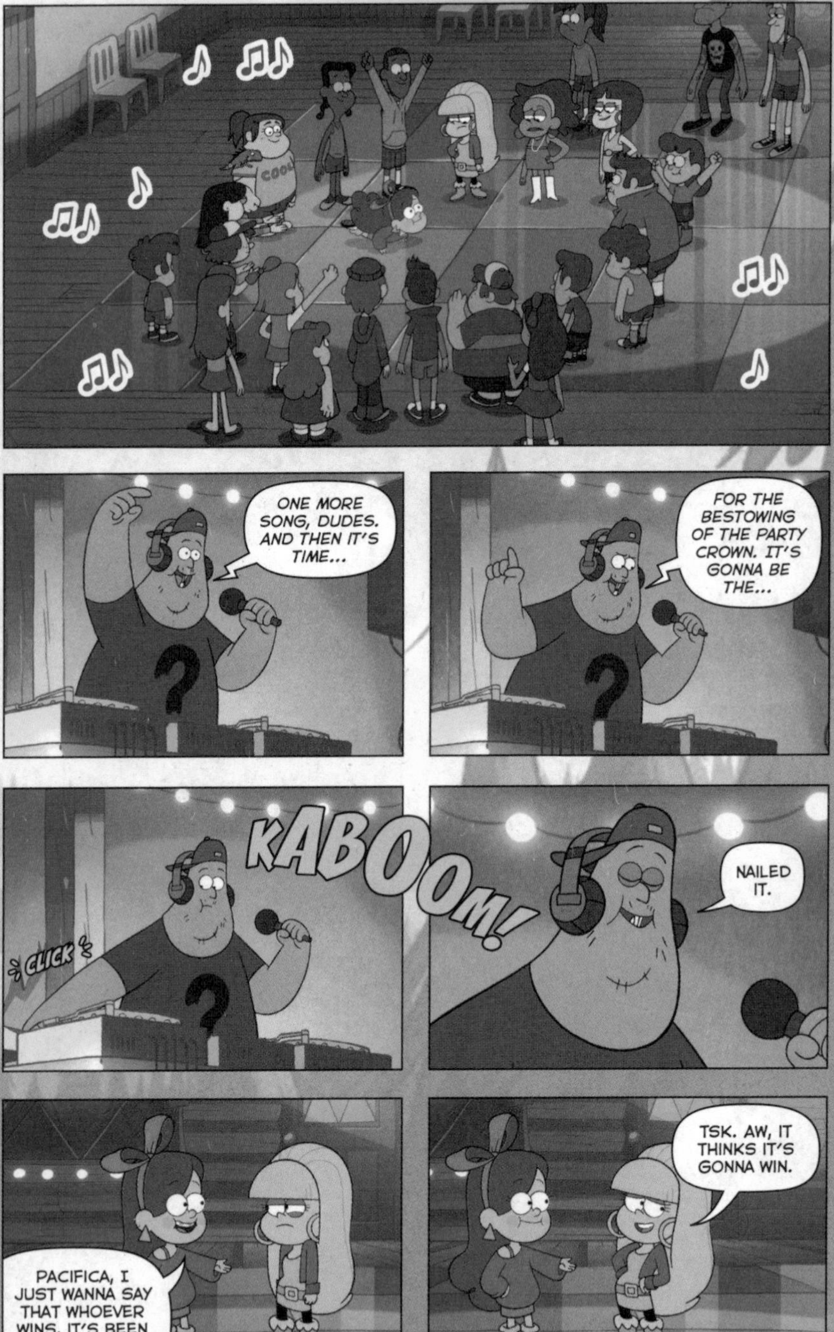

COOL
ONE MORE SONG, DUDES. AND THEN IT'S TIME...
FOR THE BESTOWING OF THE PARTY CROWN. IT'S GONNA BE THE...
KABOOM!
CLICK
NAILED IT.
PACIFICA, I JUST WANNA SAY THAT WHOEVER WINS, IT'S BEEN A SUPER FUN PARTY.
TSK. AW, IT THINKS IT'S GONNA WIN.

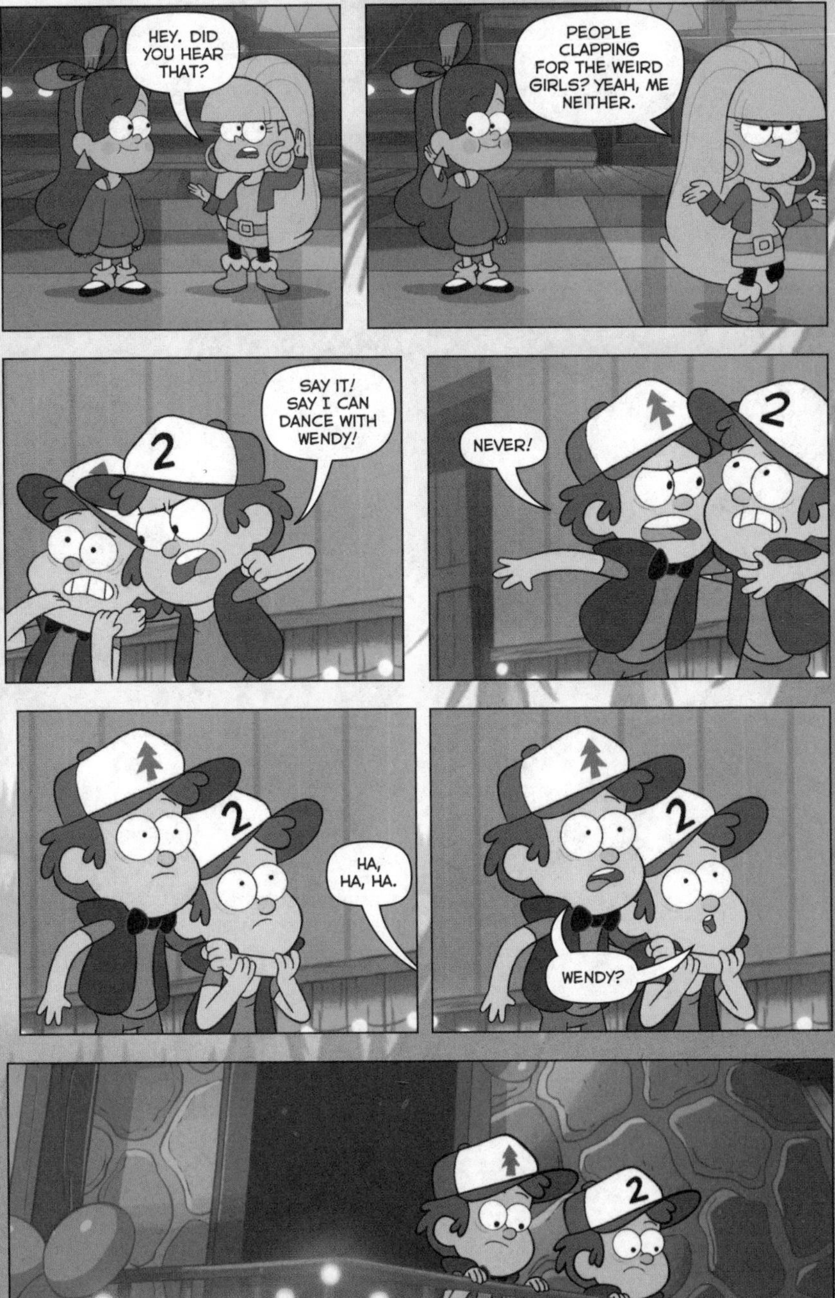
HEY. DID YOU HEAR THAT?
PEOPLE CLAPPING FOR THE WEIRD GIRLS? YEAH, ME NEITHER.
SAY IT! SAY I CAN DANCE WITH WENDY!
NEVER!
HA, HA, HA.
WENDY?

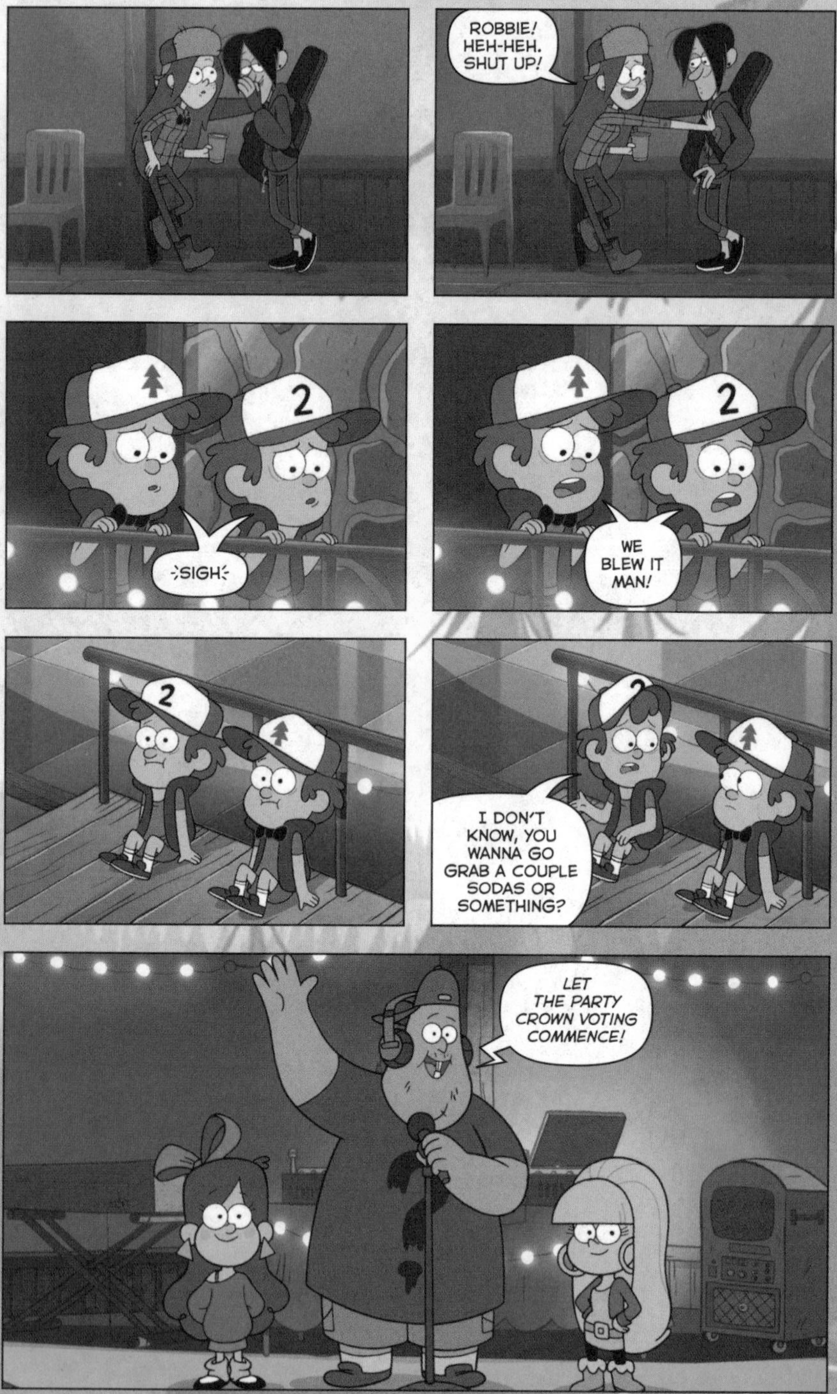
ROBBIE! HEH-HEH. SHUT UP!
SIGH
WE BLEW IT MAN!
I DON'T KNOW, YOU WANNA GO GRAB A COUPLE SODAS OR SOMETHING?
LET THE PARTY CROWN VOTING COMMENCE!

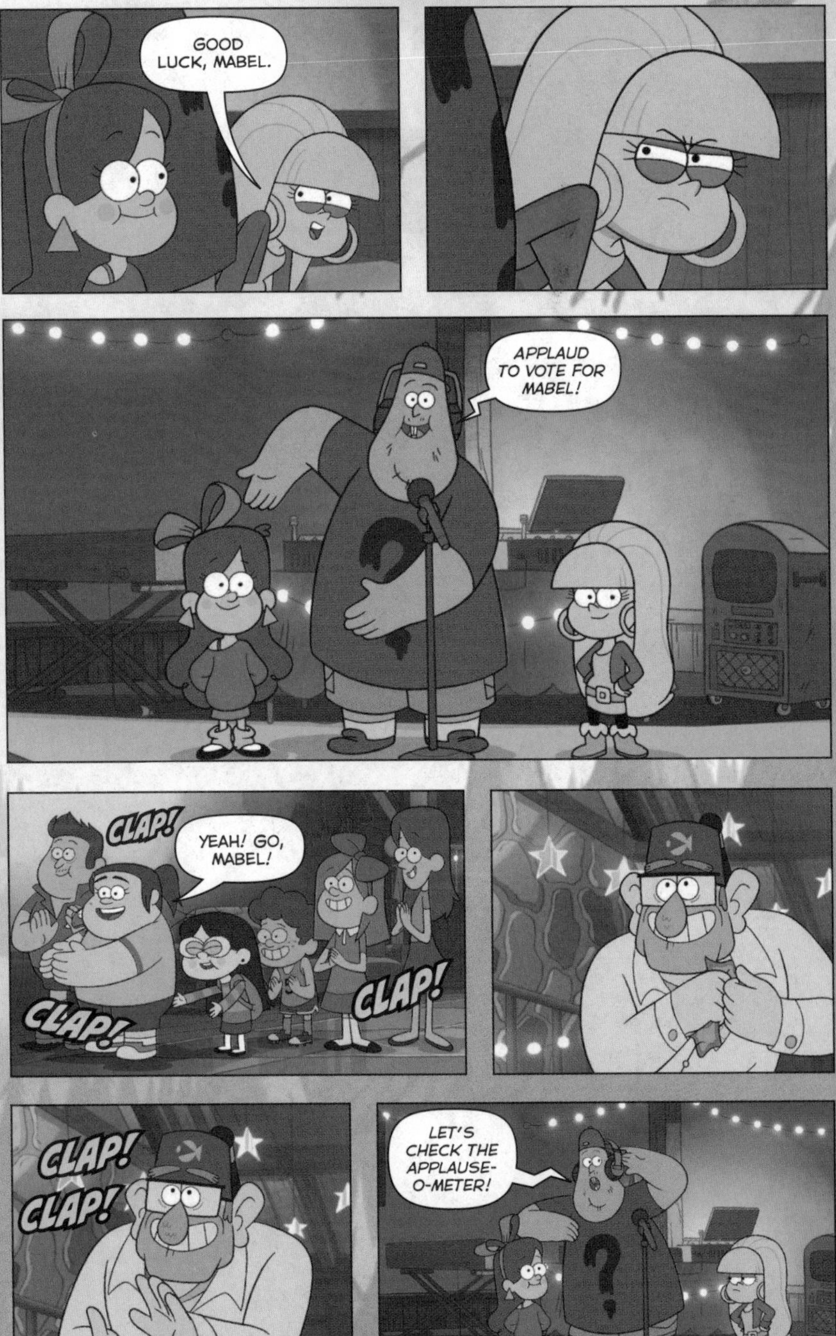
GOOD LUCK, MABEL.
APPLAUD TO VOTE FOR MABEL!
CLAP!
YEAH! GO, MABEL!
CLAP!
CLAP!
CLAP!
CLAP!
LET'S CHECK THE APPLAUSE-O-METER!

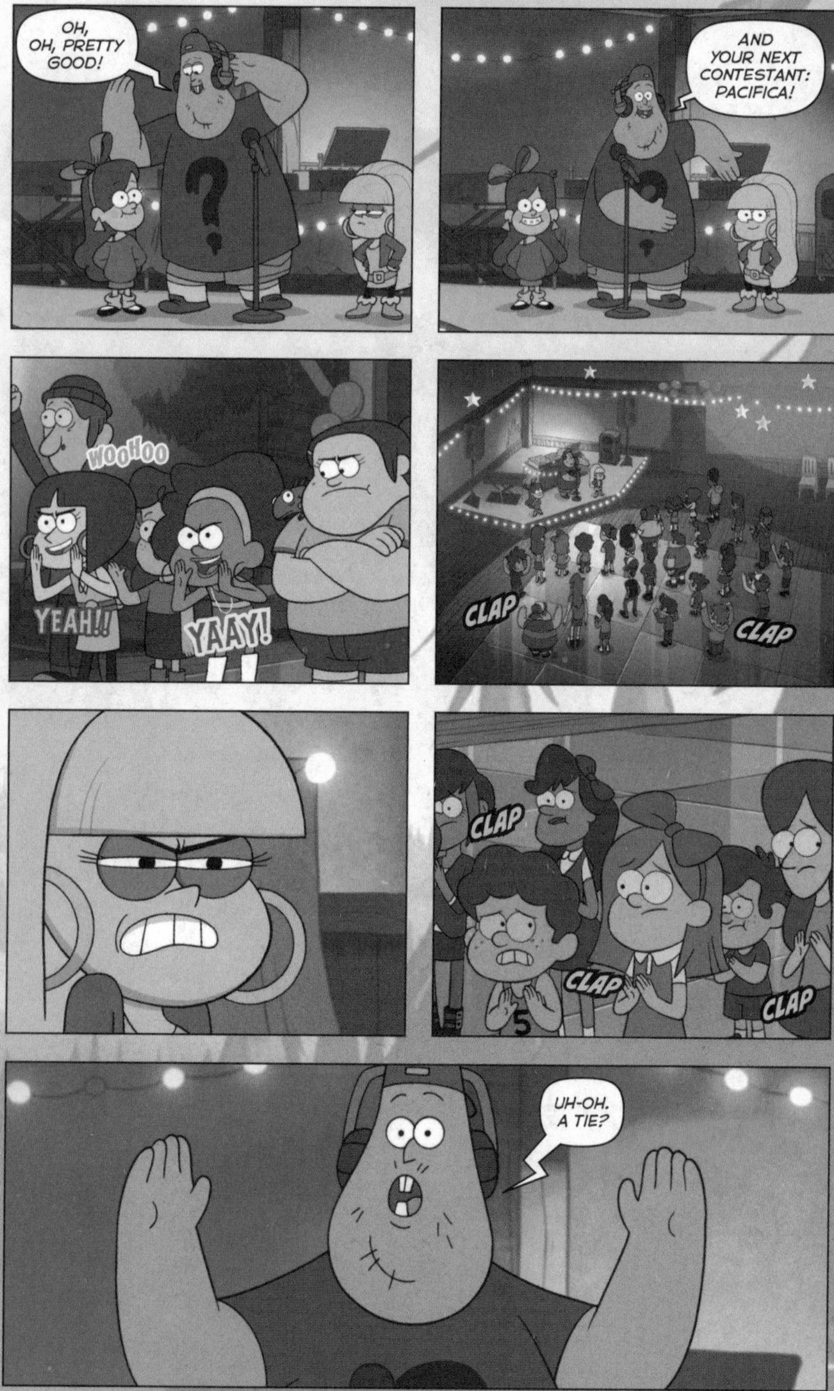
OH, OH, PRETTY GOOD!
AND YOUR NEXT CONTESTANT: PACIFICA!
WOOHOO
YEAH!!
YAAY!
CLAP
CLAP
CLAP
CLAP
CLAP
UH-OH. A TIE?

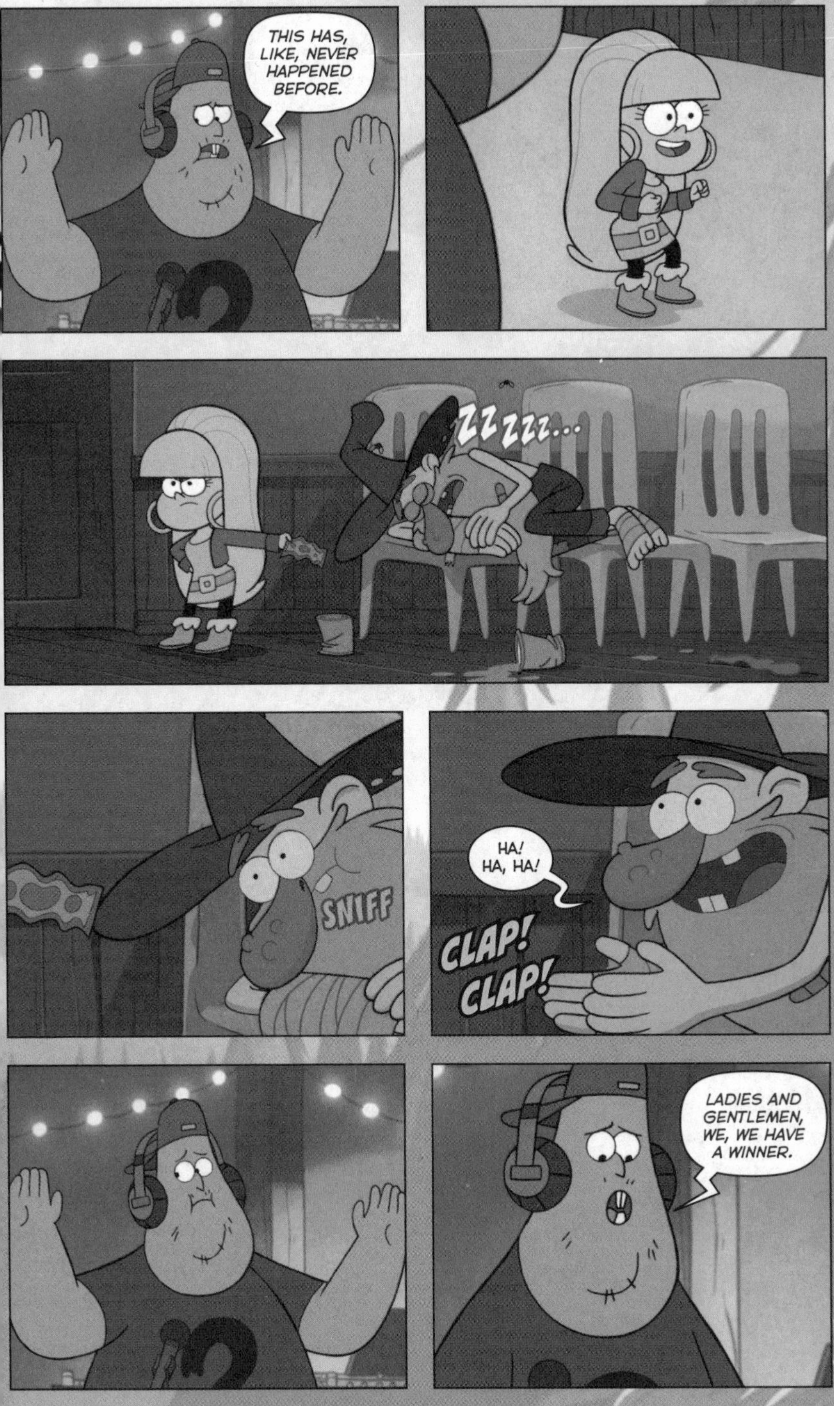
THIS HAS, LIKE, NEVER HAPPENED BEFORE.
ZZZZZ...
SNIFF
HA! HA, HA!
CLAP! CLAP!
LADIES AND GENTLEMEN, WE, WE HAVE A WINNER.

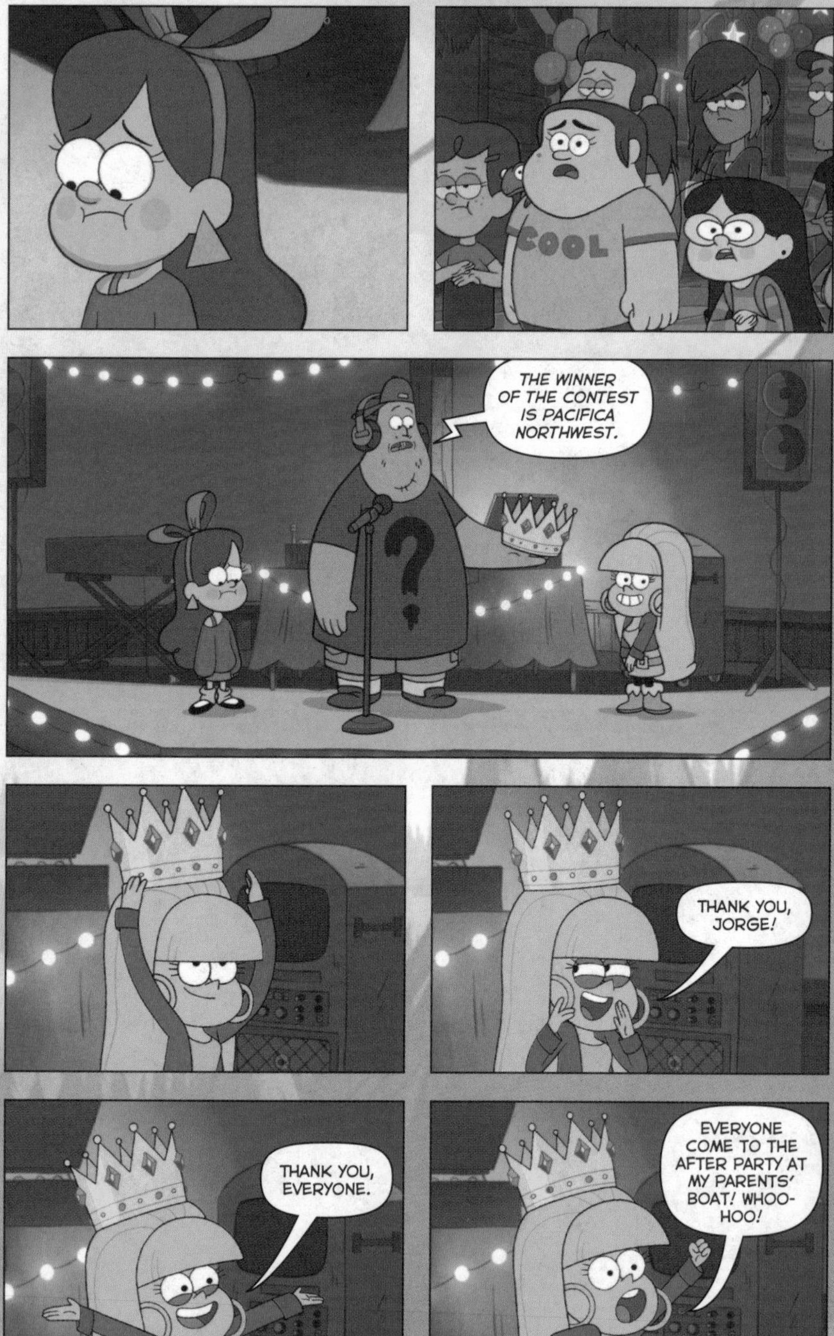
COOL
THE WINNER OF THE CONTEST IS PACIFICA NORTHWEST.
THANK YOU, JORGE!
THANK YOU, EVERYONE.
EVERYONE COME TO THE AFTER PARTY AT MY PARENTS' BOAT! WHOO-HOO!

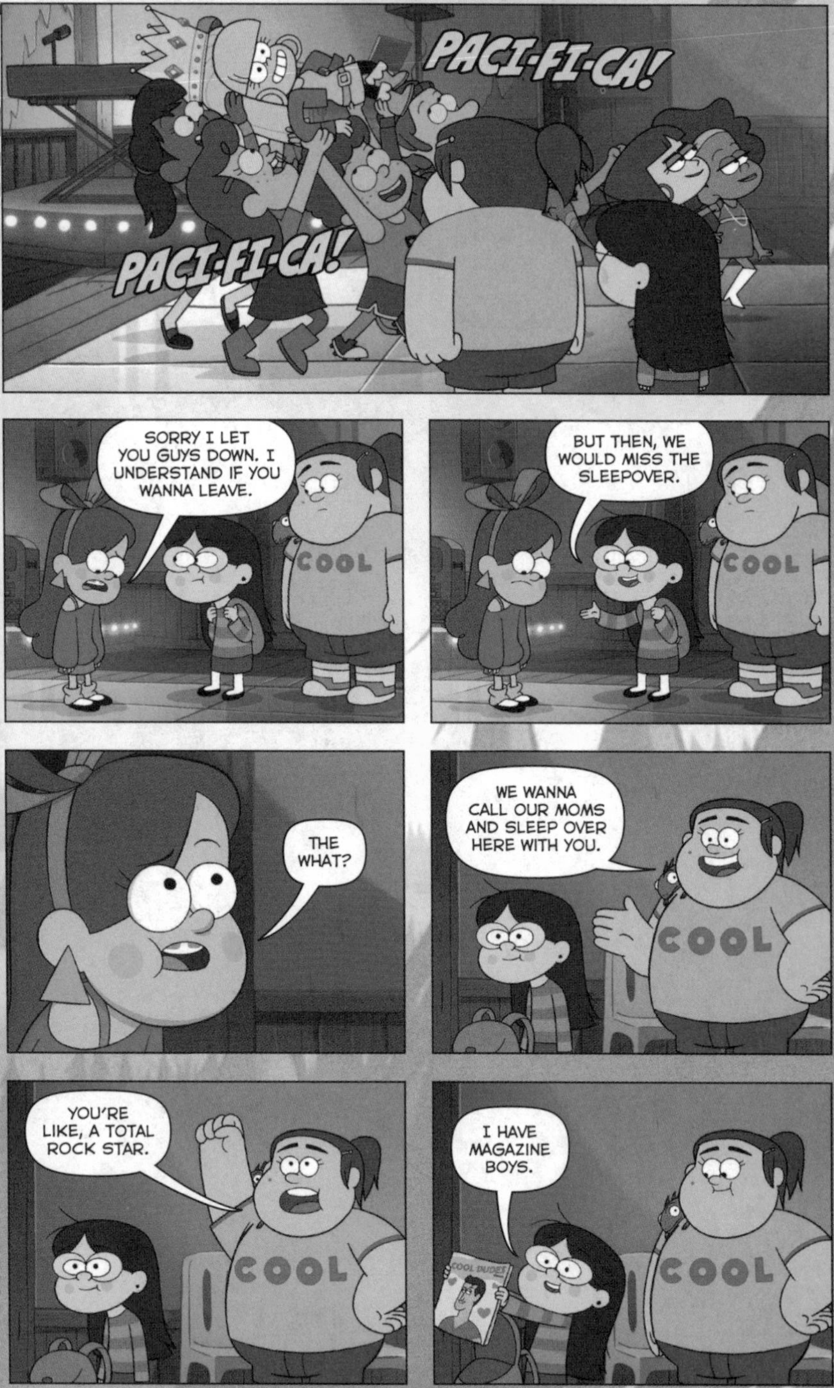
PACI-FI-CA!
PACI-FI-CA!
SORRY I LET YOU GUYS DOWN. I UNDERSTAND IF YOU WANNA LEAVE.
COOL
BUT THEN, WE WOULD MISS THE SLEEPOVER.
COOL
THE WHAT?
WE WANNA CALL OUR MOMS AND SLEEP OVER HERE WITH YOU.
COOL
YOU'RE LIKE, A TOTAL ROCK STAR.
COOL
I HAVE MAGAZINE BOYS.
COOL

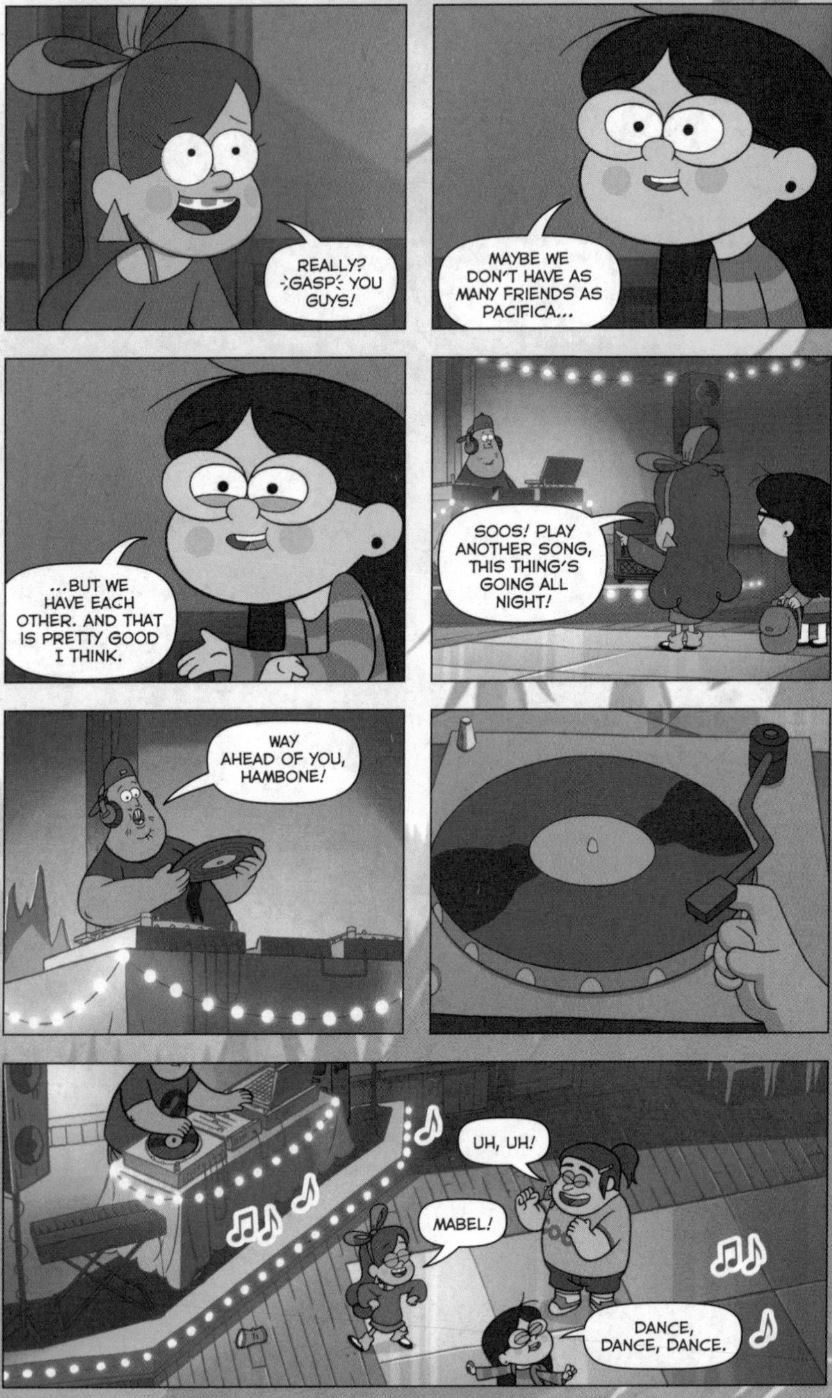
REALLY? GASP YOU GUYS!
MAYBE WE DON'T HAVE AS MANY FRIENDS AS PACIFICA...
...BUT WE HAVE EACH OTHER. AND THAT IS PRETTY GOOD I THINK.
SOOS! PLAY ANOTHER SONG, THIS THING'S GOING ALL NIGHT!
WAY AHEAD OF YOU, HAMBONE!
UH, UH!
MABEL!
DANCE, DANCE, DANCE.

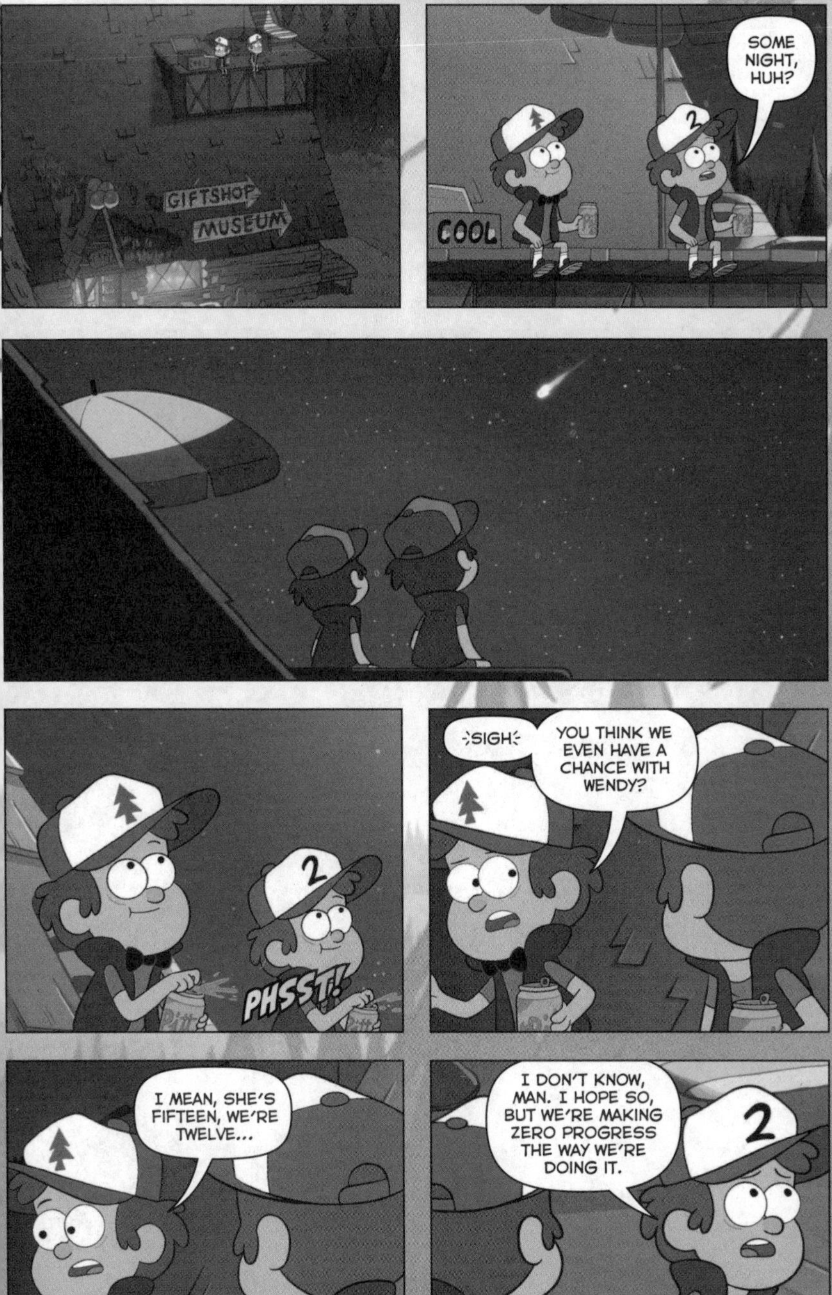
GIFTSHOP
MUSEUM
SOME NIGHT, HUH?
COOL
PHSST!
-SIGH-
YOU THINK WE EVEN HAVE A CHANCE WITH WENDY?
I MEAN, SHE'S FIFTEEN, WE'RE TWELVE...
I DON'T KNOW, MAN. I HOPE SO, BUT WE'RE MAKING ZERO PROGRESS THE WAY WE'RE DOING IT.

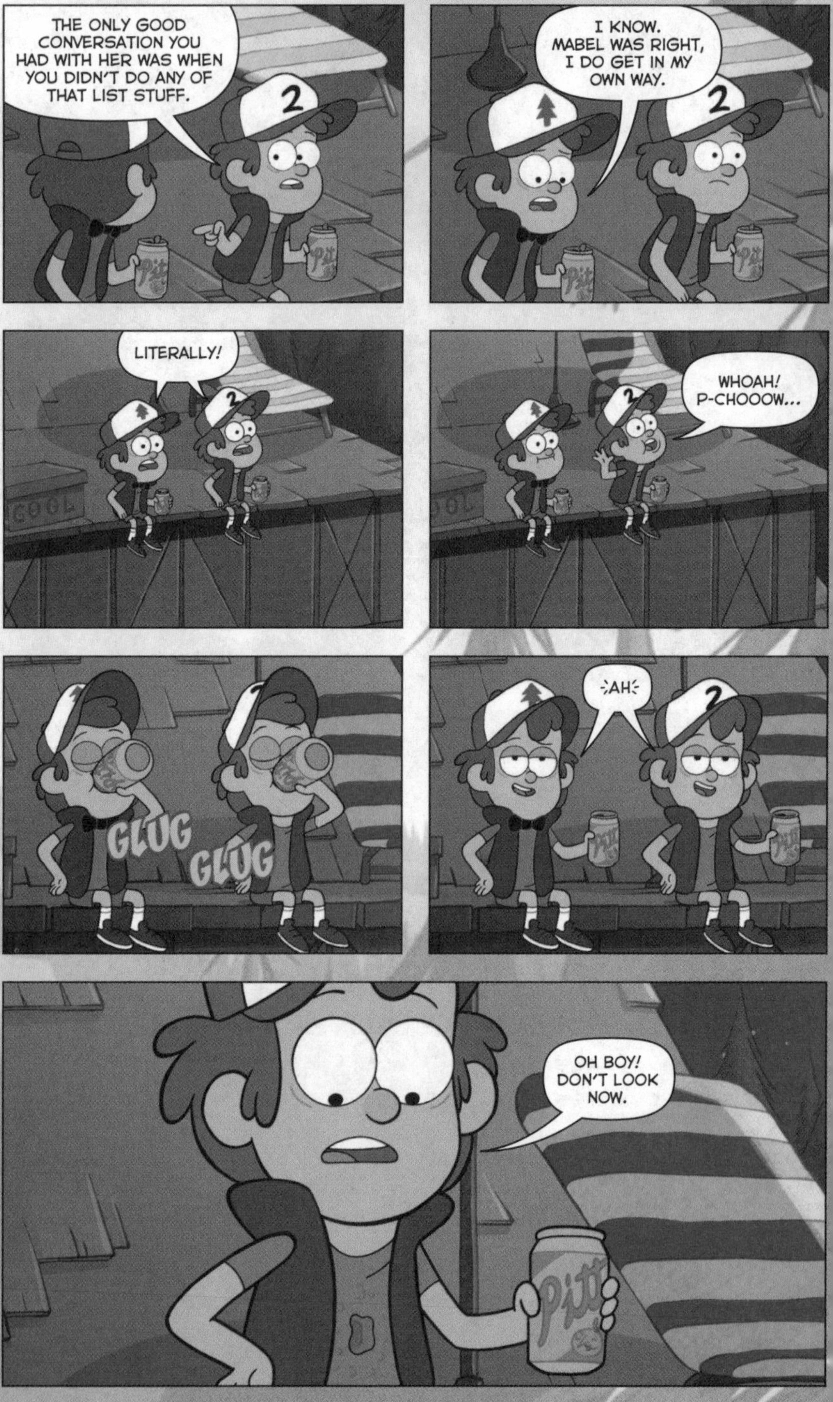
THE ONLY GOOD CONVERSATION YOU HAD WITH HER WAS WHEN YOU DIDN'T DO ANY OF THAT LIST STUFF.
I KNOW. MABEL WAS RIGHT, I DO GET IN MY OWN WAY.
LITERALLY!
WHOAH! P-CHOOOW...
GLUG
GLUG
AH
OH BOY! DON'T LOOK NOW.

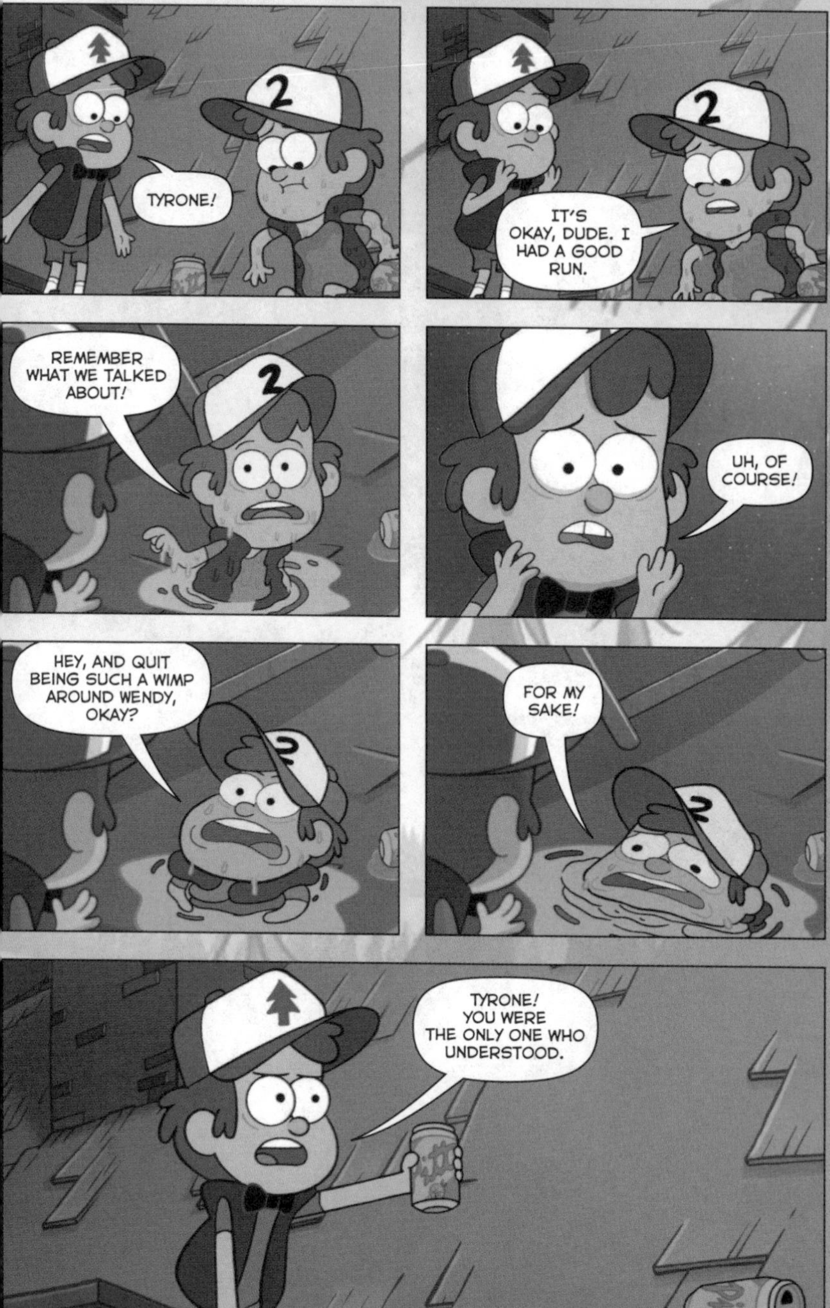
TYRONE!
IT'S OKAY, DUDE. I HAD A GOOD RUN.
REMEMBER WHAT WE TALKED ABOUT!
UH, OF COURSE!
HEY, AND QUIT BEING SUCH A WIMP AROUND WENDY, OKAY?
FOR MY SAKE!
TYRONE! YOU WERE THE ONLY ONE WHO UNDERSTOOD.

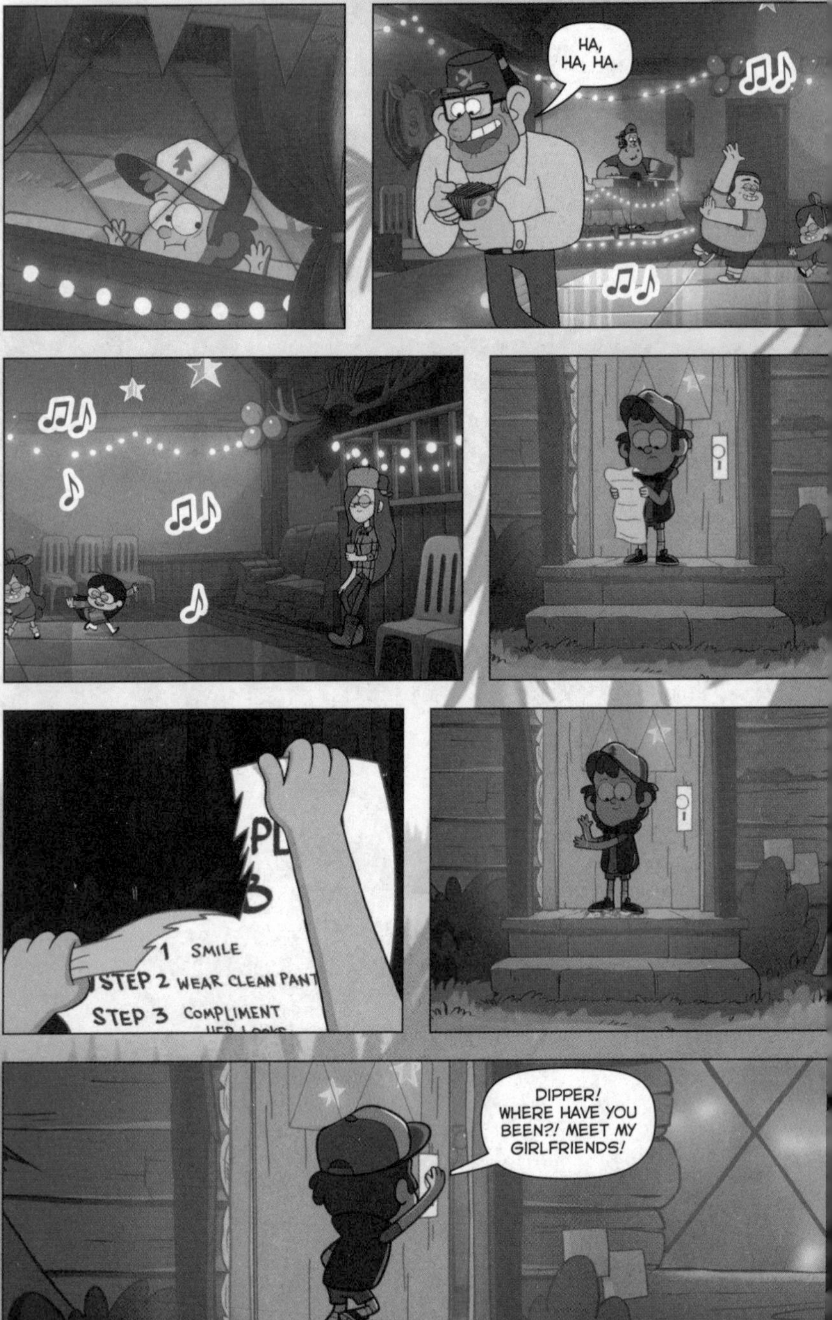
HA, HA, HA.
1 SMILE
STEP 2 WEAR CLEAN PANT
STEP 3 COMPLIMENT
DIPPER! WHERE HAVE YOU BEEN?! MEET MY GIRLFRIENDS!
THE END

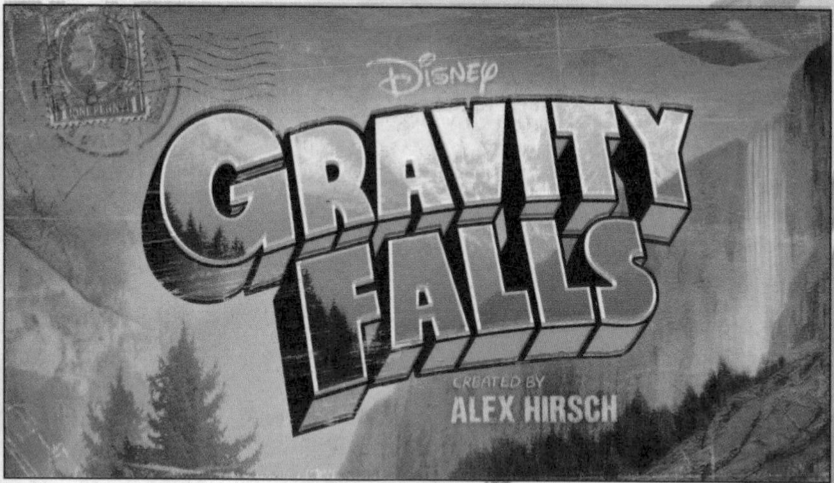
Disney
GRAVITY FALLS
CREATED BY
ALEX HIRSCH

IRRATIONAL TREASURE
EPISODE 8

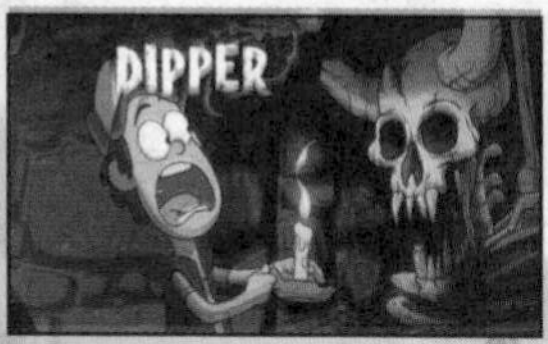
DIPPER
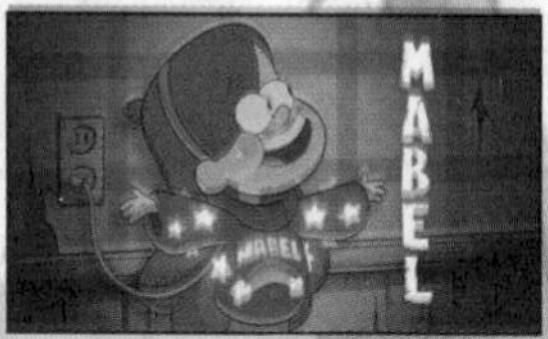
MABEL
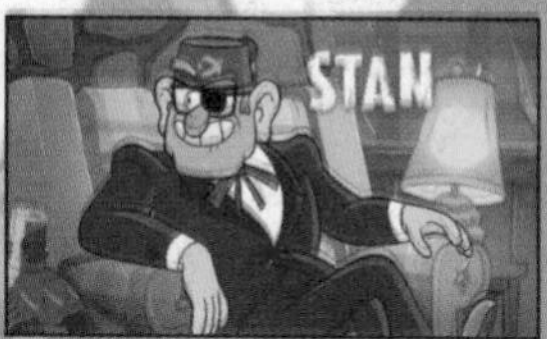
STAN

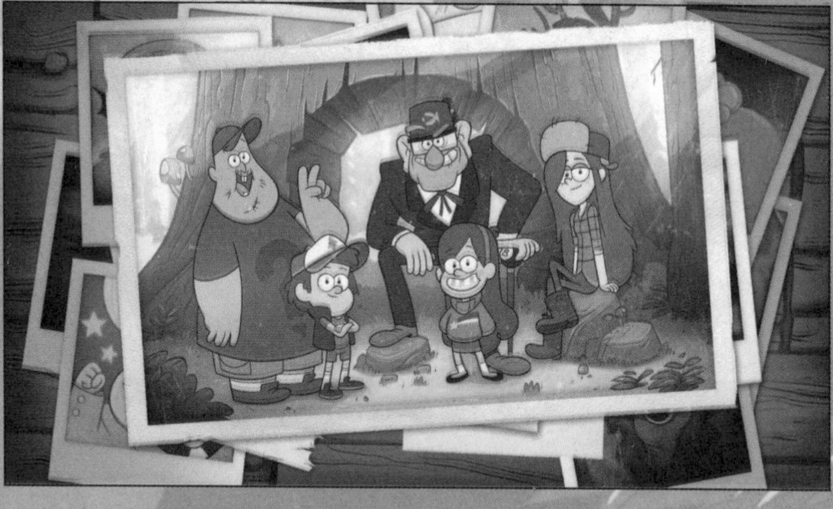

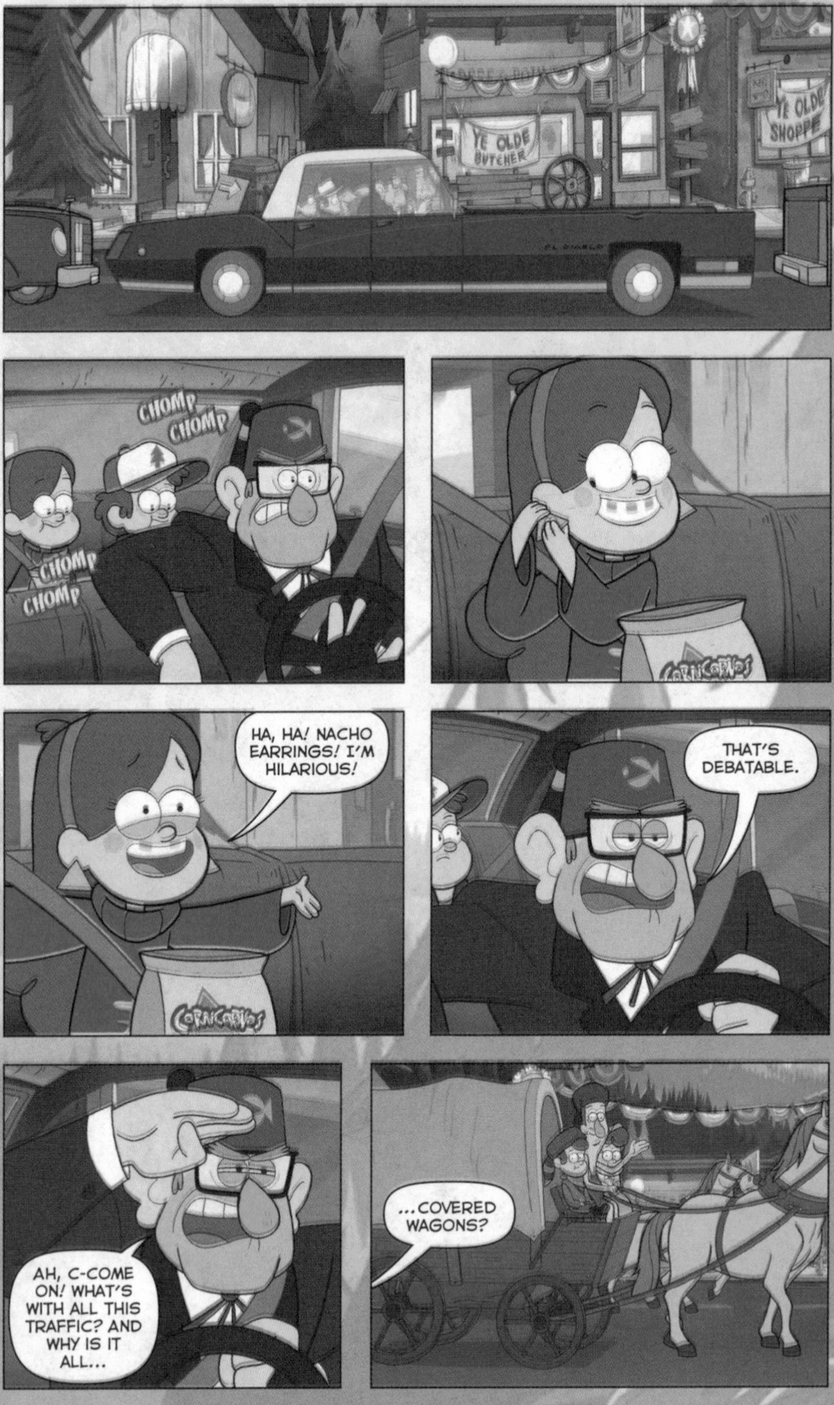
YE OLDE BUTCHER
YE OLDE SHOPPE
CHOMP CHOMP
CHOMP CHOMP
HA, HA! NACHO EARRINGS! I'M HILARIOUS!
THAT'S DEBATABLE.
AH, C-COME ON! WHAT'S WITH ALL THIS TRAFFIC? AND WHY IS IT ALL...
...COVERED WAGONS?

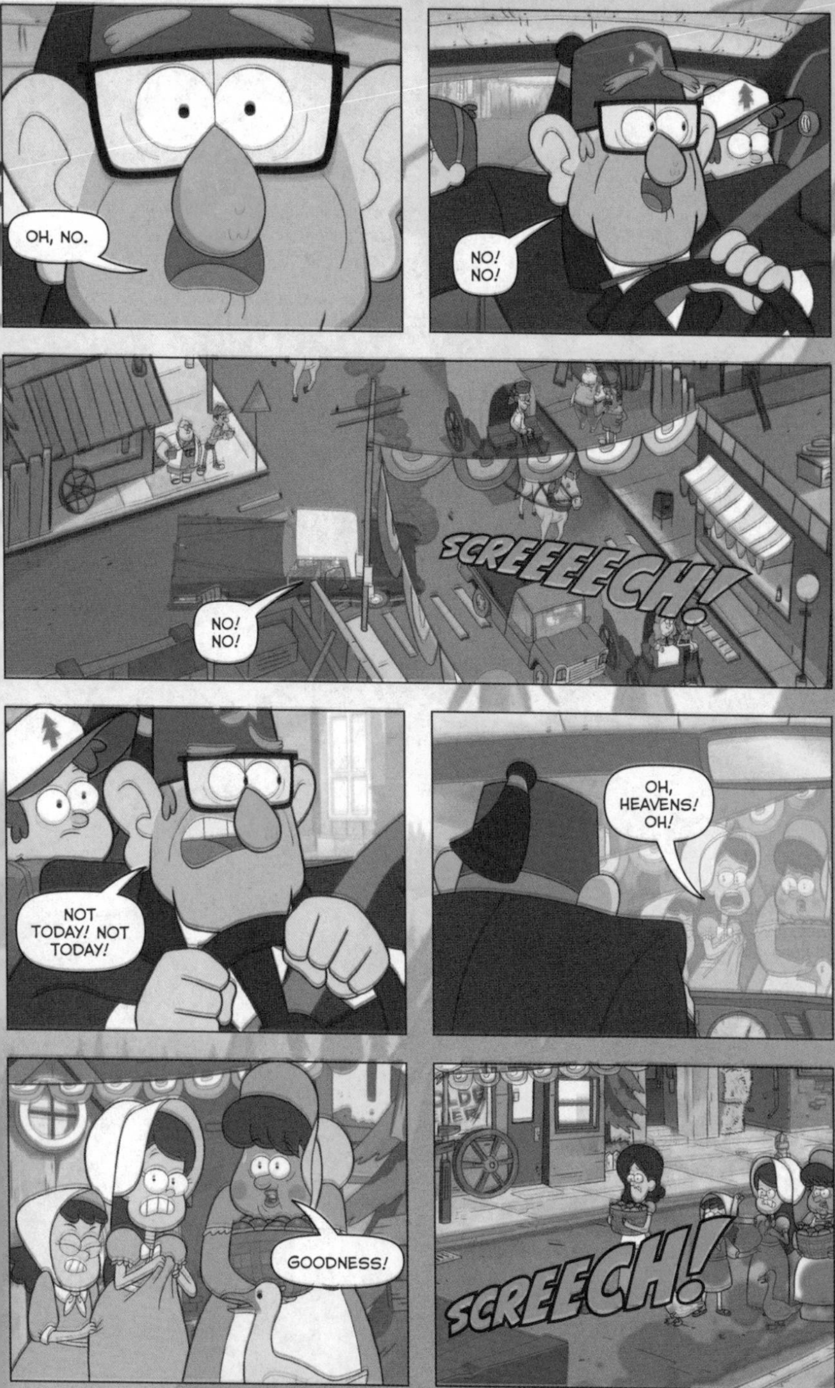
OH, NO.
NO! NO!
NO! NO!
SCREEEEECH!
NOT TODAY! NOT TODAY!
OH, HEAVENS! OH!
GOODNESS!
SCREECH!

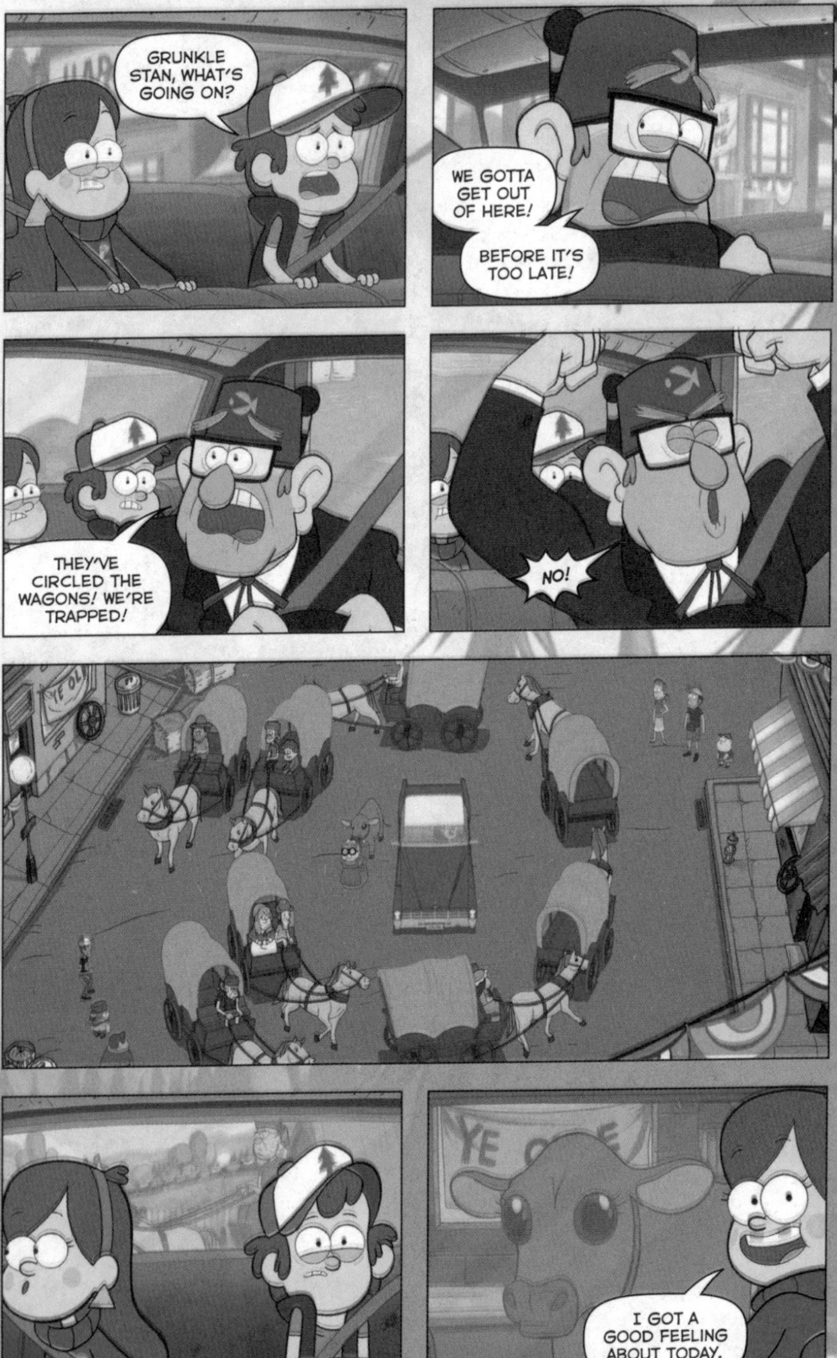
GRUNKLE STAN, WHAT'S GOING ON?
WE GOTTA GET OUT OF HERE!
BEFORE IT'S TOO LATE!
THEY'VE CIRCLED THE WAGONS! WE'RE TRAPPED!
NO!
I GOT A GOOD FEELING ABOUT TODAY.

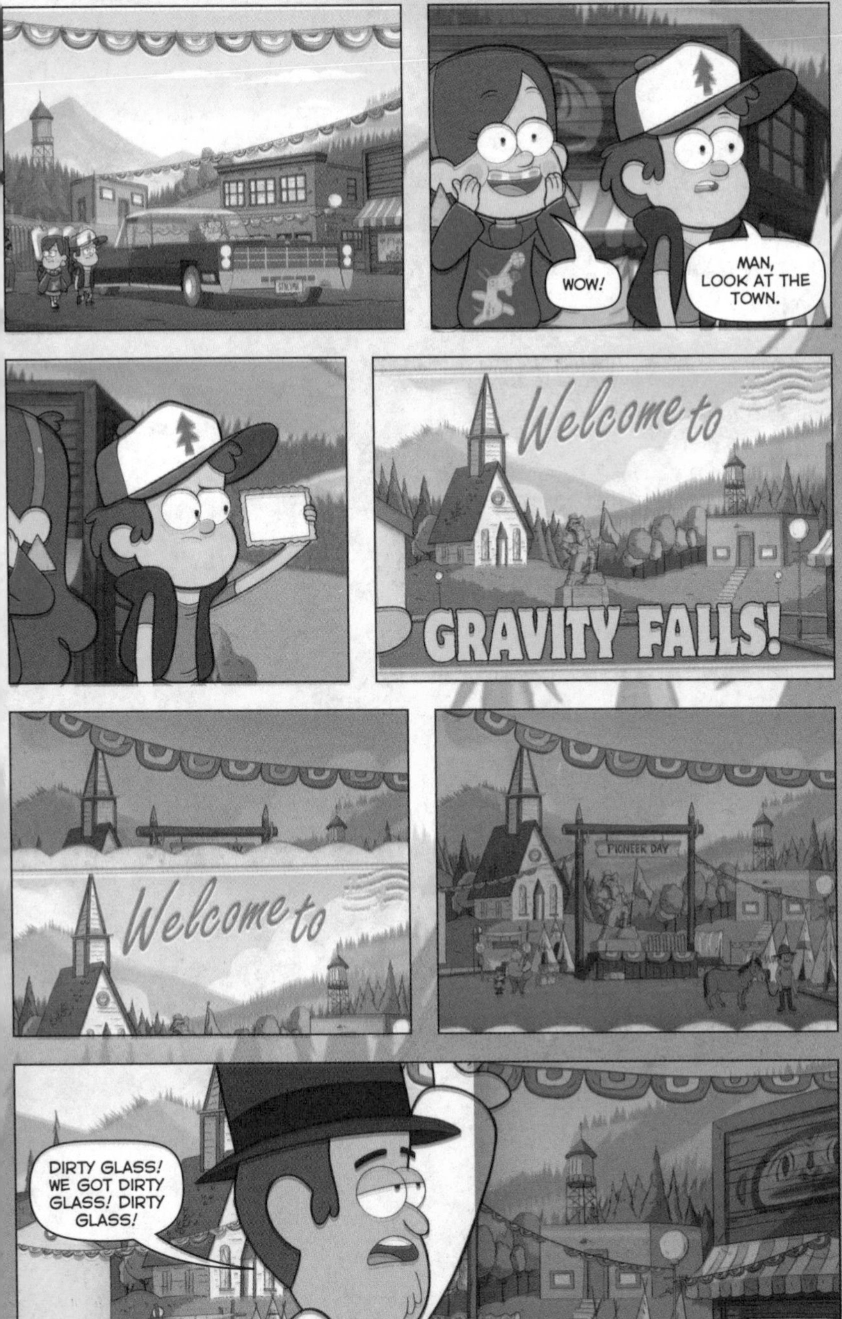
WOW!
MAN, LOOK AT THE TOWN.
Welcome to
GRAVITY FALLS!
Welcome to
PIONEER DAY
DIRTY GLASS! WE GOT DIRTY GLASS! DIRTY GLASS!
PIONEER DAY!

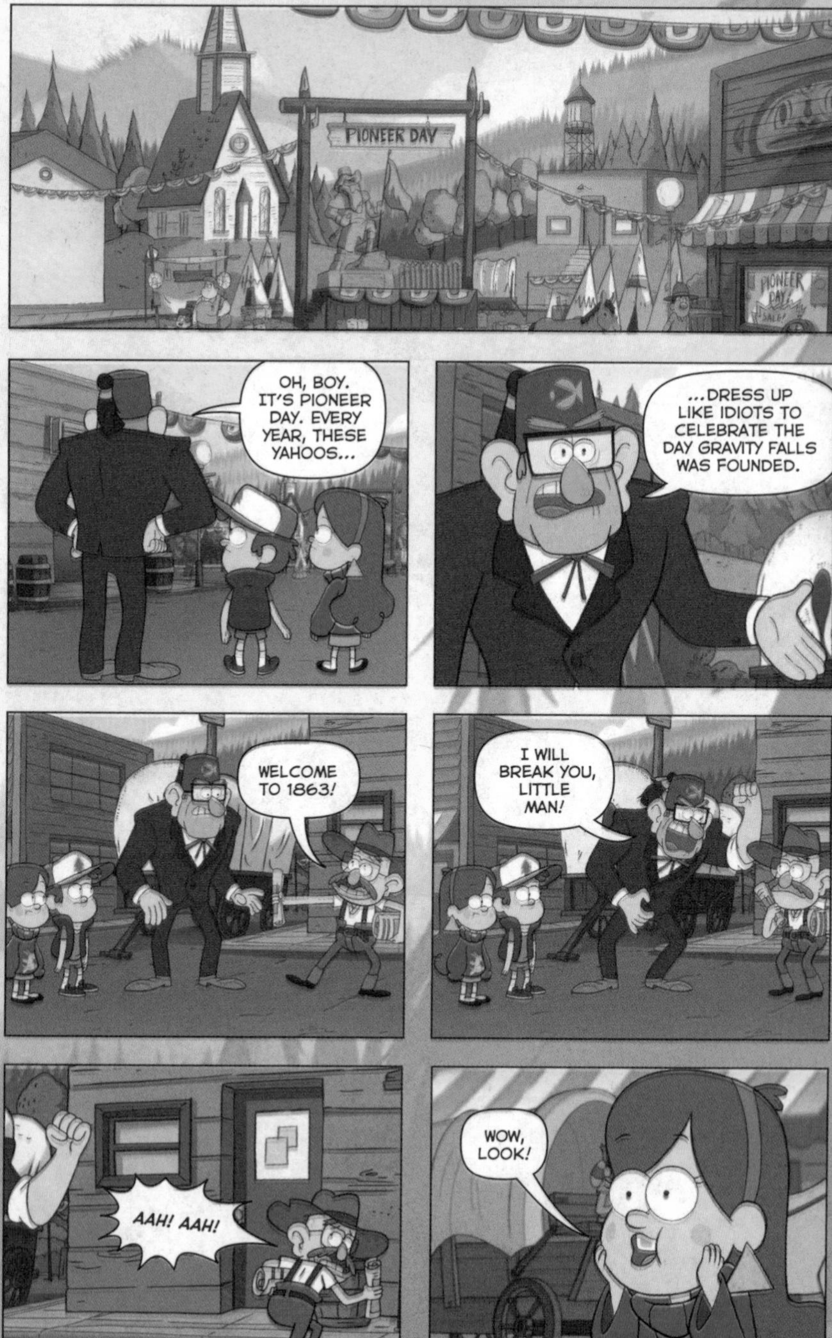
PIONEER DAY
PIONEER DAY
OH, BOY. IT'S PIONEER DAY. EVERY YEAR, THESE YAHOOS...
...DRESS UP LIKE IDIOTS TO CELEBRATE THE DAY GRAVITY FALLS WAS FOUNDED.
WELCOME TO 1863!
I WILL BREAK YOU, LITTLE MAN!
AAH! AAH!
WOW, LOOK!

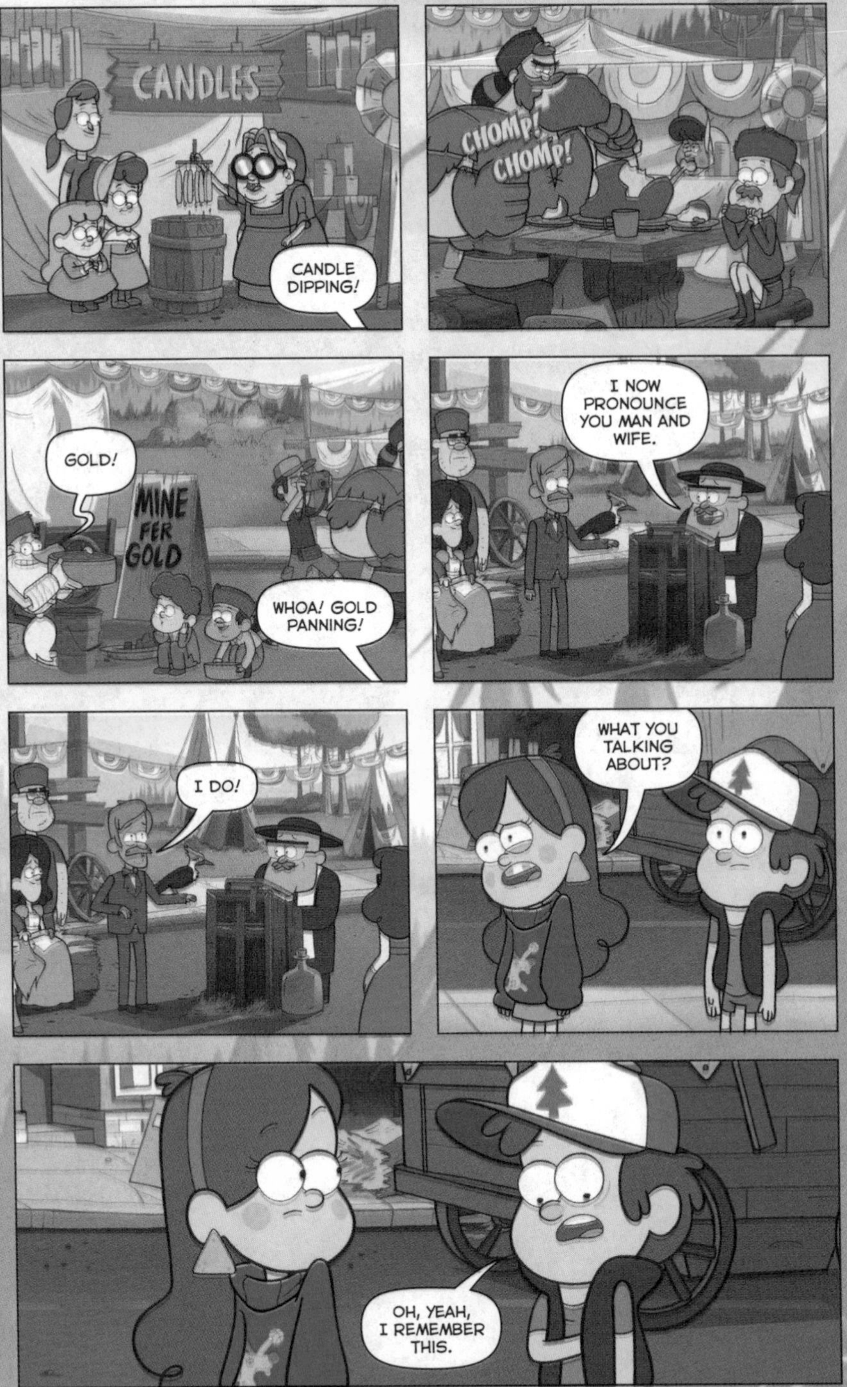
CANDLES
CANDLE DIPPING!
CHOMP! CHOMP!
GOLD!
MINE FER GOLD
WHOA! GOLD PANNING!
I NOW PRONOUNCE YOU MAN AND WIFE.
I DO!
WHAT YOU TALKING ABOUT?
OH, YEAH, I REMEMBER THIS.

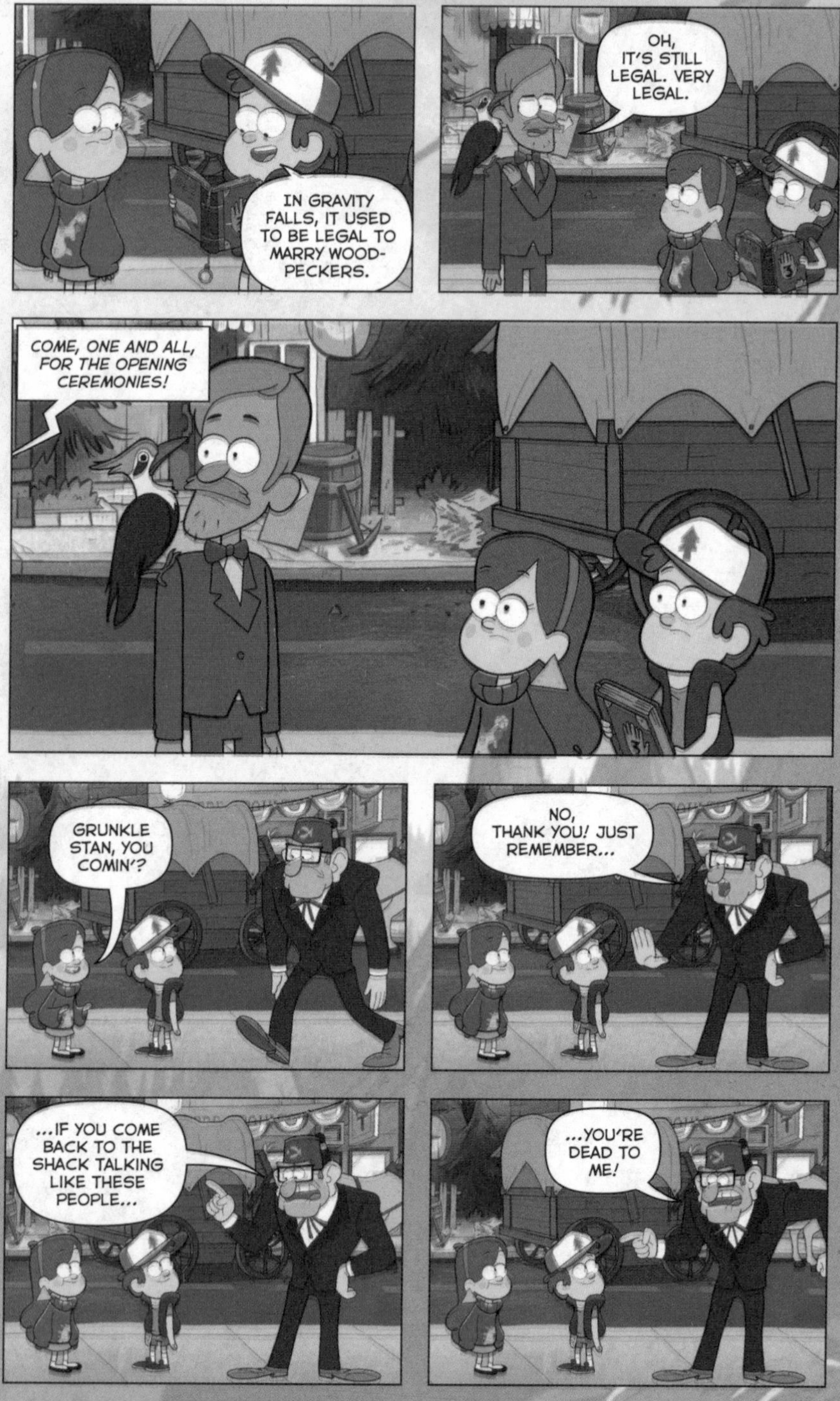
IN GRAVITY FALLS, IT USED TO BE LEGAL TO MARRY WOOD-PECKERS.
OH, IT'S STILL LEGAL. VERY LEGAL.
COME, ONE AND ALL, FOR THE OPENING CEREMONIES!
GRUNKLE STAN, YOU COMIN'?
NO, THANK YOU! JUST REMEMBER...
...IF YOU COME BACK TO THE SHACK TALKING LIKE THESE PEOPLE...
...YOU'RE DEAD TO ME!

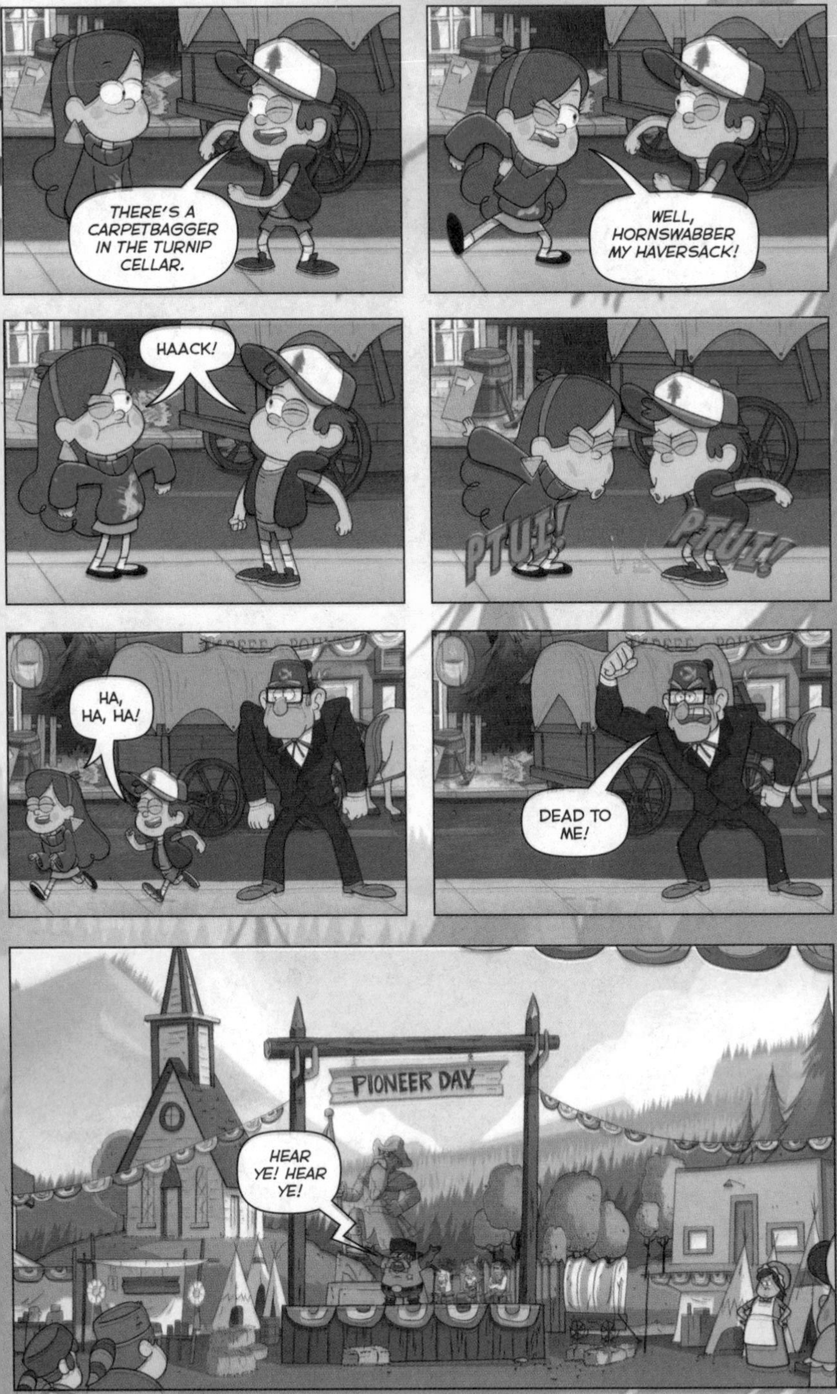
THERE'S A CARPETBAGGER IN THE TURNIP CELLAR.
WELL, HORNSWABBER MY HAVERSACK!
HAACK!
PTUI!
PTUI!
HA, HA, HA!
DEAD TO ME!
PIONEER DAY
HEAR YE! HEAR YE!

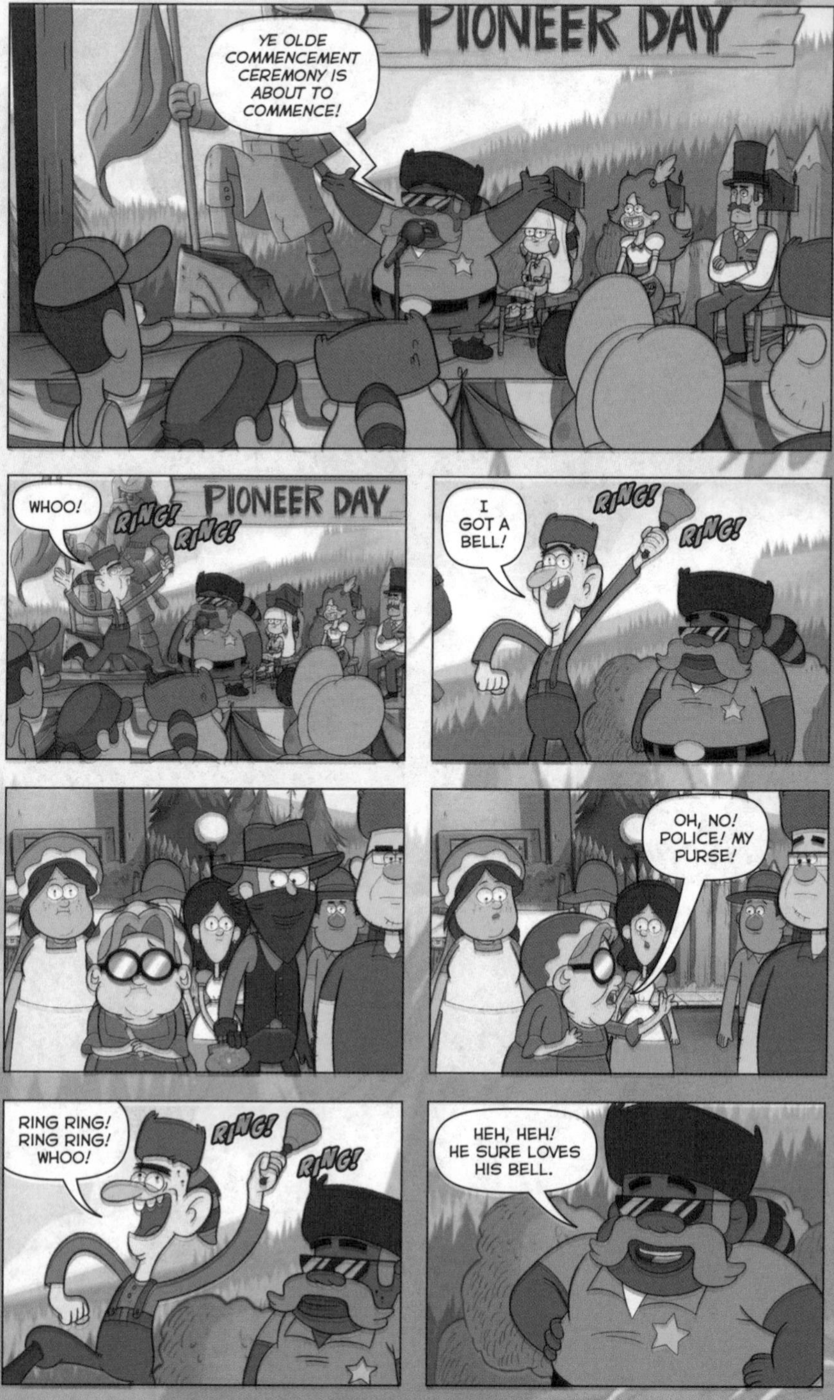
PIONEER DAY
YE OLDE COMMENCEMENT CEREMONY IS ABOUT TO COMMENCE!
PIONEER DAY
WHOO!
RING! RING!
I GOT A BELL!
RING! RING!
OH, NO! POLICE! MY PURSE!
RING RING! RING RING! WHOO!
RING! RING!
HEH, HEH! HE SURE LOVES HIS BELL.

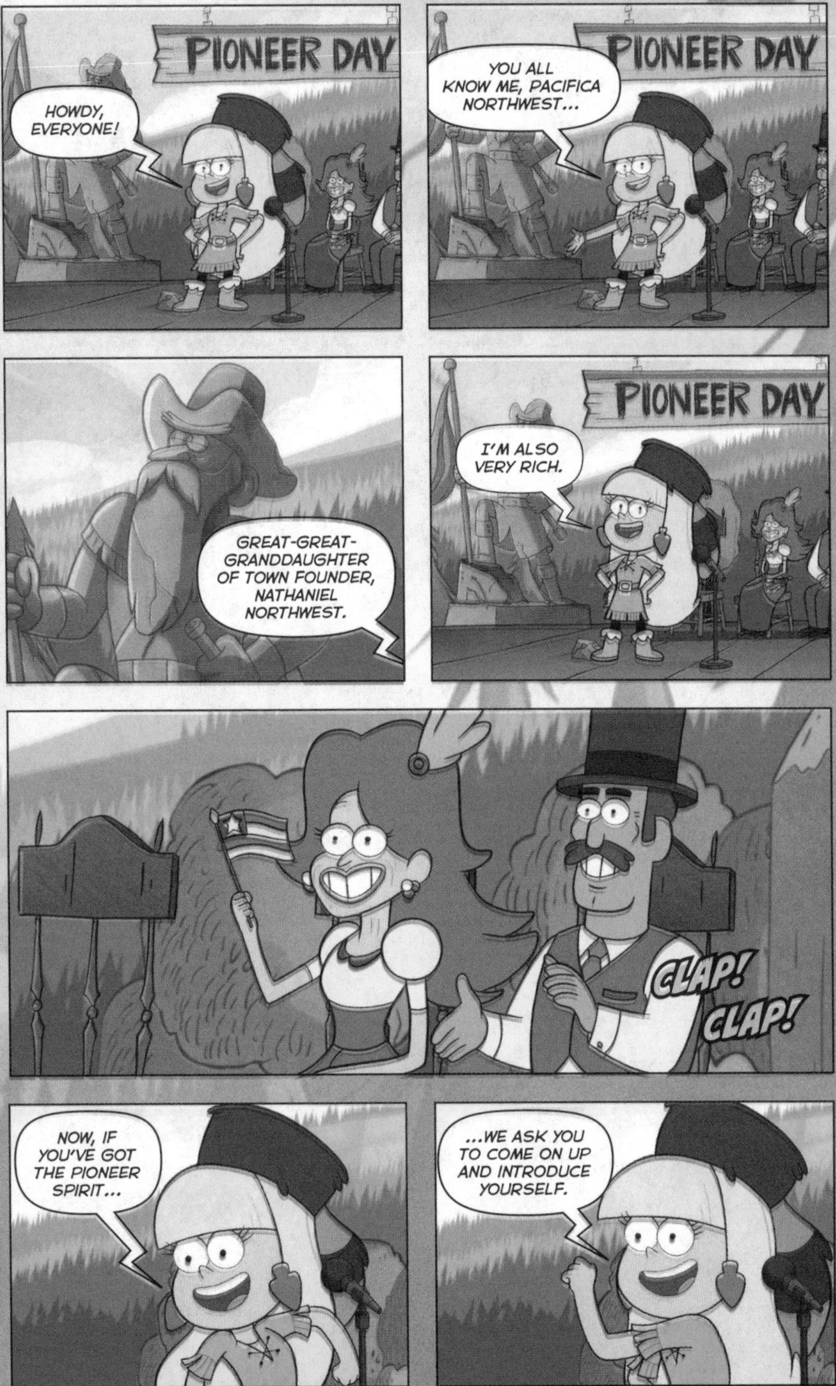
PIONEER DAY
HOWDY, EVERYONE!
PIONEER DAY
YOU ALL KNOW ME, PACIFICA NORTHWEST...
GREAT-GREAT-GRANDDAUGHTER OF TOWN FOUNDER, NATHANIEL NORTHWEST.
PIONEER DAY
I'M ALSO VERY RICH.
CLAP! CLAP!
NOW, IF YOU'VE GOT THE PIONEER SPIRIT...
...WE ASK YOU TO COME ON UP AND INTRODUCE YOURSELF.

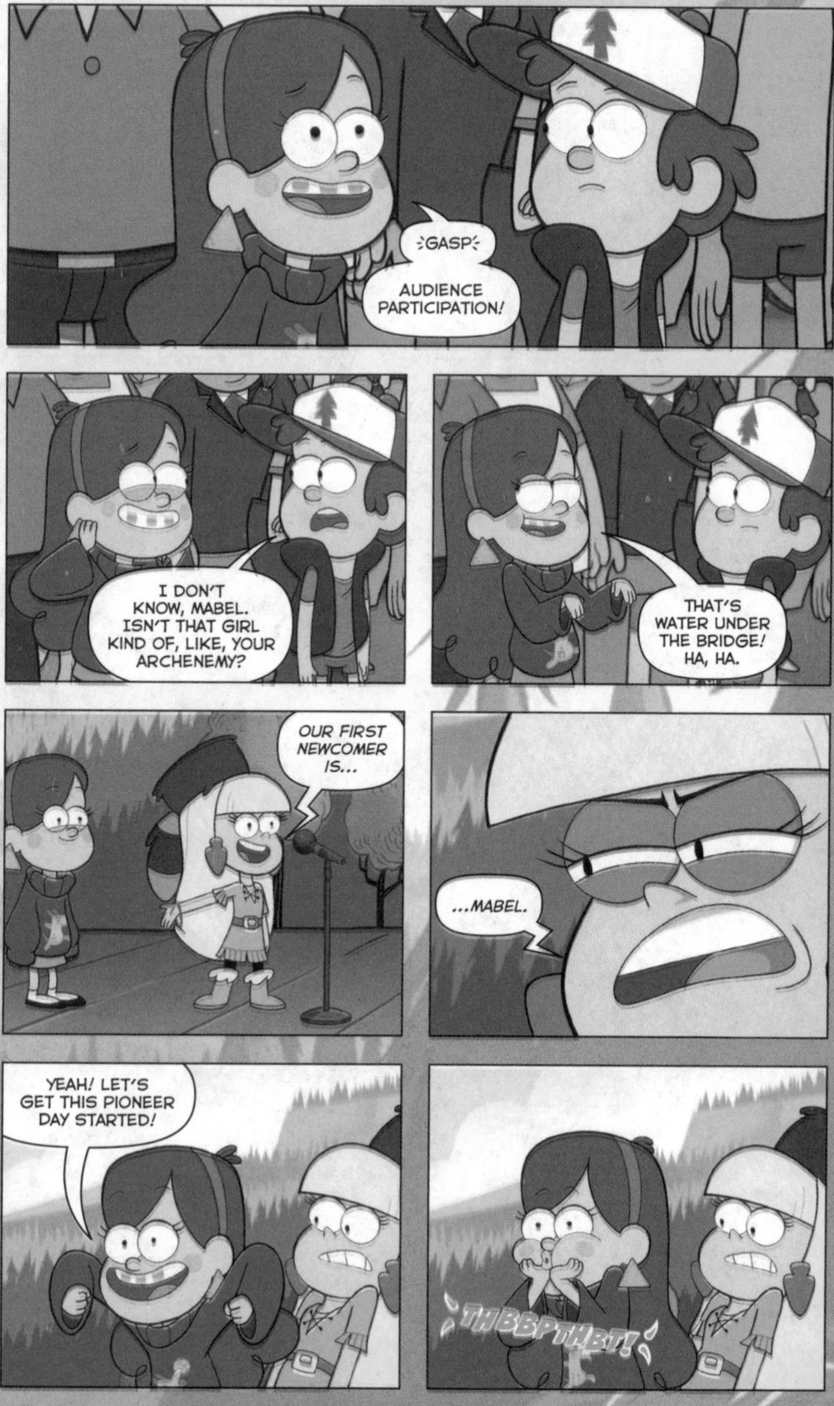
GASP
AUDIENCE PARTICIPATION!
I DON'T KNOW, MABEL. ISN'T THAT GIRL KIND OF, LIKE, YOUR ARCHENEMY?
THAT'S WATER UNDER THE BRIDGE! HA, HA.
OUR FIRST NEWCOMER IS...
...MABEL.
YEAH! LET'S GET THIS PIONEER DAY STARTED!
THBBPTHBT!

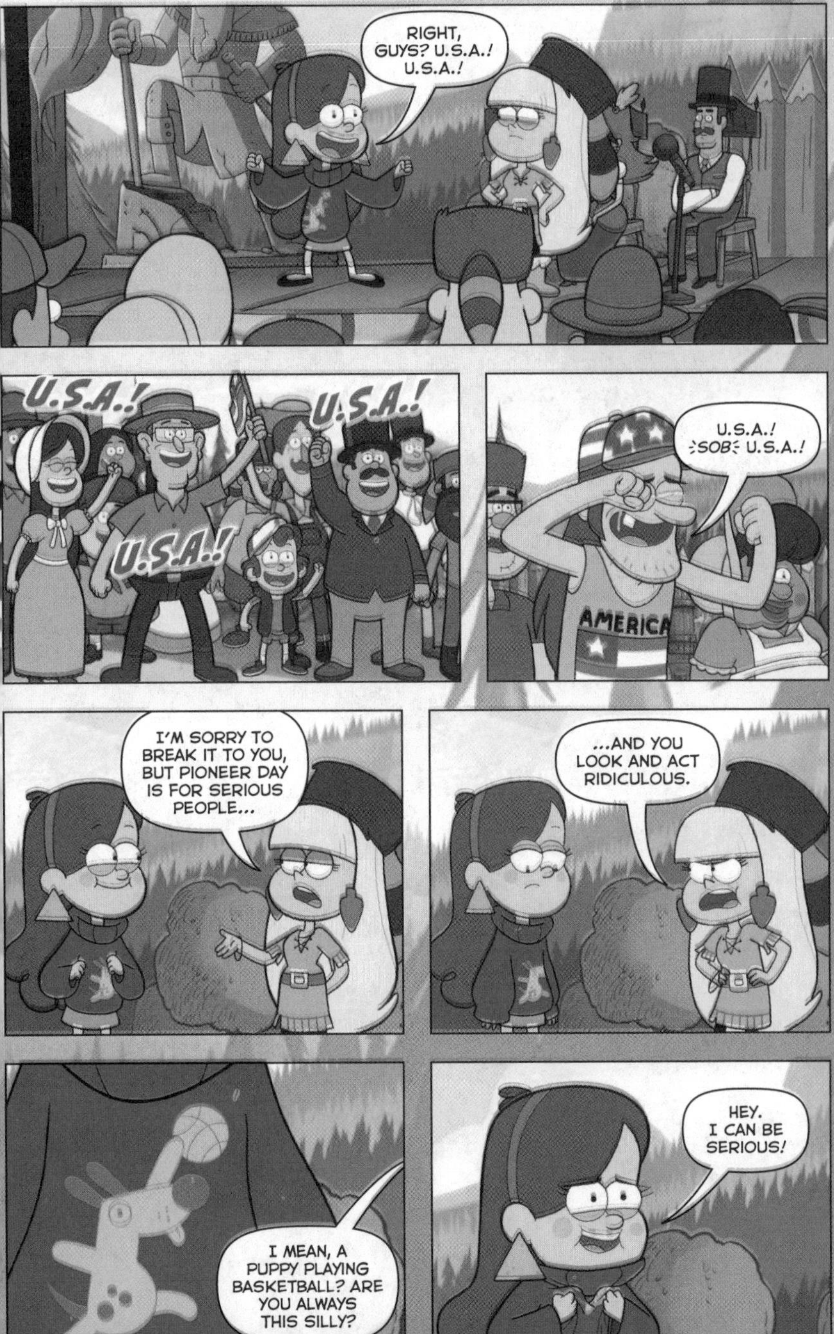
RIGHT, GUYS? U.S.A.! U.S.A.!
U.S.A.!
U.S.A.!
U.S.A.!
U.S.A.! ⁝SOB⁝ U.S.A.!
AMERICA
I'M SORRY TO BREAK IT TO YOU, BUT PIONEER DAY IS FOR SERIOUS PEOPLE...
...AND YOU LOOK AND ACT RIDICULOUS.
I MEAN, A PUPPY PLAYING BASKETBALL? ARE YOU ALWAYS THIS SILLY?
HEY. I CAN BE SERIOUS!

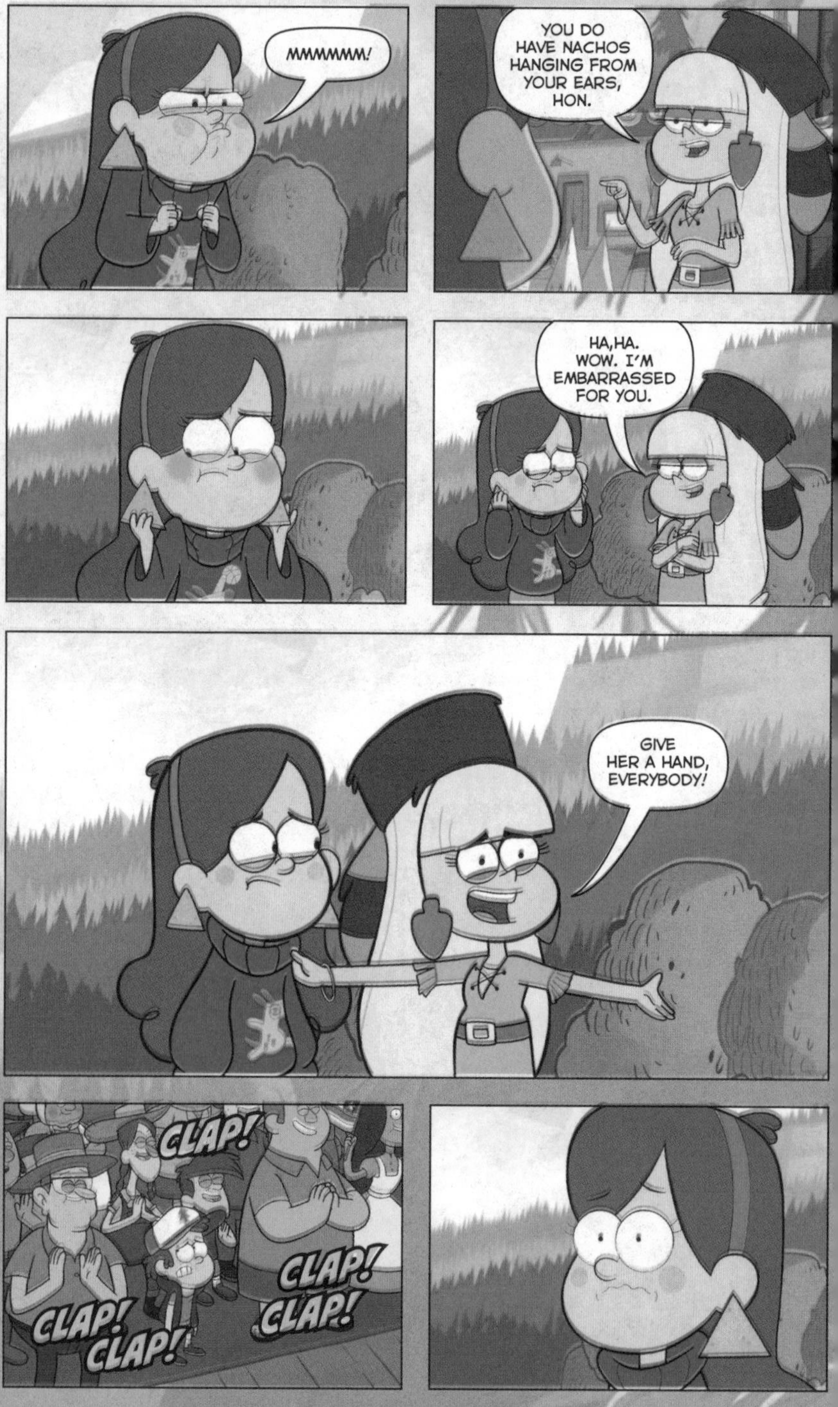
MMMMMM!
YOU DO HAVE NACHOS HANGING FROM YOUR EARS, HON.
HA,HA. WOW. I'M EMBARRASSED FOR YOU.
GIVE HER A HAND, EVERYBODY!
CLAP!
CLAP! CLAP!
CLAP! CLAP!

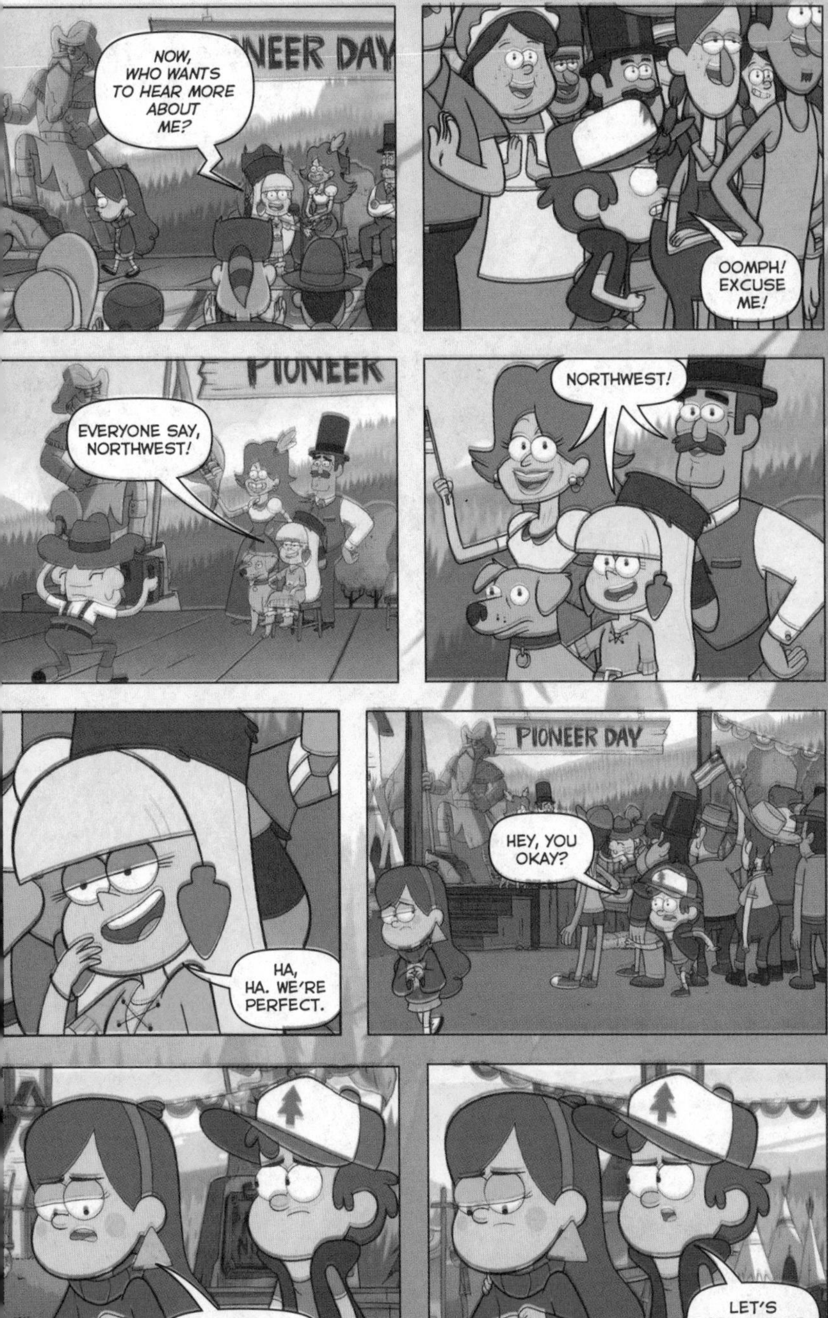
PIONEER DAY
NOW, WHO WANTS TO HEAR MORE ABOUT ME?
OOMPH! EXCUSE ME!
PIONEER
EVERYONE SAY, NORTHWEST!
NORTHWEST!
HA, HA. WE'RE PERFECT.
PIONEER DAY
HEY, YOU OKAY?
I NEED SOME OLD-TIMEY BUTTERSCOTCH.
LET'S GET OUT OF HERE.

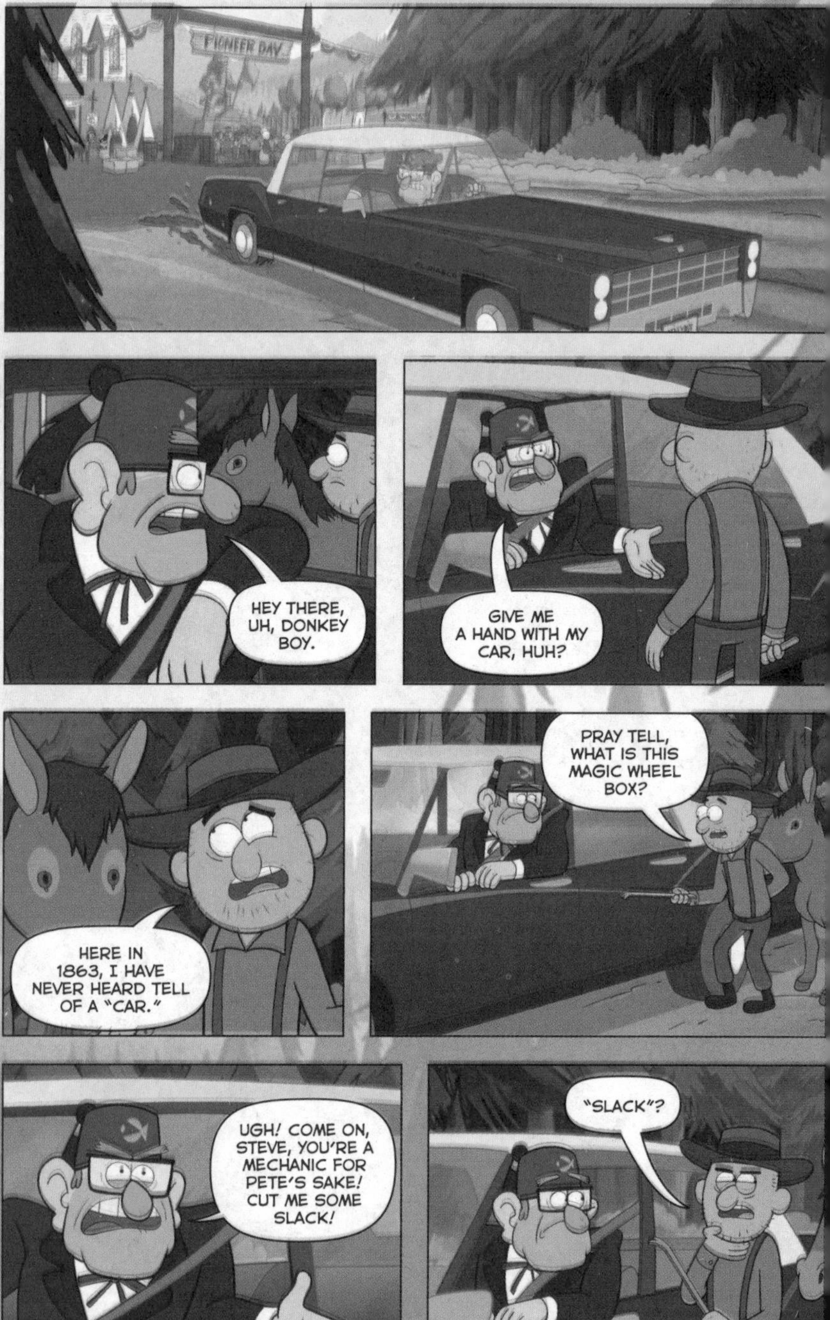

PIONEER DAY
HEY THERE, UH, DONKEY BOY.
GIVE ME A HAND WITH MY CAR, HUH?
HERE IN 1863, I HAVE NEVER HEARD TELL OF A "CAR."
PRAY TELL, WHAT IS THIS MAGIC WHEEL BOX?
UGH! COME ON, STEVE, YOU'RE A MECHANIC FOR PETE'S SAKE! CUT ME SOME SLACK!
"SLACK"?

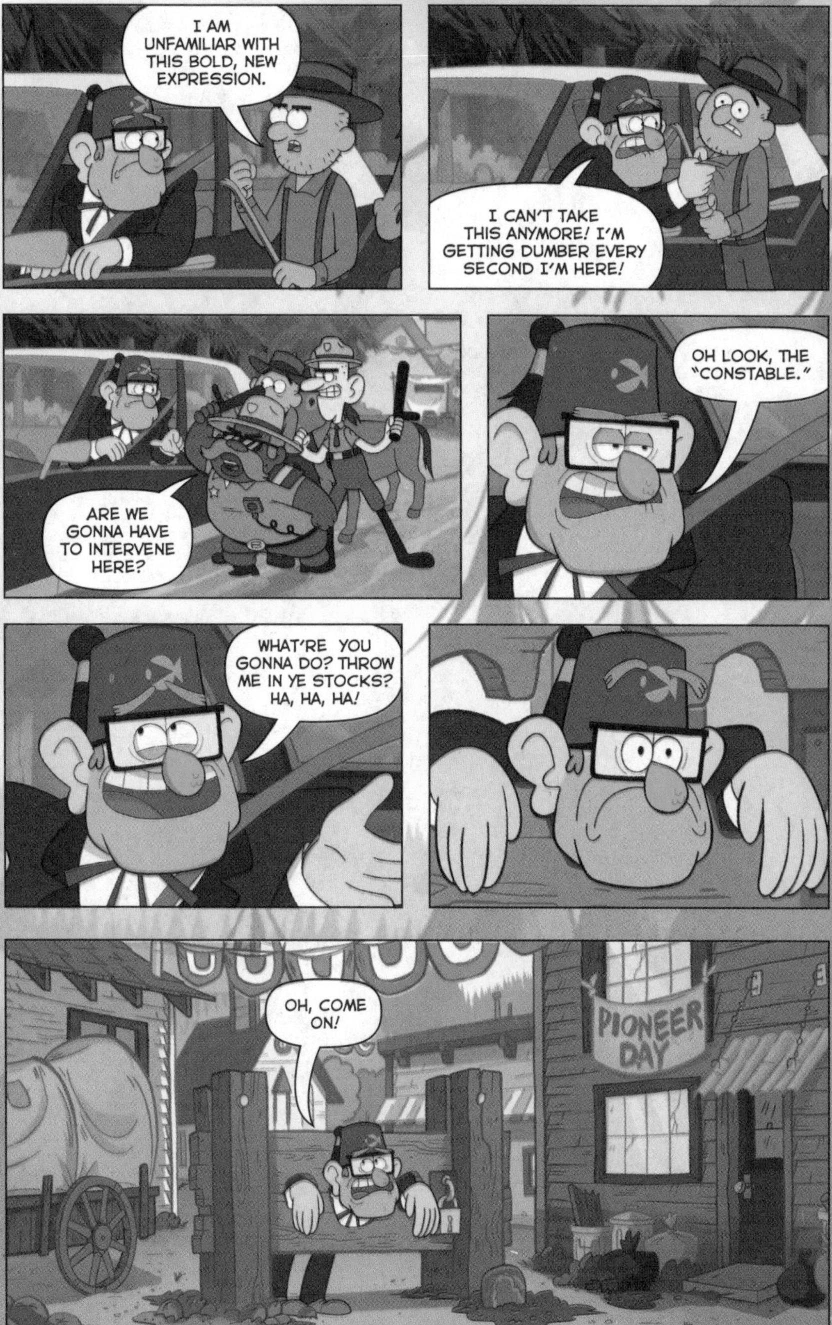
I AM UNFAMILIAR WITH THIS BOLD, NEW EXPRESSION.
I CAN'T TAKE THIS ANYMORE! I'M GETTING DUMBER EVERY SECOND I'M HERE!
ARE WE GONNA HAVE TO INTERVENE HERE?
OH LOOK, THE "CONSTABLE."
WHAT'RE YOU GONNA DO? THROW ME IN YE STOCKS? HA, HA, HA!
OH, COME ON!
PIONEER DAY

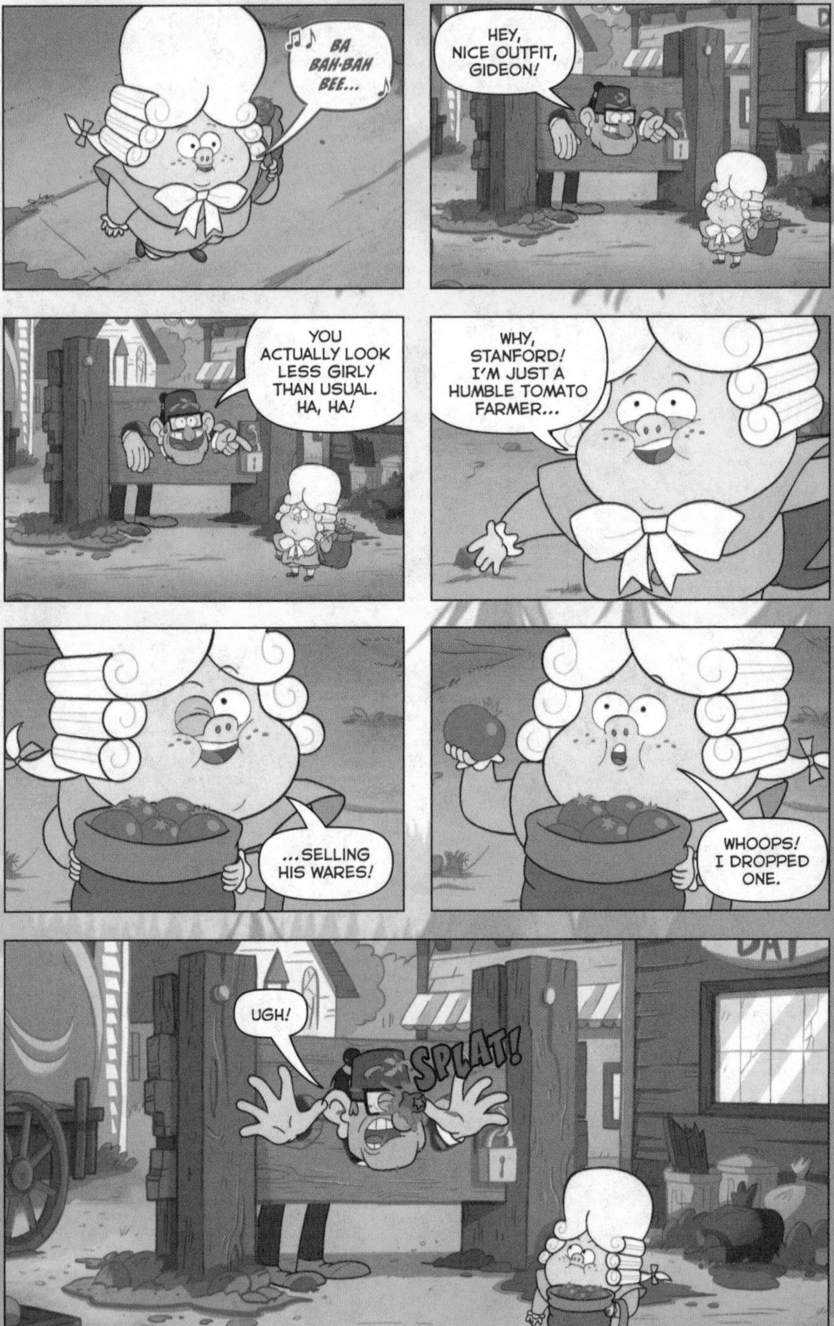

BA BAH-BAH BEE...
HEY, NICE OUTFIT, GIDEON!
YOU ACTUALLY LOOK LESS GIRLY THAN USUAL. HA, HA!
WHY, STANFORD! I'M JUST A HUMBLE TOMATO FARMER...
...SELLING HIS WARES!
WHOOPS! I DROPPED ONE.
UGH!
SPLAT!

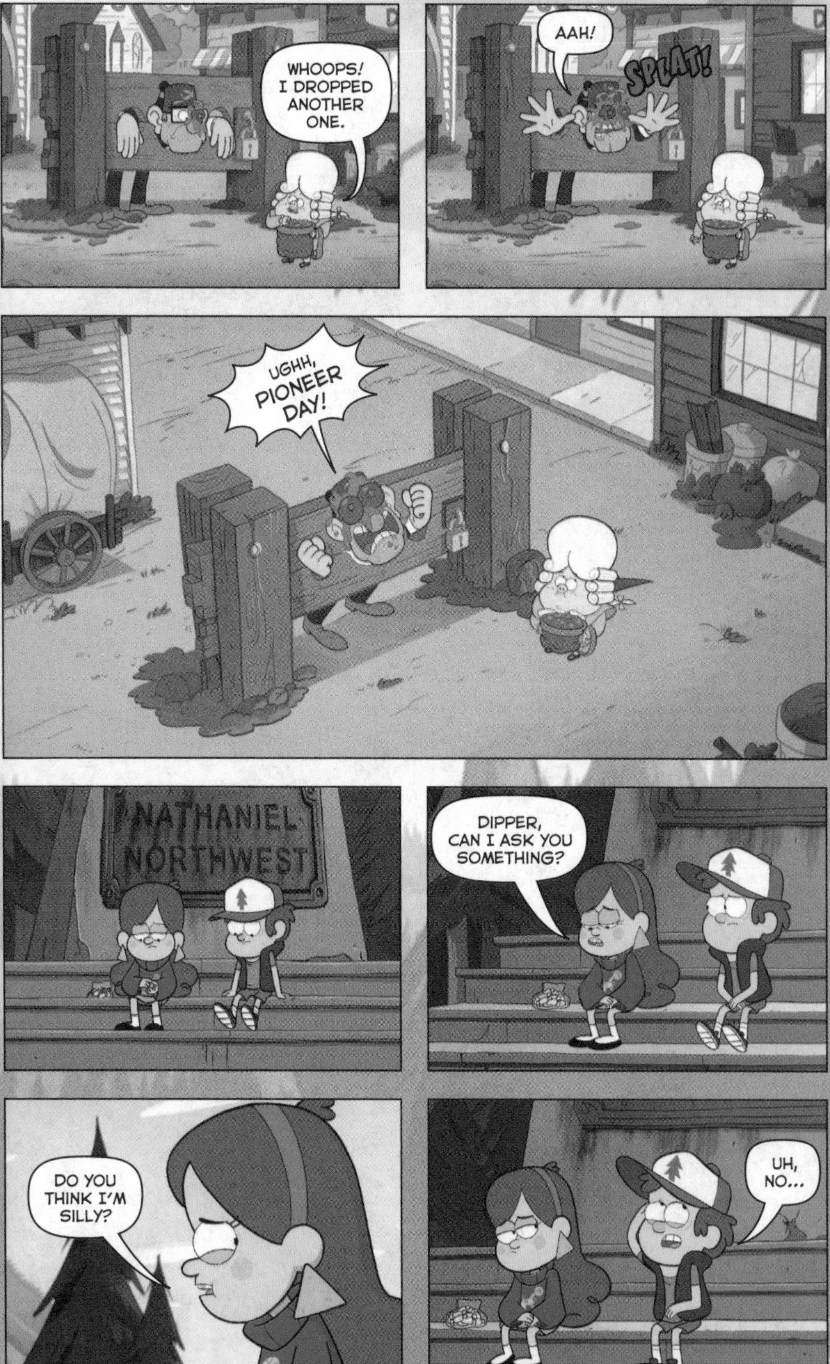
WHOOPS! I DROPPED ANOTHER ONE.
AAH!
SPLAT!
UGHH, PIONEER DAY!
NATHANIEL NORTHWEST
DIPPER, CAN I ASK YOU SOMETHING?
DO YOU THINK I'M SILLY?
UH, NO...

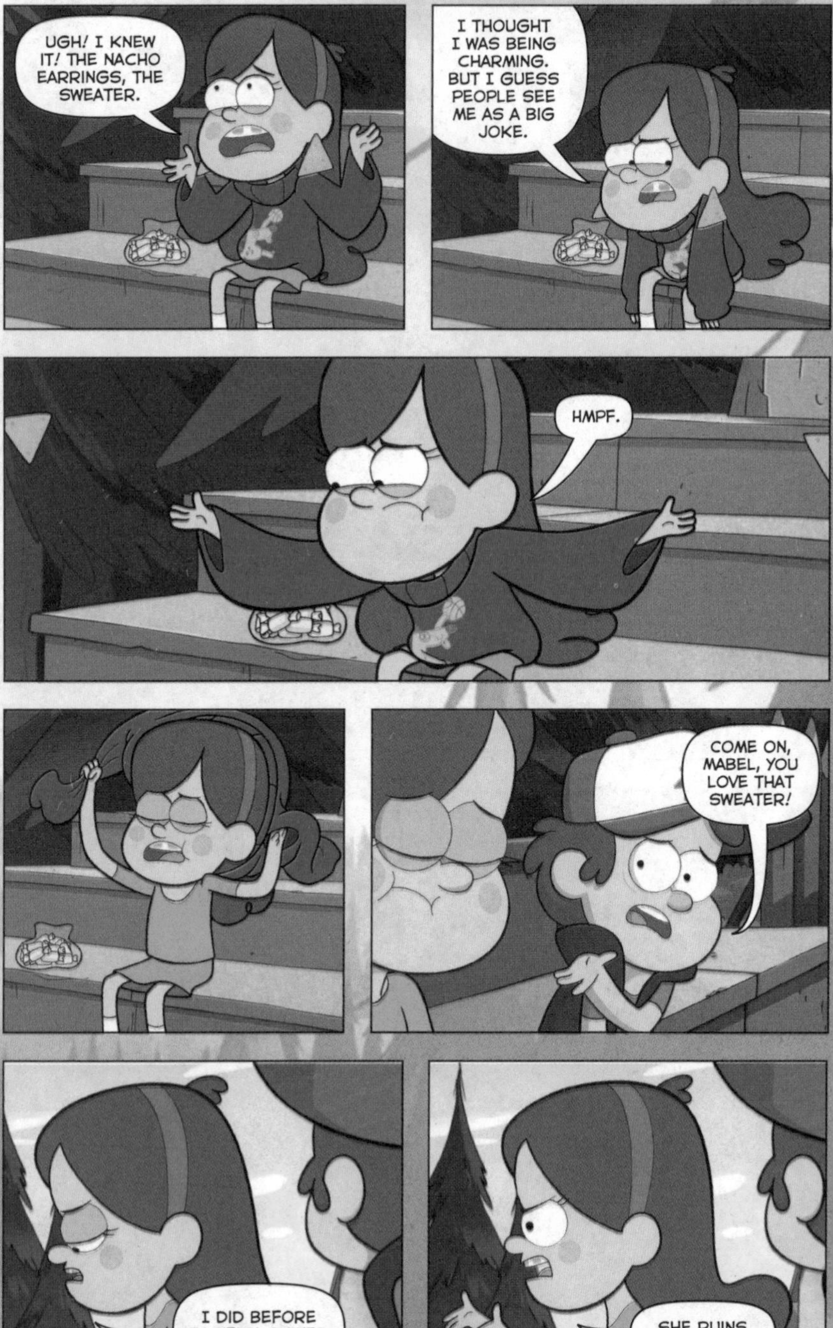
UGH! I KNEW IT! THE NACHO EARRINGS, THE SWEATER.
I THOUGHT I WAS BEING CHARMING. BUT I GUESS PEOPLE SEE ME AS A BIG JOKE.
HMPF.
COME ON, MABEL, YOU LOVE THAT SWEATER!
I DID BEFORE PACIFICA RUINED IT FOR ME.
SHE RUINS EVERYTHING!

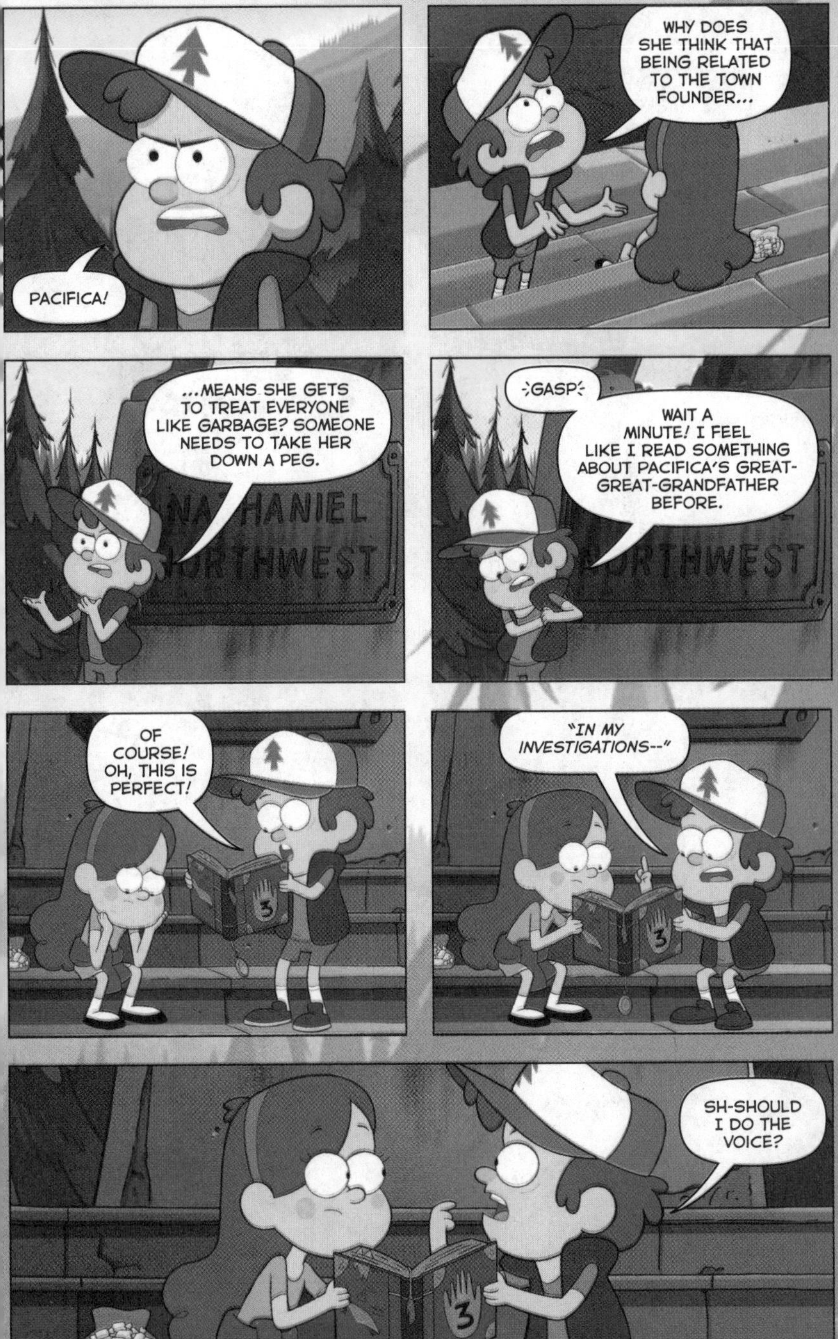
PACIFICA!
WHY DOES SHE THINK THAT BEING RELATED TO THE TOWN FOUNDER...
...MEANS SHE GETS TO TREAT EVERYONE LIKE GARBAGE? SOMEONE NEEDS TO TAKE HER DOWN A PEG.
NATHANIEL NORTHWEST
GASP
WAIT A MINUTE! I FEEL LIKE I READ SOMETHING ABOUT PACIFICA'S GREAT-GREAT-GRANDFATHER BEFORE.
OF COURSE! OH, THIS IS PERFECT!
"IN MY INVESTIGATIONS--"
SH-SHOULD I DO THE VOICE?

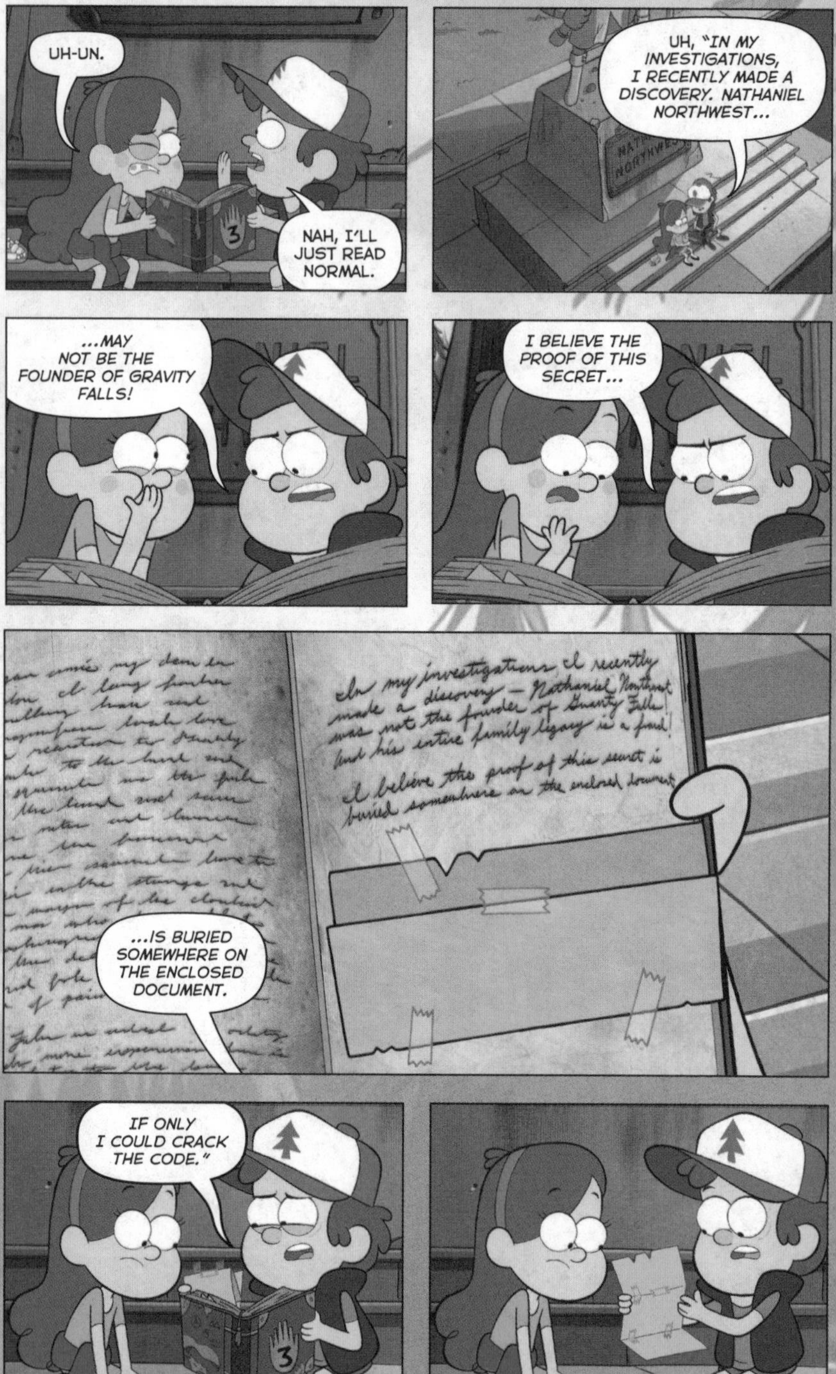
UH-UN.
NAH, I'LL JUST READ NORMAL.
UH, "IN MY INVESTIGATIONS, I RECENTLY MADE A DISCOVERY. NATHANIEL NORTHWEST...
...MAY NOT BE THE FOUNDER OF GRAVITY FALLS!
I BELIEVE THE PROOF OF THIS SECRET...
In my investigations I recently made a discovery — Nathaniel Northwest was not the founder of Gravity Falls! And his entire family legacy is a fraud!
I believe the proof of this secret is buried somewhere on the enclosed document
...IS BURIED SOMEWHERE ON THE ENCLOSED DOCUMENT.
IF ONLY I COULD CRACK THE CODE."

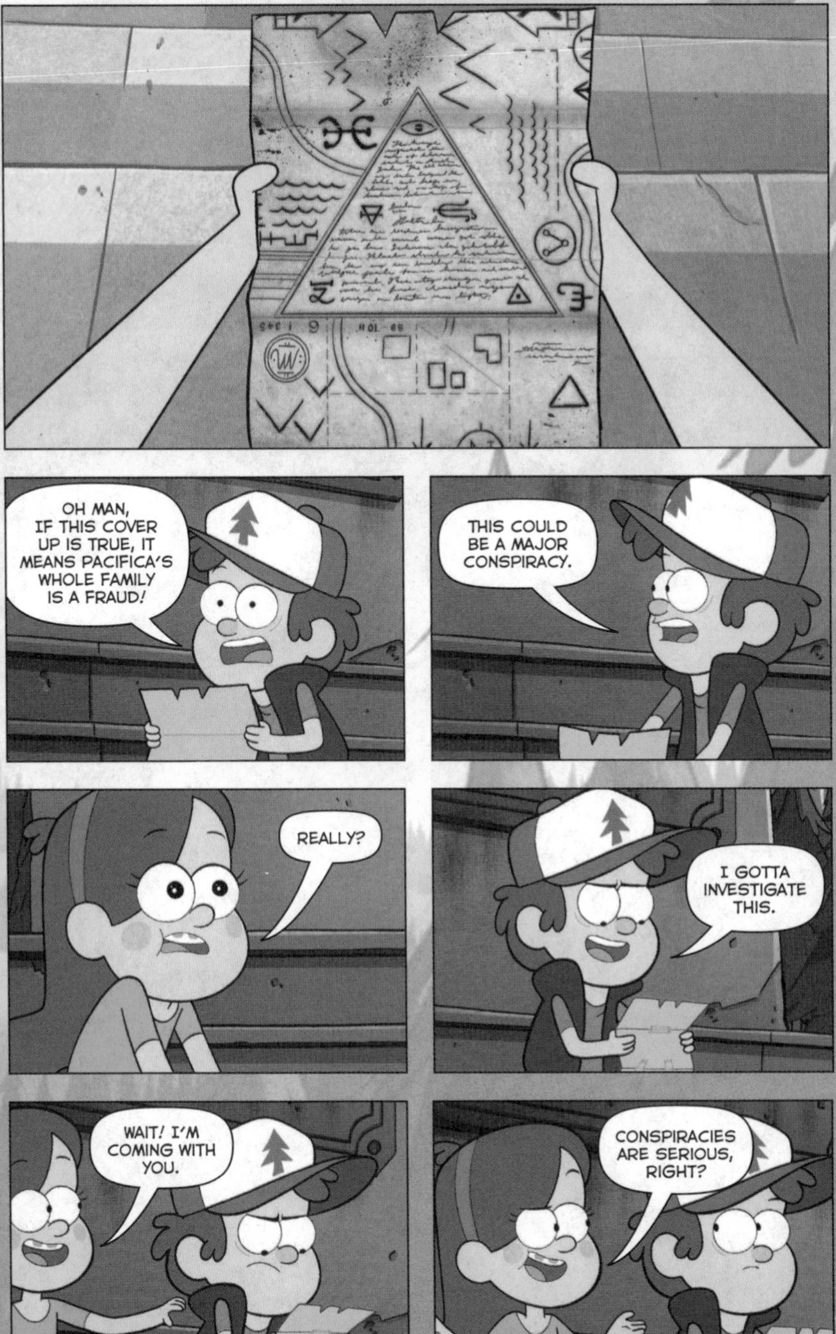
OH MAN, IF THIS COVER UP IS TRUE, IT MEANS PACIFICA'S WHOLE FAMILY IS A FRAUD!
THIS COULD BE A MAJOR CONSPIRACY.
REALLY?
I GOTTA INVESTIGATE THIS.
WAIT! I'M COMING WITH YOU.
CONSPIRACIES ARE SERIOUS, RIGHT?

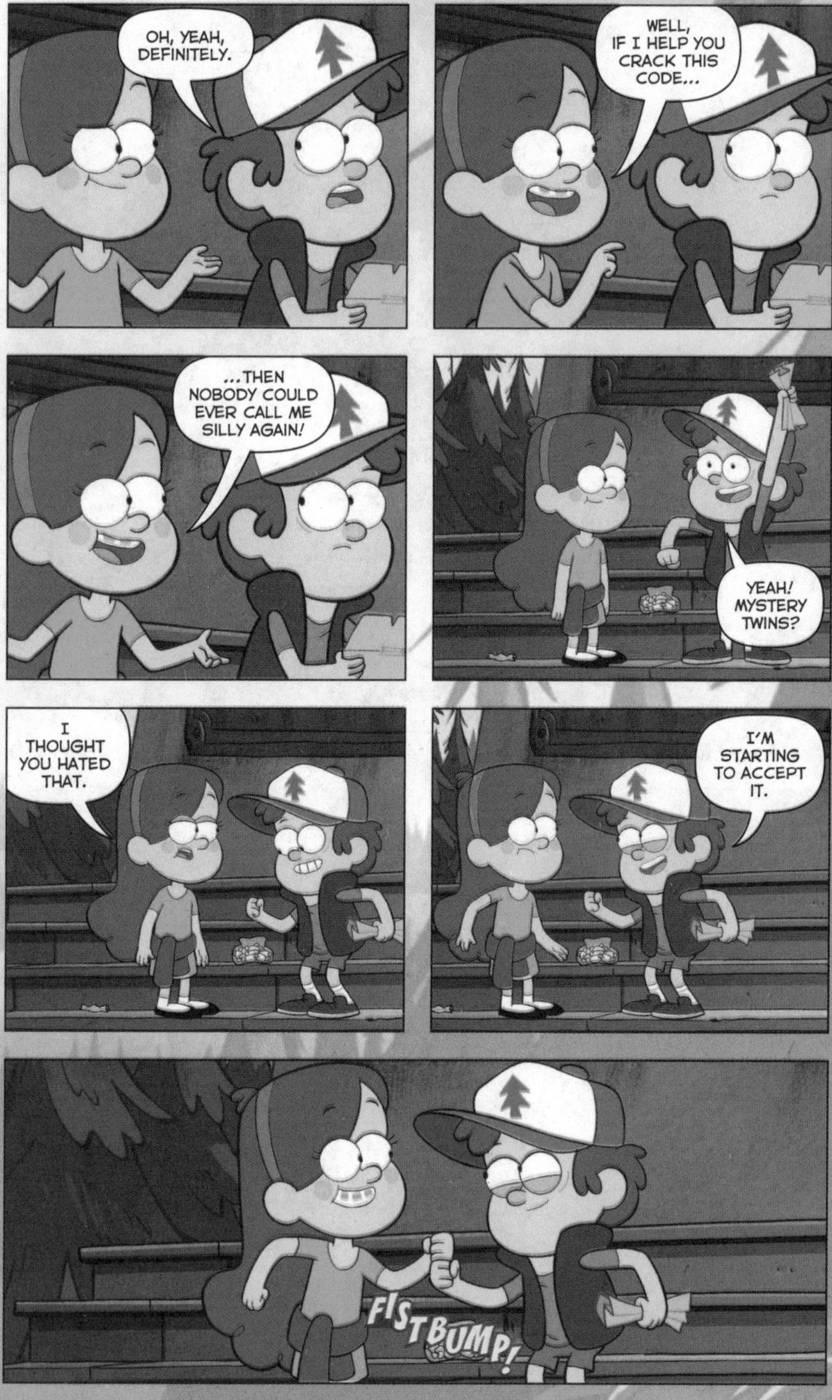
OH, YEAH, DEFINITELY.
WELL, IF I HELP YOU CRACK THIS CODE...
...THEN NOBODY COULD EVER CALL ME SILLY AGAIN!
YEAH! MYSTERY TWINS?
I THOUGHT YOU HATED THAT.
I'M STARTING TO ACCEPT IT.
FIST BUMP!

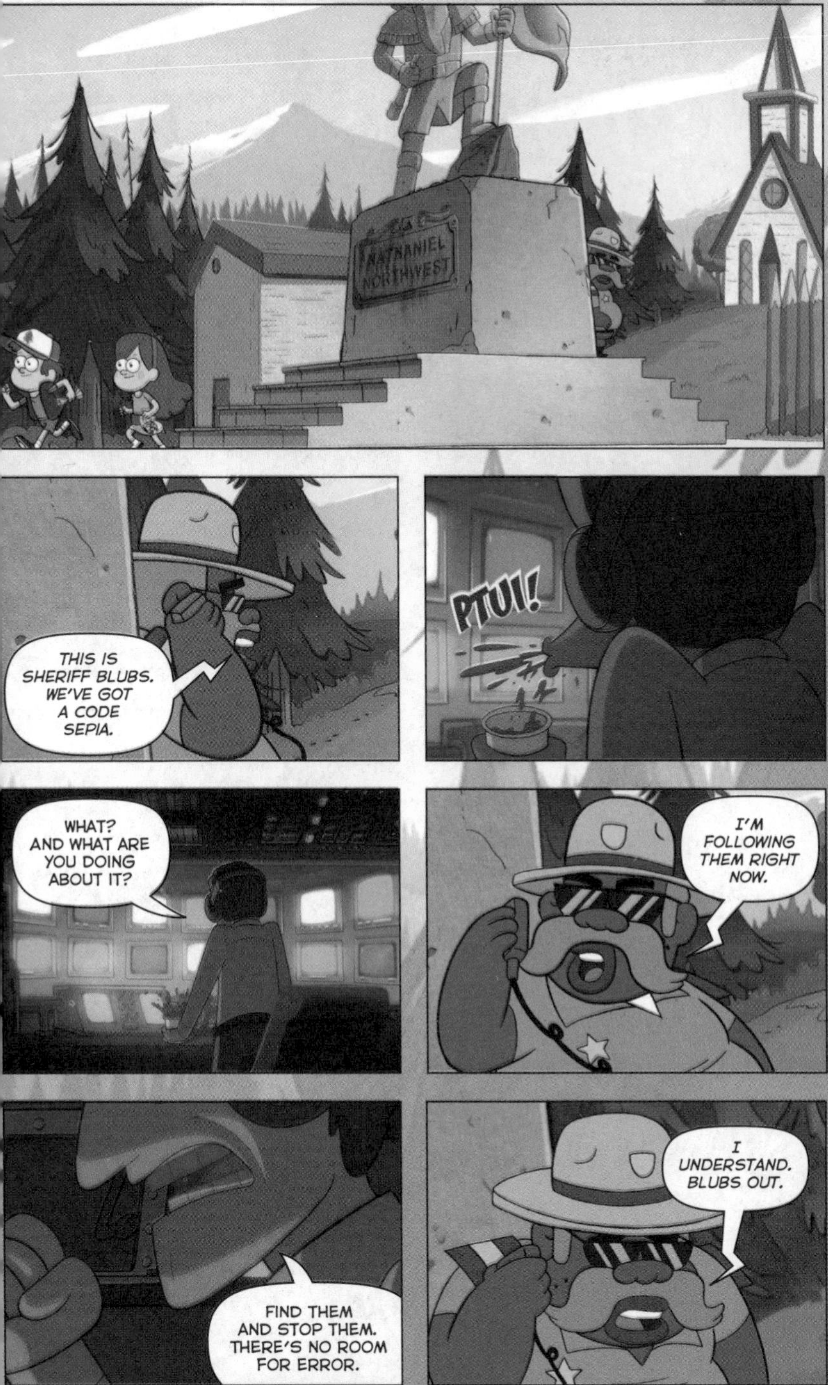
NATHANIEL NORTHWEST
THIS IS SHERIFF BLUBS. WE'VE GOT A CODE SEPIA.
PTUI!
WHAT? AND WHAT ARE YOU DOING ABOUT IT?
I'M FOLLOWING THEM RIGHT NOW.
FIND THEM AND STOP THEM. THERE'S NO ROOM FOR ERROR.
I UNDERSTAND. BLUBS OUT.

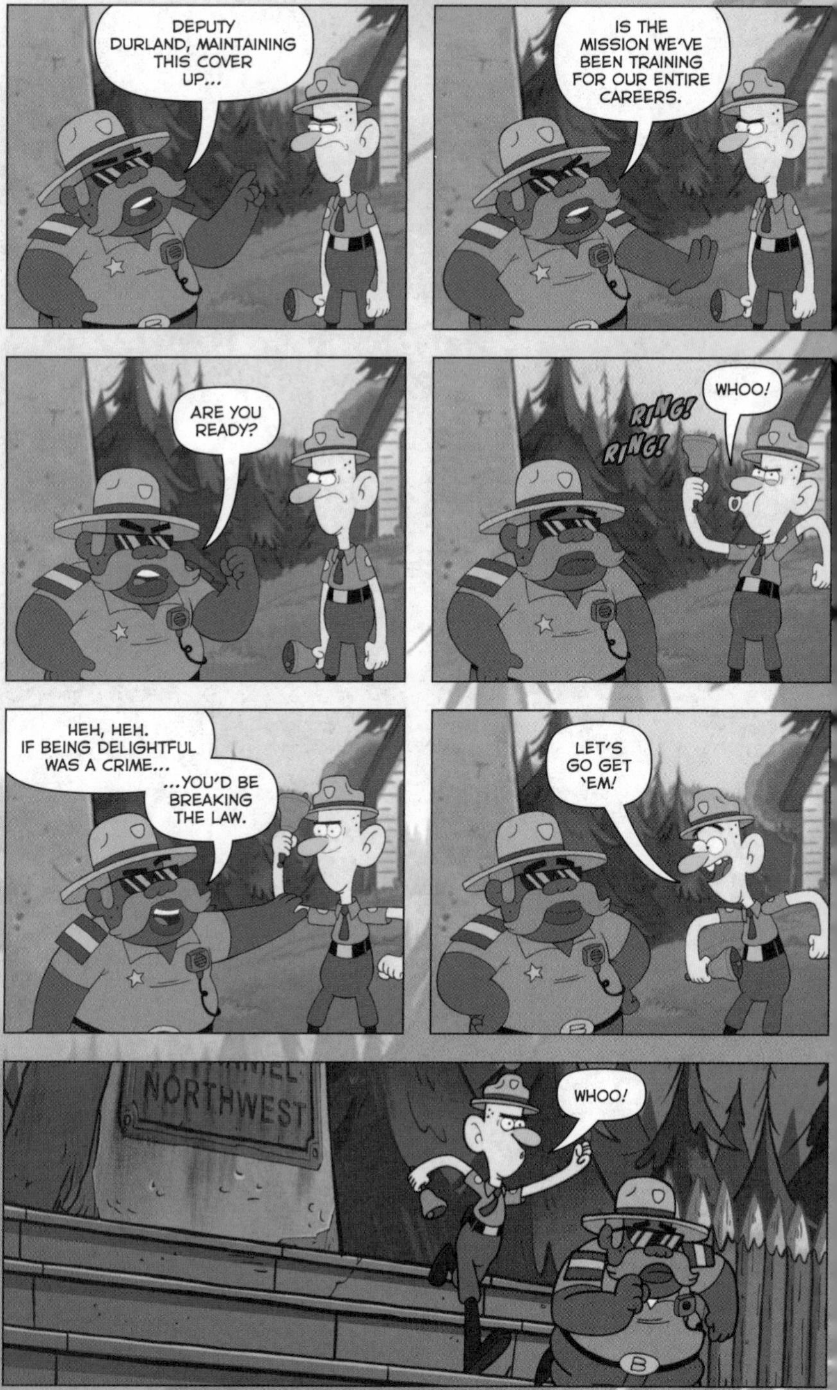
DEPUTY DURLAND, MAINTAINING THIS COVER UP...
IS THE MISSION WE'VE BEEN TRAINING FOR OUR ENTIRE CAREERS.
ARE YOU READY?
RING! RING!
WHOO!
HEH, HEH. IF BEING DELIGHTFUL WAS A CRIME...
...YOU'D BE BREAKING THE LAW.
LET'S GO GET 'EM!
NORTHWEST
WHOO!

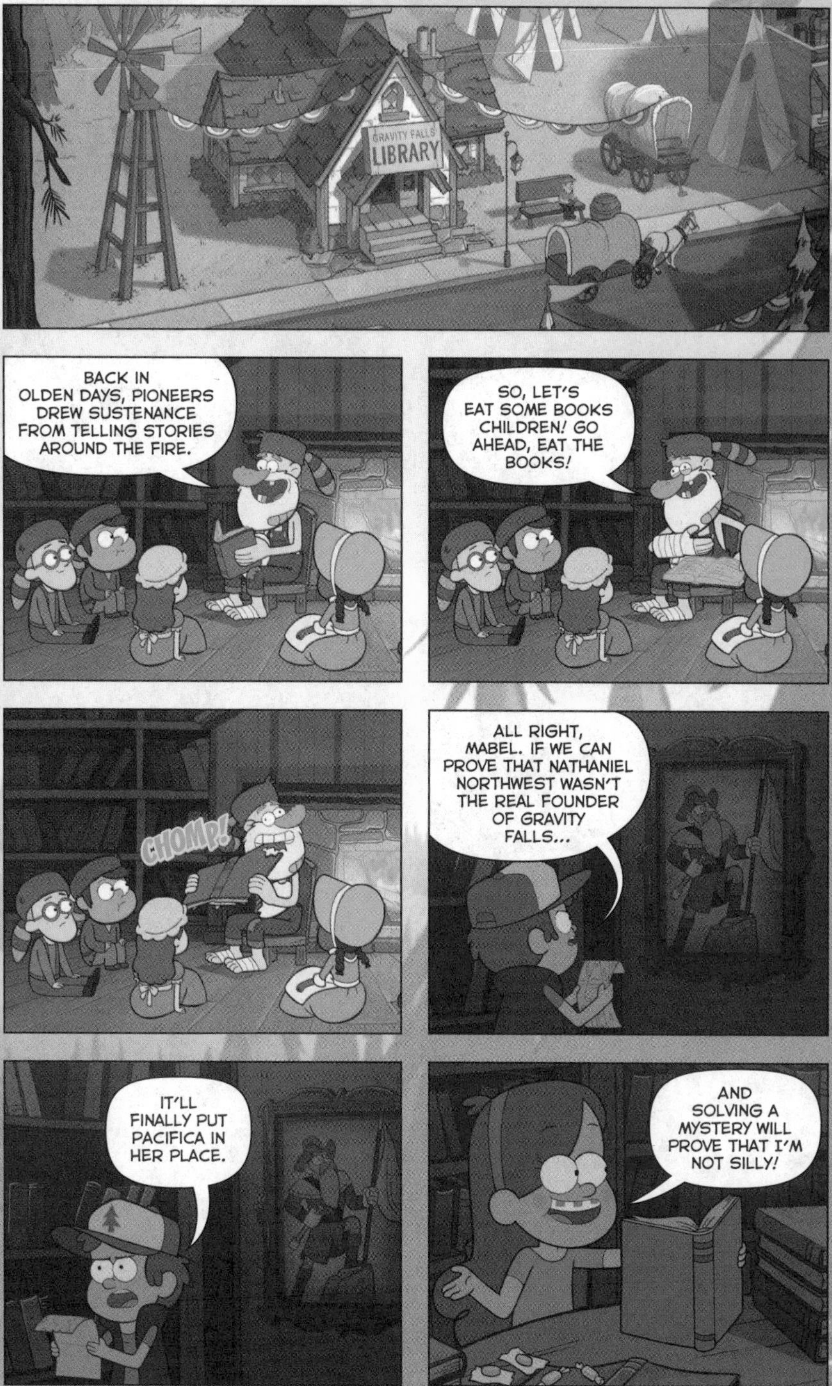
GRAVITY FALLS LIBRARY
BACK IN OLDEN DAYS, PIONEERS DREW SUSTENANCE FROM TELLING STORIES AROUND THE FIRE.
SO, LET'S EAT SOME BOOKS CHILDREN! GO AHEAD, EAT THE BOOKS!
CHOMP!
ALL RIGHT, MABEL. IF WE CAN PROVE THAT NATHANIEL NORTHWEST WASN'T THE REAL FOUNDER OF GRAVITY FALLS...
IT'LL FINALLY PUT PACIFICA IN HER PLACE.
AND SOLVING A MYSTERY WILL PROVE THAT I'M NOT SILLY!

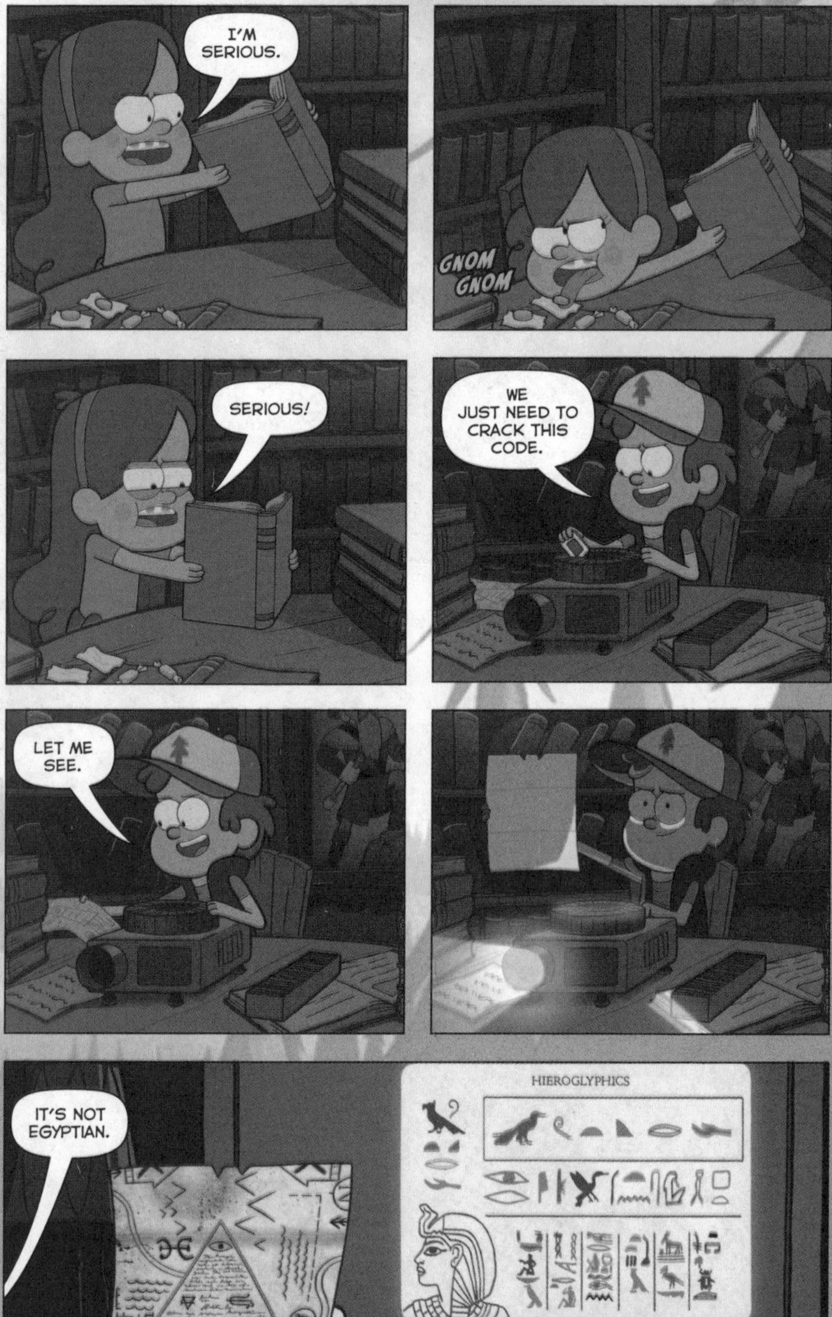
I'M SERIOUS.
GNOM GNOM
SERIOUS!
WE JUST NEED TO CRACK THIS CODE.
LET ME SEE.
IT'S NOT EGYPTIAN.
HIEROGLYPHICS

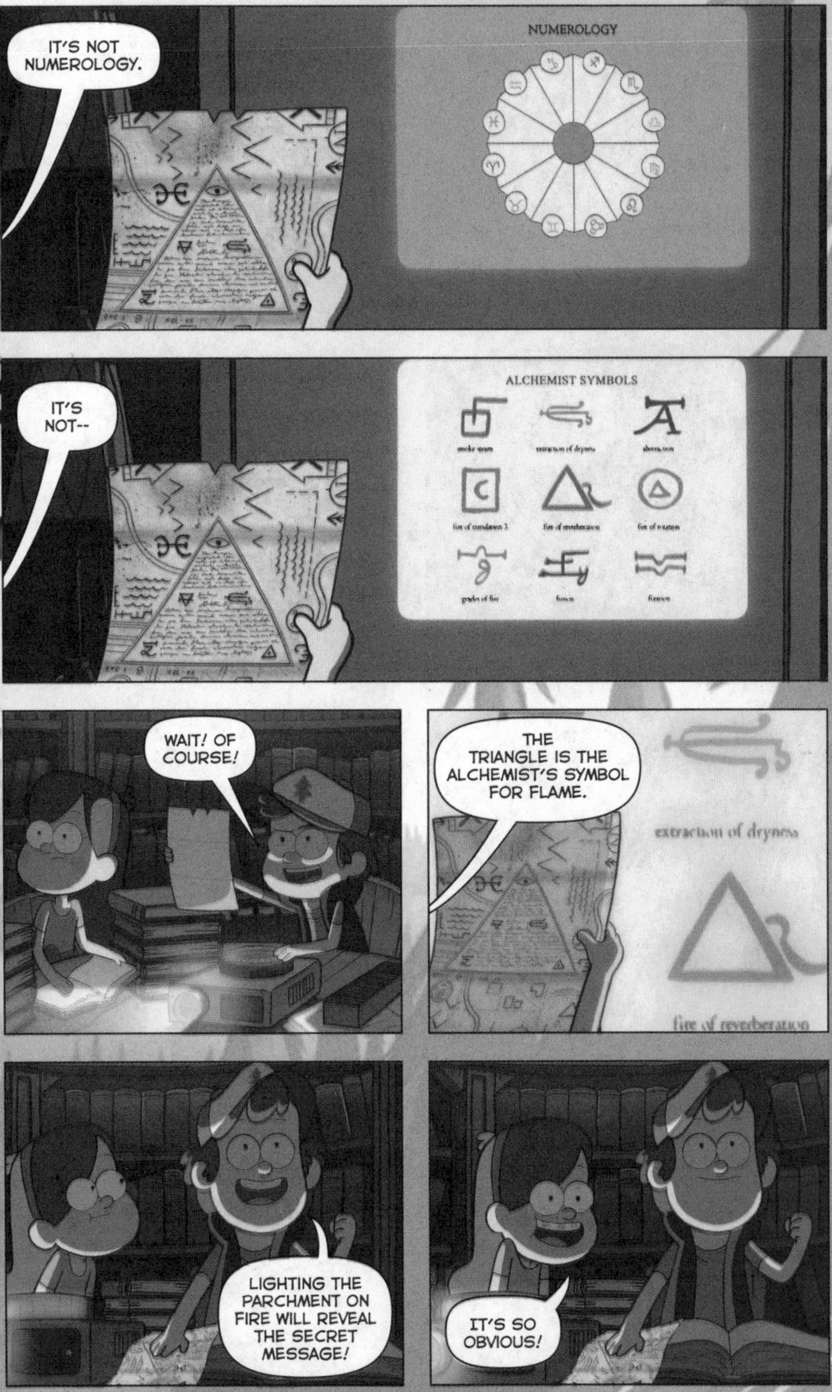

IT'S NOT NUMEROLOGY.
NUMEROLOGY
IT'S NOT--
ALCHEMIST SYMBOLS
WAIT! OF COURSE!
THE TRIANGLE IS THE ALCHEMIST'S SYMBOL FOR FLAME.
extraction of dryness
fire of reverberation
LIGHTING THE PARCHMENT ON FIRE WILL REVEAL THE SECRET MESSAGE!
IT'S SO OBVIOUS!

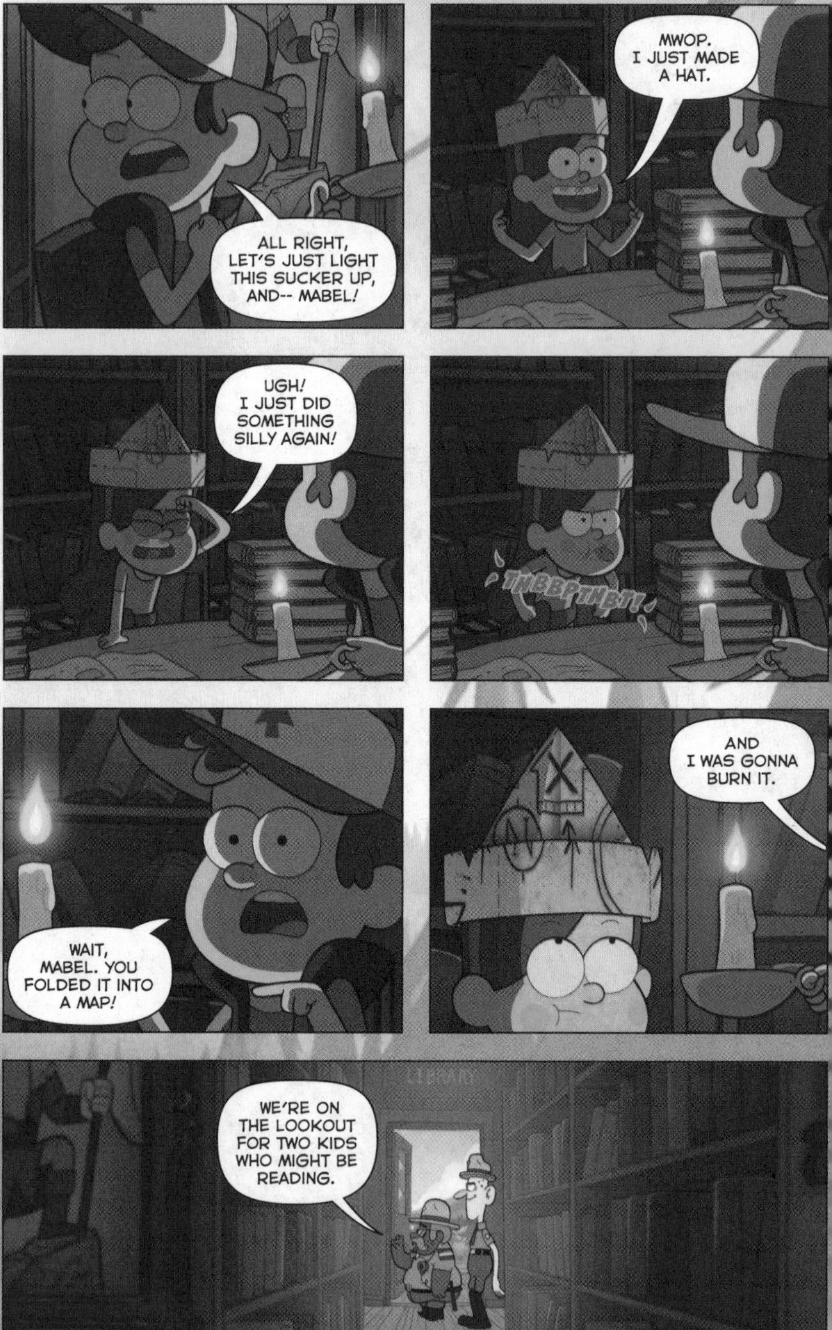

ALL RIGHT, LET'S JUST LIGHT THIS SUCKER UP, AND-- MABEL!
MWOP. I JUST MADE A HAT.
UGH! I JUST DID SOMETHING SILLY AGAIN!
THBBPTHBT!
WAIT, MABEL. YOU FOLDED IT INTO A MAP!
AND I WAS GONNA BURN IT.
LIBRARY
WE'RE ON THE LOOKOUT FOR TWO KIDS WHO MIGHT BE READING.

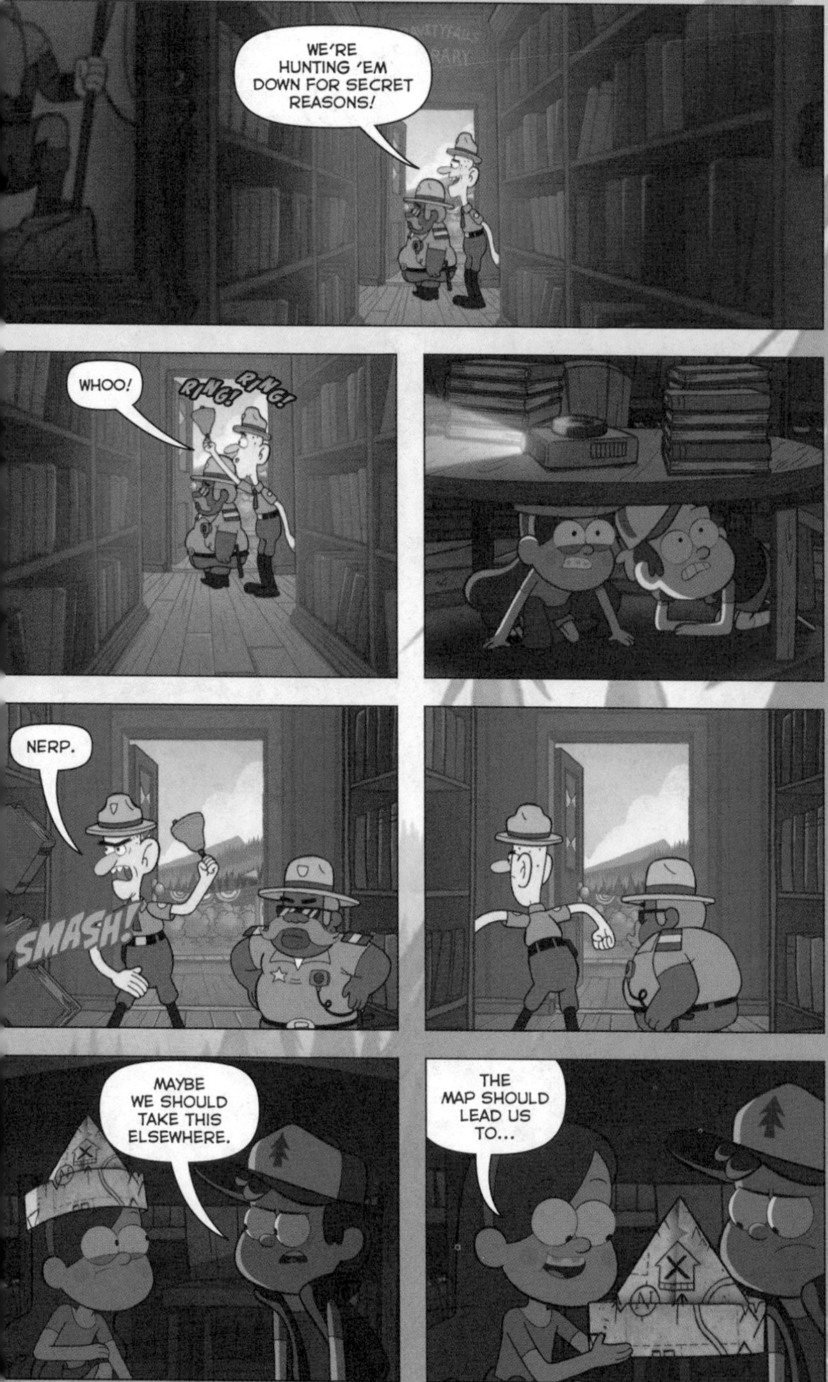
WE'RE HUNTING 'EM DOWN FOR SECRET REASONS!
WHOO!
RING! RING!
NERP.
SMASH!
MAYBE WE SHOULD TAKE THIS ELSEWHERE.
THE MAP SHOULD LEAD US TO...

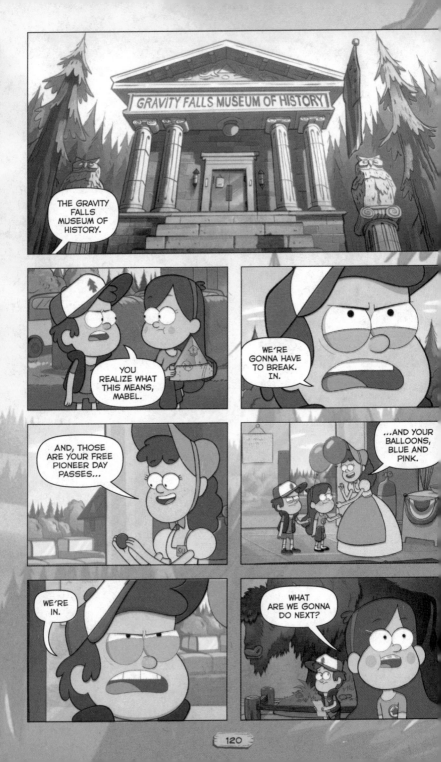

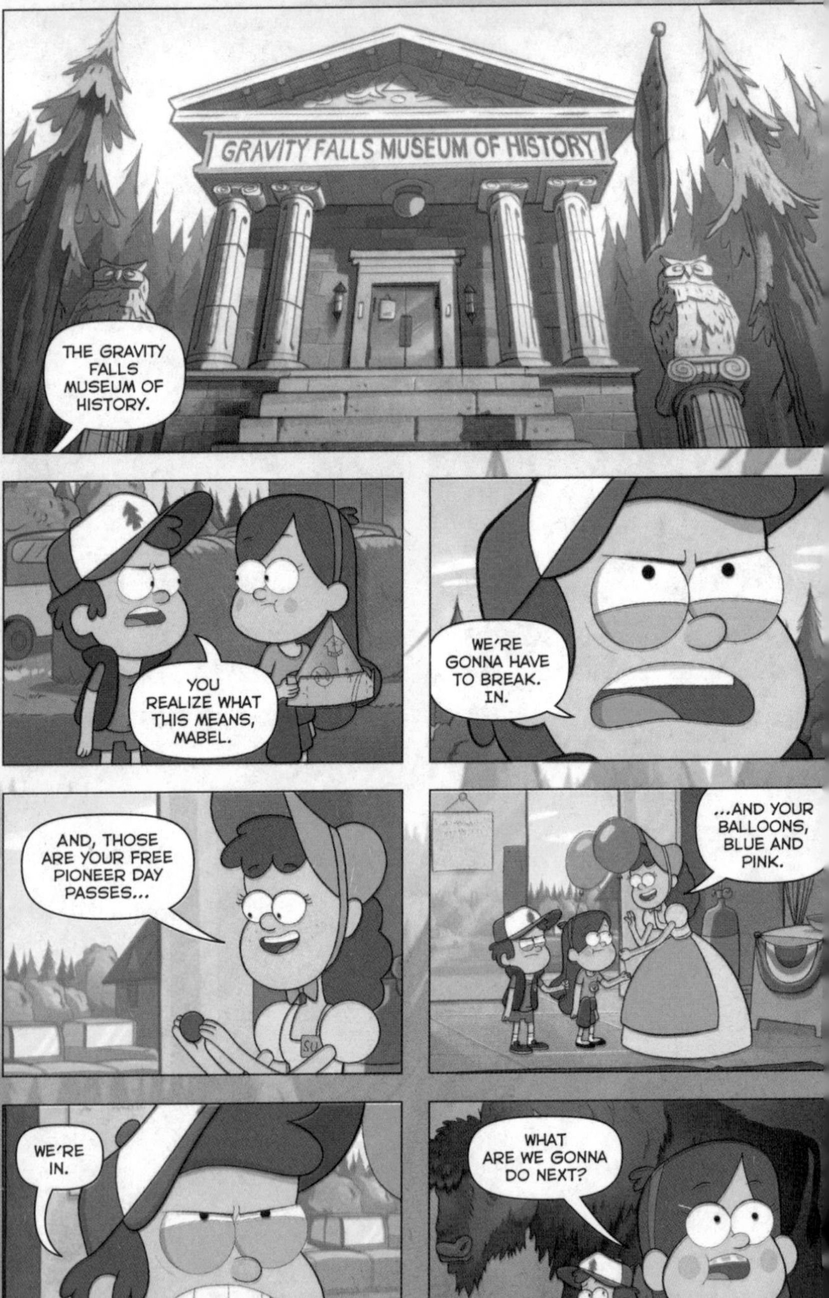
GRAVITY FALLS MUSEUM OF HISTORY
THE GRAVITY FALLS MUSEUM OF HISTORY.
YOU REALIZE WHAT THIS MEANS, MABEL.
WE'RE GONNA HAVE TO BREAK. IN.
AND, THOSE ARE YOUR FREE PIONEER DAY PASSES...
...AND YOUR BALLOONS, BLUE AND PINK.
WE'RE IN.
WHAT ARE WE GONNA DO NEXT?

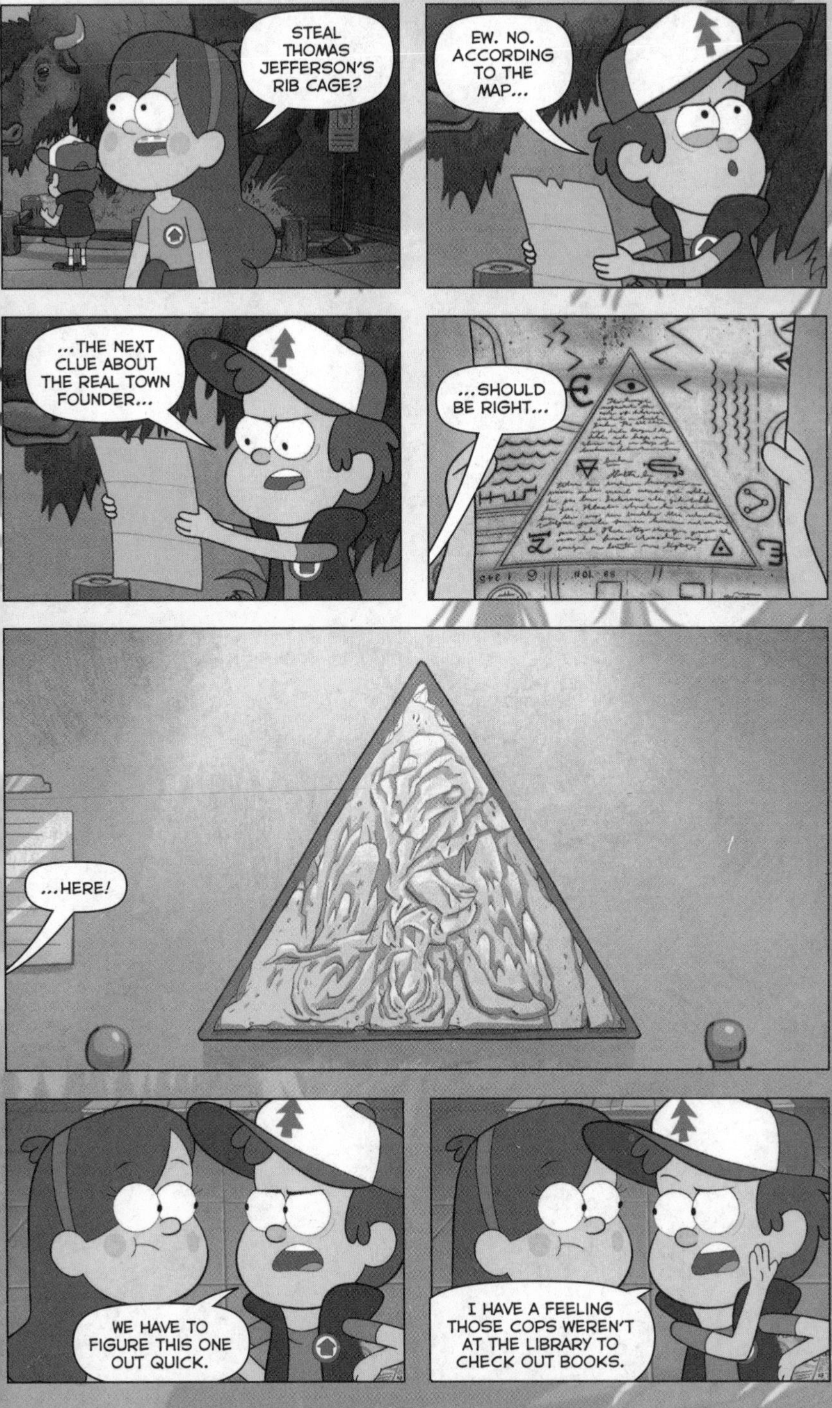
STEAL THOMAS JEFFERSON'S RIB CAGE?
EW. NO. ACCORDING TO THE MAP...
...THE NEXT CLUE ABOUT THE REAL TOWN FOUNDER...
...SHOULD BE RIGHT...
...HERE!
WE HAVE TO FIGURE THIS ONE OUT QUICK.
I HAVE A FEELING THOSE COPS WEREN'T AT THE LIBRARY TO CHECK OUT BOOKS.

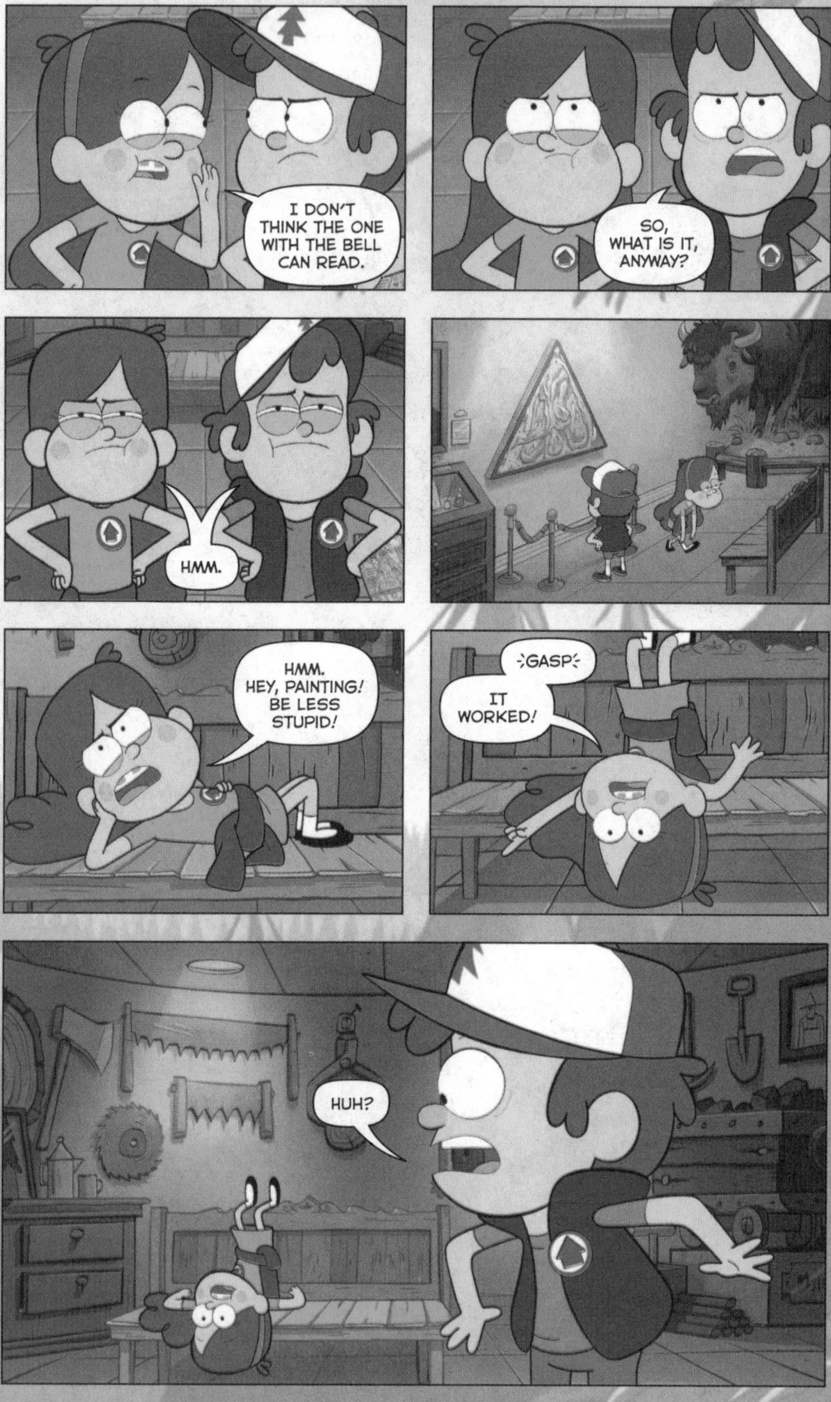
I DON'T THINK THE ONE WITH THE BELL CAN READ.
SO, WHAT IS IT, ANYWAY?
HMM.
HMM. HEY, PAINTING! BE LESS STUPID!
-GASP-
IT WORKED!
HUH?

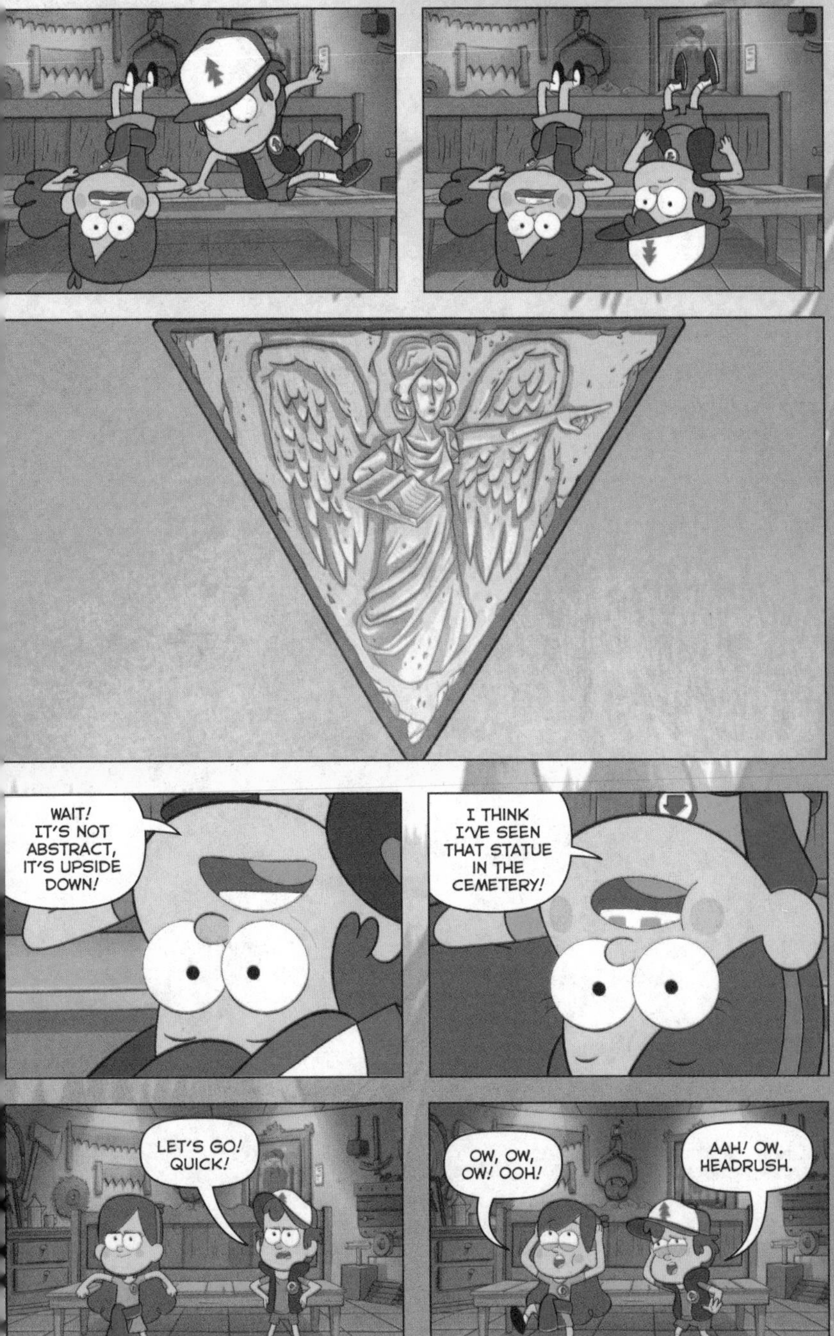
WAIT! IT'S NOT ABSTRACT, IT'S UPSIDE DOWN!
I THINK I'VE SEEN THAT STATUE IN THE CEMETERY!
LET'S GO! QUICK!
OW, OW, OW! OOH!
AAH! OW. HEADRUSH.

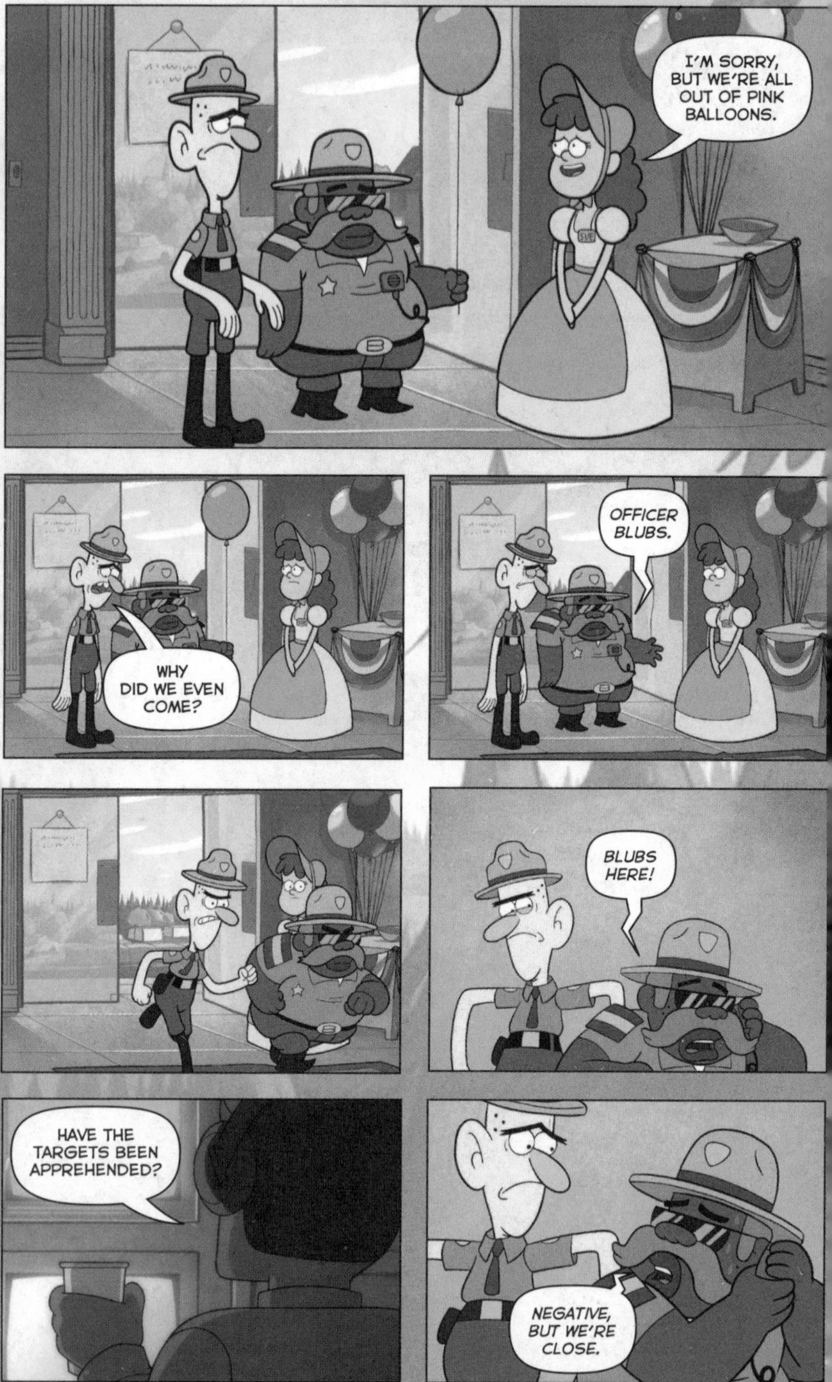
I'M SORRY, BUT WE'RE ALL OUT OF PINK BALLOONS.
WHY DID WE EVEN COME?
OFFICER BLUBS.
BLUBS HERE!
HAVE THE TARGETS BEEN APPREHENDED?
NEGATIVE, BUT WE'RE CLOSE.

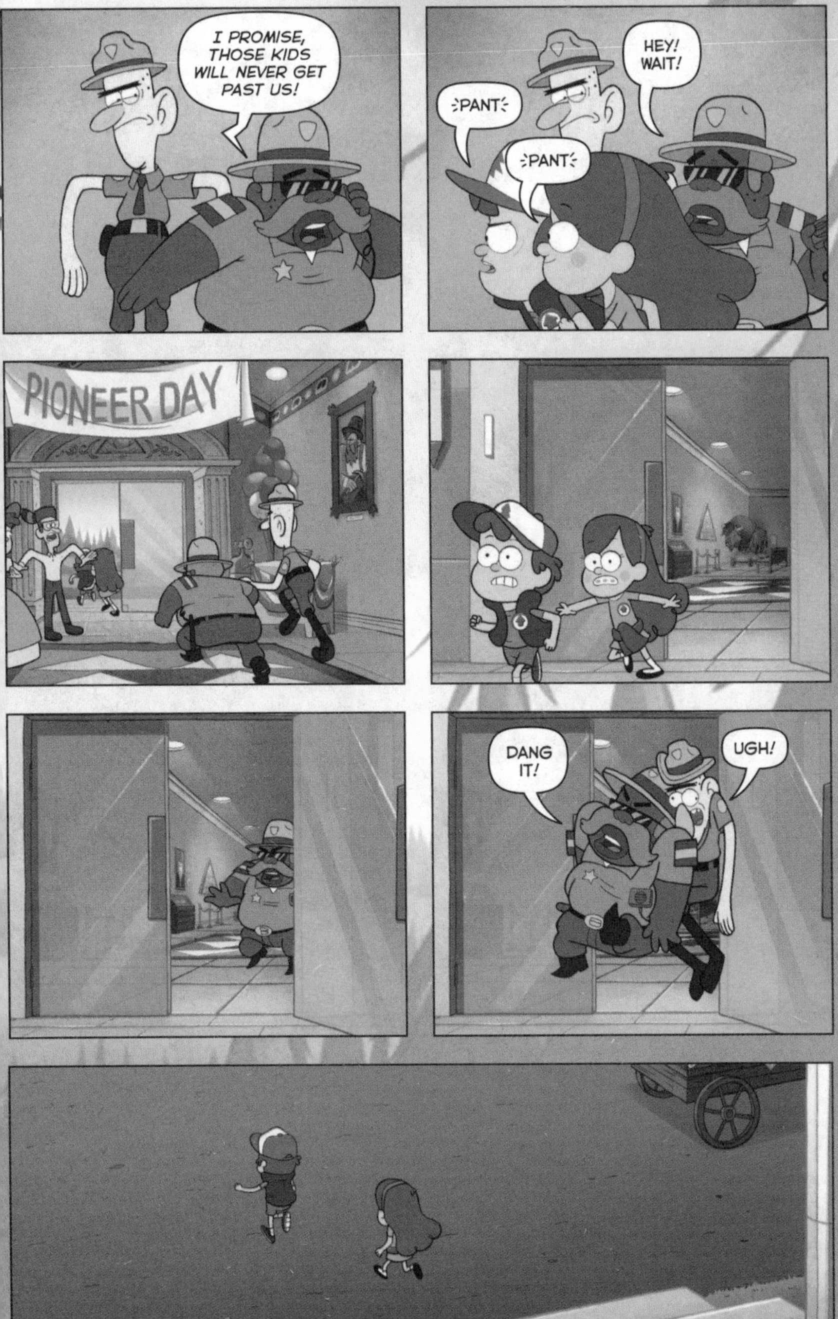
I PROMISE, THOSE KIDS WILL NEVER GET PAST US!
PANT
PANT
HEY! WAIT!
PIONEER DAY
DANG IT!
UGH!

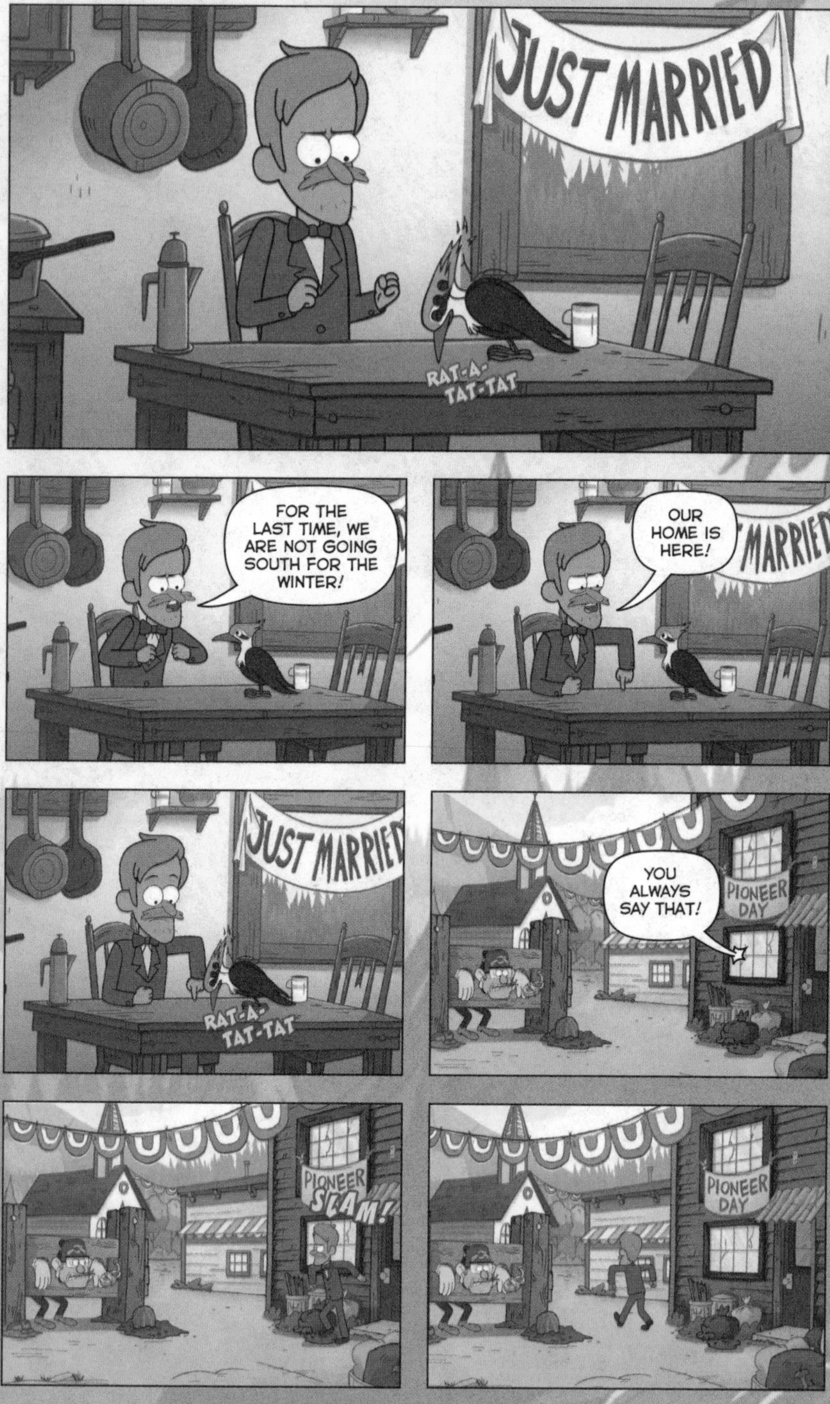
JUST MARRIED
RAT-A-TAT-TAT
FOR THE LAST TIME, WE ARE NOT GOING SOUTH FOR THE WINTER!
OUR HOME IS HERE!
JUST MARRIED
RAT-A-TAT-TAT
YOU ALWAYS SAY THAT!
PIONEER DAY
PIONEER
SLAM!
PIONEER DAY

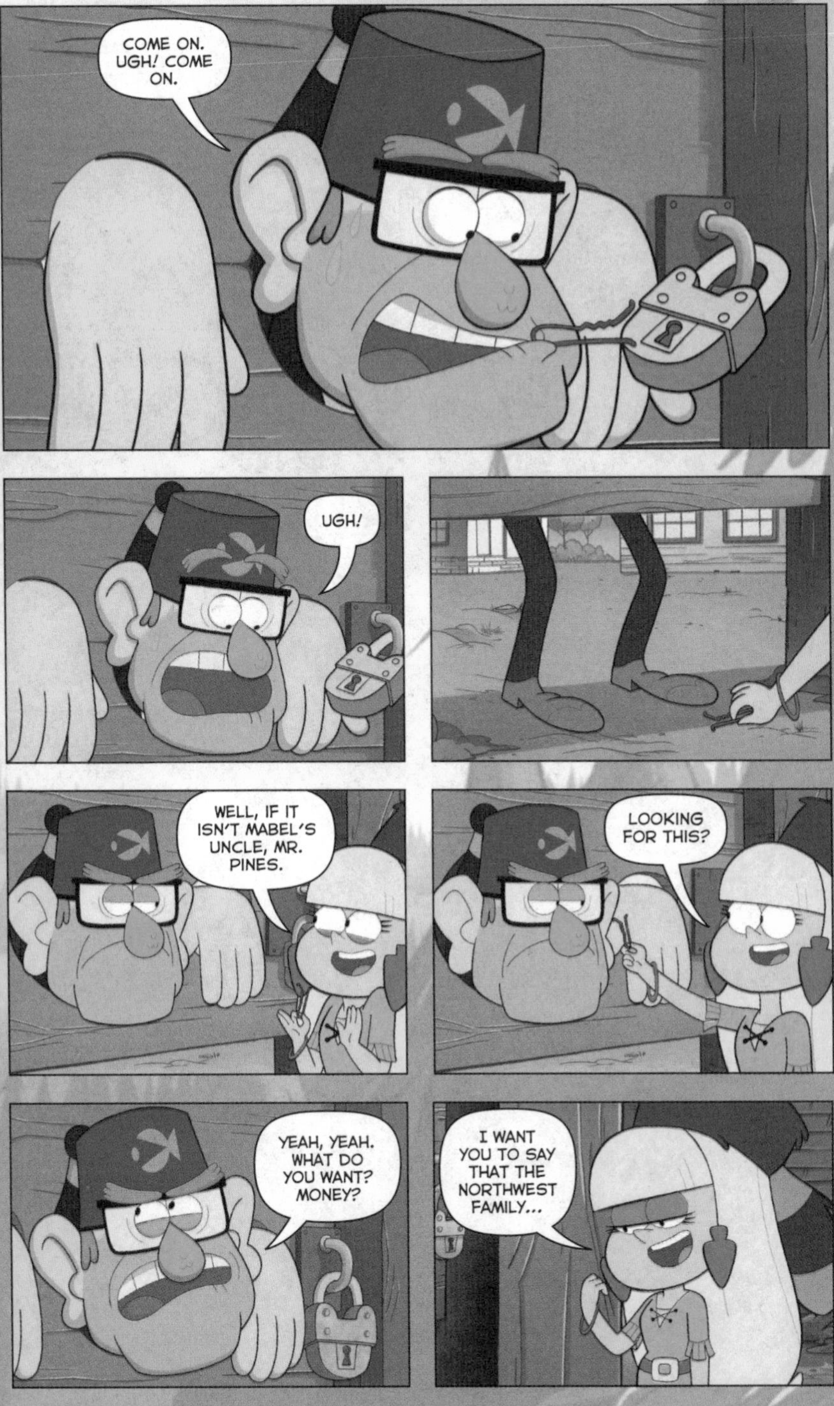
COME ON. UGH! COME ON.
UGH!
WELL, IF IT ISN'T MABEL'S UNCLE, MR. PINES.
LOOKING FOR THIS?
YEAH, YEAH. WHAT DO YOU WANT? MONEY?
I WANT YOU TO SAY THAT THE NORTHWEST FAMILY...

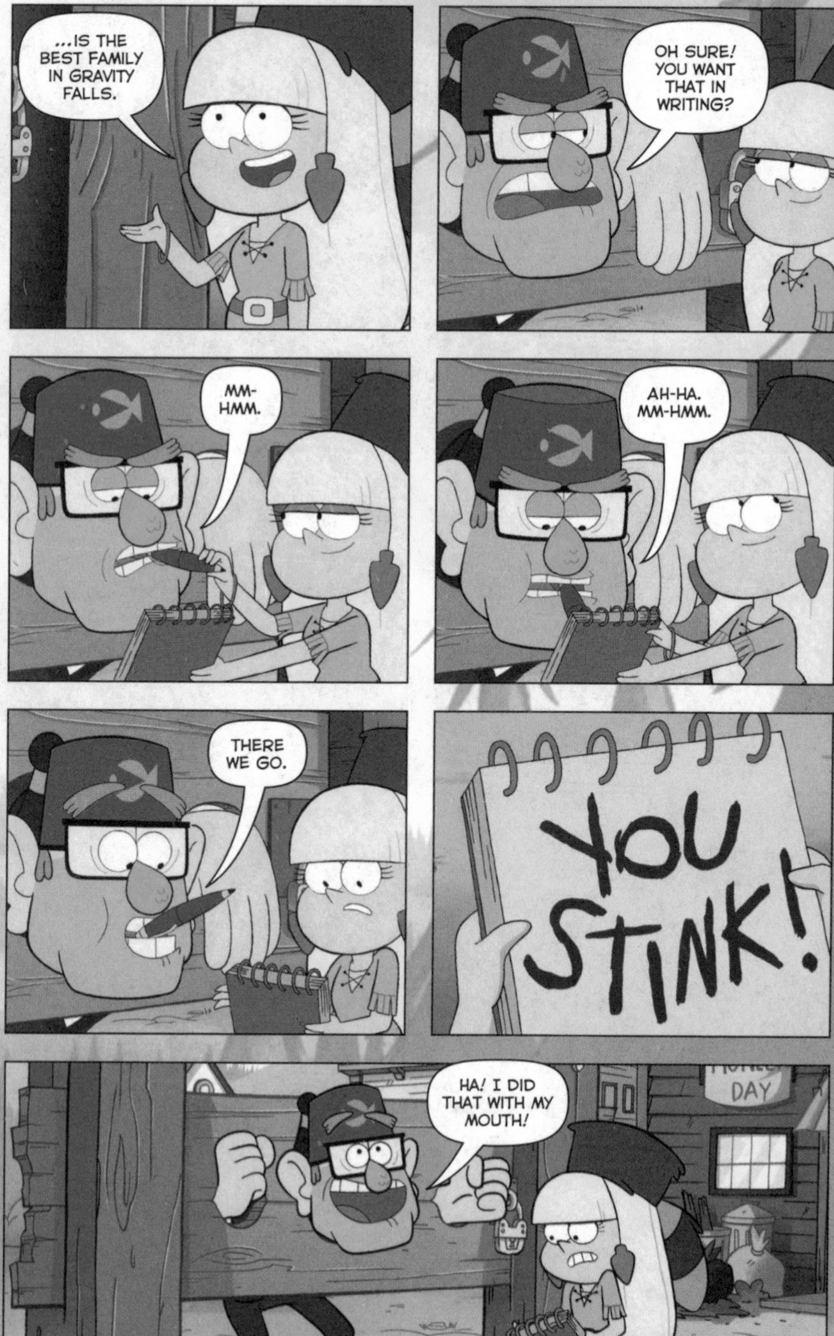

...IS THE BEST FAMILY IN GRAVITY FALLS.
OH SURE! YOU WANT THAT IN WRITING?
MM-HMM.
AH-HA. MM-HMM.
THERE WE GO.
YOU STINK!
HA! I DID THAT WITH MY MOUTH!
DAY

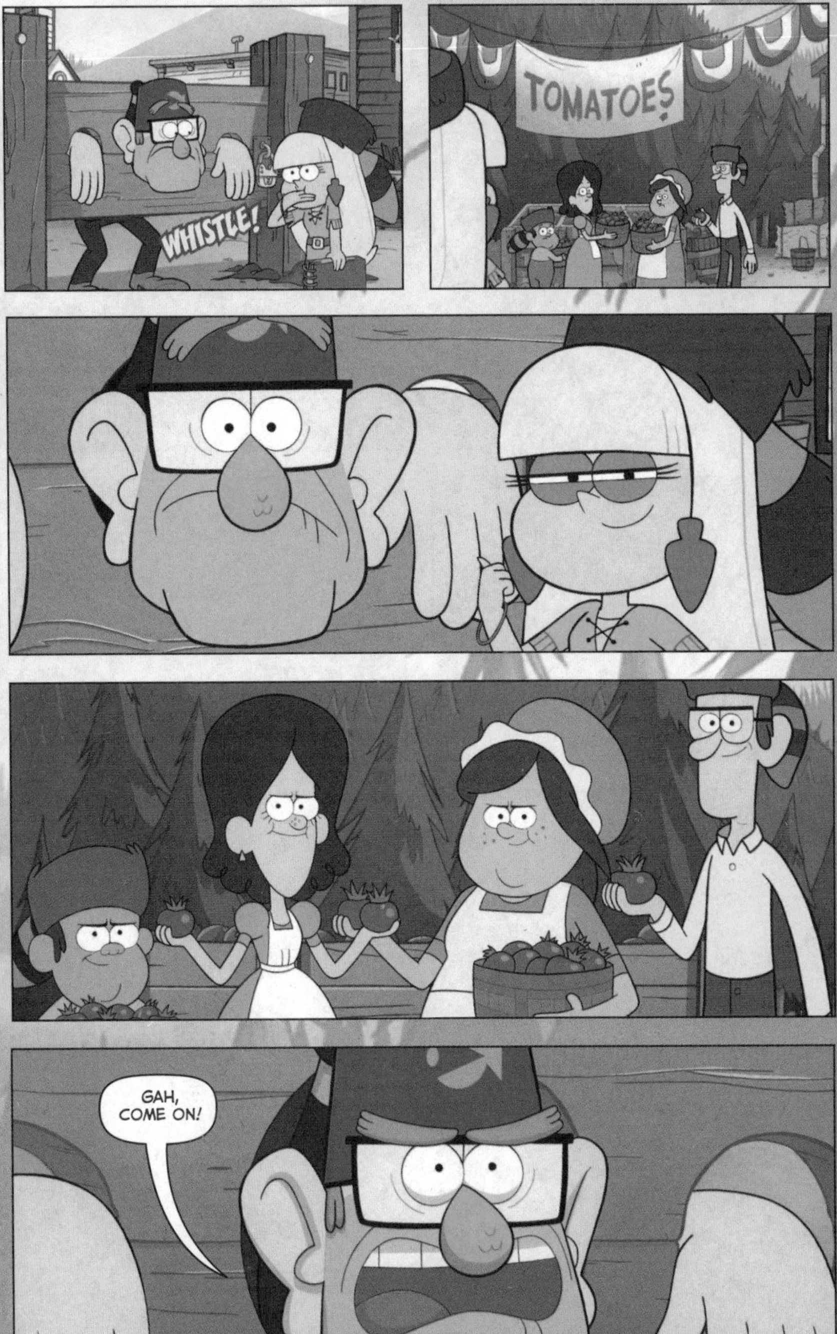
WHISTLE!
TOMATOES
GAH, COME ON!

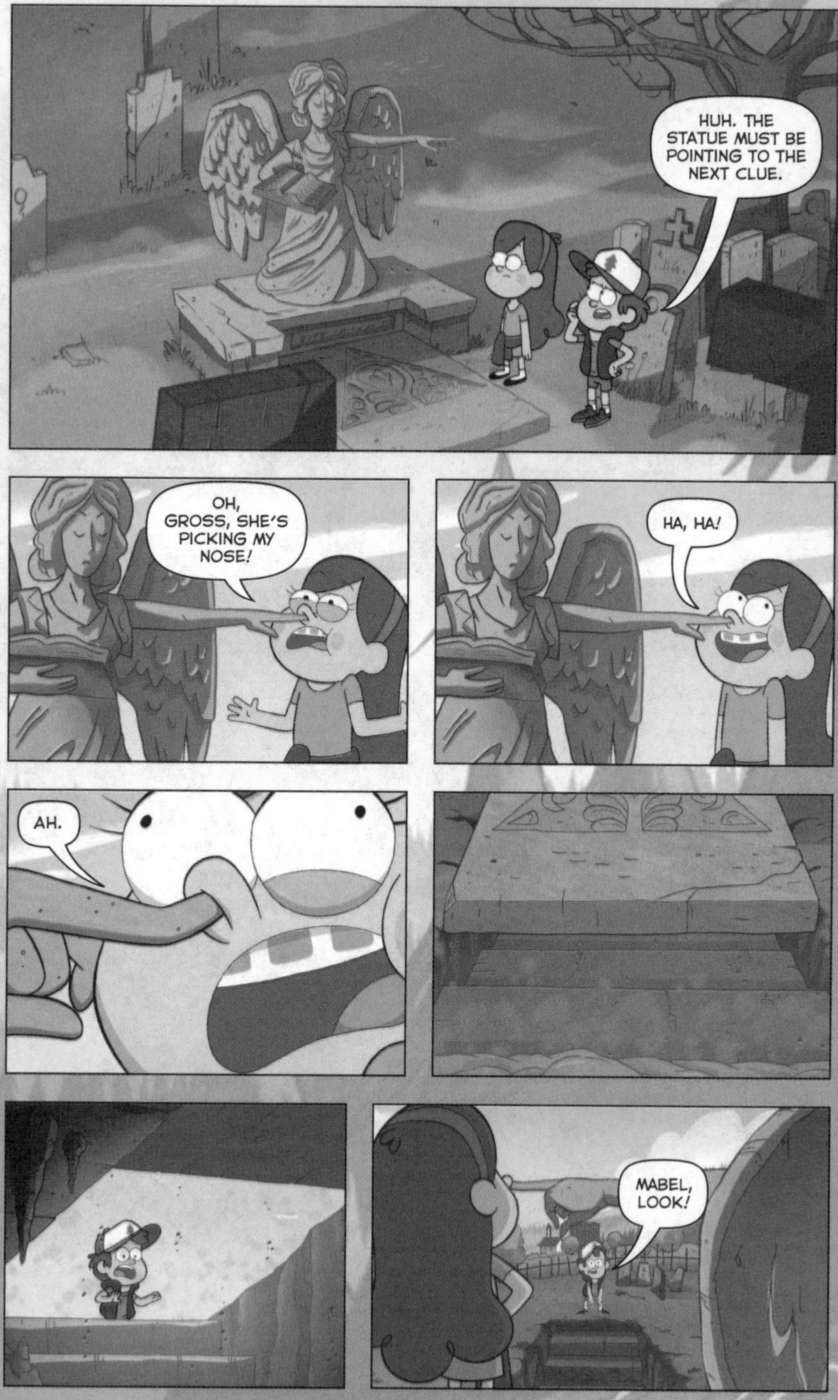
HUH. THE STATUE MUST BE POINTING TO THE NEXT CLUE.
OH, GROSS, SHE'S PICKING MY NOSE!
HA, HA!
AH.
MABEL, LOOK!

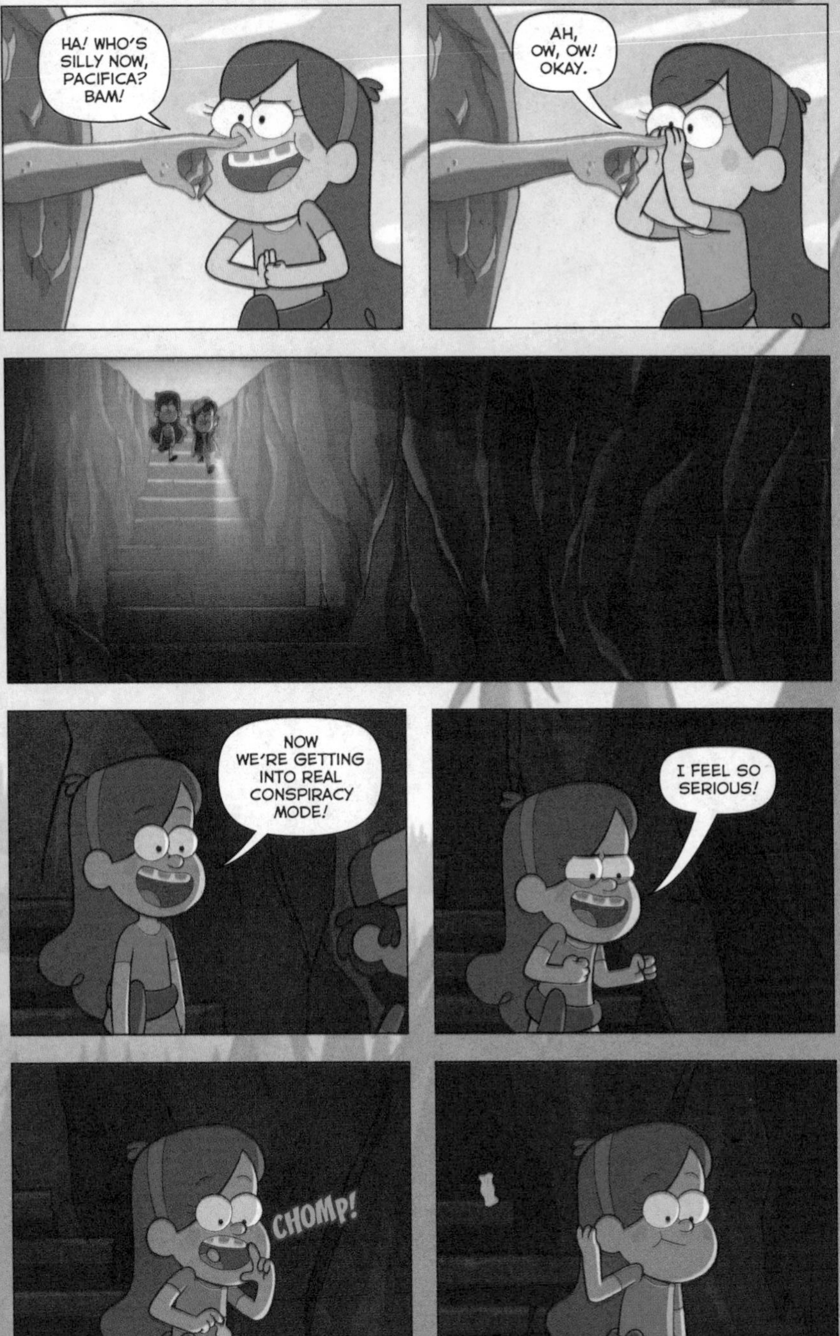
HA! WHO'S SILLY NOW, PACIFICA? BAM!
AH, OW, OW! OKAY.
NOW WE'RE GETTING INTO REAL CONSPIRACY MODE!
I FEEL SO SERIOUS!
CHOMP!

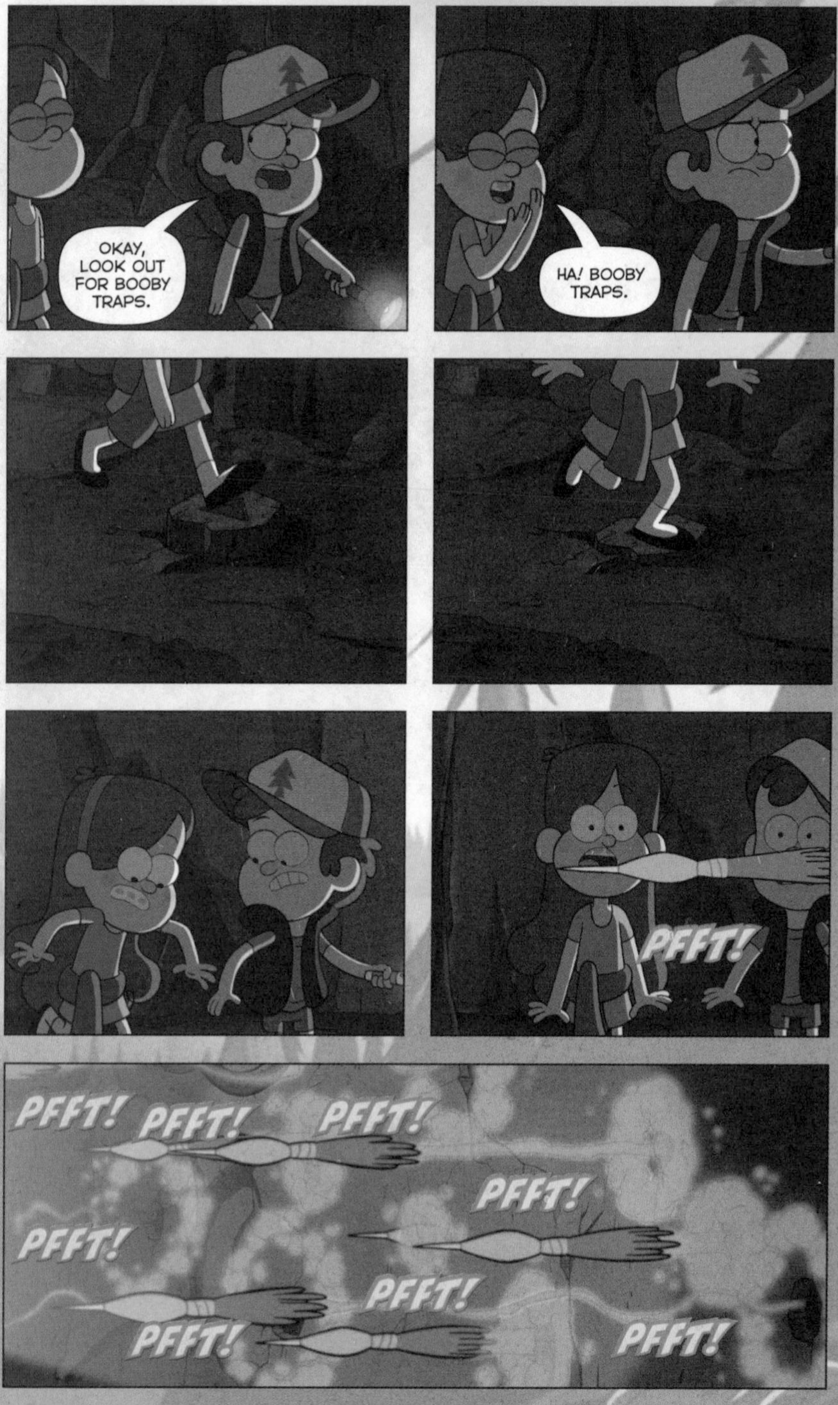
OKAY, LOOK OUT FOR BOOBY TRAPS.
HA! BOOBY TRAPS.
PFFT!
PFFT!
PFFT!
PFFT!
PFFT!
PFFT!
PFFT!
PFFT!
PFFT!

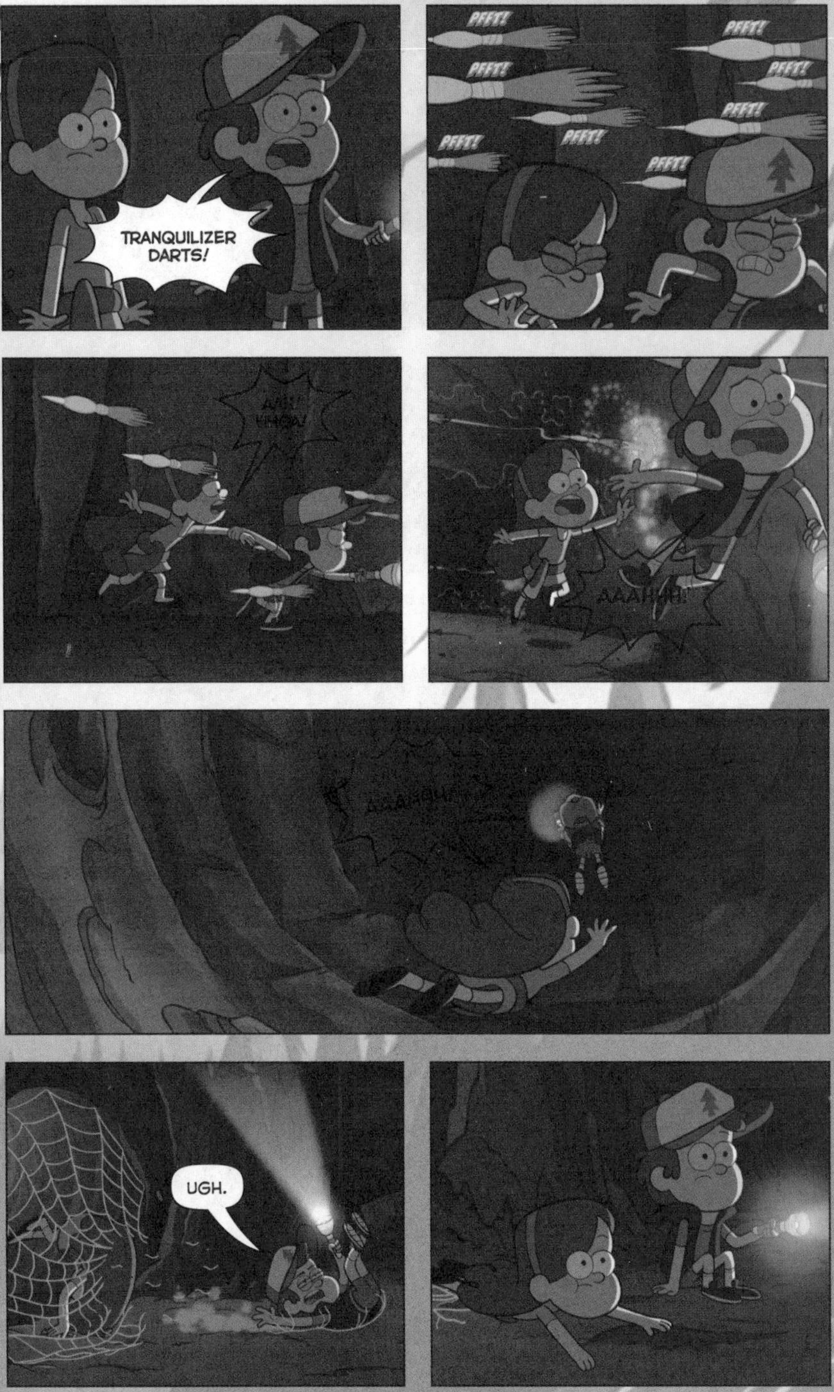
TRANQUILIZER DARTS!
PFFT!
PFFT!
PFFT!
PFFT!
PFFT!
PFFT!
PFFT!
PFFT!
PFFT!
AAAHHH!
UGH.

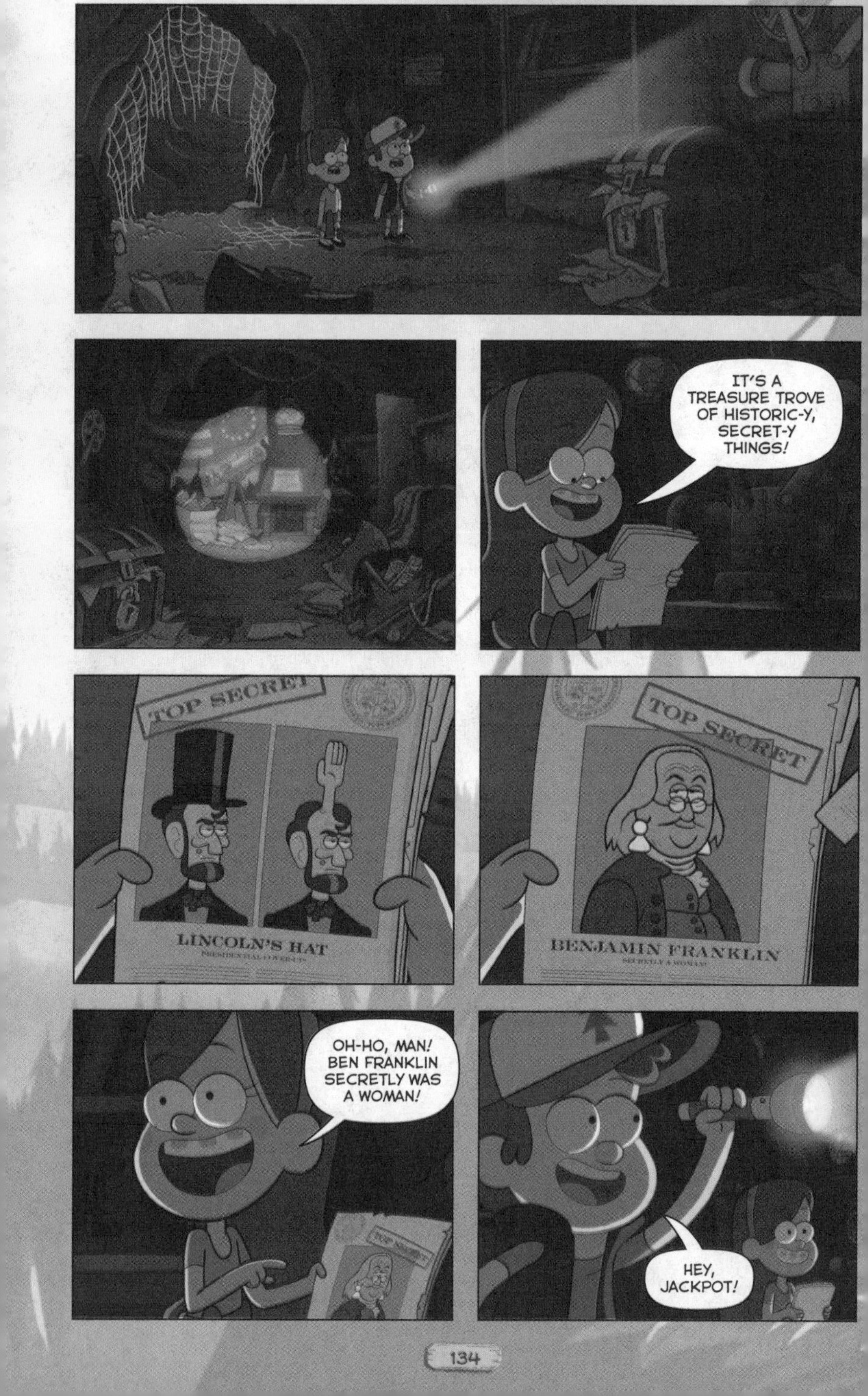
IT'S A TREASURE TROVE OF HISTORIC-Y, SECRET-Y THINGS!
TOP SECRET
LINCOLN'S HAT
TOP SECRET
BENJAMIN FRANKLIN
OH-HO, MAN! BEN FRANKLIN SECRETLY WAS A WOMAN!
TOP SECRET
HEY, JACKPOT!

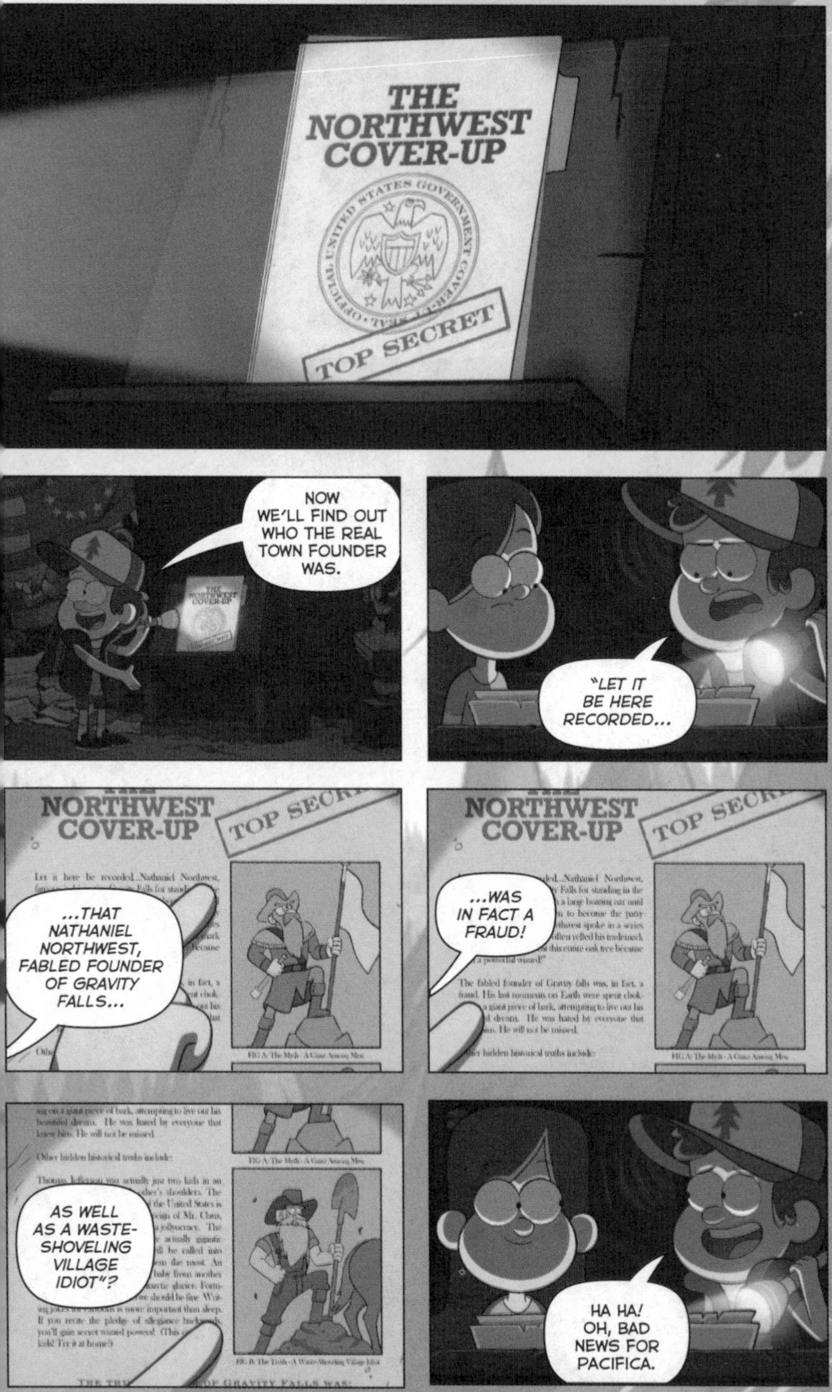
THE NORTHWEST COVER-UP
OFFICIAL UNITED STATES GOVERNMENT COVER-UP SEAL
TOP SECRET
NOW WE'LL FIND OUT WHO THE REAL TOWN FOUNDER WAS.
"LET IT BE HERE RECORDED...
NORTHWEST COVER-UP
TOP SECR
...THAT NATHANIEL NORTHWEST, FABLED FOUNDER OF GRAVITY FALLS...
NORTHWEST COVER-UP
TOP SEC
...WAS IN FACT A FRAUD!
AS WELL AS A WASTE-SHOVELING VILLAGE IDIOT"?
HA HA! OH, BAD NEWS FOR PACIFICA.

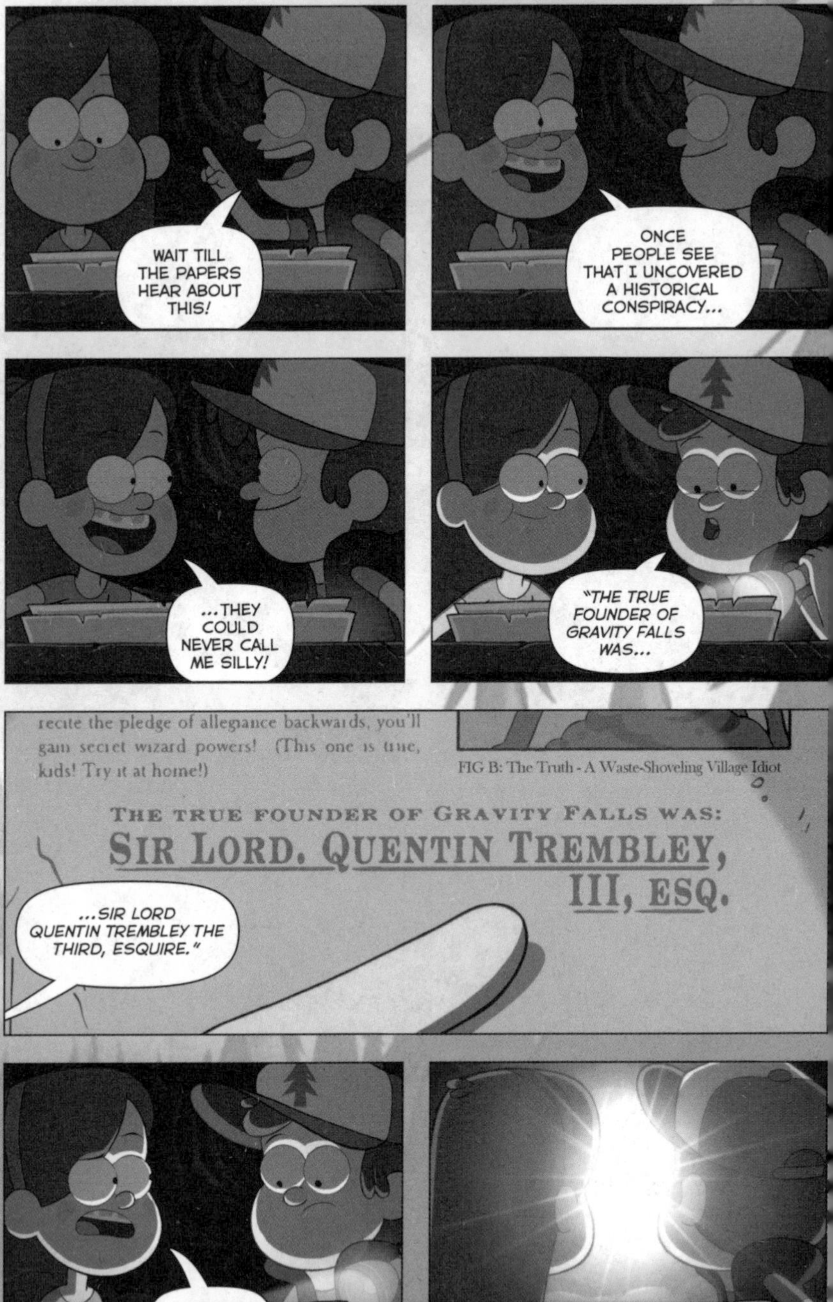

WAIT TILL THE PAPERS HEAR ABOUT THIS!
ONCE PEOPLE SEE THAT I UNCOVERED A HISTORICAL CONSPIRACY...
...THEY COULD NEVER CALL ME SILLY!
"THE TRUE FOUNDER OF GRAVITY FALLS WAS...
recite the pledge of allegiance backwards, you'll gain secret wizard powers! (This one is true, kids! Try it at home!)
FIG B: The Truth - A Waste-Shoveling Village Idiot
THE TRUE FOUNDER OF GRAVITY FALLS WAS:
SIR LORD, QUENTIN TREMBLEY, III, ESQ.
...SIR LORD QUENTIN TREMBLEY THE THIRD, ESQUIRE."
WHO'S QUENTIN TREMBLEY?

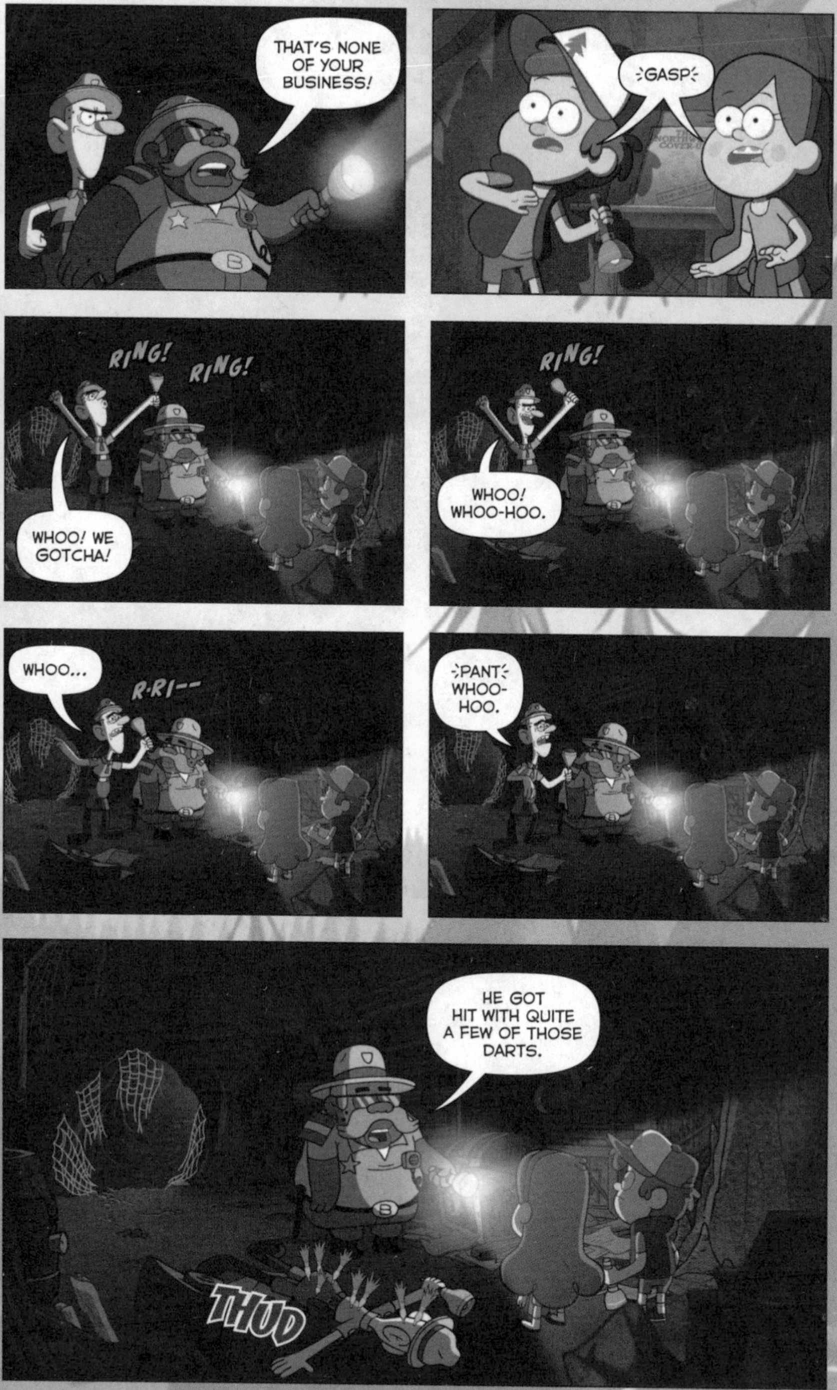
THAT'S NONE OF YOUR BUSINESS!
GASP
RING!
RING!
WHOO! WE GOTCHA!
RING!
WHOO! WHOO-HOO.
WHOO...
R-RI--
PANT WHOO-HOO.
HE GOT HIT WITH QUITE A FEW OF THOSE DARTS.
THUD

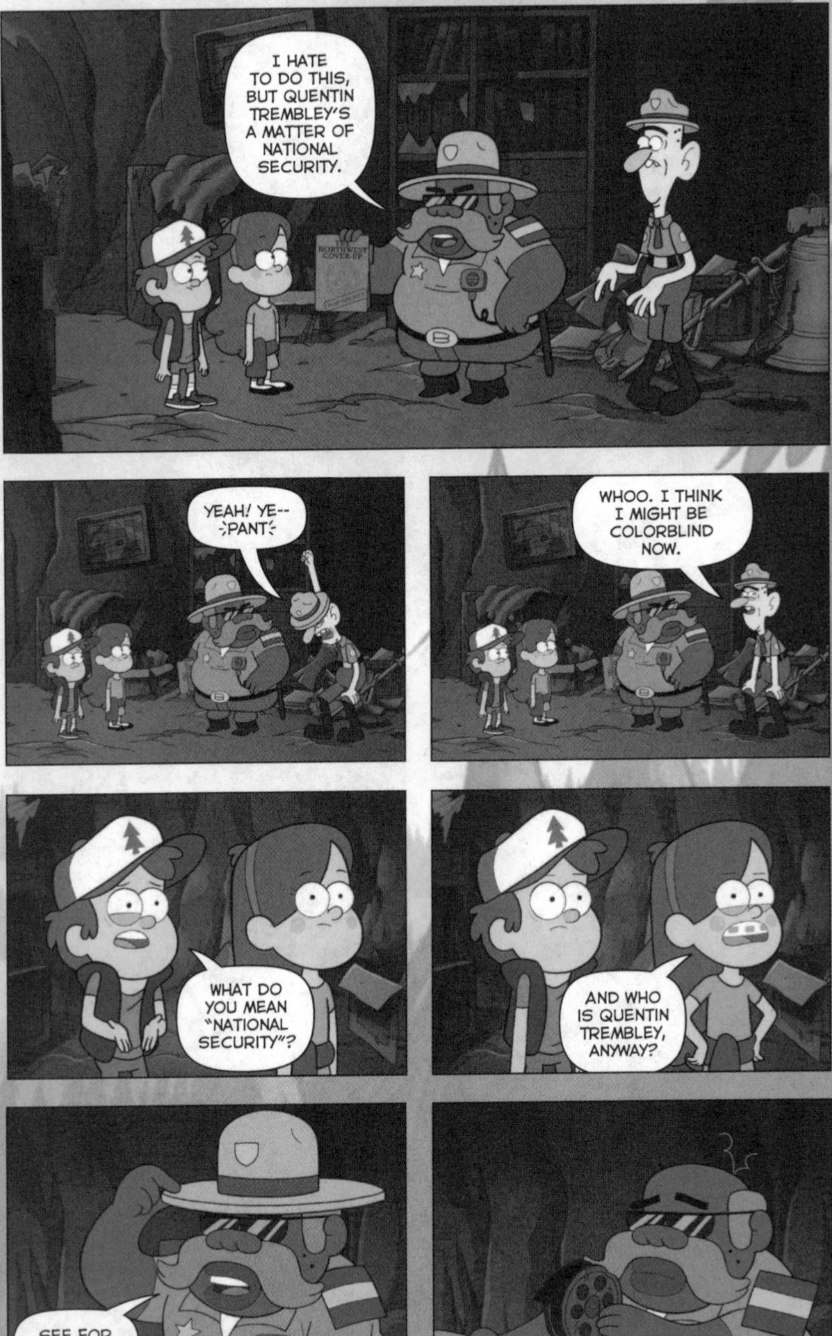
I HATE TO DO THIS, BUT QUENTIN TREMBLEY'S A MATTER OF NATIONAL SECURITY.
YEAH! YE-- PANT
WHOO. I THINK I MIGHT BE COLORBLIND NOW.
WHAT DO YOU MEAN "NATIONAL SECURITY"?
AND WHO IS QUENTIN TREMBLEY, ANYWAY?
SEE FOR YOURSELF.

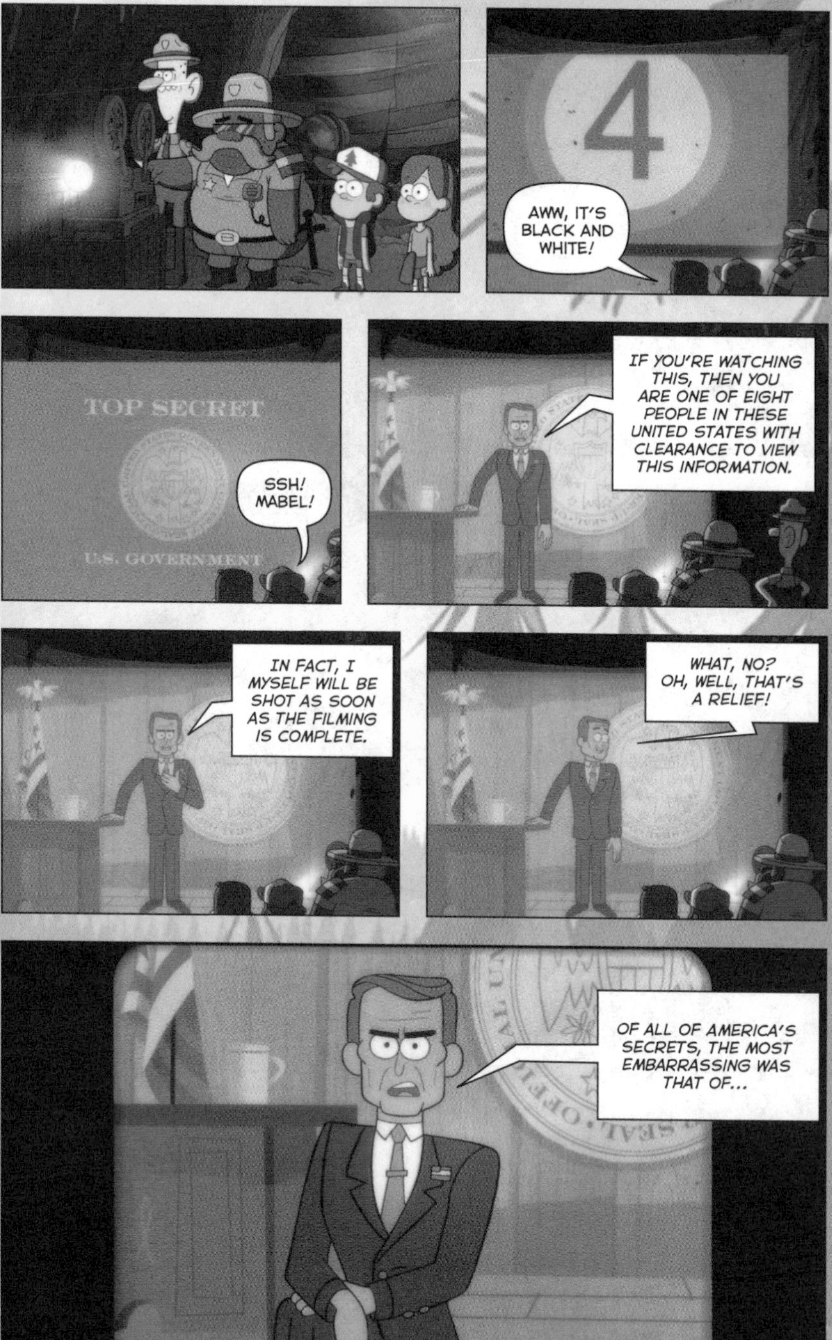
AWW, IT'S BLACK AND WHITE!
TOP SECRET
U.S. GOVERNMENT
SSH! MABEL!
IF YOU'RE WATCHING THIS, THEN YOU ARE ONE OF EIGHT PEOPLE IN THESE UNITED STATES WITH CLEARANCE TO VIEW THIS INFORMATION.
IN FACT, I MYSELF WILL BE SHOT AS SOON AS THE FILMING IS COMPLETE.
WHAT, NO? OH, WELL, THAT'S A RELIEF!
OF ALL OF AMERICA'S SECRETS, THE MOST EMBARRASSING WAS THAT OF...

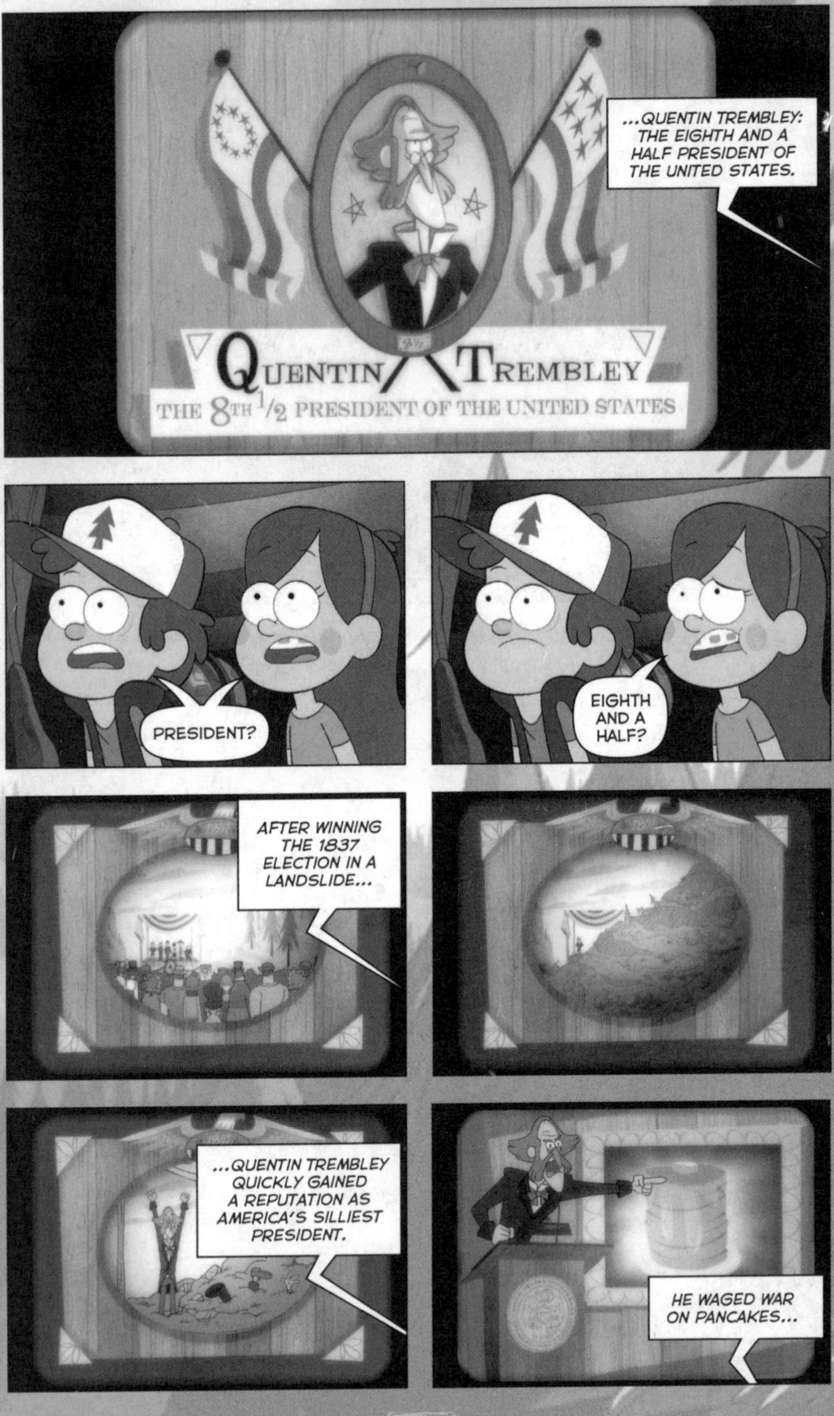
...QUENTIN TREMBLEY: THE EIGHTH AND A HALF PRESIDENT OF THE UNITED STATES.
QUENTIN TREMBLEY
THE 8TH 1/2 PRESIDENT OF THE UNITED STATES
PRESIDENT?
EIGHTH AND A HALF?
AFTER WINNING THE 1837 ELECTION IN A LANDSLIDE...
...QUENTIN TREMBLEY QUICKLY GAINED A REPUTATION AS AMERICA'S SILLIEST PRESIDENT.
HE WAGED WAR ON PANCAKES...

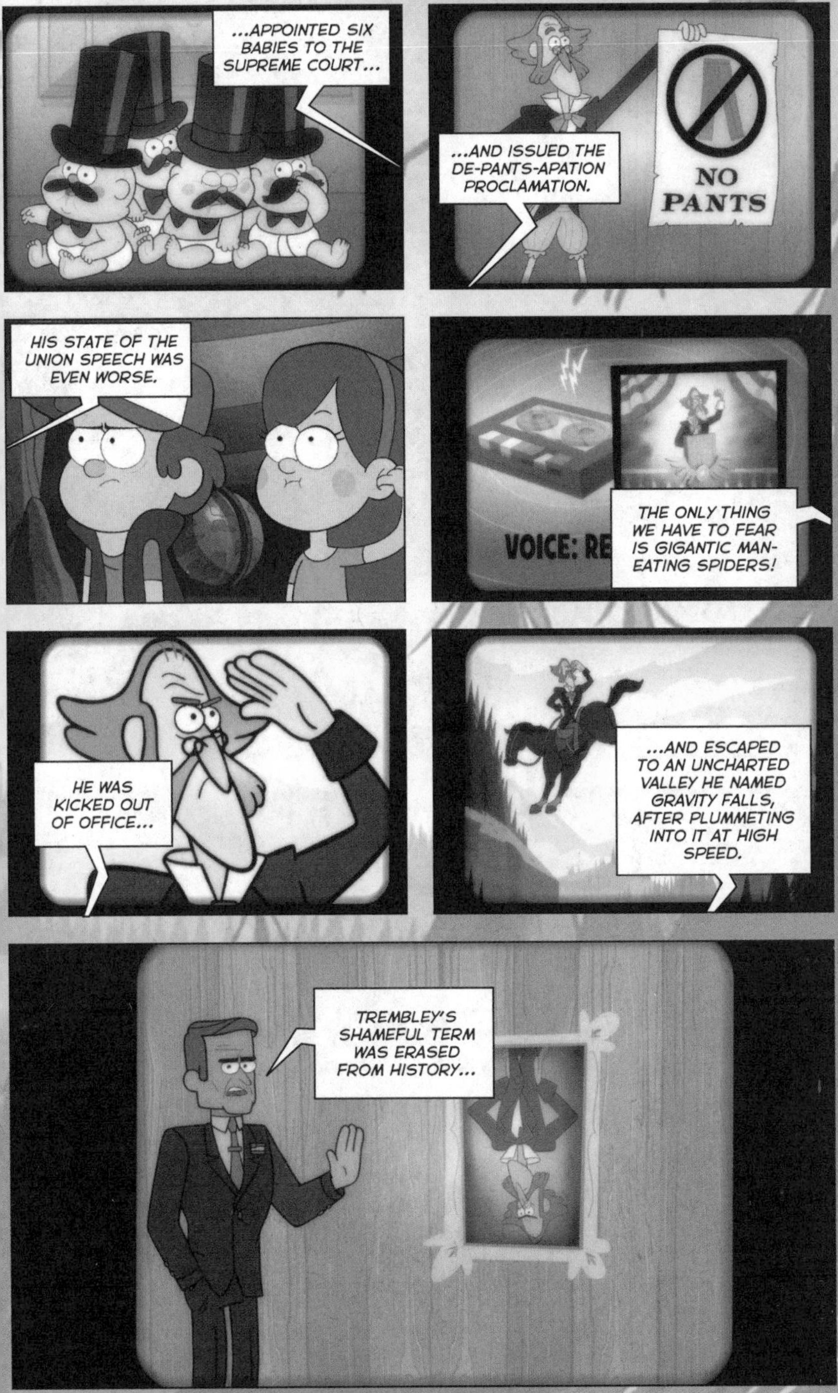
...APPOINTED SIX BABIES TO THE SUPREME COURT...
...AND ISSUED THE DE-PANTS-APATION PROCLAMATION.
NO PANTS
HIS STATE OF THE UNION SPEECH WAS EVEN WORSE.
VOICE: RE
THE ONLY THING WE HAVE TO FEAR IS GIGANTIC MAN-EATING SPIDERS!
HE WAS KICKED OUT OF OFFICE...
...AND ESCAPED TO AN UNCHARTED VALLEY HE NAMED GRAVITY FALLS, AFTER PLUMMETING INTO IT AT HIGH SPEED.
TREMBLEY'S SHAMEFUL TERM WAS ERASED FROM HISTORY...

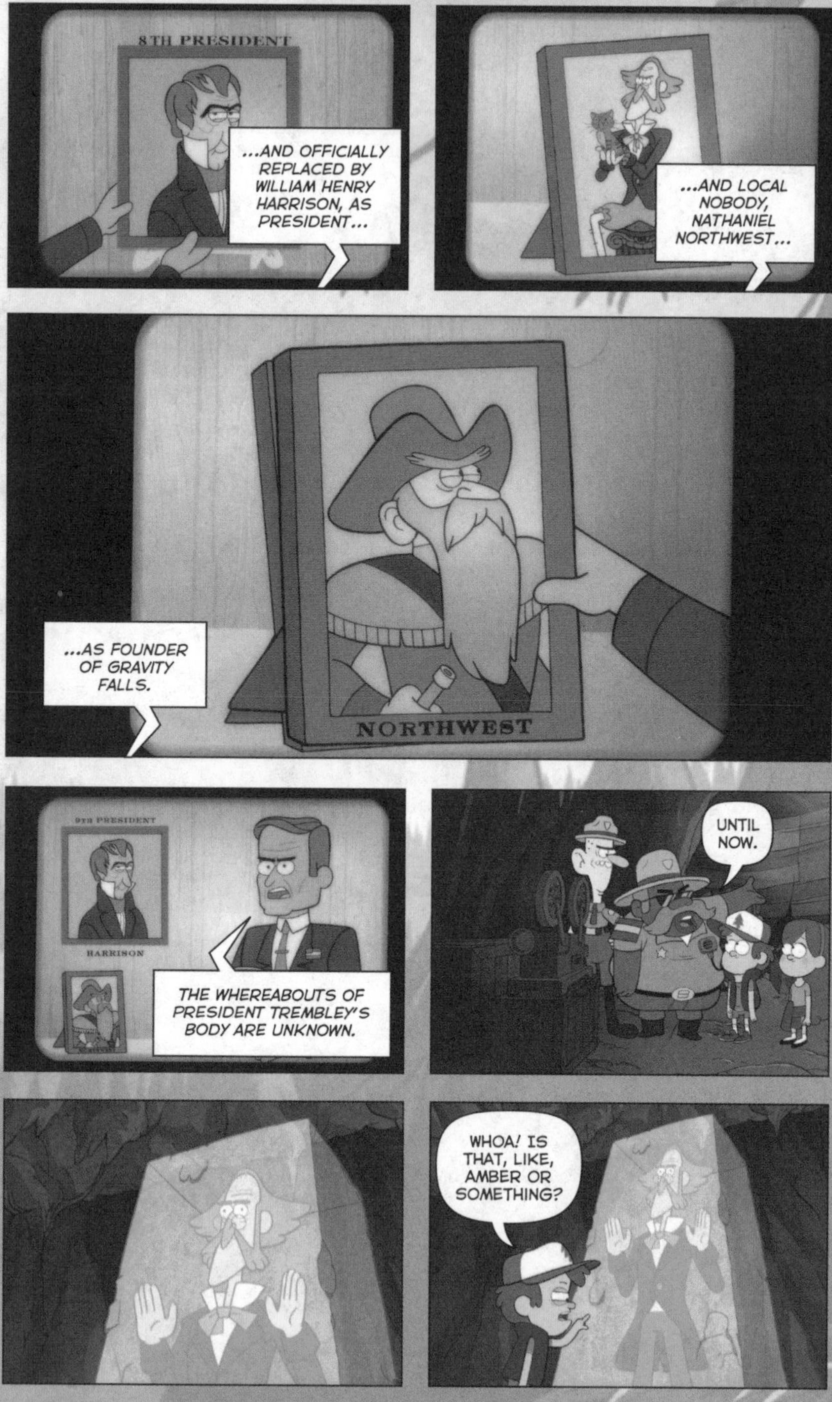
8TH PRESIDENT
...AND OFFICIALLY REPLACED BY WILLIAM HENRY HARRISON, AS PRESIDENT...
...AND LOCAL NOBODY, NATHANIEL NORTHWEST...
...AS FOUNDER OF GRAVITY FALLS.
NORTHWEST
9TH PRESIDENT
HARRISON
THE WHEREABOUTS OF PRESIDENT TREMBLEY'S BODY ARE UNKNOWN.
UNTIL NOW.
WHOA! IS THAT, LIKE, AMBER OR SOMETHING?

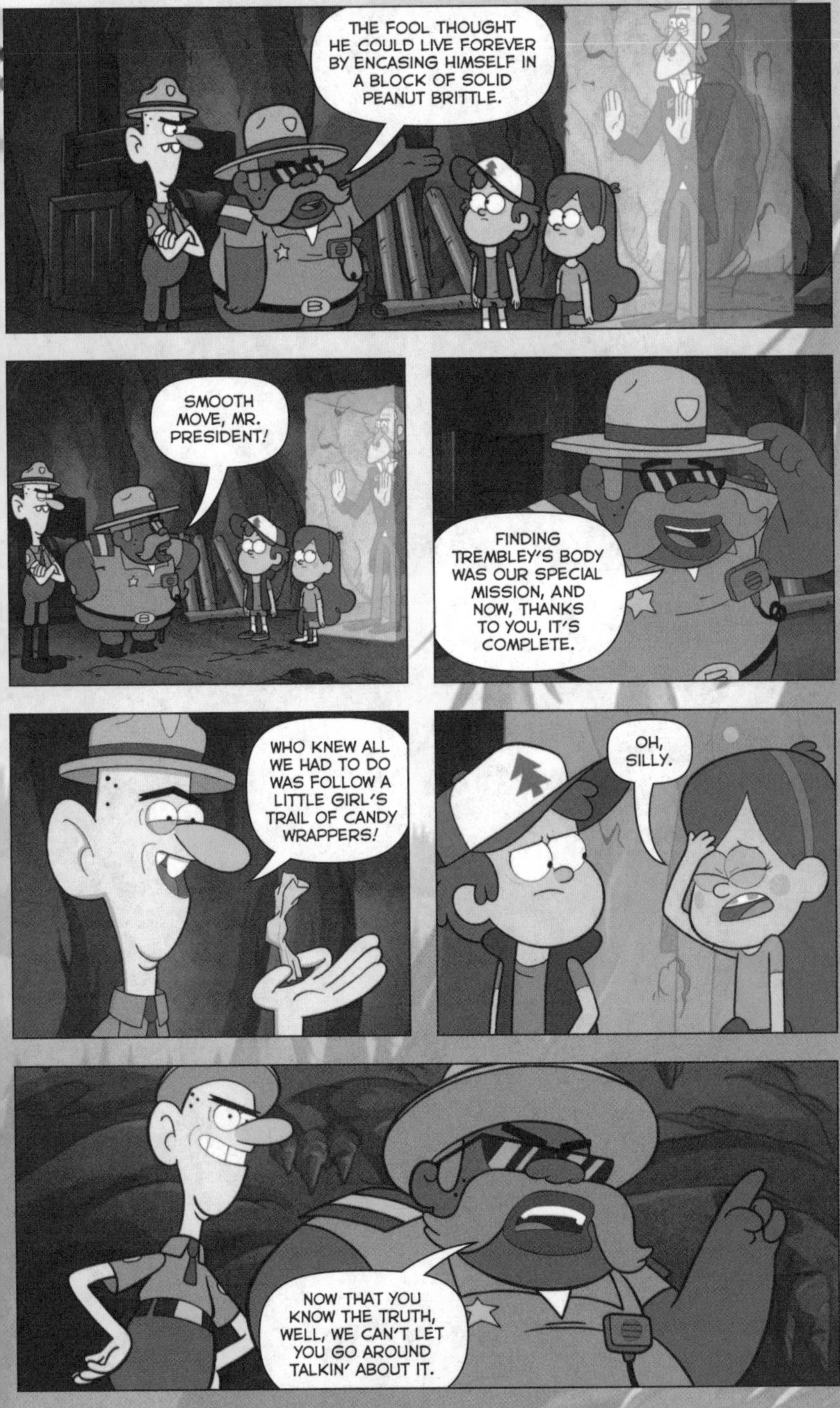
THE FOOL THOUGHT HE COULD LIVE FOREVER BY ENCASING HIMSELF IN A BLOCK OF SOLID PEANUT BRITTLE.
SMOOTH MOVE, MR. PRESIDENT!
FINDING TREMBLEY'S BODY WAS OUR SPECIAL MISSION, AND NOW, THANKS TO YOU, IT'S COMPLETE.
WHO KNEW ALL WE HAD TO DO WAS FOLLOW A LITTLE GIRL'S TRAIL OF CANDY WRAPPERS!
OH, SILLY.
NOW THAT YOU KNOW THE TRUTH, WELL, WE CAN'T LET YOU GO AROUND TALKIN' ABOUT IT.

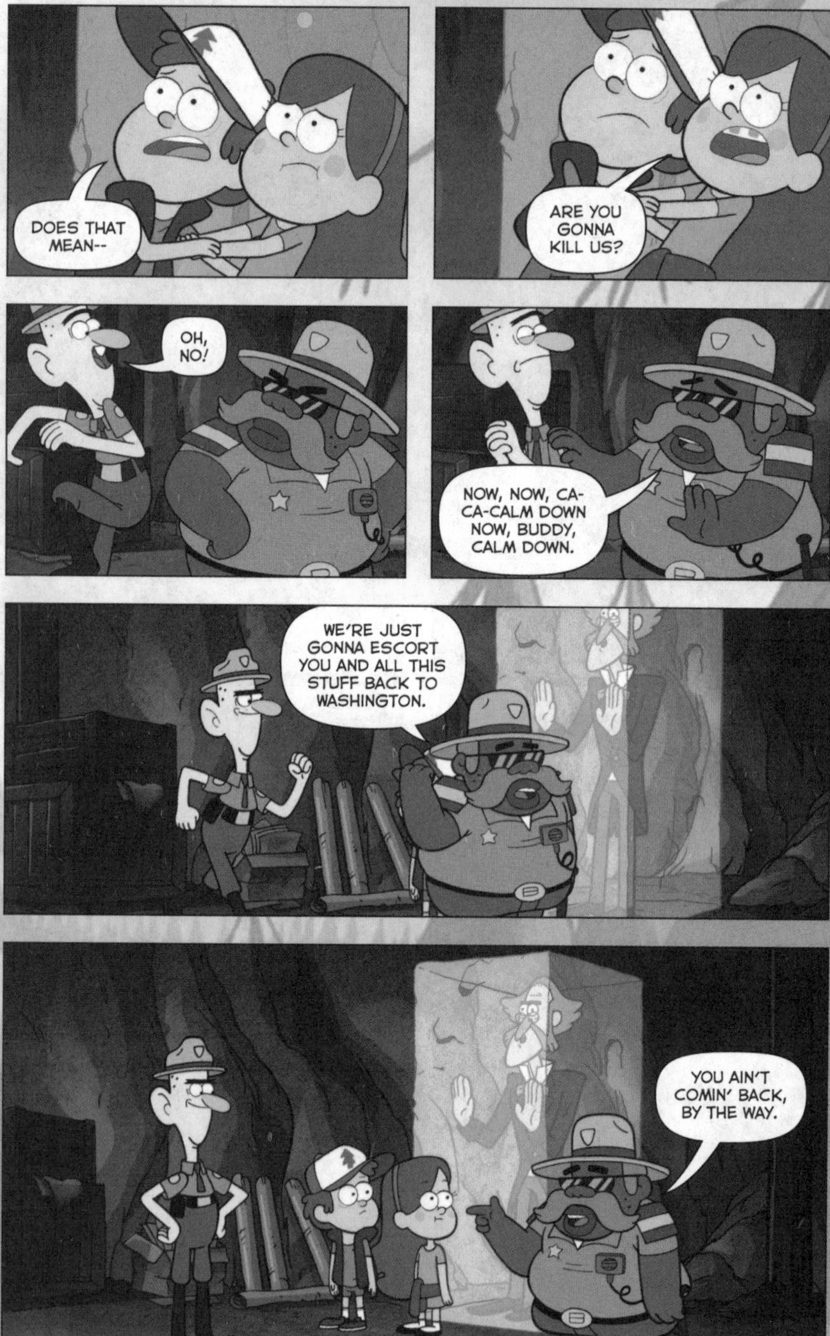
DOES THAT MEAN--
ARE YOU GONNA KILL US?
OH, NO!
NOW, NOW, CA-CA-CALM DOWN NOW, BUDDY, CALM DOWN.
WE'RE JUST GONNA ESCORT YOU AND ALL THIS STUFF BACK TO WASHINGTON.
YOU AIN'T COMIN' BACK, BY THE WAY.

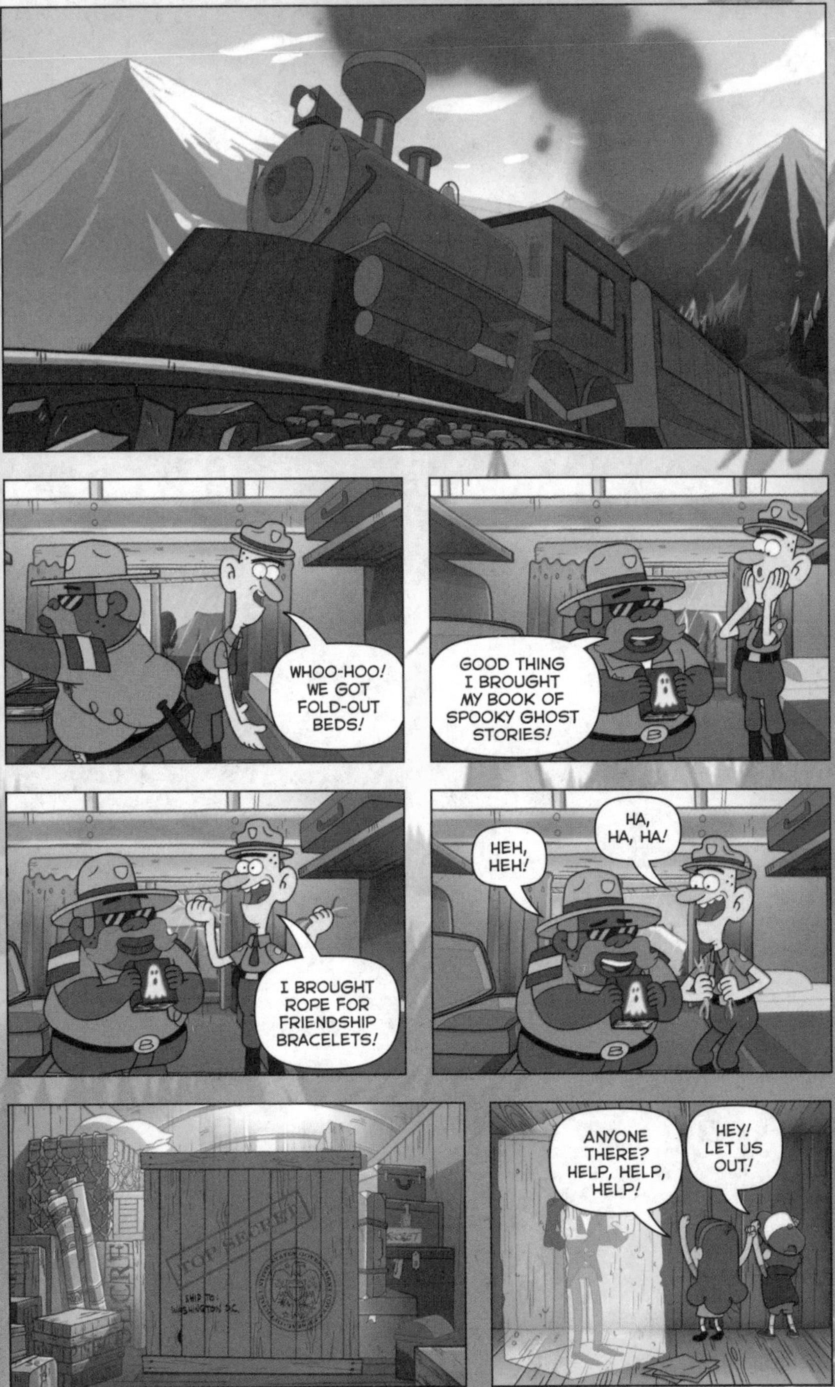
WHOO-HOO! WE GOT FOLD-OUT BEDS!
GOOD THING I BROUGHT MY BOOK OF SPOOKY GHOST STORIES!
I BROUGHT ROPE FOR FRIENDSHIP BRACELETS!
HEH, HEH!
HA, HA, HA!
TOP SECRET
ANYONE THERE? HELP, HELP, HELP!
HEY! LET US OUT!

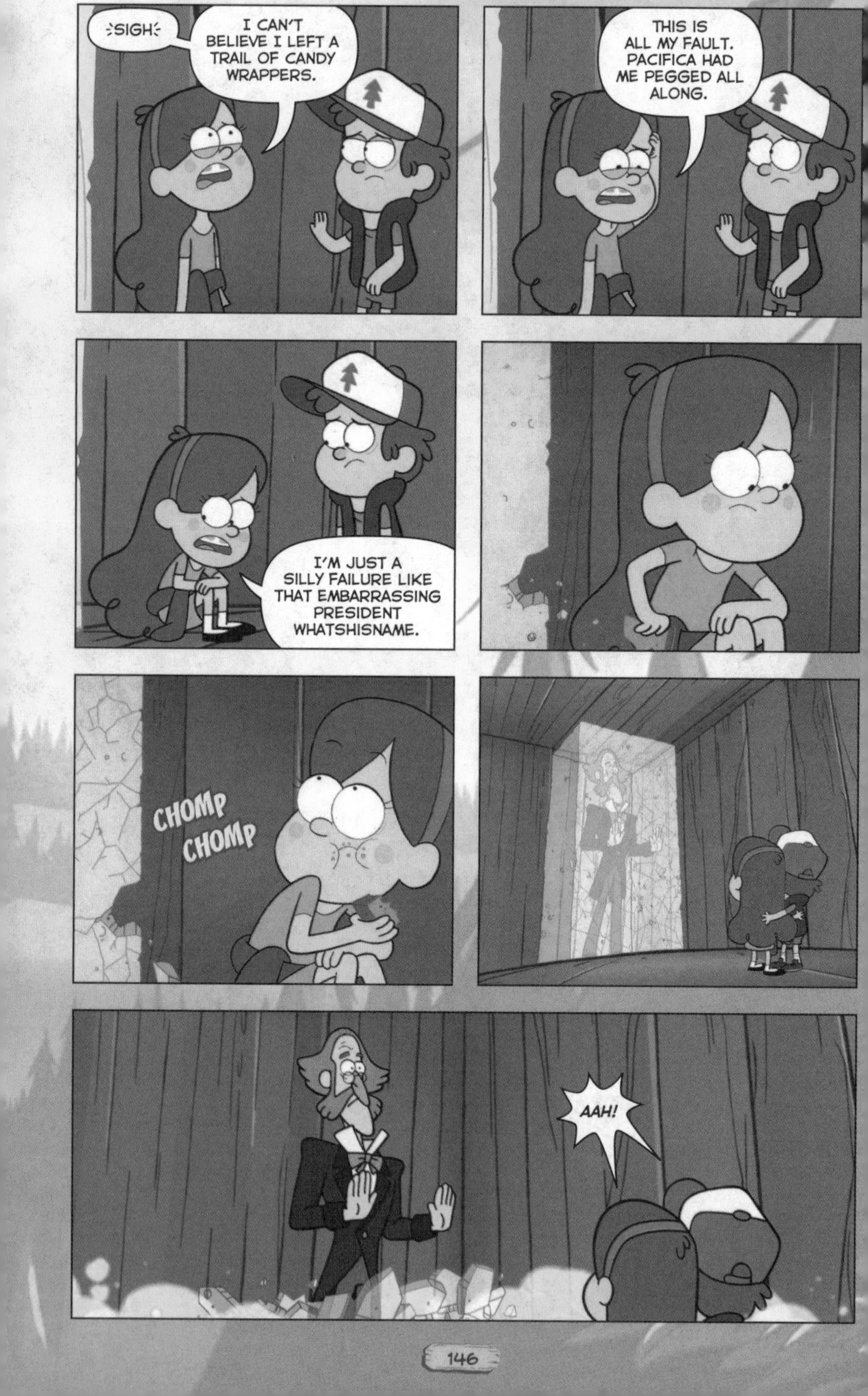
SIGH
I CAN'T BELIEVE I LEFT A TRAIL OF CANDY WRAPPERS.
THIS IS ALL MY FAULT. PACIFICA HAD ME PEGGED ALL ALONG.
I'M JUST A SILLY FAILURE LIKE THAT EMBARRASSING PRESIDENT WHATSHISNAME.
CHOMP
CHOMP
AAH!

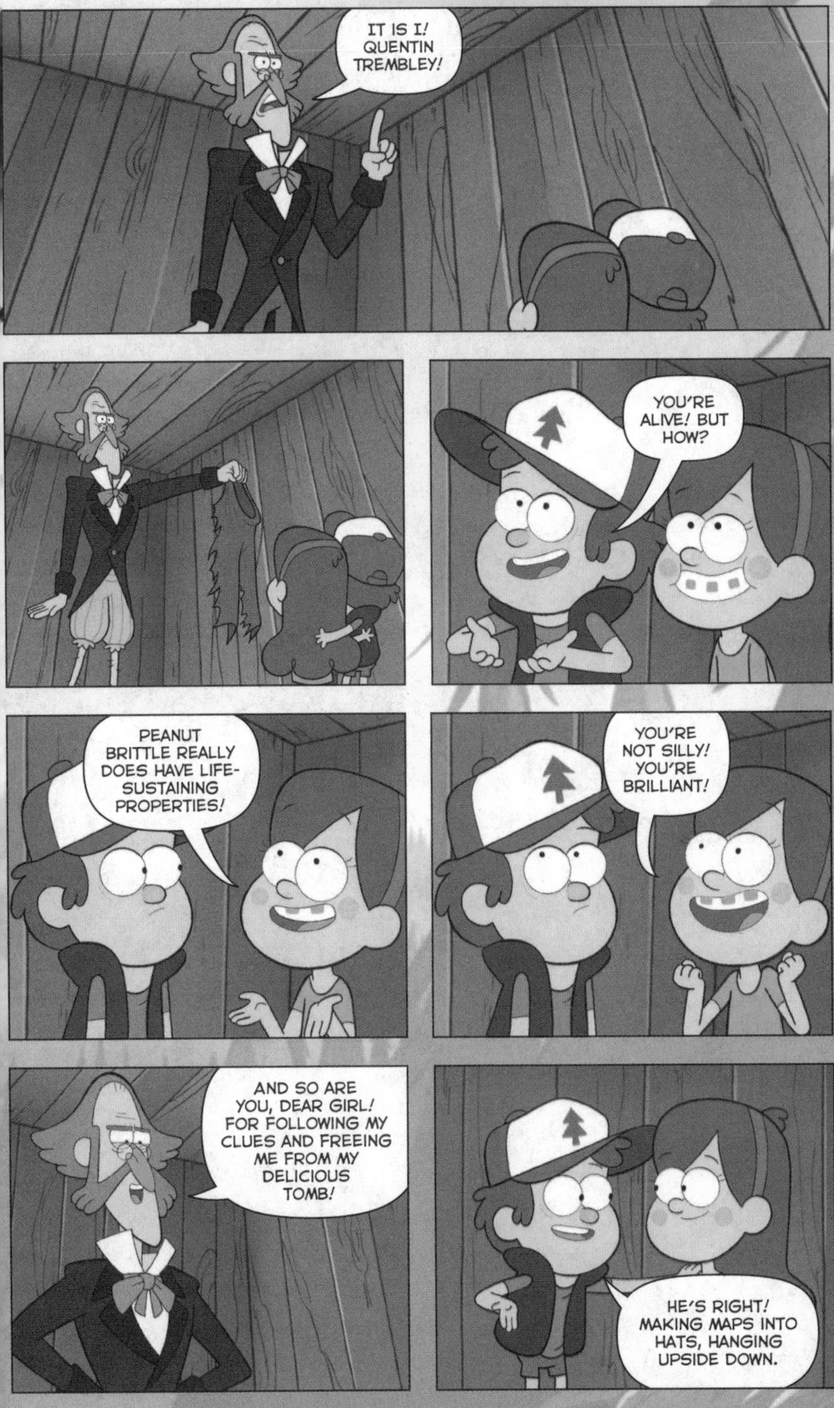
IT IS I! QUENTIN TREMBLEY!
YOU'RE ALIVE! BUT HOW?
PEANUT BRITTLE REALLY DOES HAVE LIFE-SUSTAINING PROPERTIES!
YOU'RE NOT SILLY! YOU'RE BRILLIANT!
AND SO ARE YOU, DEAR GIRL! FOR FOLLOWING MY CLUES AND FREEING ME FROM MY DELICIOUS TOMB!
HE'S RIGHT! MAKING MAPS INTO HATS, HANGING UPSIDE DOWN.

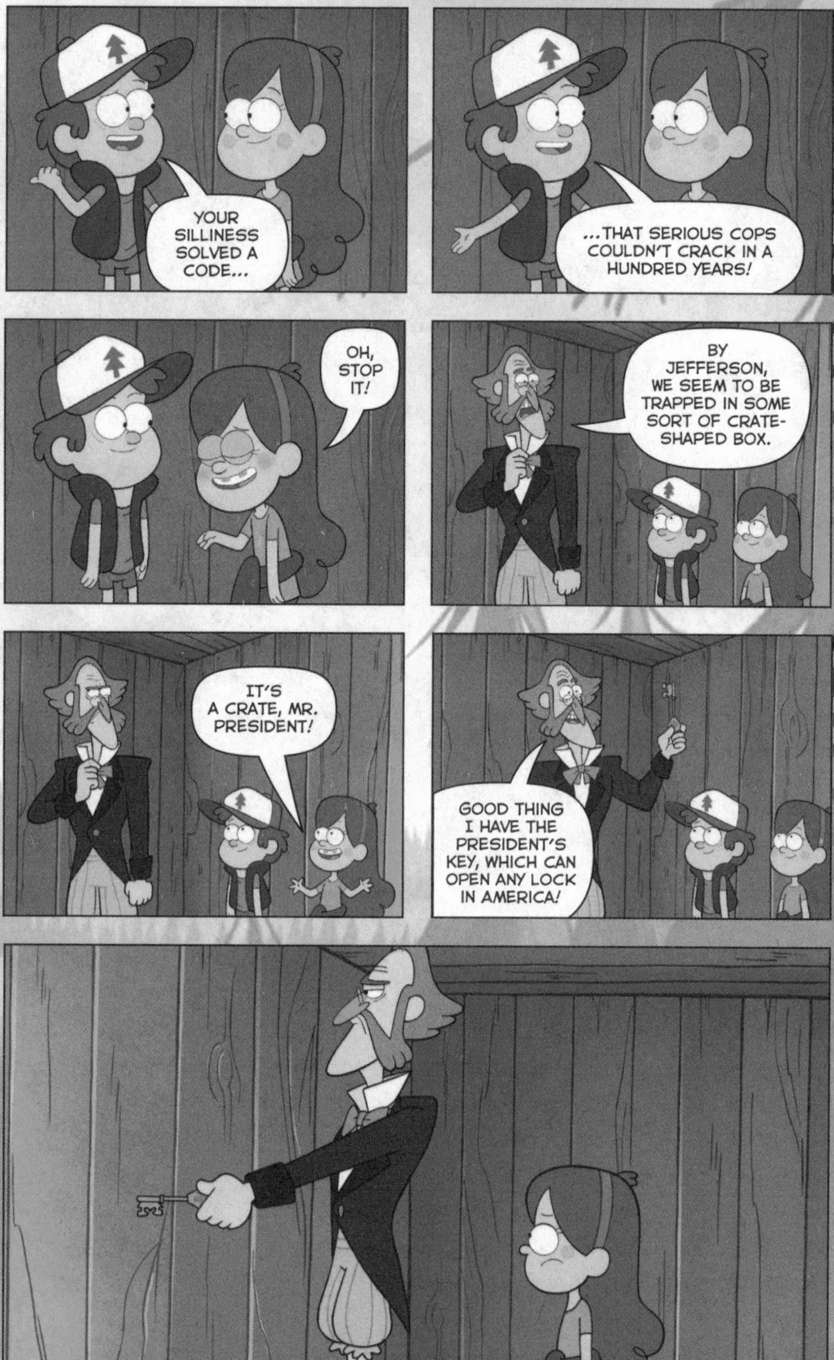
YOUR SILLINESS SOLVED A CODE...
...THAT SERIOUS COPS COULDN'T CRACK IN A HUNDRED YEARS!
OH, STOP IT!
BY JEFFERSON, WE SEEM TO BE TRAPPED IN SOME SORT OF CRATE-SHAPED BOX.
IT'S A CRATE, MR. PRESIDENT!
GOOD THING I HAVE THE PRESIDENT'S KEY, WHICH CAN OPEN ANY LOCK IN AMERICA!

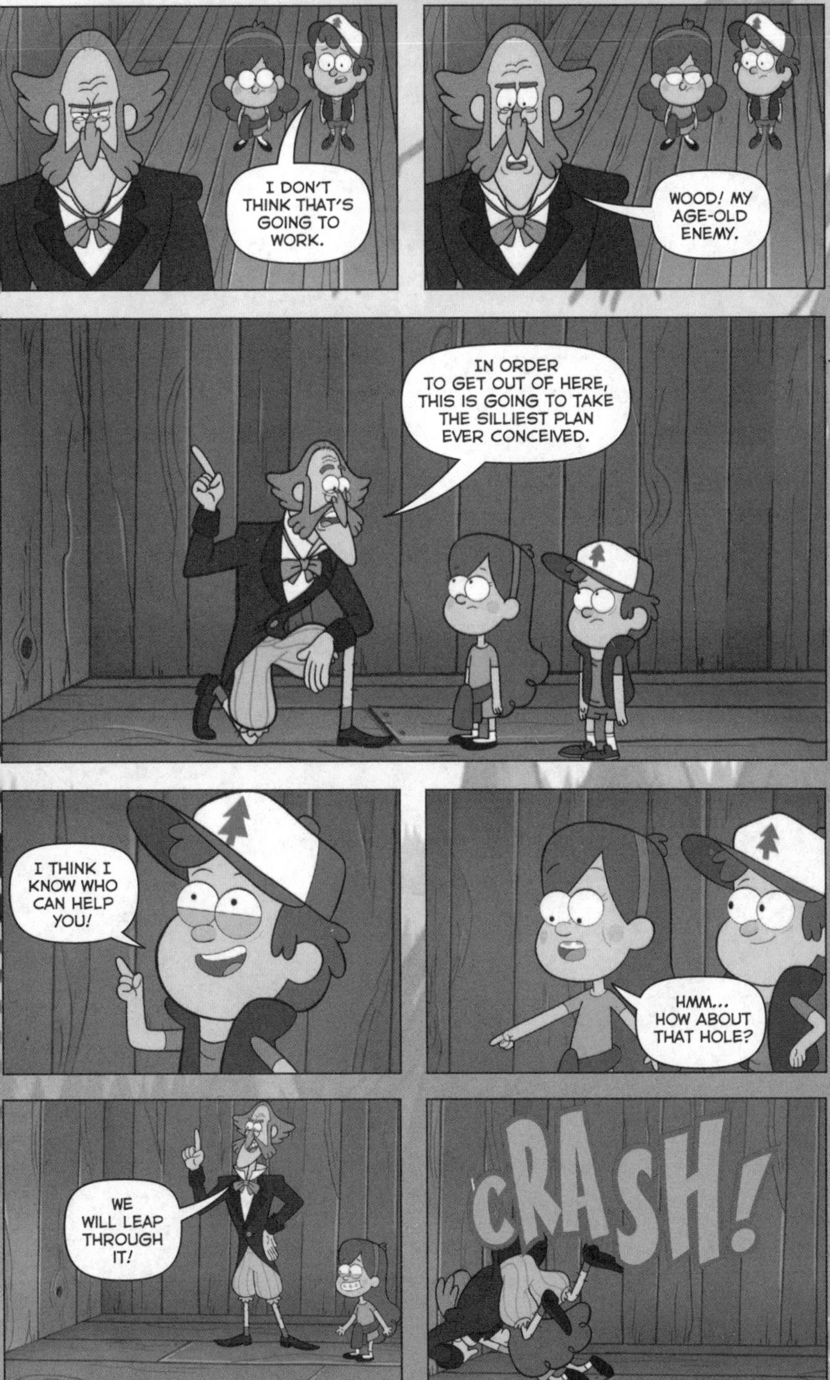
I DON'T THINK THAT'S GOING TO WORK.
WOOD! MY AGE-OLD ENEMY.
IN ORDER TO GET OUT OF HERE, THIS IS GOING TO TAKE THE SILLIEST PLAN EVER CONCEIVED.
I THINK I KNOW WHO CAN HELP YOU!
HMM... HOW ABOUT THAT HOLE?
WE WILL LEAP THROUGH IT!
CRASH!

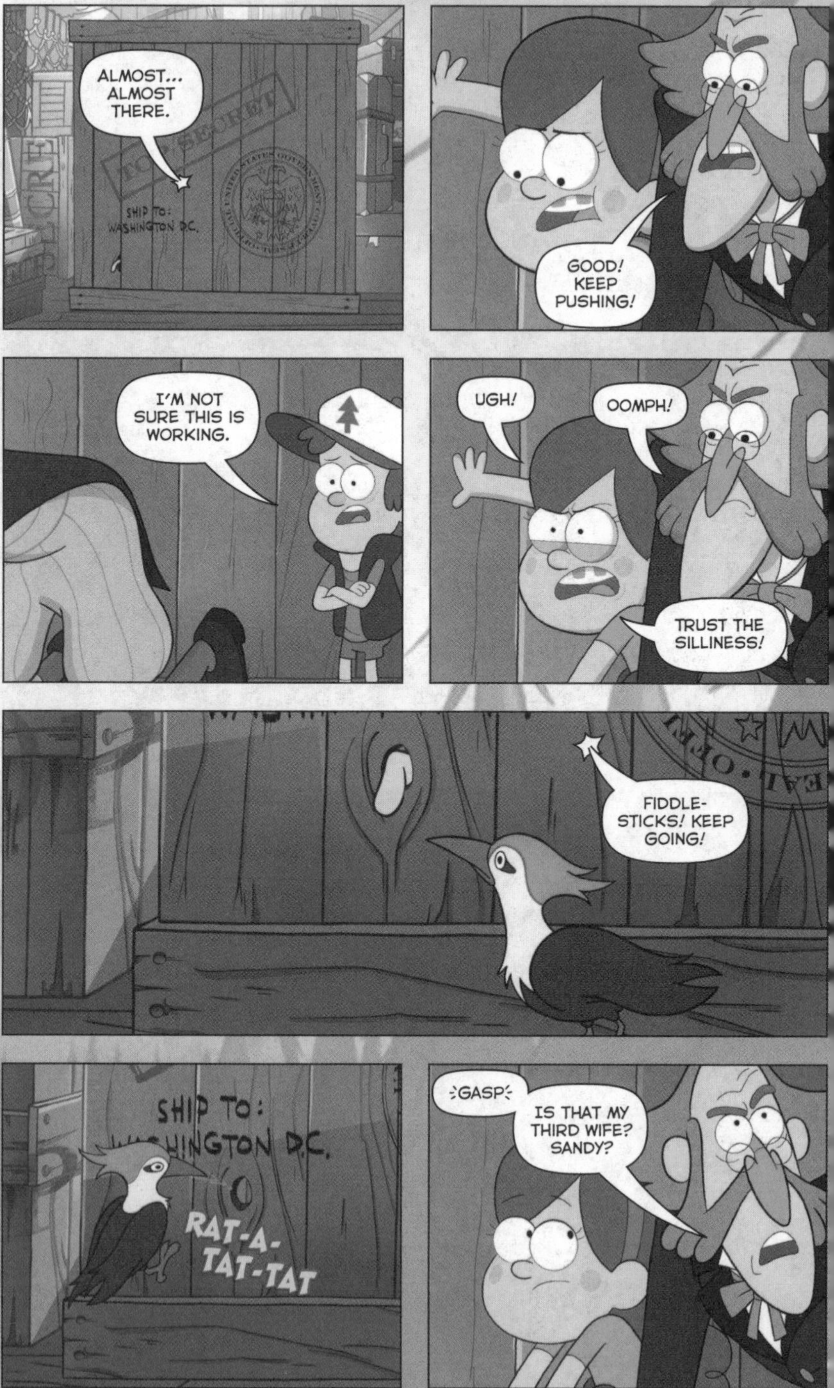
TOP SECRET
SHIP TO: WASHINGTON D.C.
ALMOST... ALMOST THERE.
GOOD! KEEP PUSHING!
I'M NOT SURE THIS IS WORKING.
UGH!
OOMPH!
TRUST THE SILLINESS!
FIDDLE-STICKS! KEEP GOING!
SHIP TO:
RAT-A-TAT-TAT
GASP
IS THAT MY THIRD WIFE? SANDY?

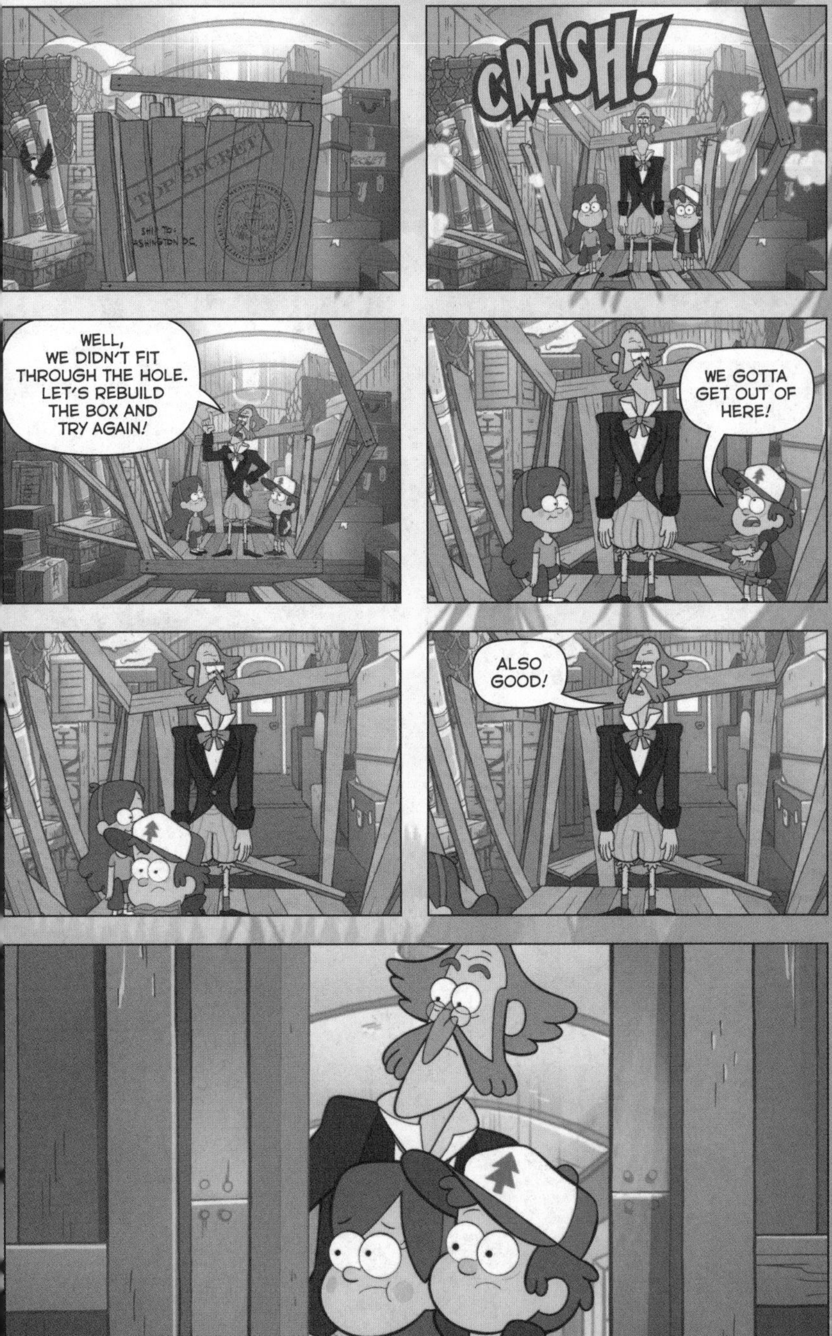
TOP SECRET
CRASH!
WELL, WE DIDN'T FIT THROUGH THE HOLE. LET'S REBUILD THE BOX AND TRY AGAIN!
WE GOTTA GET OUT OF HERE!
ALSO GOOD!

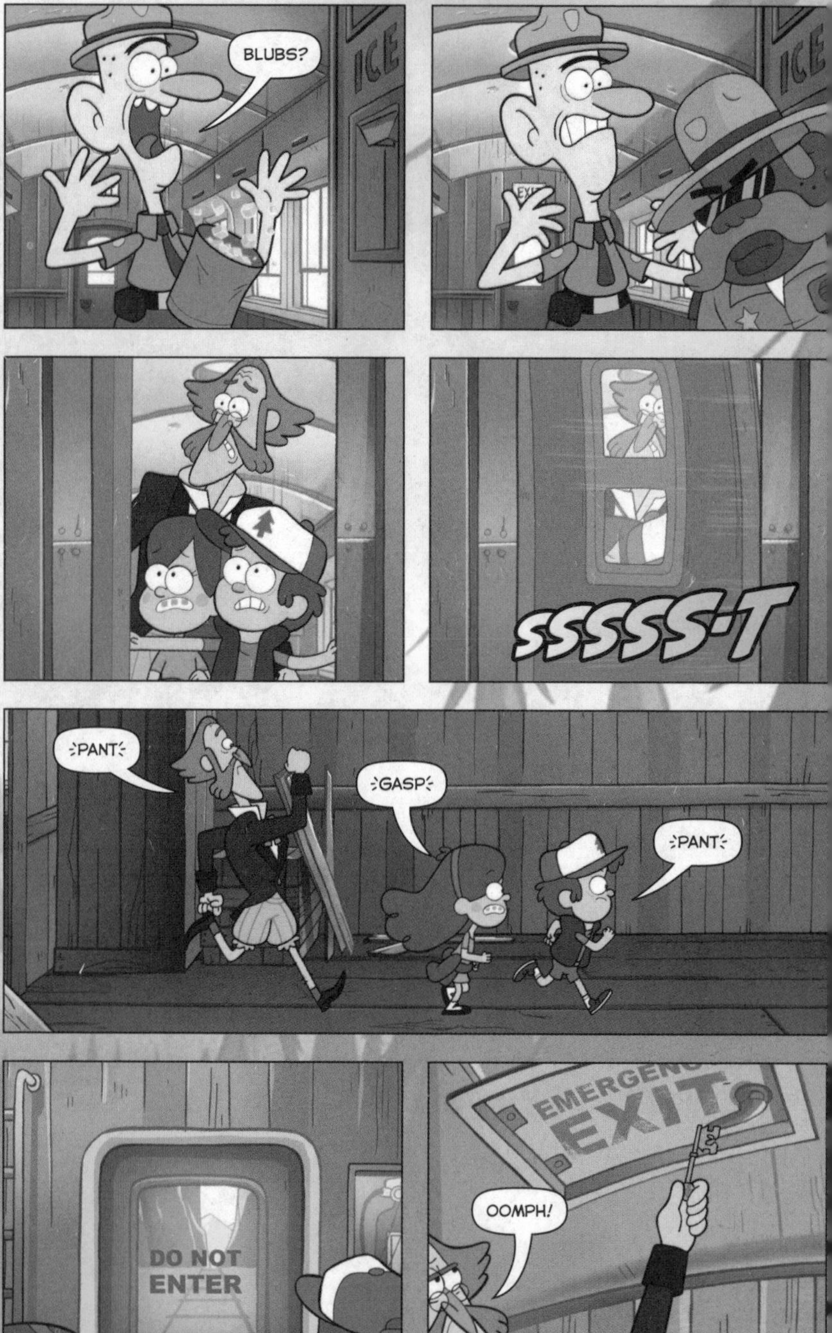

BLUBS?
ICE
ICE
SSSSS-T
PANT
GASP
PANT
DO NOT ENTER
EMERGEN
EXIT
OOMPH!

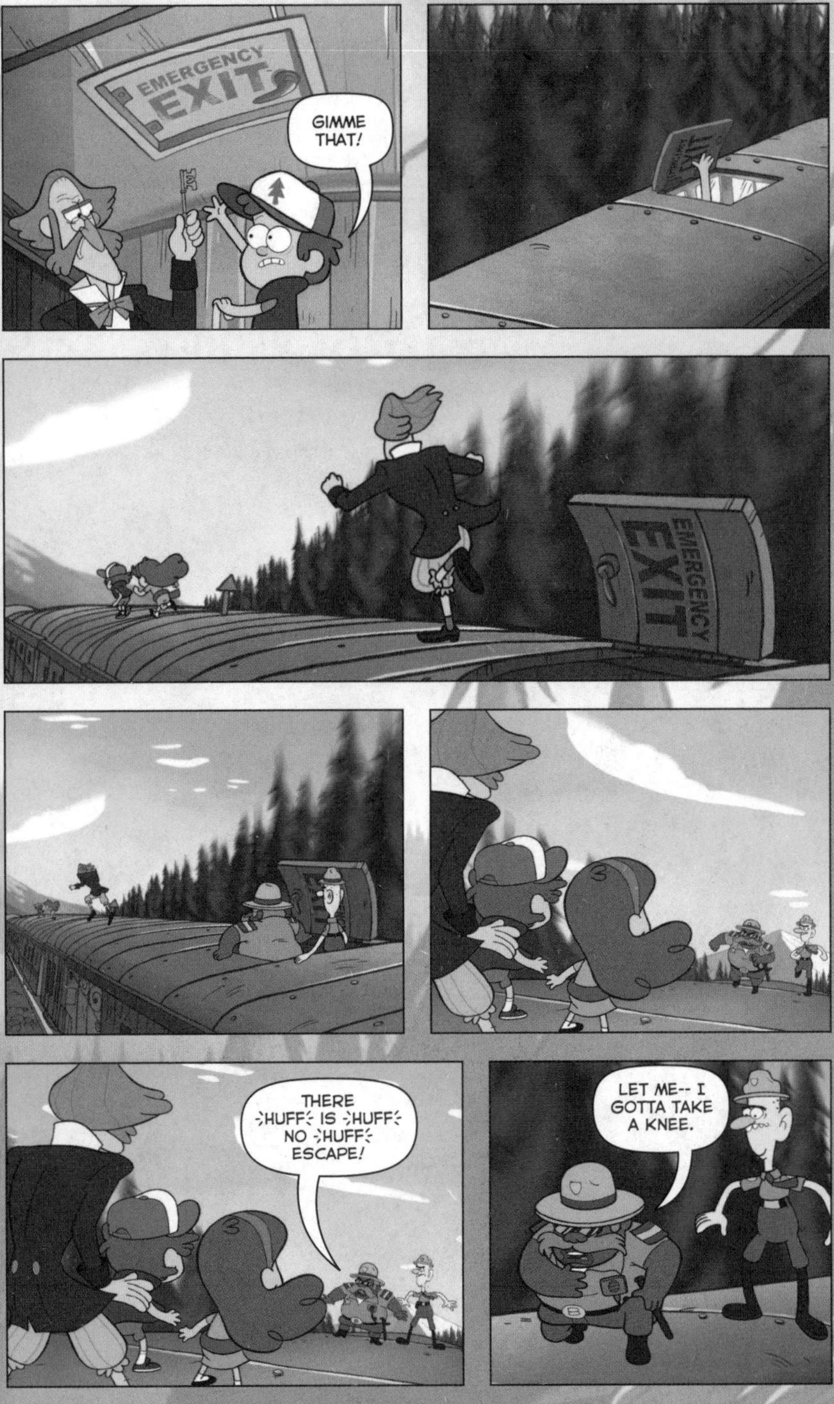
EMERGENCY EXIT
GIMME THAT!
EMERGENCY EXIT
THERE ⁏HUFF⁏ IS ⁏HUFF⁏ NO ⁏HUFF⁏ ESCAPE!
LET ME-- I GOTTA TAKE A KNEE.

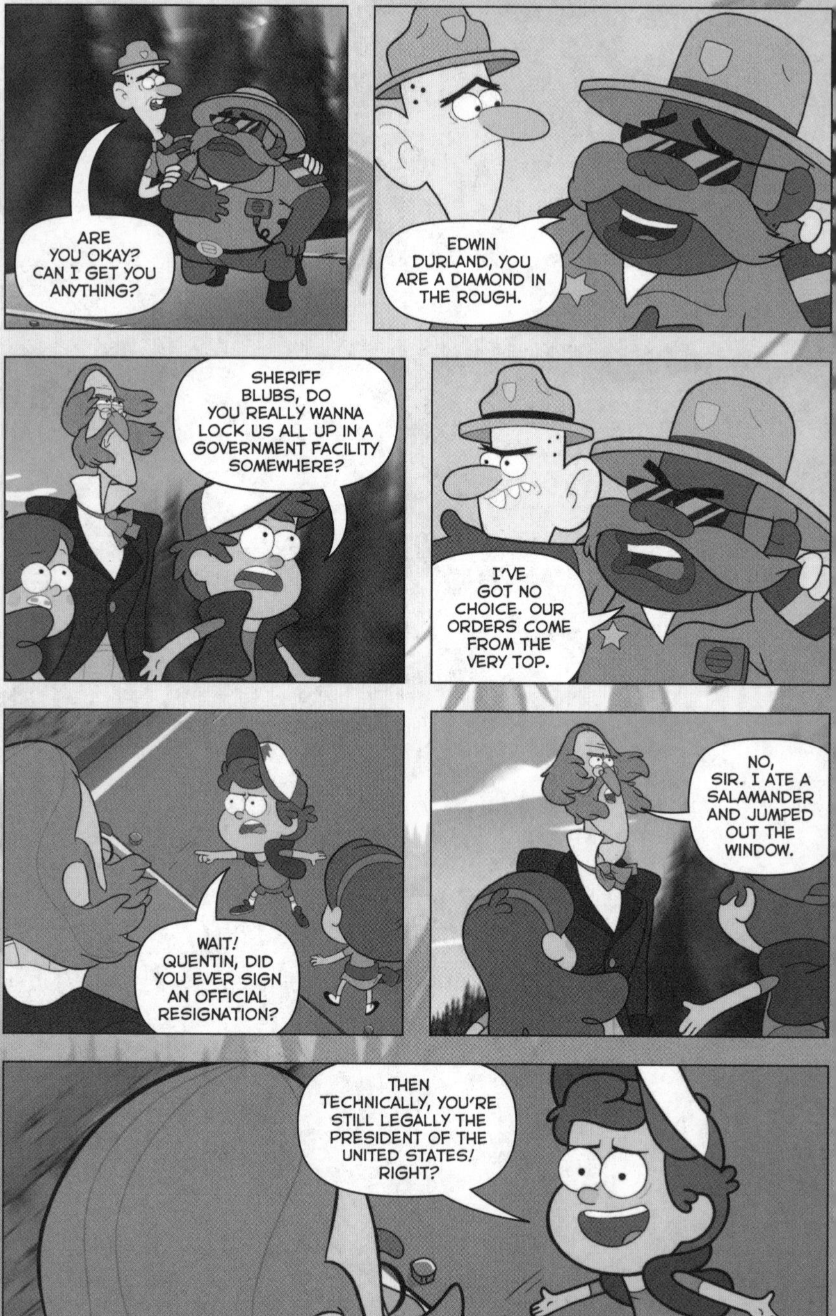

ARE YOU OKAY? CAN I GET YOU ANYTHING?
EDWIN DURLAND, YOU ARE A DIAMOND IN THE ROUGH.
SHERIFF BLUBS, DO YOU REALLY WANNA LOCK US ALL UP IN A GOVERNMENT FACILITY SOMEWHERE?
I'VE GOT NO CHOICE. OUR ORDERS COME FROM THE VERY TOP.
WAIT! QUENTIN, DID YOU EVER SIGN AN OFFICIAL RESIGNATION?
NO, SIR. I ATE A SALAMANDER AND JUMPED OUT THE WINDOW.
THEN TECHNICALLY, YOU'RE STILL LEGALLY THE PRESIDENT OF THE UNITED STATES! RIGHT?

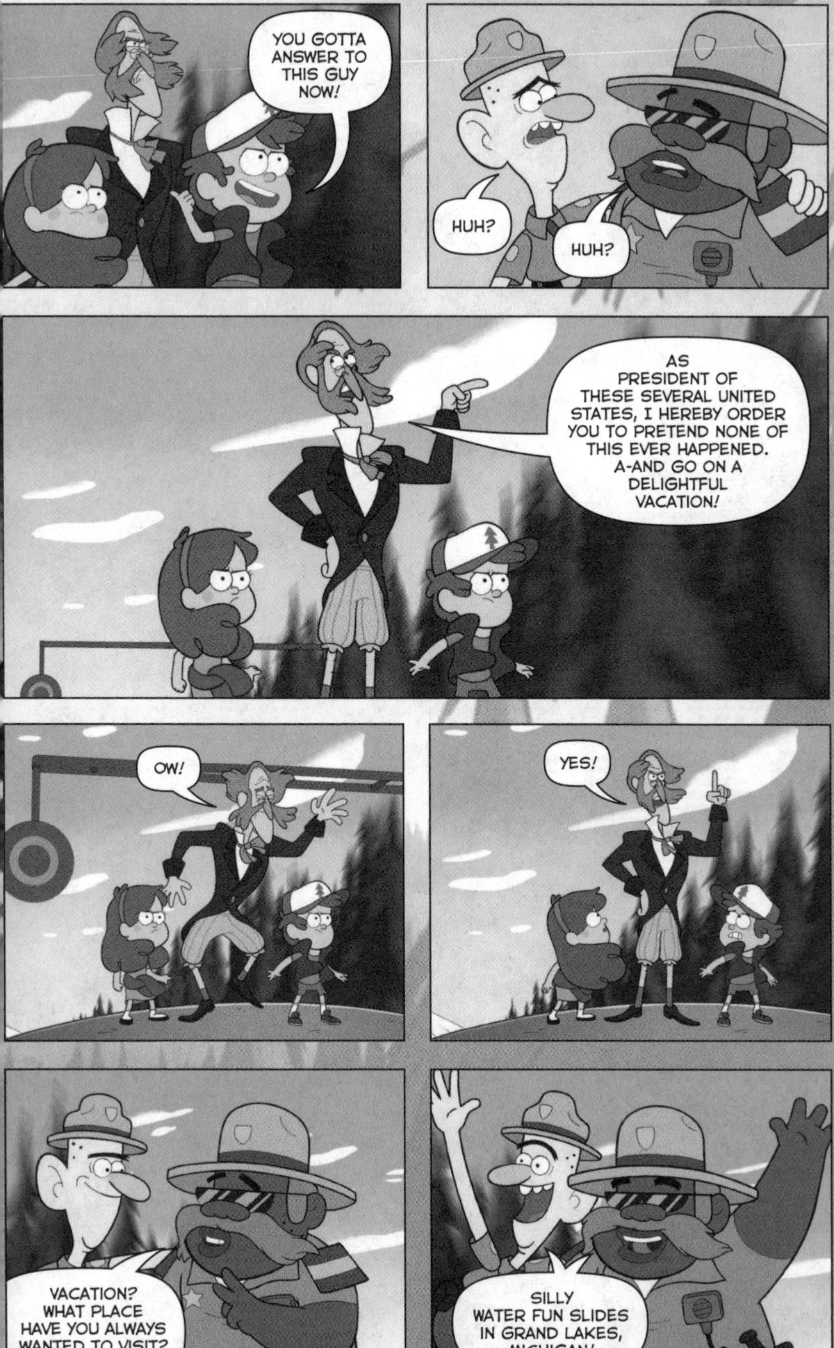

YOU GOTTA ANSWER TO THIS GUY NOW!
HUH?
HUH?
AS PRESIDENT OF THESE SEVERAL UNITED STATES, I HEREBY ORDER YOU TO PRETEND NONE OF THIS EVER HAPPENED. A-AND GO ON A DELIGHTFUL VACATION!
OW!
YES!
VACATION? WHAT PLACE HAVE YOU ALWAYS WANTED TO VISIT? ONE, TWO...
SILLY WATER FUN SLIDES IN GRAND LAKES, MICHIGAN!

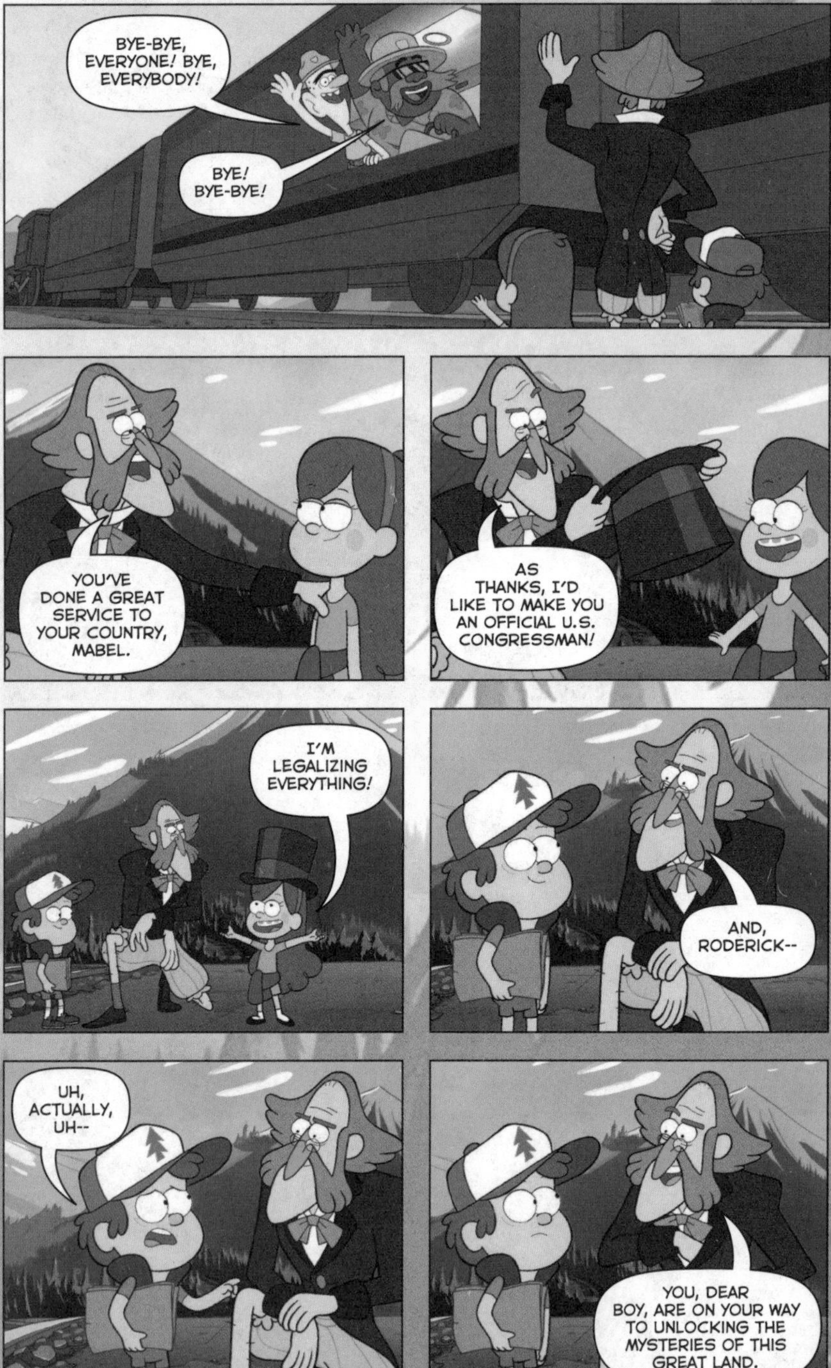
BYE-BYE, EVERYONE! BYE, EVERYBODY!
BYE! BYE-BYE!
YOU'VE DONE A GREAT SERVICE TO YOUR COUNTRY, MABEL.
AS THANKS, I'D LIKE TO MAKE YOU AN OFFICIAL U.S. CONGRESSMAN!
I'M LEGALIZING EVERYTHING!
AND, RODERICK--
UH, ACTUALLY, UH--
YOU, DEAR BOY, ARE ON YOUR WAY TO UNLOCKING THE MYSTERIES OF THIS GREAT LAND.

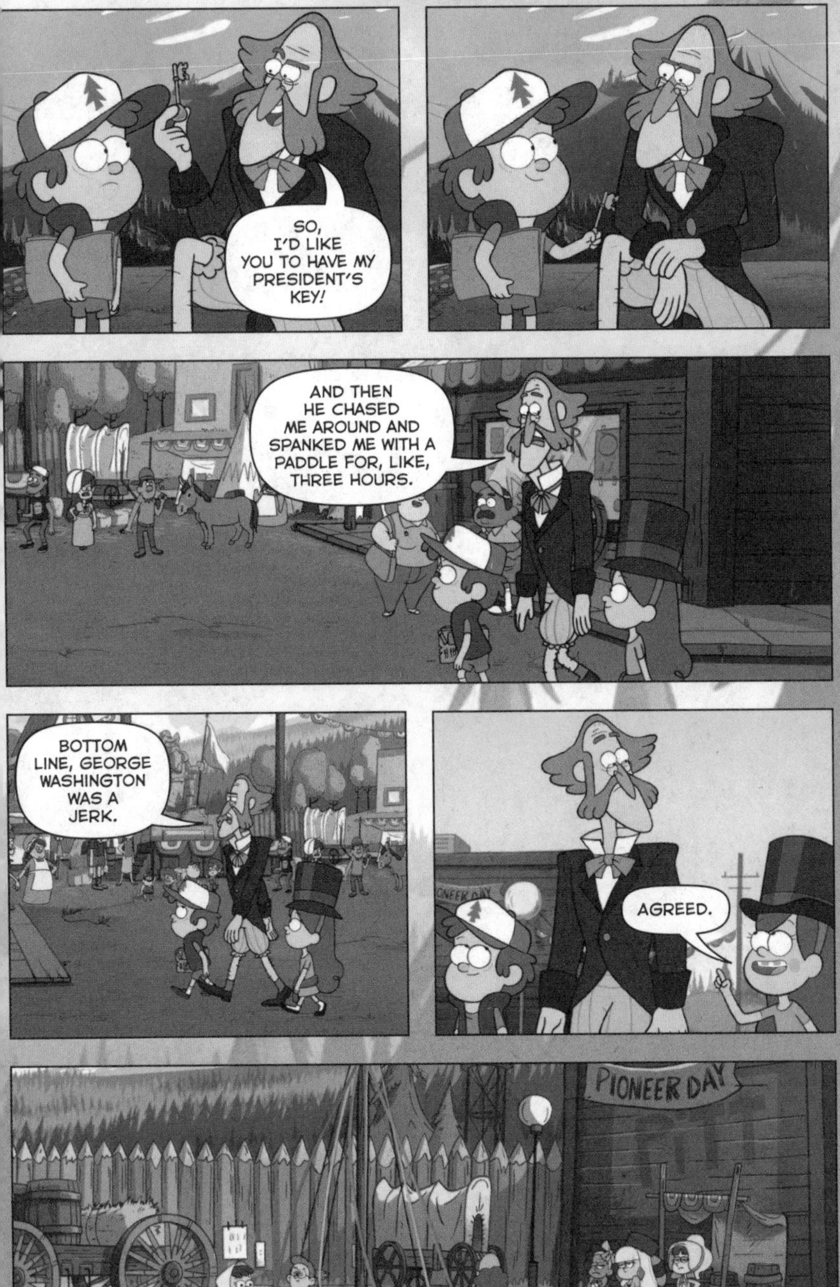
SO, I'D LIKE YOU TO HAVE MY PRESIDENT'S KEY!
AND THEN HE CHASED ME AROUND AND SPANKED ME WITH A PADDLE FOR, LIKE, THREE HOURS.
BOTTOM LINE, GEORGE WASHINGTON WAS A JERK.
AGREED.
PIONEER DAY

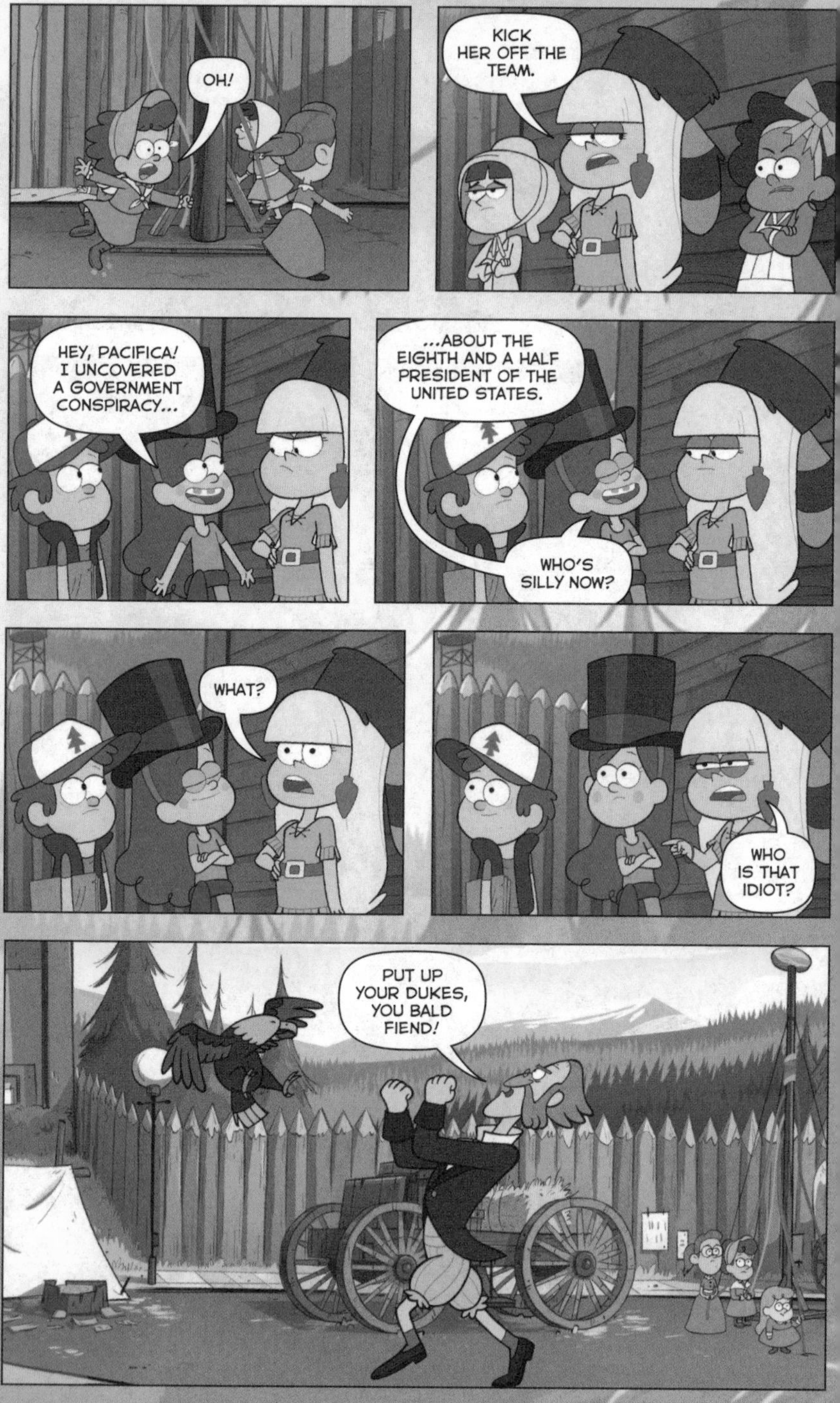
OH!
KICK HER OFF THE TEAM.
HEY, PACIFICA! I UNCOVERED A GOVERNMENT CONSPIRACY...
...ABOUT THE EIGHTH AND A HALF PRESIDENT OF THE UNITED STATES.
WHO'S SILLY NOW?
WHAT?
WHO IS THAT IDIOT?
PUT UP YOUR DUKES, YOU BALD FIEND!

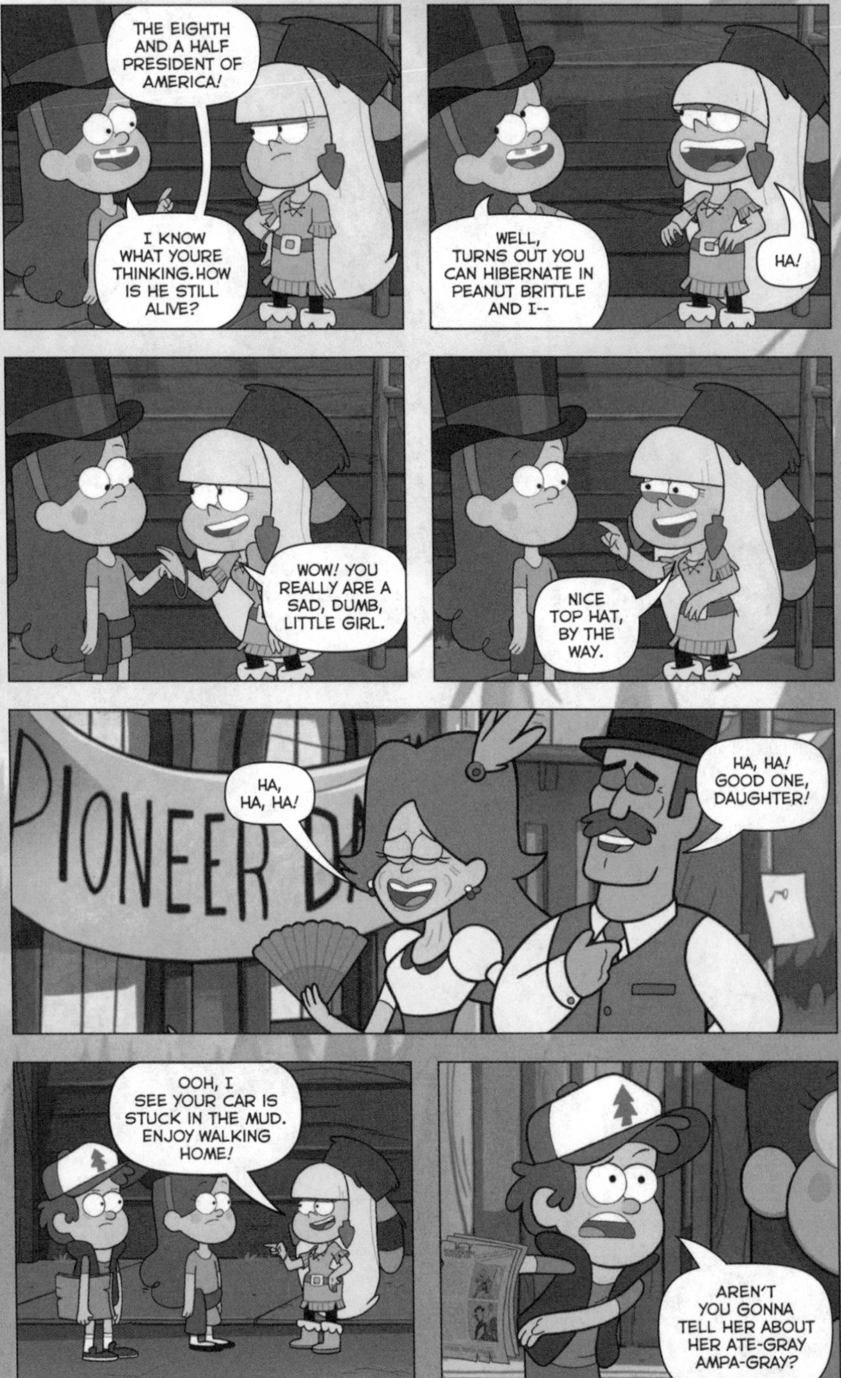
THE EIGHTH AND A HALF PRESIDENT OF AMERICA!
I KNOW WHAT YOURE THINKING. HOW IS HE STILL ALIVE?
WELL, TURNS OUT YOU CAN HIBERNATE IN PEANUT BRITTLE AND I--
HA!
WOW! YOU REALLY ARE A SAD, DUMB, LITTLE GIRL.
NICE TOP HAT, BY THE WAY.
PIONEER DA
HA, HA, HA!
HA, HA! GOOD ONE, DAUGHTER!
OOH, I SEE YOUR CAR IS STUCK IN THE MUD. ENJOY WALKING HOME!
AREN'T YOU GONNA TELL HER ABOUT HER ATE-GRAY AMPA-GRAY?

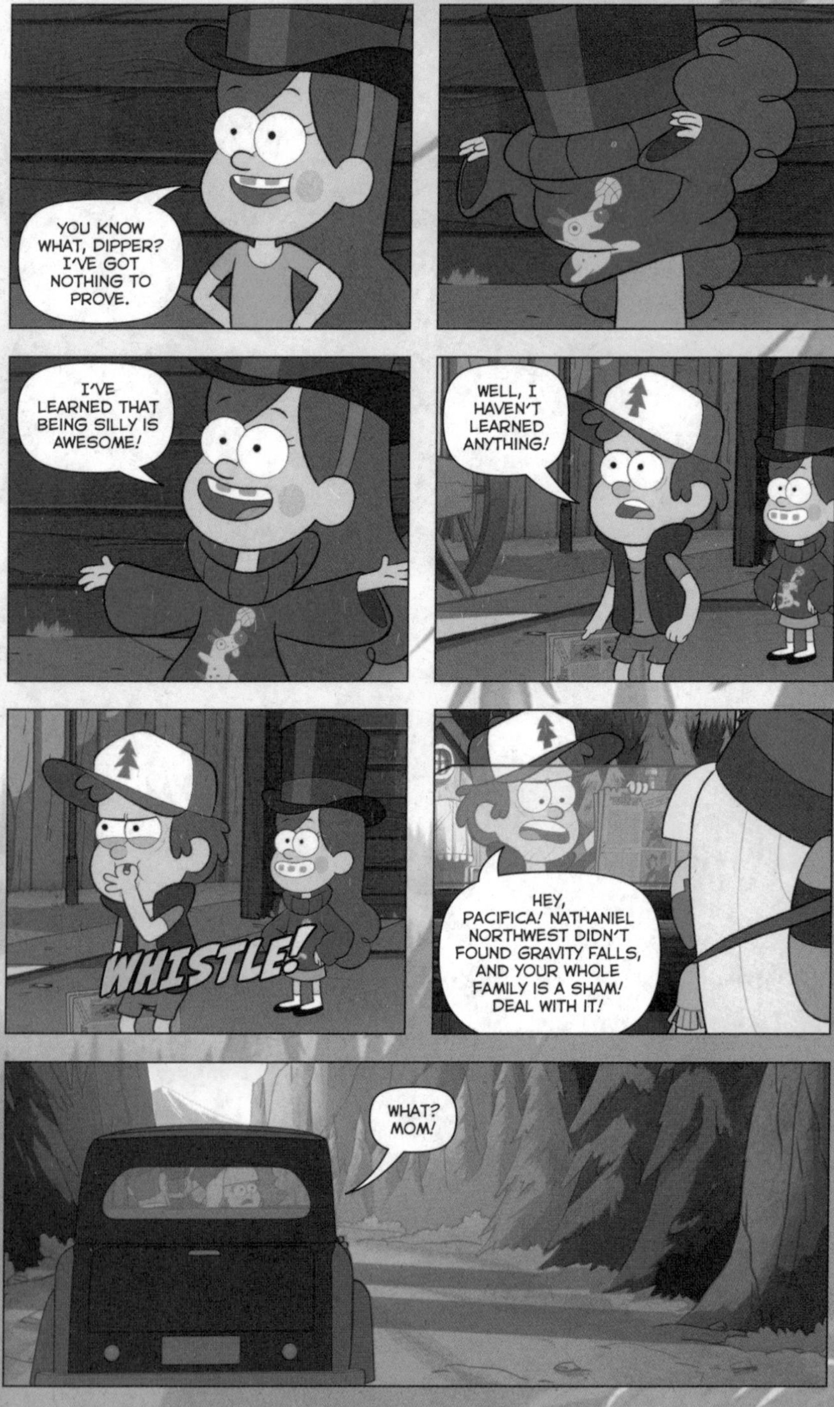
YOU KNOW WHAT, DIPPER? I'VE GOT NOTHING TO PROVE.
I'VE LEARNED THAT BEING SILLY IS AWESOME!
WELL, I HAVEN'T LEARNED ANYTHING!
WHISTLE!
HEY, PACIFICA! NATHANIEL NORTHWEST DIDN'T FOUND GRAVITY FALLS, AND YOUR WHOLE FAMILY IS A SHAM! DEAL WITH IT!
WHAT? MOM!

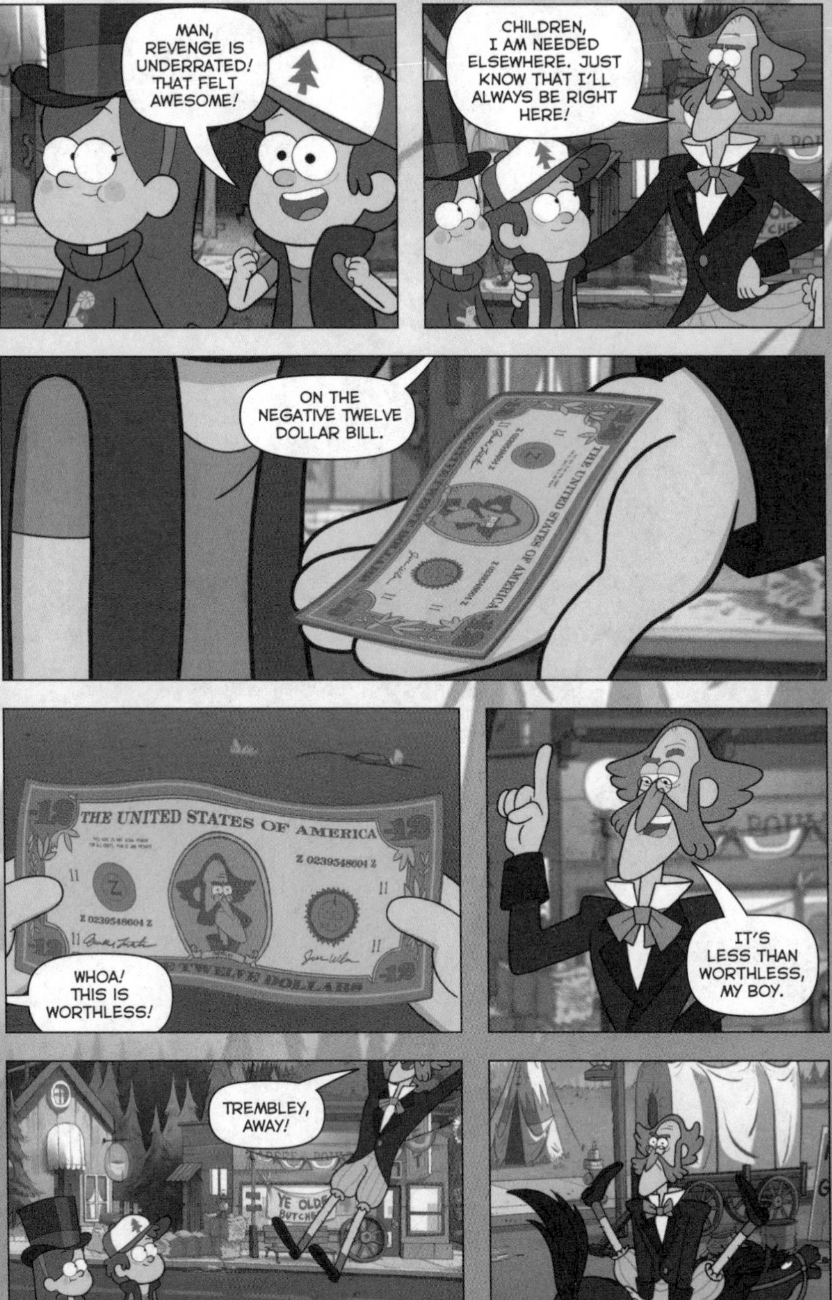
MAN, REVENGE IS UNDERRATED! THAT FELT AWESOME!
CHILDREN, I AM NEEDED ELSEWHERE. JUST KNOW THAT I'LL ALWAYS BE RIGHT HERE!
ON THE NEGATIVE TWELVE DOLLAR BILL.
THE UNITED STATES OF AMERICA
Z 0239548604 Z
WHOA! THIS IS WORTHLESS!
IT'S LESS THAN WORTHLESS, MY BOY.
TREMBLEY, AWAY!
YE OLDE BUTCHE

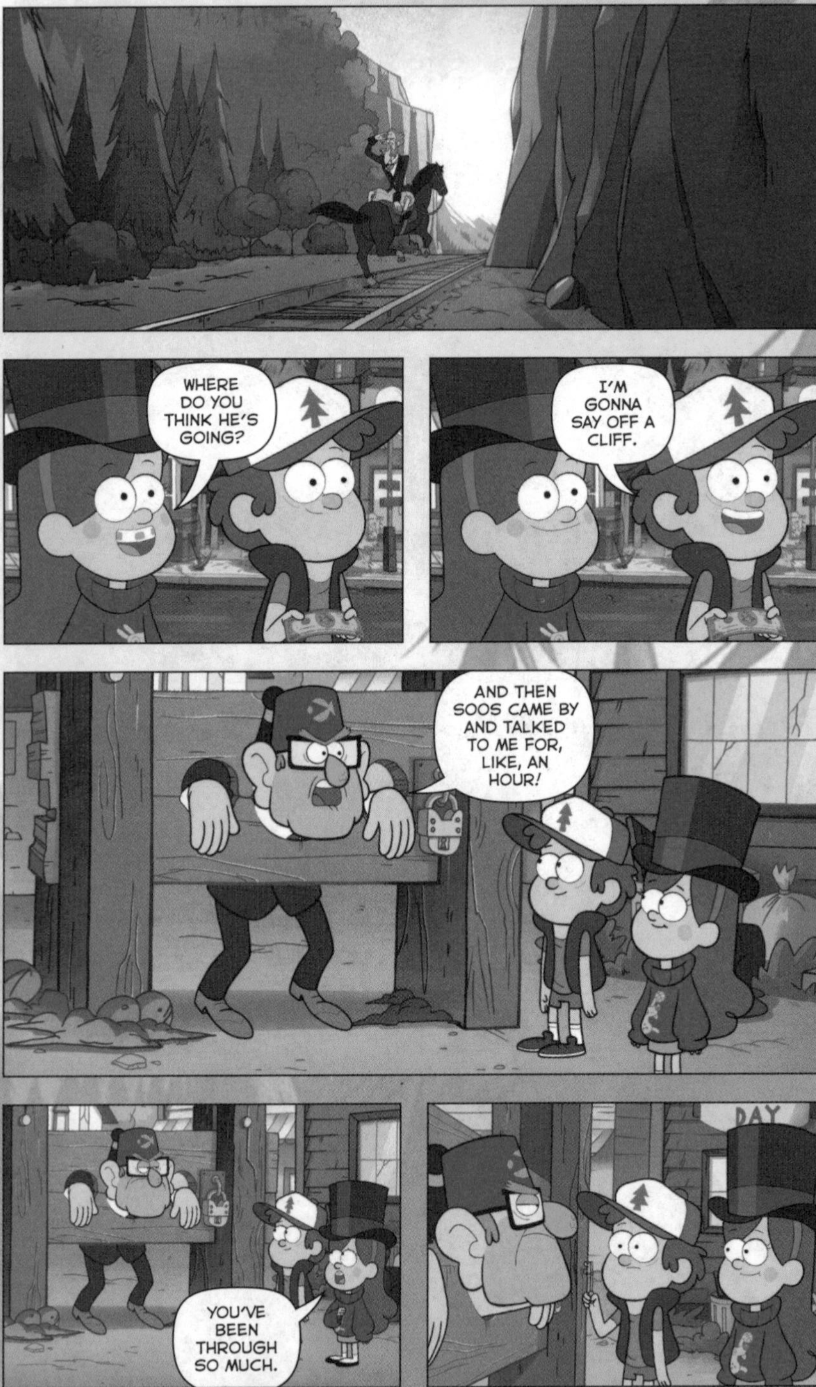
WHERE DO YOU THINK HE'S GOING?
I'M GONNA SAY OFF A CLIFF.
AND THEN SOOS CAME BY AND TALKED TO ME FOR, LIKE, AN HOUR!
YOU'VE BEEN THROUGH SO MUCH.
DAY

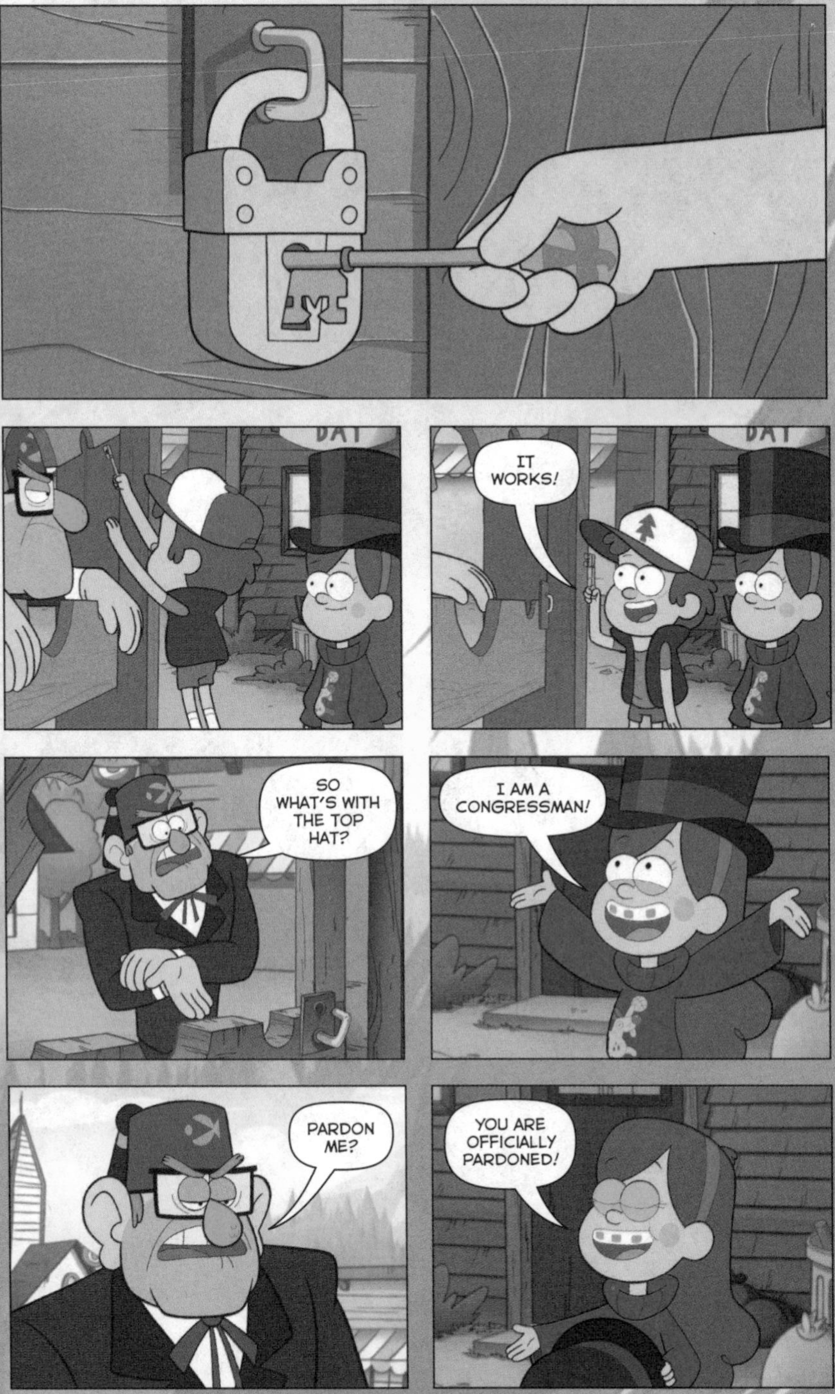

IT WORKS!
SO WHAT'S WITH THE TOP HAT?
I AM A CONGRESSMAN!
PARDON ME?
YOU ARE OFFICIALLY PARDONED!

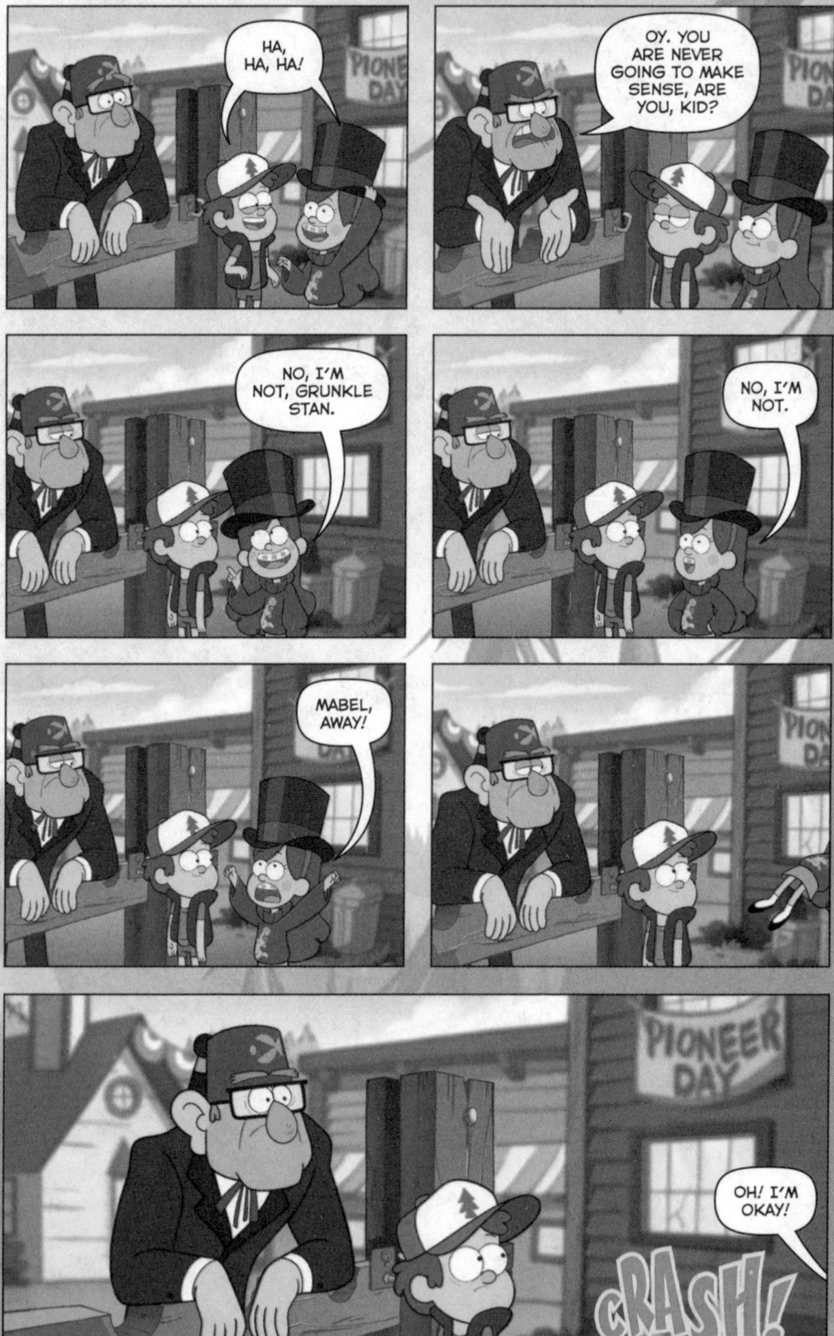
HA, HA, HA!
OY. YOU ARE NEVER GOING TO MAKE SENSE, ARE YOU, KID?
NO, I'M NOT, GRUNKLE STAN.
NO, I'M NOT.
MABEL, AWAY!
PIONEER DAY
OH! I'M OKAY!
CRASH!
THE END

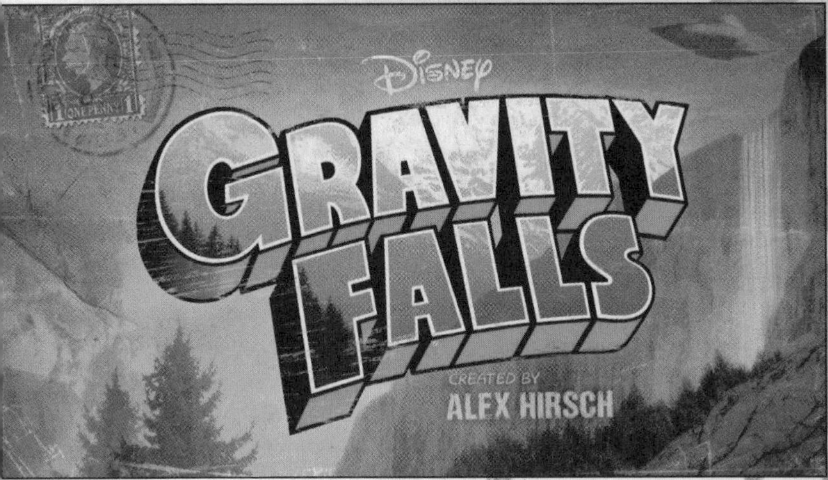
DISNEY
GRAVITY FALLS
CREATED BY
ALEX HIRSCH

THE TIME TRAVELER'S PIG
EPISODE 9

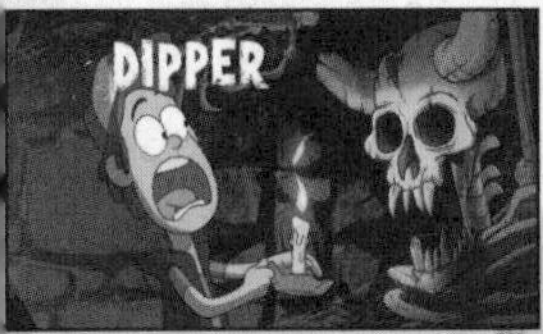
DIPPER

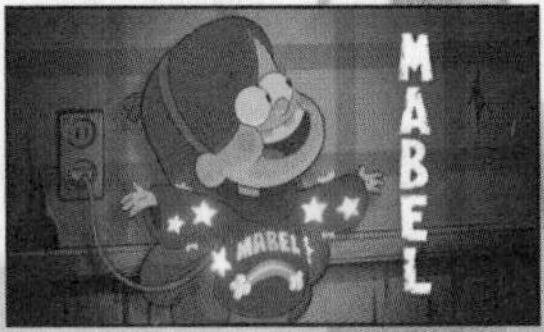
MABEL

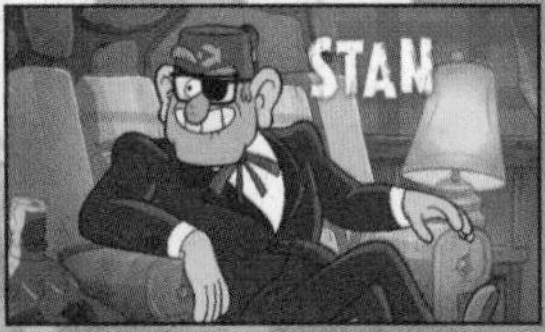
STAN

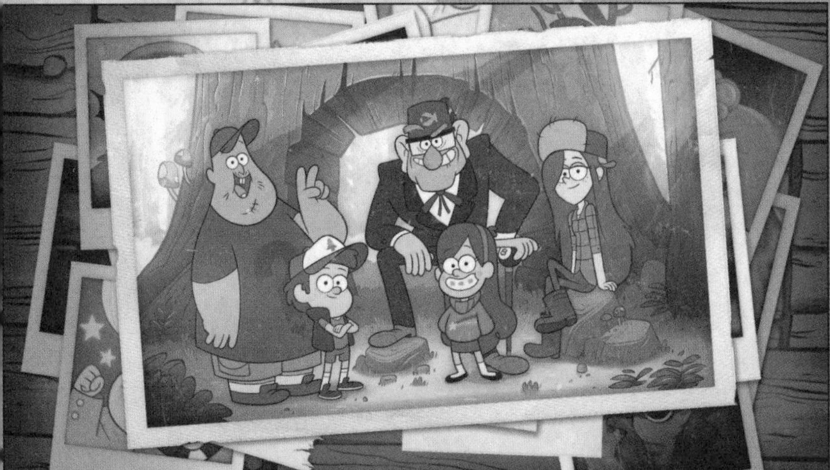

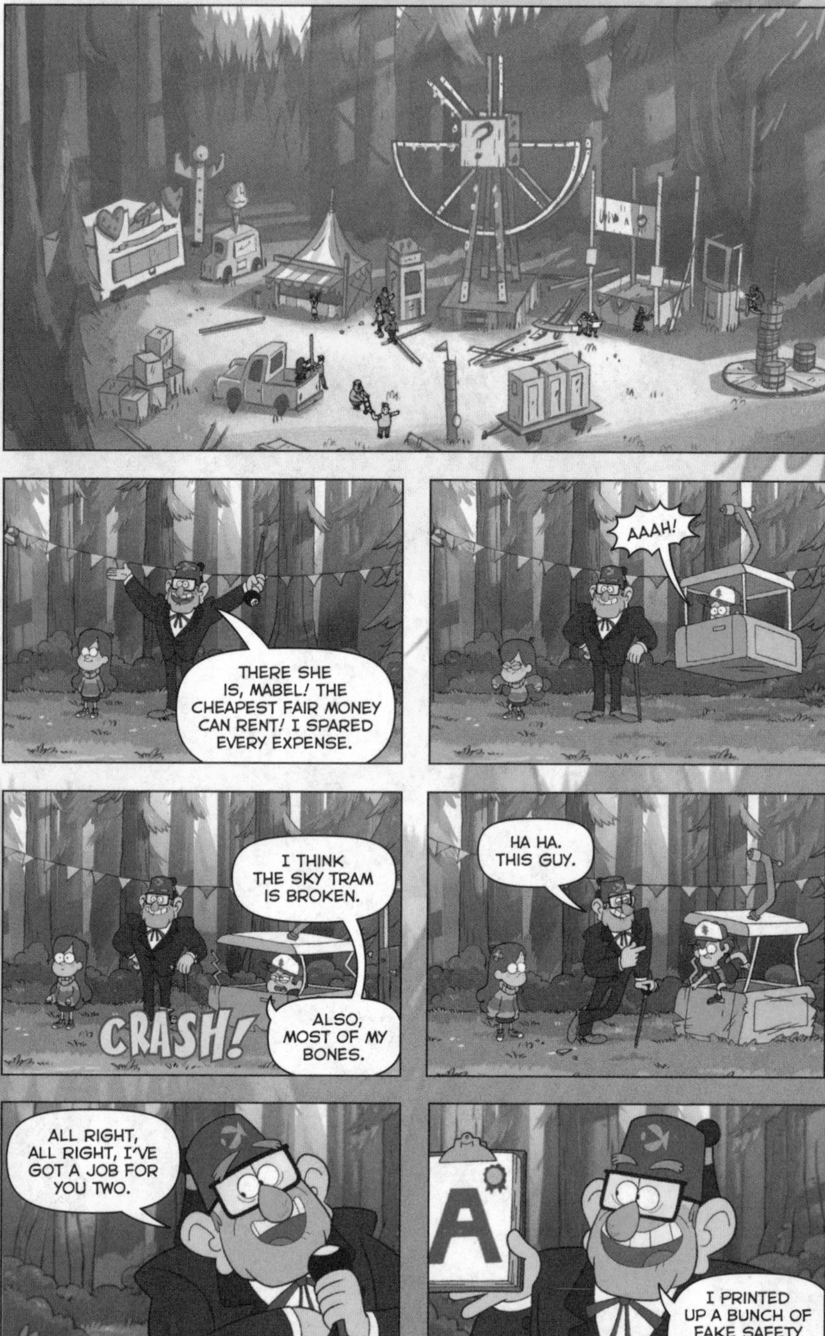
THERE SHE IS, MABEL! THE CHEAPEST FAIR MONEY CAN RENT! I SPARED EVERY EXPENSE.
AAAH!
I THINK THE SKY TRAM IS BROKEN.
CRASH!
ALSO, MOST OF MY BONES.
HA HA. THIS GUY.
ALL RIGHT, ALL RIGHT, I'VE GOT A JOB FOR YOU TWO.
A
I PRINTED UP A BUNCH OF FAKE SAFETY INSPECTION CERTIFICATES.

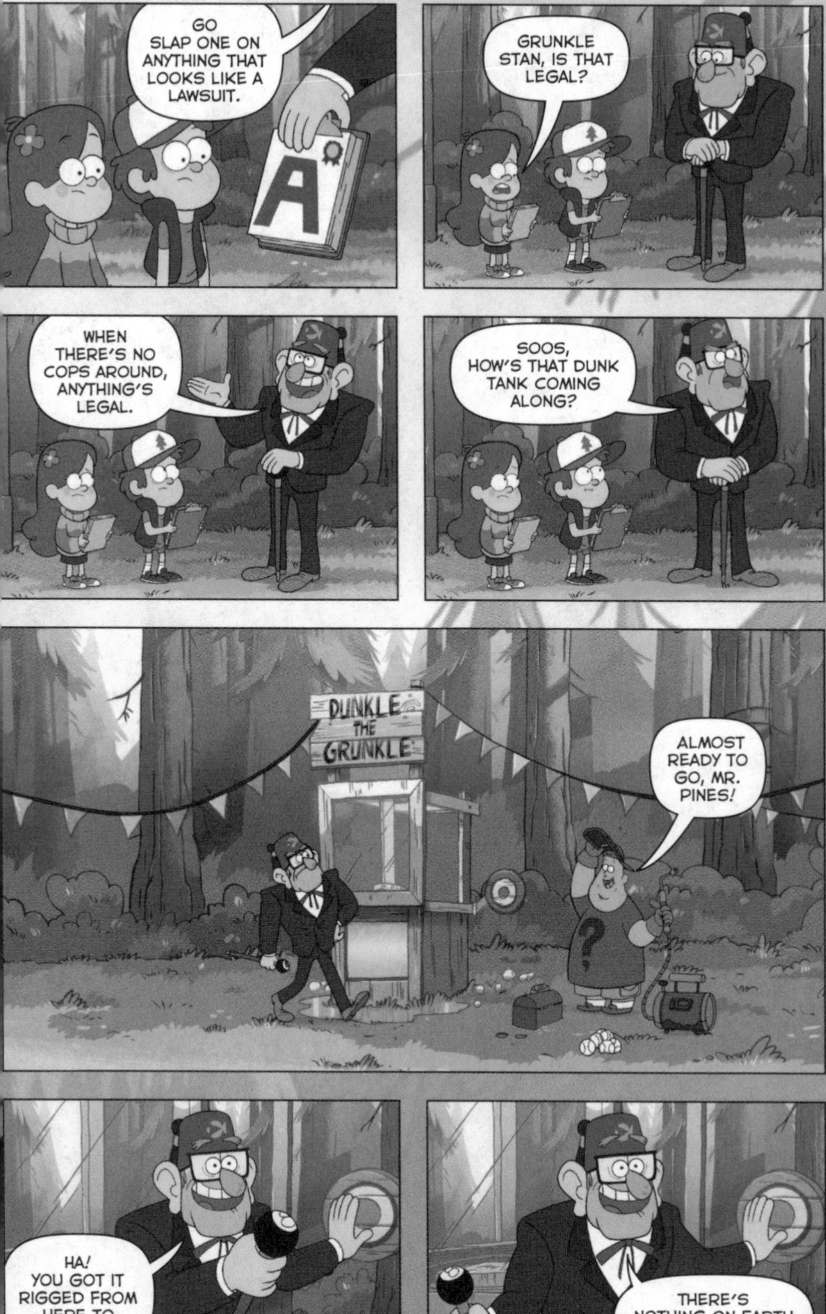
GO SLAP ONE ON ANYTHING THAT LOOKS LIKE A LAWSUIT.
A
GRUNKLE STAN, IS THAT LEGAL?
WHEN THERE'S NO COPS AROUND, ANYTHING'S LEGAL.
SOOS, HOW'S THAT DUNK TANK COMING ALONG?
DUNKLE THE GRUNKLE
ALMOST READY TO GO, MR. PINES!
HA! YOU GOT IT RIGGED FROM HERE TO TIMBUKTU!
THERE'S NOTHING ON EARTH THAT COULD KNOCK ME DOWN.

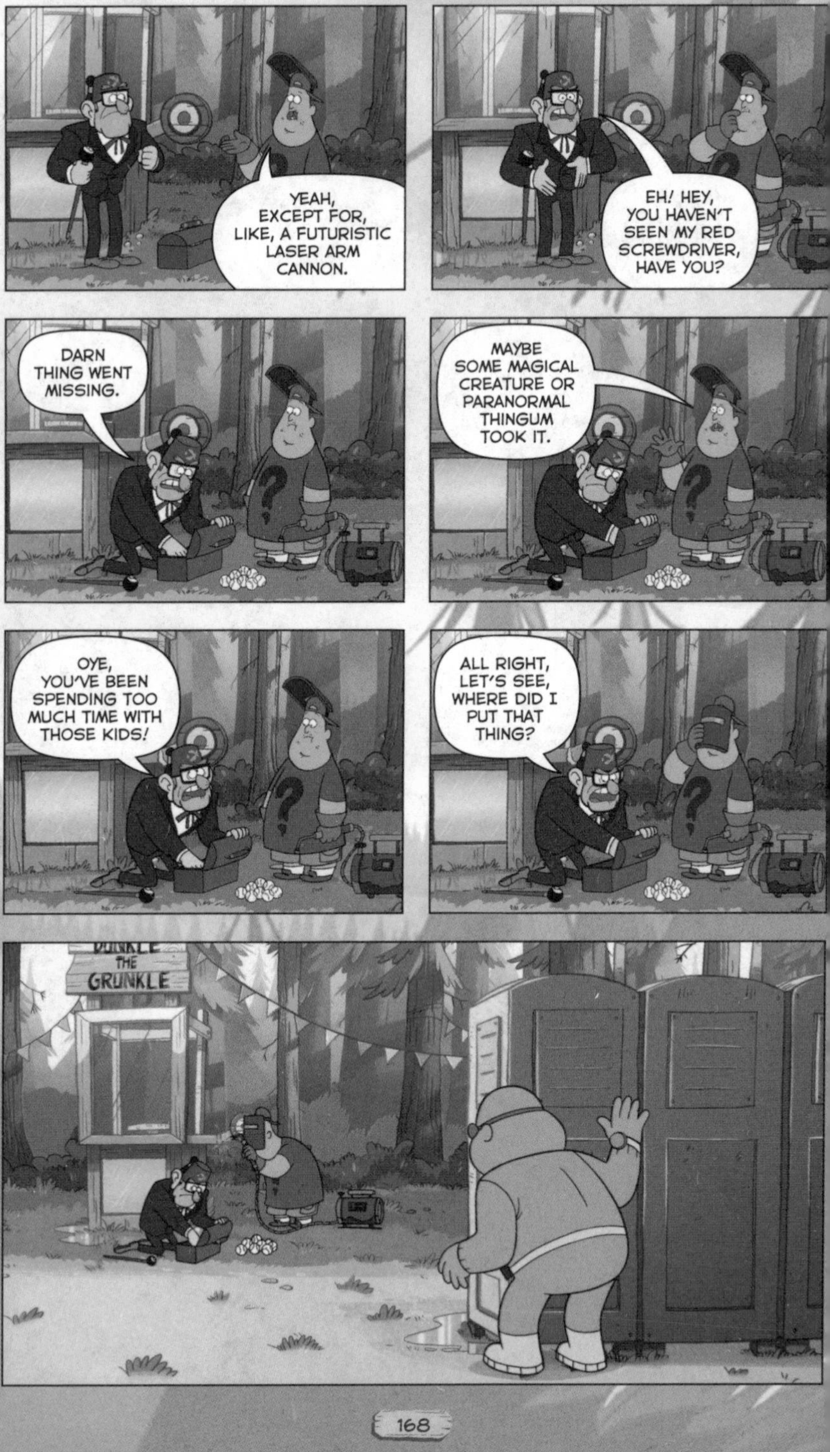
YEAH, EXCEPT FOR, LIKE, A FUTURISTIC LASER ARM CANNON.
EH! HEY, YOU HAVEN'T SEEN MY RED SCREWDRIVER, HAVE YOU?
DARN THING WENT MISSING.
MAYBE SOME MAGICAL CREATURE OR PARANORMAL THINGUM TOOK IT.
OYE, YOU'VE BEEN SPENDING TOO MUCH TIME WITH THOSE KIDS!
ALL RIGHT, LET'S SEE, WHERE DID I PUT THAT THING?
THE GRUNKLE

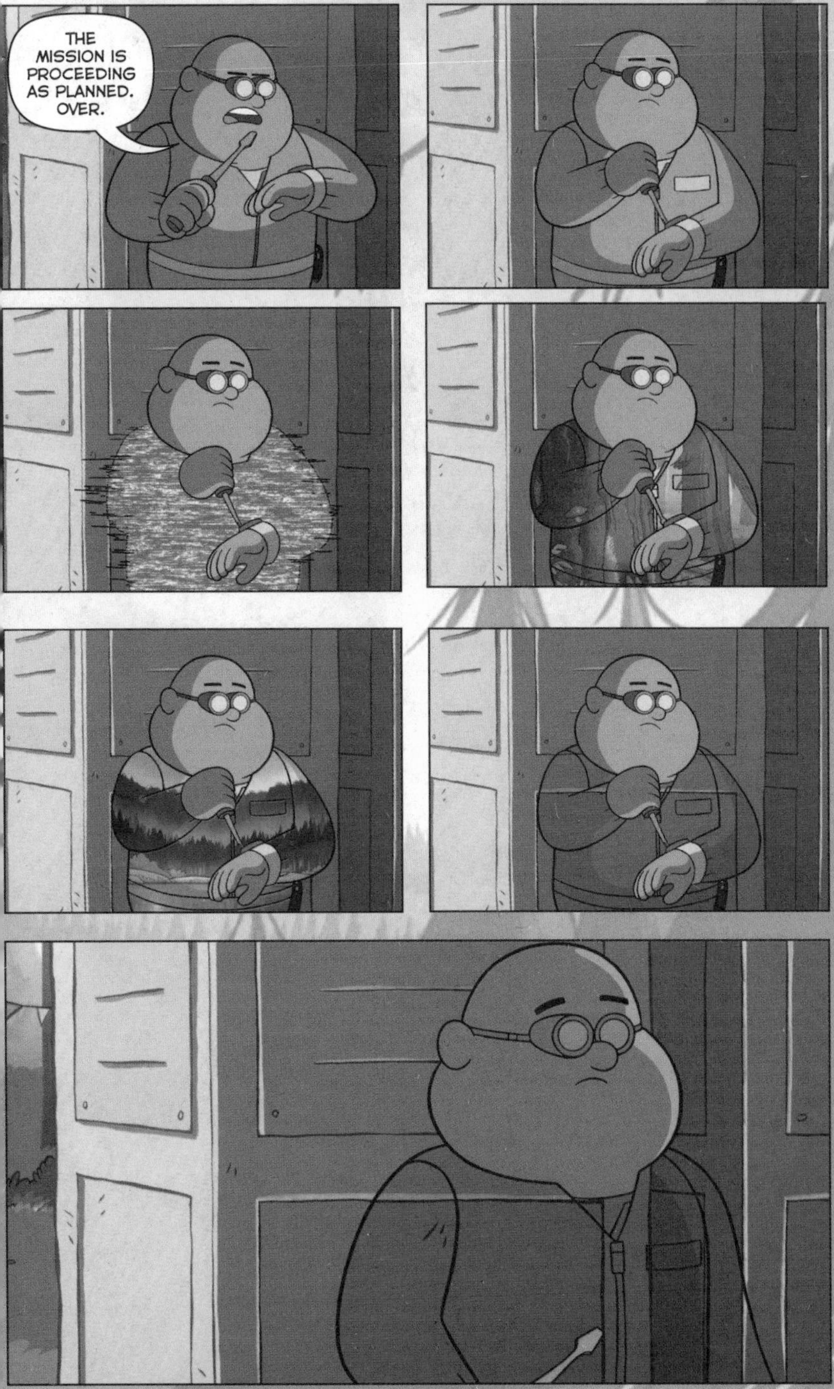
THE MISSION IS PROCEEDING AS PLANNED. OVER.

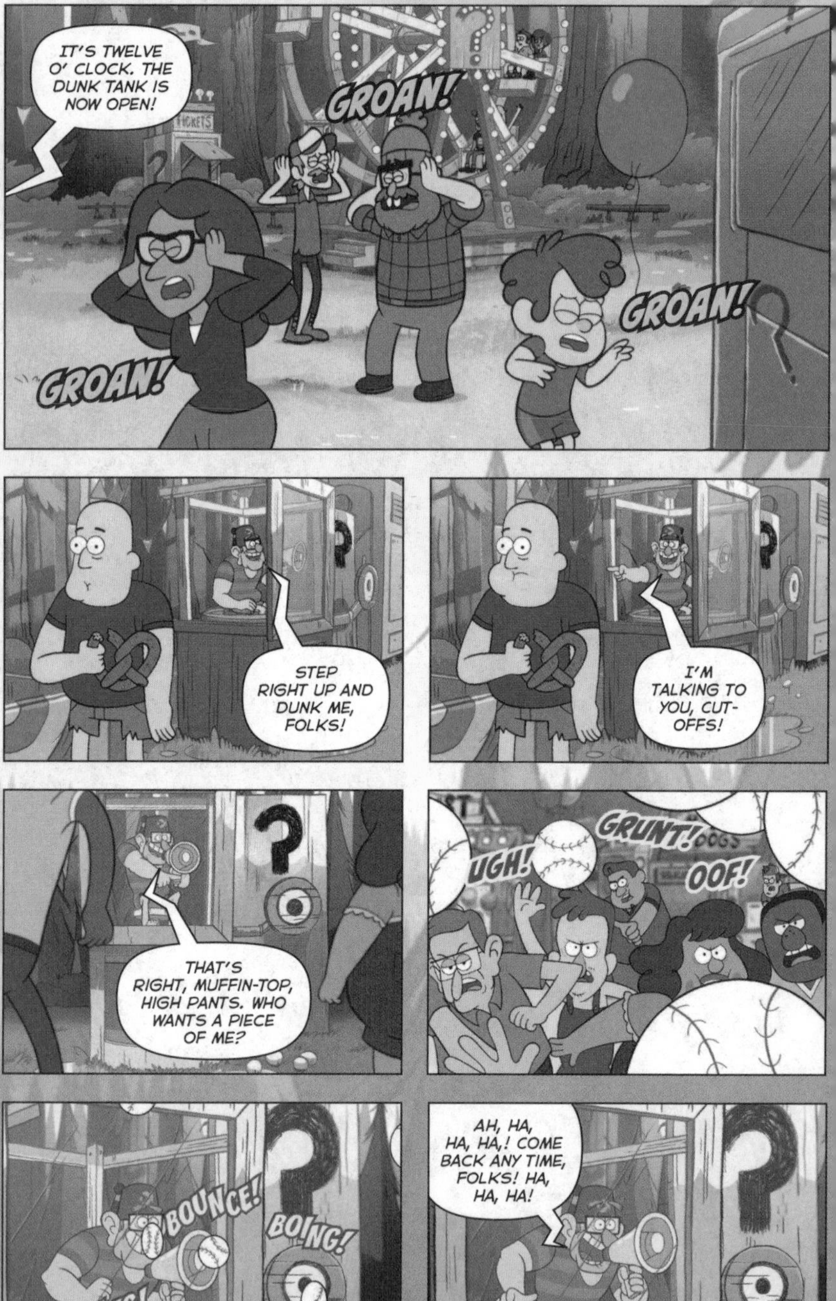
IT'S TWELVE O' CLOCK. THE DUNK TANK IS NOW OPEN!
GROAN!
GROAN!
GROAN!
STEP RIGHT UP AND DUNK ME, FOLKS!
I'M TALKING TO YOU, CUT-OFFS!
THAT'S RIGHT, MUFFIN-TOP, HIGH PANTS. WHO WANTS A PIECE OF ME?
GRUNT!
UGH!
OOF!
BOUNCE!
BOING!
BOING!
AH, HA, HA, HA,! COME BACK ANY TIME, FOLKS! HA, HA, HA!

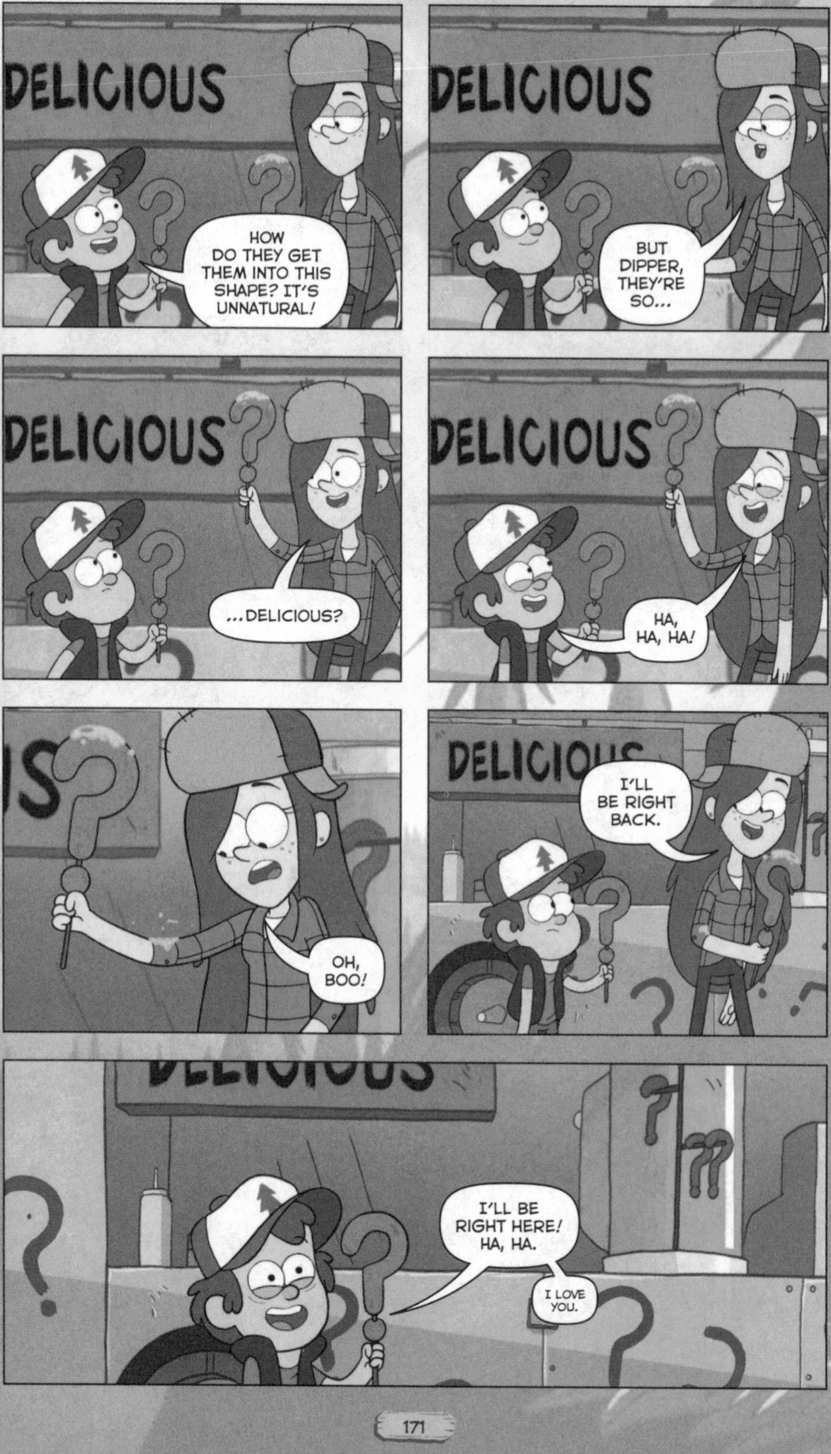
DELICIOUS
HOW DO THEY GET THEM INTO THIS SHAPE? IT'S UNNATURAL!
DELICIOUS
BUT DIPPER, THEY'RE SO...
DELICIOUS
...DELICIOUS?
DELICIOUS
HA, HA, HA!
OH, BOO!
DELICIOUS
I'LL BE RIGHT BACK.
I'LL BE RIGHT HERE! HA, HA.
I LOVE YOU.

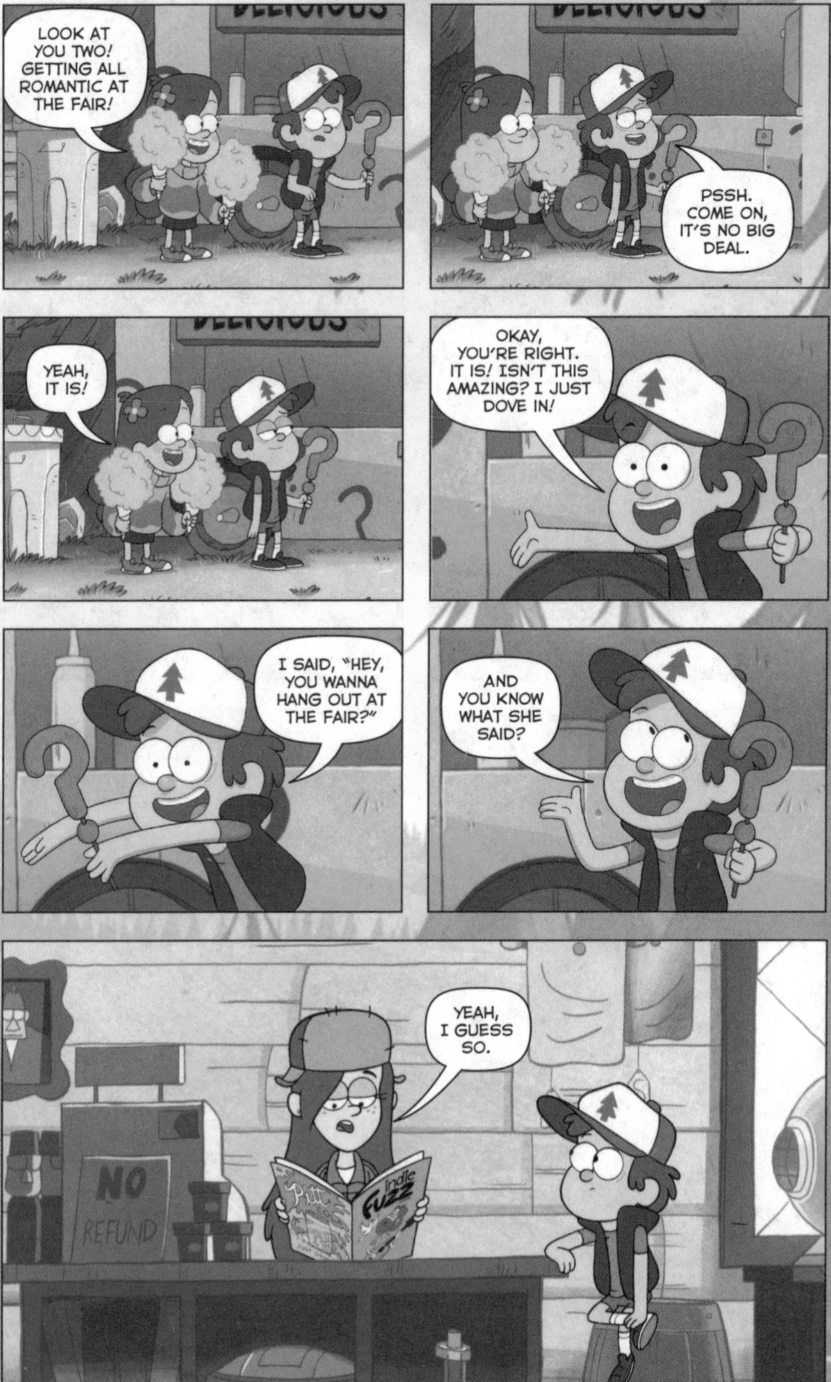
DELICIOUS
LOOK AT YOU TWO! GETTING ALL ROMANTIC AT THE FAIR!
DELICIOUS
PSSH. COME ON, IT'S NO BIG DEAL.
DELICIOUS
YEAH, IT IS!
OKAY, YOU'RE RIGHT. IT IS! ISN'T THIS AMAZING? I JUST DOVE IN!
I SAID, "HEY, YOU WANNA HANG OUT AT THE FAIR?"
AND YOU KNOW WHAT SHE SAID?
YEAH, I GUESS SO.
NO REFUND
indie FUZZ

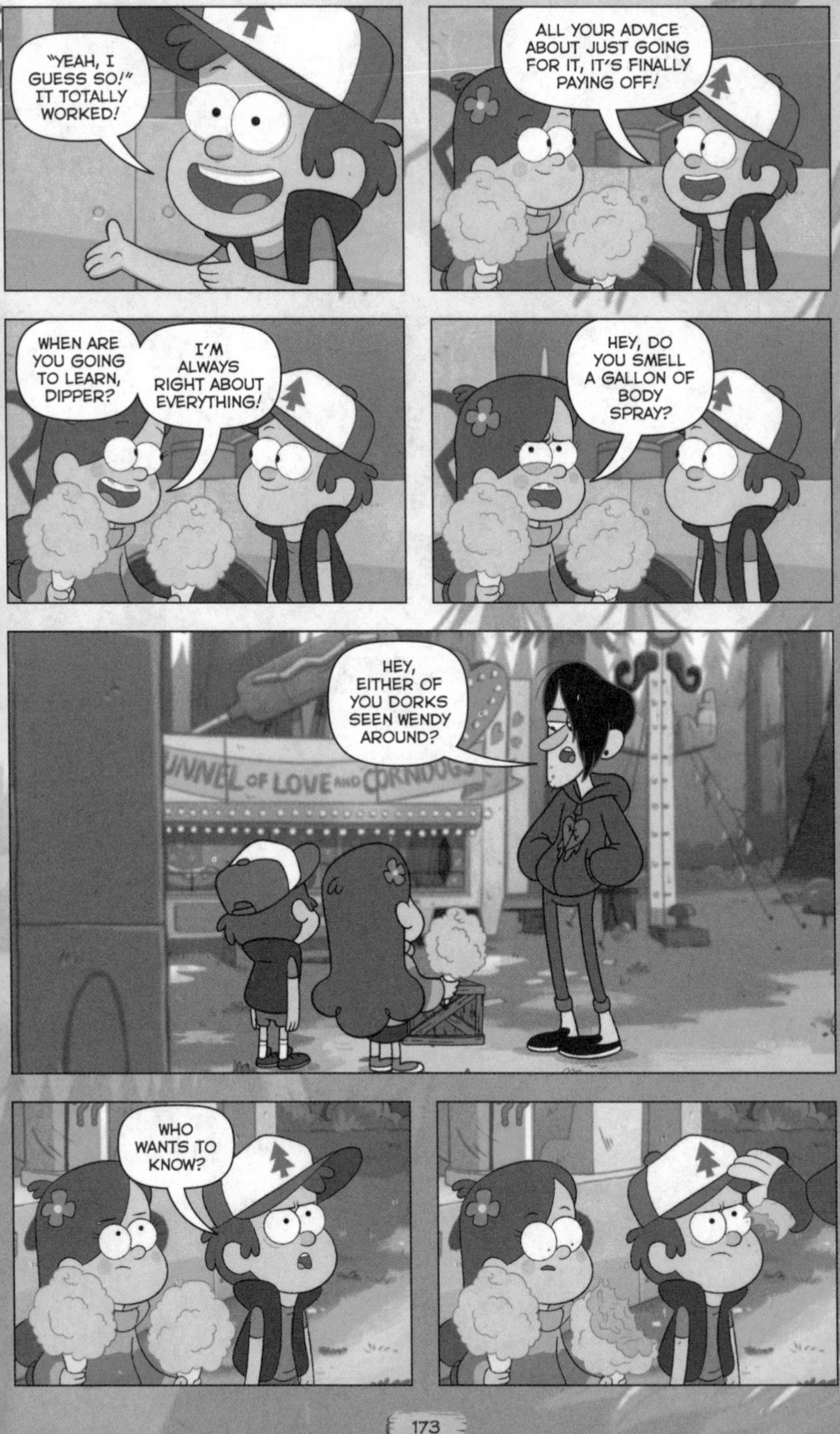
"YEAH, I GUESS SO!" IT TOTALLY WORKED!
ALL YOUR ADVICE ABOUT JUST GOING FOR IT, IT'S FINALLY PAYING OFF!
WHEN ARE YOU GOING TO LEARN, DIPPER?
I'M ALWAYS RIGHT ABOUT EVERYTHING!
HEY, DO YOU SMELL A GALLON OF BODY SPRAY?
HEY, EITHER OF YOU DORKS SEEN WENDY AROUND?
UNNEL OF LOVE AND CORNDOGS
WHO WANTS TO KNOW?

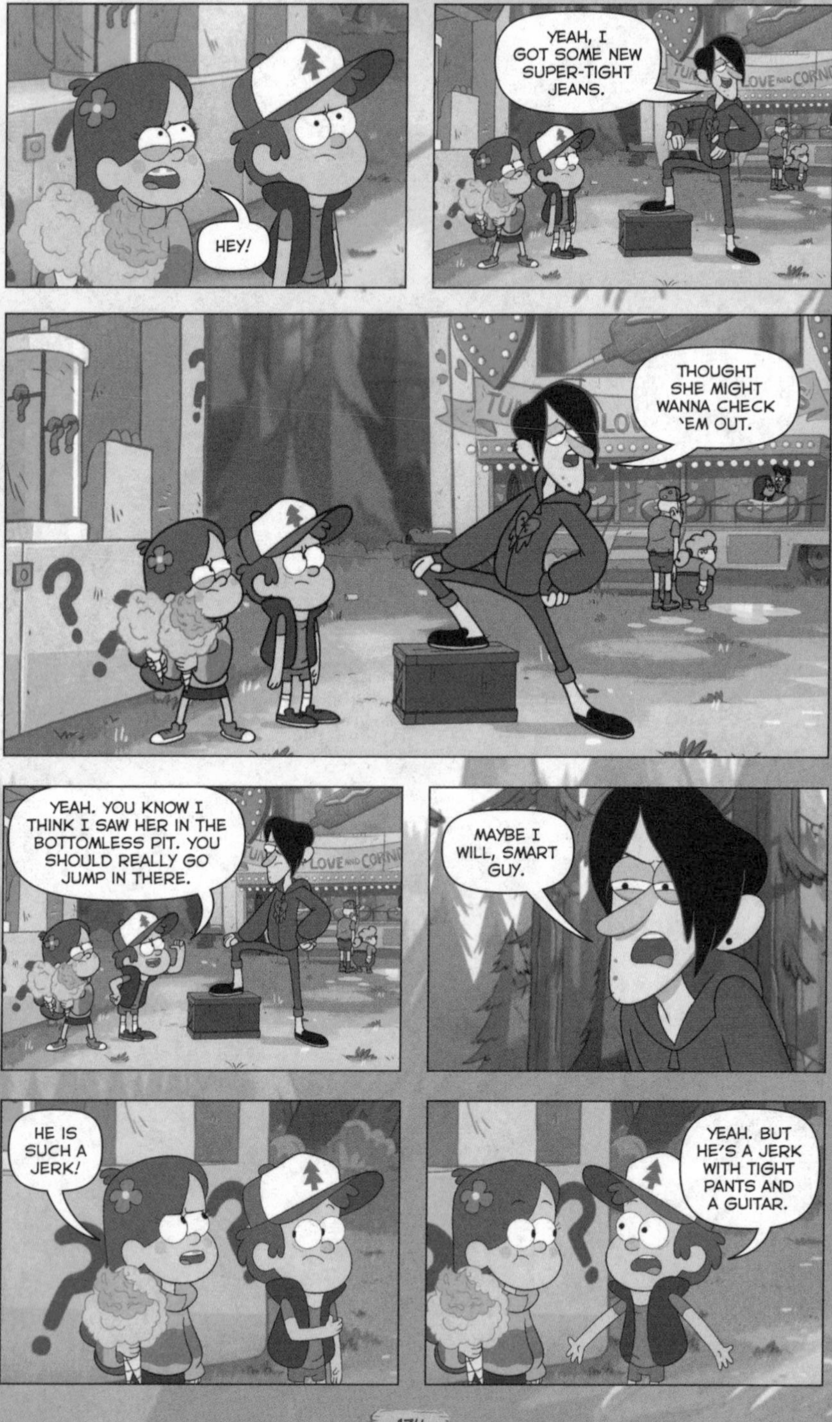
HEY!
YEAH, I GOT SOME NEW SUPER-TIGHT JEANS.
THOUGHT SHE MIGHT WANNA CHECK 'EM OUT.
YEAH. YOU KNOW I THINK I SAW HER IN THE BOTTOMLESS PIT. YOU SHOULD REALLY GO JUMP IN THERE.
MAYBE I WILL, SMART GUY.
HE IS SUCH A JERK!
YEAH. BUT HE'S A JERK WITH TIGHT PANTS AND A GUITAR.

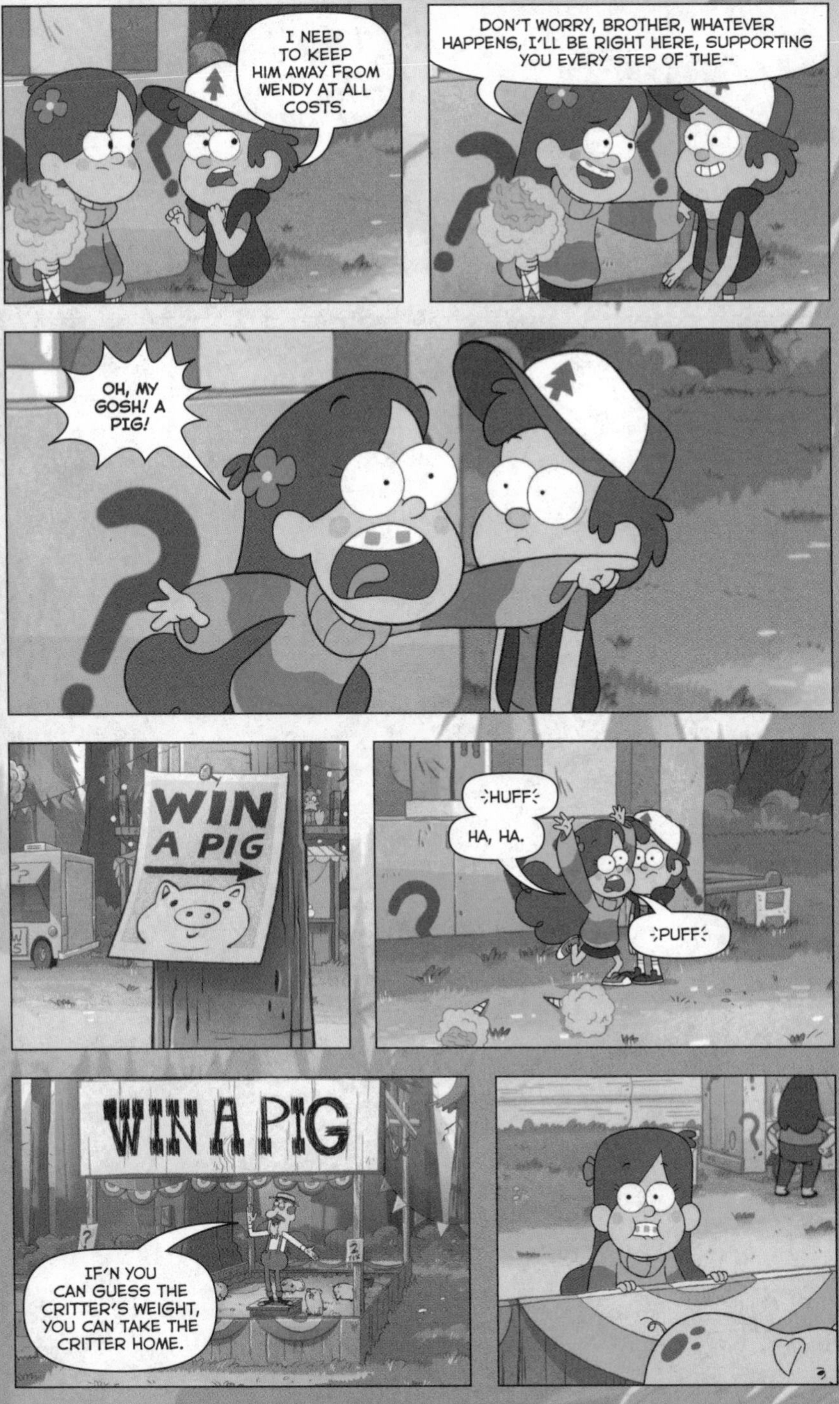
I NEED TO KEEP HIM AWAY FROM WENDY AT ALL COSTS.
DON'T WORRY, BROTHER, WHATEVER HAPPENS, I'LL BE RIGHT HERE, SUPPORTING YOU EVERY STEP OF THE--
OH, MY GOSH! A PIG!
WIN A PIG
HUFF
HA, HA.
PUFF
WIN A PIG
IF'N YOU CAN GUESS THE CRITTER'S WEIGHT, YOU CAN TAKE THE CRITTER HOME.

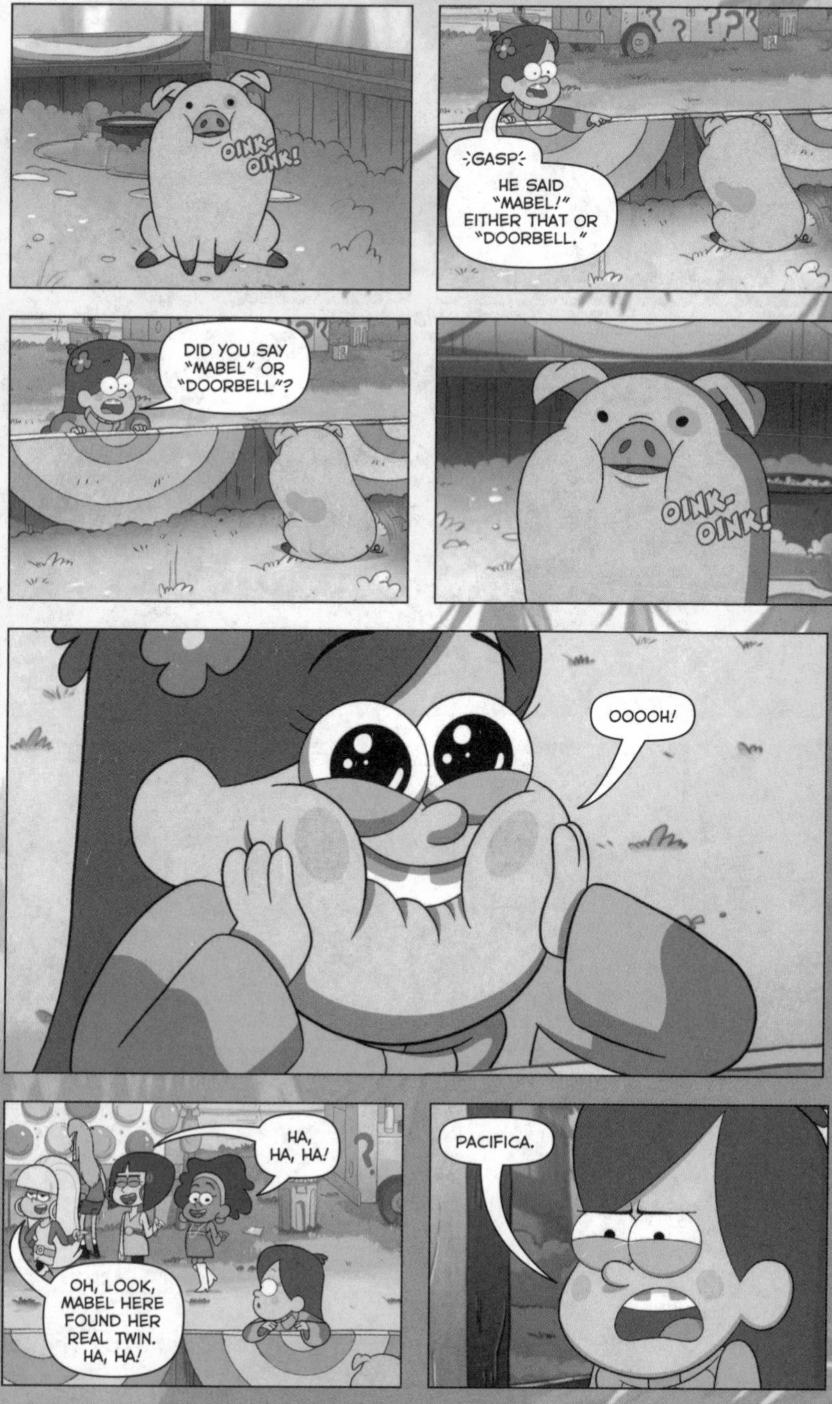
OINK-OINK!
GASP
HE SAID "MABEL!" EITHER THAT OR "DOORBELL."
DID YOU SAY "MABEL" OR "DOORBELL"?
OINK-OINK!
OOOOH!
HA, HA, HA!
OH, LOOK, MABEL HERE FOUND HER REAL TWIN. HA, HA!
PACIFICA.

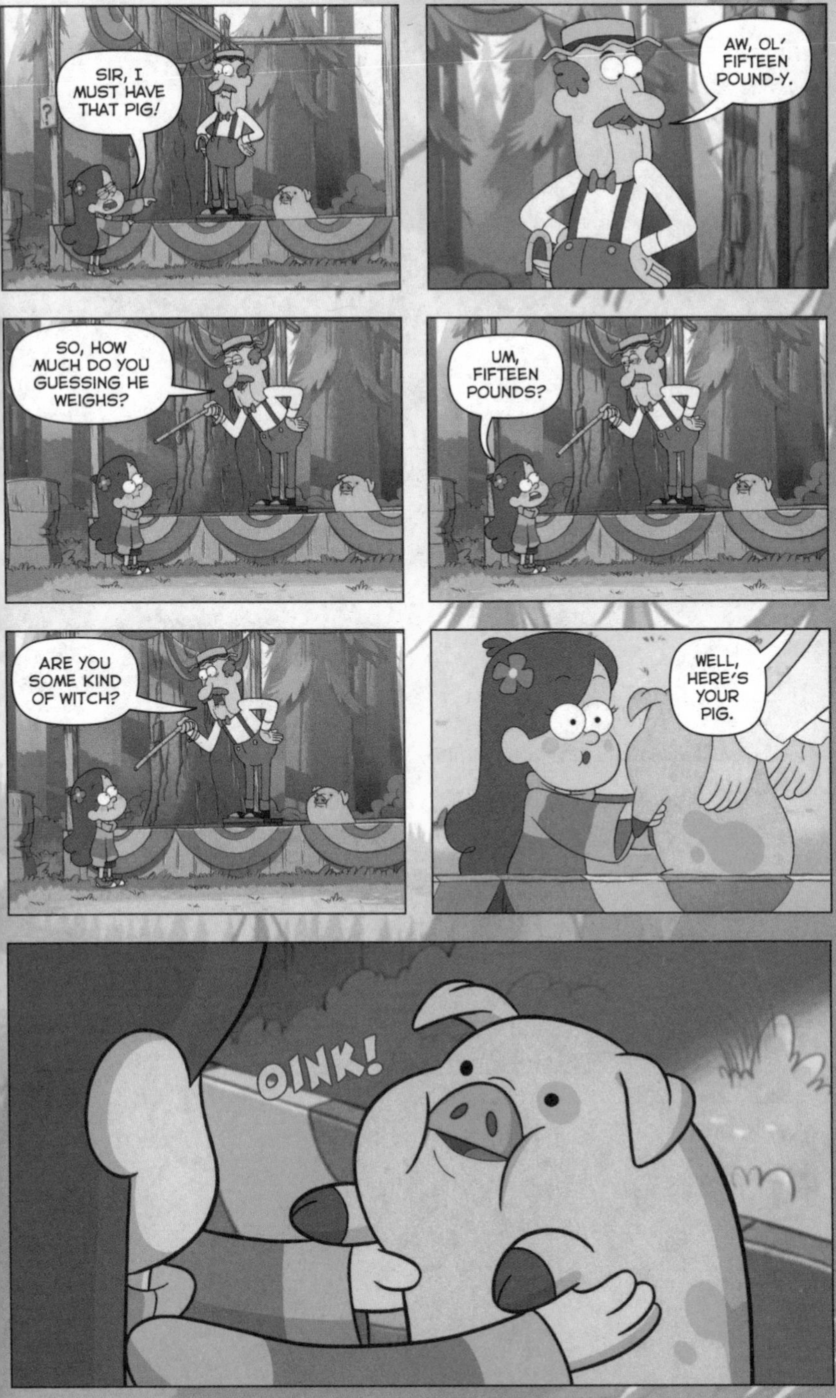
SIR, I MUST HAVE THAT PIG!
AW, OL' FIFTEEN POUND-Y.
SO, HOW MUCH DO YOU GUESSING HE WEIGHS?
UM, FIFTEEN POUNDS?
ARE YOU SOME KIND OF WITCH?
WELL, HERE'S YOUR PIG.
OINK!

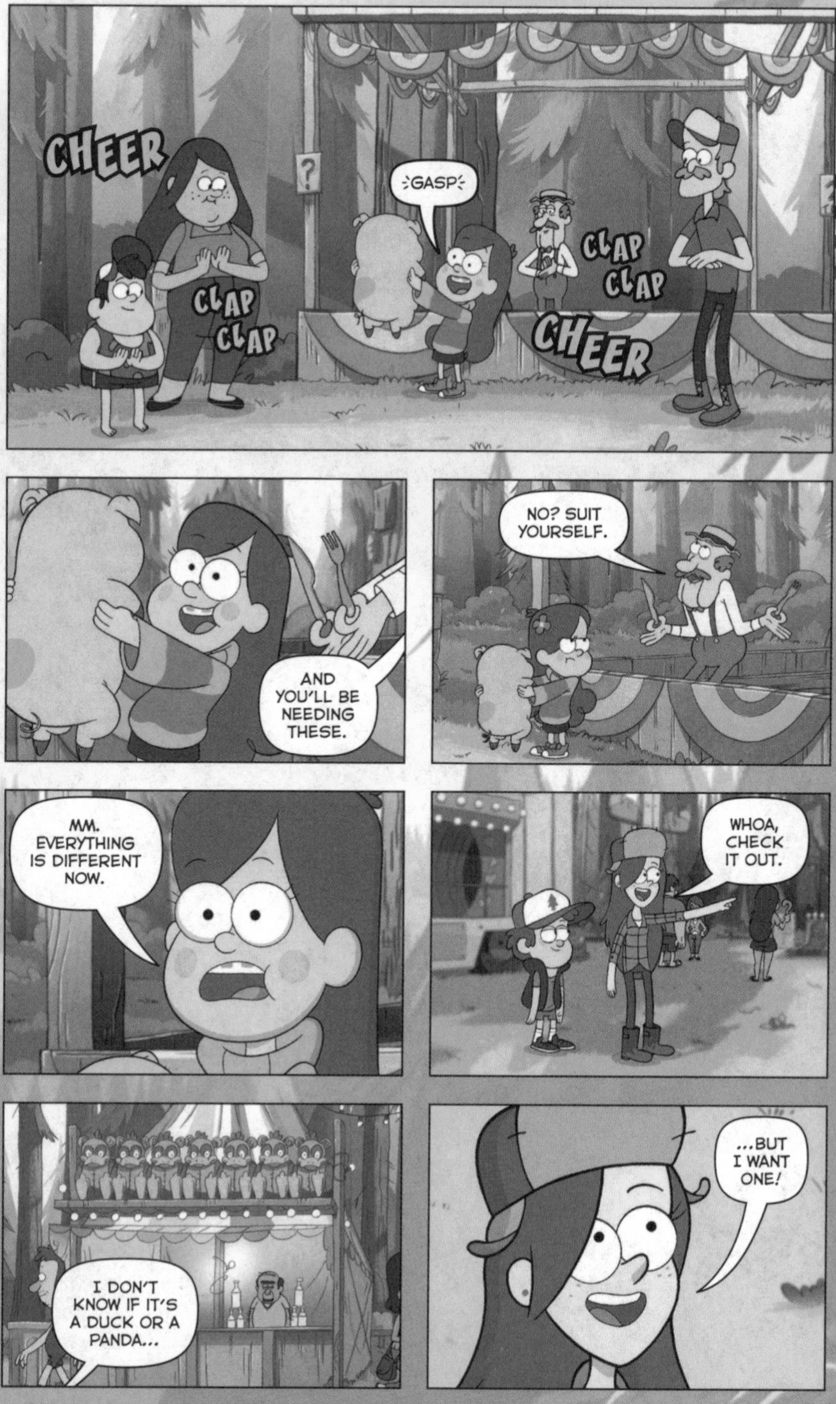
CHEER
CLAP
CLAP
GASP
CLAP
CLAP
CHEER
AND YOU'LL BE NEEDING THESE.
NO? SUIT YOURSELF.
MM. EVERYTHING IS DIFFERENT NOW.
WHOA, CHECK IT OUT.
I DON'T KNOW IF IT'S A DUCK OR A PANDA...
...BUT I WANT ONE!

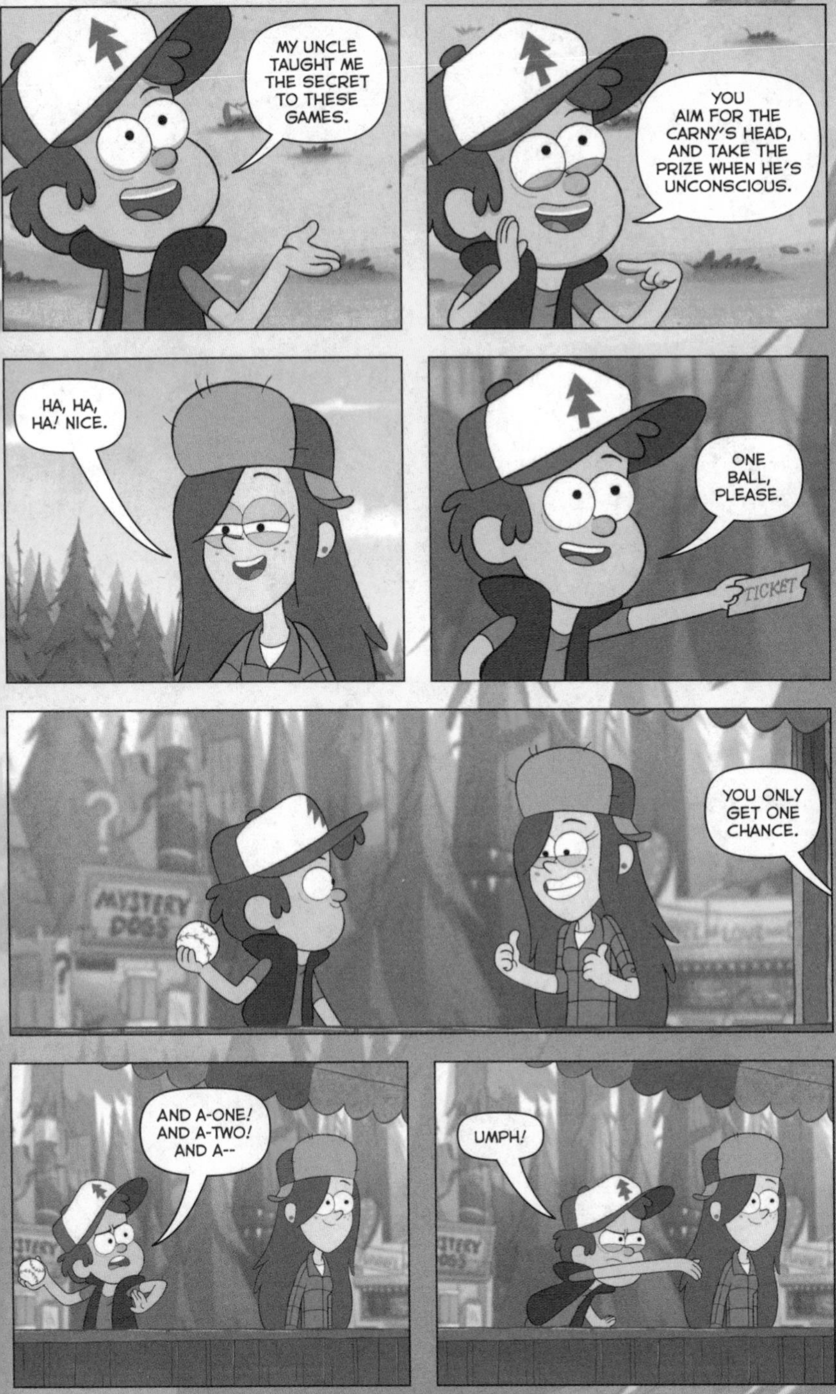
MY UNCLE TAUGHT ME THE SECRET TO THESE GAMES.
YOU AIM FOR THE CARNY'S HEAD, AND TAKE THE PRIZE WHEN HE'S UNCONSCIOUS.
HA, HA, HA! NICE.
ONE BALL, PLEASE.
TICKET
YOU ONLY GET ONE CHANCE.
MYSTERY DOGS
AND A-ONE! AND A-TWO! AND A--
UMPH!

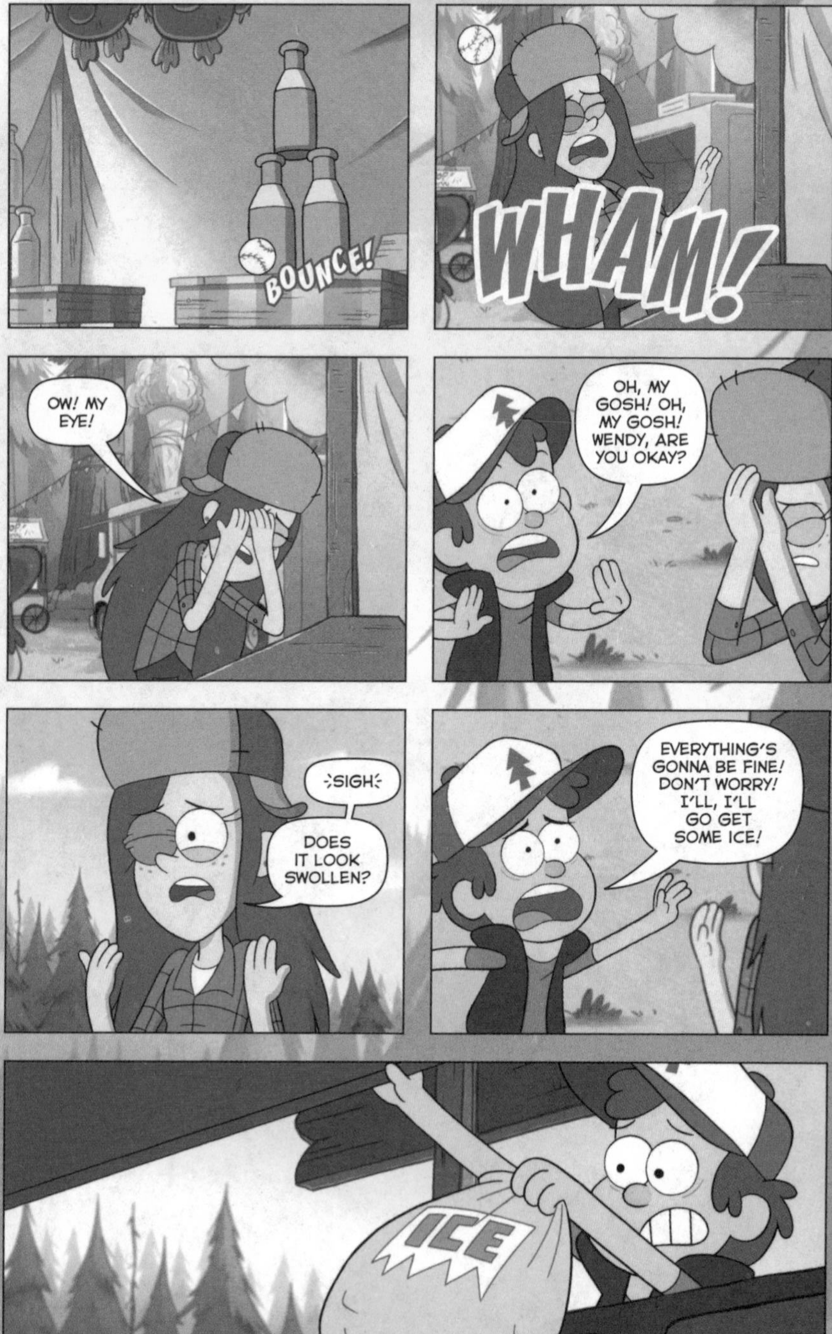
BOUNCE!
WHAM!
OW! MY EYE!
OH, MY GOSH! OH, MY GOSH! WENDY, ARE YOU OKAY?
-SIGH-
DOES IT LOOK SWOLLEN?
EVERYTHING'S GONNA BE FINE! DON'T WORRY! I'LL, I'LL GO GET SOME ICE!
ICE

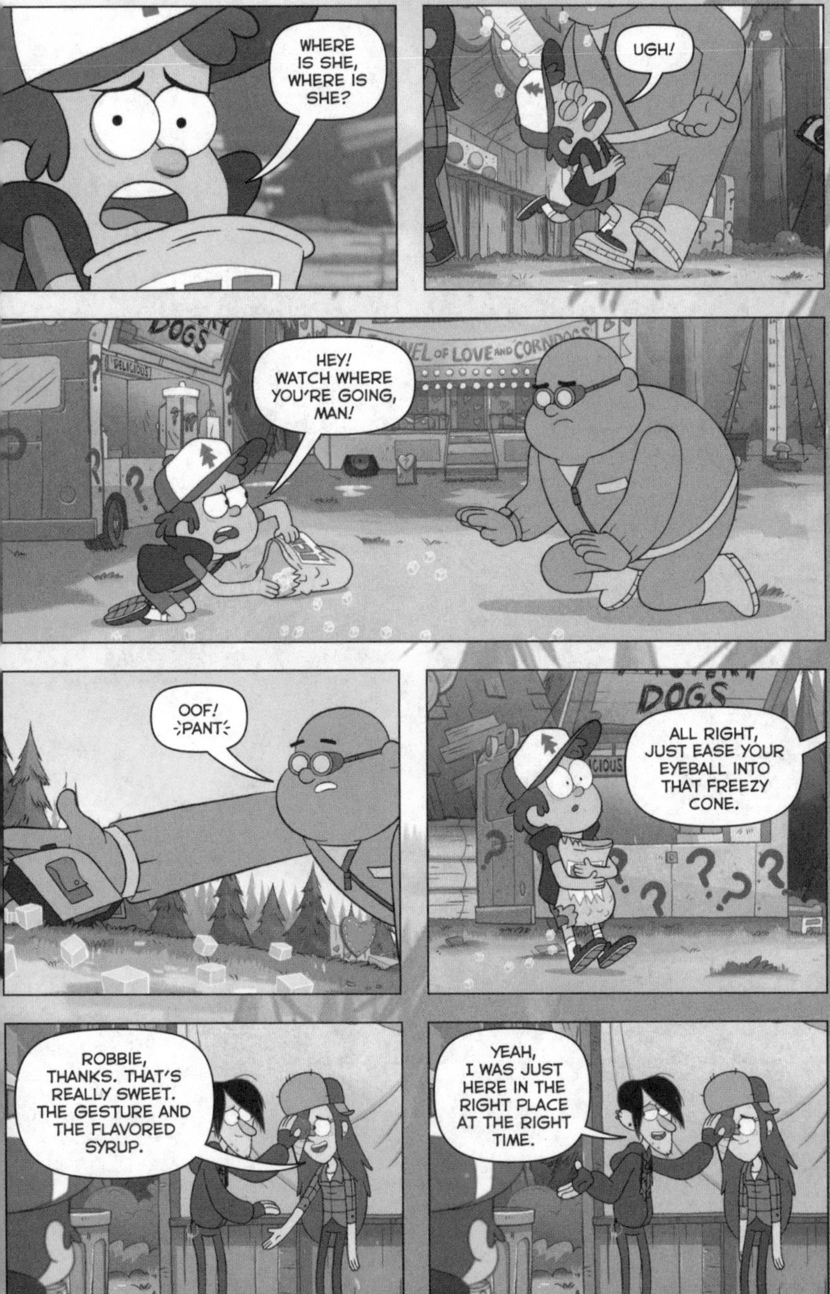
WHERE IS SHE, WHERE IS SHE?
UGH!
HEY! WATCH WHERE YOU'RE GOING, MAN!
OOF! PANT
ALL RIGHT, JUST EASE YOUR EYEBALL INTO THAT FREEZY CONE.
ROBBIE, THANKS. THAT'S REALLY SWEET. THE GESTURE AND THE FLAVORED SYRUP.
YEAH, I WAS JUST HERE IN THE RIGHT PLACE AT THE RIGHT TIME.

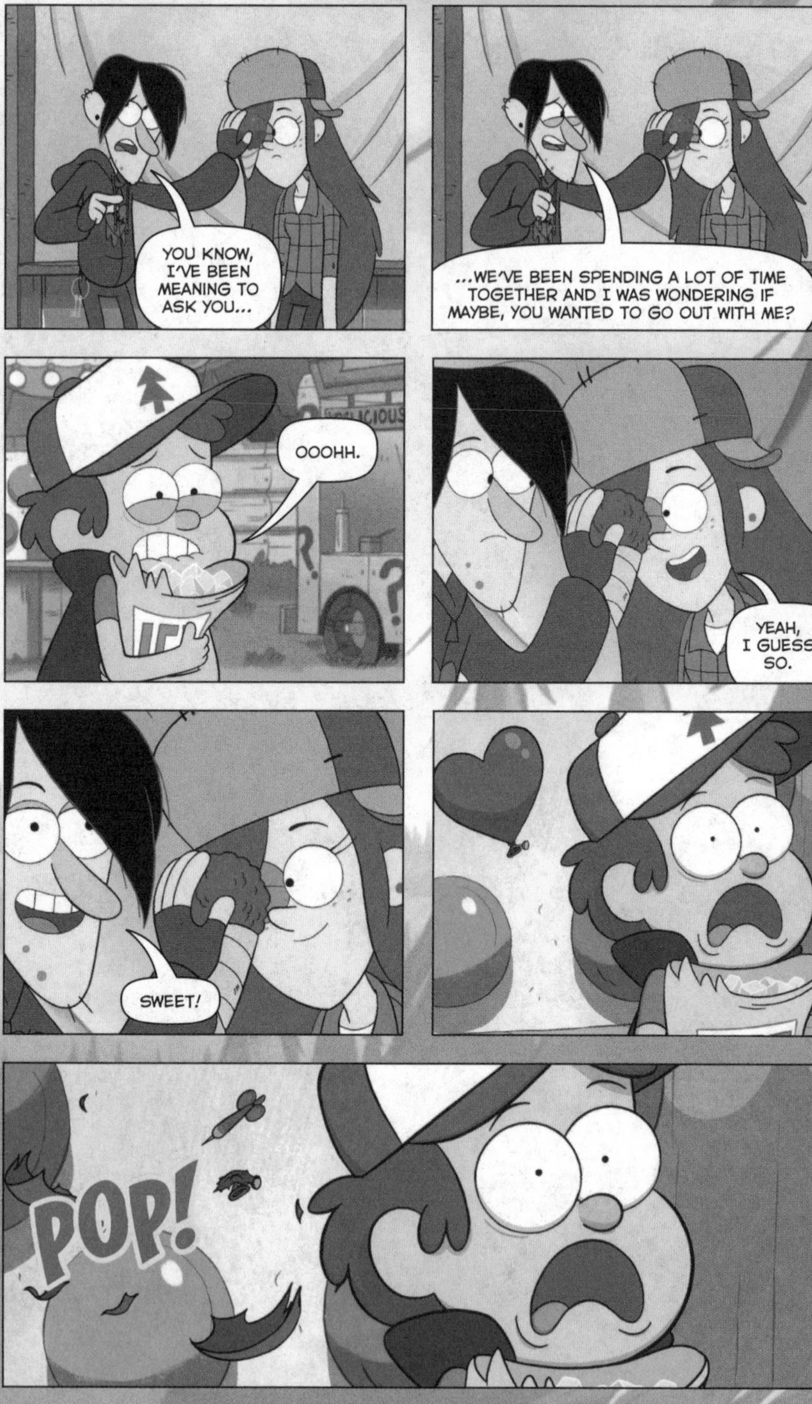
YOU KNOW, I'VE BEEN MEANING TO ASK YOU...
...WE'VE BEEN SPENDING A LOT OF TIME TOGETHER AND I WAS WONDERING IF MAYBE, YOU WANTED TO GO OUT WITH ME?
OOOHH.
YEAH, I GUESS SO.
SWEET!
POP!

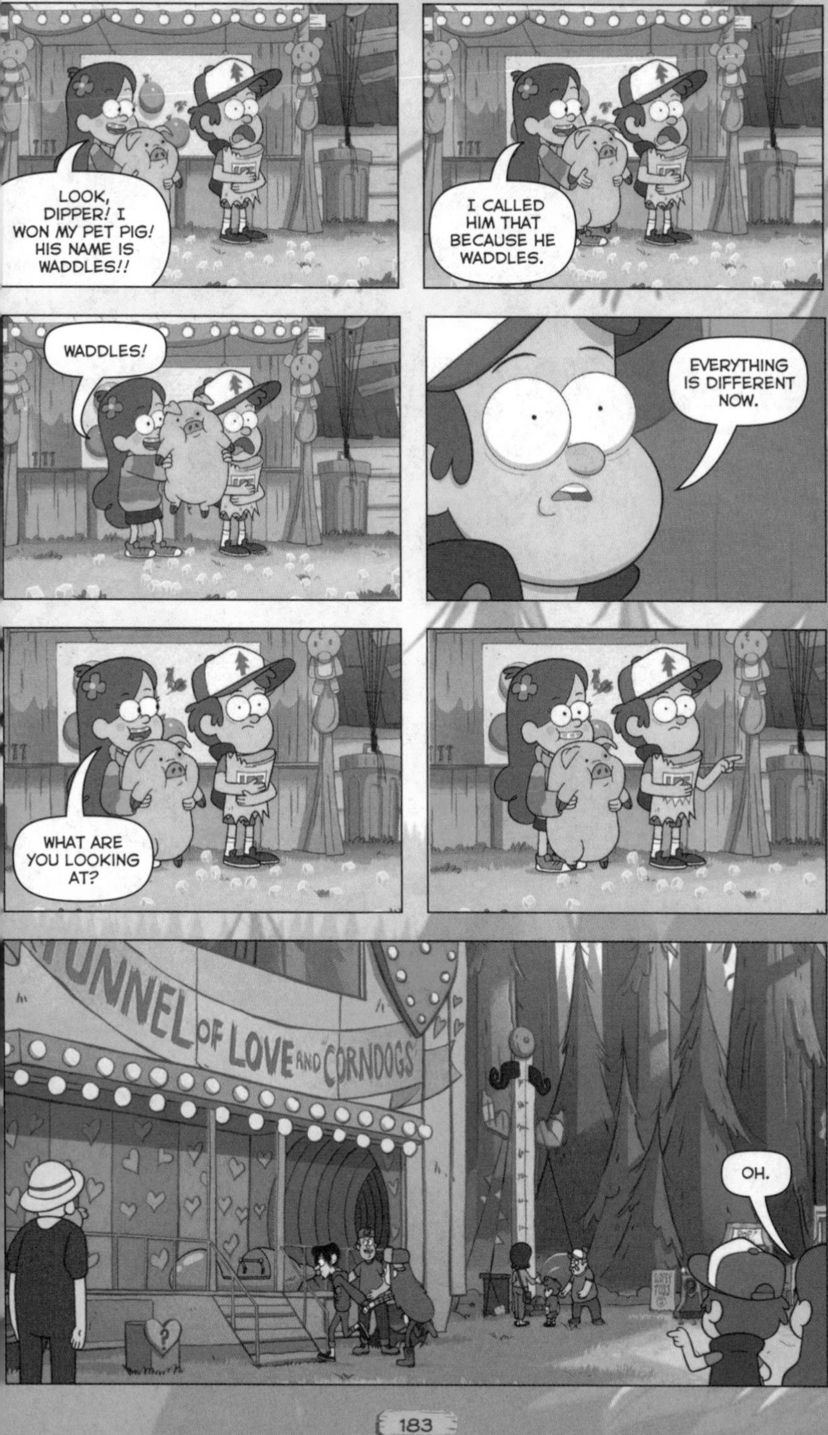

LOOK, DIPPER! I WON MY PET PIG! HIS NAME IS WADDLES!!
I CALLED HIM THAT BECAUSE HE WADDLES.
WADDLES!
EVERYTHING IS DIFFERENT NOW.
WHAT ARE YOU LOOKING AT?
TUNNEL OF LOVE AND CORNDOGS
OH.

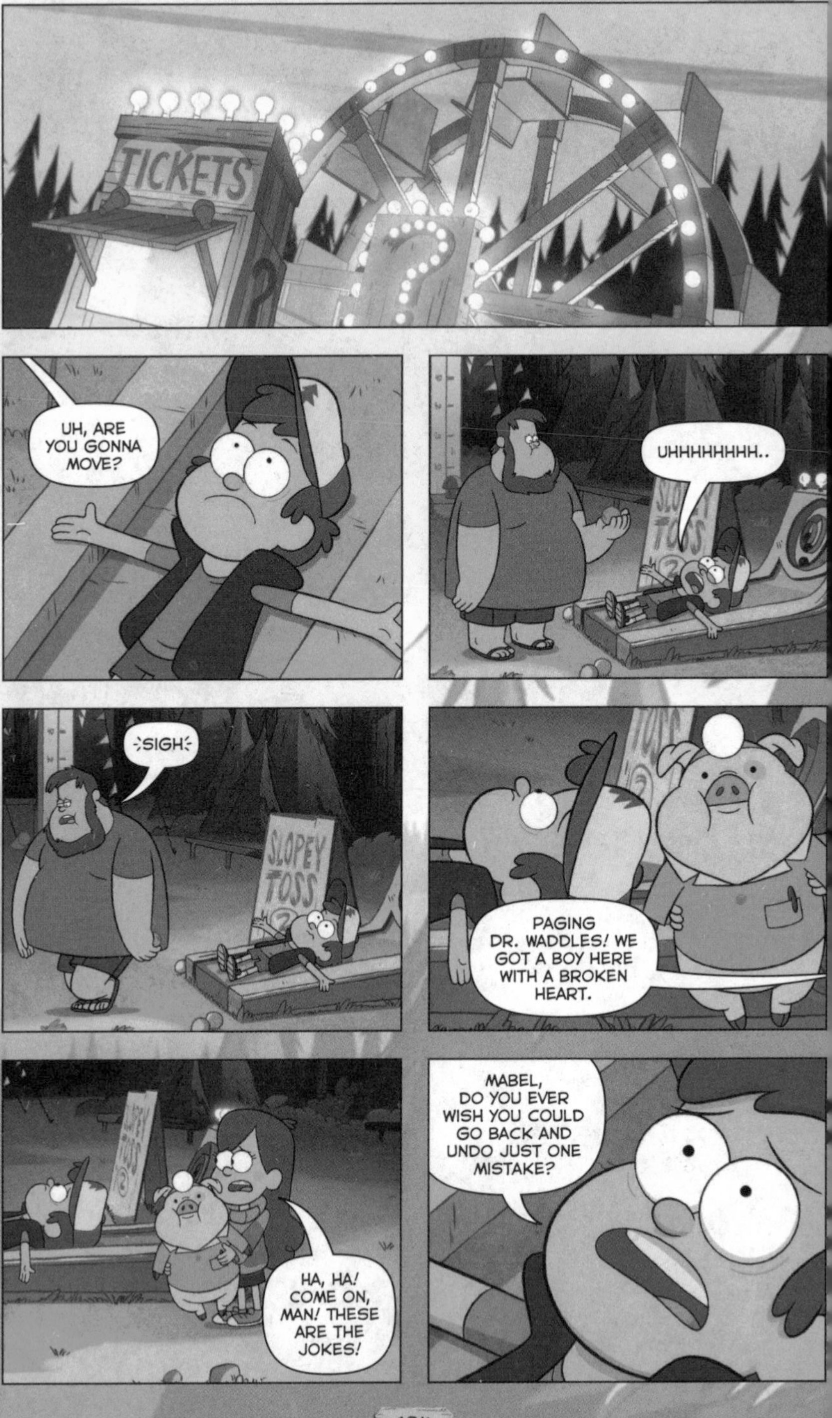
TICKETS
UH, ARE YOU GONNA MOVE?
UHHHHHHHH..
SLOPEY TOSS
SIGH
SLOPEY TOSS
PAGING DR. WADDLES! WE GOT A BOY HERE WITH A BROKEN HEART.
HA, HA! COME ON, MAN! THESE ARE THE JOKES!
MABEL, DO YOU EVER WISH YOU COULD GO BACK AND UNDO JUST ONE MISTAKE?

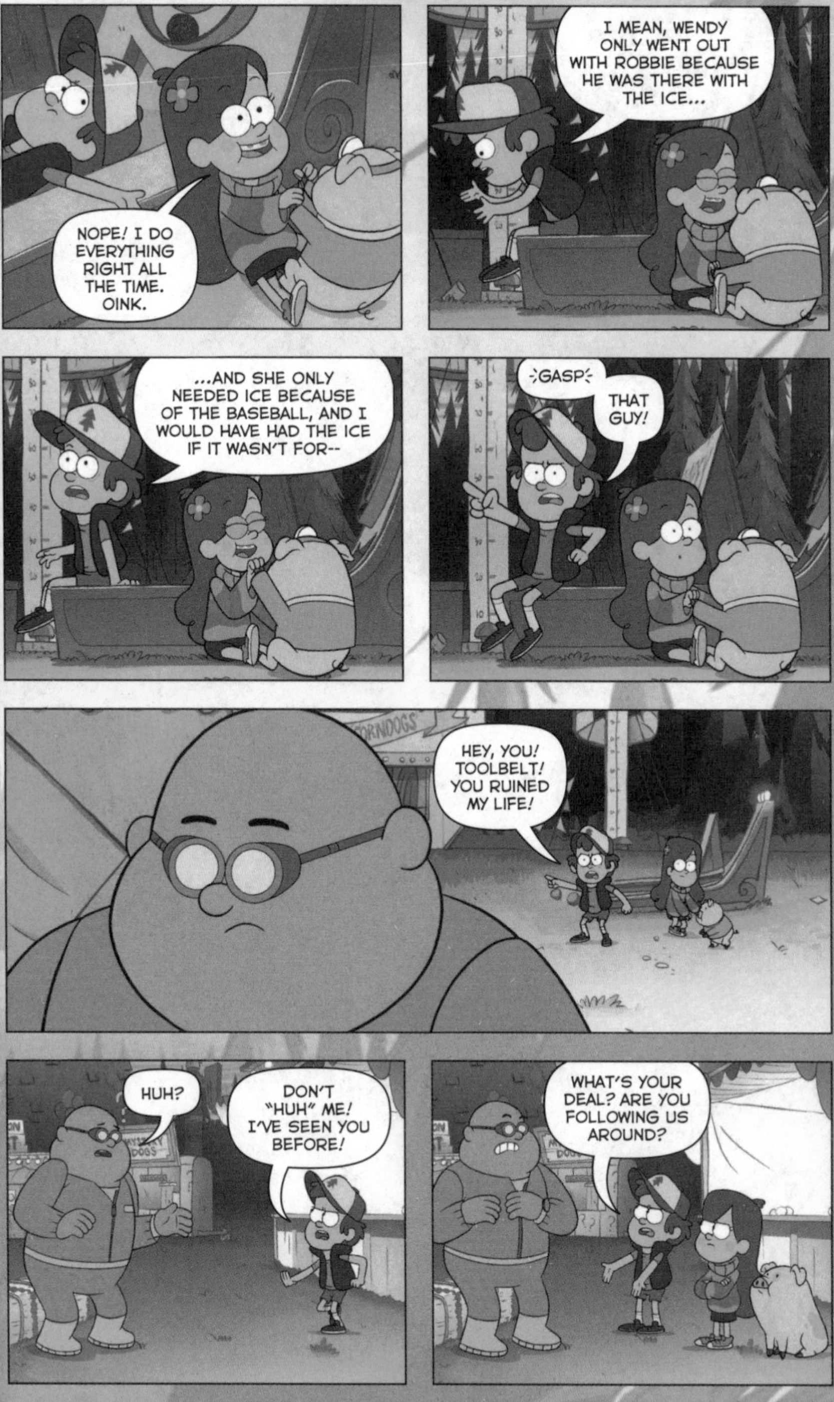
NOPE! I DO EVERYTHING RIGHT ALL THE TIME. OINK.
I MEAN, WENDY ONLY WENT OUT WITH ROBBIE BECAUSE HE WAS THERE WITH THE ICE...
...AND SHE ONLY NEEDED ICE BECAUSE OF THE BASEBALL, AND I WOULD HAVE HAD THE ICE IF IT WASN'T FOR--
GASP
THAT GUY!
CORNDOGS
HEY, YOU! TOOLBELT! YOU RUINED MY LIFE!
HUH?
DON'T "HUH" ME! I'VE SEEN YOU BEFORE!
WHAT'S YOUR DEAL? ARE YOU FOLLOWING US AROUND?

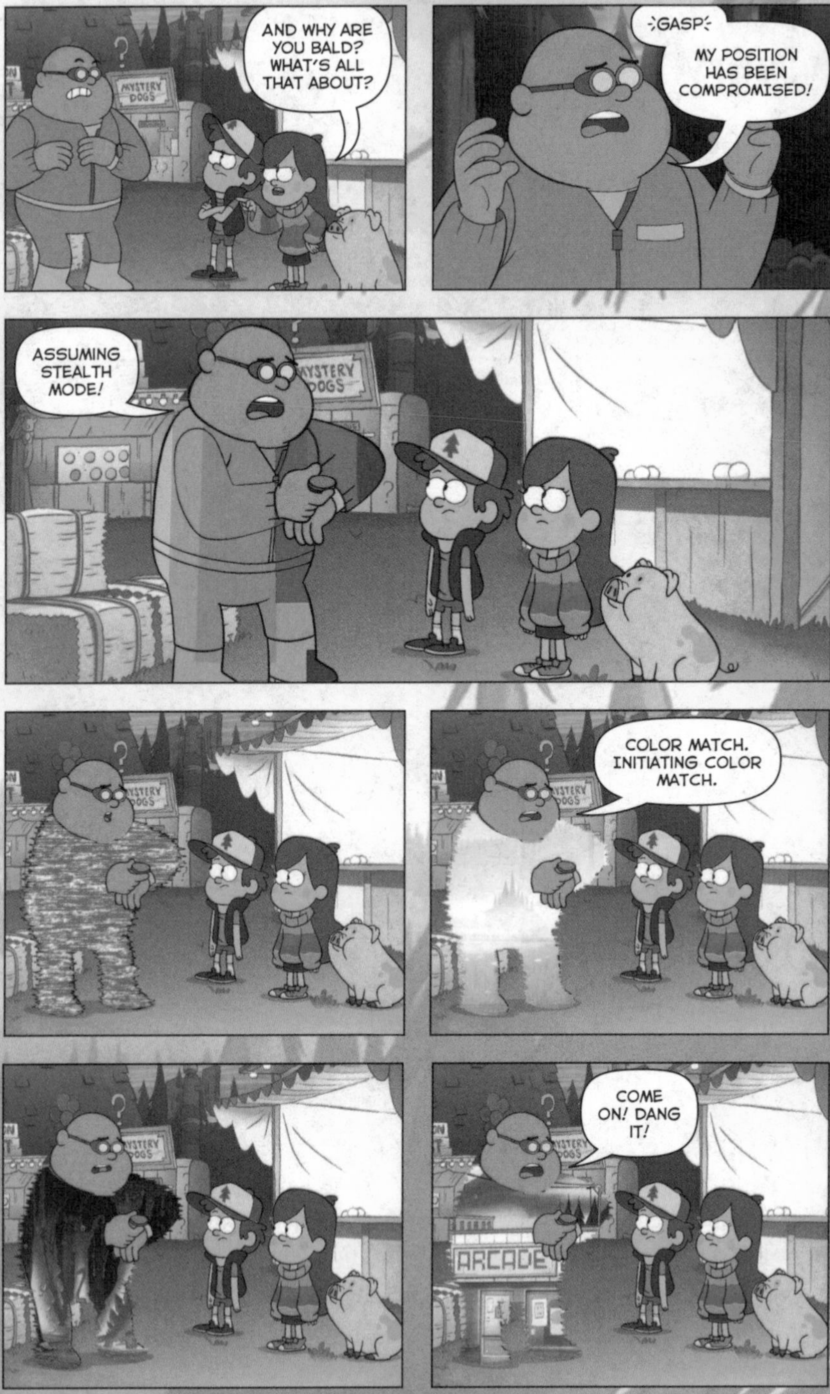
AND WHY ARE YOU BALD? WHAT'S ALL THAT ABOUT?
MYSTERY DOGS
GASP
MY POSITION HAS BEEN COMPROMISED!
ASSUMING STEALTH MODE!
COLOR MATCH. INITIATING COLOR MATCH.
COME ON! DANG IT!
ARCADE

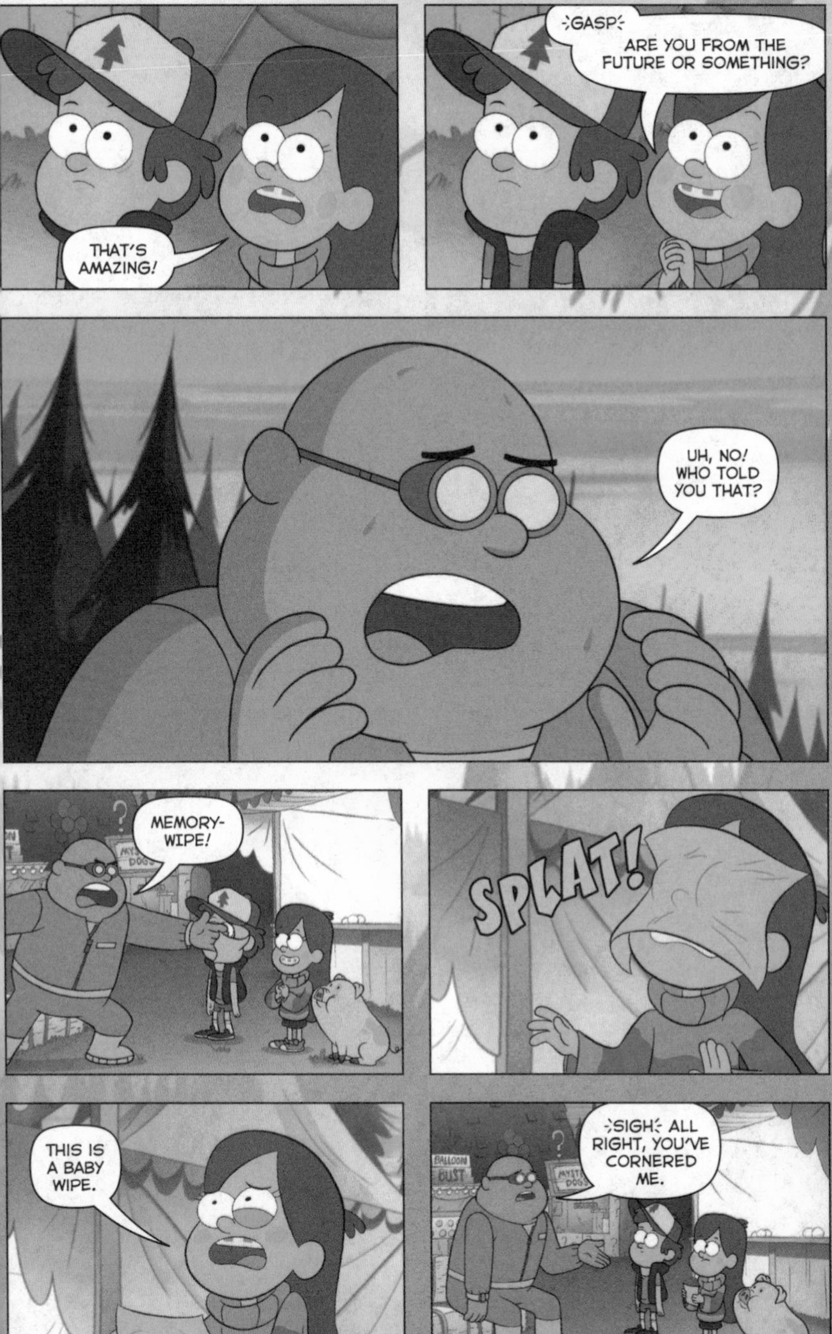
THAT'S AMAZING!
-GASP- ARE YOU FROM THE FUTURE OR SOMETHING?
UH, NO! WHO TOLD YOU THAT?
MEMORY-WIPE!
SPLAT!
THIS IS A BABY WIPE.
-SIGH- ALL RIGHT, YOU'VE CORNERED ME.

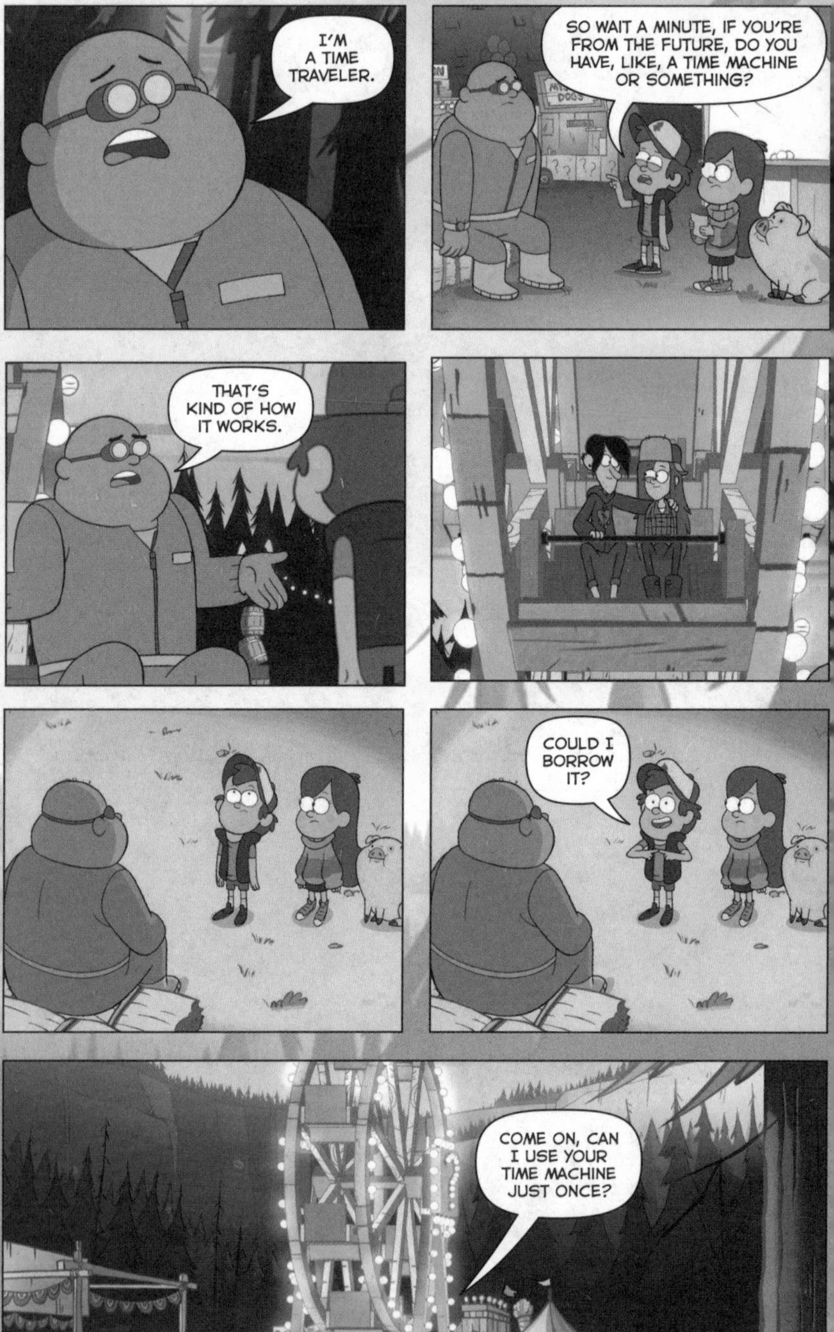
I'M A TIME TRAVELER.
SO WAIT A MINUTE, IF YOU'RE FROM THE FUTURE, DO YOU HAVE, LIKE, A TIME MACHINE OR SOMETHING?
THAT'S KIND OF HOW IT WORKS.
COULD I BORROW IT?
COME ON, CAN I USE YOUR TIME MACHINE JUST ONCE?

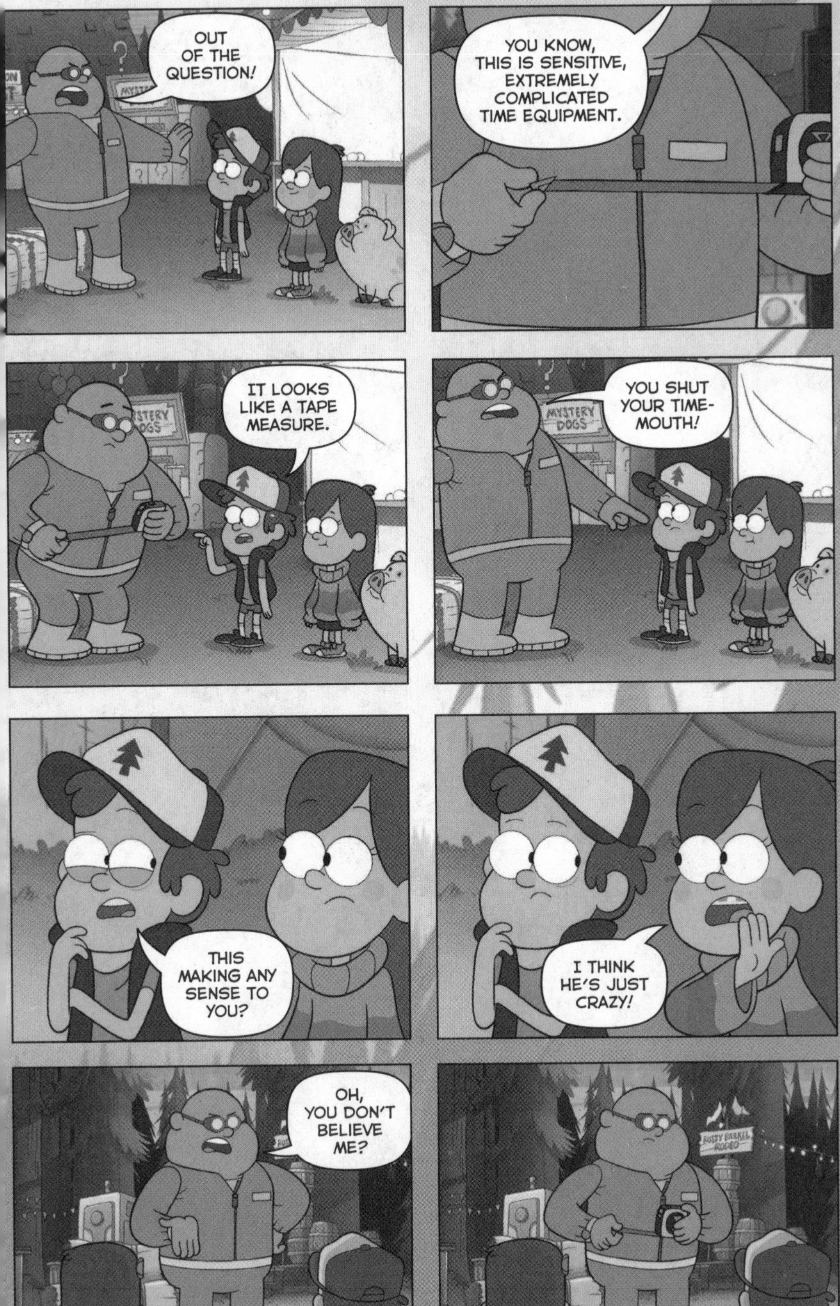

MYSTERY
OUT OF THE QUESTION!
YOU KNOW, THIS IS SENSITIVE, EXTREMELY COMPLICATED TIME EQUIPMENT.
MYSTERY DOGS
IT LOOKS LIKE A TAPE MEASURE.
MYSTERY DOGS
YOU SHUT YOUR TIME-MOUTH!
THIS MAKING ANY SENSE TO YOU?
I THINK HE'S JUST CRAZY!
OH, YOU DON'T BELIEVE ME?
RUSTY BARREL RODEO

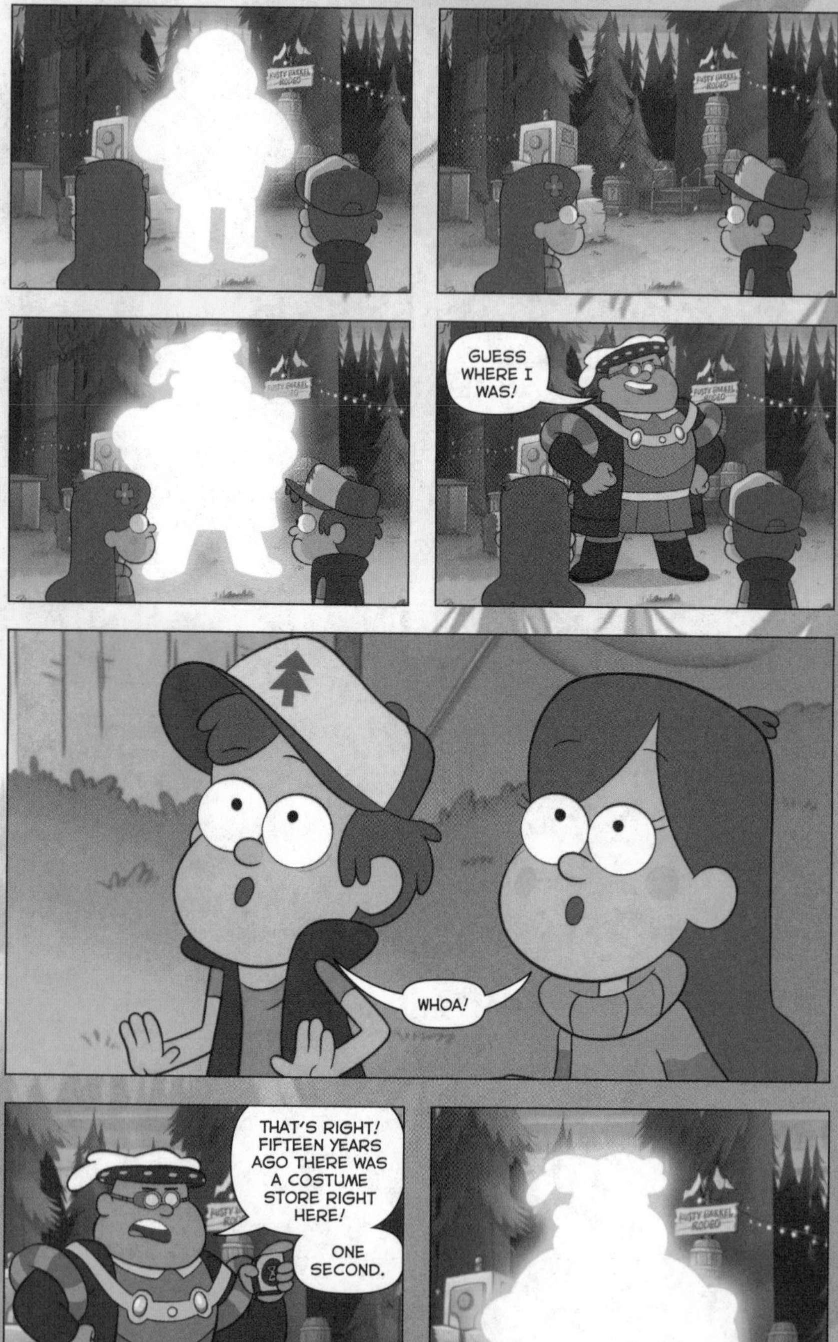
GUESS WHERE I WAS!
WHOA!
THAT'S RIGHT! FIFTEEN YEARS AGO THERE WAS A COSTUME STORE RIGHT HERE!
ONE SECOND.

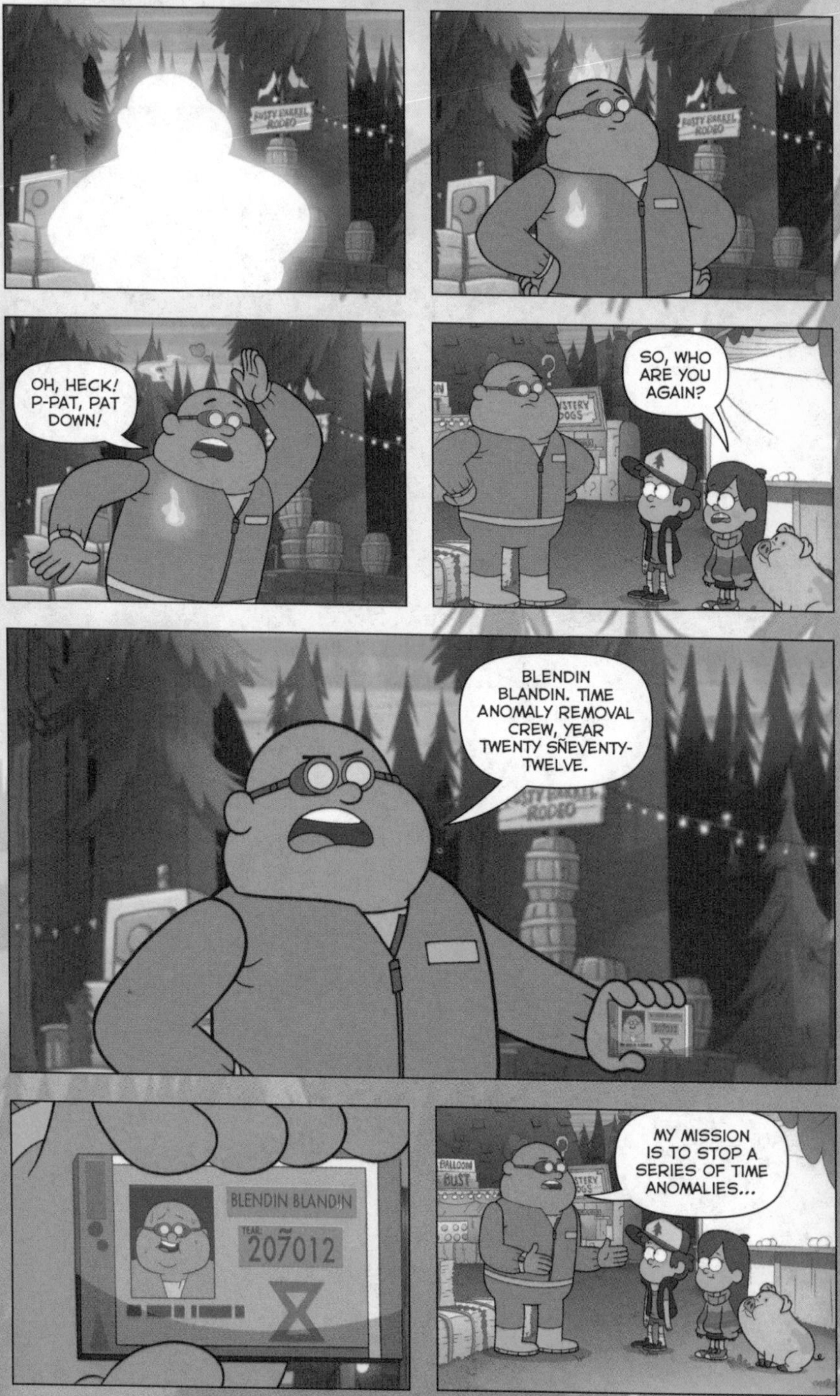
OH, HECK! P-PAT, PAT DOWN!
SO, WHO ARE YOU AGAIN?
BLENDIN BLANDIN. TIME ANOMALY REMOVAL CREW, YEAR TWENTY SÑEVENTY-TWELVE.
BLENDIN BLANDIN
207012
MY MISSION IS TO STOP A SERIES OF TIME ANOMALIES...

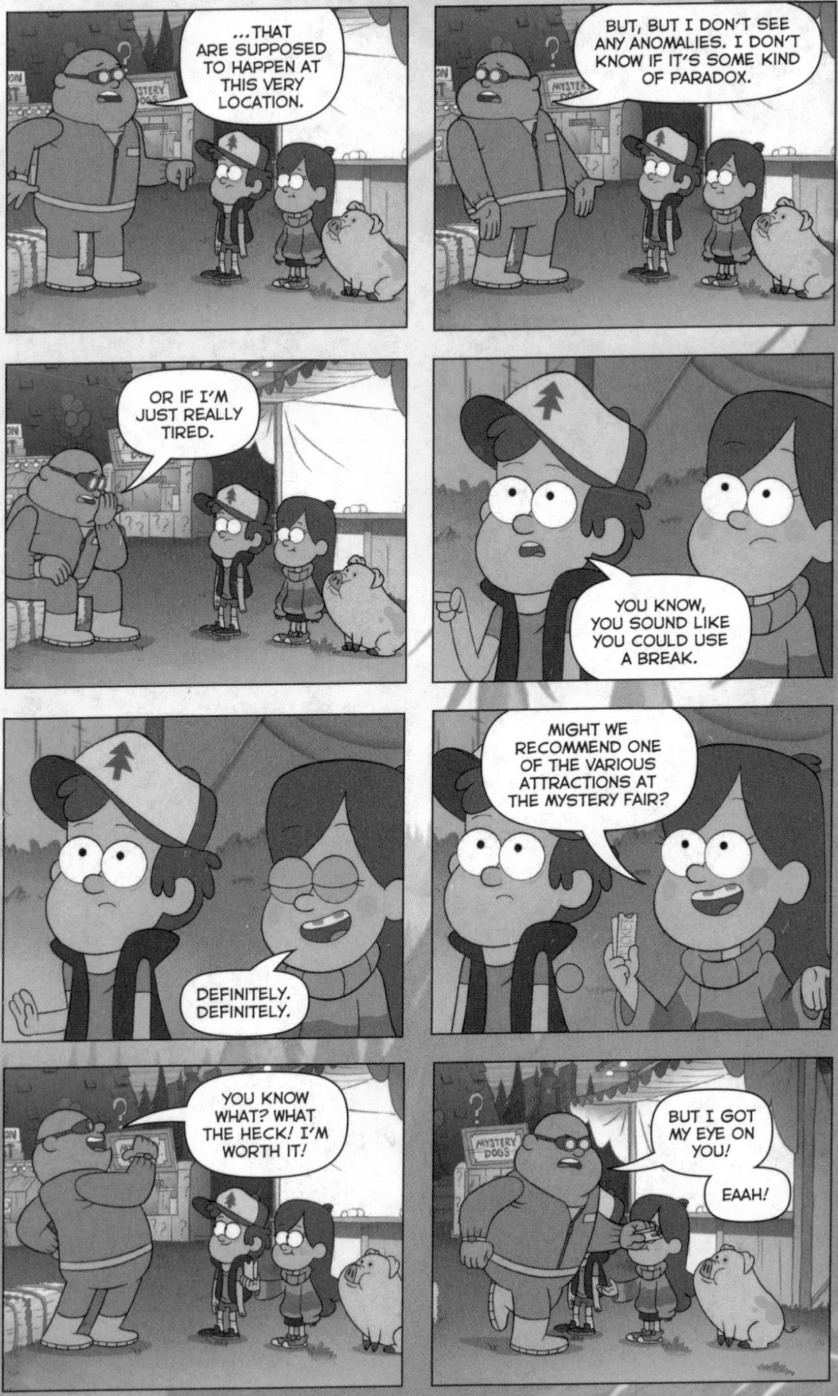
...THAT ARE SUPPOSED TO HAPPEN AT THIS VERY LOCATION.
MYSTERY DOGS
BUT, BUT I DON'T SEE ANY ANOMALIES. I DON'T KNOW IF IT'S SOME KIND OF PARADOX.
OR IF I'M JUST REALLY TIRED.
YOU KNOW, YOU SOUND LIKE YOU COULD USE A BREAK.
DEFINITELY. DEFINITELY.
MIGHT WE RECOMMEND ONE OF THE VARIOUS ATTRACTIONS AT THE MYSTERY FAIR?
TICKET
YOU KNOW WHAT? WHAT THE HECK! I'M WORTH IT!
MYSTERY DOGS
BUT I GOT MY EYE ON YOU!
EAAH!

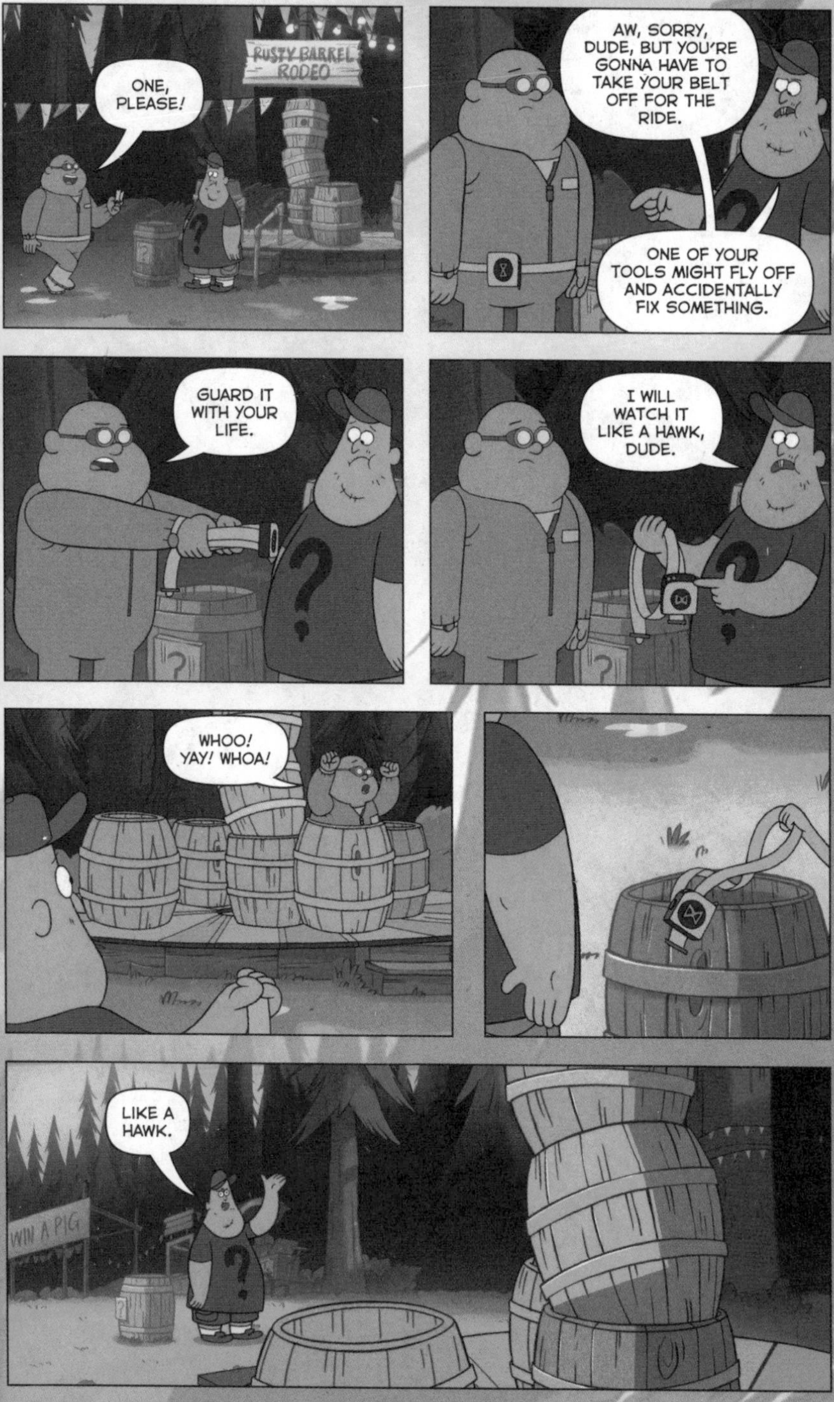
RUSTY BARREL RODEO
ONE, PLEASE!
AW, SORRY, DUDE, BUT YOU'RE GONNA HAVE TO TAKE YOUR BELT OFF FOR THE RIDE.
ONE OF YOUR TOOLS MIGHT FLY OFF AND ACCIDENTALLY FIX SOMETHING.
GUARD IT WITH YOUR LIFE.
I WILL WATCH IT LIKE A HAWK, DUDE.
WHOO! YAY! WHOA!
LIKE A HAWK.
WIN A PIG

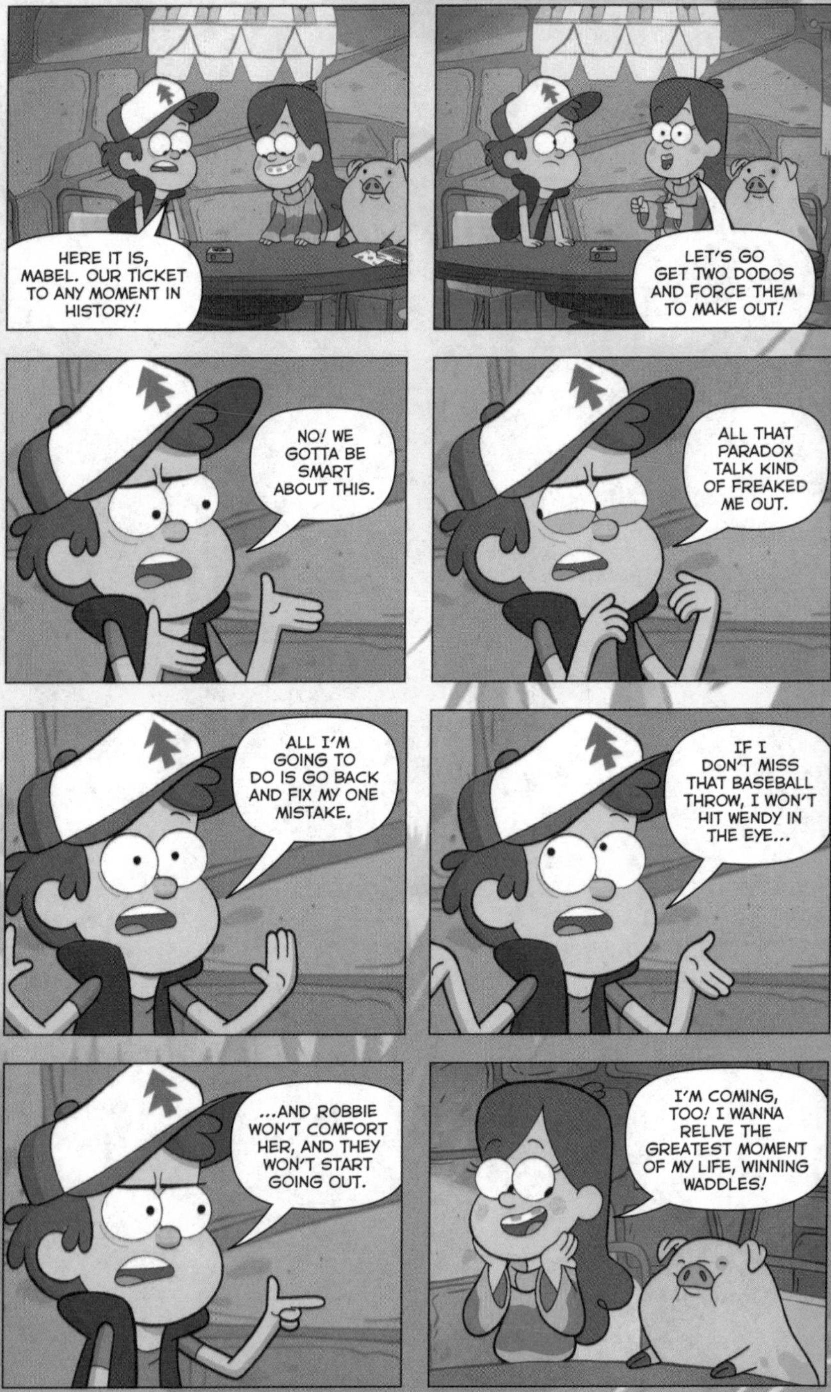
HERE IT IS, MABEL. OUR TICKET TO ANY MOMENT IN HISTORY!
LET'S GO GET TWO DODOS AND FORCE THEM TO MAKE OUT!
NO! WE GOTTA BE SMART ABOUT THIS.
ALL THAT PARADOX TALK KIND OF FREAKED ME OUT.
ALL I'M GOING TO DO IS GO BACK AND FIX MY ONE MISTAKE.
IF I DON'T MISS THAT BASEBALL THROW, I WON'T HIT WENDY IN THE EYE...
...AND ROBBIE WON'T COMFORT HER, AND THEY WON'T START GOING OUT.
I'M COMING, TOO! I WANNA RELIVE THE GREATEST MOMENT OF MY LIFE, WINNING WADDLES!

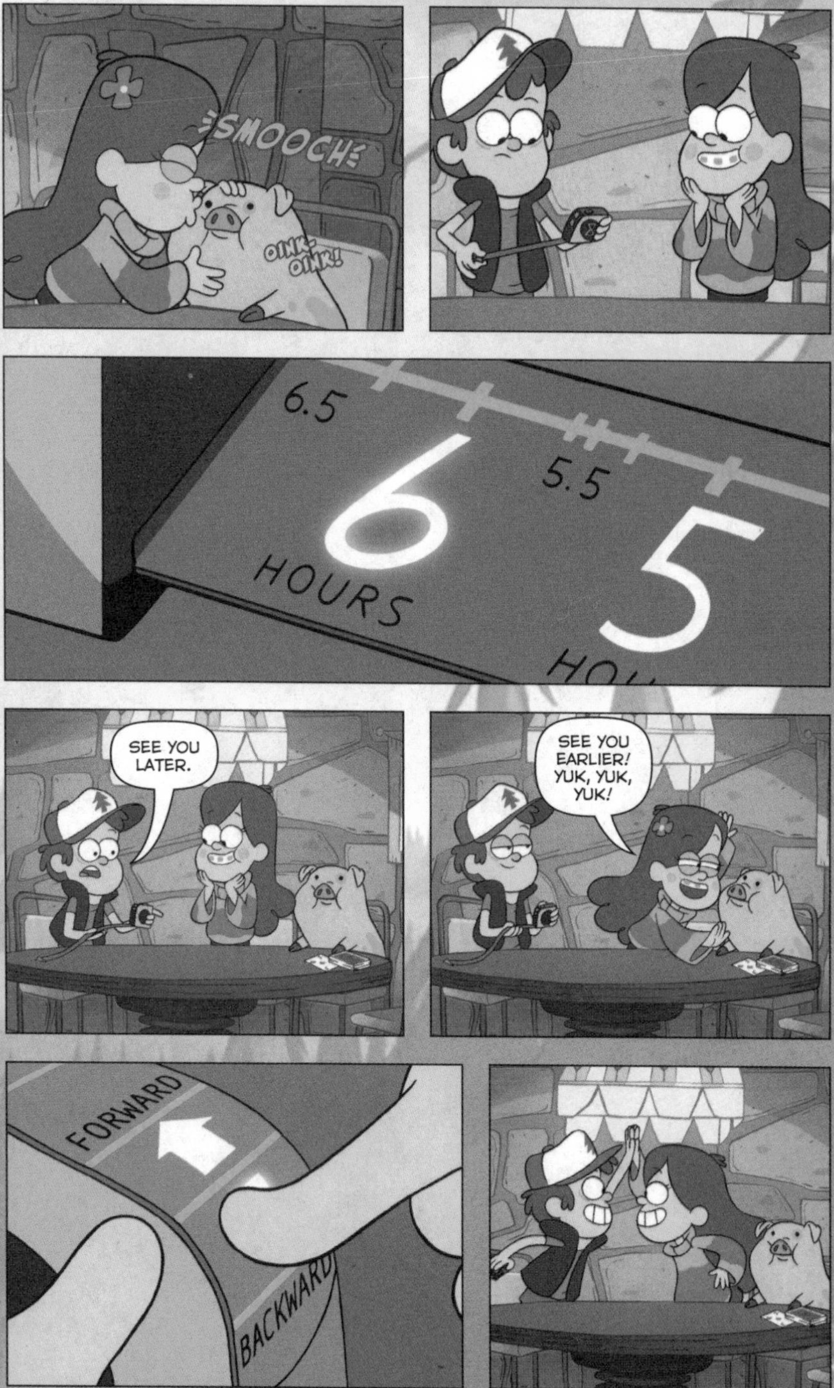
SMOOCH
OINK-OINK!
6.5
5.5
6
HOURS
5
SEE YOU LATER.
SEE YOU EARLIER! YUK, YUK, YUK!
FORWARD
BACKWARD

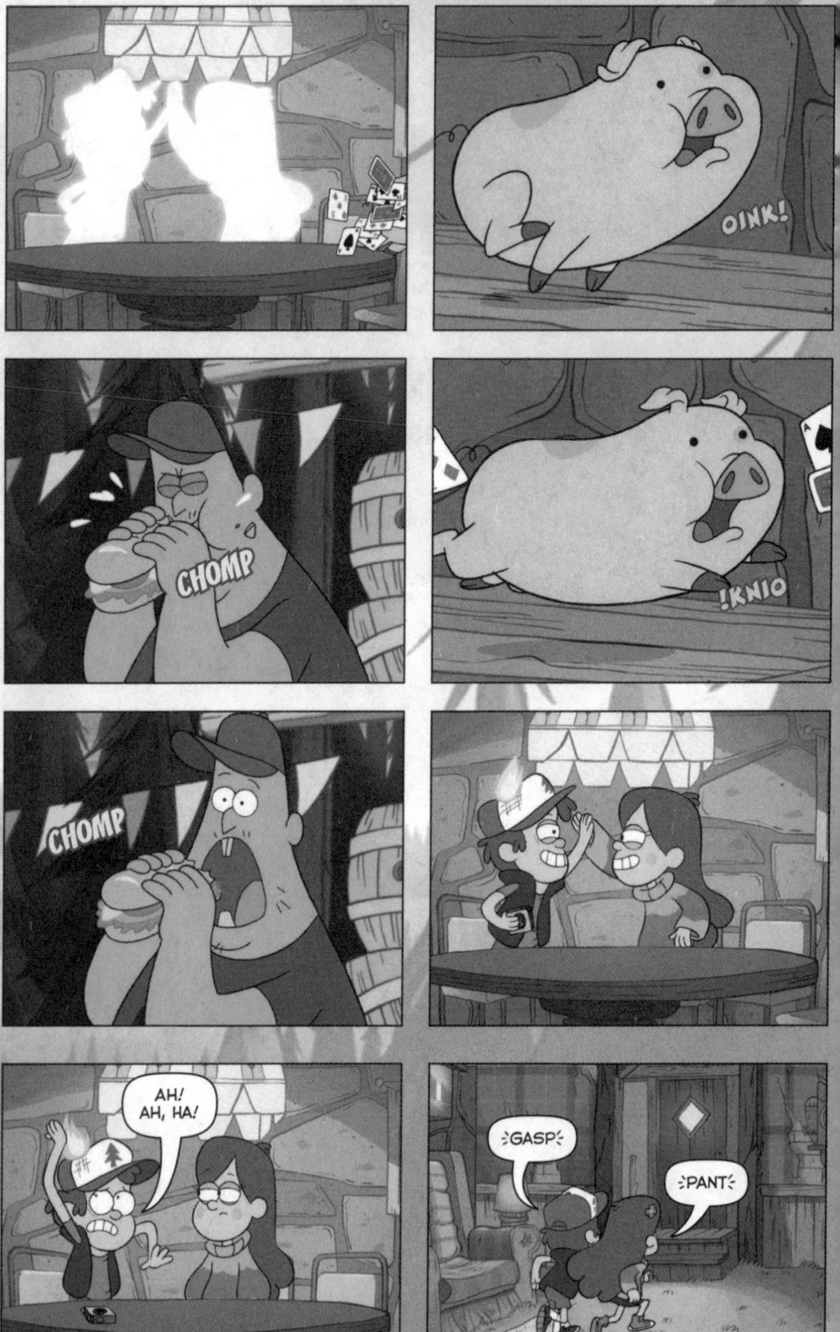
OINK!
CHOMP
!KNIO
CHOMP
AH!
AH, HA!
GASP
PANT

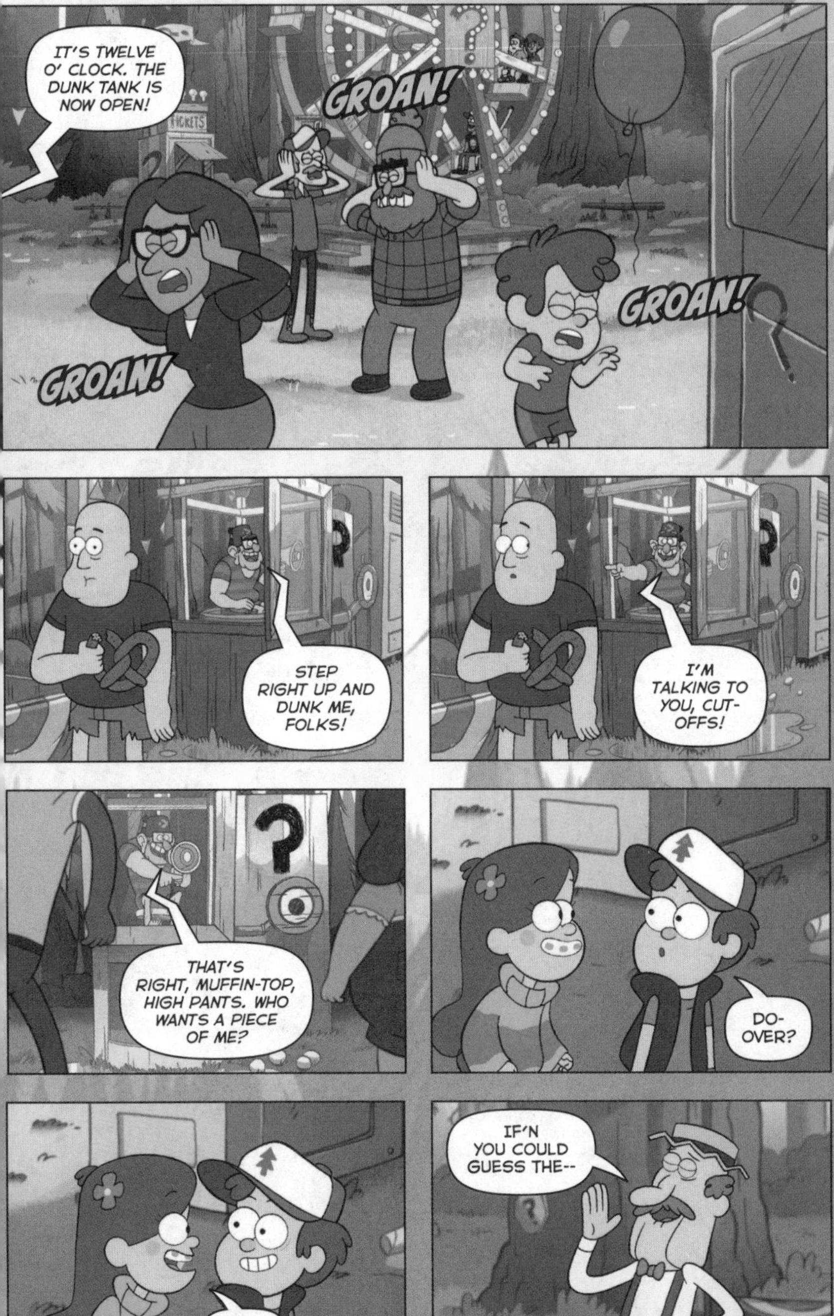
IT'S TWELVE O' CLOCK. THE DUNK TANK IS NOW OPEN!
GROAN!
GROAN!
GROAN!
STEP RIGHT UP AND DUNK ME, FOLKS!
I'M TALKING TO YOU, CUT-OFFS!
THAT'S RIGHT, MUFFIN-TOP, HIGH PANTS. WHO WANTS A PIECE OF ME?
DO-OVER?
DO-OVER!
IF'N YOU COULD GUESS THE--

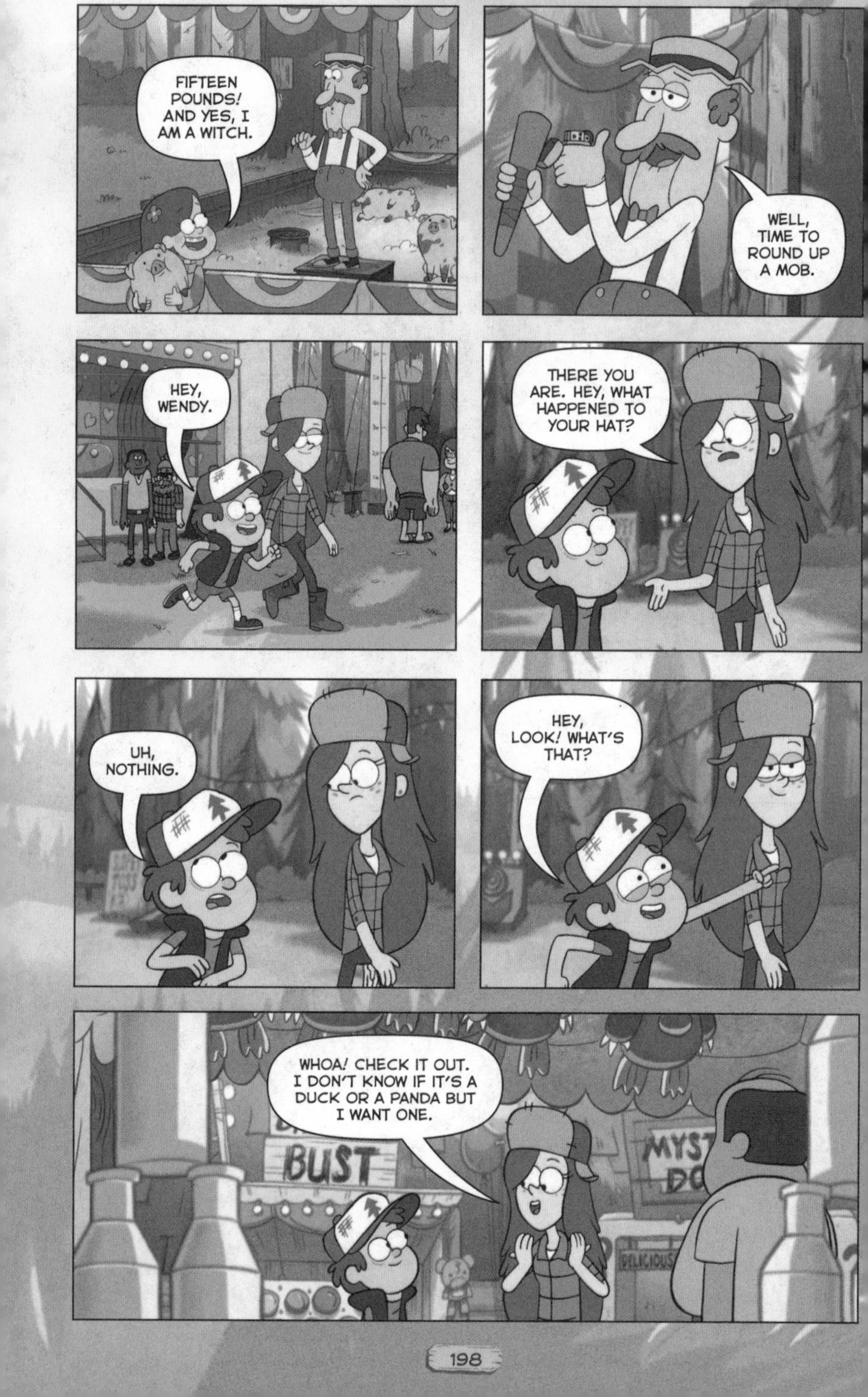
FIFTEEN POUNDS! AND YES, I AM A WITCH.
WELL, TIME TO ROUND UP A MOB.
HEY, WENDY.
THERE YOU ARE. HEY, WHAT HAPPENED TO YOUR HAT?
UH, NOTHING.
HEY, LOOK! WHAT'S THAT?
WHOA! CHECK IT OUT. I DON'T KNOW IF IT'S A DUCK OR A PANDA BUT I WANT ONE.
BUST

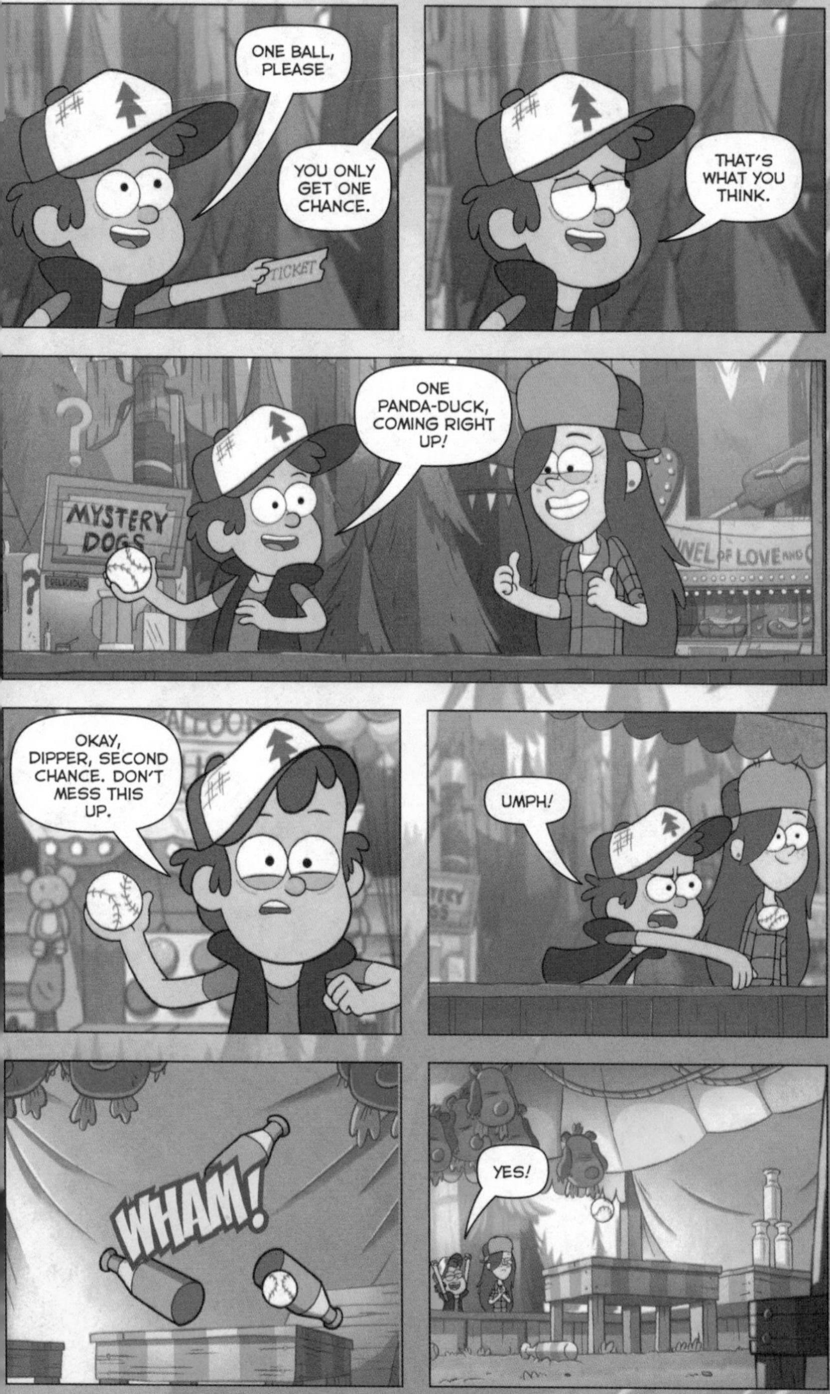
ONE BALL, PLEASE
YOU ONLY GET ONE CHANCE.
TICKET
THAT'S WHAT YOU THINK.
ONE PANDA-DUCK, COMING RIGHT UP!
MYSTERY DOGS
OKAY, DIPPER, SECOND CHANCE. DON'T MESS THIS UP.
UMPH!
WHAM!
YES!

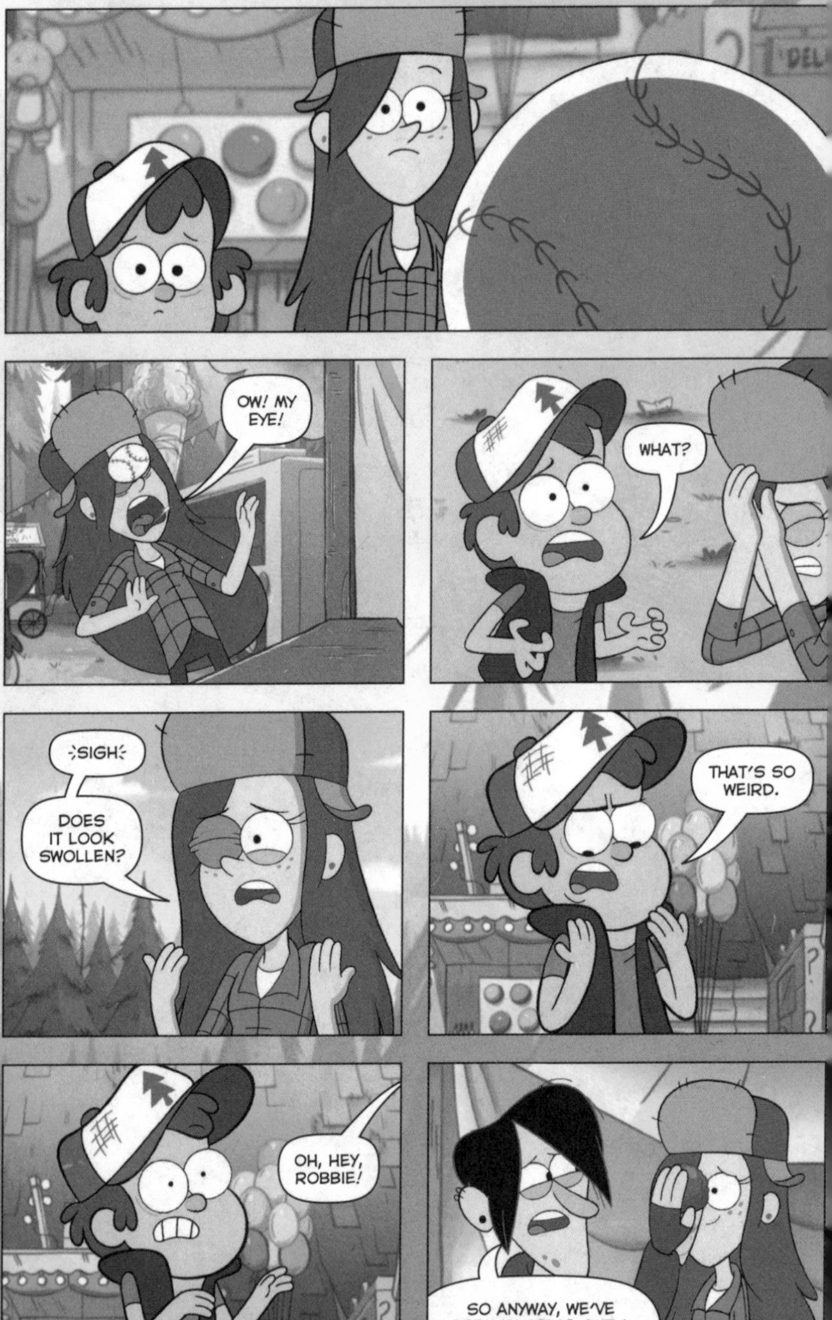
OW! MY EYE!
WHAT?
SIGH
DOES IT LOOK SWOLLEN?
THAT'S SO WEIRD.
OH, HEY, ROBBIE!
SO ANYWAY, WE'VE BEEN HANGING OUT A LOT, AND I'VE BEEN WONDERING...

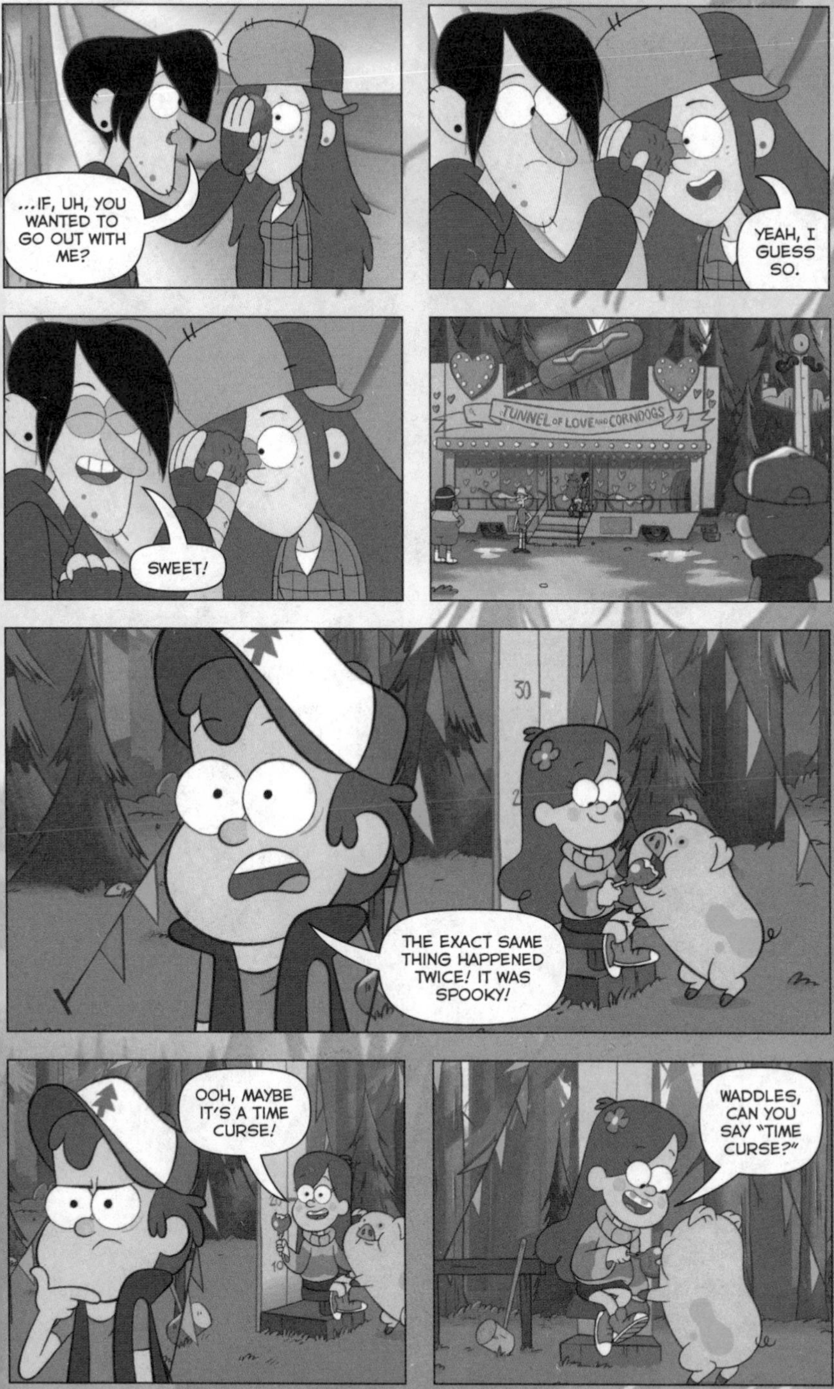
...IF, UH, YOU WANTED TO GO OUT WITH ME?
YEAH, I GUESS SO.
SWEET!
TUNNEL OF LOVE AND CORNDOGS
30
THE EXACT SAME THING HAPPENED TWICE! IT WAS SPOOKY!
OOH, MAYBE IT'S A TIME CURSE!
WADDLES, CAN YOU SAY "TIME CURSE?"

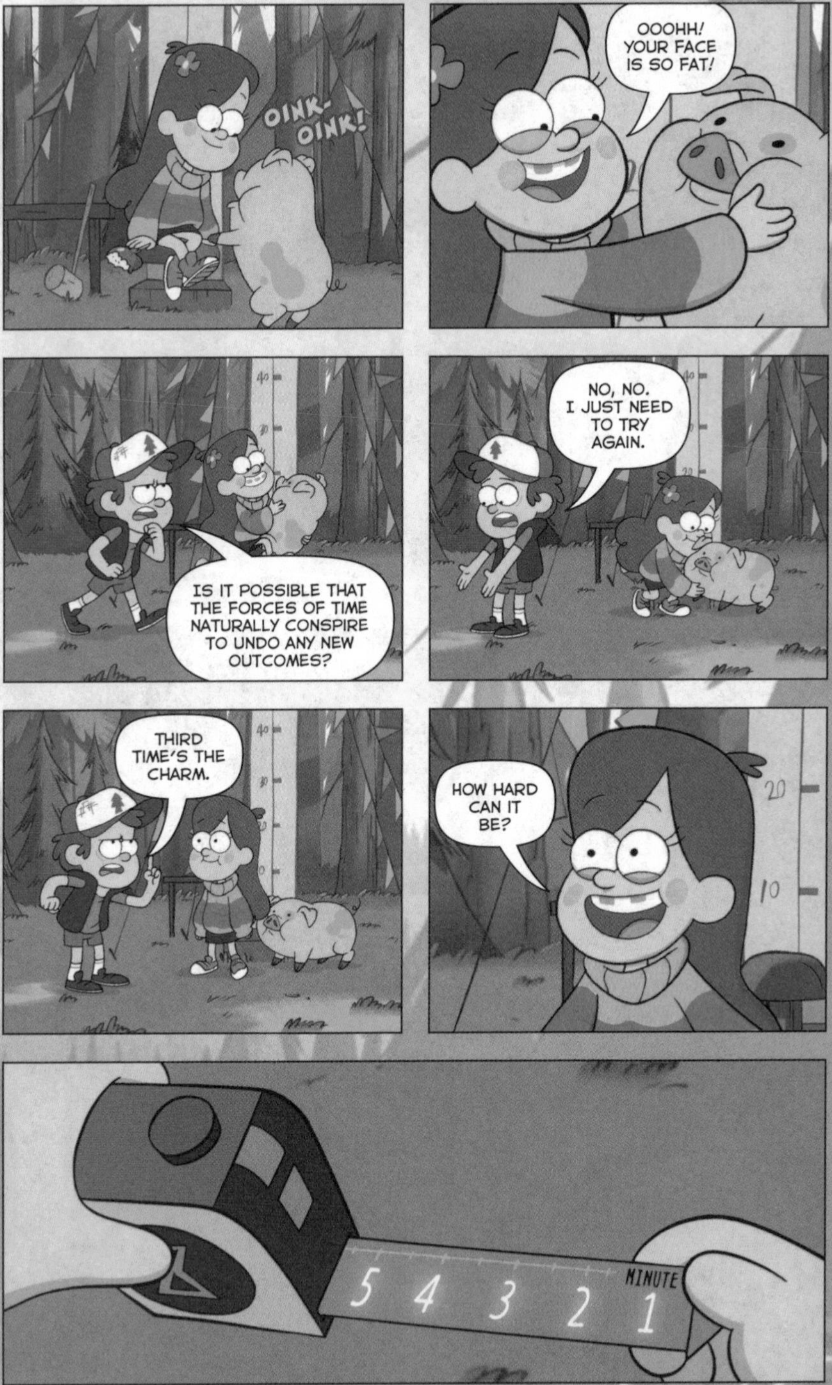
OINK-OINK!
OOOHH! YOUR FACE IS SO FAT!
IS IT POSSIBLE THAT THE FORCES OF TIME NATURALLY CONSPIRE TO UNDO ANY NEW OUTCOMES?
NO, NO. I JUST NEED TO TRY AGAIN.
THIRD TIME'S THE CHARM.
HOW HARD CAN IT BE?
MINUTE
5 4 3 2 1

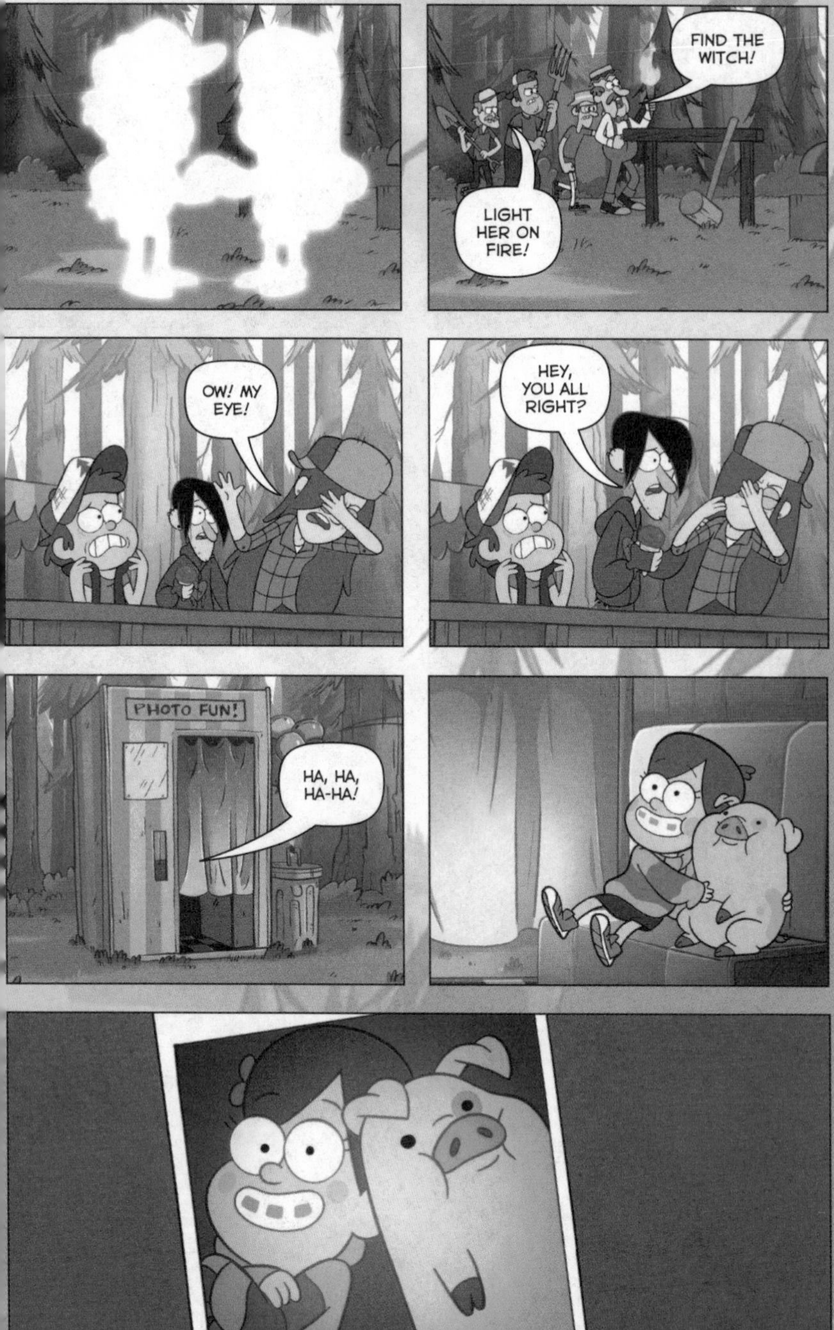
FIND THE WITCH!
LIGHT HER ON FIRE!
OW! MY EYE!
HEY, YOU ALL RIGHT?
PHOTO FUN!
HA, HA, HA-HA!

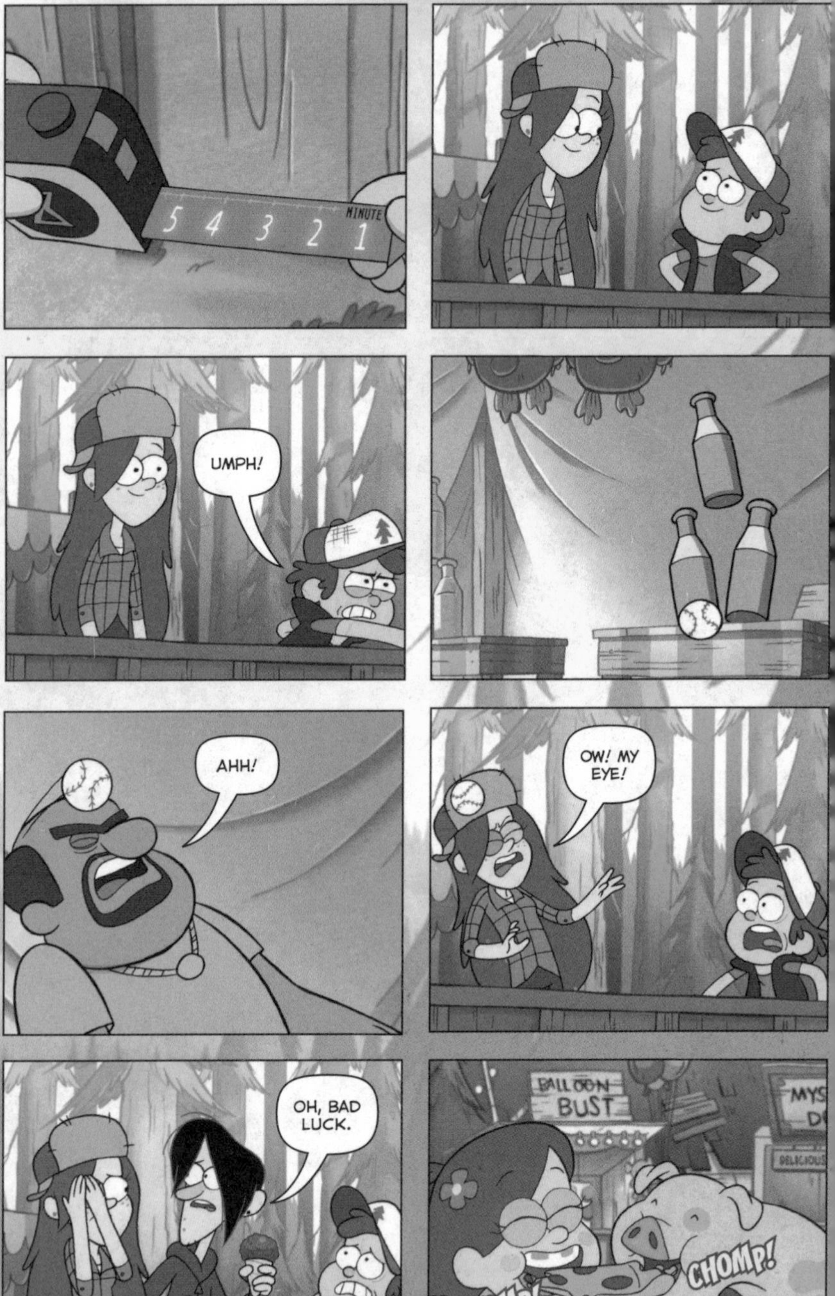

5 4 3 2 1
MINUTE
UMPH!
AHH!
OW! MY EYE!
OH, BAD LUCK.
BALLOON BUST
CHOMP!
CHOMP!

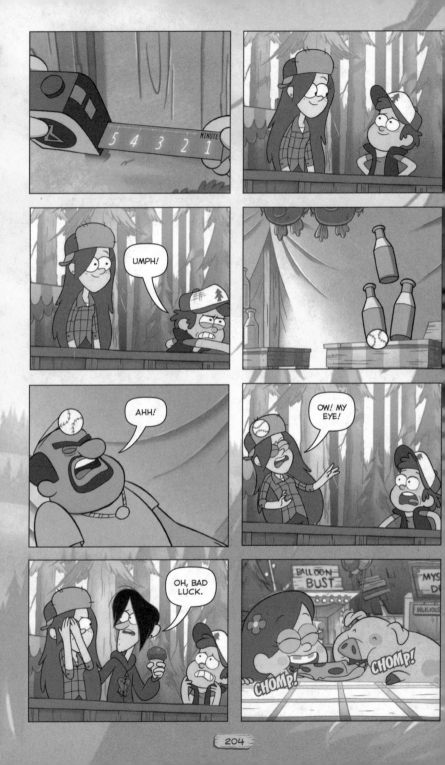

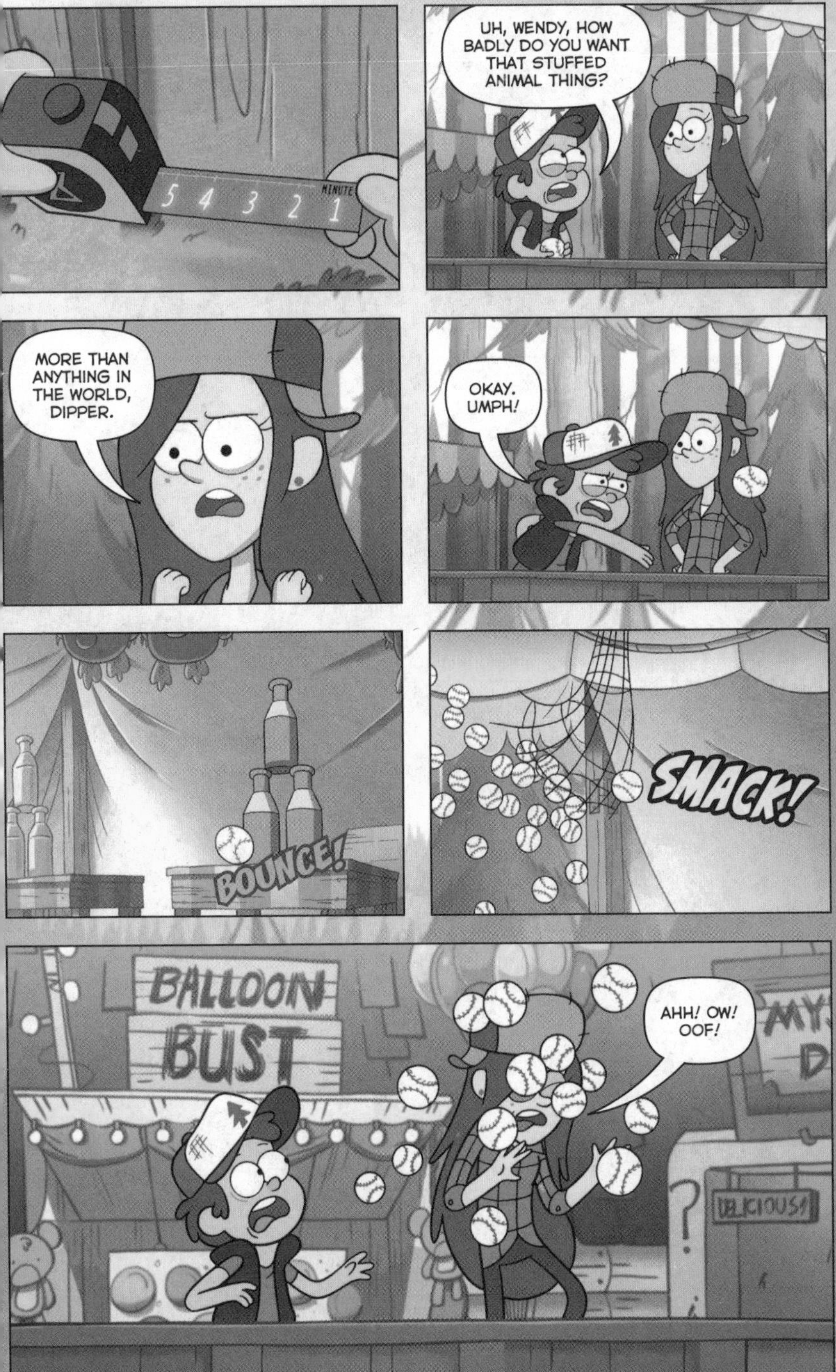
5 4 3 2 1
MINUTE
UH, WENDY, HOW BADLY DO YOU WANT THAT STUFFED ANIMAL THING?
MORE THAN ANYTHING IN THE WORLD, DIPPER.
OKAY. UMPH!
BOUNCE!
SMACK!
BALLOON BUST
AHH! OW! OOF!
DELICIOUS!

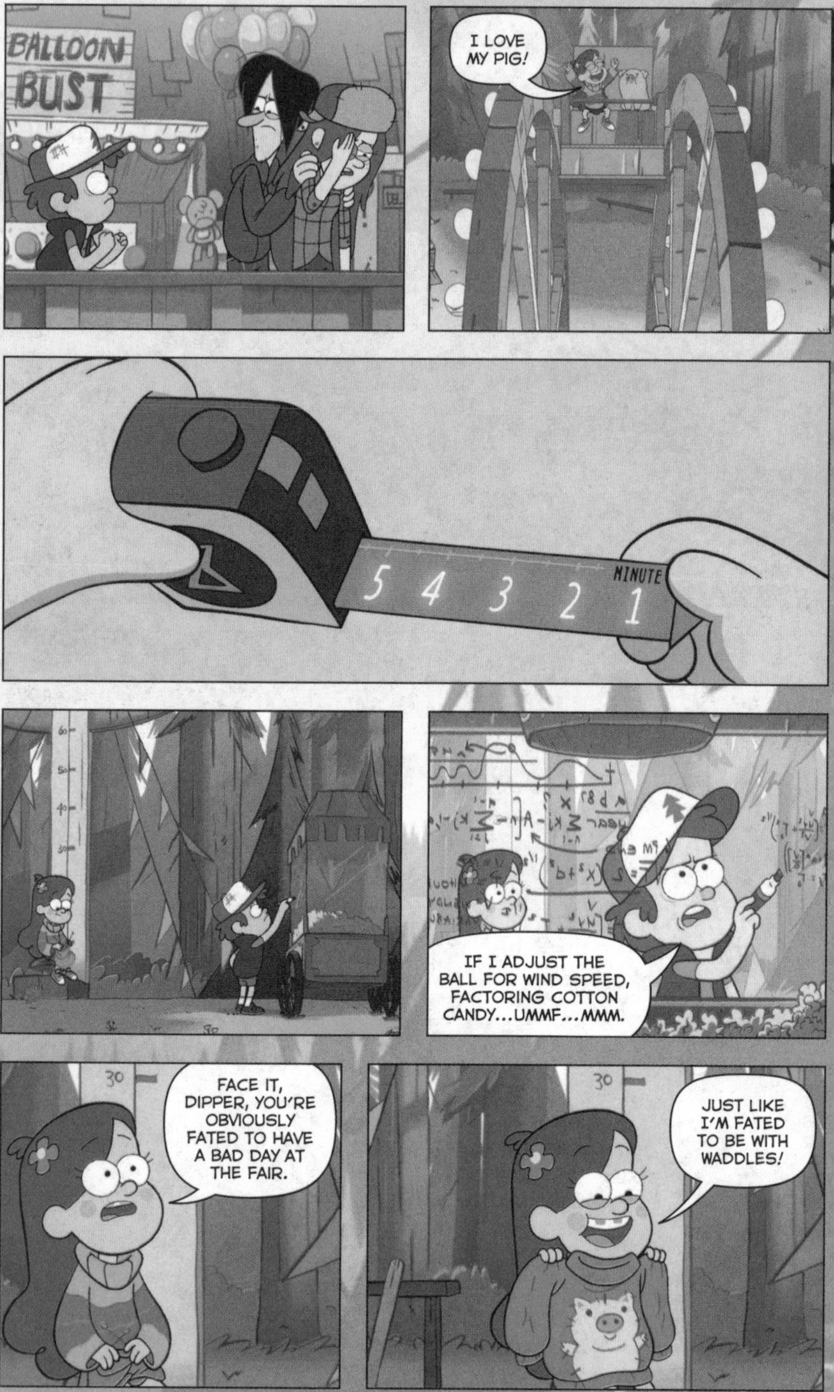
BALLOON BUST
I LOVE MY PIG!
MINUTE
5 4 3 2 1
IF I ADJUST THE BALL FOR WIND SPEED, FACTORING COTTON CANDY...UMMF...MMM.
FACE IT, DIPPER, YOU'RE OBVIOUSLY FATED TO HAVE A BAD DAY AT THE FAIR.
JUST LIKE I'M FATED TO BE WITH WADDLES!

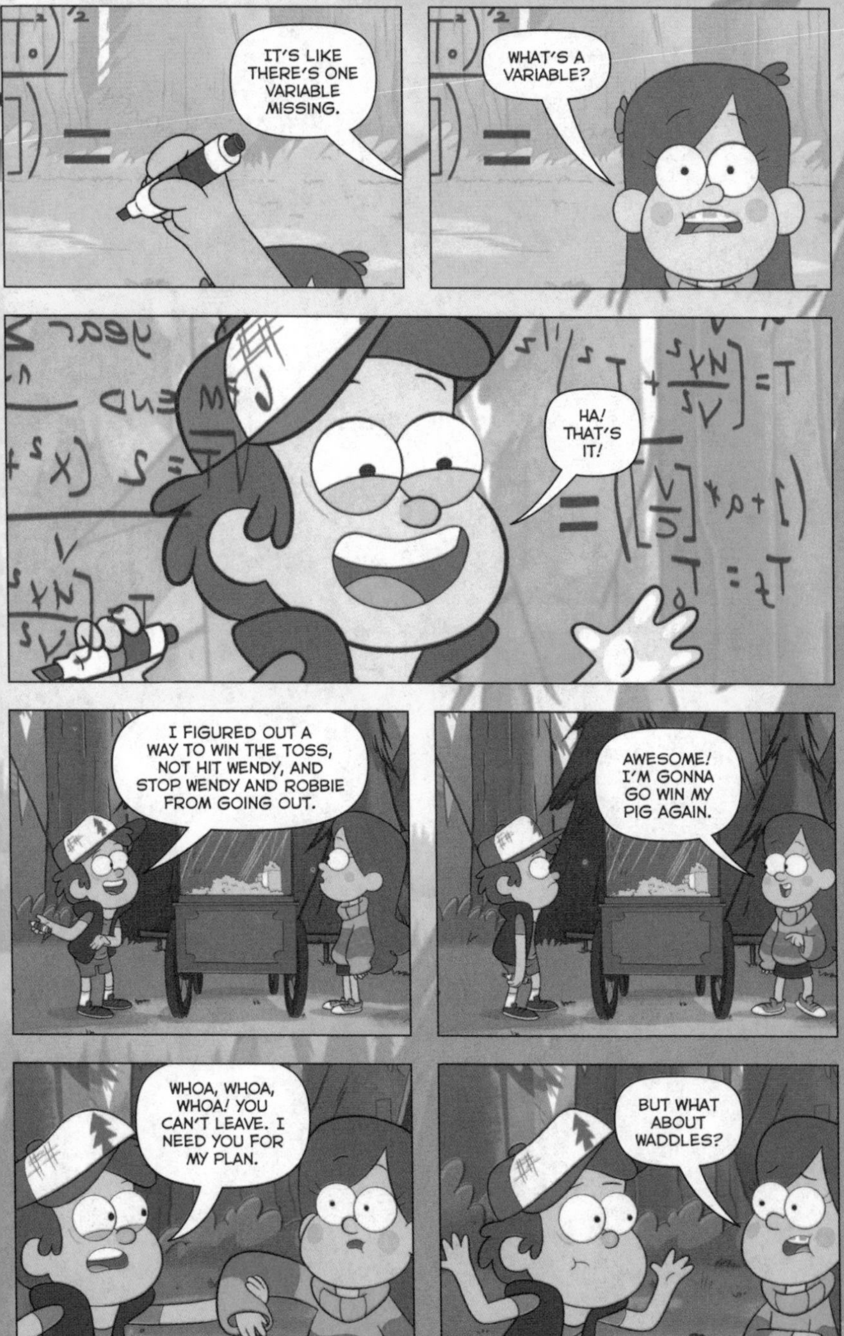
IT'S LIKE THERE'S ONE VARIABLE MISSING.
WHAT'S A VARIABLE?
HA! THAT'S IT!
I FIGURED OUT A WAY TO WIN THE TOSS, NOT HIT WENDY, AND STOP WENDY AND ROBBIE FROM GOING OUT.
AWESOME! I'M GONNA GO WIN MY PIG AGAIN.
WHOA, WHOA, WHOA! YOU CAN'T LEAVE. I NEED YOU FOR MY PLAN.
BUT WHAT ABOUT WADDLES?

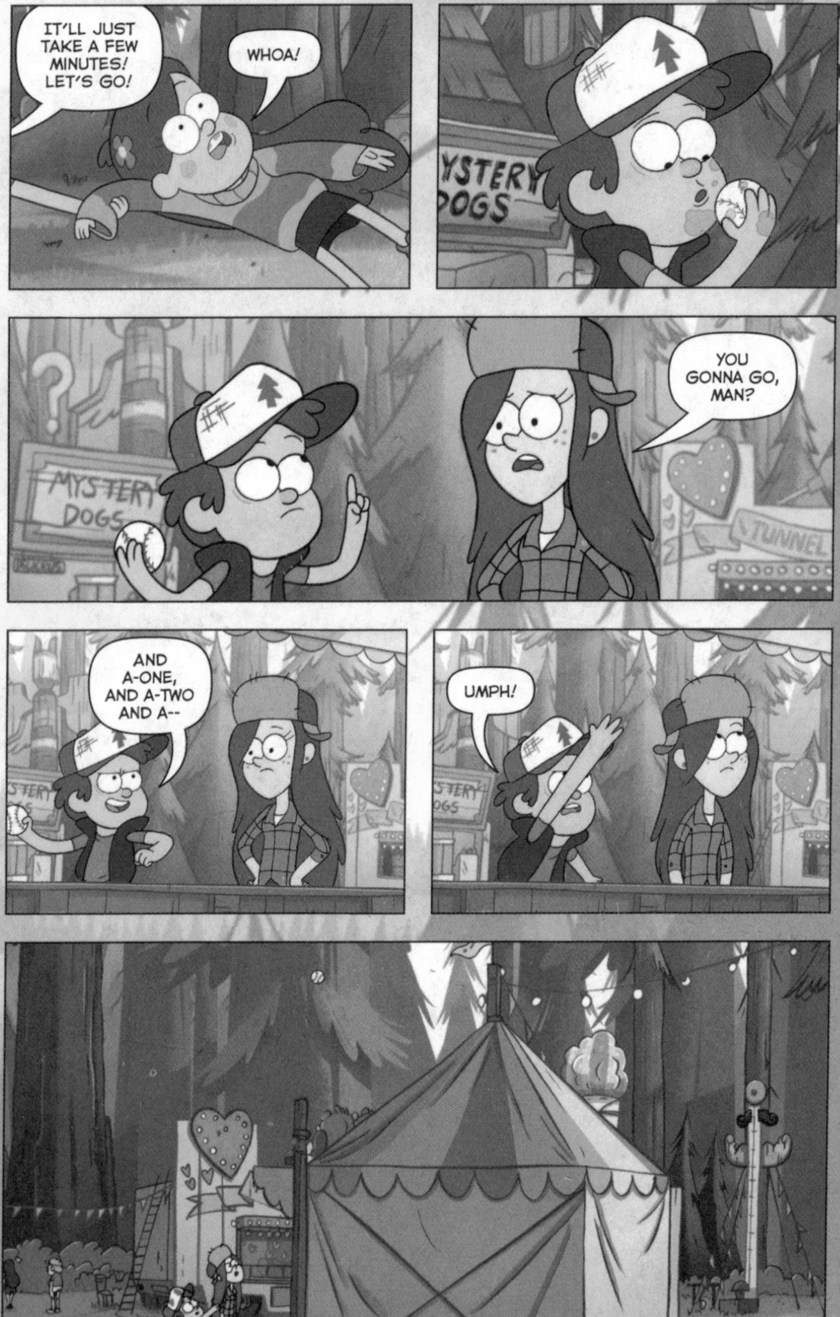
IT'LL JUST TAKE A FEW MINUTES! LET'S GO!
WHOA!
YSTERY
OGS
MYSTERY
DOGS
YOU GONNA GO, MAN?
TUNNEL
AND A-ONE, AND A-TWO AND A--
UMPH!

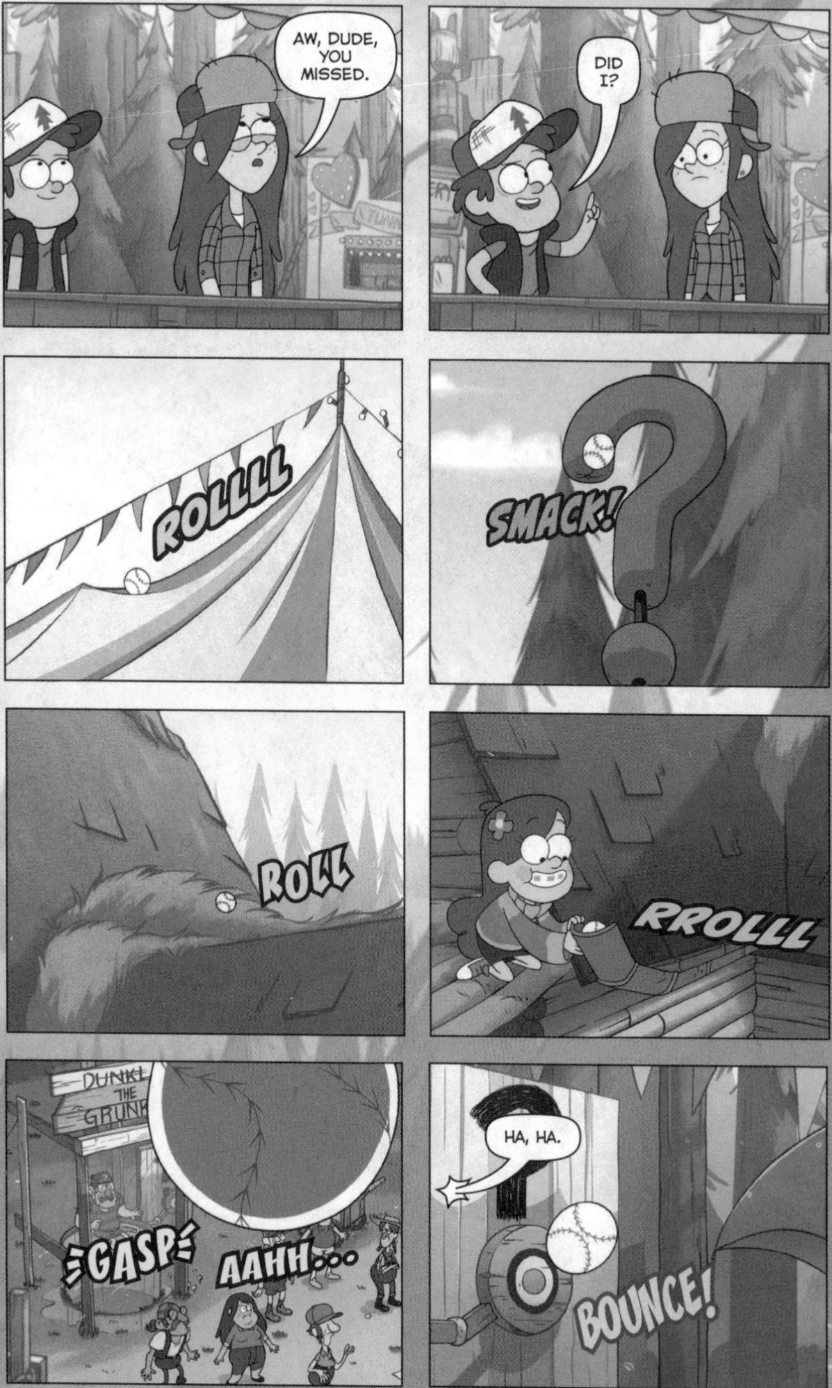
AW, DUDE, YOU MISSED.
DID I?
ROLLLL
SMACK!
ROLL
RROLLL
DUNK THE GRUNK
GASP
AAHH...
HA, HA.
BOUNCE!

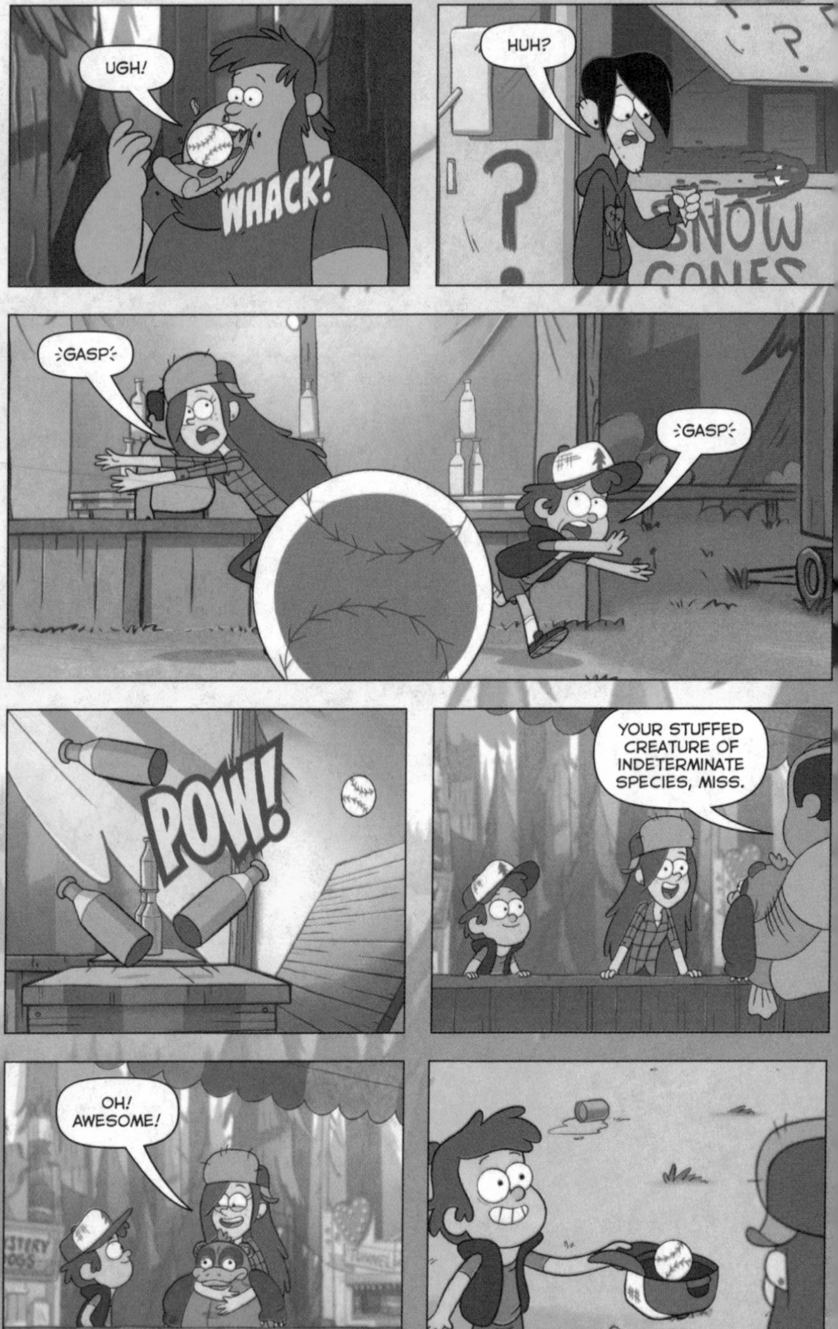
UGH!
WHACK!
HUH?
SNOW CONES
GASP
GASP
POW!
YOUR STUFFED CREATURE OF INDETERMINATE SPECIES, MISS.
OH! AWESOME!

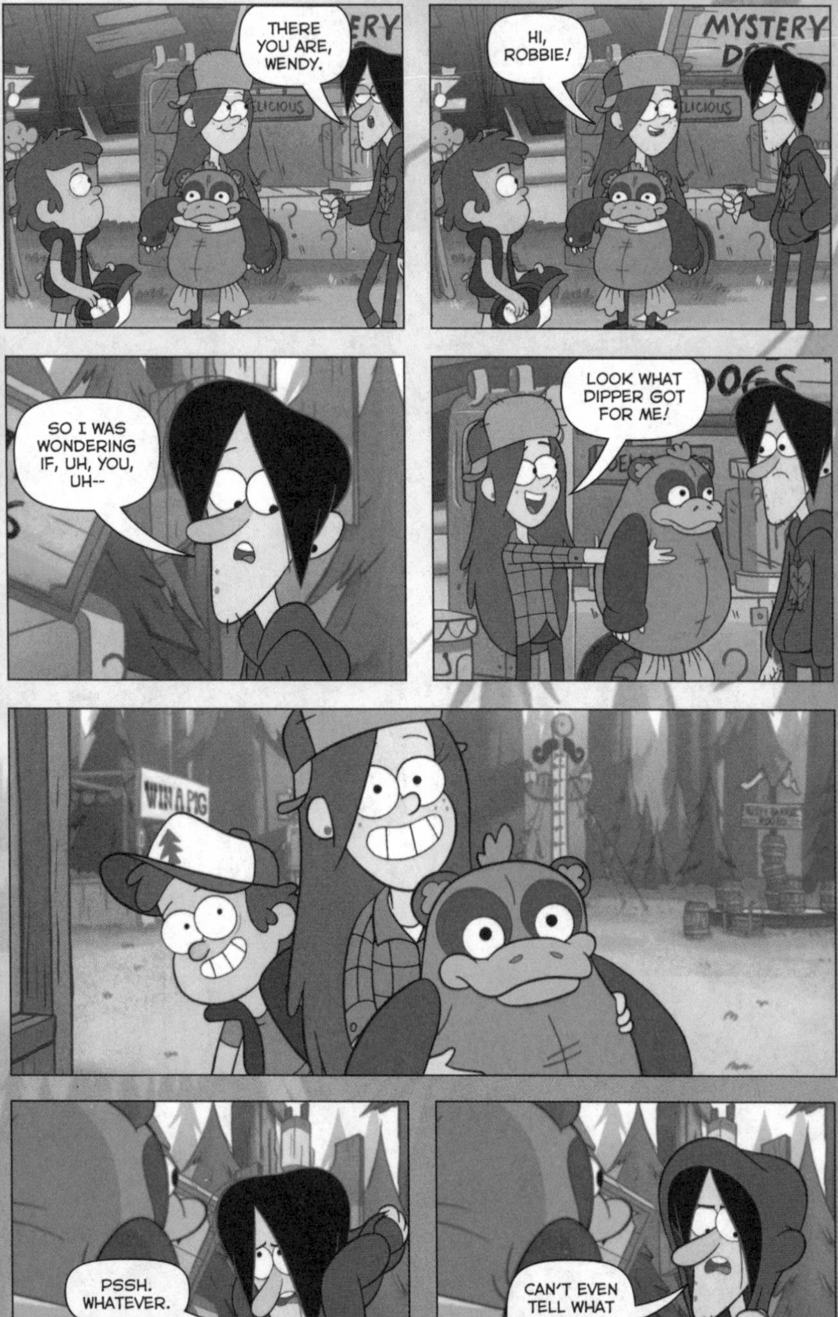
THERE YOU ARE, WENDY.
HI, ROBBIE!
SO I WAS WONDERING IF, UH, YOU, UH--
LOOK WHAT DIPPER GOT FOR ME!
WIN A PIG
PSSH. WHATEVER.
CAN'T EVEN TELL WHAT SPECIES IT IS.

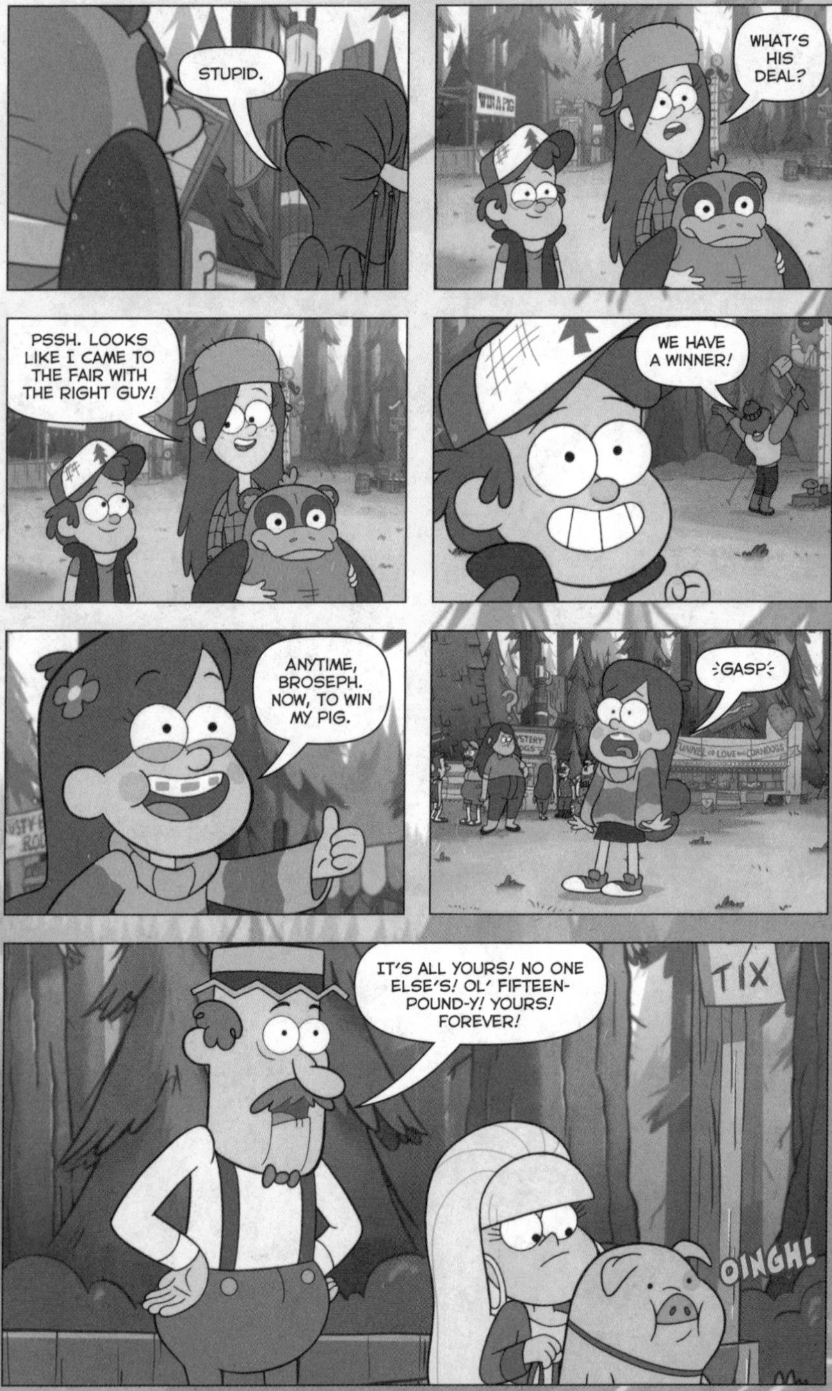
STUPID.
WHAT'S HIS DEAL?
PSSH. LOOKS LIKE I CAME TO THE FAIR WITH THE RIGHT GUY!
WE HAVE A WINNER!
ANYTIME, BROSEPH. NOW, TO WIN MY PIG.
GASP
IT'S ALL YOURS! NO ONE ELSE'S! OL' FIFTEEN-POUND-Y! YOURS! FOREVER!
TIX
OINGH!

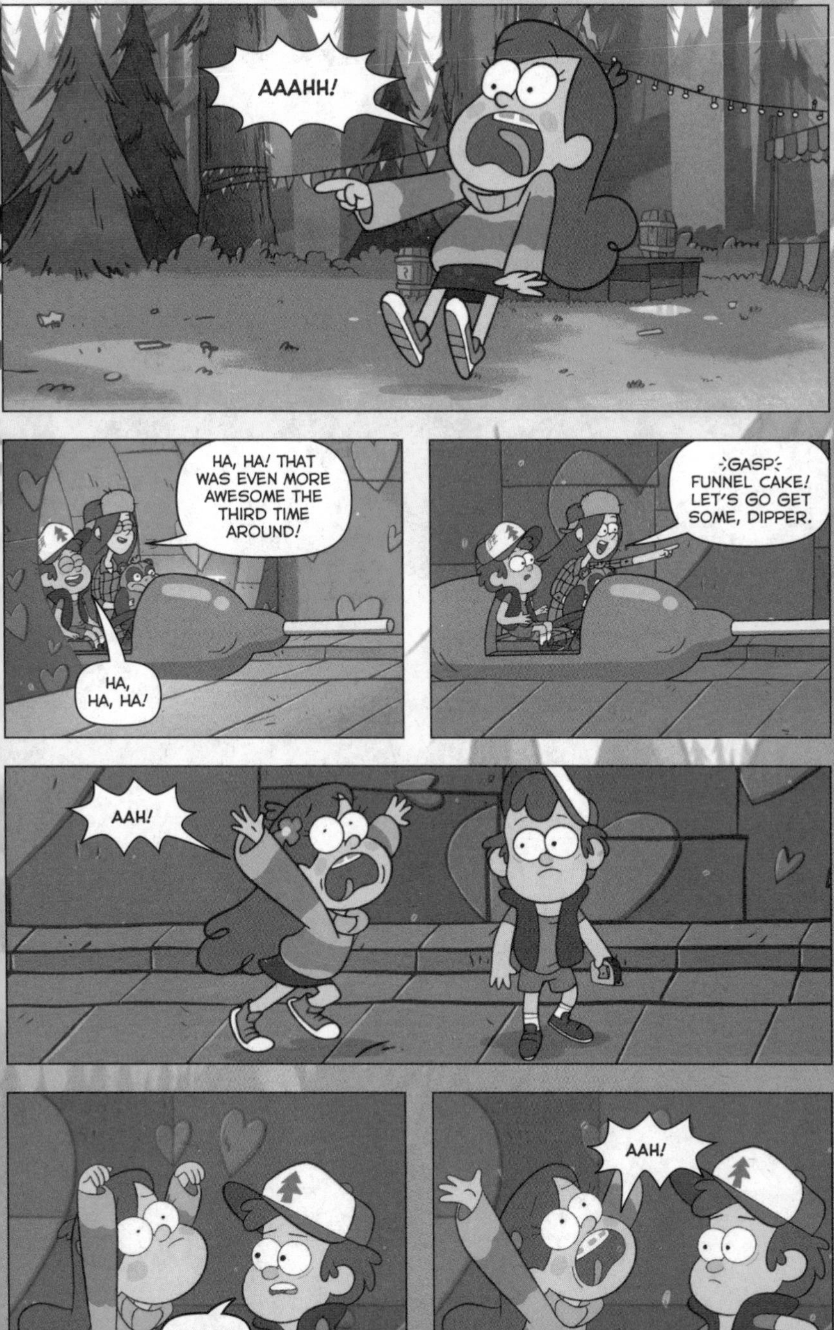
AAAHH!
HA, HA! THAT WAS EVEN MORE AWESOME THE THIRD TIME AROUND!
HA, HA, HA!
GASP
FUNNEL CAKE! LET'S GO GET SOME, DIPPER.
AAH!
WHAT'S WR--
AAH!

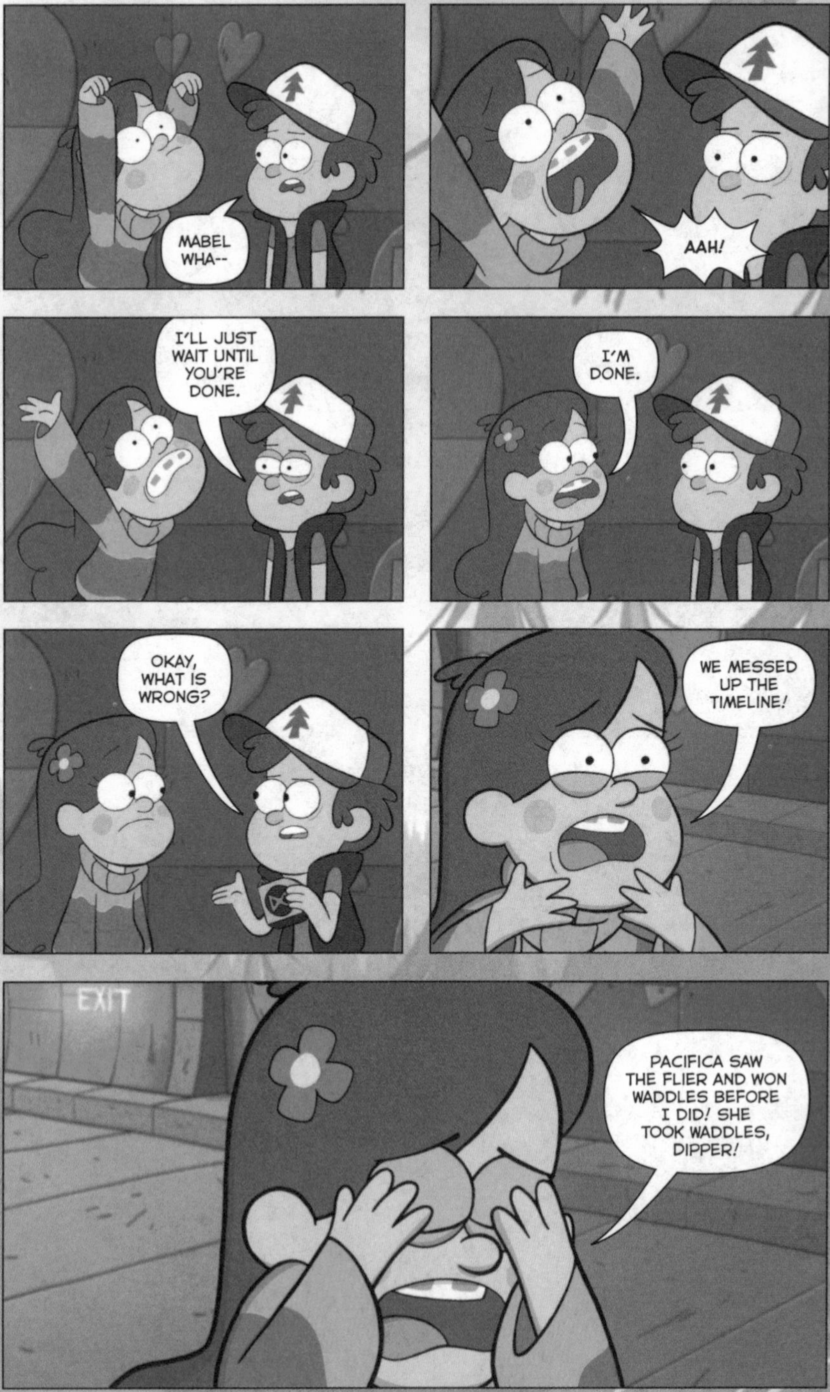
MABEL WHA--
AAH!
I'LL JUST WAIT UNTIL YOU'RE DONE.
I'M DONE.
OKAY, WHAT IS WRONG?
WE MESSED UP THE TIMELINE!
EXIT
PACIFICA SAW THE FLIER AND WON WADDLES BEFORE I DID! SHE TOOK WADDLES, DIPPER!

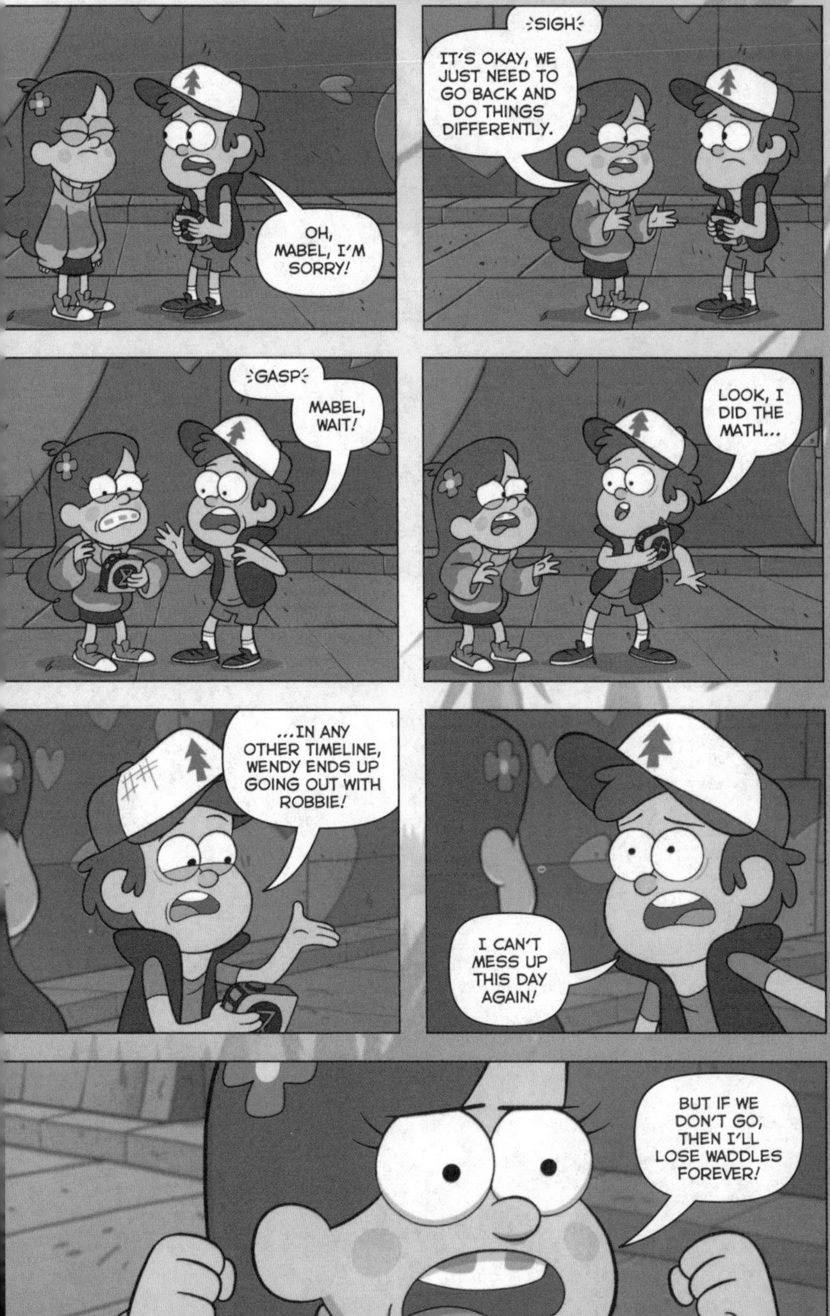

OH, MABEL, I'M SORRY!
-SIGH-
IT'S OKAY, WE JUST NEED TO GO BACK AND DO THINGS DIFFERENTLY.
-GASP-
MABEL, WAIT!
LOOK, I DID THE MATH...
...IN ANY OTHER TIMELINE, WENDY ENDS UP GOING OUT WITH ROBBIE!
I CAN'T MESS UP THIS DAY AGAIN!
BUT IF WE DON'T GO, THEN I'LL LOSE WADDLES FOREVER!

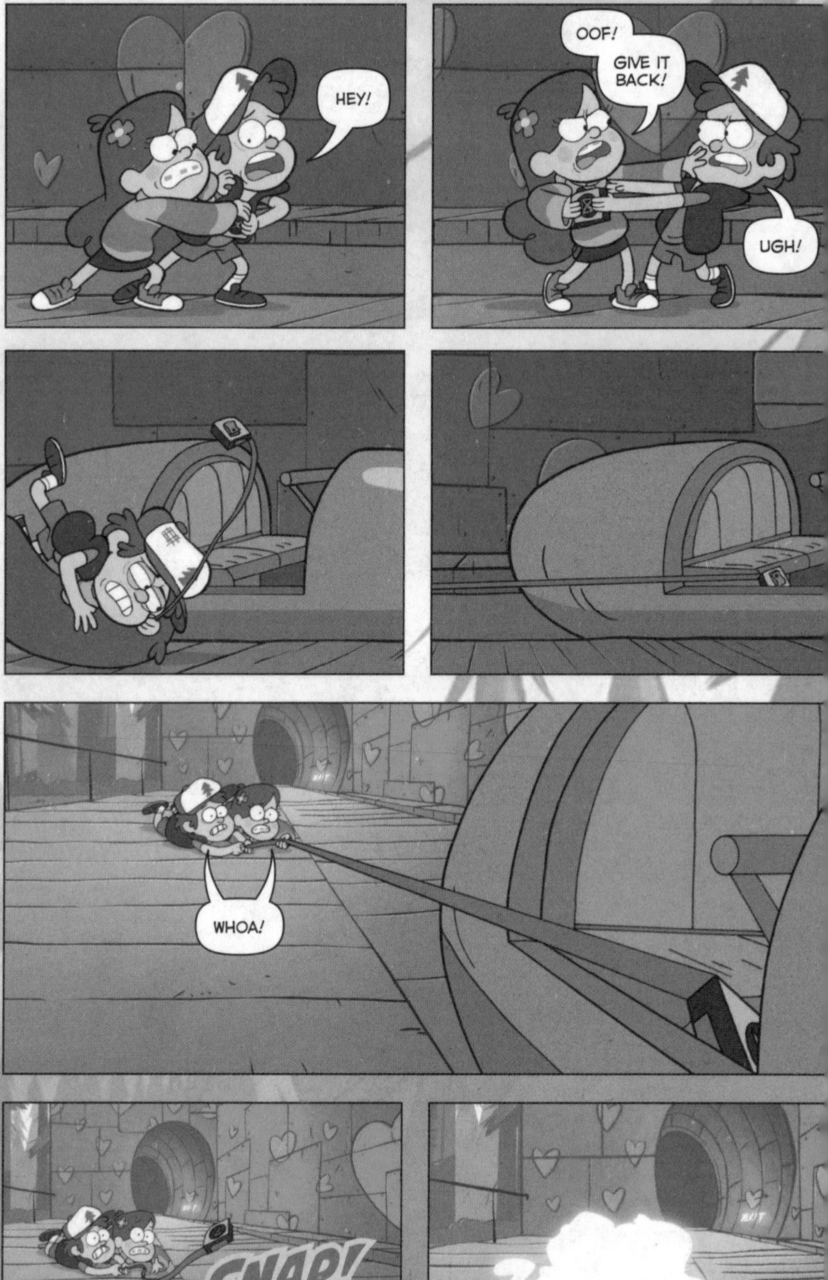
HEY!
OOF!
GIVE IT BACK!
UGH!
WHOA!
SNAP!

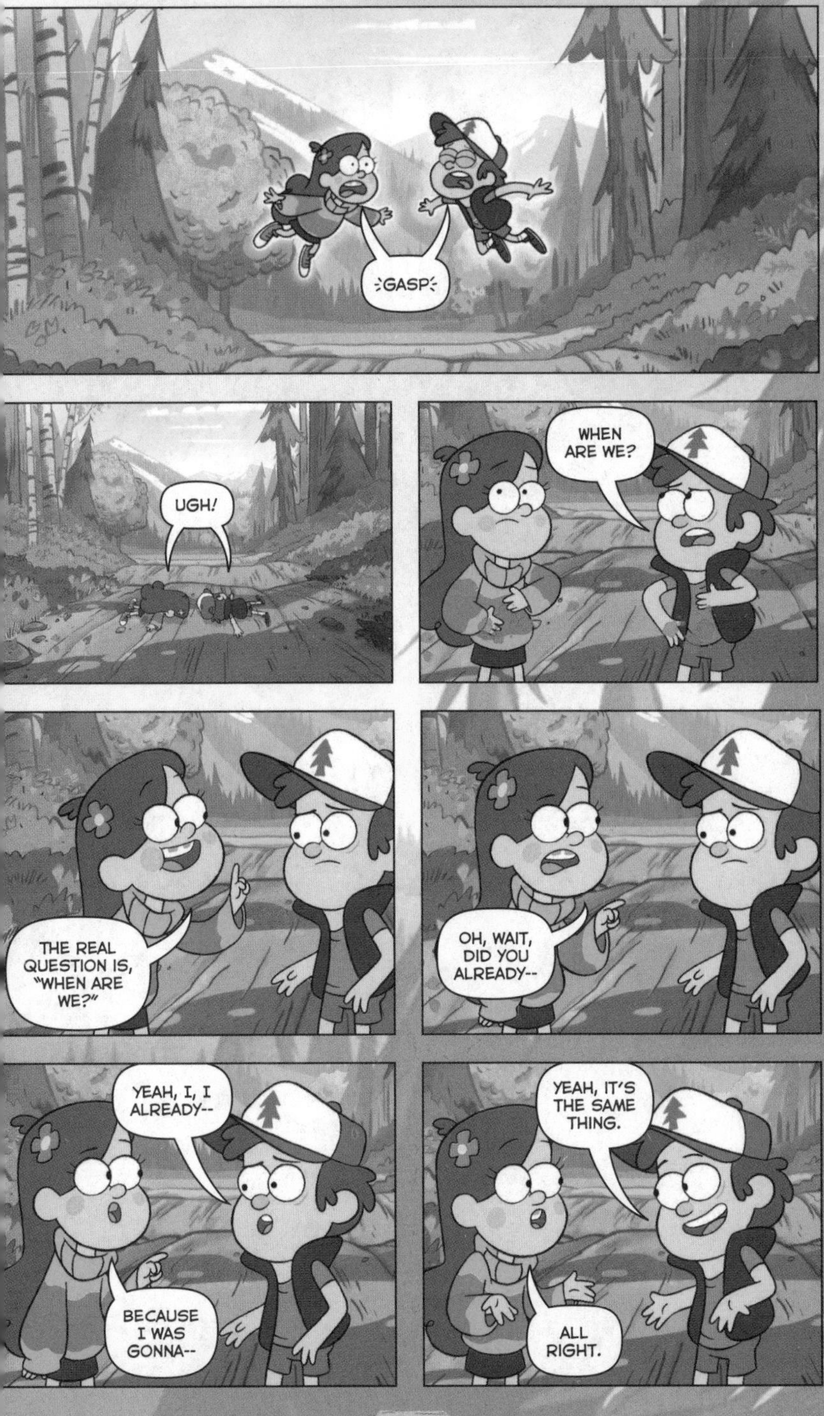
GASP
UGH!
WHEN ARE WE?
THE REAL QUESTION IS, "WHEN ARE WE?"
OH, WAIT, DID YOU ALREADY--
YEAH, I, I ALREADY--
BECAUSE I WAS GONNA--
YEAH, IT'S THE SAME THING.
ALL RIGHT.

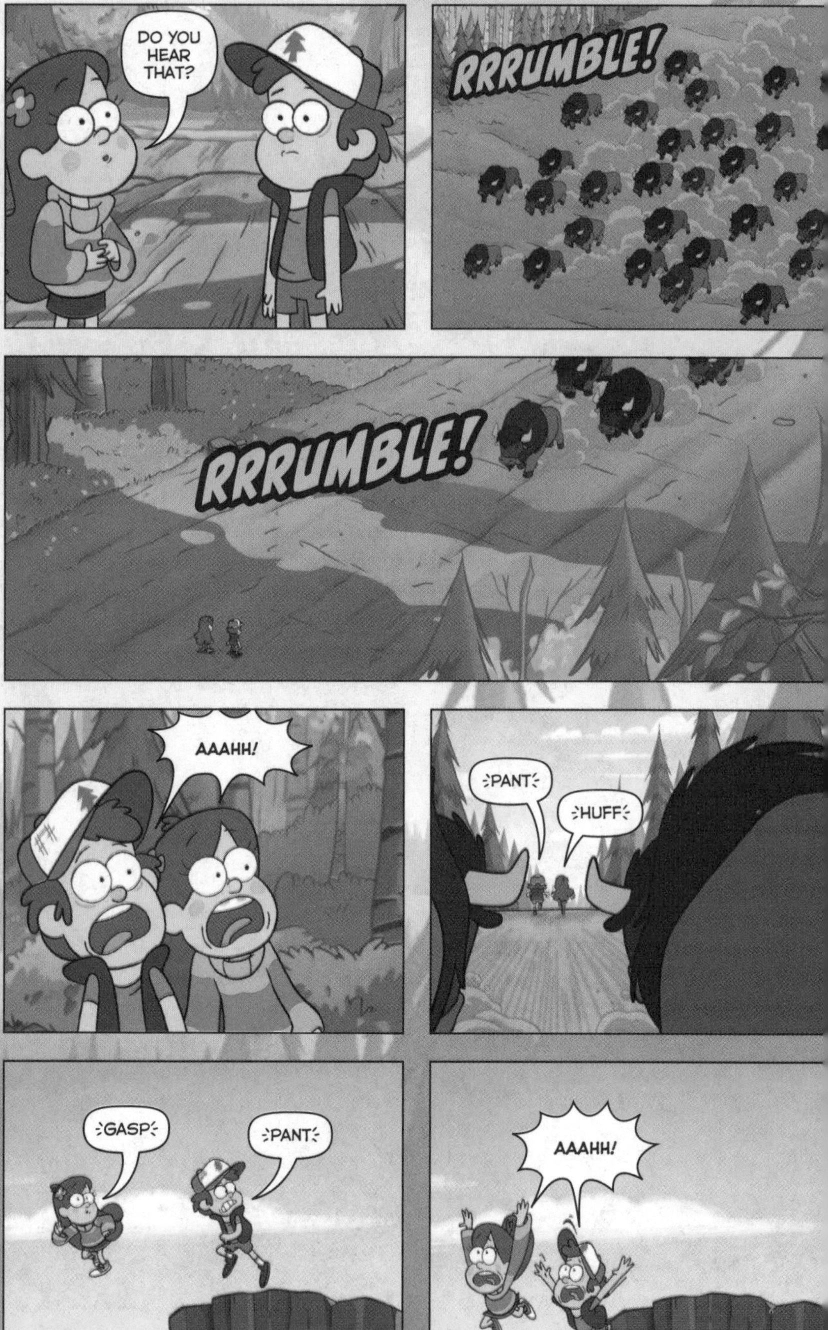

DO YOU HEAR THAT?
RRRUMBLE!
RRRUMBLE!
AAAHH!
PANT
HUFF
GASP
PANT
AAAHH!

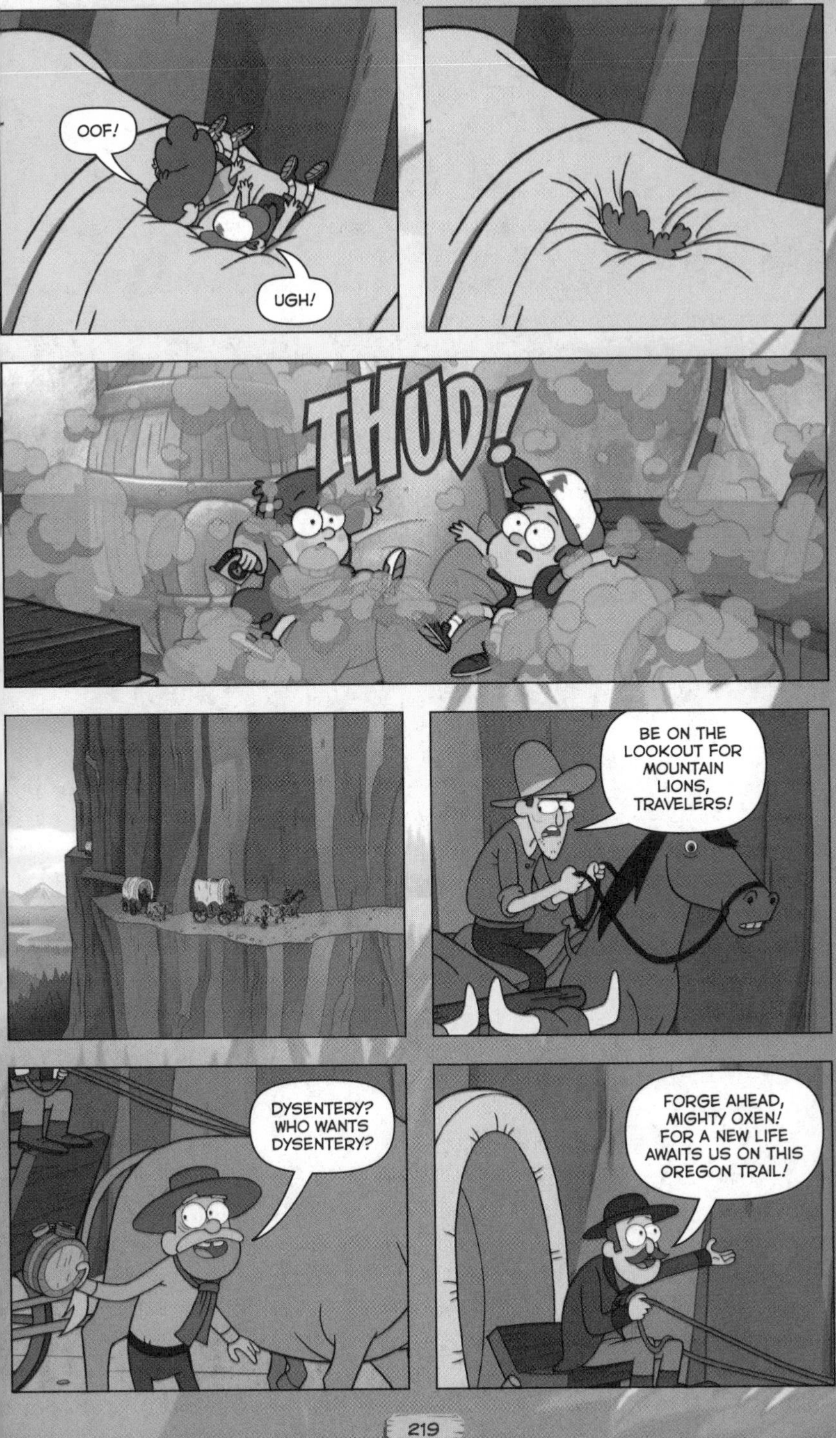
OOF!
UGH!
THUD!
BE ON THE LOOKOUT FOR MOUNTAIN LIONS, TRAVELERS!
DYSENTERY? WHO WANTS DYSENTERY?
FORGE AHEAD, MIGHTY OXEN! FOR A NEW LIFE AWAITS US ON THIS OREGON TRAIL!

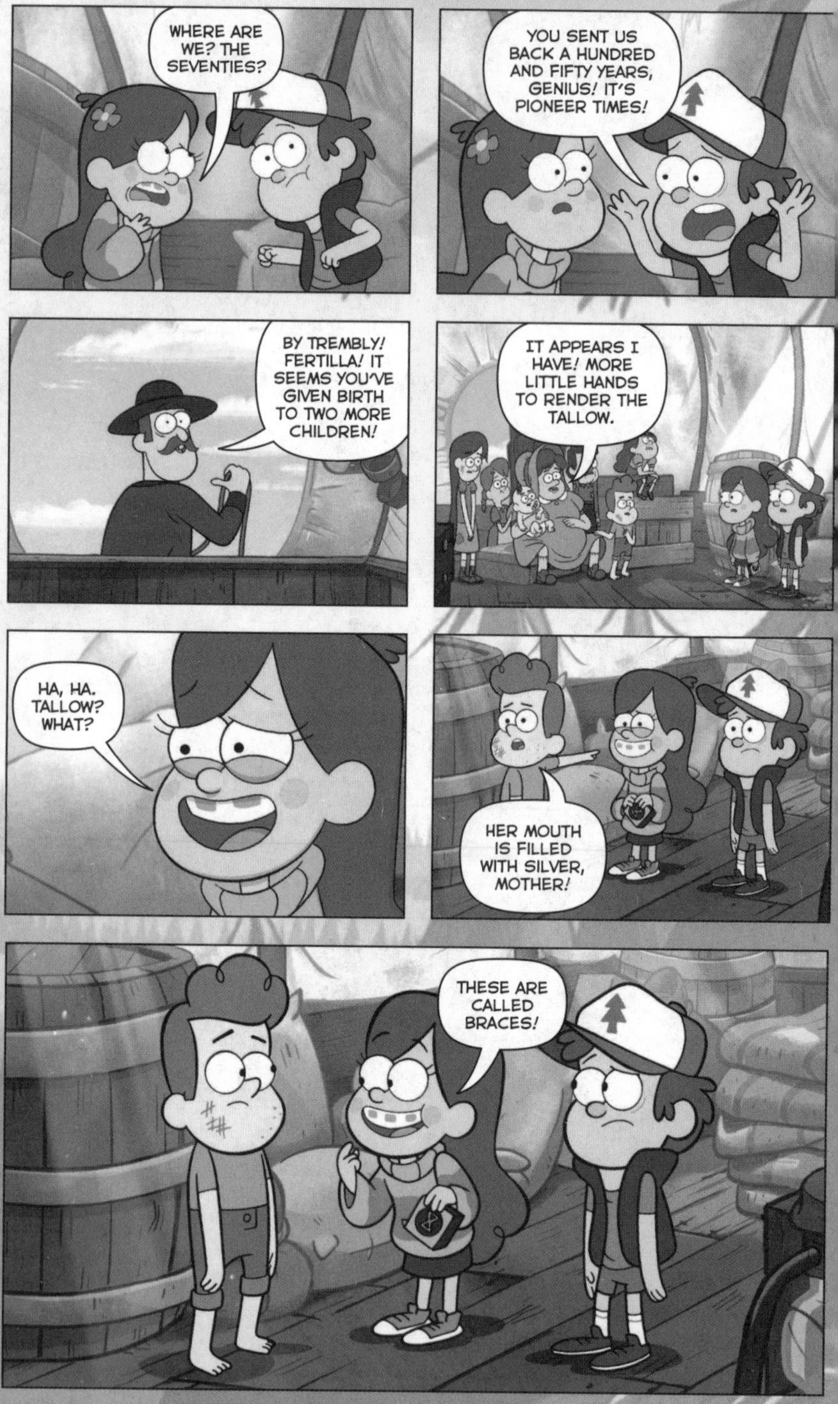
WHERE ARE WE? THE SEVENTIES?
YOU SENT US BACK A HUNDRED AND FIFTY YEARS, GENIUS! IT'S PIONEER TIMES!
BY TREMBLY! FERTILLA! IT SEEMS YOU'VE GIVEN BIRTH TO TWO MORE CHILDREN!
IT APPEARS I HAVE! MORE LITTLE HANDS TO RENDER THE TALLOW.
HA, HA. TALLOW? WHAT?
HER MOUTH IS FILLED WITH SILVER, MOTHER!
THESE ARE CALLED BRACES!

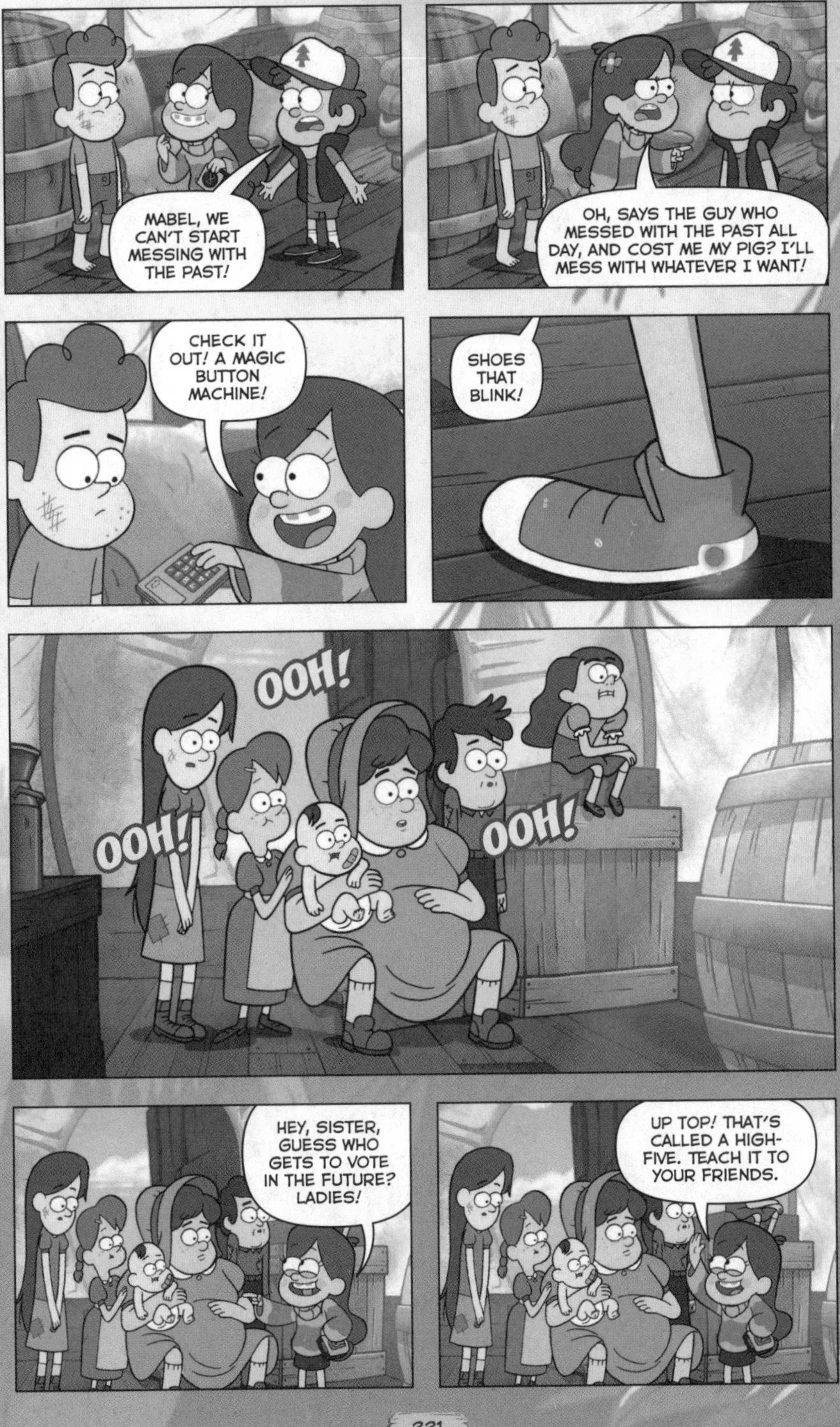
MABEL, WE CAN'T START MESSING WITH THE PAST!
OH, SAYS THE GUY WHO MESSED WITH THE PAST ALL DAY, AND COST ME MY PIG? I'LL MESS WITH WHATEVER I WANT!
CHECK IT OUT! A MAGIC BUTTON MACHINE!
SHOES THAT BLINK!
OOH!
OOH!
OOH!
HEY, SISTER, GUESS WHO GETS TO VOTE IN THE FUTURE? LADIES!
UP TOP! THAT'S CALLED A HIGH-FIVE. TEACH IT TO YOUR FRIENDS.

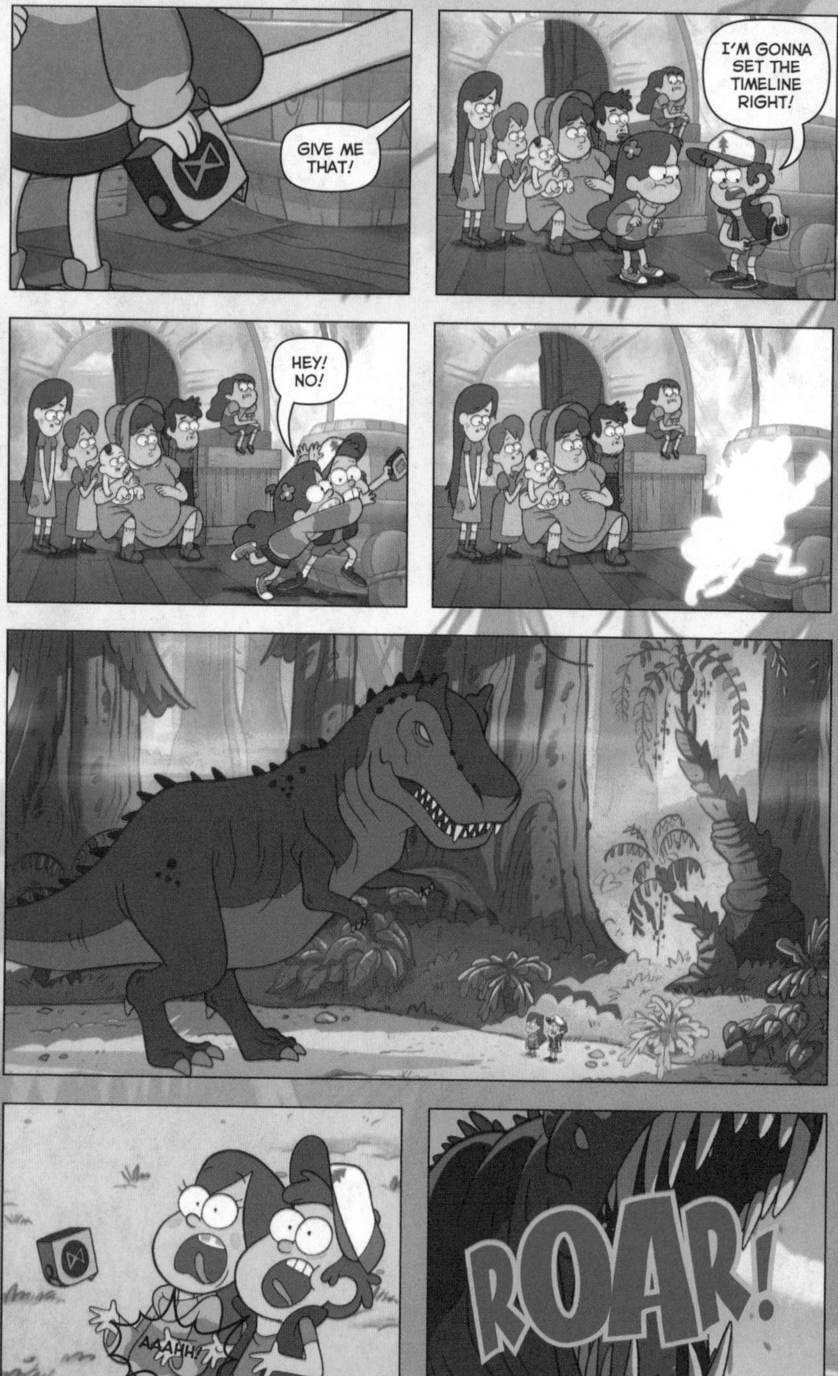
GIVE ME THAT!
I'M GONNA SET THE TIMELINE RIGHT!
HEY! NO!
AAAHH!
ROAR!

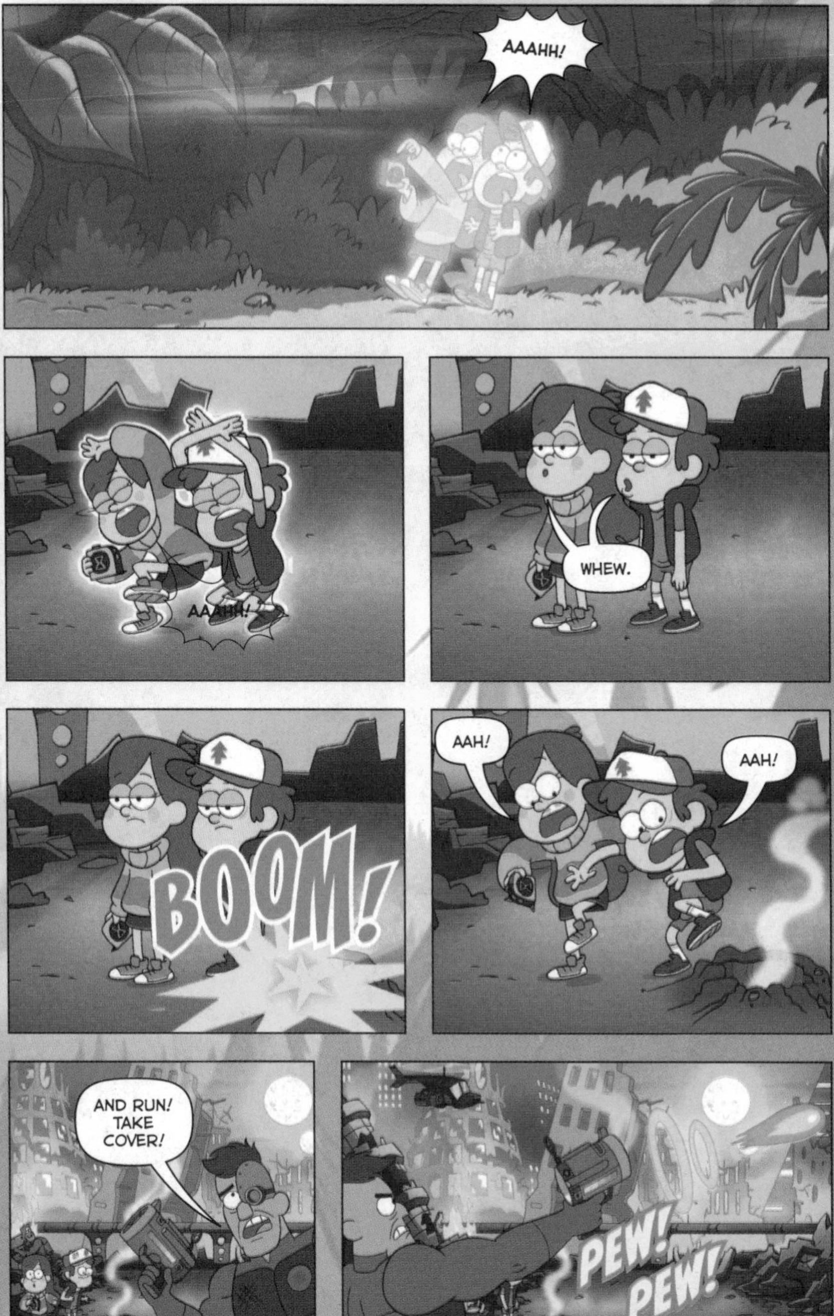
AAAHH!
AAAHH!
WHEW.
BOOM!
AAH!
AAH!
AND RUN! TAKE COVER!
PEW! PEW!

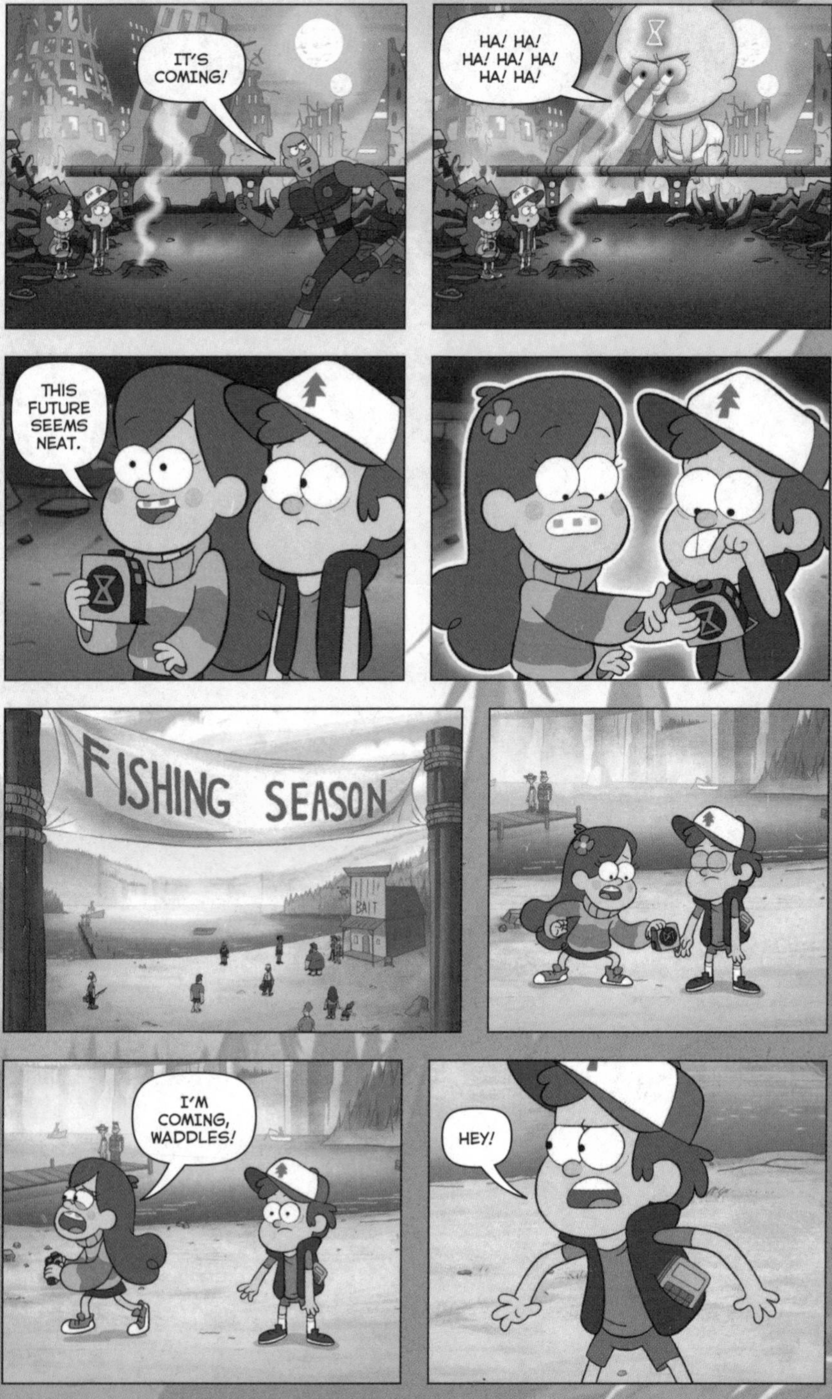
IT'S COMING!
HA! HA! HA! HA! HA! HA! HA!
THIS FUTURE SEEMS NEAT.
FISHING SEASON
BAIT
I'M COMING, WADDLES!
HEY!

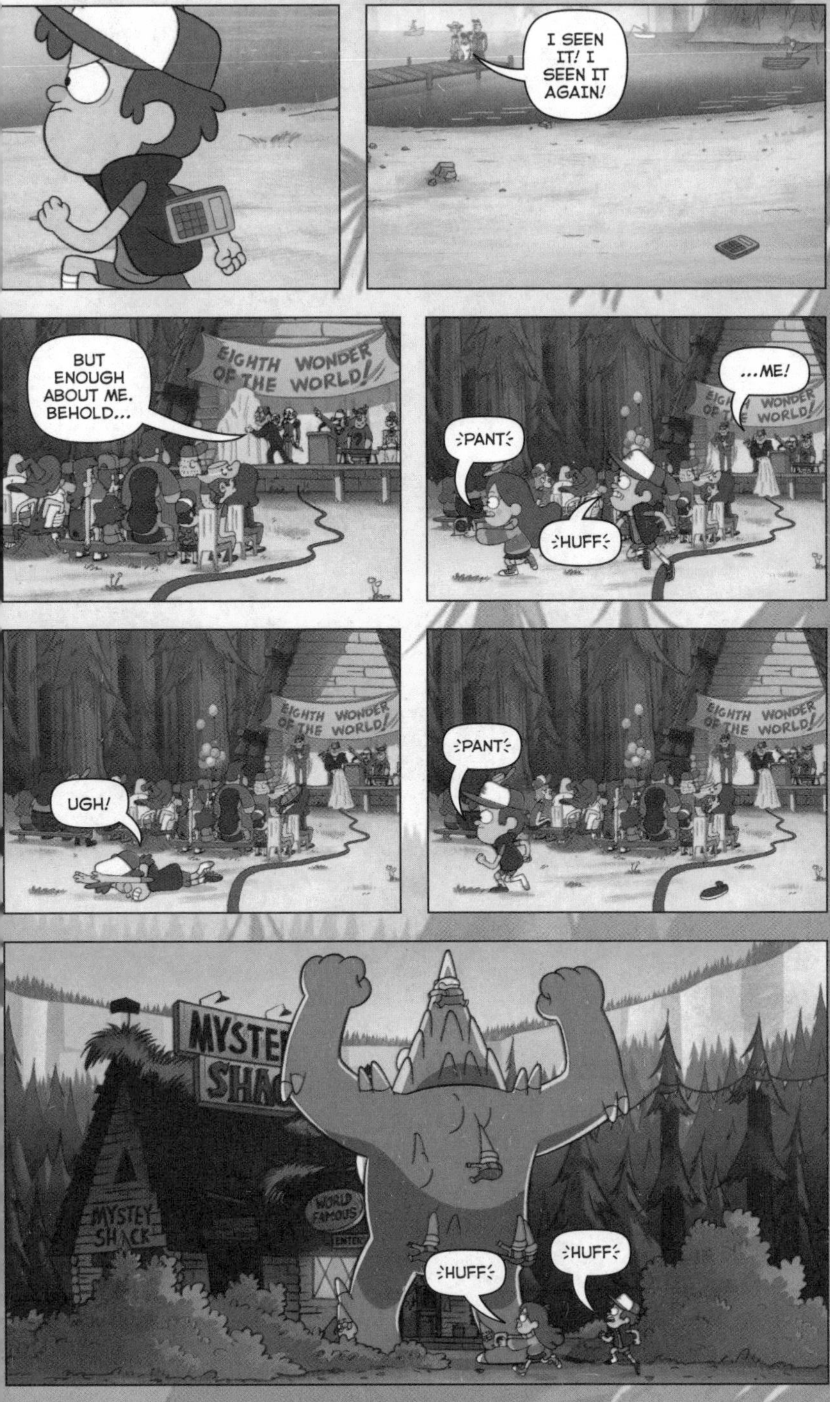
I SEEN IT! I SEEN IT AGAIN!
EIGHTH WONDER OF THE WORLD!
BUT ENOUGH ABOUT ME. BEHOLD...
EIGHTH WONDER OF THE WORLD!
...ME!
PANT
HUFF
EIGHTH WONDER OF THE WORLD!
UGH!
EIGHTH WONDER OF THE WORLD!
PANT
MYSTE
SHAC
MYSTEY SHACK
WORLD FAMOUS
ENTER
HUFF
HUFF

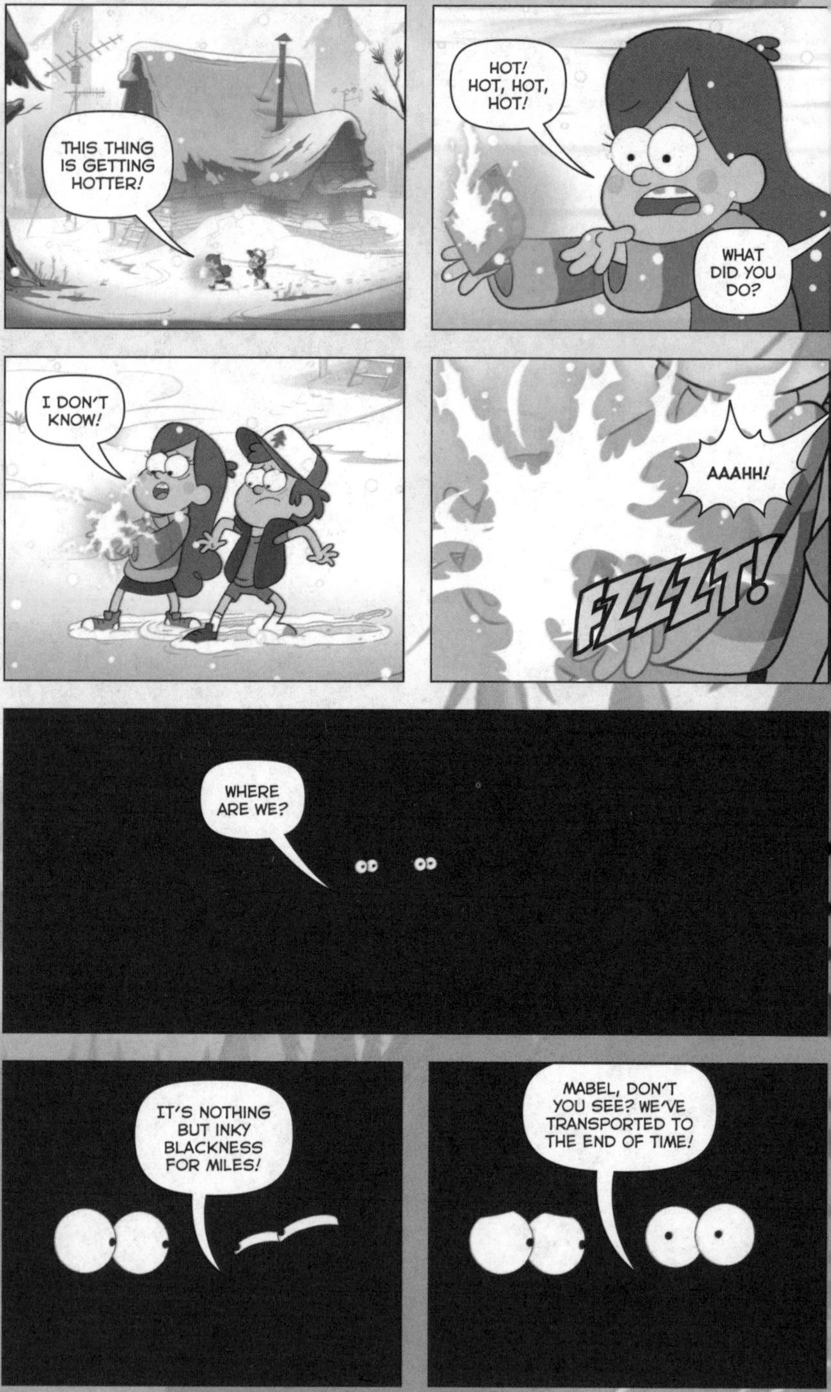
THIS THING IS GETTING HOTTER!
HOT! HOT, HOT, HOT!
WHAT DID YOU DO?
I DON'T KNOW!
AAAHH!
FZZZT!
WHERE ARE WE?
IT'S NOTHING BUT INKY BLACKNESS FOR MILES!
MABEL, DON'T YOU SEE? WE'VE TRANSPORTED TO THE END OF TIME!

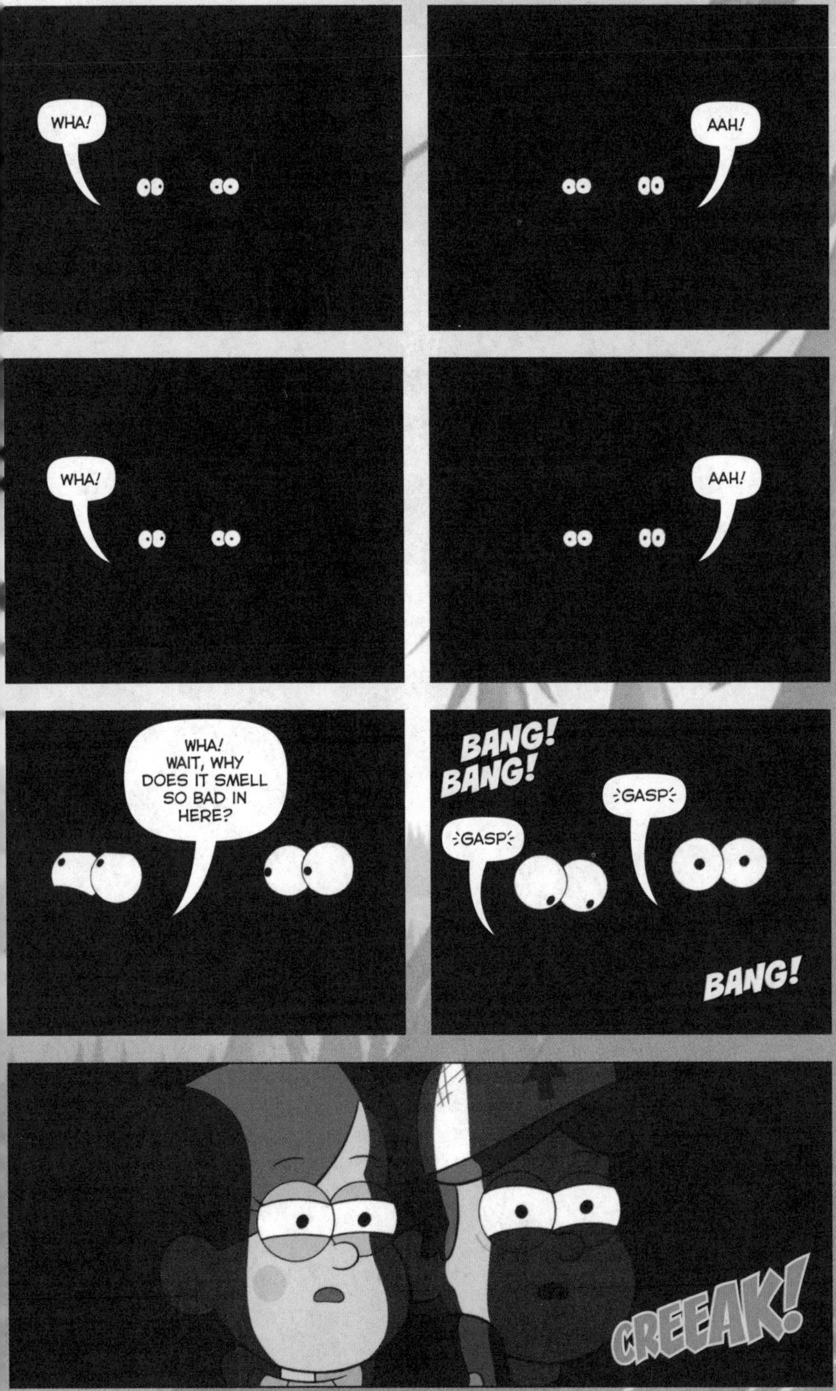
WHA!
AAH!
WHA!
AAH!
WHA! WAIT, WHY DOES IT SMELL SO BAD IN HERE?
BANG! BANG!
GASP
GASP
BANG!
CREEAK!

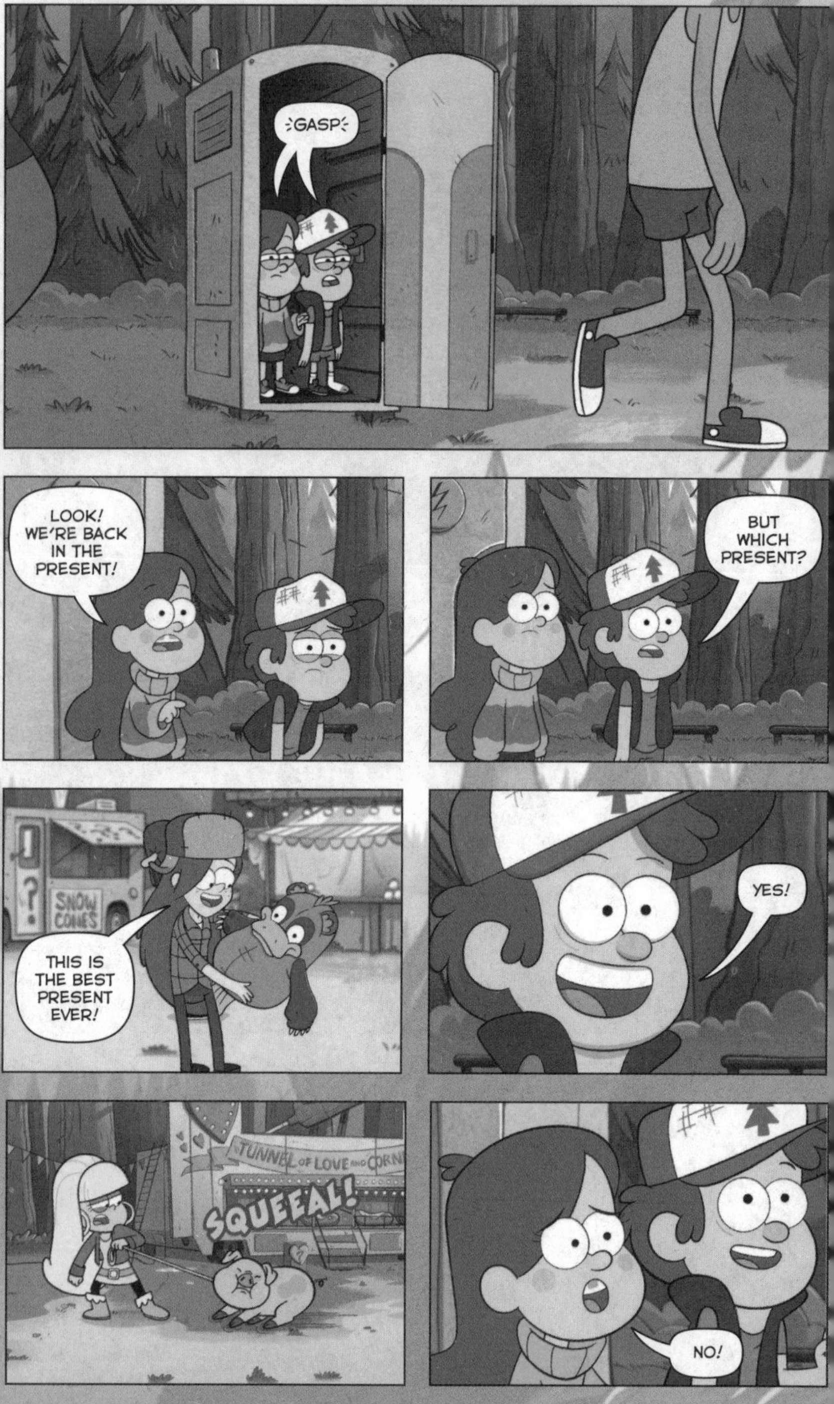
GASP
LOOK! WE'RE BACK IN THE PRESENT!
BUT WHICH PRESENT?
SNOW CONES
THIS IS THE BEST PRESENT EVER!
YES!
TUNNEL OF LOVE AND CORN
SQUEEAL!
NO!

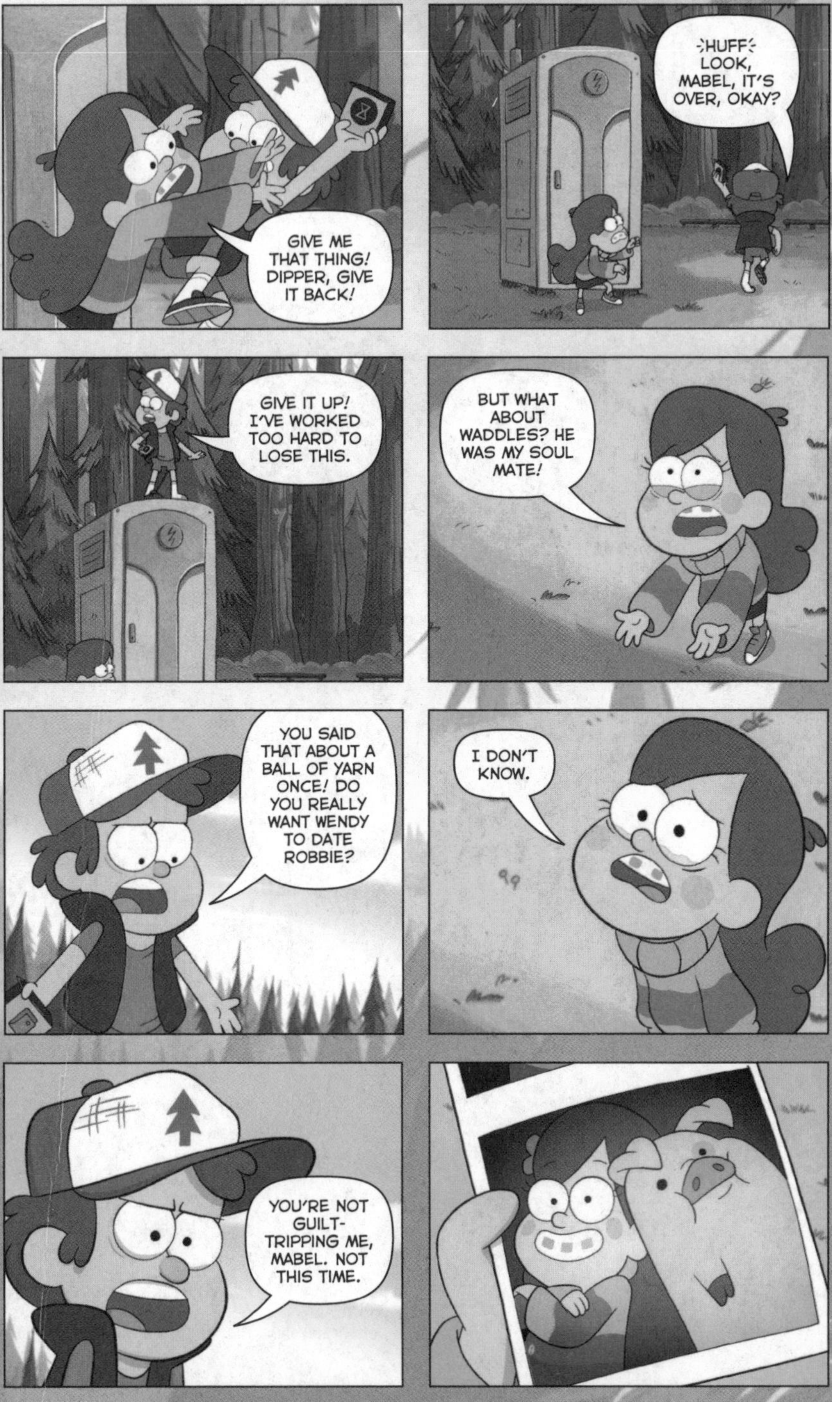
GIVE ME THAT THING! DIPPER, GIVE IT BACK!
-HUFF- LOOK, MABEL, IT'S OVER, OKAY?
GIVE IT UP! I'VE WORKED TOO HARD TO LOSE THIS.
BUT WHAT ABOUT WADDLES? HE WAS MY SOUL MATE!
YOU SAID THAT ABOUT A BALL OF YARN ONCE! DO YOU REALLY WANT WENDY TO DATE ROBBIE?
I DON'T KNOW.
YOU'RE NOT GUILT-TRIPPING ME, MABEL. NOT THIS TIME.

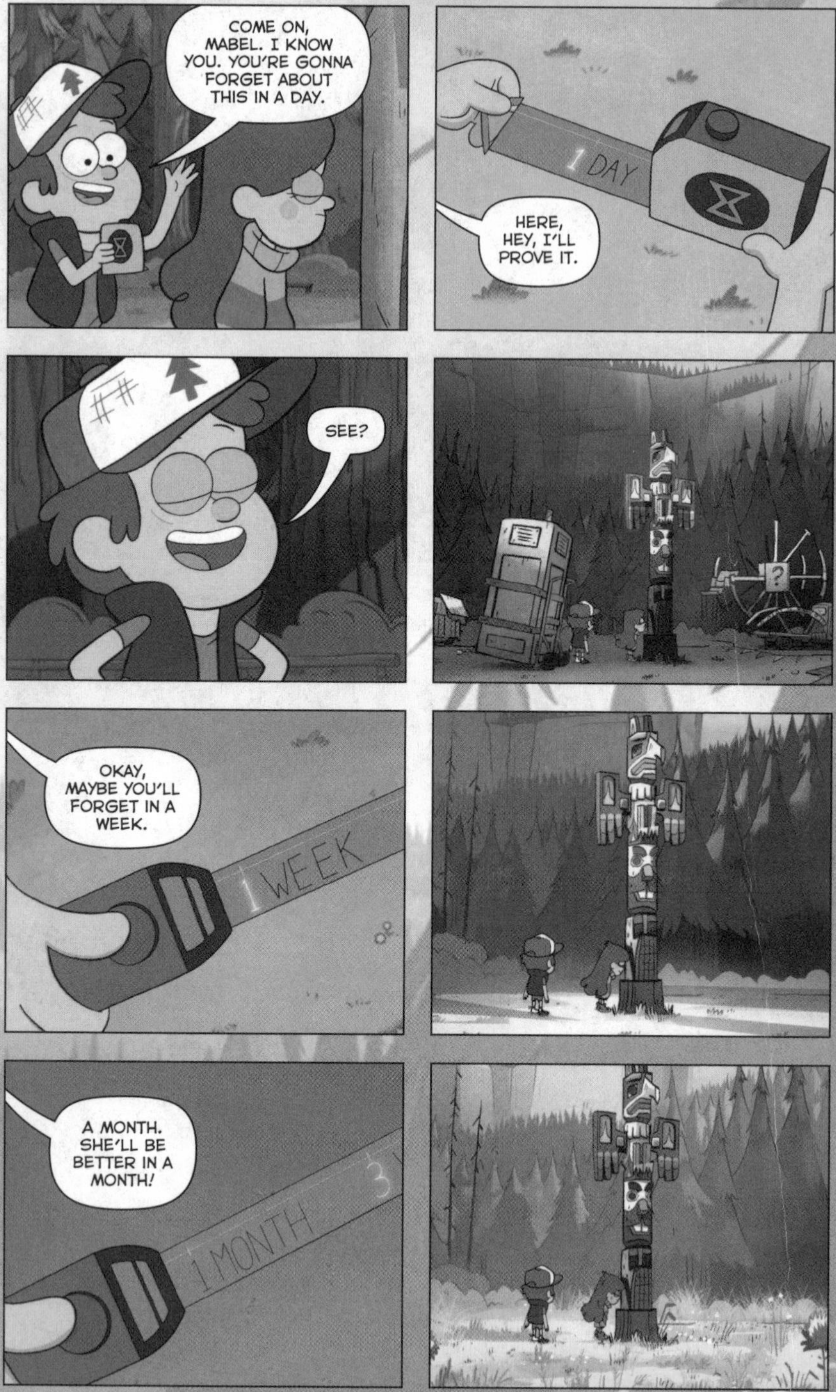
COME ON, MABEL. I KNOW YOU. YOU'RE GONNA FORGET ABOUT THIS IN A DAY.
1 DAY
HERE, HEY, I'LL PROVE IT.
SEE?
OKAY, MAYBE YOU'LL FORGET IN A WEEK.
1 WEEK
A MONTH. SHE'LL BE BETTER IN A MONTH!
1 MONTH

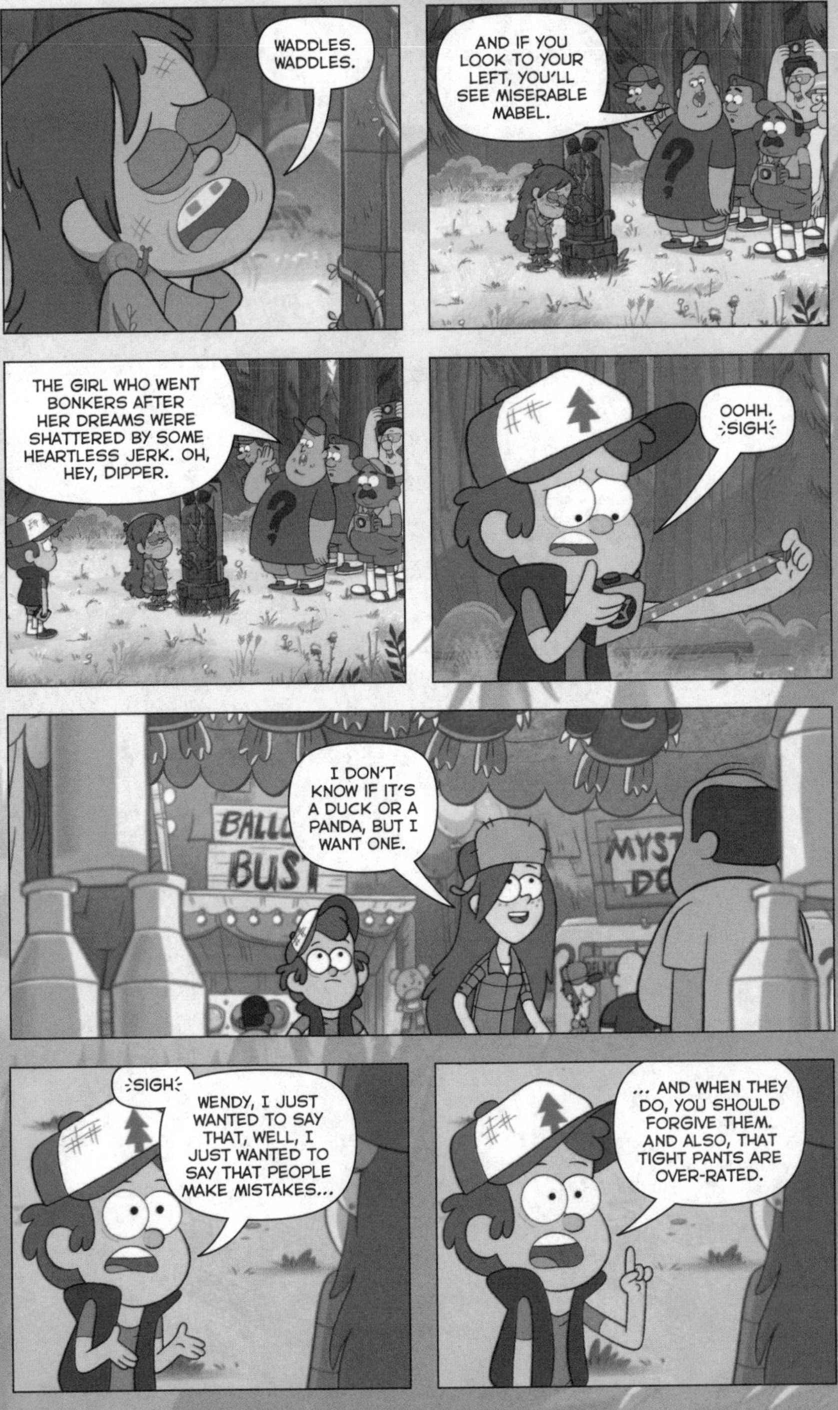
WADDLES. WADDLES.
AND IF YOU LOOK TO YOUR LEFT, YOU'LL SEE MISERABLE MABEL.
THE GIRL WHO WENT BONKERS AFTER HER DREAMS WERE SHATTERED BY SOME HEARTLESS JERK. OH, HEY, DIPPER.
OOHH. SIGH
BALLO
BUST
I DON'T KNOW IF IT'S A DUCK OR A PANDA, BUT I WANT ONE.
MYST
DO
SIGH
WENDY, I JUST WANTED TO SAY THAT, WELL, I JUST WANTED TO SAY THAT PEOPLE MAKE MISTAKES...
... AND WHEN THEY DO, YOU SHOULD FORGIVE THEM. AND ALSO, THAT TIGHT PANTS ARE OVER-RATED.

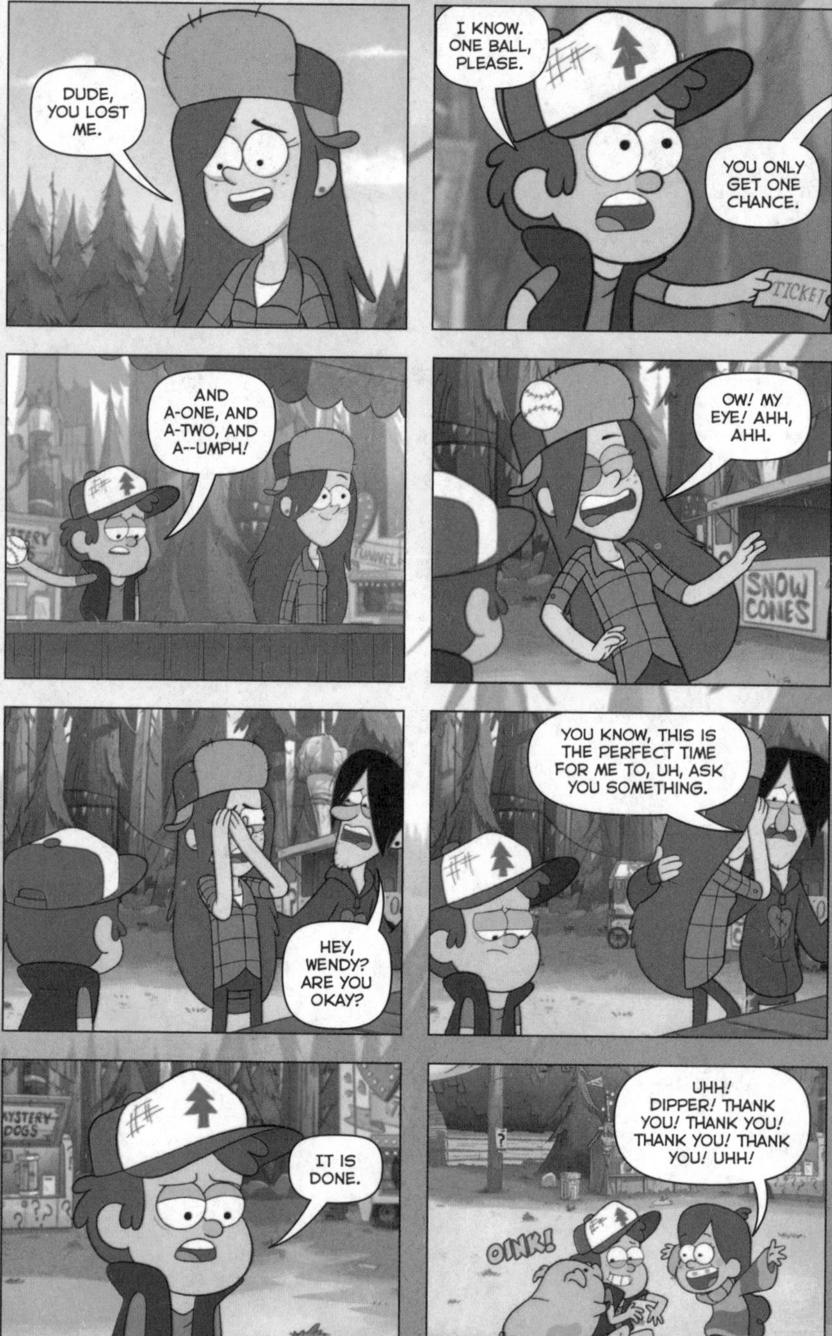
DUDE, YOU LOST ME.
I KNOW. ONE BALL, PLEASE.
YOU ONLY GET ONE CHANCE.
TICKET
AND A-ONE, AND A-TWO, AND A--UMPH!
OW! MY EYE! AHH, AHH.
SNOW CONES
HEY, WENDY? ARE YOU OKAY?
YOU KNOW, THIS IS THE PERFECT TIME FOR ME TO, UH, ASK YOU SOMETHING.
IT IS DONE.
UHH! DIPPER! THANK YOU! THANK YOU! THANK YOU! THANK YOU! UHH!
OINK!

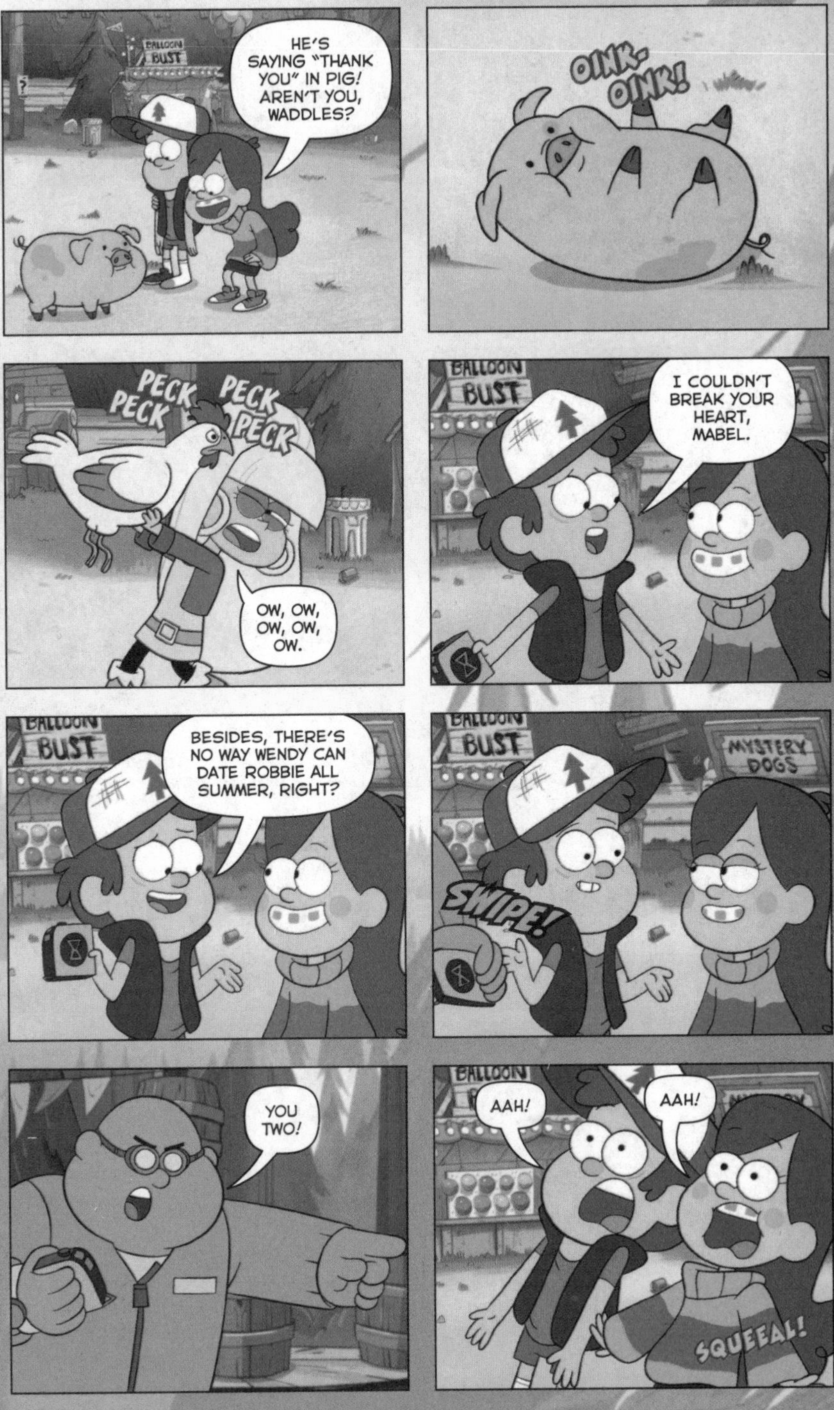
BALLOON BUST
HE'S SAYING "THANK YOU" IN PIG! AREN'T YOU, WADDLES?
OINK-OINK!
PECK PECK PECK PECK
OW, OW, OW, OW, OW.
BALLOON BUST
I COULDN'T BREAK YOUR HEART, MABEL.
BALLOON BUST
BESIDES, THERE'S NO WAY WENDY CAN DATE ROBBIE ALL SUMMER, RIGHT?
BALLOON BUST
MYSTERY DOGS
SWIPE!
YOU TWO!
BALLOON
AAH!
AAH!
SQUEEAL!

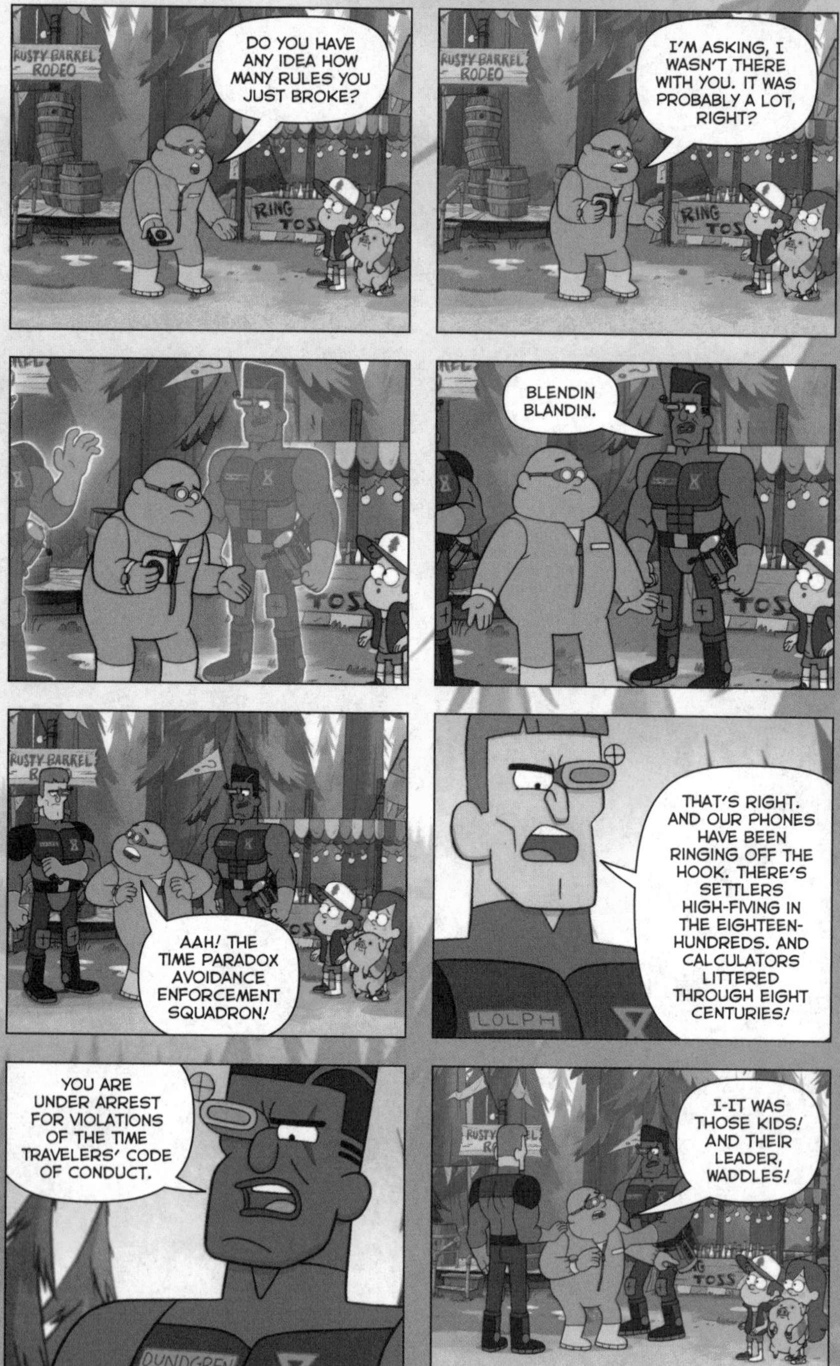
RUSTY BARREL RODEO
DO YOU HAVE ANY IDEA HOW MANY RULES YOU JUST BROKE?
RING TOS
I'M ASKING, I WASN'T THERE WITH YOU. IT WAS PROBABLY A LOT, RIGHT?
BLENDIN BLANDIN.
AAH! THE TIME PARADOX AVOIDANCE ENFORCEMENT SQUADRON!
THAT'S RIGHT. AND OUR PHONES HAVE BEEN RINGING OFF THE HOOK. THERE'S SETTLERS HIGH-FIVING IN THE EIGHTEEN-HUNDREDS. AND CALCULATORS LITTERED THROUGH EIGHT CENTURIES!
LOLPH
YOU ARE UNDER ARREST FOR VIOLATIONS OF THE TIME TRAVELERS' CODE OF CONDUCT.
DUNDGREN
I-IT WAS THOSE KIDS! AND THEIR LEADER, WADDLES!

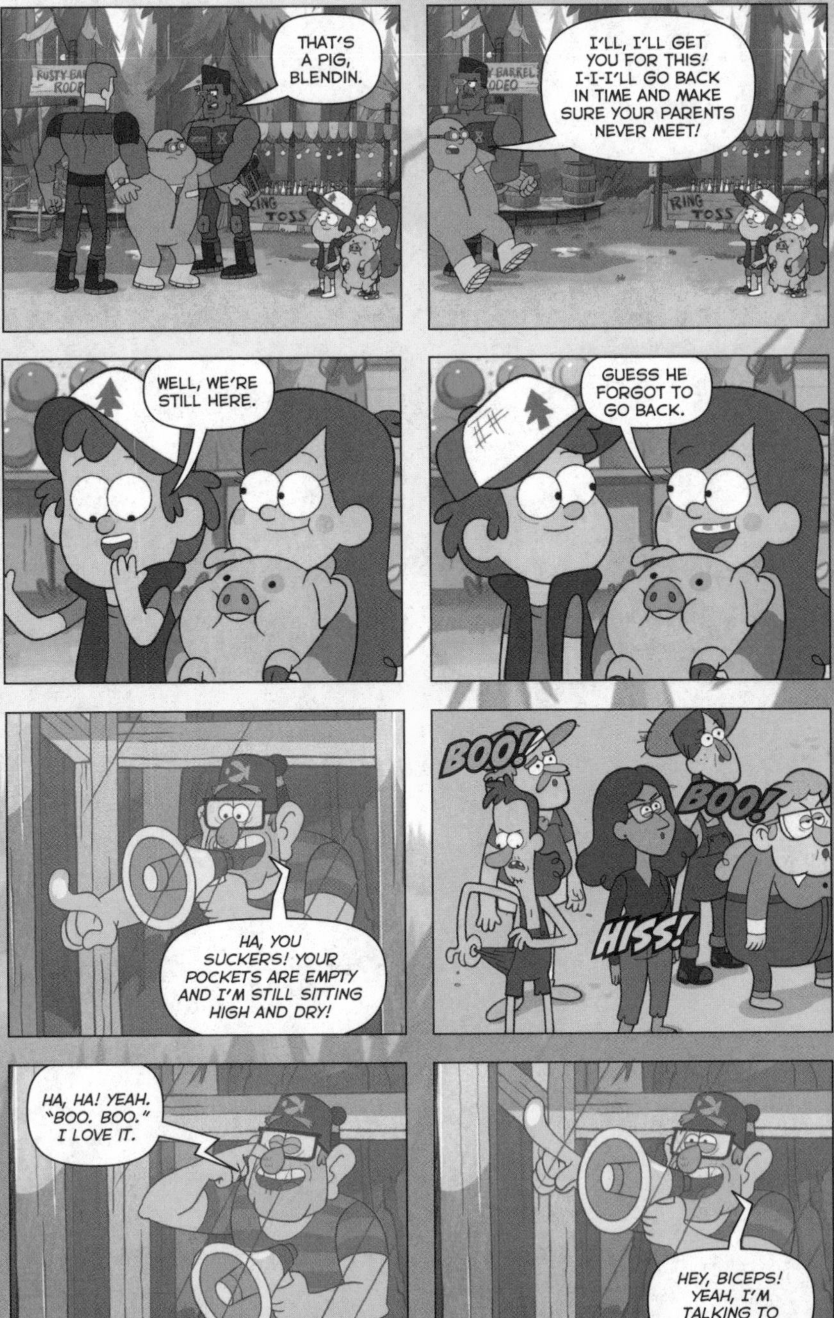

THAT'S A PIG, BLENDIN.
I'LL, I'LL GET YOU FOR THIS! I-I-I'LL GO BACK IN TIME AND MAKE SURE YOUR PARENTS NEVER MEET!
RING TOSS
WELL, WE'RE STILL HERE.
GUESS HE FORGOT TO GO BACK.
HA, YOU SUCKERS! YOUR POCKETS ARE EMPTY AND I'M STILL SITTING HIGH AND DRY!
BOO!
BOO!
HISS!
HA, HA! YEAH. "BOO. BOO." I LOVE IT.
HEY, BICEPS! YEAH, I'M TALKING TO YOU, HAIRCUT.

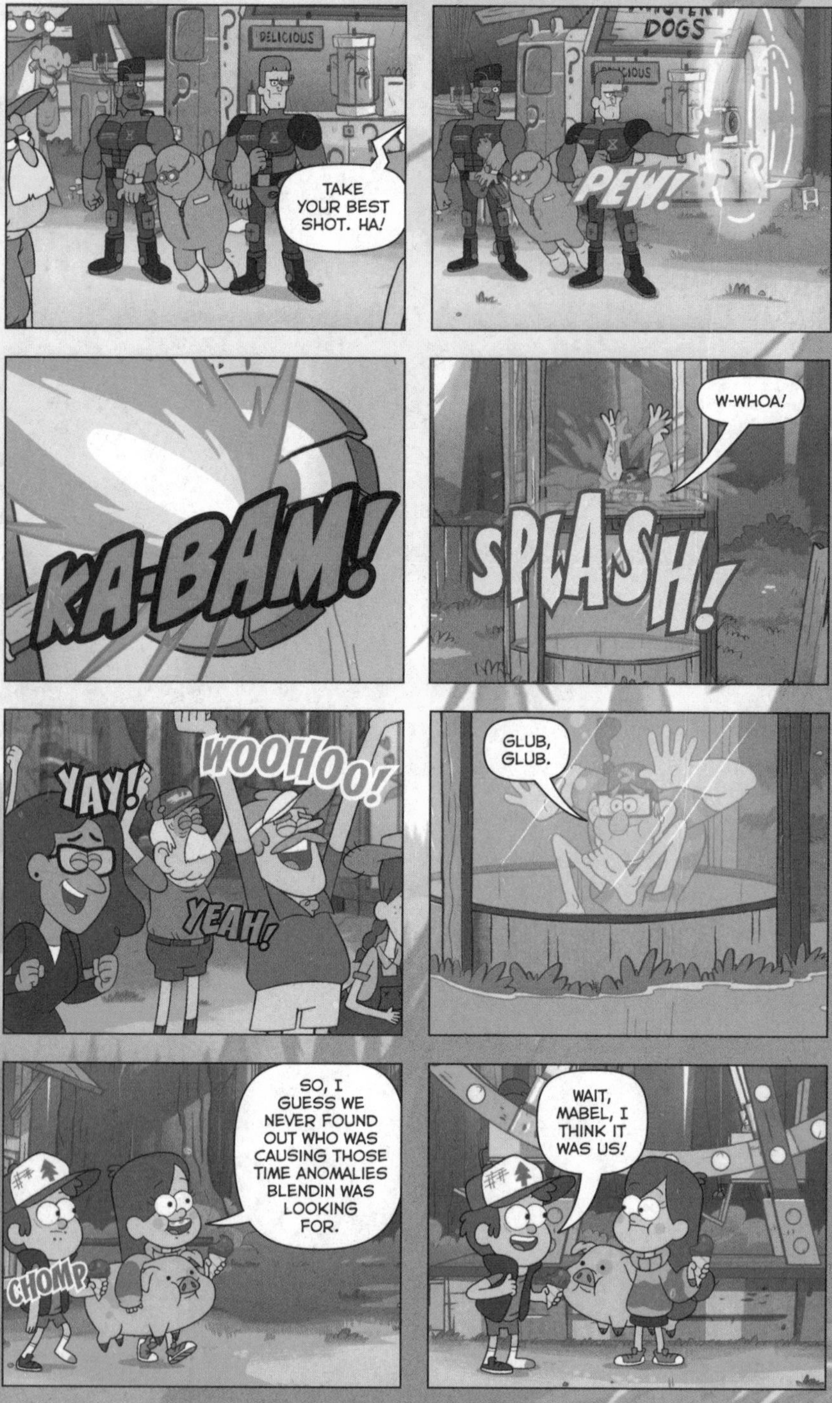
DELICIOUS
TAKE YOUR BEST SHOT. HA!
DOGS
PEW!
KA-BAM!
W-WHOA!
SPLASH!
YAY!
WOOHOO!
YEAH!
GLUB, GLUB.
SO, I GUESS WE NEVER FOUND OUT WHO WAS CAUSING THOSE TIME ANOMALIES BLENDIN WAS LOOKING FOR.
CHOMP
WAIT, MABEL, I THINK IT WAS US!

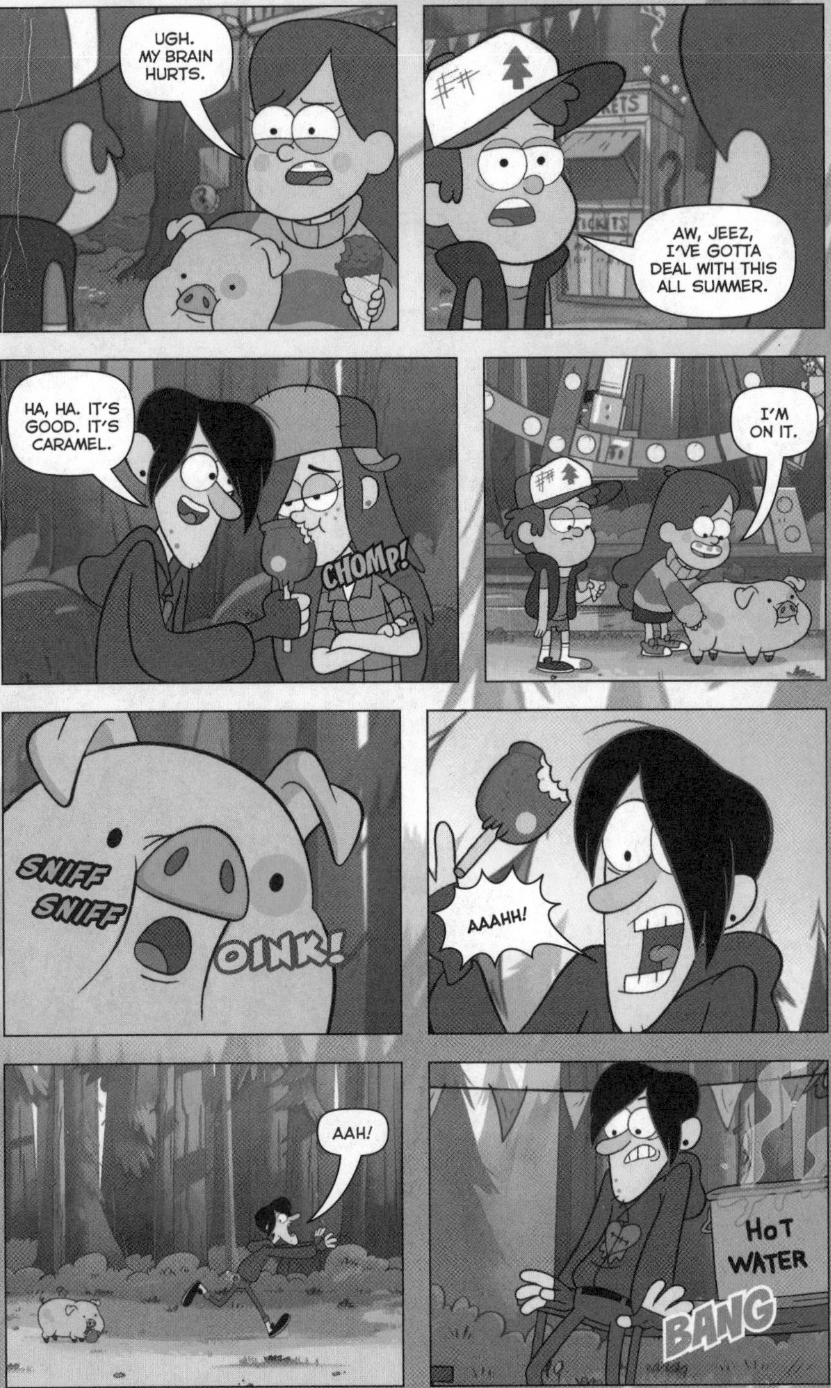
UGH. MY BRAIN HURTS.
AW, JEEZ, I'VE GOTTA DEAL WITH THIS ALL SUMMER.
HA, HA. IT'S GOOD. IT'S CARAMEL.
CHOMP!
I'M ON IT.
SNIFF SNIFF
OINK!
AAAHH!
AAH!
HOT WATER
BANG

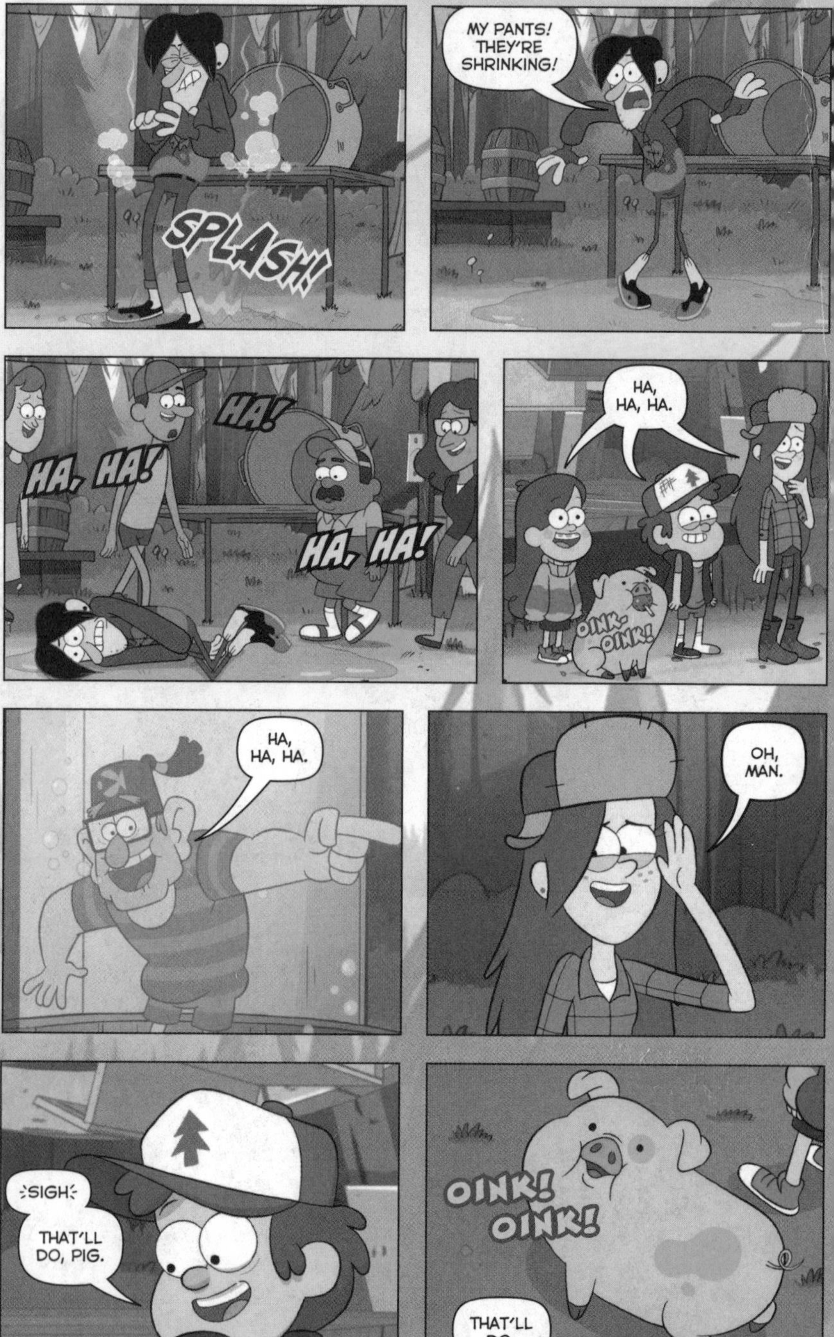
SPLASH!
MY PANTS! THEY'RE SHRINKING!
HA, HA!
HA!
HA, HA!
HA, HA, HA.
OINK-OINK!
HA, HA, HA.
OH, MAN.
-SIGH-
THAT'LL DO, PIG.
OINK! OINK!
THAT'LL DO.
THE END